AF575758

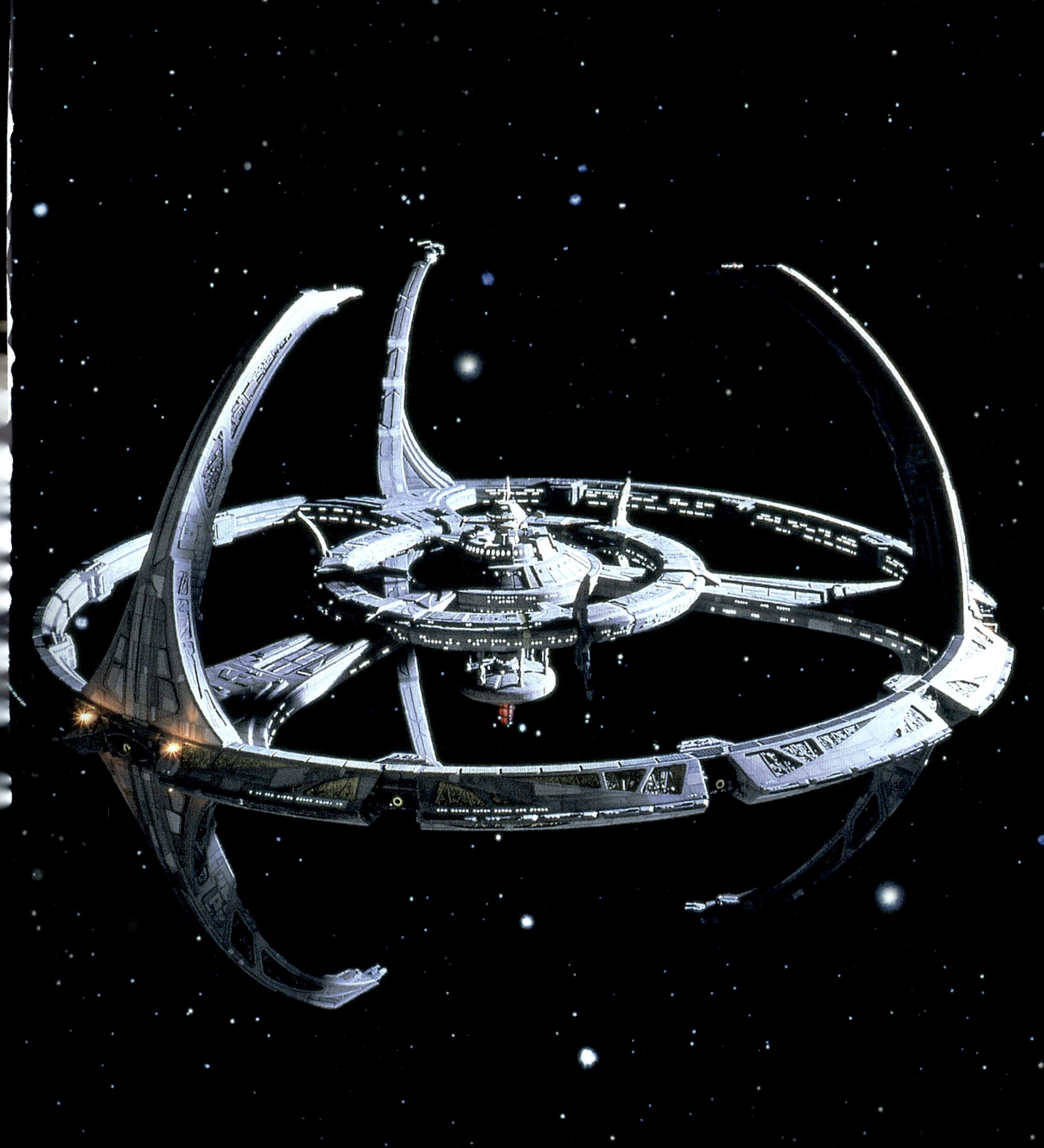

General Editor: **Ben Robinson**
Project Manager: **Jo Bourne**
Editor: **Simon Hugo**
Sub-editor: **Alice Peebles**
Designer: **Katy Everett**

With thanks to the team at CBS: John Van Citters, Marian Cordry and Risa Kessler

Published by **Hero Collector Books**, a division of Eaglemoss Ltd. 2021
Eaglemoss Ltd., Premier Place, 2 & A Half Devonshire Square, EC2M 4UJ, London, UK
Eaglemoss France, 144 Avenue Charles de Gaulle, 92200 Neuilly-Sur-Seine, France

First published by **Hero Collector Books** in 2020

Second printing 2021

To order back issues: Order online at
www.shop.eaglemoss.com

ISBN 978-1-85875-951-7

Printed in Spain
10 9 8 7 6 5 4 3 2

www.herocollector.com

STAR TREK™

DEEP SPACE 9

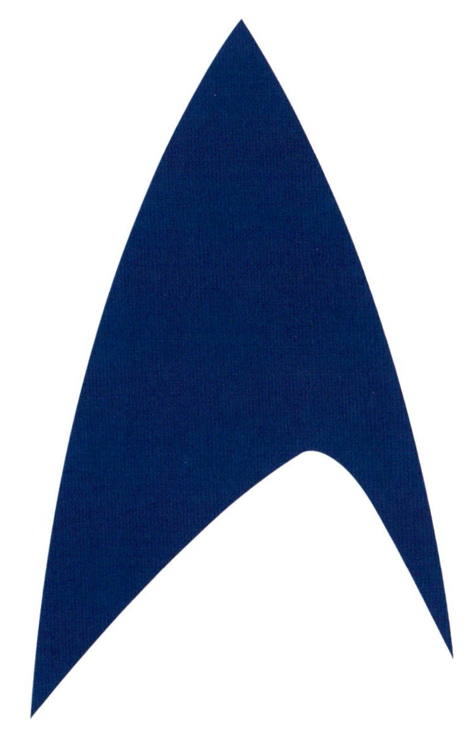

ILLUSTRATED HANDBOOK

CONTENTS

ACKNOWLEDGMENTS

Most of the material in this book originally appeared in the *STAR TREK Fact Files,* an extraordinary, heavily illustrated reference work that was delivered in weekly instalments before the Internet was widespread. It covered every aspect of the *STAR TREK* universe, including Deep Space 9, the *U.S.S. Defiant*, and the station's runabouts. We'd like to thank the talented team of artists who worked on it: Stuart Wagland, Ian Fulwood, Peter Harper, and more than anyone, Rob Garrard, who created the illustrations you will find on the following pages. The CG renders in this book were produced by Rob Bonchune, Adam 'Mojo' Lebowitz, Doug Drexler, and Ed Giddings, who built our model of Deep Space 9.

Reconstructing the names of the people who wrote the text is beyond us, but the *Fact Files* would never have been possible without the hard work of Jenny Cole, Tim Gaskill, Tim Leng, and Marcus Riley.

Of course, we owe a massive debt to the *STAR TREK: DEEP SPACE NINE Technical Manual,* written by Rick Sternbach and Doug Drexler, which revealed many unknown details about the station and its history. Rick, Doug, and Mike and Denise Okuda have always been a great help to us and we are profoundly grateful.

No list of acknowledgments would be complete without mentioning Gene Roddenberry, who brought *STAR TREK* into being, and the talented production teams who followed in his footsteps. We are particularly grateful to Ira Steven Behr and the writing team who brought Deep Space 9 to life.

Finally, we'd like to thank our friends at CBS Consumer Products: Risa Kessler, who did the deals that made all this possible; Guy Vardaman, Paul Ruditis, and Tim Gaskill, who handled the original approvals; and Marian Cordry and John Van Citters, who run the show today.

FOREWORD

Deep Space 9 was radically unlike anything we had seen before: a Cardassian ore-processing plant that had been converted into an administrative center and trading post, before Starfleet came in and refitted it with their technology. It not only looked different, it worked differently. The technology was mostly Cardassian, with elements of Starfleet, Bajoran, and even Ferengi cultures thrown in. This book covers all the elements of the station we saw during the show's seven years on air, plus the auxiliary vehicles Starfleet posted there: the *Danube*-class runabouts and Starfleet's first true warship, the *U.S.S. Defiant.*

As with the other volumes in this series, you will find isometric drawings of all the key locations, with detailed artworks of areas such as ops and the Promenade that show you exactly how everything was connected, and illustrations showing uniforms, phasers, tricorders, and some of the Alpha Quadrant's weapons in the war agains the Dominion. You'll see CG renders of the station and the ships, including the *Defiant's* rarely seen shuttles.

As you read this book, our hope is that you will get a real sense of Deep Space 9 as a place that hundreds of people called home, with all the things that entails. You won't just find out about the details of the station's weapons and shields, youll discover what kind of living quarters are available and where to find the holosuites.

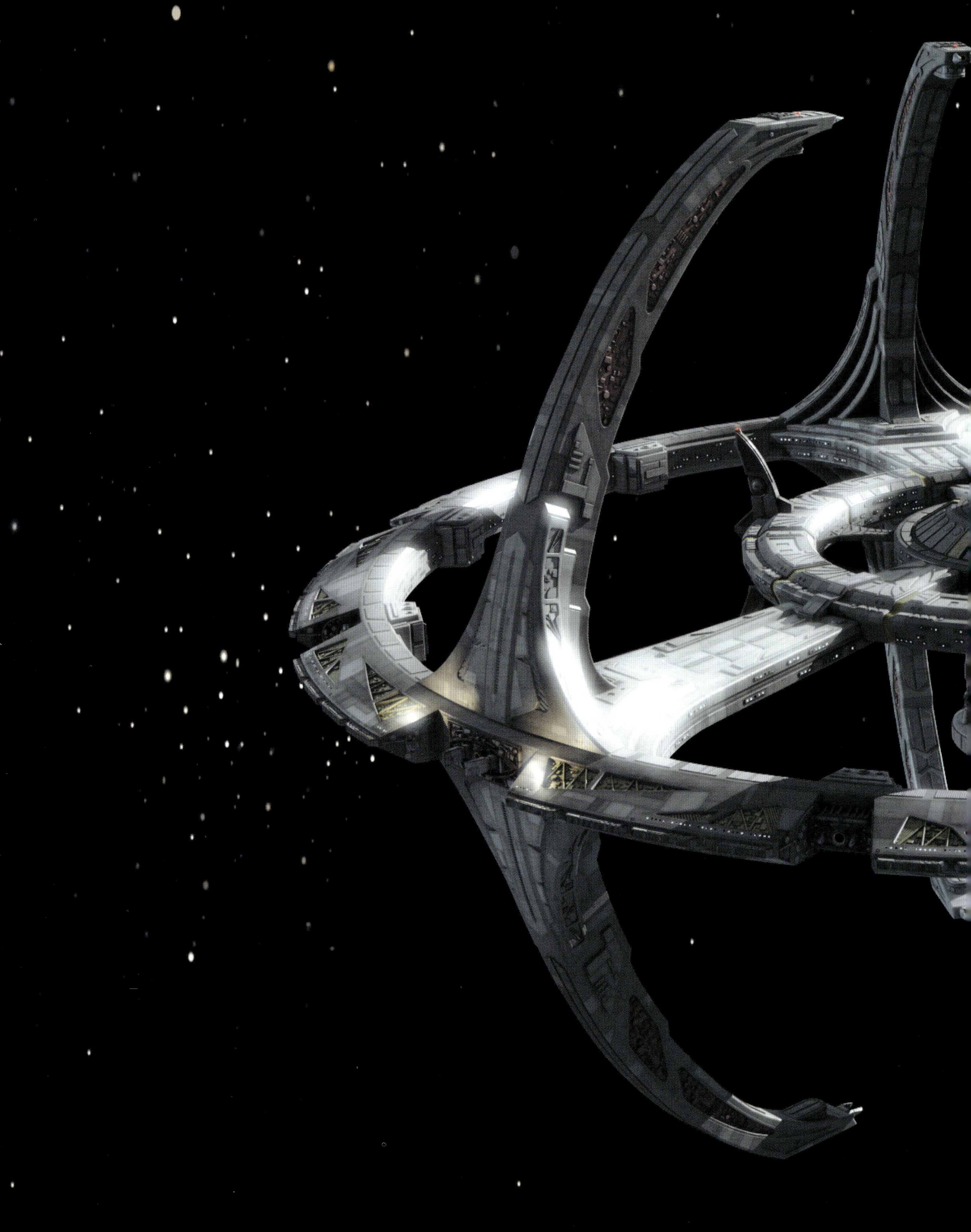

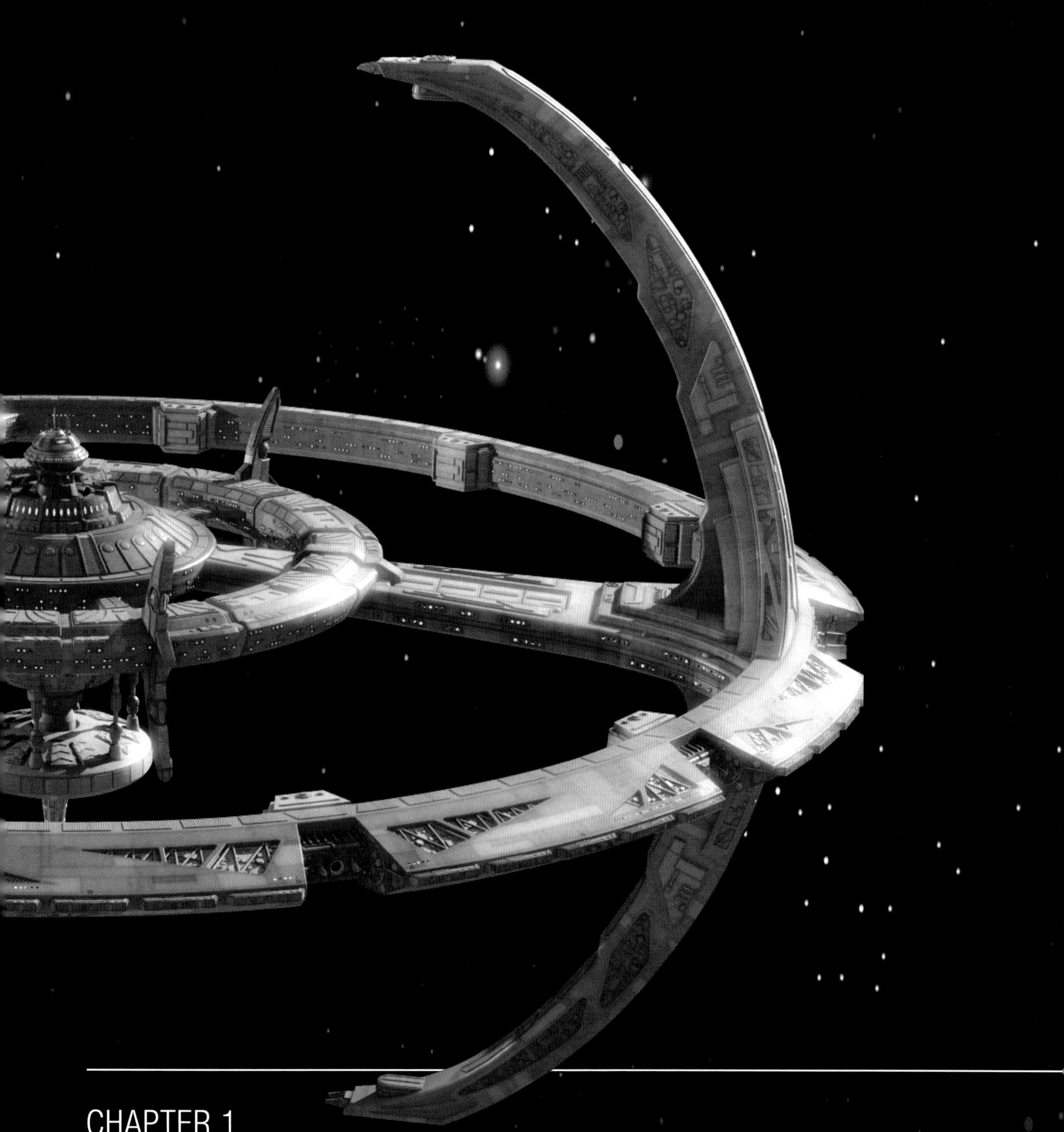

CHAPTER 1

DEEP SPACE 9

CONSTRUCTION AND REFIT

Originally known as Terok Nor, the space station Deep Space 9 was built by the Cardassians using Bajoran slave labor. It was upgraded with Starfleet systems and additional defenses after the liberation of Bajor.

The Cardassian station that would later become Deep Space 9 was built to a standard Cardassian design. Construction was completed in 2346, but the station was not in full service until 2351. Thereafter it served as both an ore-processing facility and the orbital headquarters for the occupation of Bajor. Its Cardassian name was Terok Nor, and its identical sister stations included Empok Nor in the Trivas system.

THE CENTRAL CORE

Most of the raw materials used to build the station were found in the Bajoran system, but some had to be mined from asteroids closer to Cardassia Prime. Cardassian-run facilities on Bajor were used to construct the hull plating, power conduits, and parts of the fusion generator.

Construction took place above Bajor, starting with the midcore. Here the Cardassians established a temporary command center, along with basic habitable spaces for the Bajoran workforce. Next came the lower core, where more permanent residences and work areas were set up, and preparations began for installing the fusion reactors. The upper core came third, and the temporary command center relocated here once its systems were operational.

Completing the core involved building and activating the fusion generator. Ever mindful of attacks from the Bajoran Resistance, the Cardassians also installed reactive shield armor and shield emitters at this point. When the fusion generator was functional, work began on the Promenade, and the command center made its final move to the ops module, which had been prefabricated on Cardassia. Last of all, turbolift interlinks were connected and atmospheric integrity was established throughout the core.

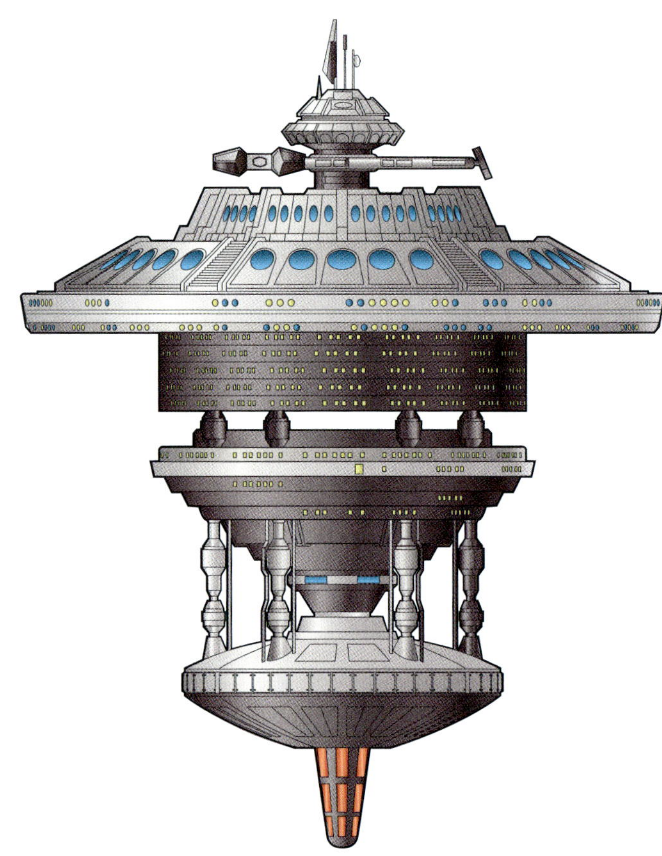

The central core was constructed in three stages, starting with the midcore. It was fully operational before work began on the two outer rings and the docking pylons.

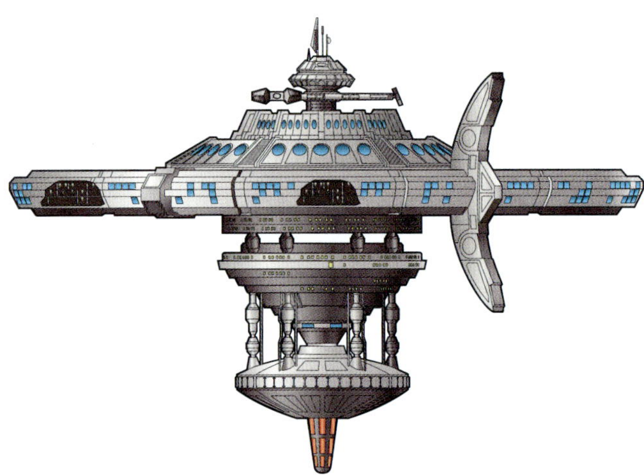

Once the core was complete, the habitat ring was built out from crossover bridges radiating from the core. The weapons sails were installed as completed units.

RINGS AND PYLONS

The inner ring (known as the habitat ring) was built next, along with the crossover bridges that connected it to the central core. The weapons sails were manufactured as separate modules in nearby orbit and connected to the habitat ring as they became available. The bridges were then built out to their fullest extent and the docking pylons took shape around them. The pylons were completed by the installation of ore-processing equipment, leaving only the construction of the outer ring (known as the docking ring) before the station was fully formed.

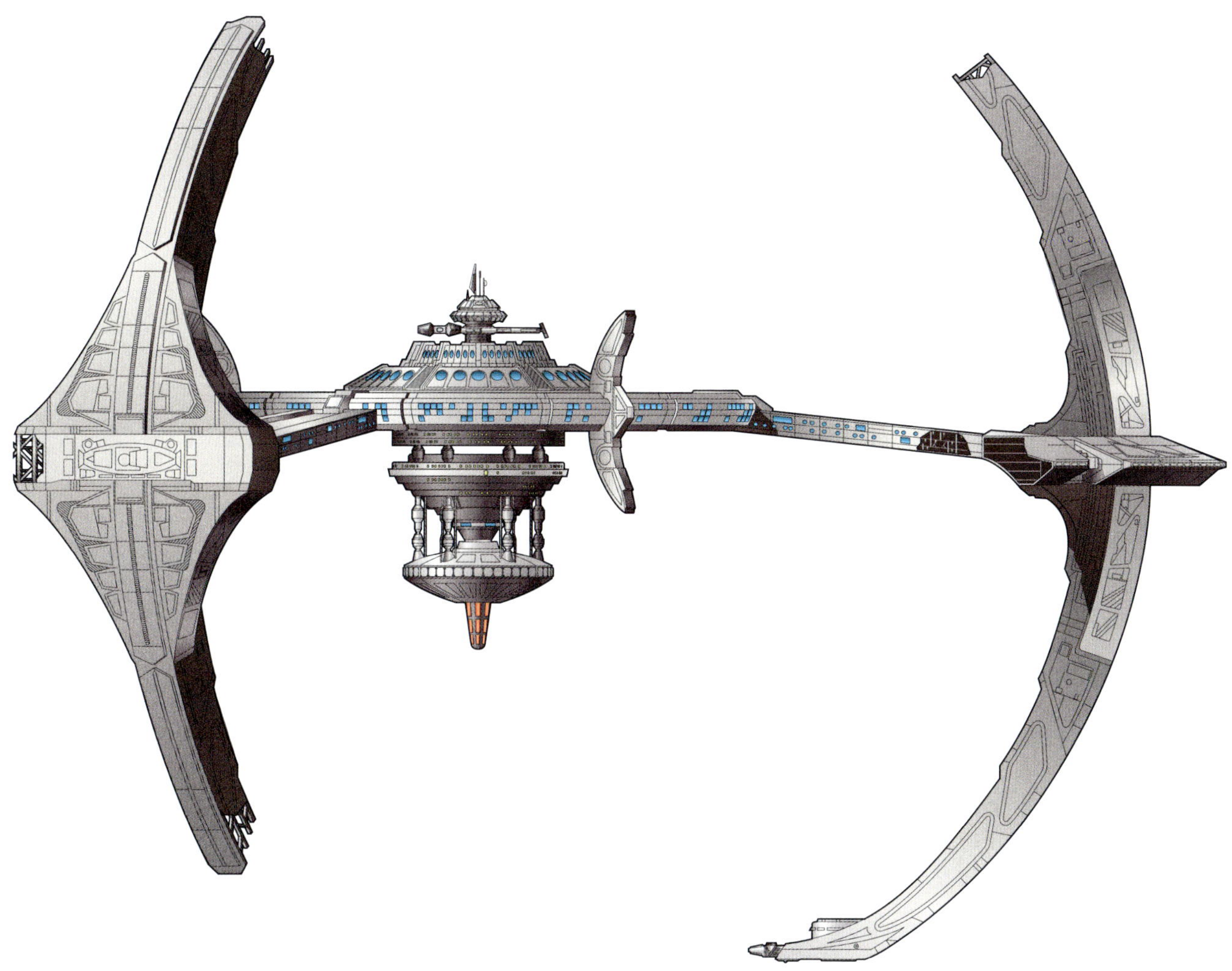

Later stages of construction saw the crossover bridges extended and the docking pylons branch off from them. The docking ring was built once the pylons were complete.

AFTER THE OCCUPATION

When the Cardassians pulled out of Bajor in 2369, they also abandoned Terok Nor. Starfleet moved in at the invitation of the the Bajoran provisional government and began a major refit of the station. Under the supervision of chief of operations Miles O'Brien, its systems were made compatible with Starfleet equipment and safety standards were greatly improved. The EPS network was upgraded with input controllers, step-up plasma phase inverters, and level limiters, and the original computer core was augmented with a set of adaptive interfaces.

Now known as Deep Space 9, the station retained no ore-processing functions, and sections of the habitat ring previously occupied by laborers were repurposed as landing bays for six Starfleet runabouts. The docking ports were modified to accept a greater range of craft, and the communications system was upgraded with new subspace transceivers and antennae. The atmospheric controls were adjusted to produce a cooler environment than the one favored by Cardassians, and the replicators were reprogrammed with a far wider range of cuisine.

Perhaps the most important upgrades, however, were those made to the weapons and shields. When the Cardassians vacated the station, they deliberately left it all but defenseless. The possibility that they might try to retake it by force was a real one, and so the first priority was establishing a new defensive shield. Once this was achieved, a gradual process of upgrading the weapons systems got underway.

WARTIME UPGRADES

At first, enhancing the station's arsenal proved a long and slow affair, but the threat of war with the Dominion focused minds and resources. By the end of the war, Deep Space 9 was equipped with rotary phaser cannons, microtorpedo launchers, and large retractable phaser arrays mounted on electrohydraulic ramps. In general, Starfleet weapons were installed in the same locations as their Cardassian precursors, but improved levels of automation meant that the former Cardassian weapons monitoring rooms were now surplus to requirements.

Despite Starfleet's many upgrades over the years, some facets of the station always proved resistant to change. The nature of the original build prevented the use of anti-grav cargo lifts and some holographic systems, while the integral plasma distribution manifolds made use of beta-matrix compositors that could only be replaced using parts salvaged from other Cardassian facilities.

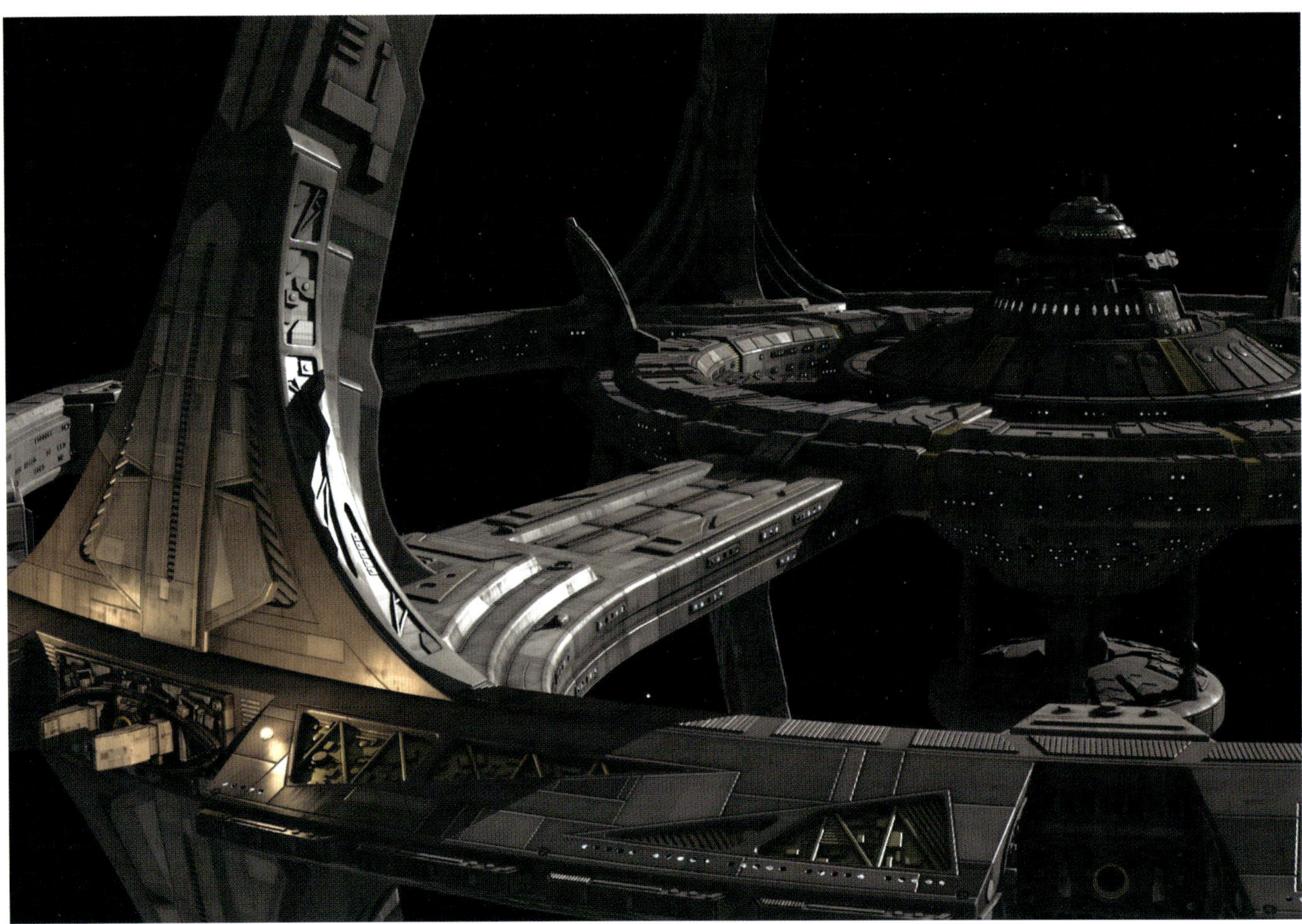

OPERATIONAL HISTORY

Deep Space 9 began life as a Cardassian ore-processing plant, but under joint Bajoran and Federation control, it became the key strategic outpost at the mouth of a stable wormhole.

For most of the 2350s and 2360s, Deep Space 9 was a Cardassian ore-processing plant in orbit of Bajor. It played a major role in the Cardassians' strip-mining of Bajor, refining the planet's rich deposits of uridium before they were shipped throughout the Cardassian Union. Then known as Terok Nor, the station was also the Cardassians' administrative base in the Bajor system. By 2362, it was under the command of a Cardassian gul called Dukat, as part of his remit as the prefect of Bajor.

Several independent businesses operated from Terok Nor's Promenade, including a bar run by the Ferengi Quark. But for the most part, workers on the station were Bajoran prisoners and conscripts, detailed to work in ore processing. Life was very hard for these slaves, who were forced to live on the station in pens, and were provided with minimal food and no medical care. At first, the Bajoran sector of the station lacked even environmental controls, and so its inhabitants had to burn their few possessions for warmth.

Some Bajorans fared better than others, serving on work details that saw them seconded to the businesses on the Promenade. Others were granted extra rations and even private quarters – but only in exchange for satisfying the desires of their oppressors. Loathing for the Cardassians naturally ran deep, and a well-organized Bajoran Resistance did its best to disrupt and undermine the running of Terok Nor. In its first year of service, the station was targeted by the Higa Metar resistance group, but its biological weapon failed to activate until the occupation was over.

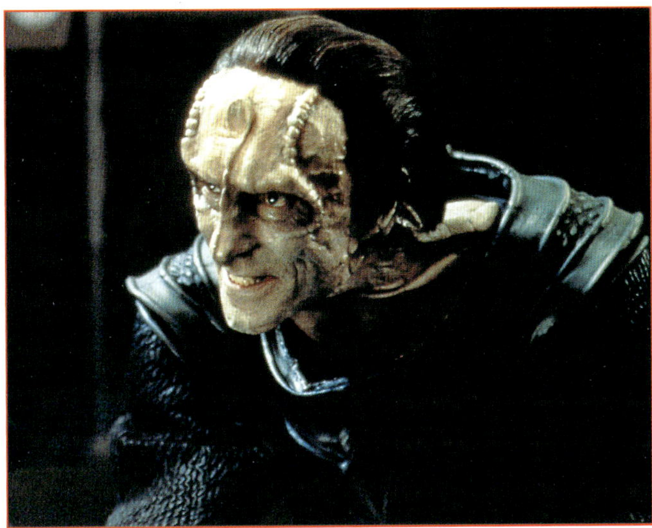
As the prefect of Bajor, Gul Dukat was in charge of the station when it was known as Terok Nor. He bitterly opposed his government's decision to quit the planet in 2369.

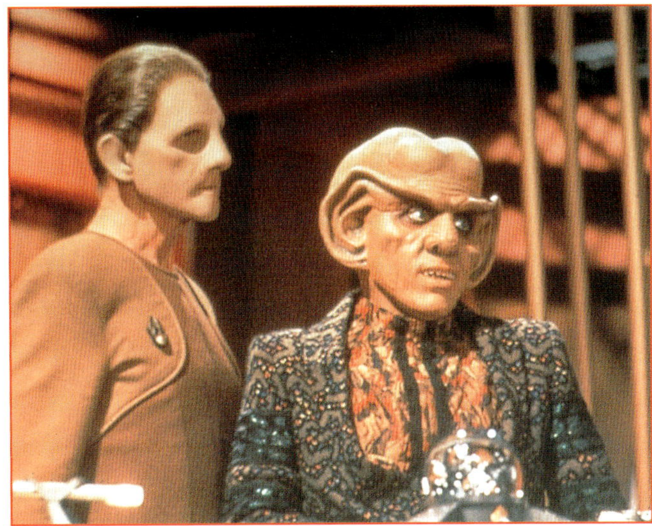
The station's Ferengi bar owner, Quark, and security chief, Odo, maintained a mutually antagonistic relationship for more than a decade.

In 2363, Gul Dukat encountered the mysterious shape-shifter Odo, who lived at the Bajoran Institute of Science. Two years later, he assigned Odo to investigate a murder on the station, having remembered his unique capacity for disguise. Though the case was never solved, Dukat kept Odo in place as station security chief, and the "Constable" quickly earned a reputation for his fairness and sense of justice. When the Cardassians finally abandoned the station in 2369, Odo was hailed by the Bajorans as one of the occupation's heroes, and he continued in the same role – now with a Bajoran uniform and deputies.

CARDASSIAN WITHDRAWAL

The Cardassian Union's exit from Bajor proved almost as painful as the occupation itself. Having stripped the planet of all they wanted, they determined to leave none of what was left for the Bajorans. Cardassian troops burned and poisoned vast tracts of agricultural land, looted cities, and gutted Terok Nor as they withdrew. Only one Cardassian remained on the station – the exiled Elim Garak, who ran a tailor's shop on the Promenade.

Without the resources or desire to stand alone, the new Bajoran provisional government turned to the Federation for immediate aid and the longer-term goal of membership. As a result, Starfleet took responsibility for the day-to-day running of Terok Nor, which was renamed Deep Space 9. The new commander of the station was Benjamin Sisko, a Human officer who had lost his wife in the Battle of Wolf 359, so now had sole care of his teenage son, Jake. His senior staff included science officer Jadzia Dax, medical officer Dr. Julian Bashir, and chief of operations Miles O'Brien, formerly of the *U.S.S. Enterprise* NCC-1701-D. As Deep Space 9 remained sovereign territory of Bajor, it was also crewed by members of the Bajoran Militia – with the hero of the Resistance, Major Kira Nerys, chief among them as Commander Sisko's second-in-command.

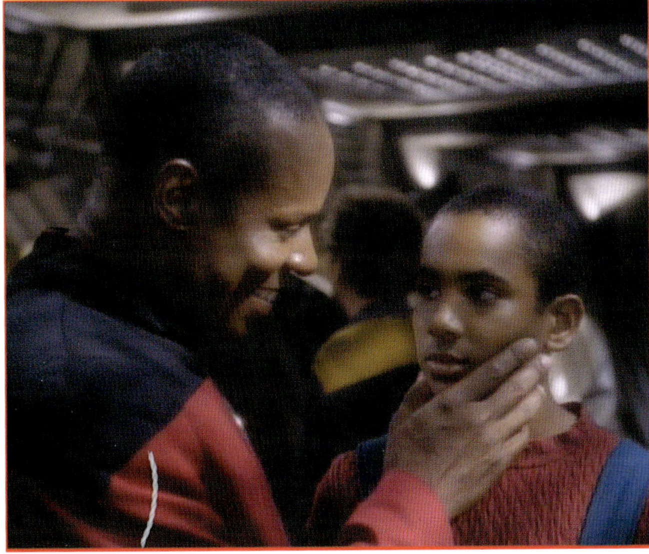
Neither Benjamin nor Jake Sisko was impressed when they came aboard Deep Space 9 in 2369, but Ben hid his doubts behind a smile for the benefit of his teenage son.

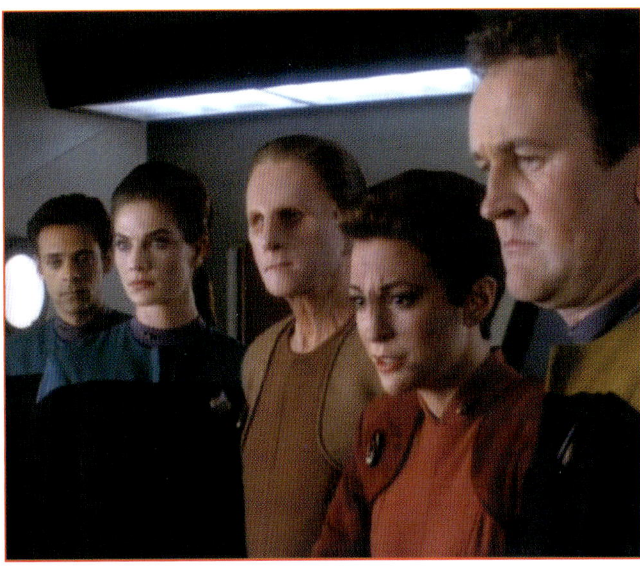
Senior station staff from 2369 (left to right): Dr. Julian Bashir, science officer Jadzia Dax, security chief Odo, Major Kira Nerys, and chief of operations Miles O'Brien.

DISCOVERY OF THE WORMHOLE

At first, Sisko was unhappy with his posting to Deep Space 9, and still harbored resentment over the death of his wife. But his outlook changed when he encountered the alien species living inside a previously undiscovered wormhole close to Bajor. This species, which the Bajorans viewed as their gods, gave Sisko a glimpse of their complex, nonlinear relationship with time, and challenged him to explain the nature of his own existence. This experience allowed him to come to terms with his own past and embrace the future. It also fulfilled an ancient Bajoran prophecy about the discovery of the "Celestial Temple,"and from then on Sisko was regarded by a majority of Bajor's believers as the foretold Emissary of the Prophets.

The discovery of the wormhole had more than spiritual implications, too. As a stable conduit linking Bajoran space to the distant Gamma Quadrant in a matter of moments, it was set to become a major route for trade and exploration, and staking a claim to its location was key to Bajor's future interests. Sisko ordered the station to be moved out of orbit to a fixed position at the mouth of the wormhole, and in so doing secured its new strategic significance.

NEW BEGINNINGS

From its new location in the Denorios belt, Deep Space 9 quickly flourished as a center of commerce, research, and also religion, as many Bajorans sought closeness to the Prophets and their flesh-and-blood Emissary. Starfleet set about upgrades to facilities and defenses throughout the station, and most doubts about the Federation's motives in Bajoran space were swiftly dispelled. Not everyone was convinced, however, and before 2369 was out, a Bajoran terrorist group attempted to destroy the wormhole, in the hope that a return to strategic insignificance would cause Starfleet to lose interest in the region.

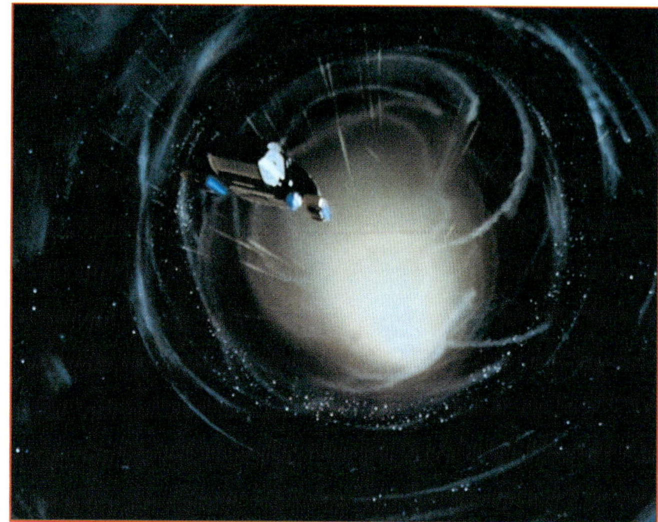

The only known stable wormhole in the entire galaxy was discovered by Commander Sisko and Lieutenant Dax in the runabout U.S.S. *Rio Grande* NCC-72452 in 2369.

More political intrigue was quick to follow when Vedek Bareil, one of two leading candidates for Bajor's highest office, was the target of an assassination attempt on the station. Then, as 2370 began, a Bajoran separatist group known as the Circle briefly took control of Deep Space 9, aiming to overthrow the provisional government and expel all non-Bajorans from the planet. Both failed bids for power were linked to Bareil's political opponent, Vedek Winn, but she was able to avoid scandal and was soon elected to the powerful position of Kai.

NEW THREATS

in 2370, the Federation also signed a border treaty that left several of its colonies in a demilitarized zone close to the Cardassian border. As the Starfleet outpost closest to these colonies, Deep Space 9 had a large part to play

BAJORAN CONSPIRACY

In late 2369, Winn Adami lured her fellow Bajoran vedek, Bareil Antos, to Deep Space 9 and convinced one of her supporters to make an attempt on his life. The following year, Bajoran provisional government minister Jaro Essa promised Winn the hallowed position of Kai, if she helped him sever Bajor's ties to the Federation.

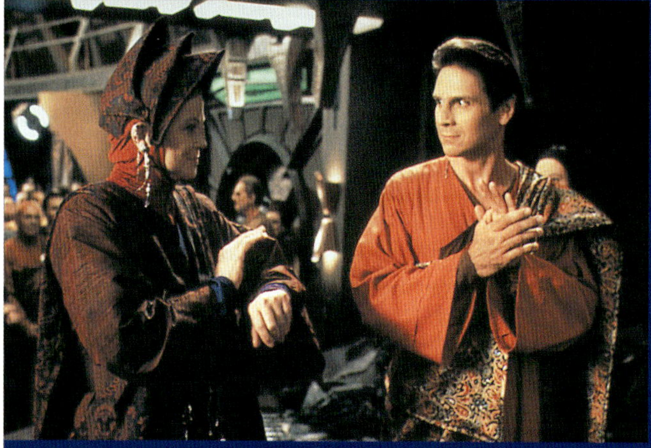

Vedek Winn manufactured a controversy around schoolteaching on Deep Space 9 to draw her rival, Vedek Bareil, out of monastic seclusion and onto the station.

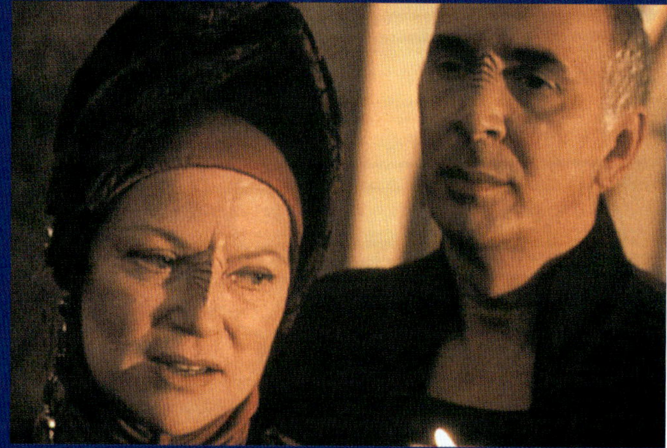

A seasoned political survivor, Winn plotted with Minister Jaro, only to turn publicly against him when scandal threatened to engulf their jointly conceived plans.

DOMINION OCCUPATION

When the Dominion took control of Deep Space 9 in late 2373, the Cardassians revived its original name of Terok Nor. It was overseen by a ruling council including Gul Dukat, the Vorta Weyoun, and Odo – whom the Vorta revered as one of the Founders. Quark continued to run his bar for Cardassian and Jem'Hadar soldiers.

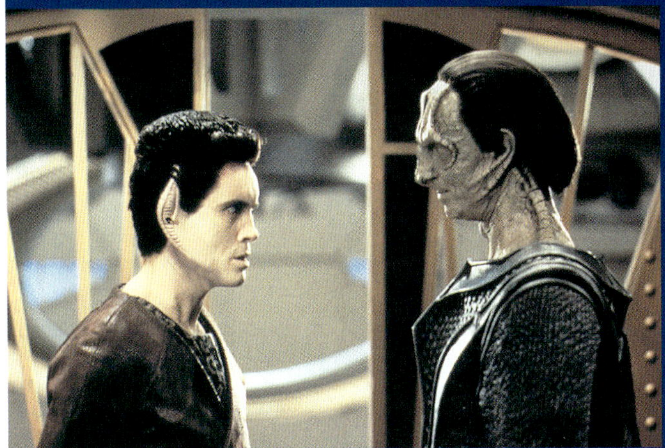

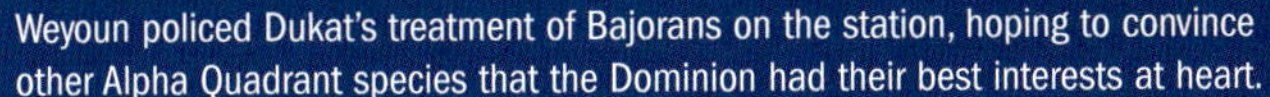

Weyoun policed Dukat's treatment of Bajorans on the station, hoping to convince other Alpha Quadrant species that the Dominion had their best interests at heart.

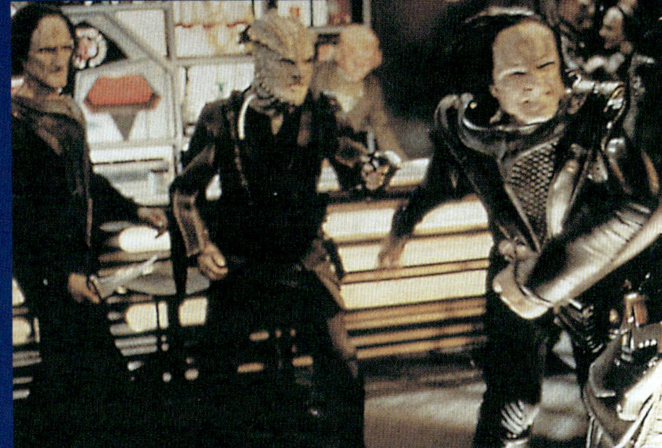

Despite Weyoun's attempted shows of unity, some Cardassians openly vented their frustrations with Dominion membership after a few glasses of *kanar* at Quark's.

in combating a newly militant faction of the colonists and their sympathizers, who launched attacks on Federation and Cardassian targets alike. Known as the Maquis, the group attracted several high-profile Federation defectors, including Deep Space 9's own chief of Starfleet security, Michael Eddington, who worked as a double agent under Sisko for some time. For a while, the Maquis posed the most pressing threat to the station, but they were swiftly overshadowed – and eventually completely destroyed – by an even greater danger...

THE DOMINION

As the preeminent power bloc in the Gamma Quadrant, the Dominion saw the wormhole as a threat and an opportunity for expansion. In late 2370, its bred-for-purpose military wing, the Jem'Hadar, traveled into the Alpha Quadrant for the first time and gave notice at Deep Space 9 that no further expansion into Dominion territory would be tolerated. Moments later, a Jem'Hadar ship destroyed the *Galaxy*-class starship *U.S.S. Odyssey* in the Gamma Quadrant.

Starfleet's response to this new threat saw Deep Space 9's defensive weaponry greatly enhanced, and a starship assigned to the station. The experimental *U.S.S. Defiant* NX-74205 was Starfleet's first warship, originally designed to combat the Borg. It was also the first Federation ship to have a cloaking device, under a one-off agreement with the Romulans. Sisko took the *Defiant* into the Gamma Quadrant to contact the Dominion's leaders – but it was Odo and Kira who learned that these "Founders" belonged to the same shape-shifting species as Odo himself.

SHIFTING ALLIANCES

Fear of the Dominion grew throughout 2371, causing the Romulan and Cardassian secret services to launch a joint attack against the Founders. When this Alpha Quadrant fleet was completely destroyed, it left the Federation and the Klingon Empire standing alone against the growing possibility of invasion. However, by the end of the year, it was apparent that the Founders were already posing as senior figures in both administrations. These agents stoked paranoia wherever possible, causing a year-long Federation-Klingon War, and a failed military coup on Earth. This unrest saw Starfleet's only Klingon officer, Lieutenant Commander Worf, assigned to Deep Space 9 for his strategic expertise, and the recently promoted Captain Sisko briefly reassigned from the station to head up Starfleet Security on Earth.

The war ended in early 2373, when Odo exposed the Founders' infiltrator high up in the Klingon ranks. But it was not long before the Founders established a foothold on Deep Space 9 itself – by capturing and replacing Dr. Bashir with one of their own. The deception was exposed, and

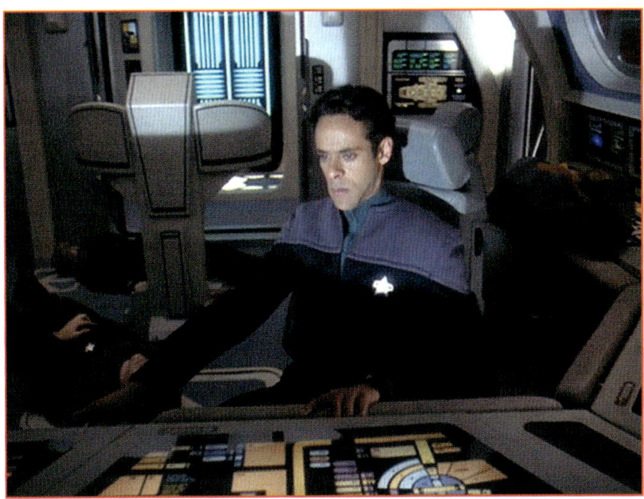

The Founder posing as Dr. Bashir stole a runabout and killed its crew in an attempt to wipe out resistance to the Dominion by destroying Bajor's sun.

BATTLE STATION

After Deep Space 9 was retaken from the Dominion by a combined Federation and Klingon fleet, it became a crucial base for battle planning and mobilizing allied forces against the Cardassians and the Jem'Hadar. Even the highly secretive Romulans established a base on the station when they finally entered the war.

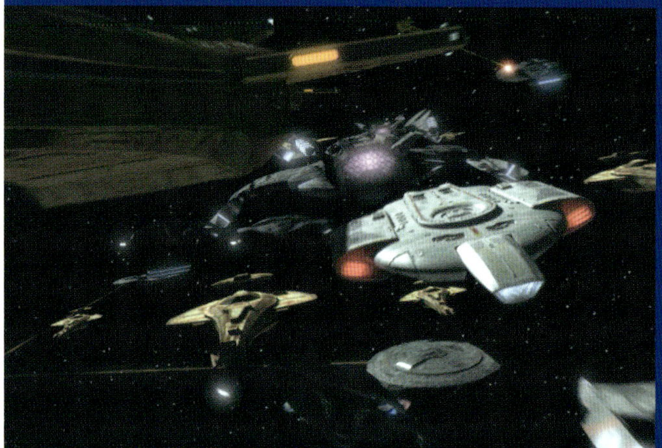

Around 600 Federation vessels massed against a fleet twice as large to reclaim Deep Space 9. The battle was later joined by welcome Klingon reinforcements.

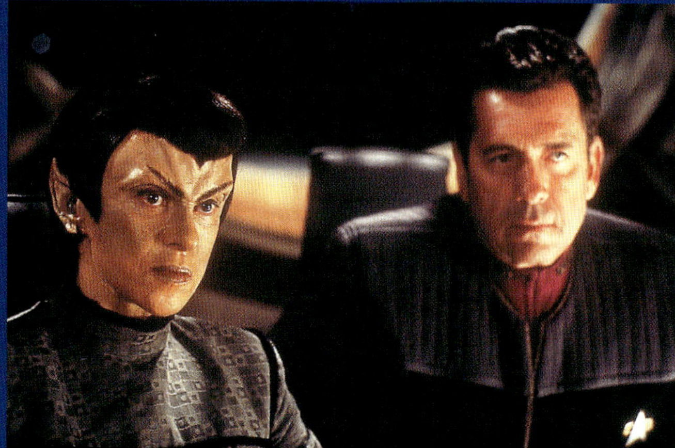

Romulan senator Cretak and Starfleet Command flag officer Admiral William Ross were both familiar faces on Deep Space 9 in the latter days of the Dominion War.

the real Bashir escaped Dominion imprisonment. But this did not stop a full Jem'Hadar invasion of the Alpha Quadrant that saw the Cardassian Union join the Dominion – and the Maquis completely wiped out.

SURRENDERING THE STATION

With Jem'Hadar forces gathering in Cardassian space, the *Defiant* laid a minefield at the entrance to the wormhole and Sisko convinced Bajor to sign a nonaggression pact with the Dominion. This meant all Bajorans evacuating *Deep Space 9* ahead of inevitable Jem'Hadar retaliation for the minefield. When the attack came, augmented by Cardassian warships, Starfleet had no choice but to abandon the station. Sisko vowed to return, and left behind a program that sabotaged all of the command systems.

As 2374 began, Deep Space 9 was once again under the control of Gul Dukat, along with his Dominion handler, the Vorta Weyoun. Elsewhere, a Federation-Klingon alliance was engaged in all-out war with the Jem'Hadar, with the station's former command crew running frequent combat missions out of Starbase 375. Kira, Odo, Quark, and Jake Sisko all remained on Deep Space 9, with Odo consenting to join its new ruling council. Quark's brother Rom also remained onboard, operating alongside Kira as a spy and saboteur for Sisko and the Federation.

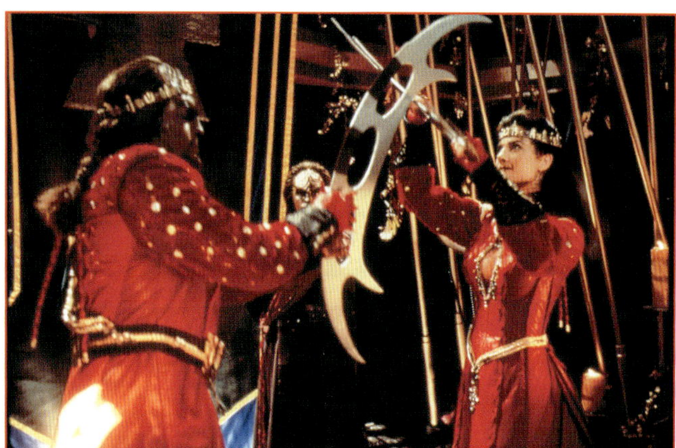

Deep Space 9 officers Worf and Jadzia Dax were married on the station by Lady Sirella, Mistress of the House of Martok, in a traditional Klingon ceremony in 2374.

OPERATION RETURN

After several months, Starfleet approved a plan to retake Deep Space 9. Led by Sisko and the *Defiant*, the operation was timed to stop the Cardassians from deactivating the minefield and allowing countless Jem'Hadar reinforcements through. However, despite the last-minute assistance of the Klingon fleet, the strike came too late and the mines were destroyed *en masse*. Dominion control of the station – and the Alpha Quadrant – seemed assured. But when Sisko made a last stand against the Jem'Hadar in the wormhole, the Prophets refused to let him die, and instead used their powers to neutralize the oncoming fleet. With the station's weapons sabotaged by Nog and Kira, all Dominion forces then left the station, with the exception of Gul Dukat – who was seemingly driven out of his mind by defeat and the death of his daughter during the evacuation.

THE BEGINNING OF THE END

With Deep Space 9 once again under joint Federation and Bajoran control, it played host to the wedding of Dax and Worf. Dukat was charged with war crimes, but escaped the station before his trial could begin. Meanwhile, the war with the Dominion continued to rage, as Jem'Hadar forces conquered Alpha Quadrant strongholds such as Betazed, in the heart of Federation territory.

Sisko was determined that the Romulans must be brought into the war and abandon the neutrality they had affected ever since the Tal Shiar's disastrous attack on the Founders in 2371. To that end, Sisko used Deep Space 9 as the backdrop to a deception that achieved this goal, but at the cost of several lives, plus his own sense of honor, decency, and moral certainty.

Soon after this, a joint Federation, Klingon, and Romulan fleet scored a major victory against the Dominion in the Chin'toka system – only for tragedy to strike back at the station. Dukat, under the influence of a Pah-wraith (the ancient, incorporeal enemies of the Prophets), murdered Jadzia Dax and sealed the wormhole, cutting the Bajorans off from their Celestial Temple. Devastated by the loss of his dear friend, Captain Sisko then went on an extended leave of absence from Starfleet and returned home – to New Orleans on Earth – with Jake.

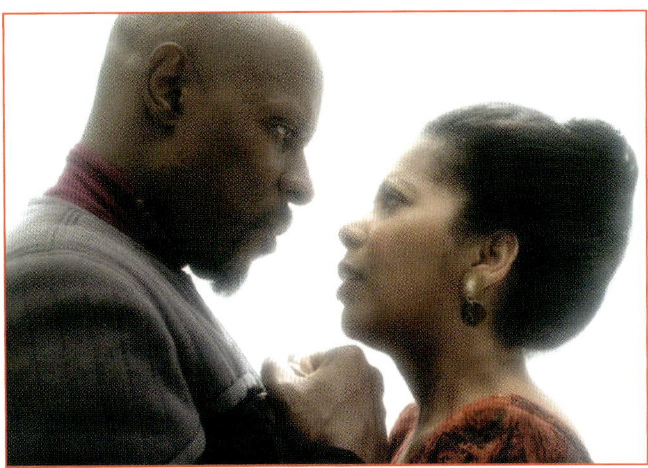

Benjamin Sisko and Kasidy Yates-Sisko shared a last embrace in the Celestial Temple, after which she was able to tell Jake and the Deep Space 9 crew about his fate.

WAR AND PEACE

For the first two months of 2375, Deep Space 9 was under the command of the newly promoted Colonel Kira (who was by now in a romantic relationship with Odo). Meanwhile, on Earth, Sisko had a vision that led him to discover that his birth mother was one of the Prophets, and that he had always been destined to become their Emissary. His revelation also resulted in a way to reopen the Bajoran wormhole. When he returned to the station, he was accompanied by Starfleet ensign Ezri Dax, a Trill who was newly joined with the Dax symbiont previously hosted by Jadzia. She then joined the station staff as a counselor, with a promotion to lieutenant, junior grade.

Later on in the year, Sisko married the freighter captain Kasidy Yates on Deep Space 9, with Jake as his best man. Not long after, Kasidy became pregnant with their child. These moments lightened the growing darkness of the war, as Earth was attacked by the Dominion's new allies, the Breen, and Dr. Bashir learned that Section 31 – the Federation's secretive black ops unit – had infected Odo with a deadly virus so the shape-shifter could unwittingly transmit it to the Founders.

Bashir worked tirelessly to find a remedy, and when he finally did so, it played a large part in restoring peace to the Alpha Quadrant. With the Cardassians in open revolt against the Dominion and Odo's people ravaged by the virus, in 2375, the Founders signed a peace treaty on board Deep Space 9 in exchange for the cure, officially ending the war.

As this took place, however, another battle was raging on Bajor. In the planet's Fire Caves, Sisko was in a fight to the death with Dukat, as yet still possessed by the Pah-wraith. He saved the planet and the wormhole aliens from being destroyed by the Pah-wraiths, but sacrificed his corporeal existence in the process. The Prophets allowed Sisko to appear before Kasidy one last time, before he took his place beside them in the Celestial Temple. From then on, life on Deep Space 9 continued without the captain – but with Colonel Kira in the command office chair.

MOVE ALONG HOME

After the Dominion War, Chief O'Brien left Deep Space 9 to teach engineering at Starfleet Academy, while Odo returned to The Great Link where the Founders existed as a single, liquid form. Worf accepted a post as Federation ambassador to the Klingon Empire, while Kira, Bashir, and Dax remained onboard the station.

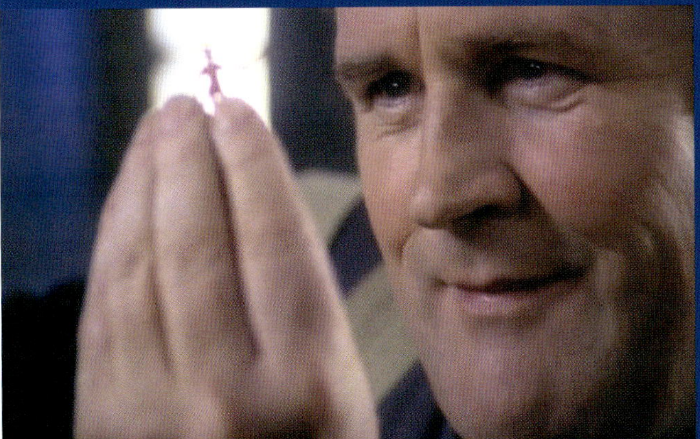

Before returning to Earth, Chief O'Brien reminisced about his friendship with Dr. Bashir, including many happy hours spent recreating historic battles in miniature.

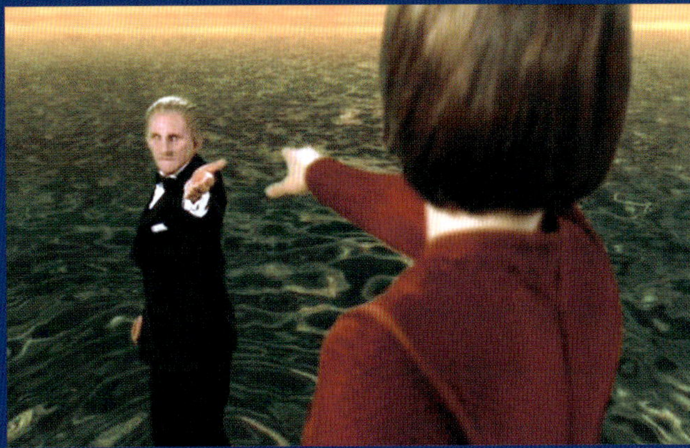

Colonel Kira accompanied Odo on his return to The Great Link. As the lovers said their final farewells, the shape-shifter morphed his Bajoran uniform into a tuxedo.

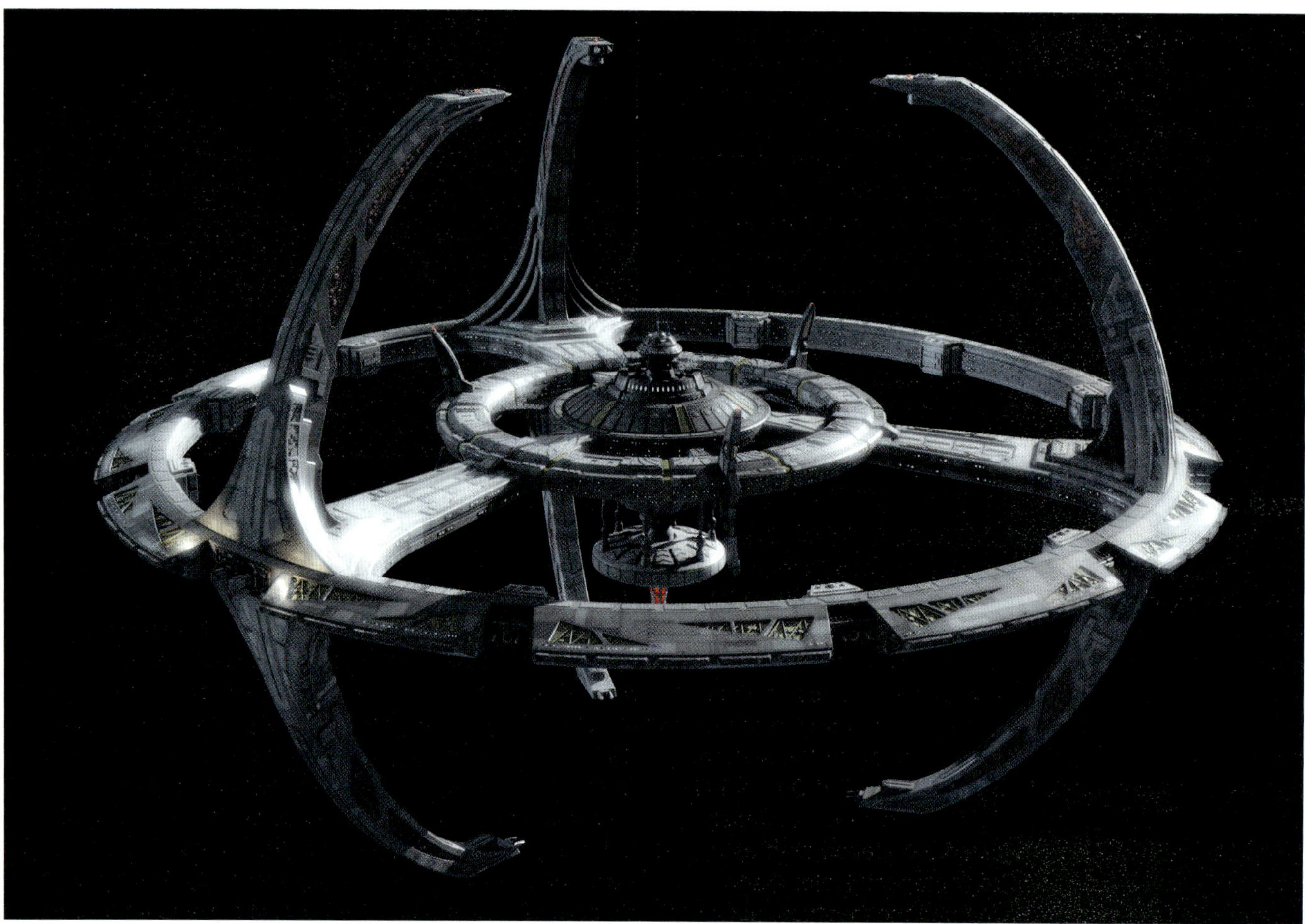

ANNOTATED EXTERIOR VIEWS

Cardassian design had little in common with Federation norms – functionally or aesthetically. Even Starfleet engineers found that detailed labeling of key features and locations helped make sense of a station like Deep Space 9.

Measuring 1451.82 meters across and 969.26 meters tall (from the tips of the upper docking pylons to those of the lower ones), Deep Space 9 was one of the largest civilian-inhabited space stations known to the Federation in the late 24th century. It comprised 98 levels divided into 19 sections linked by access conduits made of two metre thick duranium, a substance impenetrable to most known scanning techniques. In official Starfleet parlance, it was designated a "hybrid planar-columnar tri-radial structure", and in layperson's terms it was a circular multistory tower encircled by two concentric rings and six perimeter docking pylons.

Visually, the station bore very little resemblance to the average Federation starbase, which was hardly surprising, given that it was built by the Cardassians as a base for refining uridium ore. Its external architecture was a blend of rugged functionality and an aesthetic sensibility found only in the Cardassian Union – primarily featuring bold curves and distorted triangular shapes.

When the Cardassians abandoned the station as part of their withdrawal from Bajoran space in 2369, it was dilapidated on the inside, with many key systems stripped out or sabotaged. But the superstructure remained intact, having been designed and built for a long operational life. And so its new custodians – Starfleet and the Bajorans – kept it in service with barely any changes to its external appearance. New armaments were eventually fitted, but these were usually retracted inside the hull.

PORT ELEVATION

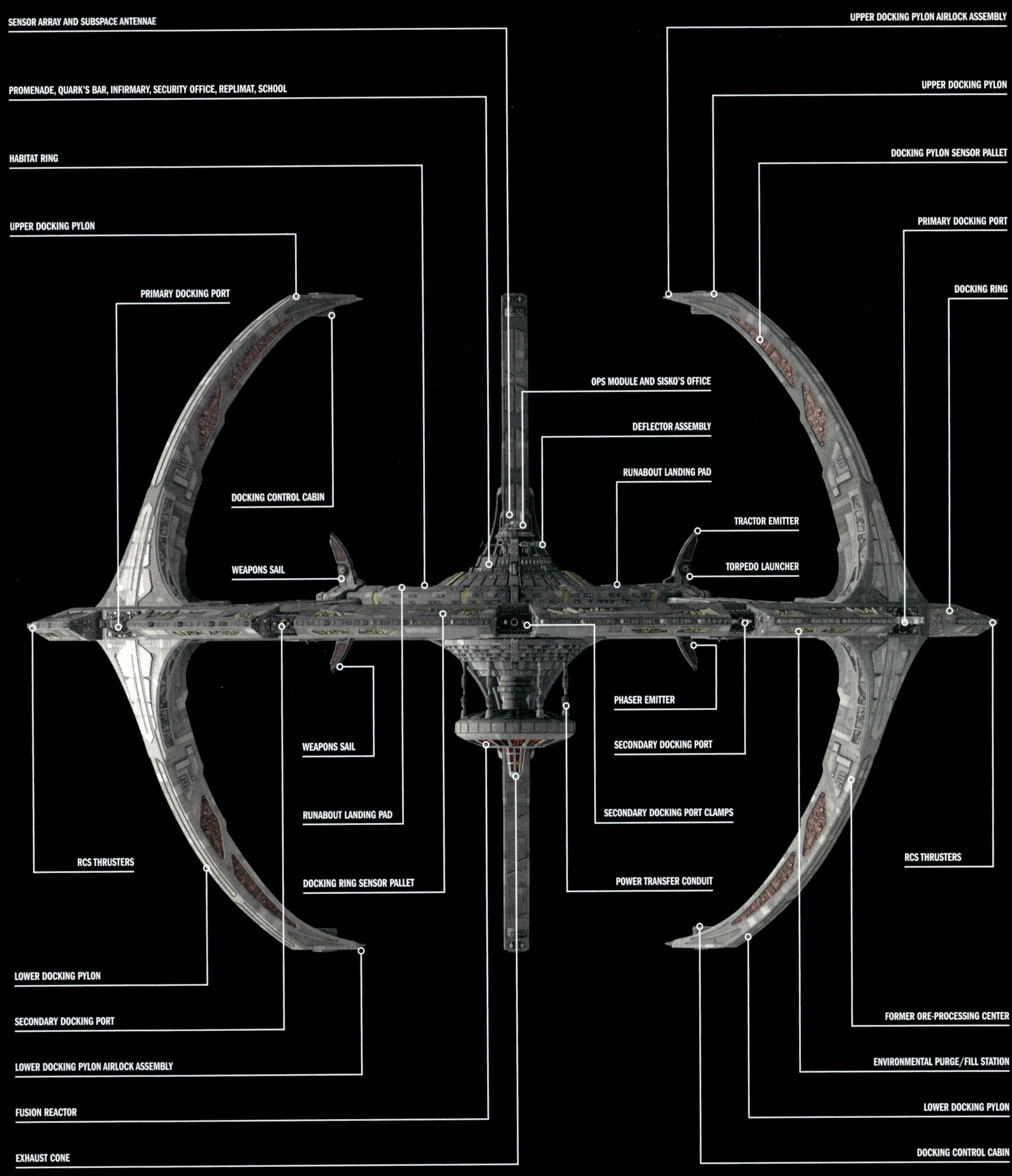

DORSAL VIEW

PROMENADE, QUARK'S BAR, INFIRMARY, SECURITY OFFICE, REPLIMAT, SCHOOL
OPS MODULE AND SISKO'S OFFICE
SECONDARY DOCKING PORT
RUNABOUT LANDING PAD
ENVIRONMENTAL PURGE/FILL STATION
CROSSOVER BRIDGE
RCS THRUSTERS
PRIMARY DOCKING PORT
TRACTOR EMITTER AND WEAPONS SAIL
SECONDARY DOCKING PORT
HABITAT RING
RCS THRUSTERS
TRACTOR EMITTER AND WEAPONS SAIL
PRIMARY DOCKING PORT CLAMPS
DEFLECTOR
RUNABOUT LANDING PAD
SENSOR ARRAY AND SUBSPACE ANTENNAS
UPPER DOCKING PYLON

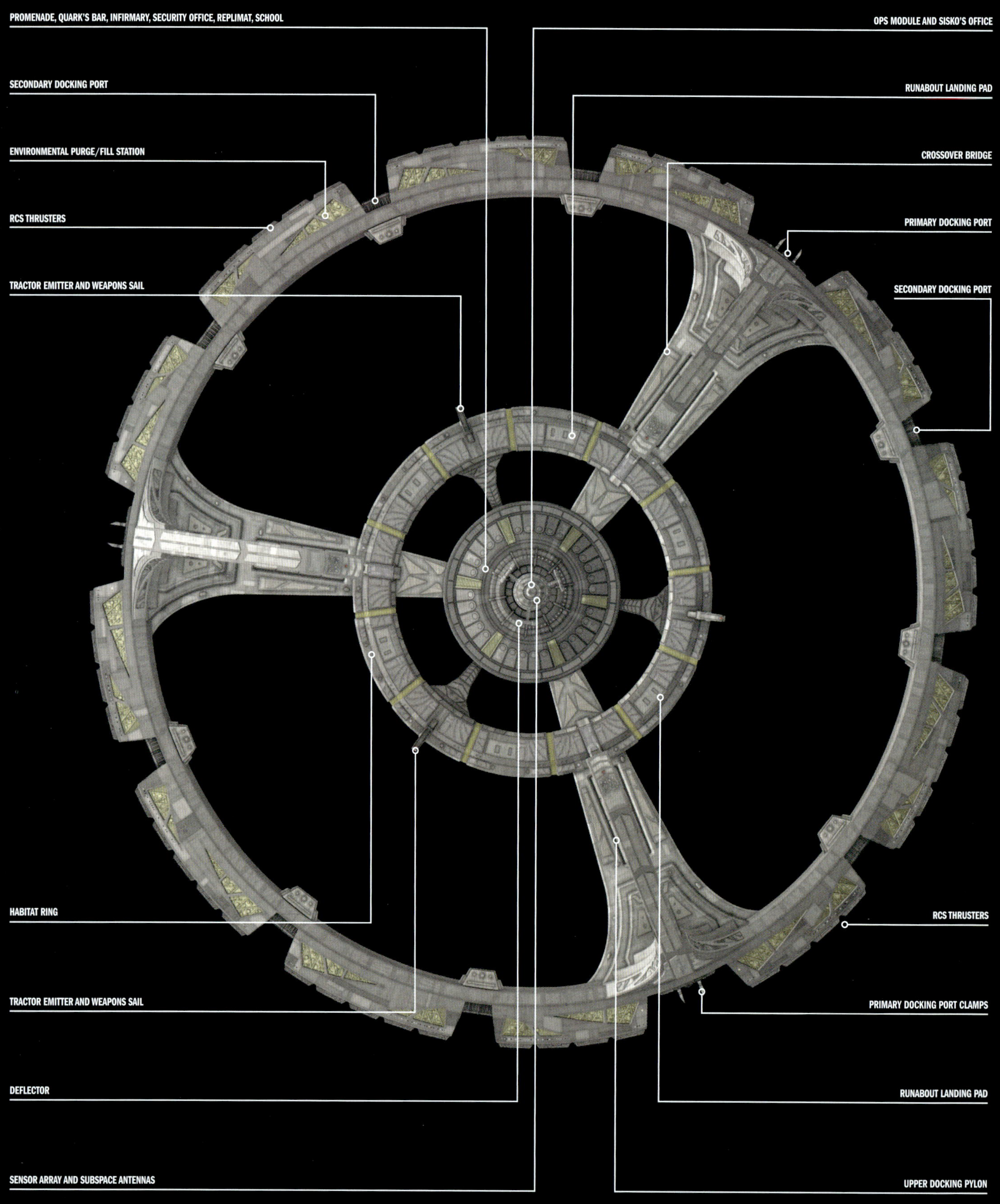

VENTRAL VIEW

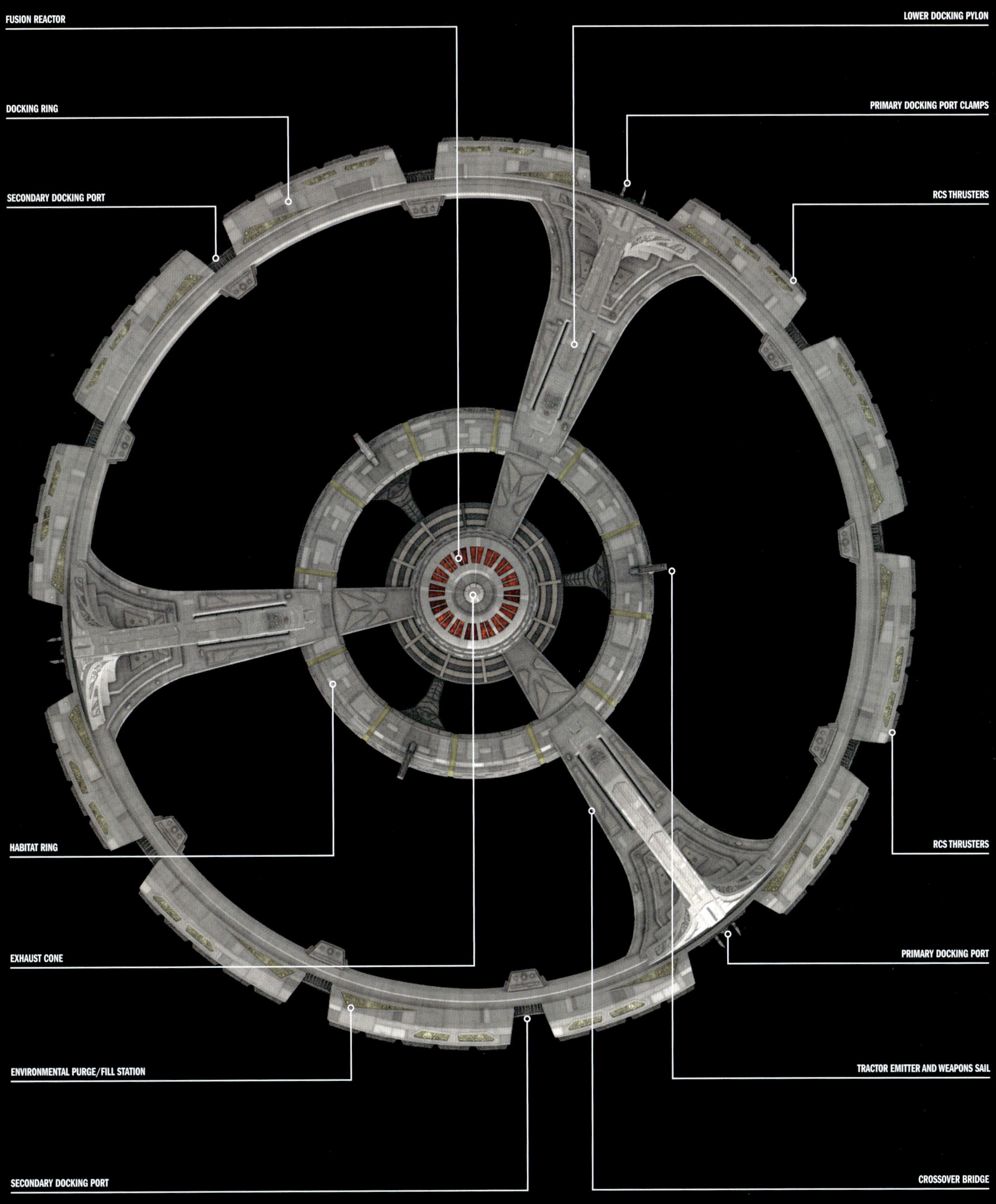

THE BAJORAN WORMHOLE

The first known stable wormhole in the galaxy was discovered on Stardate 46397.1 by officers stationed on Deep Space 9. In the years that followed, it shaped the fortunes of the space station and the entire Alpha Quadrant.

In quantum theory, a wormhole is a subspace tunnel that directly links two points in normal spacetime that would otherwise be further (potentially much further) apart. By the late 23th century, Federation scientists accepted that wormholes not only occurred naturally across the galaxy, but also that they could sometimes be artificially created by improperly balanced warp drive systems. In both cases, however, it was understood that wormholes always existed in a constant state of flux, with their entry and exit points frequently relocating in time, space, or both. As such, they presented rich opportunities for research, but no practical application as shortcuts for interstellar travel – given that neither the intended destination nor the likelihood of a route back could ever be guaranteed.

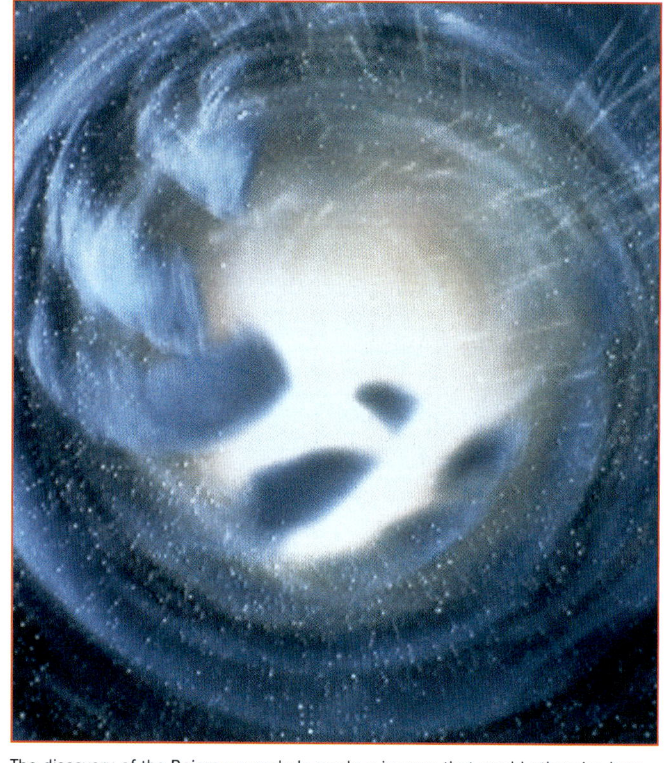

The discovery of the Bajoran wormhole made a journey that would otherwise have taken almost 70 years at maximum warp achievable in just a few brief moments.

HISTORIC DISCOVERY

This all changed in 2369, with the discovery of the first known stable wormhole by the Starfleet officers Lieutenant Jadzia Dax and Commander Benjamin Sisko. Boasting fixed points at both ends, the Bajoran wormhole had one entry/exit in the Denorios belt – around 160 million kilometers from Bajor in the Alpha Quadrant – and another 70,000 light years away in the Gamma Quadrant. Traveling between the two points via the wormhole took just a matter of moments.

Despite its stable nature, the wormhole had never been recorded before 2369, because of its distance from standard flight routes. At least two Bajoran ships did encounter the phenomenon in the 22nd century, but one registered it only as a hazard to be avoided, while the other was lost inside it until 2372. Other unexplained events in the region over the centuries were ascribed by the Bajorans to their gods, who were known as the Prophets. In fact, the Bajorans' religious beliefs were remarkably close to the truth. Data from the wormhole suggested that it was created artificially, and its creators were most likely the incorporeal beings whom Sisko encountered inside it.

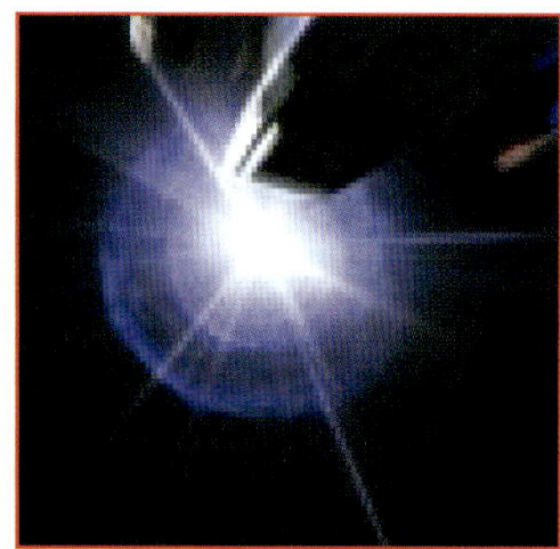

When a ship approached, the wormhole burst open, growing from a single point of light to a swirling mouth-like vortex.

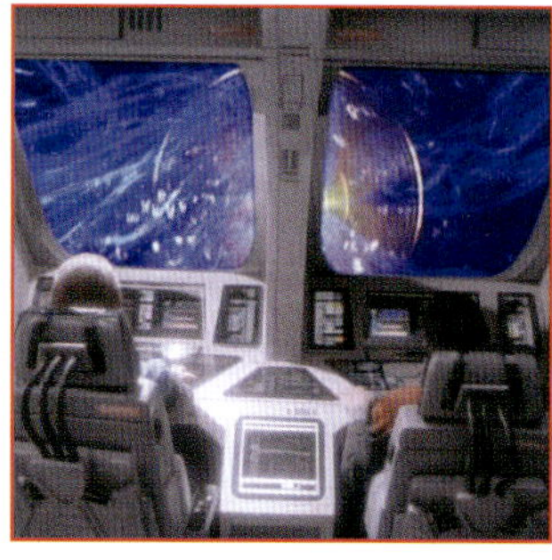

Dax and Sisko's first, unscheduled trip through the phenomenon was a bumpy ride, but future journeys were smoother.

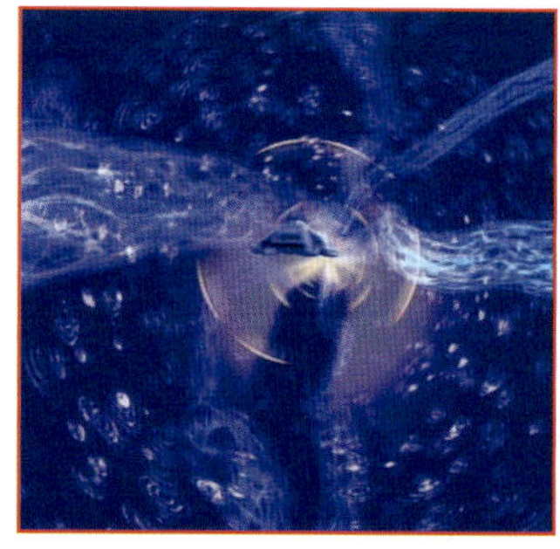

The wormhole's interior existed beyond normal space, allowing it to encompass any size of ship – or even entire fleets.

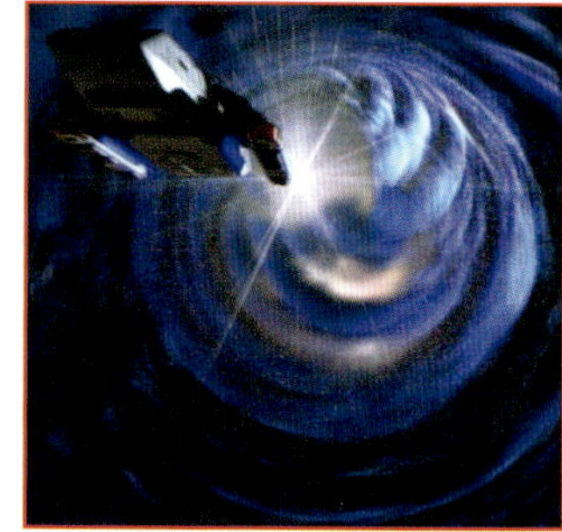

On exiting the wormhole, ships emerged from the same visually stunning space-time disturbance witnessed upon entry.

This powerful species was known to Starfleet as the wormhole aliens, but to religious Bajorans they were the Prophets themselves, and the wormhole their Celestial Temple. In time, it was proved that the beings had indeed been guiding Bajor's path for millennia – using methods that could easily be mistaken for divine intervention.

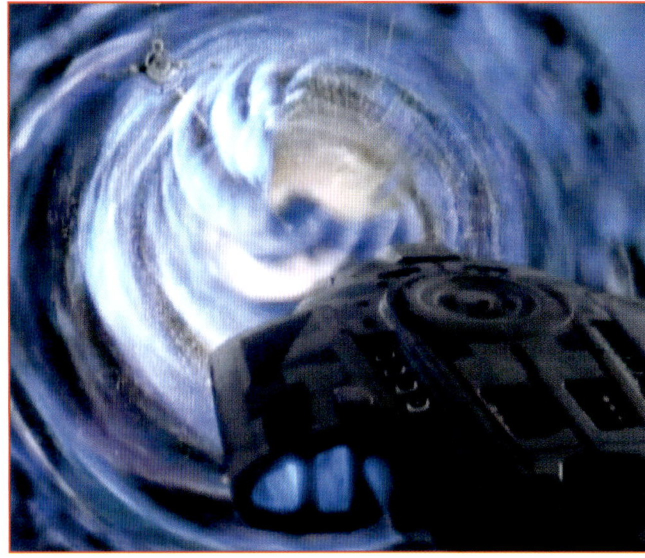
Cardassian scientists and crew on the *U.S.S. Defiant* observed that the theta-band carrier wave from an experimental relay station destabilized the wormhole in 2371.

PHYSICAL CHARACTERISTICS

The functioning of the wormhole relied on stable verteron particles, which are self-sustaining in nature. Therefore, it exhibited none of the usual quantum fluctuations found in the vicinity of a naturally occurring wormhole. The verteron particles enabled a ship to travel through the phenomenon at impulse power, but not at warp speeds, which would, in theory, have disastrous consequences for the speeding ship – and potentially for the wormhole itself.

At "rest," the wormhole was invisible to the naked eye. If not known, its precise location could be found by scanning the area for neutrino disturbances and high proton levels. When a ship did traverse the exact coordinates in either the Alpha or Gamma Quadrants, the wormhole would manifest briefly in that location as a turbulent, cloudlike vortex with a glowing center. Once the ship was inside, the mouth of the wormhole would close up again, as if having swallowed the ship.

Inside the wormhole, ribbons of light flowed across and around the passing ship, carrying it on a subspace current toward its inexorable destination. On returning to normal space, an equivalent vortex would appear to disgorge the ship on the other side of the galaxy.

COMMUNICATIONS

Until 2371, there was no way to send subspace messages through the wormhole, as the conduit was only activated by the presence of physical vessels. Deep Space 9's chief of operations, Miles O'Brien, had experimented with soliton pulses sent between the station and a relay station placed in the Gamma Quadrant, but without success. Cardassian scientists then proposed a similar project using a more precise kind of transceiver coil, only for tests to create a brief but dangerous subspace inversion.

It was only when fragments from a stray comet passed through the wormhole, leaving a trace amount of silithium behind, that communications were finally established, using the Cardassian technology. The silithium served to create a subspace filament along the wormhole's length just sufficient to carry messages between the Alpha and Gamma Quadrants, without affecting the transit of vessels through the conduit. This link was only severed when the wormhole itself briefly disappeared in late 2374.

OUT OF THE UNKNOWN

When Deep Space 9 was relocated to the Denorios belt, it became the first port of call for Gamma Quadrant species traveling through the wormhole. The station's first visitors from across the Galaxy were Tosk and the hunters chasing him. Soon after, a delegation from the Wadi was the first to be formally received.

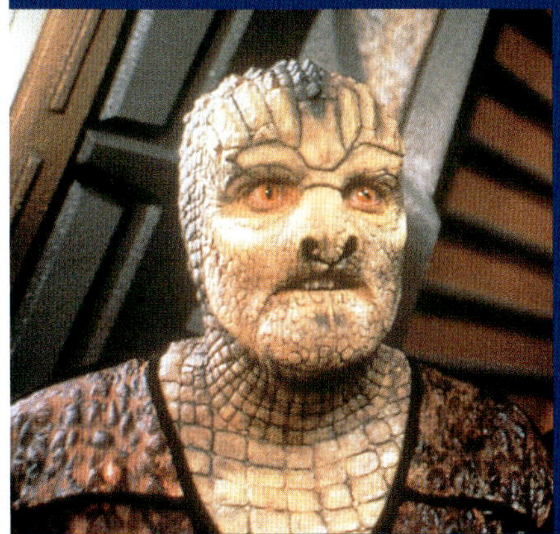
Tosk was the willing prey in a ruthless hunt, bound by rules that prevented him from explaining this.

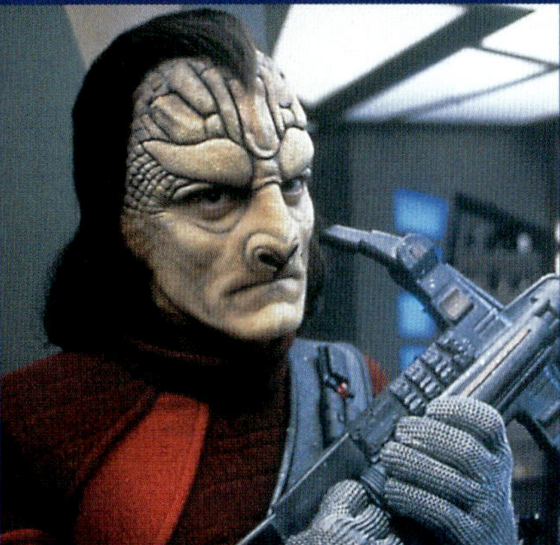
Tosk's pursuers were natives of his own planet. Chief O'Brien helped Tosk flee DS9 to keep the hunt going.

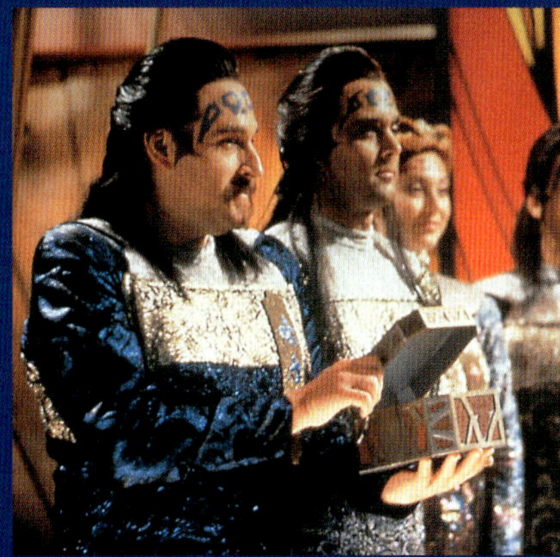
The Wadi's love of immersive games caused chaos when they visited the station.

FUSION POWER GENERATION

Deep Space 9 relied on a 790-terawatt nuclear fusion reactor in its lower core to power all station systems. Immediately above this were the robust deuterium storage tanks that fueled the reactor chambers.

The nuclear fusion reactor that powered all systems on Deep Space 9 was fueled by deuterium. An essential power source for many starships and starbases, this unusual isotope of hydrogen could not be replicated, but could be generated by a process called electrocentrifugal fractioning. When fused into heavier helium nuclei inside the reactor, it released energy in the same way as a star.

STORAGE TANKS

On Deep Space 9, the deuterium stocks were held in six storage tanks with a total capacity of 76,000m^3, located on level 30 in the lower core. These were supported by six smaller surge tanks on level 32. Both tank types were made from alternating layers of spin-cast anodium arkenide and plasma-expanded polysilica boronite insulating foam, with walls up to 3.61cm thick. The deuterium in the tanks was kept deep-frozen until needed, at which point it was warmed until it became a thick, slow-moving liquid known as slush deuterium. It was then fed through conduits that shaped the isotope into pellets before it was introduced to the power-generation chambers.

REACTION CHAMBERS

Found beneath the storage tanks at the lower core base, the six fusion chambers that made up the nuclear reactor were made from an extremely durable, gamma-welded rodinium pentacarbide alloy. When the deuterium pellets were fed into the reactor, they were bombarded by lasers in order to accelerate their nuclei and initiate the fusion reaction. The resulting plasma explosions were contained within the chambers, before being channeled into the first stage of the station's power-distribution EPS network.

At full power, the reactor could generate an impressive 790 terawatts of energy. However, two of the six chambers did not conform to Starfleet safety tolerances, and so the station operated at just two-thirds of its maximum capacity from 2369 onwards. This was more than sufficient, given that it no longer operated as an ore-processing center. Nevertheless, Starfleet also installed auxiliary generators to supplement the core's reduced output.

SAFETY SYSTEMS

The generator core also housed vital cooling and safety systems. These included: a series of heat-dissipation sinks along the lowest face of the core, to vent excess heat into space; and a conical emergency vent system below this, to eject superheated plasma from the fusion chambers and deuterium from the feeder system in the event of an overload. In standard operation, the flow of deuterium was controlled by the station's computer core and monitored at the engineering station in ops – from where computer control could also be overridden.

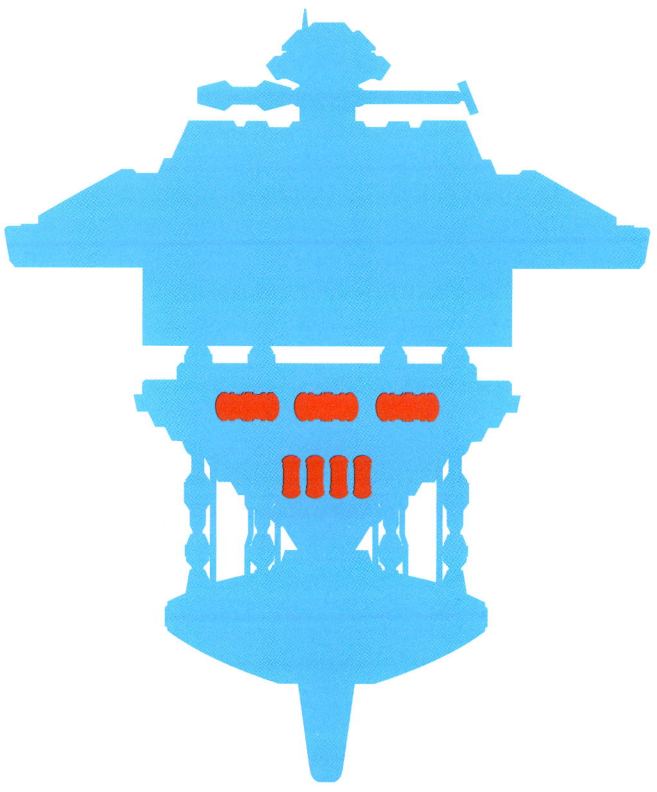

The main deuterium storage tanks formed a horizontal ring around the center of the station. The smaller surge tanks were aligned vertically two levels further down.

INSPECTION SCHEDULE

The potential for failures within the deuterium storage and distribution system posed one of the biggest threats to the station. Starfleet protocols required that each of the main storage tanks – and all pumps and conduits leading to and from them – be inspected for degraded insulation, microfractures, and other signs of wear every 3,400 hours on a rotating schedule. As the secondary surge tanks were used less intensively, these were inspected only once every 6,400 hours.

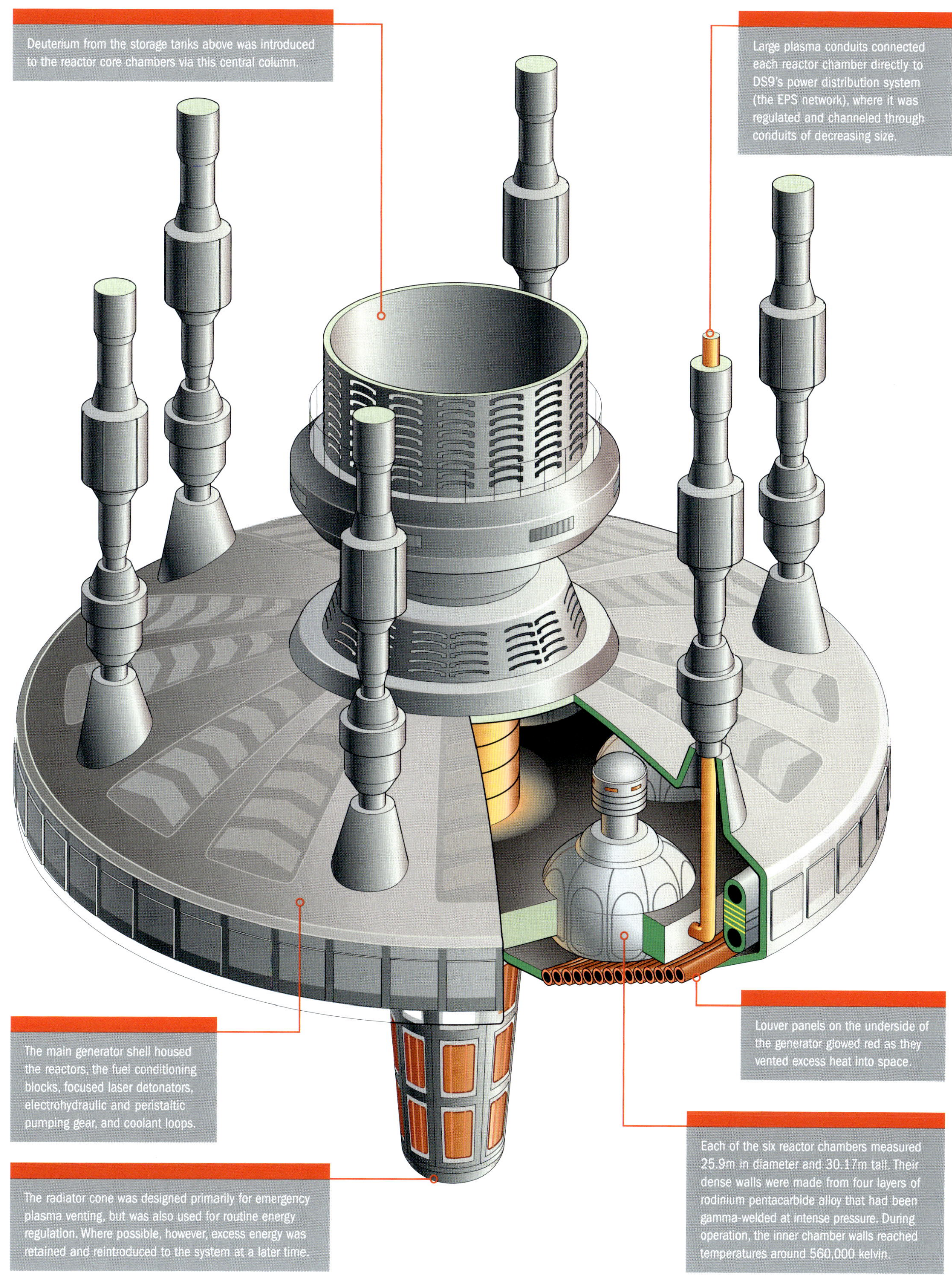
Deuterium from the storage tanks above was introduced to the reactor core chambers via this central column.
Large plasma conduits connected each reactor chamber directly to DS9's power distribution system (the EPS network), where it was regulated and channeled through conduits of decreasing size.
The main generator shell housed the reactors, the fuel conditioning blocks, focused laser detonators, electrohydraulic and peristaltic pumping gear, and coolant loops.
Louver panels on the underside of the generator glowed red as they vented excess heat into space.
The radiator cone was designed primarily for emergency plasma venting, but was also used for routine energy regulation. Where possible, however, excess energy was retained and reintroduced to the system at a later time.
Each of the six reactor chambers measured 25.9m in diameter and 30.17m tall. Their dense walls were made from four layers of rodinium pentacarbide alloy that had been gamma-welded at intense pressure. During operation, the inner chamber walls reached temperatures around 560,000 kelvin.

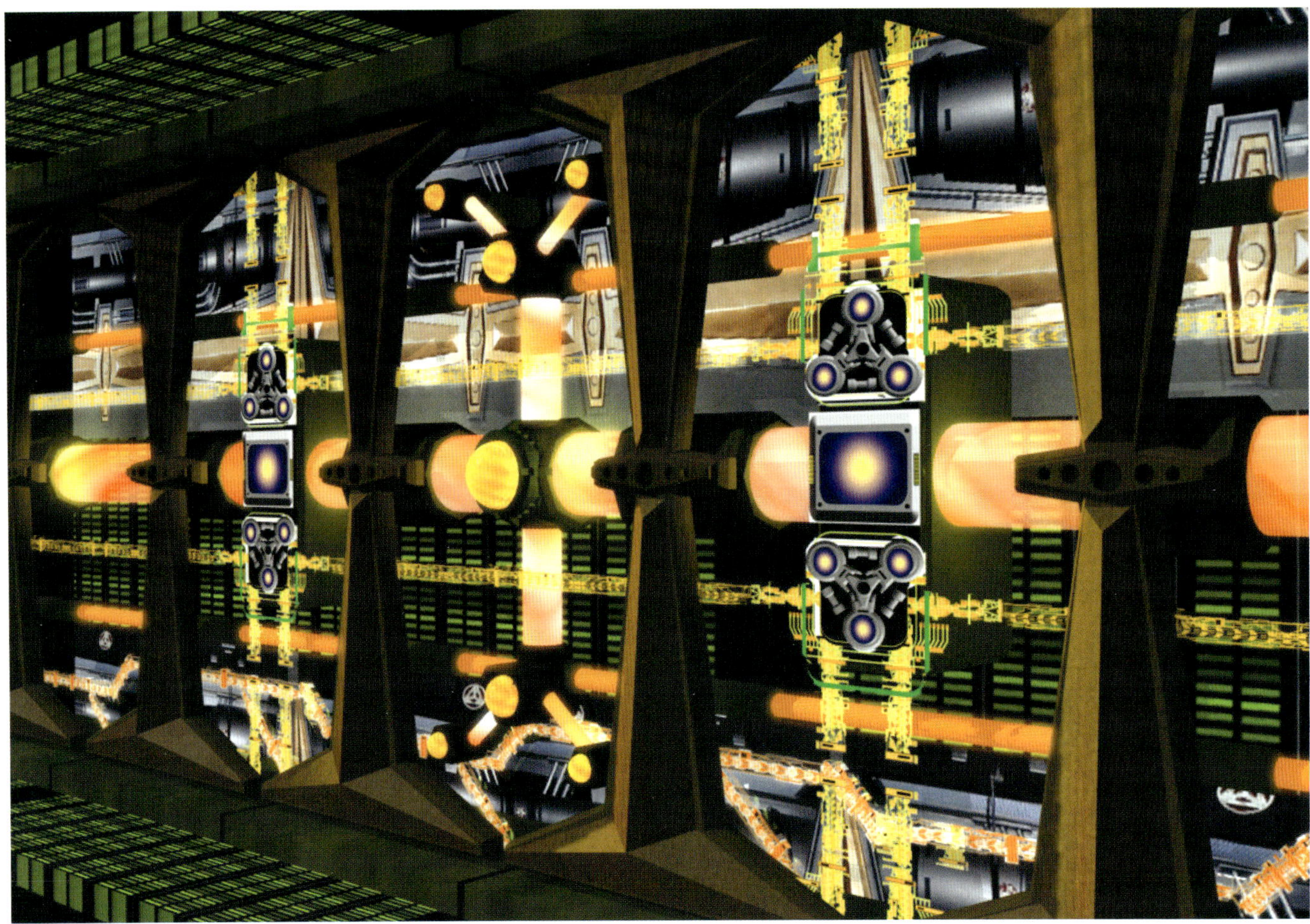

THE EPS NETWORK

A complex maze of conduits carried plasma around Deep Space 9, powering everything from the shields to the Promenade shops. The Cardassians knew it as the ion-energy network, but to Starfleet it was the electroplasma system.

The super-heated plasma from the fusion reactor that powered Deep Space 9 was distributed throughout the station by the electroplasma system, known as the EPS network. Built by the Cardassians as part of Terok Nor's original specification, the network was too deeply integrated to be replaced by Federation technology after the Cardassians abandoned the station, and so it was simply augmented to make it compatible with Starfleet equipment and safety standards.

FIVE-STAGE SYSTEM

The network comprised 651 stepped-energy EPS conduits, which reduced the plasma flow and temperature in five stages to provide different systems with the appropriate levels of power. The first- and second-stage conduits were the largest, and served as trunk routes throughout the station and were made of toranium duranite. The third-stage conduits carried power to the weapons and shields; the fourth stage was for systems with medium to heavy power requirements; and the fifth fed everyday equipment, such as internal lighting and replicators.

STAGE BY STAGE

Each of the six first-stage conduits measured more than one kilometer long and 1.89 meters across. They were fed directly from the six fusion reaction chambers, with five plasma-flow constrictors in each conduit equalizing the reactor's energy surges into a steady stream of plasma

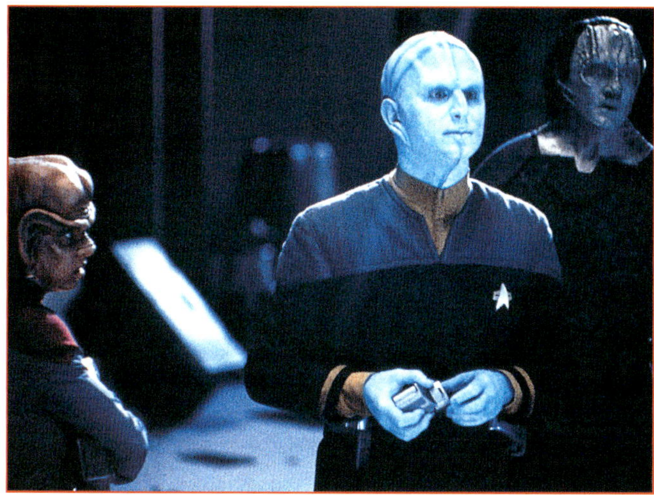

Chief O'Brien's salvage team on Empok Nor included Starfleet's first Ferengi cadet, Nog, the ill-fated Bolian Boq'ta, and Deep Space 9's resident Cardassian, Garak.

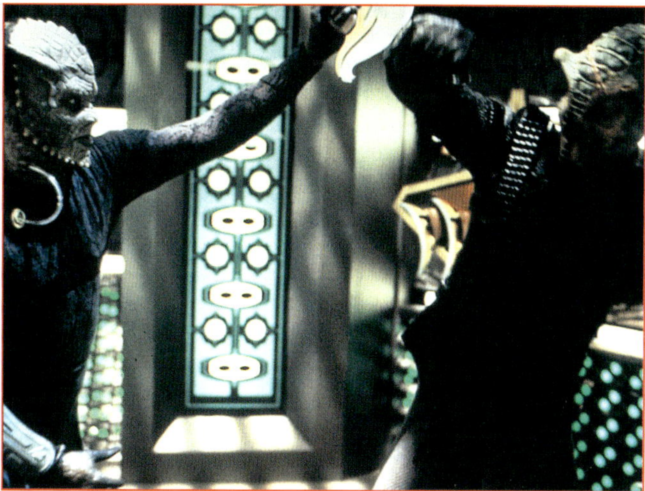

The holosuites above Quark's bar were the only civilian equipment on the station to require more energy than the low-powered, fifth-stage EPS conduits provided.

with a consistent temperature. They were also interlinked, so that power could be transferred between them according to demand across the network.

The six second-stage conduits were much smaller, at just over 85m long and a meter across. These routed power from the first-stage conduits up into the station's lower core. They were reinforced against sabotage, and were spread out, with built-in redundancies, for the same reason. They fed into the third-stage conduits, which comprised 18 larger branches running through the lower core and midcore, and 27 smaller branches carrying cooler, lower-pressure plasma to the upper core, the habitat ring, and the docking ring. Of the large branches, half extended out to the weapons and shield generators, and half powered ore-processing systems in the docking plyons. Collectively, this stage of the network was known as the multiuse pregrid.

All 162 of the fourth-stage conduits ran off the multiuse pregrid, and most ended in multiphase, alternating-current taps that were used for industrial equipment. Fifth-stage conduits also flowed from the pregrid, providing the lowest level of power for use in residential quarters, laboratories, cargo bays, and shops. By this stage in the process, the temperature of the plasma in the system was reduced to 8,192 kelvin, from an initial temperature of more than 200,000 kelvin in the first-stage conduits.

MAINTAINING THE NETWORK

The EPS network relied on Cardassian plasma-distribution manifolds with beta-matrix compositors that could not be replicated. When one of these parts failed in 2373, Chief O'Brien led a dangerous mission to gather spares from the abandoned Cardassian station Empok Nor.

Soon after this, Captain Sisko ordered the sabotage of all nonessential power systems on Deep Space 9, before surrendering the station to the Dominion. Repairs carried out by the Cardassians immediately thereafter returned the EPS network to its original specifications, and when Starfleet regained control of the station some months later, all safety and compatibility upgrades had to be reinstalled.

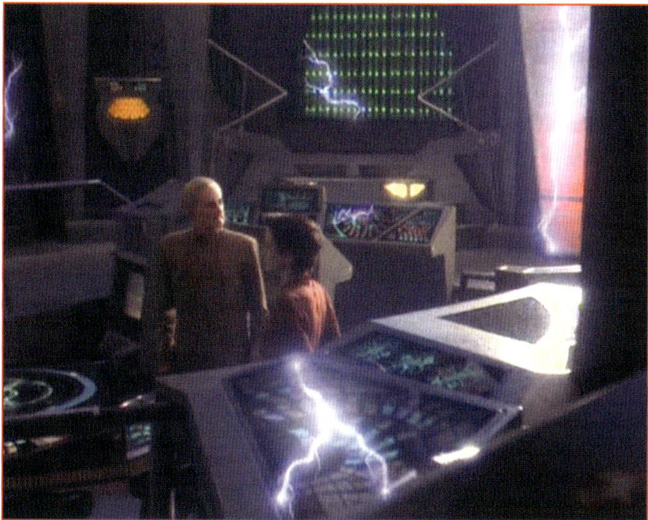

Major Kira activated Sisko's sabotage program in ops as she and Odo awaited the arrival of the Dominion, following Starfleet's tactical withdrawal in late 2373.

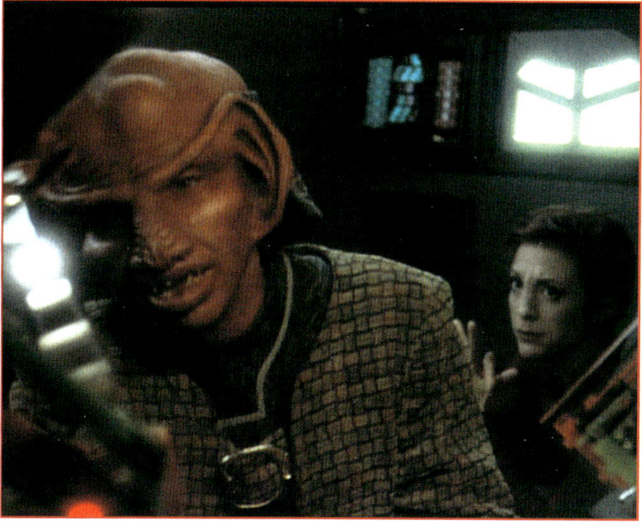

When Starfleet set out to reclaim Deep Space 9 from the Dominion in 2374, Rom deactivated its weapons by accessing one of the second-stage EPS conduits.

THE RCS THRUSTERS

Unlike a starship, Deep Space 9 had no need for impulse or warp engines. Instead, it relied on 54 lower-powered thrusters to maintain and adjust its position in space.

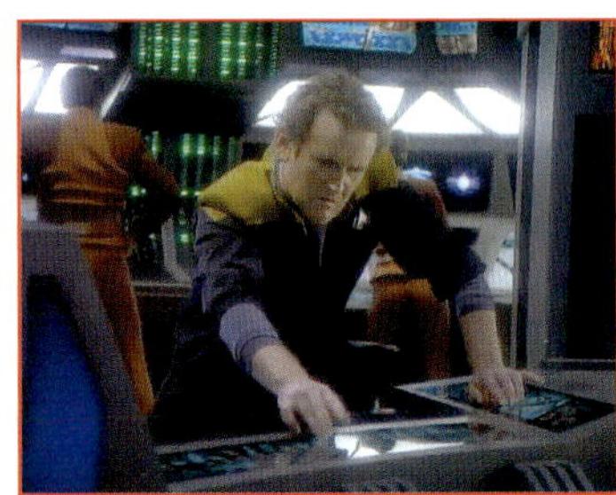
Chief O'Brien assumed manual control over the thrusters and inertial dampers when he was tasked with moving the station in 2369.

In its original incarnation as an ore-processing station, Deep Space 9 maintained a synchronous orbit around Bajor, using thrusters located around the perimeter of the docking ring. The Cardassians referred to this as the axial vector stabilization system, but in Starfleet parlance it was a reaction control system, or RCS.

STANDARD OPERATION

The RCS thruster network was made up of 54 protean-cycle fusion units similar to those used for station-keeping and low-velocity maneuvers on Federation starships. Each unit had its own fuel manifold assembly, ignition chamber and accelerator, exhaust director, and exhaust vents. Together, they were powered by slush deuterium that was channeled to the manifold assemblies from the station core through anti-backflow transfer pipes. This fuel was then pumped into the center of the ignition chambers via micronozzles, where fusion was controlled by annular positron beams. Finally, the resulting energy release was expelled through the exhaust vents to generate thrust. Each RCS unit had six independent exhaust vents for maximum vector control.

This process was sufficient to keep the station in a stable orbit above Bajor – with a constant velocity and altitude – for the first 23 years of its service life. Though the power of the system could be boosted, there was no need to do so. Any excess energy created by the deuterium fusion process was automatically recycled within the system and used for fuel pumping, positron beam generation, and the like. And though the system was monitored from ops, it was wholly computer-controlled, with only maintenance and repairs requiring the intervention of Cardassian engineers.

RELOCATING THE STATION

This state of affairs changed entirely in 2369, soon after the Cardassians had withdrawn from Bajoran space. The discovery of a stable wormhole to the Gamma Quadrant in the Denorios belt, just 160 million kilometers from Bajor, made the region a prime target for Cardassian exploitation once again. With the station now under joint Starfleet and Bajoran control, its second-in-command, Major Kira Nerys, ordered a rapid relocation to the Denorios belt to secure free and fair access to the phenomenon.

SUBSPACE FIELD GENERATION

Moving Deep Space 9 from Bajor to the mouth of the wormhole was made more challenging by the fact that, when Starfleet came aboard the station, just six of its 54 RCS thrusters were fully operational. A subspace field around the station reduced its inertial mass, enabling it to move at speed despite this reduced power.

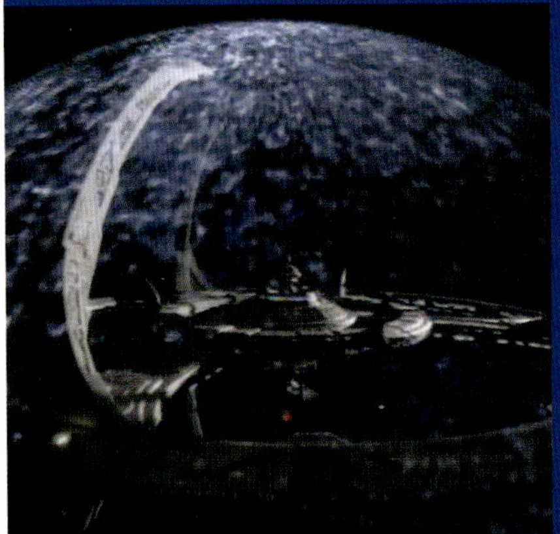
A partial subspace field around DS9 was enough to break orbit, but risked the station's structural integrity.

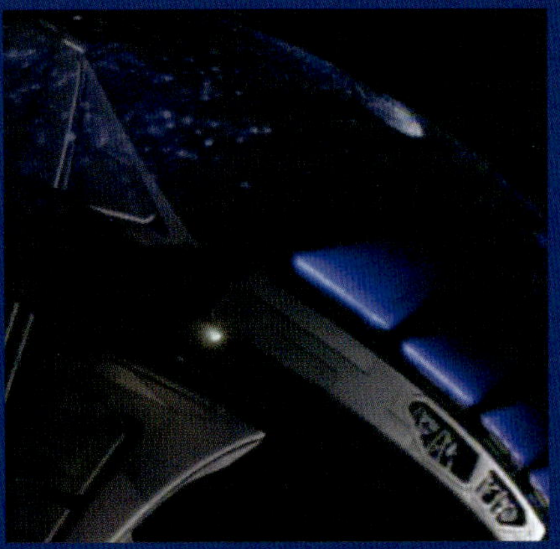
When the thrusters fired, the field started to collapse – leaving seconds before it would be torn apart.

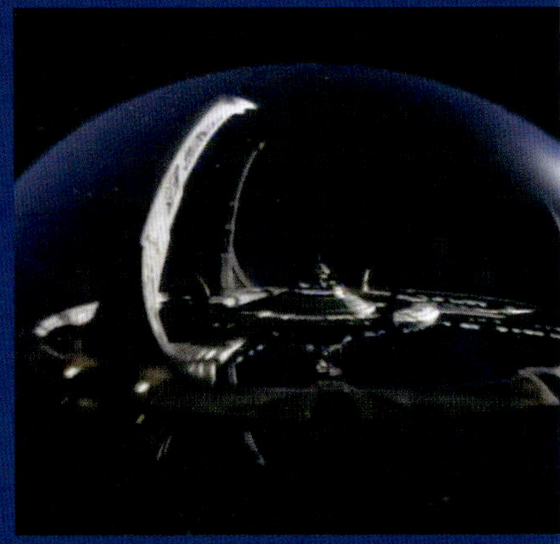
Manual transfer of power from the inertial dampers brought the field stability within flight tolerances.

DOCKING RING CUTAWAY

A cutaway view of the docking ring reveals the inner workings of an RCS unit. Ignition chambers were located behind the exhausts, which glowed blue when working at full power. A spherical fuel manifold assembly was positioned in between each pair of ignition chambers, completing each single fusion unit.

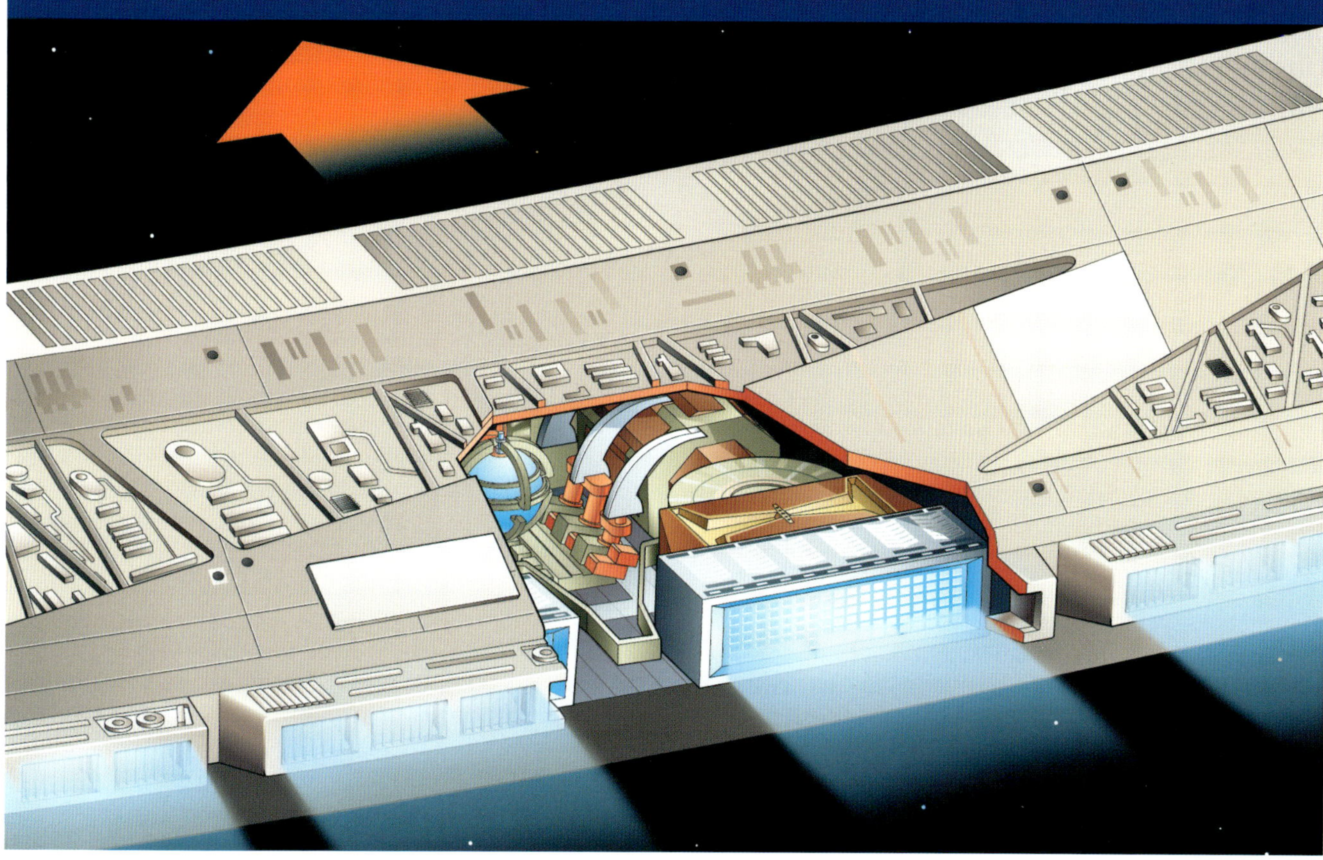

As the station was not designed for such a journey – let alone at speed – using the orbital facility to stake a claim to the wormhole seemed impossible. At full power, it should have taken at least two Earth months to make the journey using the RCS thrusters alone. Not only did the units lack the kind of high-speed accelerators and driver coils found in equivalent Starfleet technology, but also the sheer mass of the station's superstructure made breaking out of orbit a significant challenge in itself.

The solution to all of this was devised by the station's new science officer, Lieutenant Jadzia Dax. She proposed modifying the defensive shield generators to emit a low-level subspace field around the station, thereby reducing its inertial mass in normal space. With less mass to push, the unmodified EPS thrusters could, in theory, accomplish the entire journey in less than one Bajoran day. Chief of operations Miles O'Brien oversaw the modifications, and made additional corrections *en route* to stop the station from breaking apart under stress. Despite having to fight against the unfamiliar Cardassian computer system, he managed to transfer energy from the inertial dampers to the rapidly degrading subspace field, and the mission was a success. Thereafter, the RCS thruster network served to maintain the station's position relative to the wormhole.

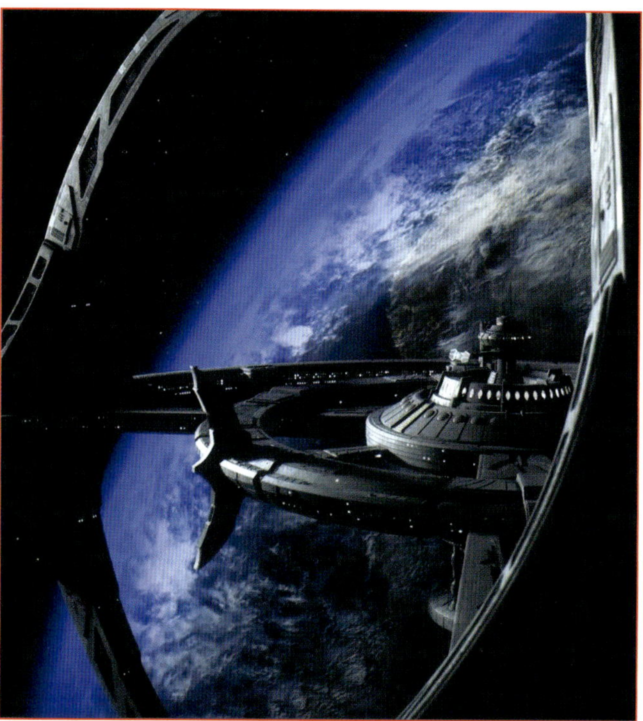

The newly-completed Terok Nor in orbit of Bajor in 2346: RCS thrusters maintained its synchronous orbit, with the central core aligned parallel with Bajor's polar axis.

TACTICAL SYSTEMS

Under Starfleet supervision, Deep Space 9 was transformed from sitting duck to battle station, complete with rotary cannons and torpedo launchers to spare.

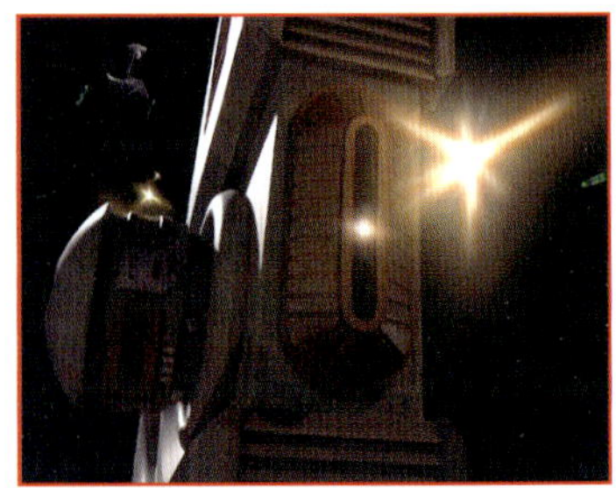
The station's newly enhanced weapons sails were immediately field-tested when Klingon ships attacked in force at the start of 2372.

When the Cardassians pulled out of Bajoran space in 2369, they removed or destroyed most of the weaponry installed on Deep Space 9. As an ore-processing facility above a securely occupied world, the station had limited strategic importance and was never heavily armed. But when the Federation first established a presence there, its ability to defend itself had been reduced to just six photon torpedoes and de-energized phasers, which could be fired just a couple of times using a pulse compression wave.

For the station's first military engagement, its new chief of operations, Miles O'Brien, created a high-energy thoron field and an ingenious arrangement of duranium shadows, first to mask the lack of defenses and then suggest the presence of a vast array of armaments. But such tactics were desperate stopgap measures only, and the discovery of the Bajoran wormhole meant that Deep Space 9 needed to be prepared for all tactical eventualities.

INITIAL UPGRADES

The station's original defenses were three weapons sails, each projecting above and below the habitat ring, for a field of fire covering the entire surrounding area. Each sail was designed to fire photon torpedoes from its tips and phaser blasts from banks located closer to the middle of each sail. The structures also included weapons monitoring rooms for maintenance and manual control over all tactical systems.

Starfleet's first significant upgrade to these sails was to replace the already stripped-out Cardassian phaser system with the same kind of phaser packs found on Federation

RETRACTABLE TORPEDO LAUNCHER AND PHASER PACK

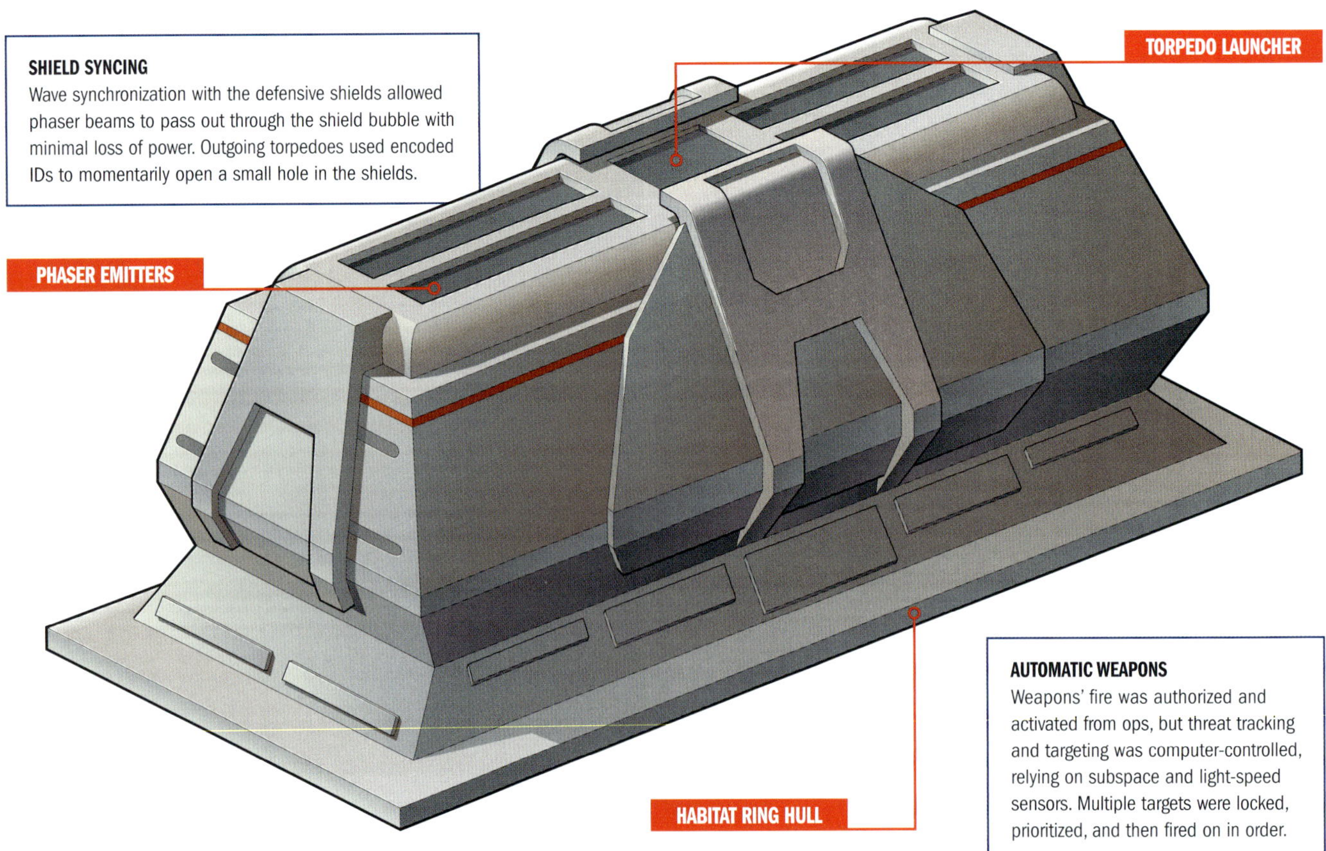

SHIELD SYNCING
Wave synchronization with the defensive shields allowed phaser beams to pass out through the shield bubble with minimal loss of power. Outgoing torpedoes used encoded IDs to momentarily open a small hole in the shields.

AUTOMATIC WEAPONS
Weapons' fire was authorized and activated from ops, but threat tracking and targeting was computer-controlled, relying on subspace and light-speed sensors. Multiple targets were locked, prioritized, and then fired on in order.

RETRACTABLE TORPEDO LAUNCHER

UPPER DOCKING PYLON HULL

TORPEDO LAUNCHER

ELECTROHYDRAULIC RAM

WEAPONS SAIL (UPPER HALF)

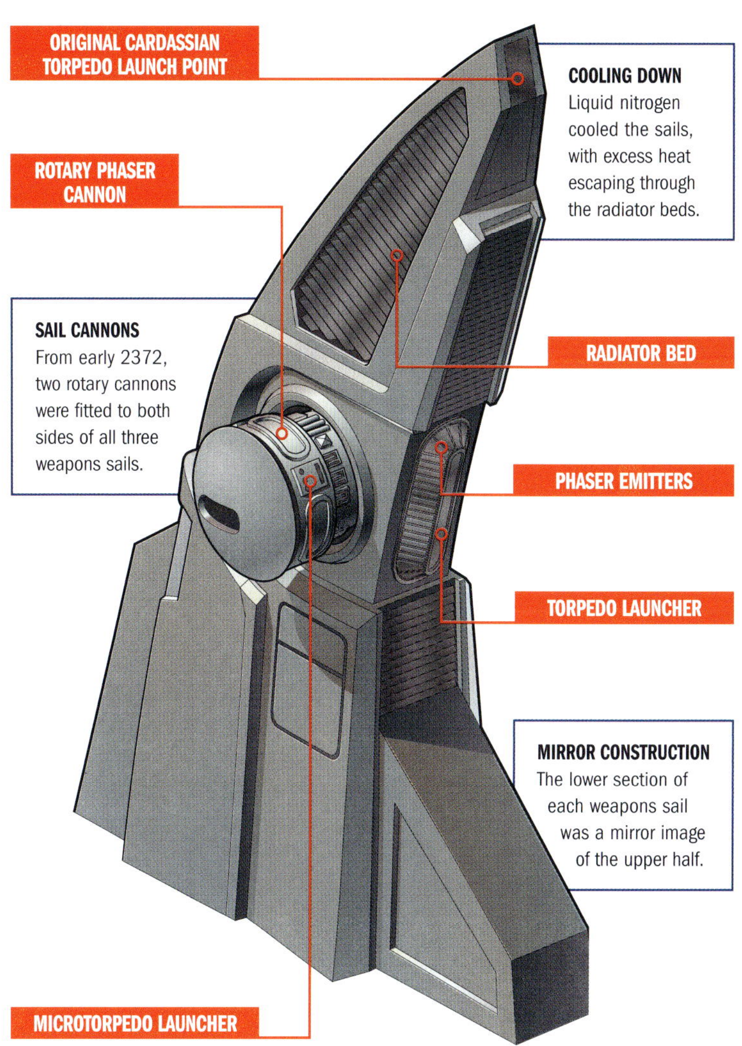

starships. Constructed from duranium, these initial packs were bonded to the rodinium sails in the same location as the original Cardassian emitters. Their operation was far more automated than the systems they replaced, and so the weapons monitoring rooms adjacent to them became redundant and sat empty for some time.

The Starfleet phaser packs also linked to newly installed photon torpedo launchers, fed from the original torpedo magazine by new loader elevators. The magazine was kept fully stocked with Mark IV torpedo casings. Deuterium and anti-deuterium supplies were stored above and below, ready to be loaded into the casings to create an active matter-antimatter warhead. These reactants could be loaded into four casings simultaneously, for volleys of six torpedoes per weapons sail every 2.3 seconds.

PREPARING FOR WAR

By the start of 2372, the Dominion was recognized as the biggest threat to the Alpha Quadrant, with Deep Space 9 in the front line of any Jem'Hadar incursion through the wormhole. Maintenance crews set about further upgrading the station's weapons systems, which actually saw their first deployment against the Klingons at the start of the Dominion-engineered Federation-Klingon War. These new defenses included rotary phaser cannons and microtorpedo launchers built into the space previously occupied by the weapons monitoring rooms, and six additional torpedo launchers at previously unarmed points on the hull.

Unlike the previous upgrades, these new weapons were not mounted directly on the hull exterior, but were more securely integrated within recessed bays, emerging on electrohydraulic rams only when required. Three of the new torpedo launchers were located on the habitat ring, equidistant from the weapons sails and with integrated phaser emitters; and three covered previous close-range blind spots where the docking ring met the docking pylons.

TAKING STOCK

By the end of the Dominion War, Deep Space 9's defenses totaled 48 phaser cannons and 24 torpedo launchers on 12 retractable rotary mounts; 36 phaser emitters and 12 torpedo launchers across six stationary phaser packs and the sail tips; and six retractable weapons platforms. The photon torpedo stocks were augmented by vastly more powerful quantum torpedoes, with the station's entire torpedo complement exceeding 5,000 units.

COUNTERINSURGENCY PROGRAM

The Cardassians' extreme measures to keep Bajoran slaves in line were carefully laid on Terok Nor – and then carelessly forgotten about when the occupiers withdrew from Bajor and the station in 2369.

The Bajorans who lived and worked on Deep Space 9 when it was the ore-processing station Terok Nor were cowed and demoralized by their Cardassian overseers. Nevertheless, station commander Gul Dukat did not rule out the possibility of an organized uprising. As a result, he installed a number of countermeasures on the station, designed to contain and, if necessary, kill any insurgents before they could inspire others to revolt.

The first stage of the counterinsurgency program sealed the relevant section of the station and activated a recorded message from Dukat, promising leniency in exchange for immediate surrender. The program would also notify ops of the emergency, and a security code could be used to end the lockdown before it escalated further.

If no code was entered, the program assumed the station had been overrun, and took control of all systems. Much of the station would be flooded with neurocine gas, while ops was secured by a force field. If breached, a self-destruct sequence began, which could only be stopped by Dukat.

Attempts to tamper with the counterinsurgency program itself would cause an automated disruptor to materialize at the nearest replicator, set to target all non-Cardassians. Unknown to Dukat, his superiors had also added an extra level of security, rescinding his authority if he tried to leave the station, on the assumption that he was deserting.

When the Cardassians abandoned Terok Nor in 2369, they left the counterinsurgency program in place. Two years later its accidental activation almost destroyed the station.

THE ENEMY WITHIN

Dukat's counterinsurgency program was buried deep in the station's computer systems, and left unnamed to evade detection by saboteurs. When Jake Sisko and Chief O'Brien tried to delete the dormant and seemingly innocuous file in 2371, it activated, trapping them in an ore-processing unit, along with Commander Sisko.

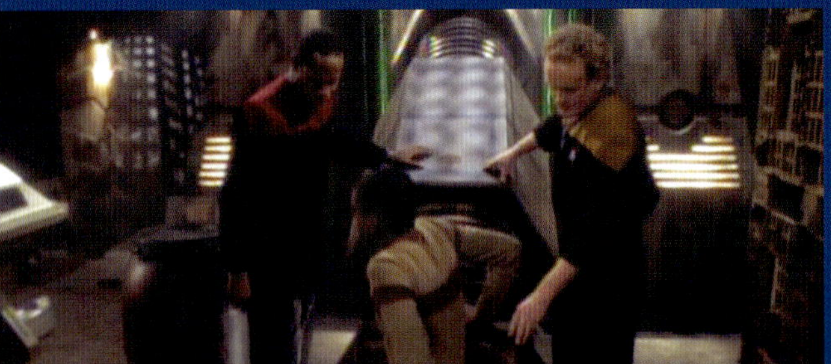

O'Brien and the two Siskos made their escape from ore-processing before it was flooded with gas, but this triggered a far bigger lockdown across the station.

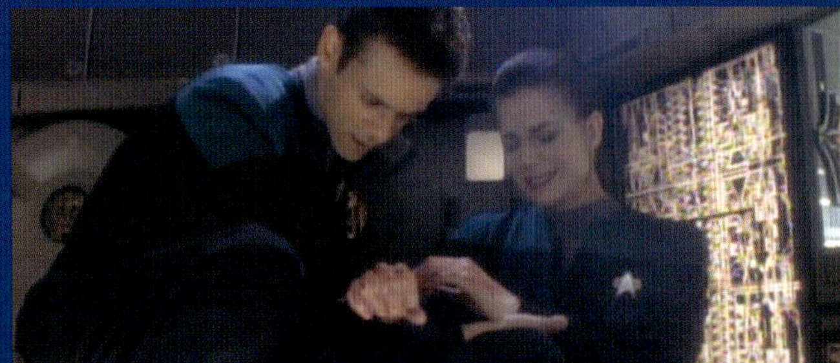

Attempts to regain control of ops saw Lieutenant Commander Dax burned by a newly erected force field, and the next level of countermeasures initiated.

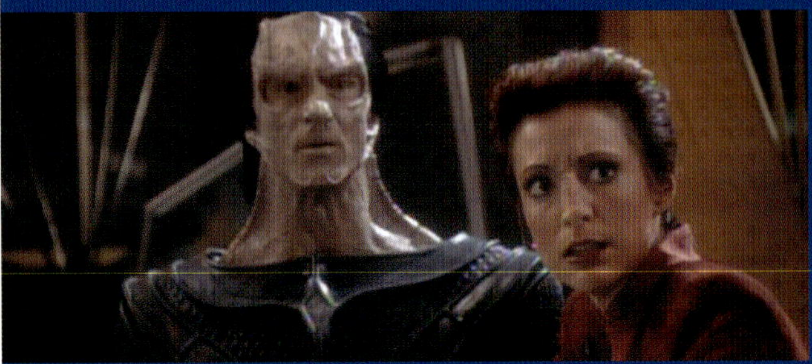

Having received word of the situation, Gul Dukat arrived to offer assistance – for a price. But he also became trapped as the self-destruct system counted down.

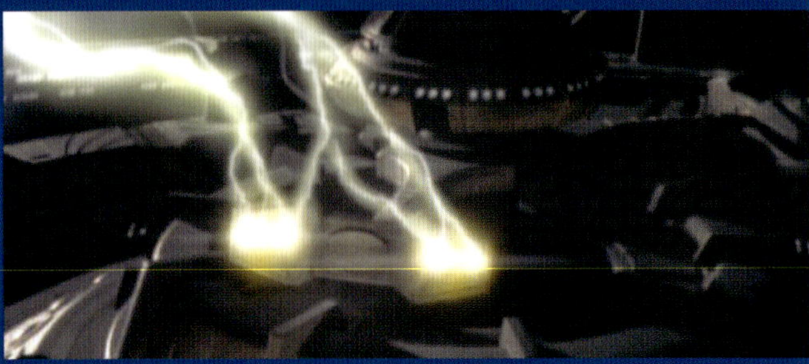

Destruction by fusion-reactor overload was averted only when Commander Sisko diverted the overload power away from the station into the deflector shields.

REPLICATED DISRUPTOR UNIT

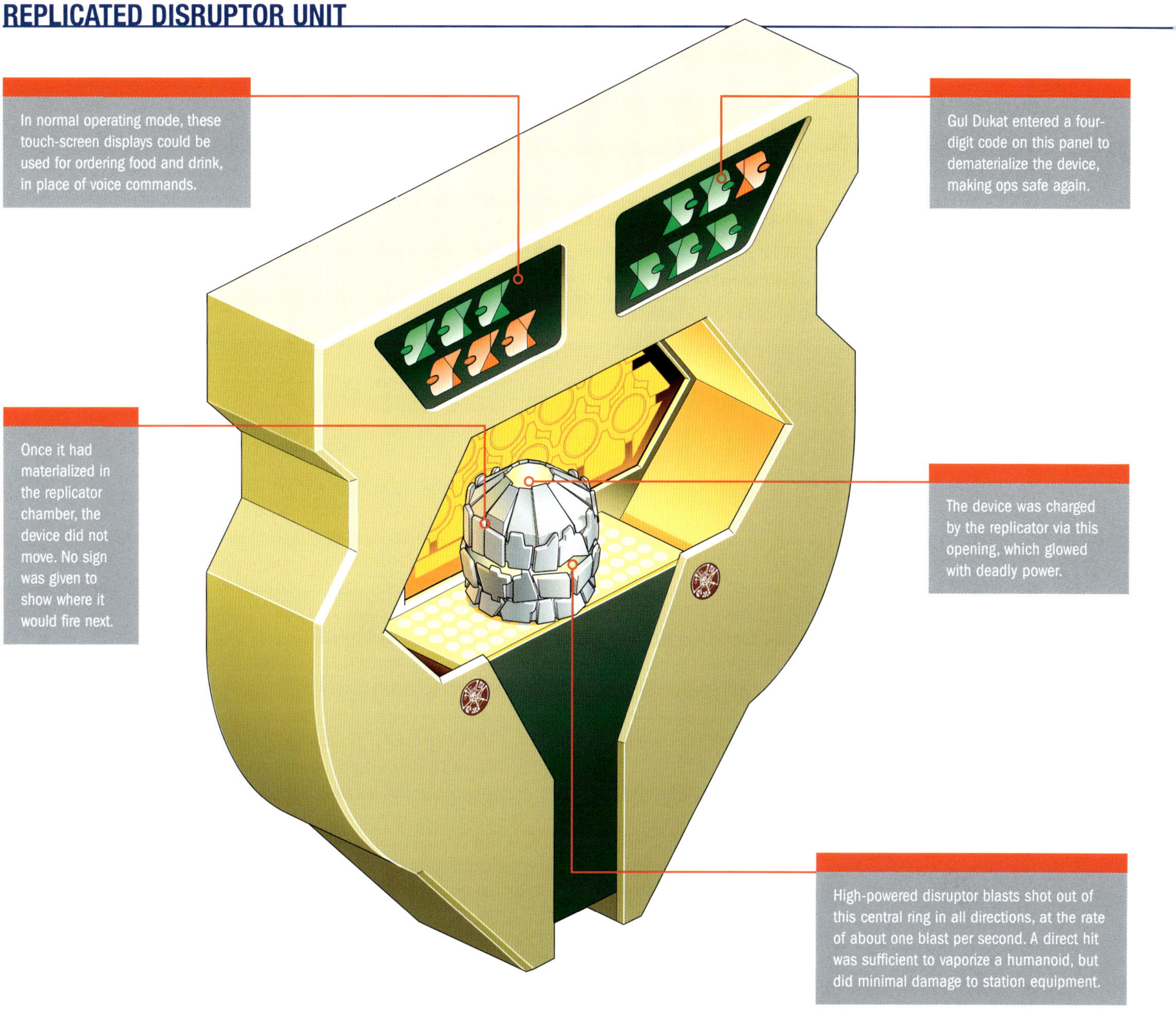

In normal operating mode, these touch-screen displays could be used for ordering food and drink, in place of voice commands.

Gul Dukat entered a four-digit code on this panel to dematerialize the device, making ops safe again.

Once it had materialized in the replicator chamber, the device did not move. No sign was given to show where it would fire next.

The device was charged by the replicator via this opening, which glowed with deadly power.

High-powered disruptor blasts shot out of this central ring in all directions, at the rate of about one blast per second. A direct hit was sufficient to vaporize a humanoid, but did minimal damage to station equipment.

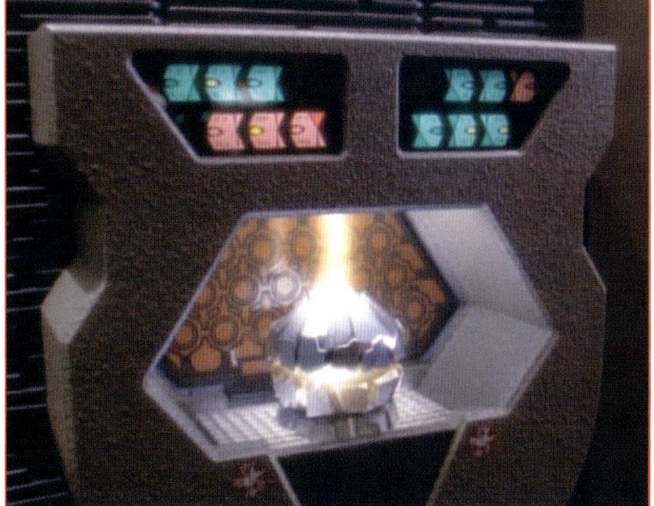

As soon as the replicator had created the automated phaser unit, it used a beam of energy to transfer power to the weapon from the station's EPS network.

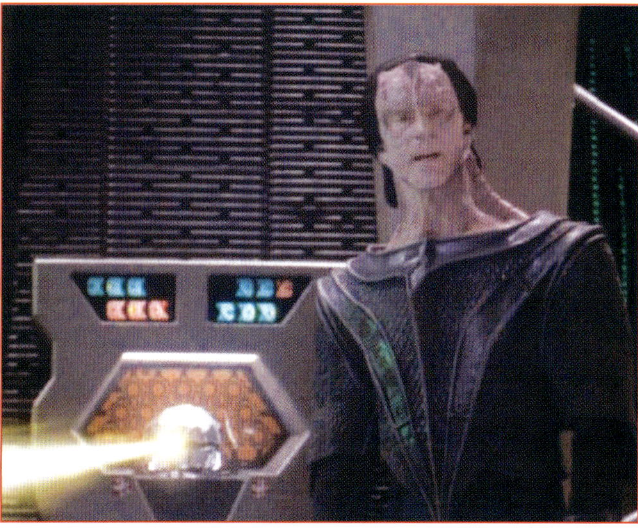

Gul Dukat had no fear of standing with his back to the active weapon, as he knew it was programmed not to target the station's original Cardassian masters.

DEFENSIVE SHIELDS

Deep Space 9 relied on unusual Cardassian technology to protect it from everyday space debris and attack by directed energy weapons and photon torpedoes.

Throughout its service life, Deep Space 9 continued to use the defensive shield network installed by the Cardassians when the station was built in the 2340s. Though similar in principle to the shields used on *Galor*-class warships, the system was unusual in various ways.

GRAVITON EMISSIONS

The shields worked by creating a bubble of gravitational energy around the station to repel everything from space debris to phaser fire and photon torpedoes. Unlike most starship defenses, this effect was achieved by means of three overlapping polarized graviton emissions from highly localized discharge waveguides. When a force or object came into contact with these intersecting emissions, the electromotive power was sufficient to rebound the impact safely away from the station.

The primary source of the gravitron emissions was an array of three shield generators connected to horizontal booms at the top of the station core, just below the ops module. These were supplemented by a series of short-range secondary shield emitters at the station's perimeter, located at regular intervals around the docking ring.

The main generators were powered by nine dedicated EPS conduits with two-thirds redundancy, to ensure shield stability and continuity in the event of mechanical failure or combat damage. The conduits fed directly into beds of regenerative duralumin-gesselium ayanaminide, which produced graviton streams when energized. As standard, this maintained a power output of 450.5 megawatts, but 2,579.3 megawatts could be achieved for short bursts, using nine phase-locked capacitance banks.

POWER DISTRIBUTION

Once the graviton streams had been generated, they were transmitted along waveguides in each of the three emitter booms. When they reached the terminating emitter blocks, the streams were separated into 454 distinct waveguides and routed to a rapid-switching controller. Polarization was completed here, as the the controller determined vectors for each waveguide and directed it to the appropriate part of the shield as a graviton pulse.

The graviton emitters generated an enormous amount of heat, and so each emitter was fitted with four passive thermal-projection radiators and two active liquid sodium

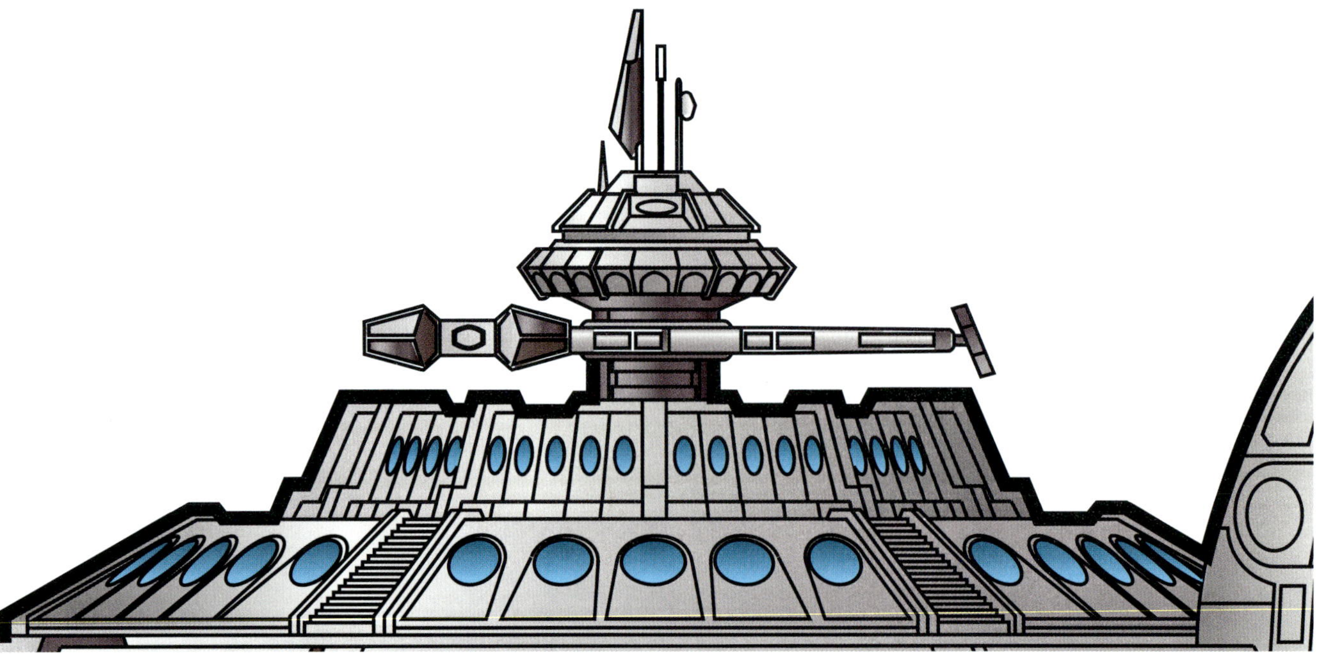

The shield generators and emitters were located in between ops and the Promenade. When the Federation first established a presence on Deep Space 9 in 2369, the shields had been rendered inoperable by the departing Cardassians. The hardware was subsequently repaired rather than replaced, and upgraded with Starfleet control systems.

coolant loops tied to the station's main fusion reactor. In an emergency, these loops could also dissipate excess heat by routing it to the phasers.

IN COMBAT

If one of the station's main shield emitters was damaged or destroyed in battle, the remaining two were sufficient to maintain a complete defensive bubble by redirecting some of their graviton pulses. In the most dire circumstances, a single generator/emitter combination could theoretically protect the station for around a minute at most.

When the shield came under attack from heavy phaser or disruptor fire, its strength would decline over time until it eventually failed altogether. By focusing fire on one area of the shields, an enemy could more easily penetrate the defensive bubble momentarily, but minor breaches were easily sealed by redirecting gravitons around the network.

Assuming a steady supply of EPS energy from the reactor core, draining the shields entirely required more firepower than most attackers possessed. This meant that the only guaranteed ways they could render the shields inoperable were to: destroy the shield generators and emitters; shut down the reactor core; or match their own energy weapons' frequency to the precise harmonics of the shields. All three options were more likely to be achieved by internal sabotage rather than frontal attack, and the latter was specifically guarded against by computer-controlled randomization of the shield harmonics at split-second intervals.

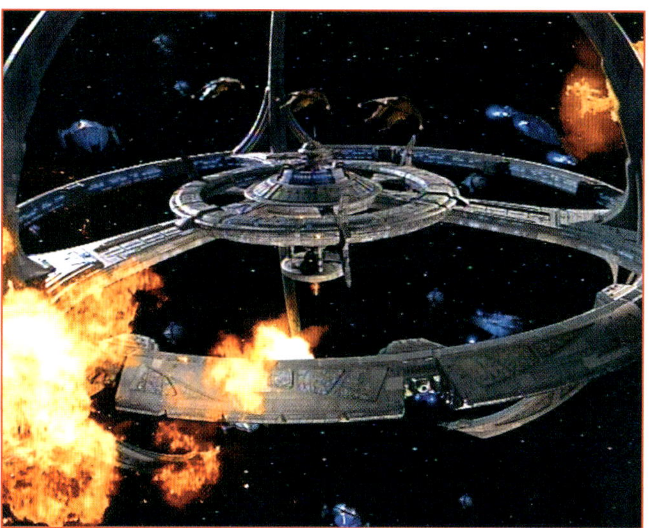

In 2373, a sustained Dominion attack on one section of Deep Space 9's docking ring was enough to disable the main shields and force an evacuation of the station.

SAFE PASSAGE

Conversely, outgoing energy weapons (those fired by the station through the bubble) had to be precisely locked to the ever-changing graviton emission harmonics to stop them from rebounding with disastrous results. Outgoing torpedoes and vessels (such as runabouts) passing through the shields also required uninhibited movement, and so carried identifying transponders with encoded IDs that momentarily opened windows in the defensive bubble.

PROTECTIVE BUBBLE

The defensive bubble was an oblate spheroid that extended far enough beyond the bounds of the station to protect any ships docked at its perimeter or pylons. In standard operation it was invisible to the naked eye, but when placed under significant stress, parts of it could be discerned as a translucent blue energy field.

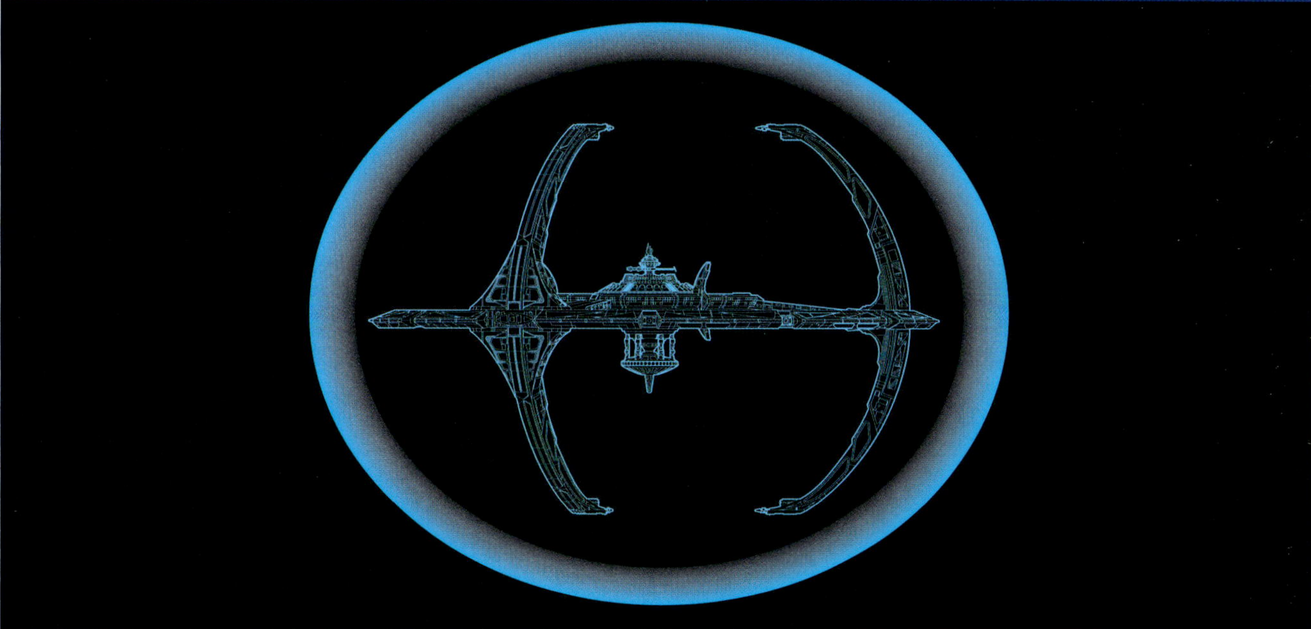

The defensive shields were not kept active at all times, primarily because of the significant demands this would have placed on the station's plasma energy network. But there were also other considerations, such as the fact that long-distance sensor capability was reduced by up to 15 percent when the graviton bubble was operational.

AUTO-DESTRUCT SYSTEMS

In the last resort, Deep Space 9 could be destroyed from within by its own command crew. If the order was given, a series of explosions would vaporize the entire station.

The Cardassians equipped Deep Space 9 with an auto-destruct system when they built it as Terok Nor. Then, when Starfleet and Bajor took control of the station in 2369, a second auto-destruct system was installed, creating a two-stage safeguard against enemy capture. The Cardassian system worked by overloading the station's fusion generator to bring about a huge explosion equivalent to a warp core breach. Starfleet's upgrade added ordnance at key points to ensure that no data or equipment would survive an auto-destruct procedure, no matter how far from the fusion generator.

UNCONTROLLED ENERGY

Overloading the fusion generator was achieved by greatly increasing the flow of deuterium to the reaction chambers and channelling additional electroplasmic energy into the laser-pulse detonators. The lasers would then fuse the extra deuterium, releasing a vast amount of energy. Built-in safety systems would work to contain this reaction, but soon be overwhelmed. Once these containment fields failed, the generator would explode and the shock wave would fuse any remaining deuterium held in reserve. This would not only pull the station apart but also vaporize much of the debris. In theory, the explosive yield would be just short of 12,000 isotons – equivalent to roughly 780 photon torpedoes.

The ordnance added by Starfleet comprised more than 50 matter-antimatter devices located around the station. These were effectively static photon torpedoes, set to go off just after the main fusion reaction. The momentary delay made sure that the shock wave caused by the explosions at the station's perimeter did not counteract the central blast. Starfleet also reconfigured the station's shields to reflect explosive shock waves back toward the superstructure in the event of an auto-destruct activation.

Together, the Cardassian and Starfleet systems were intended to vaporize Deep Space 9 in its entirety. But, if for any reason the fusion reactor could not be overloaded, the additional ordnance was enough to at least break up the structure of the station. By itself, the original system was not without its flaws, and when it was triggered by an old program in 2371, the station's new, non-Cardassian personnel successfully redirected its energy.

COUNTERMEASURES

There were two ways to interfere with the fusion reactor overload. The first was to manually disengage the laser-pulse detonators. In this case, while deuterium would still be fed into the reaction matrix, it would not be fused with the helium atoms in the chambers, meaning no nuclear reaction would occur.

The second approach, as used by station staff in 2371, was to channel the energy released by the reactor overload

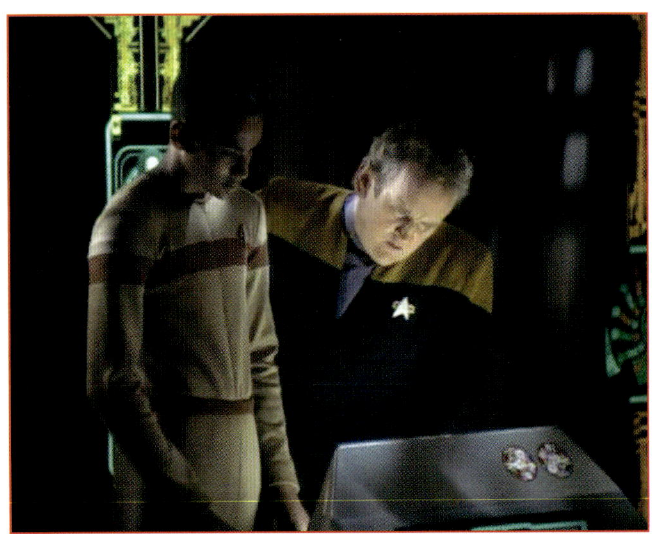

Jake Sisko and Chief O'Brien had to consider their options in 2371, after an outdated Cardassian counterinsurgency program initiated the original auto-destruct system.

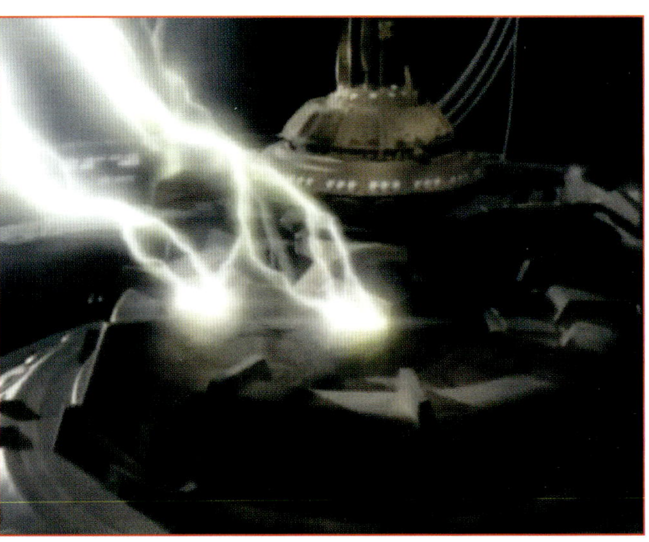

Vast amounts of energy from a fusion generator overload were safely redirected into Deep Space 9's upgraded deflector shields, before dispersing into space.

STARFLEET ORDNANCE

Starfleet installed auto-destruct warheads at key structural points around the station. A total of 52 devices were located across the habitat ring, outer docking ring, docking pylons, and crossover bridges.

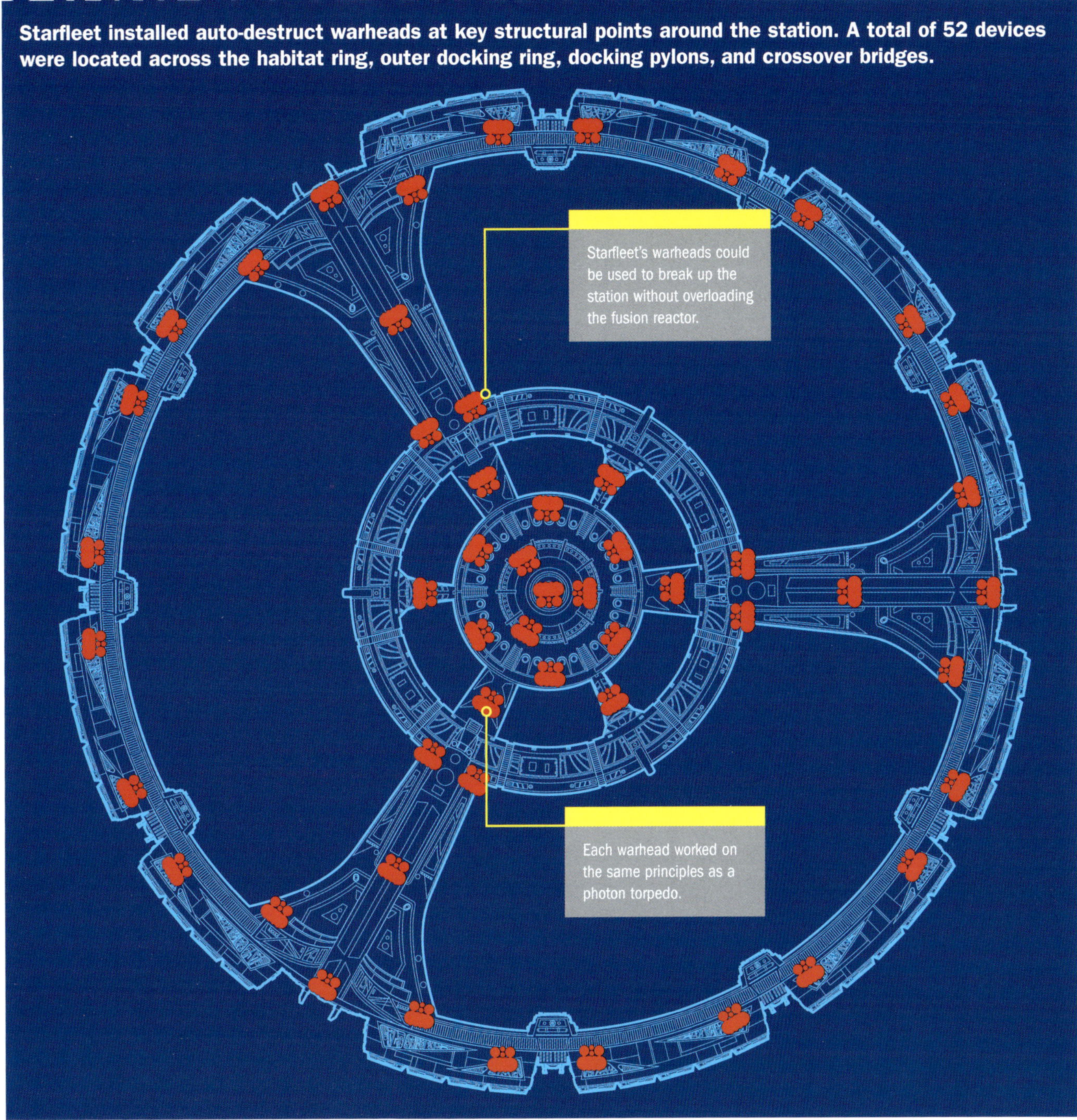

through the deflector shield and into space before it could reach the deuterium reserves. This prevented the intended cascade effect and drained the reaction chambers, which then shut down, leaving the station unharmed.

On activation, the original system initiated a countdown, allowing either the Cardassian crew to evacuate, or any other occupying force to surrender. In theory, the station's commanding officer could stop the countdown at any time, but if computer analysis suggested the commander was no longer working in the interests of Cardassian Central Command, their deactivation codes would be ignored.

When Starfleet and the Bajoran Provisional Government assumed control of the station, new software was installed that required command authorization from both a Starfleet and a Bajoran officer before the auto-destruct sequence could begin. The system would verify the officers' place in the chain of command (taking casualties and other losses into account), and then accept instructions for the length of the countdown. Warning messages would then sound throughout the station, indicating the time remaining until the explosive reactions began.

Starfleet simulations demonstrated that this system, if used properly, should allow enough time for all civilians and station personnel to evacuate the station. However, in most scenarios – where the potential for auto-destruct would be foreseen – advance warnings would give nonessential personnel far more time to leave the station long before the final countdown began.

COMMUNICATIONS AND SENSORS

Hundreds of well-protected sensors and dozens of communications transceivers dotted the surface of Deep Space 9. Many dated from its earliest days, while others were wormhole-specific upgrades.

Deep Space 9's communications and sensor systems were often considered in tandem because their main functions were intricately linked. Both relied on relay pallets located around the station, and were coordinated from ops, where precise calibrations were monitored, and irregularities detected and analyzed.

Like any other space station, Deep Space 9 relied on its sensor and communications arrays to collect and share data from the immediate vicinity. Uniquely, however, the station also played a vital role in gathering and relaying signals from inside and beyond the Bajoran wormhole. As this phenomenon was unknown when the station was in orbit of Bajor under Cardassian control, all of the sensor technology specifically for this purpose was Federation-issue, ingeniously integrated with the original systems.

Routine functionality included wideband filter protocols, which scanned the wormhole for radiometric anomalies, quantum fluctuations, and changes in neutrino levels that indicated the phenomenon was about to open. And from mid-2371 onwards, it became possible to receive sensor readings and communications from the other side of the wormhole, thanks to a subspace filament fortuitiously left behind by fragments from a stray comet.

SENSOR SYSTEMS

When the station was originally built as Terok Nor, most of the sensors were dedicated to monitoring its planetary orbit and the arrival and departure of mining vessels. Inset sections of the hull denoted their positions, and a hafnium-duranide coating protected them against exposure to open space. A small number of sensors also related to defense, but this was not a priority deep within occupied territory. By the time of the Dominion War, 473 Cardassian long-range sensors remained in place, augmented by 109 Federation and Bajoran additions. Together, these included: broad- and narrow-beam active subspace scanners; passive subspace interferometers; subspace seismicity sensors; and warp-activity detectors with threat analysis preprocessors.

Starfleet protocols ensured constant sensor coverage thanks to multiple backups and rotating maintenance schedules. Sensors relating to defense were installed in triplicate, with two out of three operating at any one time.

DEEP SPACE 9 COMBADGES

Starfleet and Bajoran Militia personnel wore different designs of combadge, but both styles were fashioned as emblems of their organizations. On Deep Space 9, both kinds were configured to the same frequencies, allowing all wearers to communicate over distance with each other, as well as with the station computer.

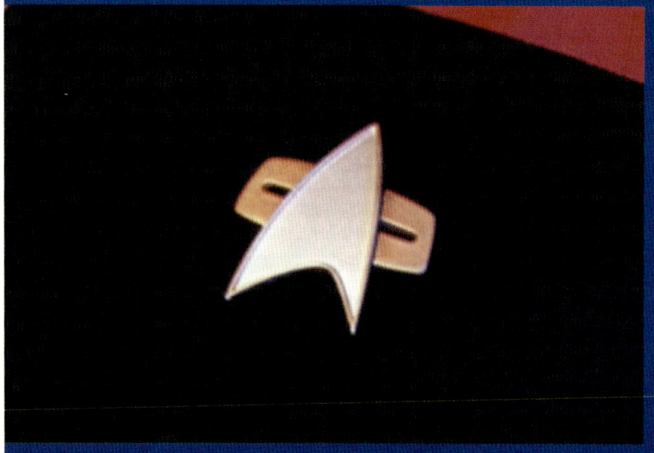

The appearance of the Starfleet combadge was updated in 2371. It was made from micromilled duranium and plasma-bonded alloys of silver and gold.

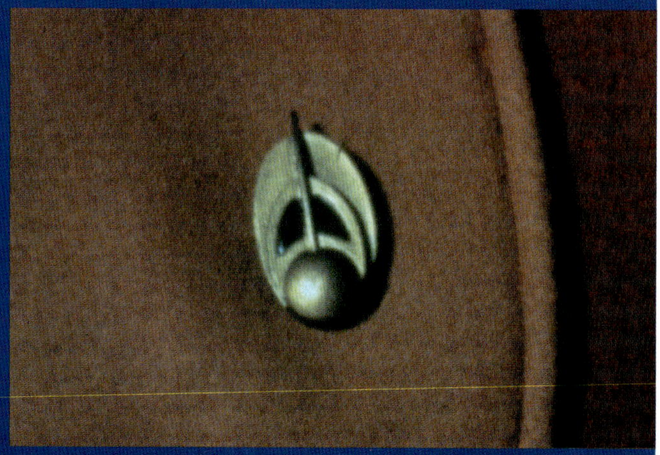

Bajoran combadges contained a densified sarium krellide power cell and were made from the same pressure-molded hafnium beritite used in Bajoran jewelry.

The addition of force-field generators around key sensors also added to their lifespans on the hull. These operated separately from the main deflector shield, powered by the station's EPS network.

COMMUNICATIONS SYSTEMS

As with the sensor network, the station's communications hardware was improved by Starfleet over the years. The number of subspace transceivers was increased from 24 to 30, with radio frequency (RF) transceivers going from 21 to 33. Though RF was dated in relation to subspace technology, it continued to serve a purpose in the vicinity of the wormhole, which could cause subspace fluctuations.

At standard power, the communications network had an operating range of 1.6 billion kilometers, with the potential to boost to 3.4 billion km in an emergency. However, most communications were relatively short-range – either with nearby ships or with Bajor – with long-range transmissions going via subspace relay stations.

INTRASTATION COMMUNICATIONS

Personal communications were handled by two separate systems, one public and one reserved for official station operations. Both used the same system of 4,750 Optical Data Network (ODN) lines and terminal nodes, but the former relied mostly on the original Cardassian parts of the network, while Starfleet and Bajoran Militia comms also made use of extensive upgrades made after 2369.

REPURPOSED RELAYS

Chief of operations Miles O'Brien knew the station's communications and sensor relays better than anyone. In 2372, he was forced to adapt them into one giant chroniton emitter by a Pah-wraith that had possessed his wife, Keiko. Its plan to kill the wormhole aliens with a chroniton beam was foiled at the last minute.

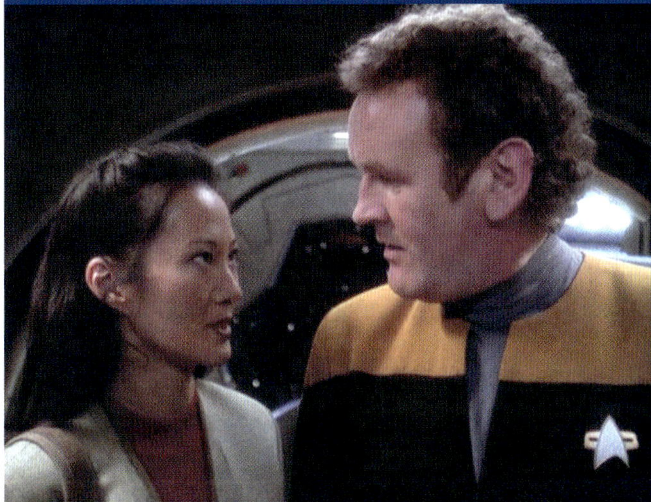

The Pah-wraith promised to kill Keiko if Chief O'Brien didn't follow its orders. He had no choice but to make seemingly harmless changes to the station's systems.

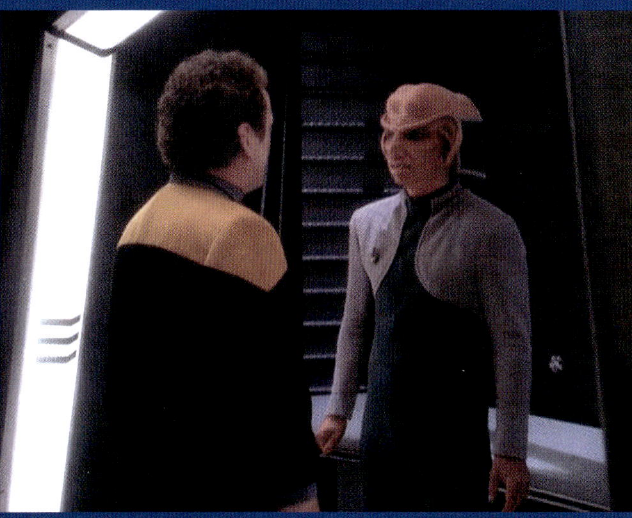

When his work aroused suspicion, O'Brien had to implicate Rom as a saboteur. The wise Ferengi then helped the chief to see the purpose of the modifications.

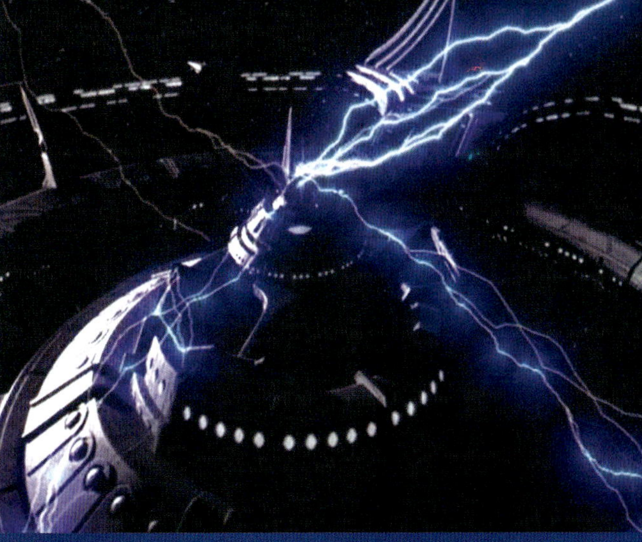

O'Brien continued to play along with the Pah-wraith's demands, taking "Keiko" to the mouth of the wormhole in a runabout before activating the chroniton beam.

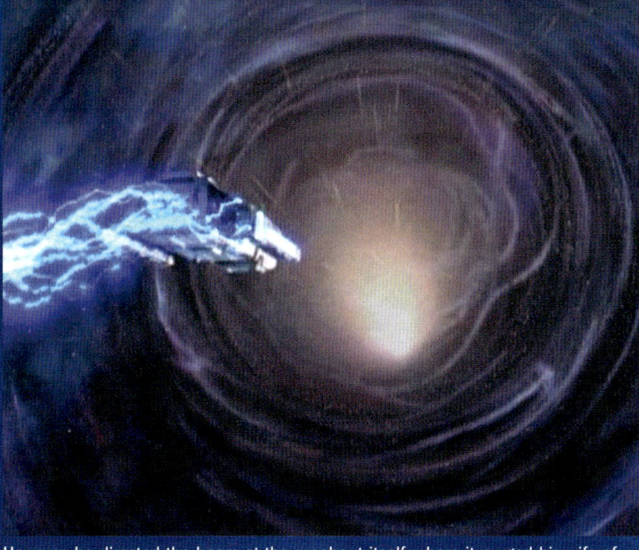

However, he directed the beam at the runabout itself, where it purged his wife of the malevolent spirit, leaving her - and the wormhole aliens - totally unharmed.

SUBSPACE RELAYS

Deep Space 9's ability to communicate with Earth and other distant locations was vital to its effectiveness. The Federation's subspace relay network made this possible.

Like all deep space stations, DS9 relied on a network of subspace relays to communicate over long distances. These relays were sometimes located on planets and other stations, but the majority hung isolated in space, far from any kind of Federation outpost or settlement.

The nearest Federation subspace relay to Deep Space 9 was around 20 light years away, in the direction of Earth. A string of relays, all roughly the same distance apart, then traced a line to Starfleet Command and the public comms networks on Earth. This single thread was just a small part of a much larger tapestry that linked the entire Federation through subspace communication channels.

RISKS AND RIVALS

Prior to the Cardassian withdrawal from Bajoran space in 2369, there had been an extensive network of Cardassian subspace relays in the sector, but Starfleet and the Bajoran Militia worked to take these out of commission in the years that followed. Naturally, the Federation's own relays were vulnerable to attack, malfunction, and accidental damage, and so they were closely monitored at all times. When the Dominion War broke out in 2373, the Jem'Hadar targeted the Federation's relays, along with the equivalent network in the Klingon Empire. Defending both was a top priority for the allied Alpha Quadrant powers, as communication lines were essential to a coordinated war effort.

THROUGH THE WORMHOLE

One way in which Deep Space 9 was unique in the network was that it housed a relay for sending/receiving messages to/from the Gamma Quadrant. Though technically more than 70,000 light years away from the relay station with which it connected, the Bajoran wormhole allowed the two to behave as if they were much closer together. The wormhole did not have to be active for the communications link to operate; a subspace filament along its length enabled messages to traverse quadrants even faster than ships passing through the artificially created spacetime tunnel.

After this first expansion of the network to the Gamma Quadrant, further relays followed, broadening the reach of Starfleet communications still further. This was swiftly curtailed, however, by the outbreak of the Dominion War.

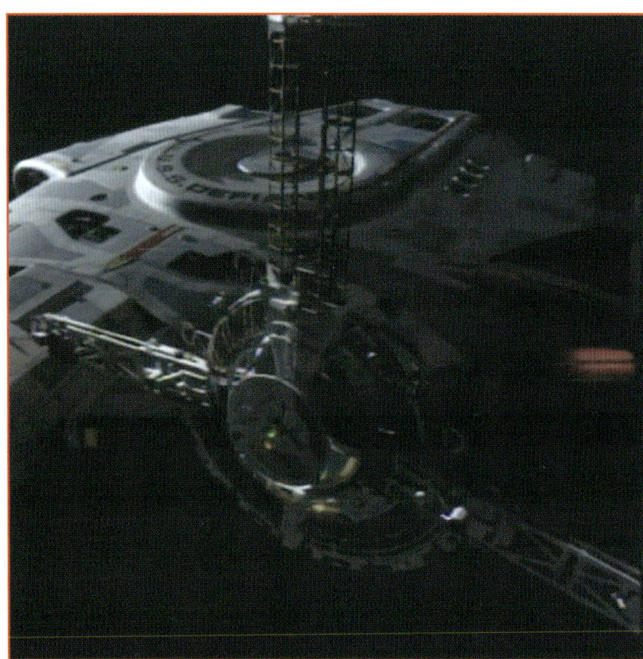

The *U.S.S. Defiant* deployed the first Alpha Quadrant-built relay on the far side of the wormhole in 2372, as part of a rare Federation-Bajoran-Cardassian collaboration.

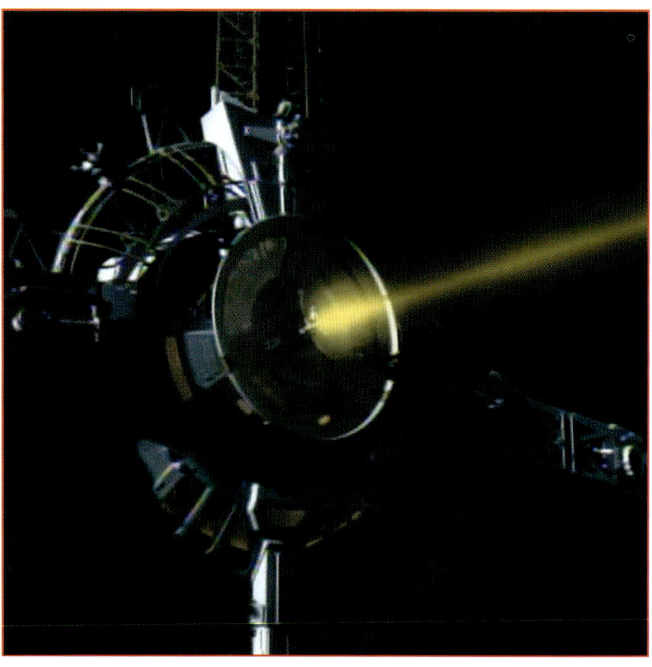

Testing the new relay station with a theta-band carrier wave not only created a visible beam, but also a dangerous gravity surge, forcing the *Defiant* to abandon the trial.

LONG-DISTANCE CALLING

The subspace relay network functioned by boosting the strength of communication signals at intervals, counteracting any degradation before it resulted in unrecoverable data loss. Permanent relays boosted subspace messages throughout charted Federation space, while exploratory vessels left a trail of temporary relays as they journeyed where no one had gone before. These were later replaced by permanent relays, where necessary.

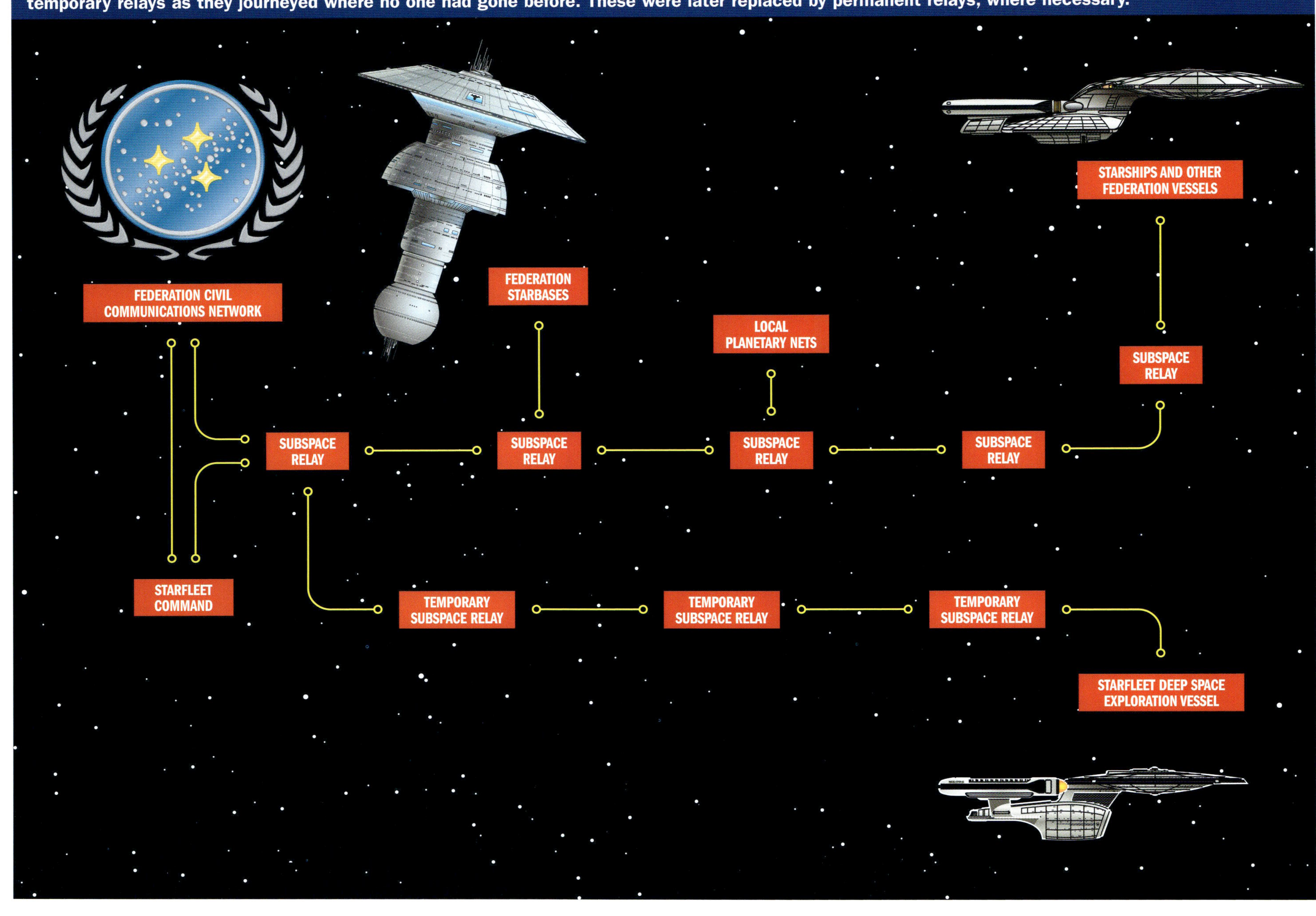

OPERATIONS CENTER

Located at the top of the central core, Deep Space 9's ops level served as a hub for Starfleet and Bajoran command officers, engineers, scientists, tactical personnel, and more.

The Operations Center, usually known as ops, was Deep Space 9's equivalent of a starship command bridge. It was where senior officers monitored and assessed threats to the station from outside, while also giving orders relating to life on the inside. It was a traffic-control base – overseeing the docking and departure of ships, as well as passage through the wormhole – a tactical control room, a conference space, a communications station, and even one of several transporter rooms.

Located at the top of the station core, on level 1, ops centered on a large command table and was overlooked by an elliptical viewscreen. On the opposite side of the room from the screen, double doors led to a private office for the exclusive use of the station commander. Possibly the single most important workstation was the engineering console, which allowed for oversight of all critical systems, including power generation, life-support, weapons, and the nearby transporter. A more hands-on approach to all these systems could be taken in the pit area directly below the viewscreen, giving direct access to the computer core, which extended to level 2. In this respect, ops was not only the station's "bridge," but also its main engineering deck.

OTHER WORKSTATIONS

Away from the operations table and engineering areas, the key workstations in ops were: science, for the analysis of sensor readings from inside and outside the station, as well as archive data retrieval; strategic operations, where Lieutenant Commander Worf took up position on joining the station crew in 2373; and a variety of monitoring and diagnostic posts that could be repurposed as required. Two turbolifts – one on either side of the room – completed the layout, providing rapid access to all areas of the station.

A platform at the top of both turbolift shafts descended with the carriage before stopping level with the floor in ops. This sealed the lift shaft until a turbolift carriage returned.

Safety railings separated the different levels of ops, which followed Cardassian ideas about hierarchy and power.

The situation table was at the heart of ops, in a direct line between the command office and the elevated viewscreen.

Ladders led down to the engineering pit, which was located immediately below the viewscreen (not shown).

Elliptical windows around the top of ops looked out on the upper docking pylons.

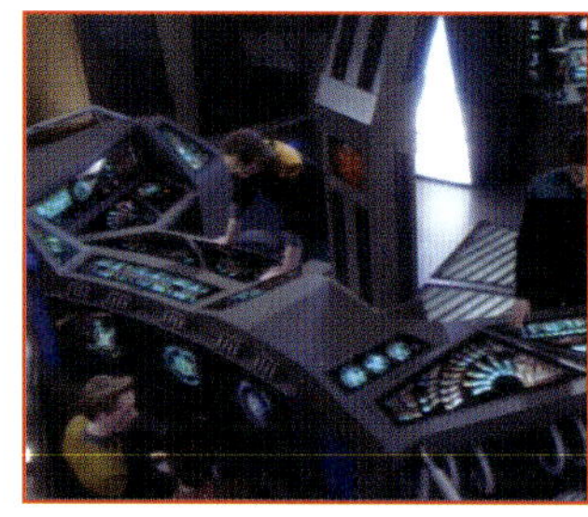

Screens on the back of the engineering workstation faced into the lower level.

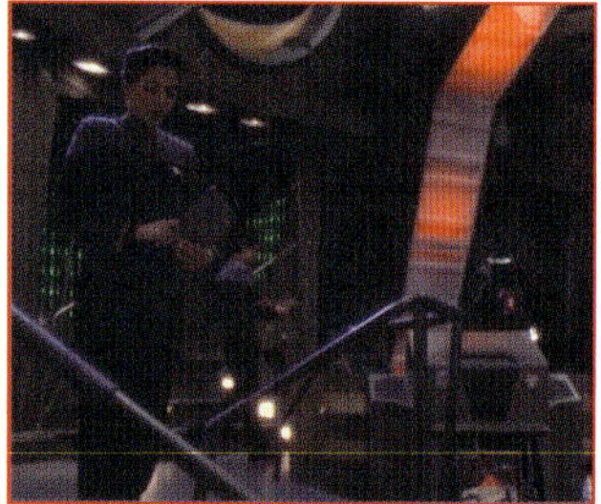

During red alerts, the lighting columns in ops glowed the appropriate color.

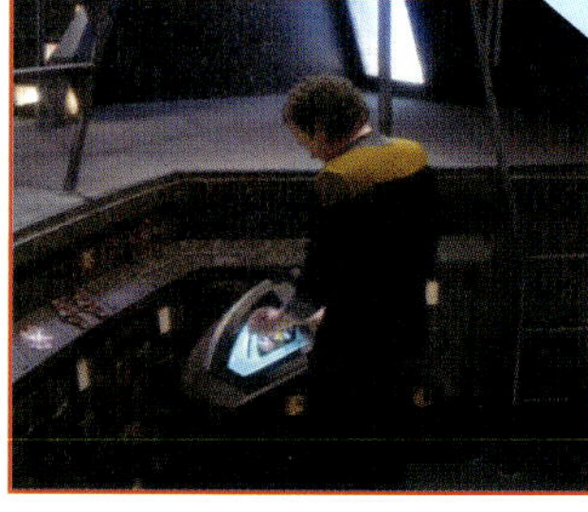

Chief O'Brien spent much of his time in the pit area below the main viewscreen.

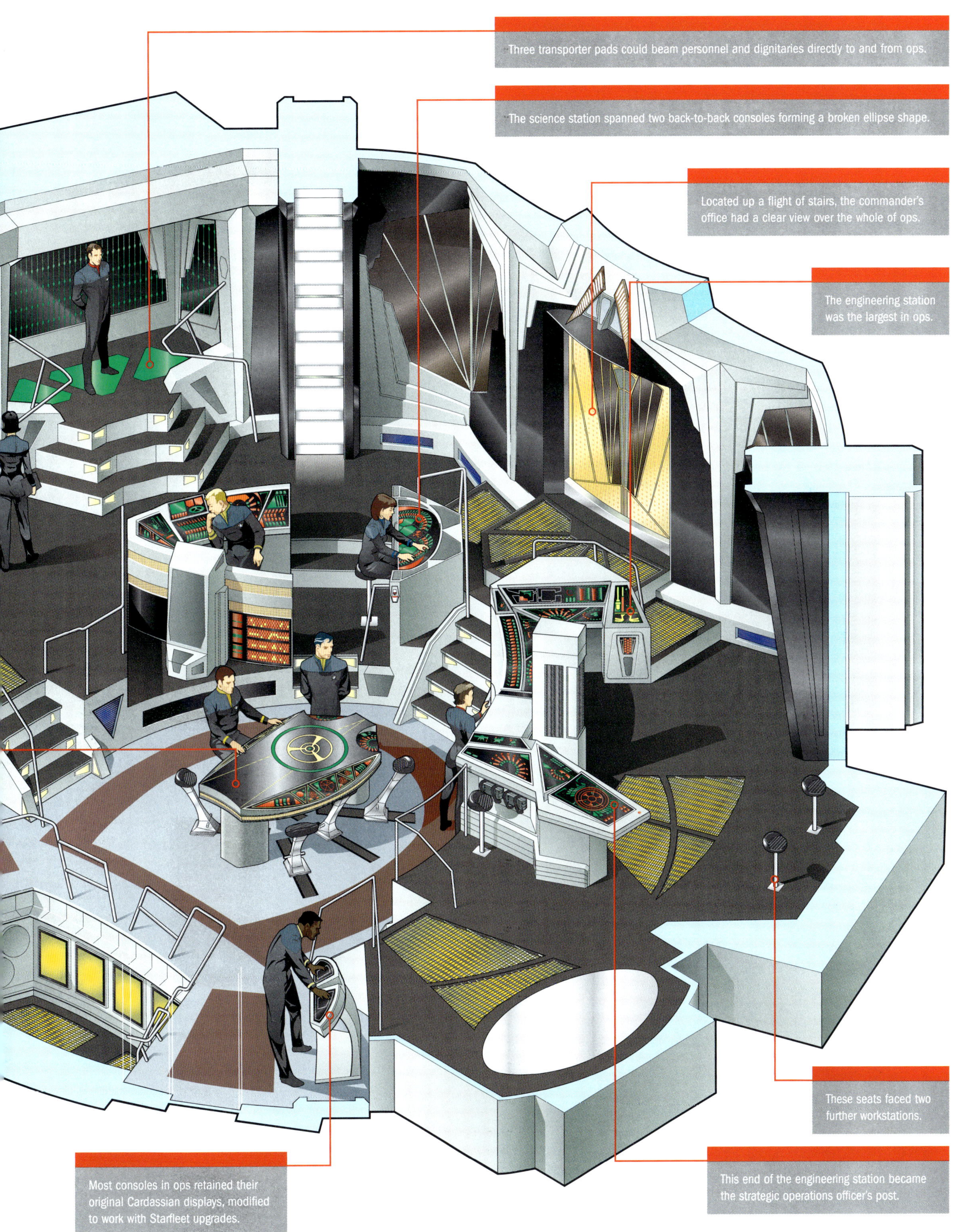
Three transporter pads could beam personnel and dignitaries directly to and from ops.
The science station spanned two back-to-back consoles forming a broken ellipse shape.
Located up a flight of stairs, the commander's office had a clear view over the whole of ops.
The engineering station was the largest in ops.
These seats faced two further workstations.
This end of the engineering station became the strategic operations officer's post.
Most consoles in ops retained their original Cardassian displays, modified to work with Starfleet upgrades.

OPERATIONS TABLE

More collegiate than the captain's chair on a starship, the table at the center of ops enabled Deep Space 9's senior staff to confer over key controls.

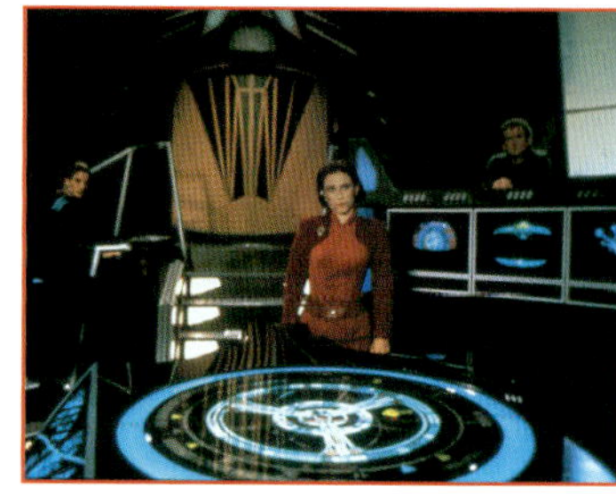

Major Kira at the operations table in 2369. All three secondary displays were active on the back of the engineering workstation.

The situation table in operations was the focus for major decision-making on Deep Space 9. It had six slide-out seats with additional standing room, and featured touch-screen command controls along its length. The displays and interface could be changed as required, allowing senior officers to respond to any situation that might arise on or outside the station. The main viewscreen was located in front of the table, and stairs on the other three sides afforded rapid access to the command office, turbolifts, and transporter pad.

MONITORING STATION

Measuring more than two meters long and over one meter wide, the operations table retained its original Cardassian-designed display screens and internal processors. From 2369 onwards, these were augmented by 18 Starfleet optronic translation buffers (15 primary and three backups) introduced to handle Federation data protocols.

The main display usually showed either, a detailed plan of the station, giving a real-time overview of all monitored activity, from cargo transfers and scheduled maintenance to security alerts; or a broader schematic of ship traffic in the immediate vicinity of the station. The angled panels around the flat tabletop featured customizable controls for changing, magnifying, and otherwise manipulating the display. Science and engineering functions could also be transferred to the table, even though these had dedicated stations elsewhere in ops. This versatility meant that any specialist could easily give briefings from the table, or monitor their station while on a command shift.

CARDASSIAN INTERFACES

With access to all command functions on Deep Space 9, the operations table was too thoroughly integrated with the computer cores to make its replacement with Federation equipment practical. Instead, Starfleet personnel rapidly had to familiarize themselves with its idiosyncratic Cardassian displays and interfaces.

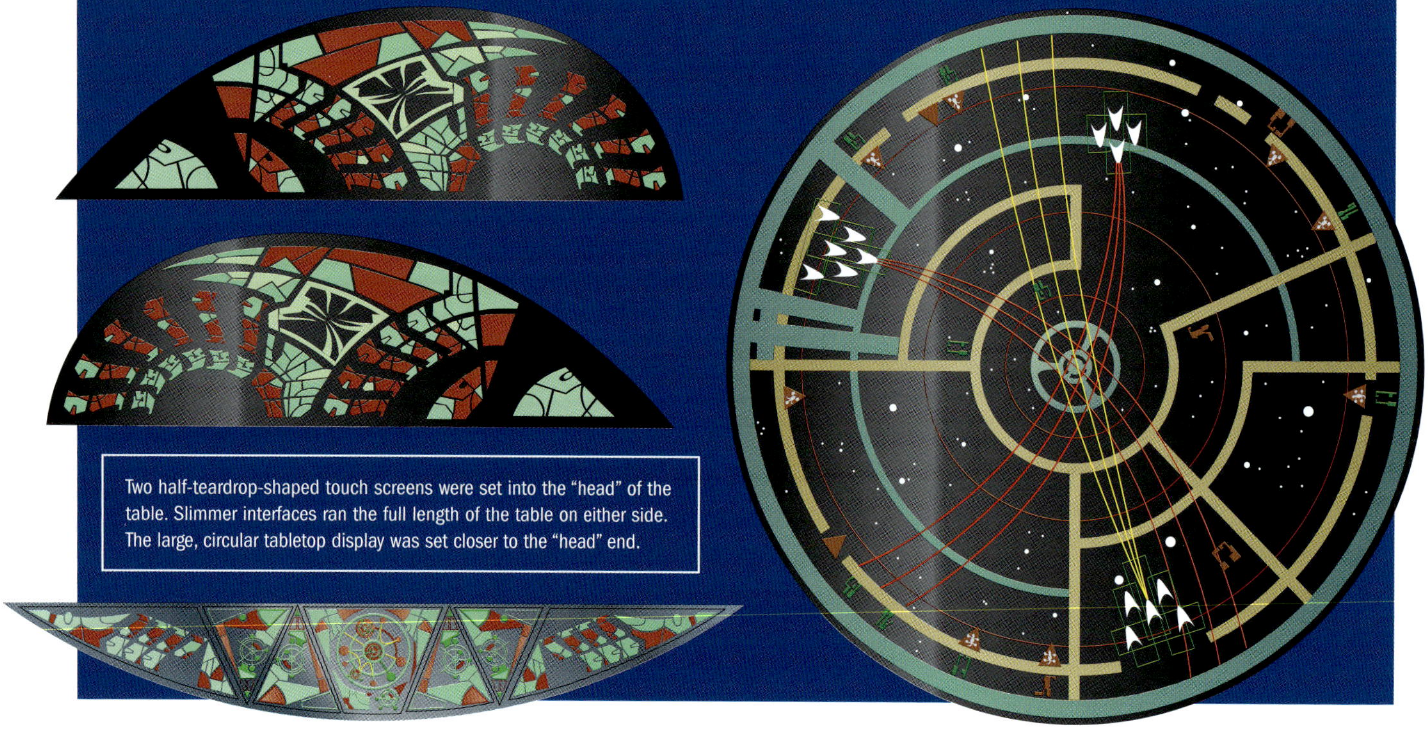

Two half-teardrop-shaped touch screens were set into the "head" of the table. Slimmer interfaces ran the full length of the table on either side. The large, circular tabletop display was set closer to the "head" end.

BATTLE STATION

Briefings around the operations table took on added import at times of crisis and war. On a quiet day, the location could be mistaken for a social hub – with officers resting cups of raktajino on displays of routine cargo traffic. But in emergencies, it was an unmatched strategic resource, just as the Cardassians had originally intended. Any ship approaching the station could be tracked visually on the large main display, while still leaving the viewscreen above free for visual communications. Three additional screens mounted on the back of the engineering workstation also came into their own in such scenarios, providing eye-level readouts for staff at the head of the operations table.

It was a sign of the robust nature of Cardassian design that the operations table outlasted the station's Terok Nor era, to the end of the Dominion War and beyond. It was not damaged during the frequent attacks on the station, even when heavily armed Klingons stormed ops in 2372.

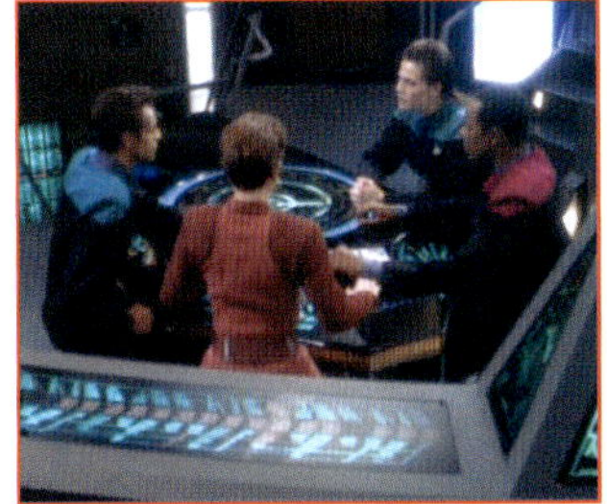

Senior staff at the operations table, as viewed from the science workstation.

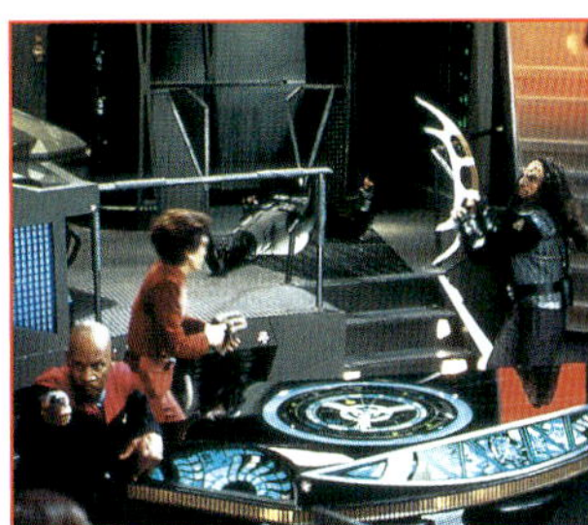

During the Klingon invasion, the operations table itself was at risk.

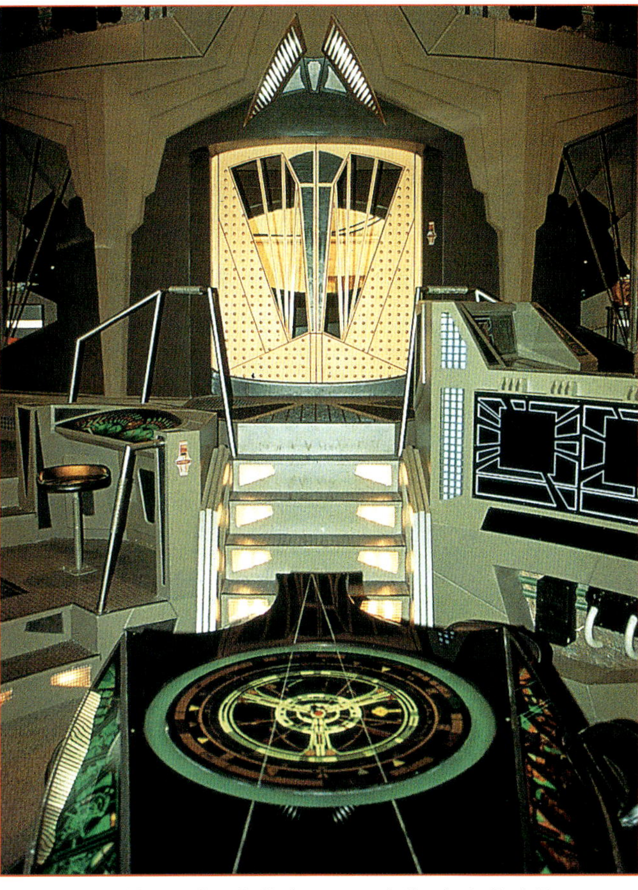

The operations table was aligned with the command office. In the Terok Nor era, the station commander would observe the table from his office door.

OVERVIEW

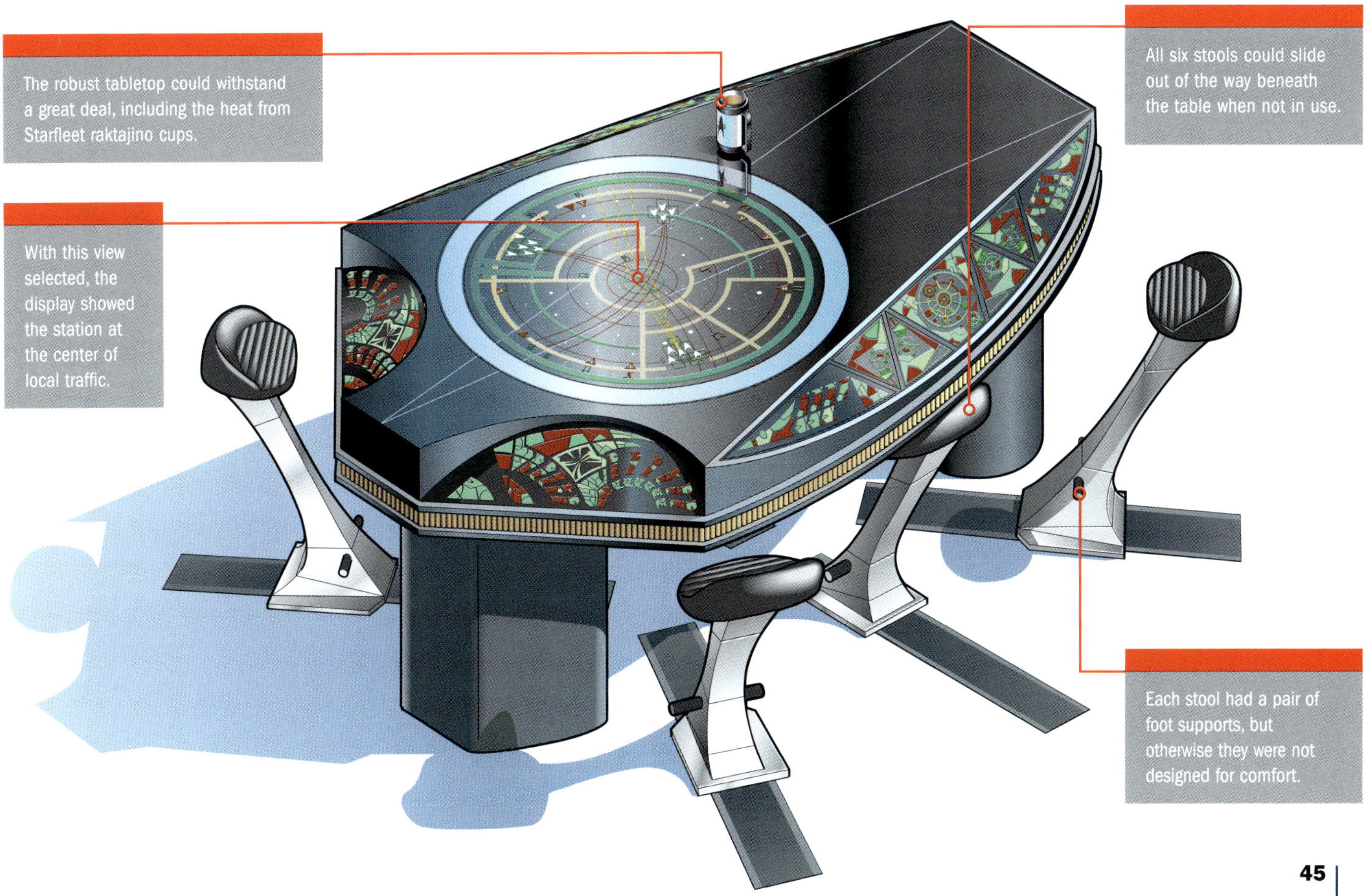

The robust tabletop could withstand a great deal, including the heat from Starfleet raktajino cups.

With this view selected, the display showed the station at the center of local traffic.

All six stools could slide out of the way beneath the table when not in use.

Each stool had a pair of foot supports, but otherwise they were not designed for comfort.

CARDASSIAN ISOLINEAR RODS

The Cardassian equivalent of the isolinear chip was integral to the running of Deep Space 9, long after its original occupiers had left. They were found in everything from handheld devices to the station's vast computer cores.

While the Federation used isolinear chips to store and process data, the Cardassian Union favored isolinear rods. This meant that, when Starfleet set about rebuilding Deep Space 9 after the Cardassian withdrawal, its technicians had to familiarize themselves with a whole new approach to computer technology – and then integrate it with their own systems. At first, this may have seemed a daunting challenge, but it soon became clear that, while superficially very different, the two competing technologies had a great deal in common.

RODS VS. CHIPS

Isolinear rods handled system software, archived data, transitory buffer data, and system communications. Like isolinear chips, they had built-in nanoprocessors. These organized and managed the data stored in each rod before passing it on as required – for example, to a display screen – via the Optical Data Network (ODN). Where they differed from the equivalent Starfleet device was primarily in their size and robustness. As their name suggested, the rods were cylindrical, measuring between 4mm and around 7cm in diameter. Their sturdy, coated housing enabled users to treat them roughly, handling them freely and even storing them loose in a drawer or pocket. This was in contrast to isolinear chips, which were all one size, rectangular, and intended for delicate handling by specialists.

The size of a Cardassian isolinear rod was determined by its purpose. Four classes were used on Deep Space 9, with the following designations:

Class 1 rods measured 4.3mm by 32.1mm. The smallest of the four classes, they were generally used in only the most compact of handheld devices.

DATA STORAGE RODS

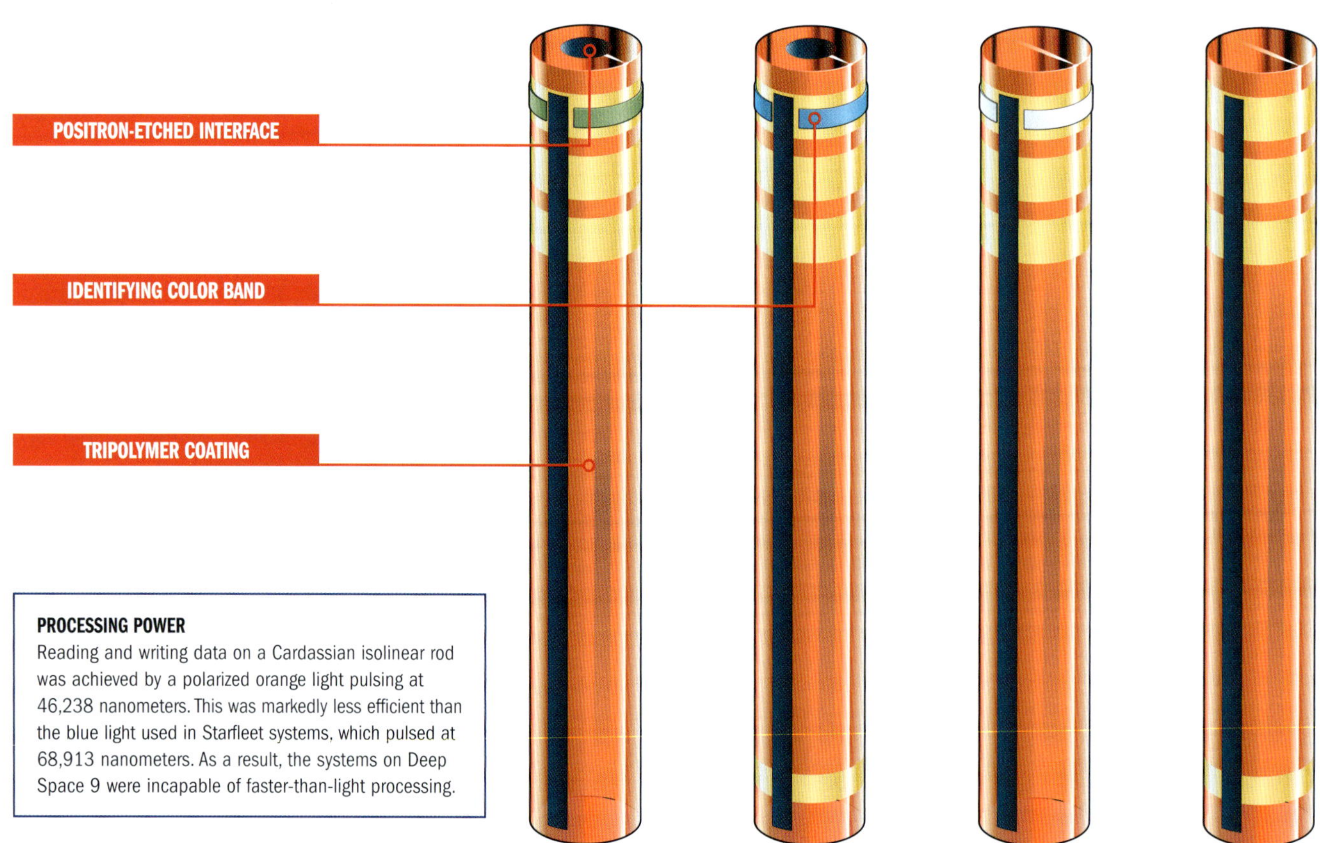

PROCESSING POWER

Reading and writing data on a Cardassian isolinear rod was achieved by a polarized orange light pulsing at 46,238 nanometers. This was markedly less efficient than the blue light used in Starfleet systems, which pulsed at 68,913 nanometers. As a result, the systems on Deep Space 9 were incapable of faster-than-light processing.

Class 2 rods measured 10.8mm by 62.6mm. They were found in larger handheld devices, such as the Cardassian PADD, which required two such rods.

Class 3 rods measured 12.7mm by 95.2mm. They were used throughout the station, such devices as consoles and free-standing podium-style computers.

Class 4 rods measured 74.3mm by 319.6mm. With the greatest capacity of the four classes, these were usually confined to use in computer cores. More than 300,000 were installed across the station's three memory cores.

For ease of identification, all four classes could be color-coded according to their purpose. Rods with a white band, for example, contained data relating to engineering, while a red band indicated library and information storage.

DRAWBACKS AND DISADVANTAGES

The ease with which data rods could be handled was not always to the intended owner's advantage. Compared to isolinear chips, they were much easier to steal without the risk of degrading their contents – and then keep safely hidden away without specialist storage requirements. The Ferengi bar owner, Quark, was among those on the station to trade sometimes in illicitly acquired rods, and his own collection included supposedly classified data that granted him access to various secure systems.

The robust coating used on all rods also inhibited their data-transfer capabilities compared to an isolinear chip's. Only the uncoated tip of the rod actually interfaced with the wider system, whereas Starfleet chips were designed so that almost their entire surface was accessible to the ODN processors. The resulting loss of transfer speed was negligible over just one rod, but created a noticeable lag when cascaded through every rod in the station's systems.

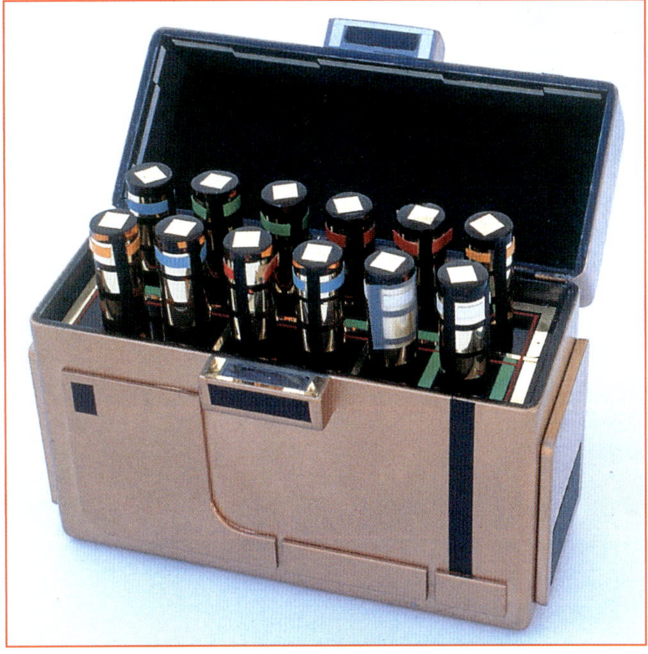

Cardassian isolinear rods were often stored in robust, custom-built containers, despite not requiring exceptionally careful management.

MANUFACTURE

Isolinear rod manufacturing was complex and exacting, since any imperfection rendered the rod useless. Once the basic structure was fabricated, a 1.2mm light-magnifying surface was positron-etched on one end of the rod to create thousands of discrete data conduits. Despite the near-identical chemical composition of rods and chips, this process was far less efficient than chip manufacture and resulted in a smaller storage capacity: on average 5.37 kiloquads per rod as opposed to 6.51 kiloquads per chip.

OPTOLYTHIC DATA RODS

Also of Cardassian design, but far rarer than standard rods, optolythic data rods were the gold standard in sensitive information storage. Because they could be inscribed with data only once, it was impossible to tamper with their contents, and their manufacture was closely regulated by the Cardassian government.

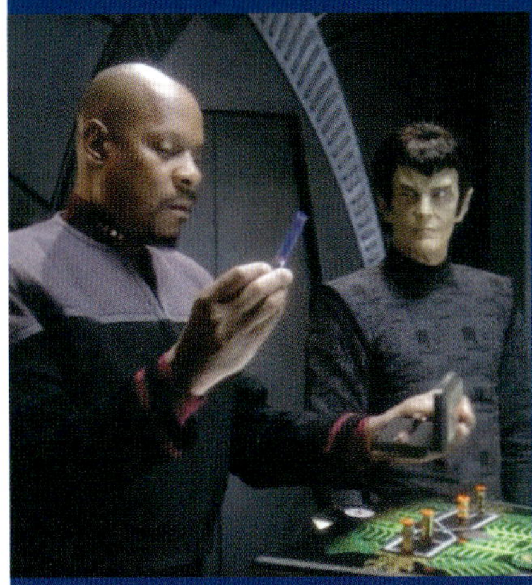

In 2374, Captain Sisko acquired a genuine, unused optolythic data rod and had it inscribed with data meant to draw the Romulans into the Dominion War.

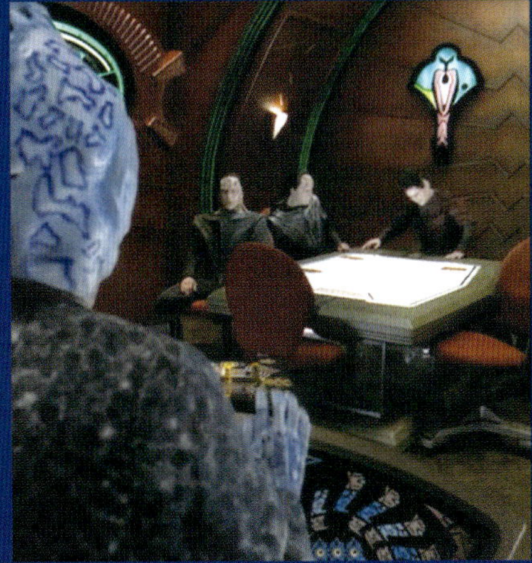

In fact, the holo-recording it contained was a brilliant fake by the master forger Grathon Tolar, depicting a secret Dominion meeting that was staged.

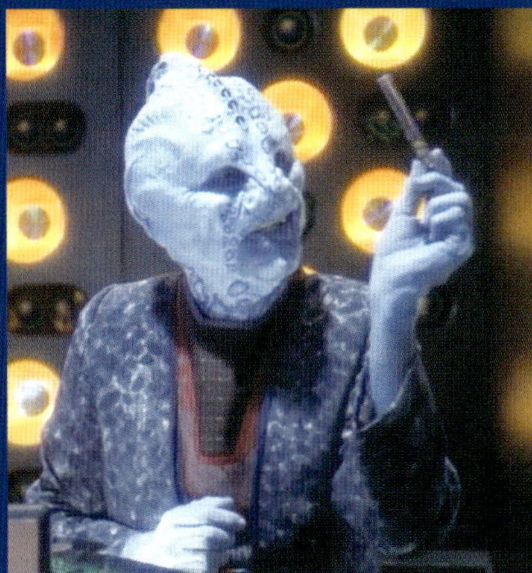

Tolar assured Sisko that his work would stand up to scrutiny, but despite both the rod being genuine, the contents were identified as false.

CARDASSIAN VIEWSCREENS

Visual communications technology in the Cardassian Union differed markedly from standard Starfleet equipment. The examples on Deep Space 9 followed the same designs found on Cardassia Prime and in Cardassian warships.

The Cardassian homeworld – Cardassia Prime – was noted for its large, outdoor viewscreens, which were used to broadcast public information and government propaganda across the planet. Shaped like an open eye, these screens were a constant reminder of the power and influence of Central Command in the average Cardassian's life. Even when not in use, they represented an all-seeing presence, watching out for enemies of the state.

ON DEEP SPACE 9

The same elliptical design was used for viewscreens of all sizes throughout the Cardassian Union, from the smallest desktop display through to the main viewers on *Galor*-class warships and stations such as Terok Nor. Many such screens were retained when that station became Deep Space 9, and they provided a very different user experience for Starfleet officers more accustomed to flat-screen and touch-screen displays.

The main way in which Cardassian screens differed from those of Starfleet was that they weren't really screens at all. No blank display panel remained when they were deactivated, only an empty surround. These frames were actually holo-emitters that generated an intangible image in two dimensions. Nevertheless, they were still referred to as "screens" because of their comparable usage as data displays, communication devices, and more.

Naturally, this style of viewscreen was also suitable for showing entertainment, and Quark sometimes displayed a similar frame in his bar. This was not the standard oval shape, however, as it more closely resembled a square.

DESKTOP COMMUNICATOR

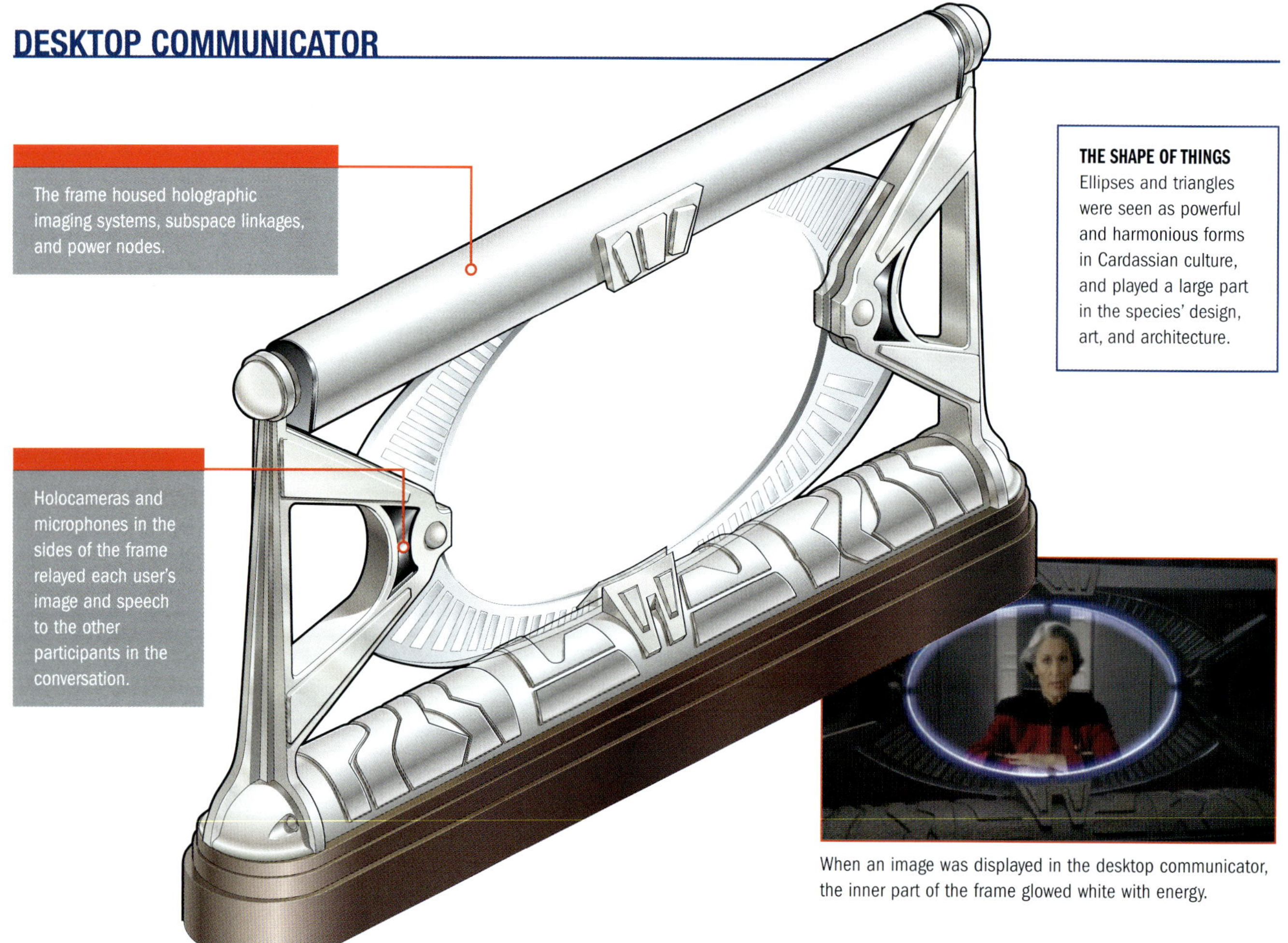

THE SHAPE OF THINGS
Ellipses and triangles were seen as powerful and harmonious forms in Cardassian culture, and played a large part in the species' design, art, and architecture.

When an image was displayed in the desktop communicator, the inner part of the frame glowed white with energy.

OPERATIONS CENTER SCREEN

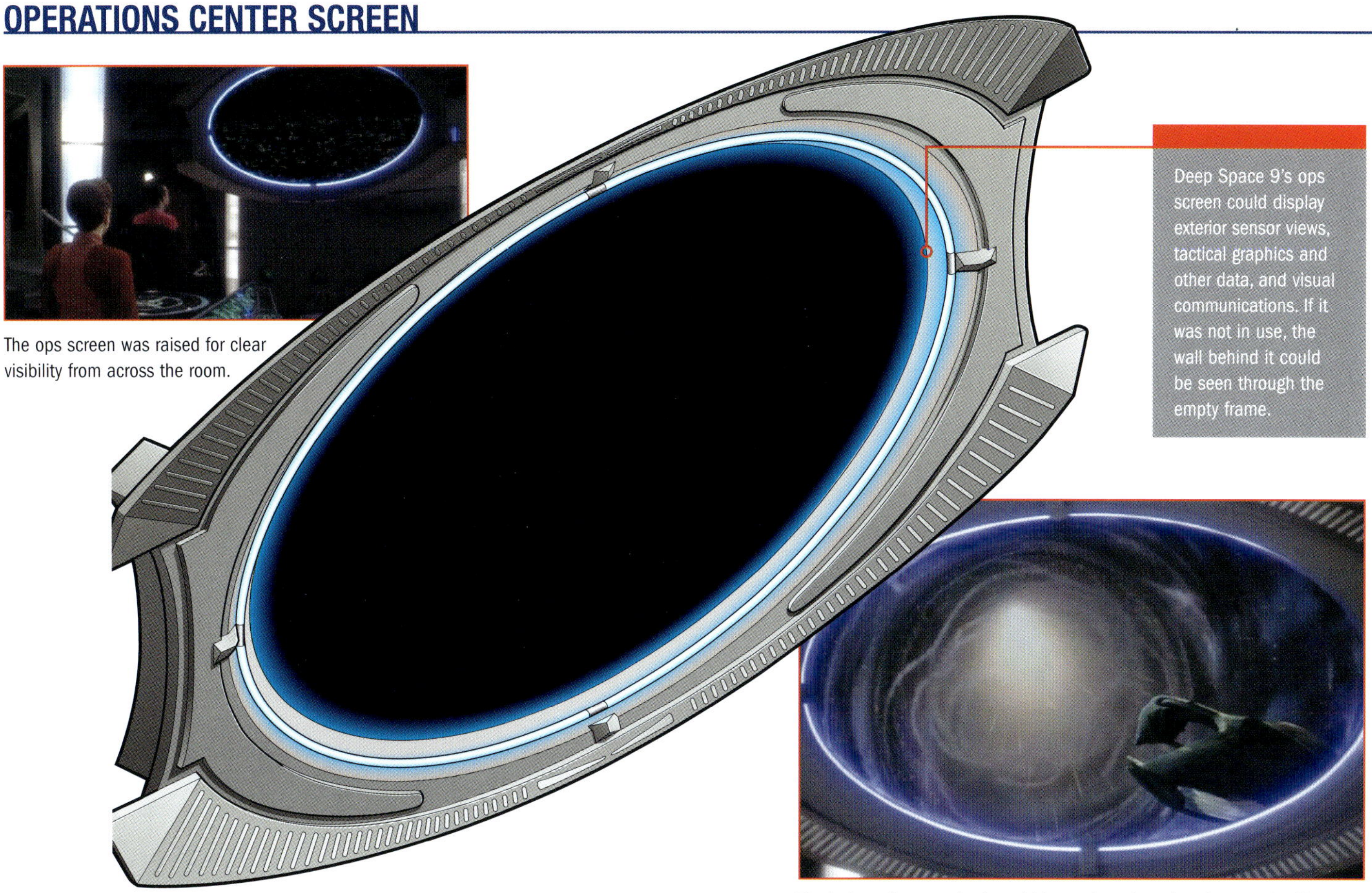

The ops screen was raised for clear visibility from across the room.

Deep Space 9's ops screen could display exterior sensor views, tactical graphics and other data, and visual communications. If it was not in use, the wall behind it could be seen through the empty frame.

The holo-emitter matrix glowed blue as it projected an image – in this case, real-time sensor observations of a Romulan warbird entering the wormhole.

STANDARD SCREEN

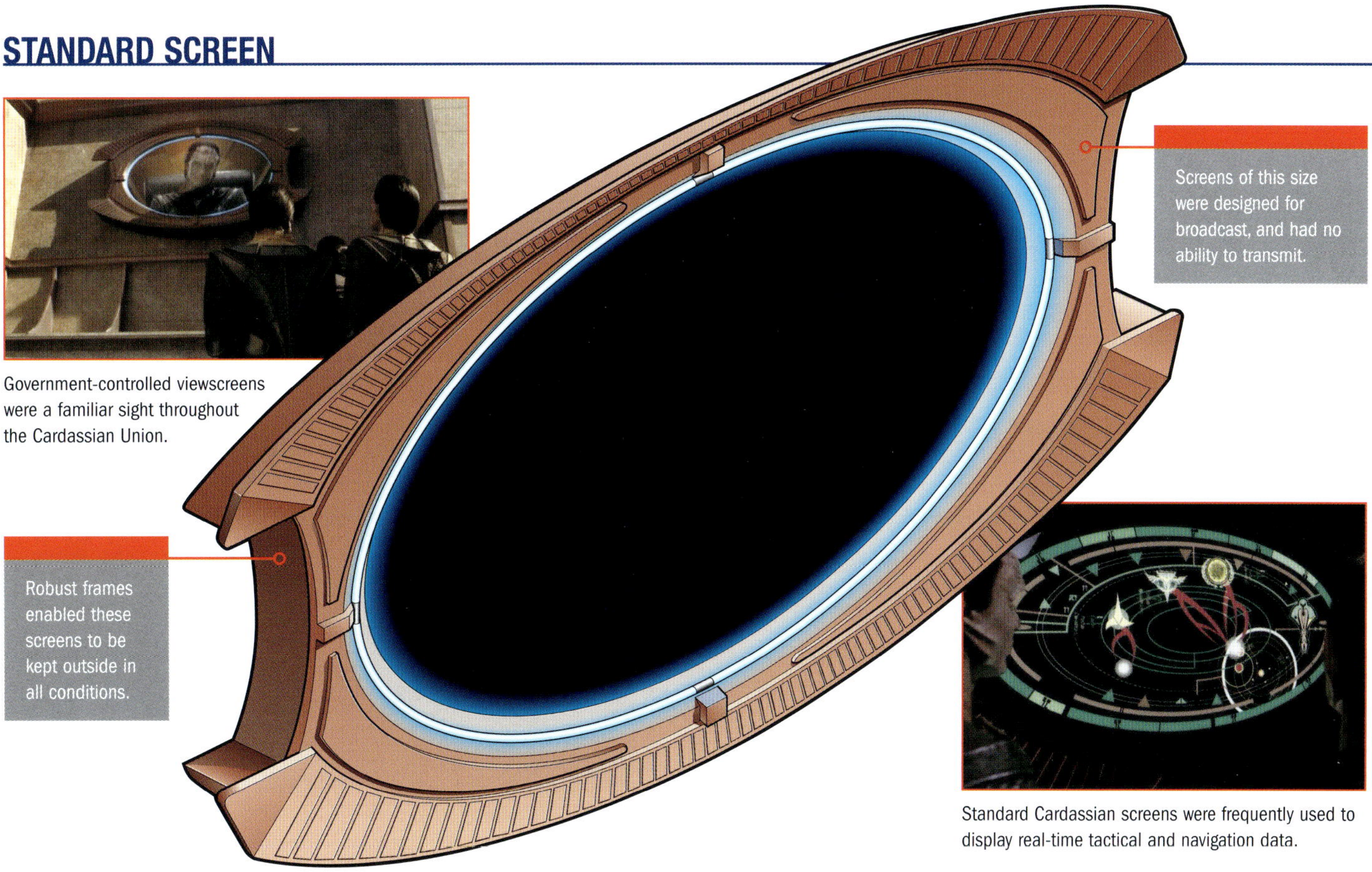

Government-controlled viewscreens were a familiar sight throughout the Cardassian Union.

Screens of this size were designed for broadcast, and had no ability to transmit.

Robust frames enabled these screens to be kept outside in all conditions.

Standard Cardassian screens were frequently used to display real-time tactical and navigation data.

COMMAND OFFICE

The station commander of Deep Space 9 had a private office adjoining ops. Its lofty position was an illustration of Cardassian architecture's respect for hierarchy.

Designed to look down on the operations center from a position of superiority (and to make subordinates look up), Deep Space 9's command office was once the sanctuary of the station's Cardassian prefect. Starting in 2369, however, it served as the office of Commander – later Captain – Benjamin Sisko.

With a curved rear wall following the shape of the upper core bulkhead, Sisko's office looked out across the station to space through a dramatic eye-shaped window. A large desk in front of the window dominated the room, facing the ornate doors that led directly to ops, while two less conspicuous side doors circumvented the control center altogether. All three doors opened only to senior staff, responding either to touch or a code.

BUILT FOR BUSINESS

To the left of the main door, two large monitor screens were built into the inner wall. These were Starfleet models, which replaced those torn out by the Cardassians when they abandoned the station. Most often used to show data, the screens could also be used for stand-up conferencing, though Sisko generally preferred to run communications channels sitting at the smaller monitor on his desk.

A small sit-down meeting area was arranged on the right of the room, from the visitor's perspective. This compensated for the fact that the desk was designed to seat only the highest-ranking Cardassian in the room. The space was hardly more welcoming, however, and was cramped for more than two people, encouraging anyone making use of it to conclude their business as quickly as possible.

PERSONAL TOUCHES

Despite the spartan nature of the office, Sisko made few efforts to humanize it. Instead, he preferred to keep it as distinct from his homely living quarters as possible, and made sure to get out of the office as often as possible. He never even had a replicator installed, so that he was forced to venture out whenever he needed refreshment.

The few luxuries he did allow himself in the room were decorative scale models – including replicas of the early 21st-century International Space Station, the 22nd-century *Daedalus*-class starship *U.S.S. Horizon* NCC-176, and his old ship, the *U.S.S. Saratoga* NCC-31911. He also kept a baseball on his desk, which came to represent the man himself when he was not on the station.

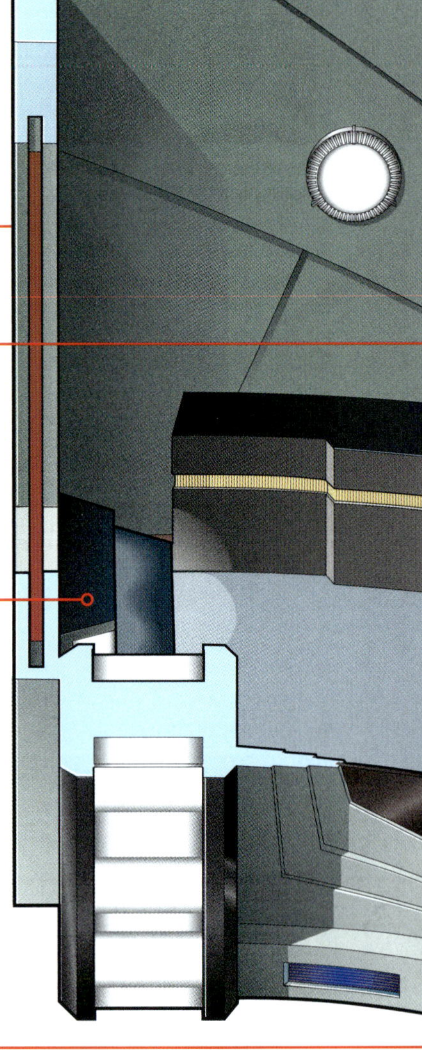

Sisko's scale models included this *Miranda*-class starship and a *Nebula*-class vessel.

The three entrances included a separate door on either side, accessed by steps.

The grand, gold-colored main doors to the office overlooked ops from atop a flight of stairs.

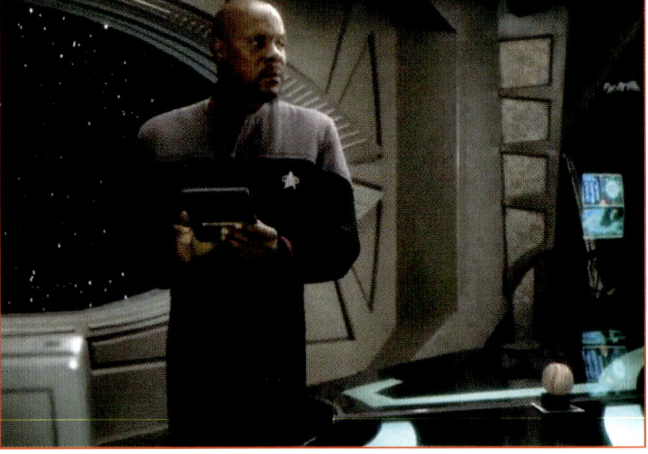

Sisko used his office to conduct a variety of station business, to communicate with senior staff at Starfleet, and to hold meetings with his crew.

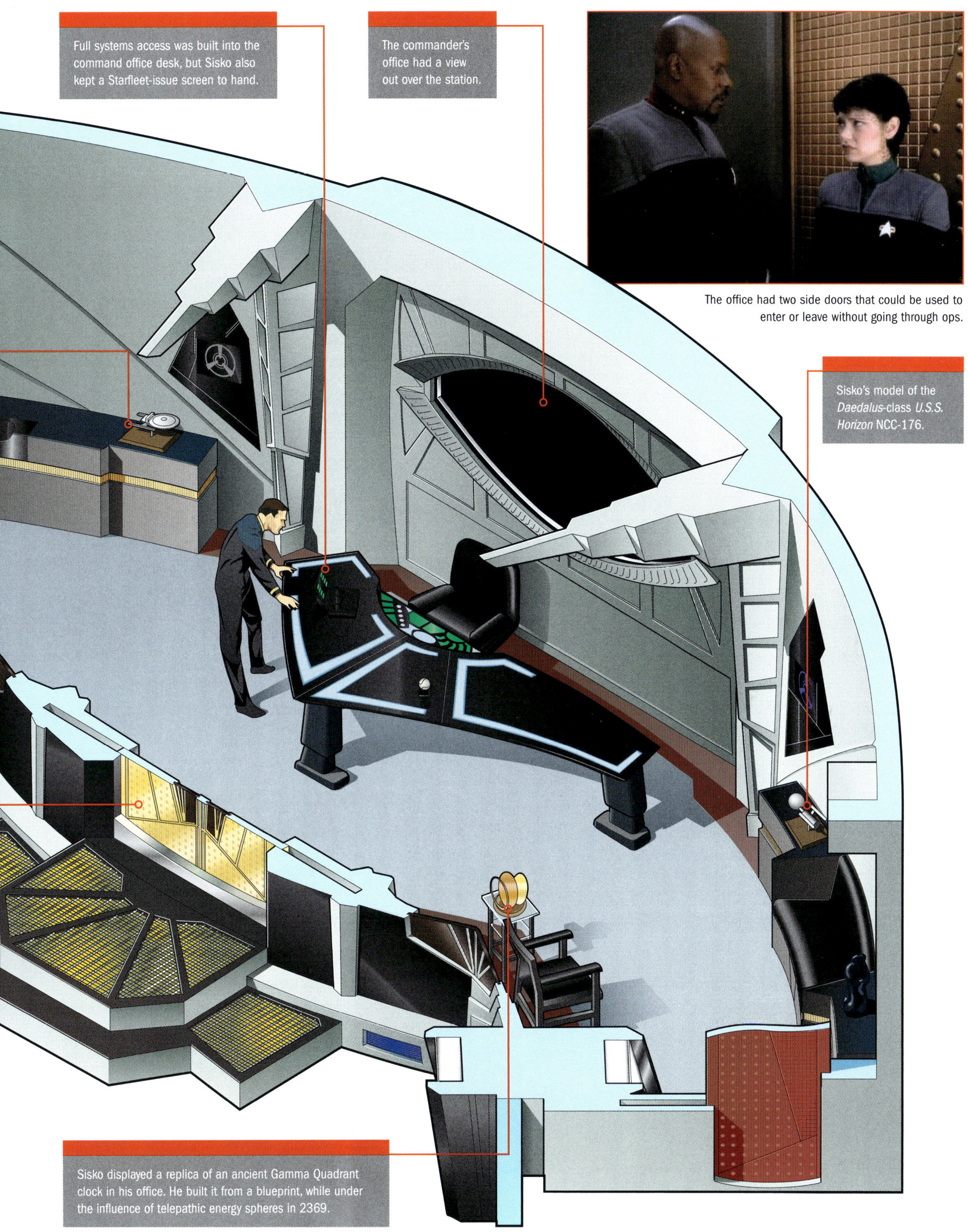

The office had two side doors that could be used to enter or leave without going through ops.

TRANSPORTER SYSTEMS

Deep Space 9's personnel transporters were used less frequently than those on a starship, but were still an essential feature of the station – along with the indispensable cargo transporters.

Though the Cardassians destroyed much equipment on their withdrawal from Terok Nor, they left behind a fully functional transporter network for cargo and personnel. As a seasoned transporter chief onboard the *U.S.S. Enterprise* NCC-1701-D, chief of operations Miles O'Brien was able to operate the unfamiliar equipment without too much trouble, but this became much easier after he installed adaptive interfaces corresponding to Bajoran and Starfleet specifications.

In its original position in orbit around Bajor, the station frequently transported Bajorans and Cardassians to and from the planet's surface. Indeed, the fact that even the cargo transporters had a default high-quantum resolution suggested that these may have been used to transport troops or large work parties *en masse*. However, once the station was relocated to the mouth of the wormhole, its distance from Bajor fell well outside the transporters' safe maximum range of 40,000km. Thereafter, most arrivals and departures on Deep Space 9 occurred via runabout pads and docking ports, and the transfer of cargo to and from docked ships monopolized the work of transporter operators. Emergency evacuation procedures were also affected, and station-to-shore beam-out protocols gave way to station-to-ship processions.

EVERYDAY USE

In total, 25 transporters were spread around the station, with 10 reserved for life-forms in the central core and the habitat ring. The remaining 15 were located in and close to the docking ring and primarily used for cargo. The inclusion of a three-pad transporter in ops allowed for officers and important visitors to be beamed directly to and from the command center, and could be configured to transport up to six humanoids at once. The more flexible cargo pads, conversely, could handle up to 1,894.5kg of living matter or 1.23 tonnes of cargo in one stream.

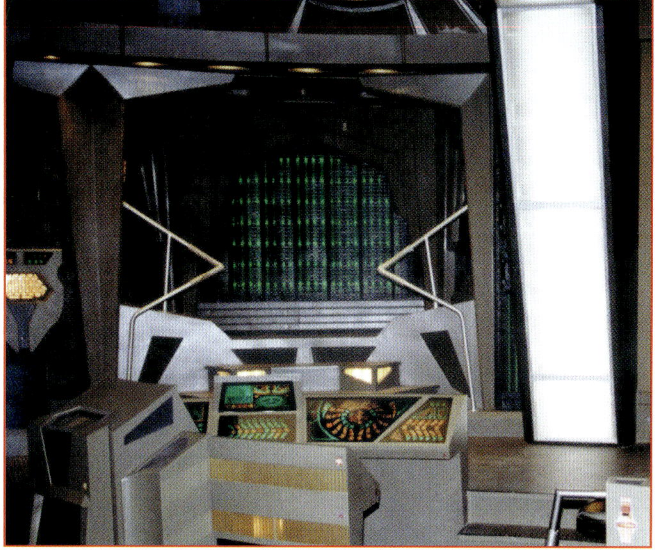
The transporter platform in ops was designed for use by up to three passengers at once, but had the capacity to transport up to six individuals or much larger objects.

All transporter operations throughout the station were supervised by either Starfleet or Bajoran security personnel, usually working alongside freighter crews. As Deep Space 9 was not technically a Federation facility, the movement of cargo incurred costs levied by the Bajorans, and these were usually calculated according to the total mass of the goods in transit and the EPS energy expended by the station as a result of their transportation.

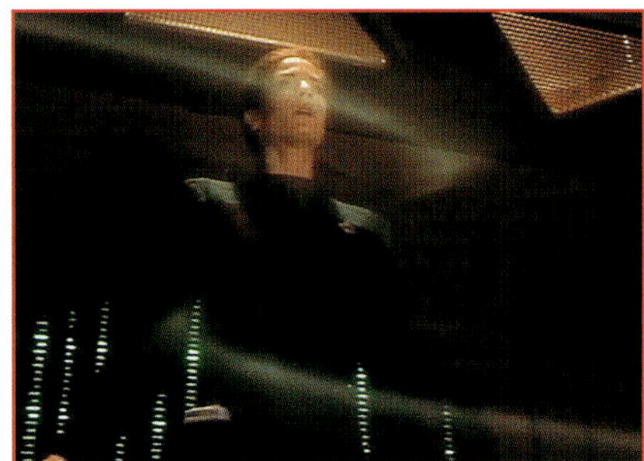
In 2369, an orb exited the wormhole and was beamed aboard Deep Space 9. On arrival in ops, it immediately dissipated to reveal Lieutenant Jadzia Dax inside.

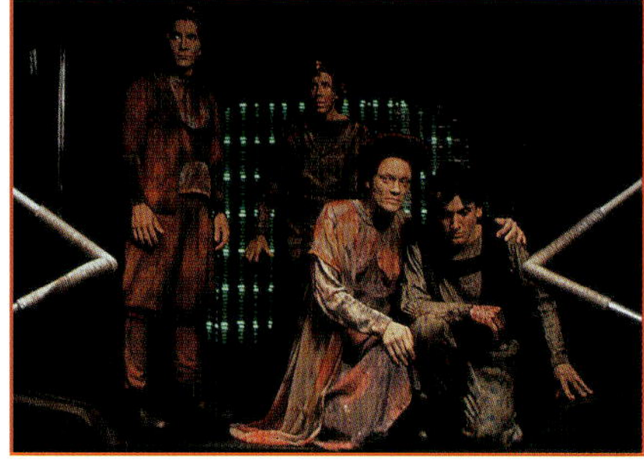
In 2370, Skrreean refugees from the Gamma Quadrant were beamed directly to ops as their badly damaged ship was brought to the station by tractor beam.

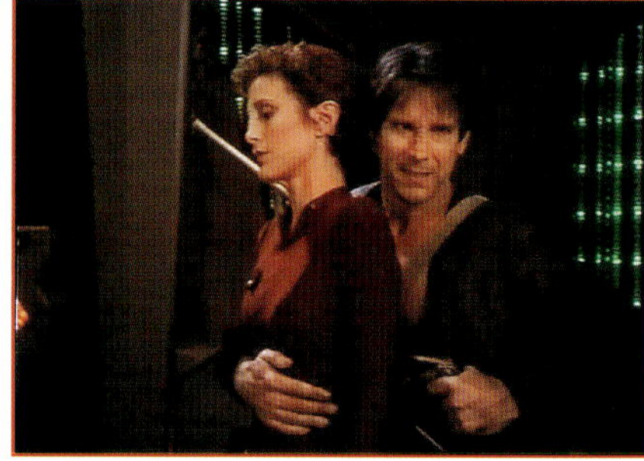
In 2374, the mirror universe counterpart of Bareil Antos hijacked the ops transporter platform to travel to Deep Space 9, where he immediately took Kira hostage.

EMERGENCY MEASURES

Transporter technology operated on a similar principle to Quark's holosuites, which generated matter from a program rather than real life. So when a transporter accident risked the loss of five crewmembers in 2372, an active holosuite program was the best place to store their patterns before they degraded in the buffer.

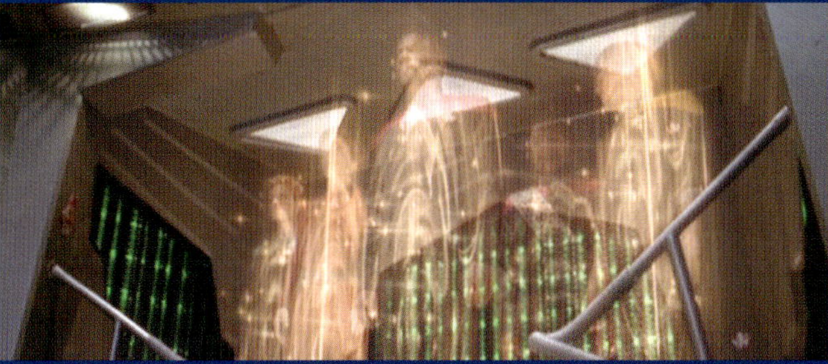

Sisko, Kira, Dax, O'Brien, and Worf were approaching the station in a sabotaged runabout when they needed emergency beam-out before the ship exploded.

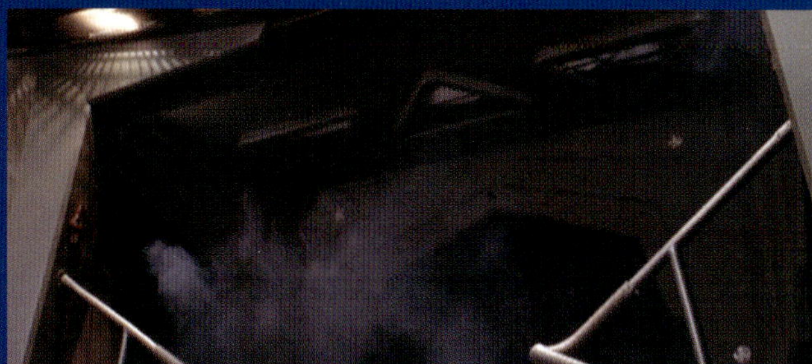

Transport was underway when the explosion occurred, releasing a blast of energy that blew out the primary energizing coils, leaving no sign of the crewmembers.

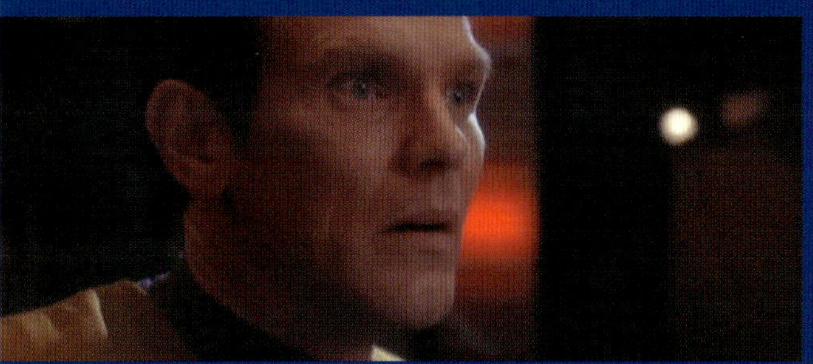

For a moment, Commander Eddington feared they were lost. In fact, their patterns were in the buffer, but would degrade if kept there until repairs were complete.

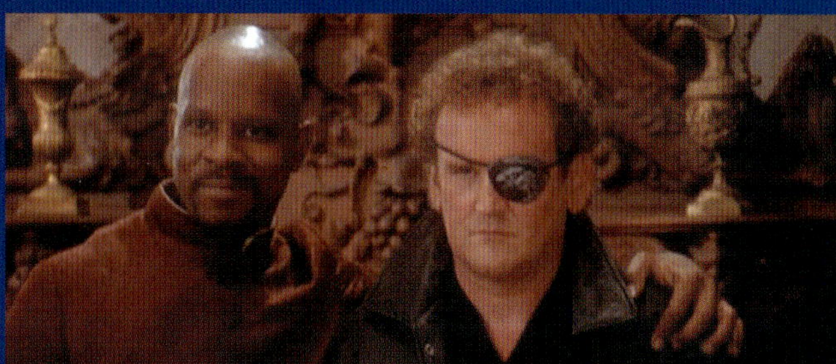

Eddington ordered the computer to make any necessary deletions to store them elsewhere, and so it saved them as characters in Dr. Bashir's 1960s spy fantasy.

TECHNICAL SPECIFICATIONS

Cardassian transporters worked along the same lines as Starfleet's equivalent technology, comprising a system of components that could not only desconstruct matter and transmit it in sequence for reintegration at a target site, but also reintegrate sequenced matter received from afar. The transporters found on Deep Space 9, however, were by no means identical to those found on a starship. Their energizing chambers were more enclosed, and bounded by field energy sustainer grids that concentrated the annular confinement beams. They also tended to be more elevated – atop a flight of three of four steps built over the phase transition coils. The nearby operating console was not part of a dedicated transporter control system, but a subset of the station's central computer core.

SAFETY MEASURES

As with all matter transportation technologies, one of the most important elements in the Cardassian system was the pattern buffer, which briefly stored the matter stream created by dematerialization prior to transmission. This allowed for the Heisenberg and Doppler compensators to correct for molecular variances in the stream, ensuring precise reintegration at the target coordinates. Buffering was usually performed in a matter of seconds, but in an emergency a humanoid pattern could be safely retained in the buffer for around four and a half minutes before it was in any serious danger of degrading.

Deep Space 9's original system also included biofilters to detect contraband devices and dangerous organisms. However, these worked from a database that included only half of the hazards identified by Federation transporters. For this reason, additional scanners were swiftly installed when Starfleet and the Bajorans assumed control of the space station in 2369.

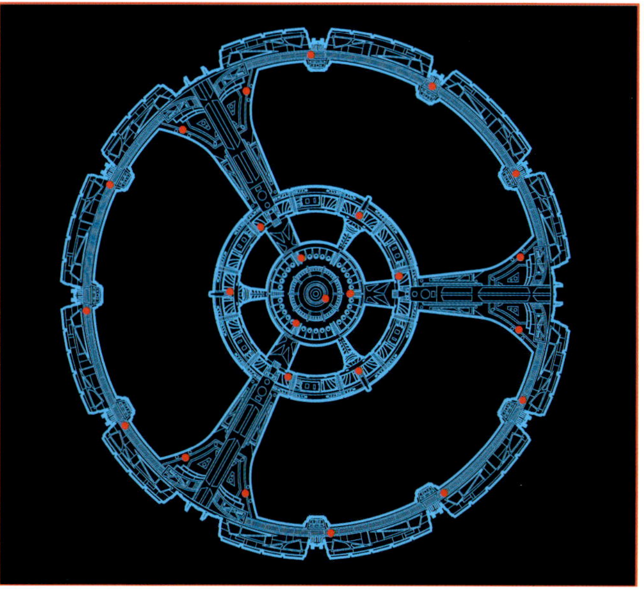

The large number of transporters on the station (marked in red) reflected its original use as an orbital facility, where Cardassians frequently beamed to and from Bajor.

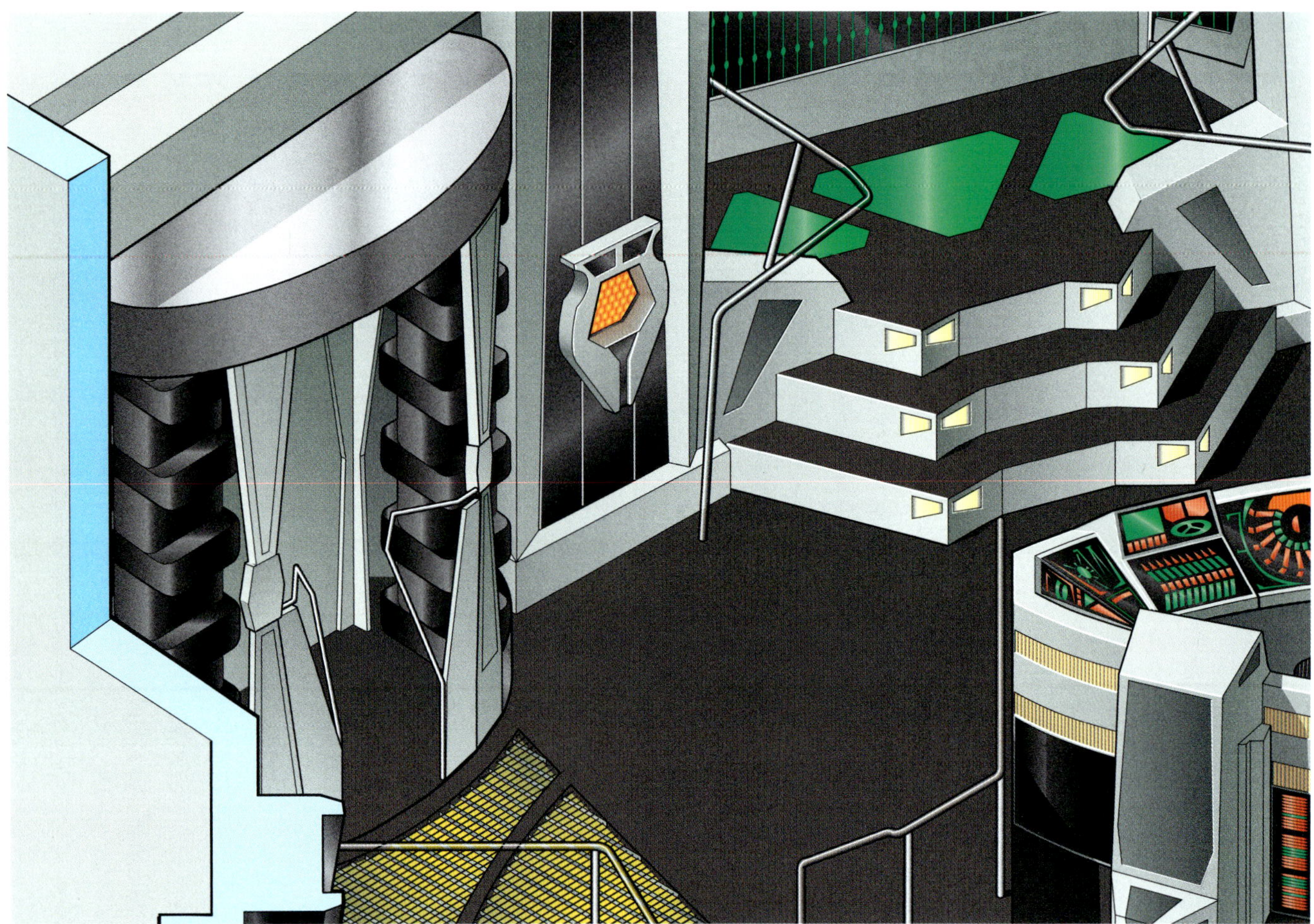

TURBOLIFT NETWORK

The turbolifts on Deep Space 9 operated on similar principles to those found onboard a Federation starship, but had a distinctly different look and a number of unusual features.

Much like a Federation starship, Deep Space 9's multilevel layout was most easily traversed using turbolifts. Numerous carriageways ran throughout the station, providing access to all 34 levels of the core, and more than 250 levels within the rings and docking pylons. Each carriage could travel both horizontally and vertically, following routes covering a total of 16.54km.

Each turbolift was powered by dedicated EPS trunking, feeding twin synchronized Maglev motors on the outside of the carriage. These motors converted the EPS energy to a multiphase alternating current to power a series of 15 Maglev coils. The direction of travel was determined by these coils, under the control of an onboard isolinear processor. The station's main computer monitored the system, but in standard operation, once a passenger had issued their command, each carriage had autonomous control over its routing, speed, and collision-avoidance measures. Peak velocity was 17m per second, making most parts of the station accessible in moments.

CARDASSIAN DESIGN

The main difference between Deep Space 9's Cardassian-designed turbolifts and the ones found on Starfleet ships was the open design of the carriages. Rather than a fully enclosed capsule, each of the station's turbolifts was more akin to a moving platform, with a back wall and a ceiling, but only safety handrails at the front. This design exposed passengers to the fast-moving surfaces of the lift-shaft interior and, as a result, each carriage was limited to six humanoid occupants at a time, to ensure that everyone could stand well back. The benefits of this system were most noticeable in ops, where there was no outer door on the turbolift shaft. This meant that an arriving officer could begin to take in the situation on the command deck while the carriage was still moving, and even leap the final meter in an emergency.

Another significant difference between Cardassian and Starfleet turbolifts was that carriages were not equipped with individual inertial damping field generators. Instead, the potentially injurious effects of such rapid transit were counteracted by an inertial damping effect provided by the EPS conduit coatings in the lift shaft, which emitted low-level polarized gravitons.

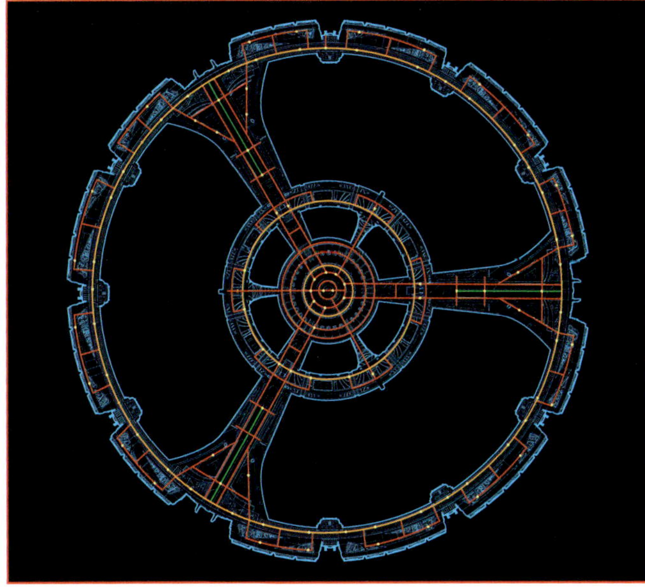

The three main turbolift carriage routes on Deep Space 9, mapped in yellow, red, and green. Key entry/exit points are marked as yellow dots.

EVERYDAY USE

Built for utility rather than enjoyment, the turbolifts were unadorned and poorly lighted. Their interiors were lined with bare duranium, built around a kelindide and toranium frame. A single oval light panel was integrated into the ceiling. To summon a turbolift, riders activated a touch pad at one of the many access points throughout the station. Heavy-duty double doors on the outside of the shaft protected against accidents when no turbolift was present, but in practice, the efficiency of the system ensured there was rarely a wait for a carriage. On entry, passengers usually requested their destination via voice command, but could also make use of a small wall-mounted panel on the wall of the carriage. Illuminated rectangular bars then indicated speed and direction of transit.

For all its quirks, the system rarely malfunctioned, and on the only notable occasion that it failed, it did so owing to a sentient computer virus that was playing havoc with all of the station's systems.

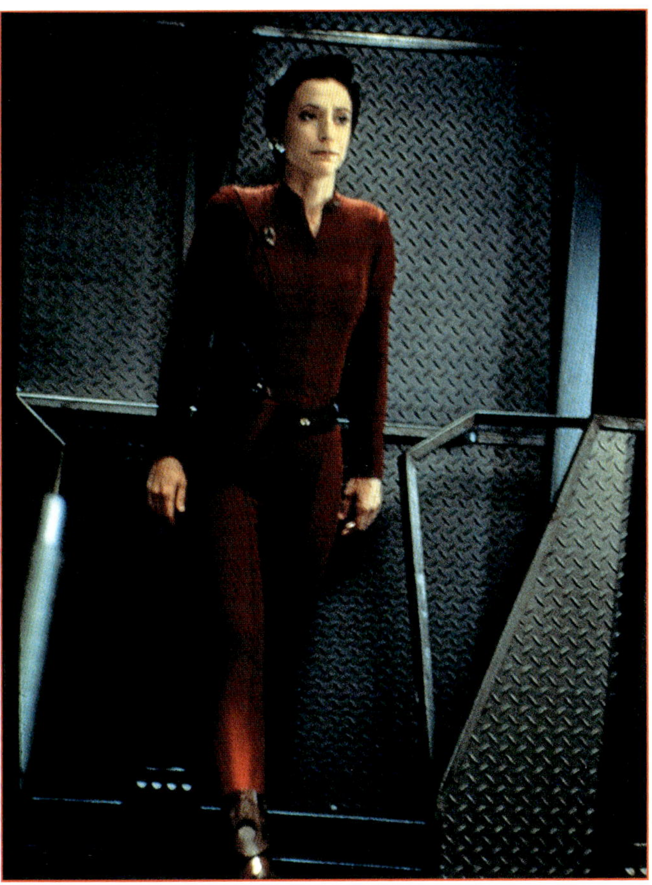

The senior staff almost always used the turbolift to enter ops. It was connected to a network of shafts that linked up with the rest of the station.

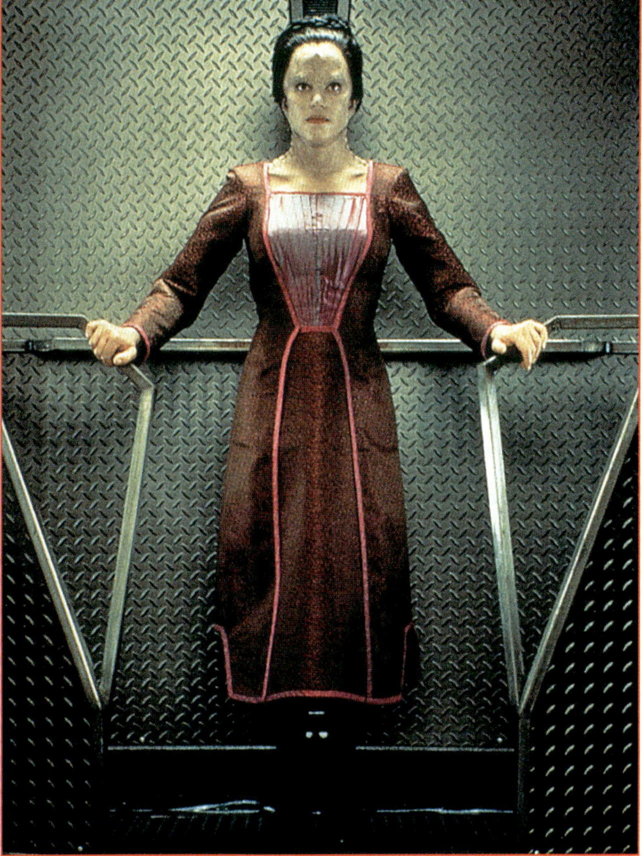

The rails at the exposed front of the station's turbolifts were angled inward to keep hands away from the lift-shaft walls. Another handrail extended along the back wall.

THE PROMENADE

The circular mall in Deep Space 9's upper core was the first port of call for many visitors to the station, and an essential part of daily life for long-term residents.

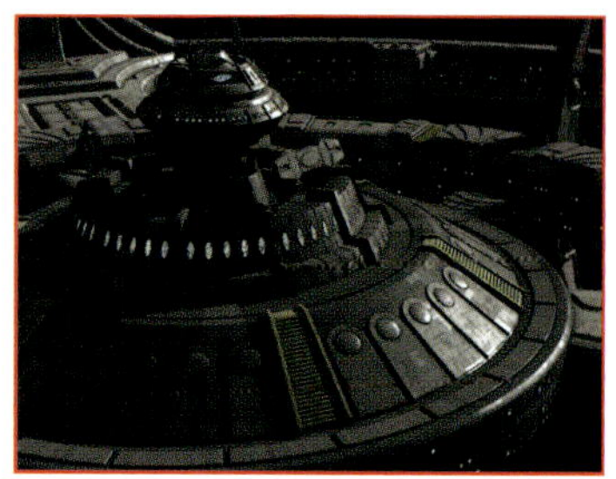

The Promenade ran aound the top of the station underneath ops.

The Promenade was at the heart of commercial and social life on Deep Space 9. Located below ops, the thoroughfare formed a circle around the upper core, and was lined with shops, eateries, and station facilities such as the security office and the infirmary. A mezzanine level looked down on the bustling scene, and out through large circular windows to the wormhole.

Security chief Odo did not usually allow weapons on the Promenade, and the main public routes leading to it had built-in weapons detectors. Sleeping on the Promenade was also prohibited, as was trading without a license. The Promenade Merchants' Association represented its many small businesses, which included Quark's Bar, Garak's Clothiers, a Bajoran jumja-stick kiosk, and Bajoran, Klingon, Bolian, and Vulcan restaurants.

The Promenade was also home to the station's Bajoran temple, and during religious festivals celebrations would extend beyond its doors.

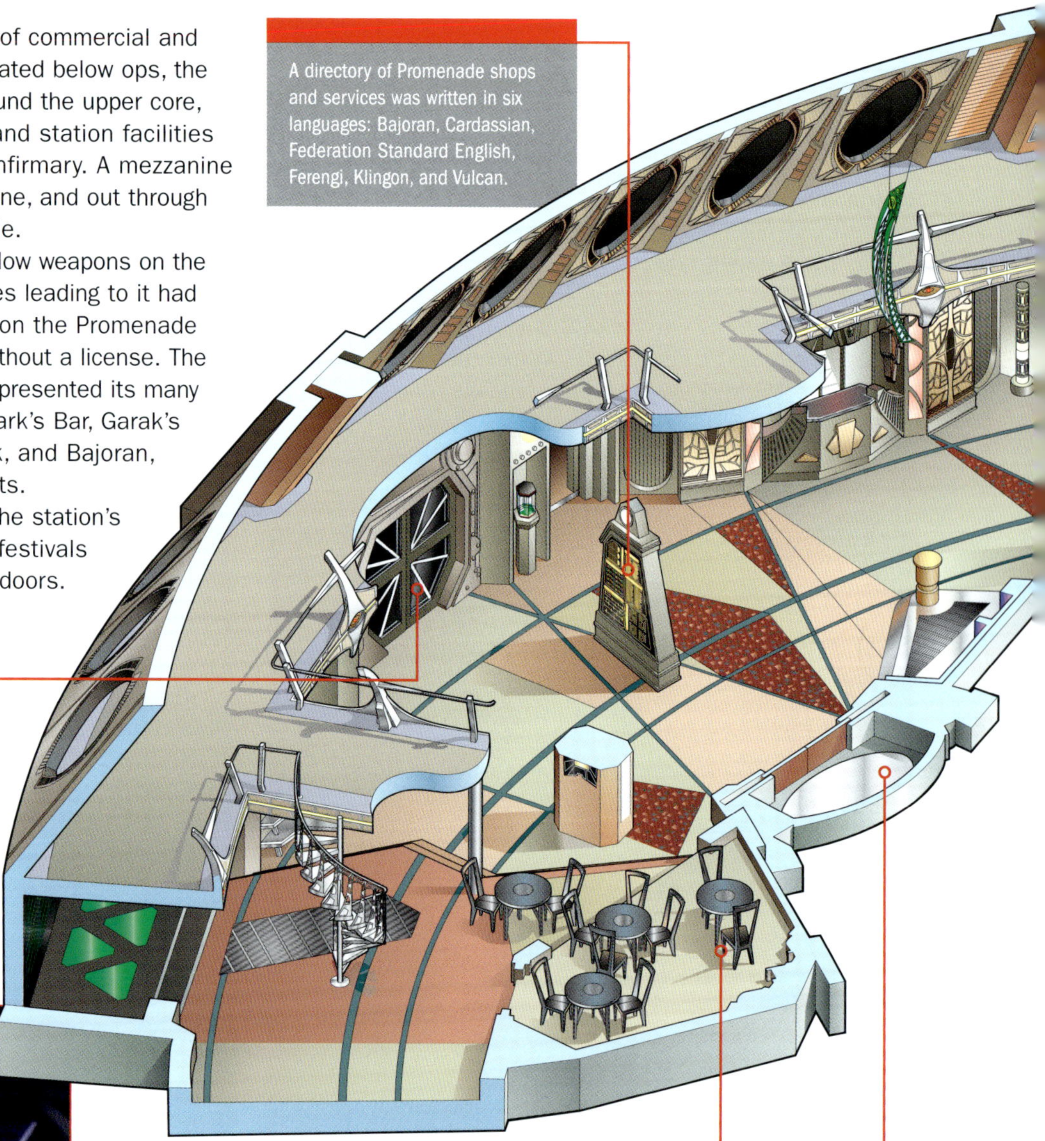

A directory of Promenade shops and services was written in six languages: Bajoran, Cardassian, Federation Standard English, Ferengi, Klingon, and Vulcan.

The security office opened onto the Promenade, enabling the public to report crimes to Odo in person – and Odo to keep a watchful eye on the public at all times.

Café-style seating and a wide range of replicated food and beverages were available at the self-service replimat.

Seven turbolift shafts connected the Promenade to the rest of the station.

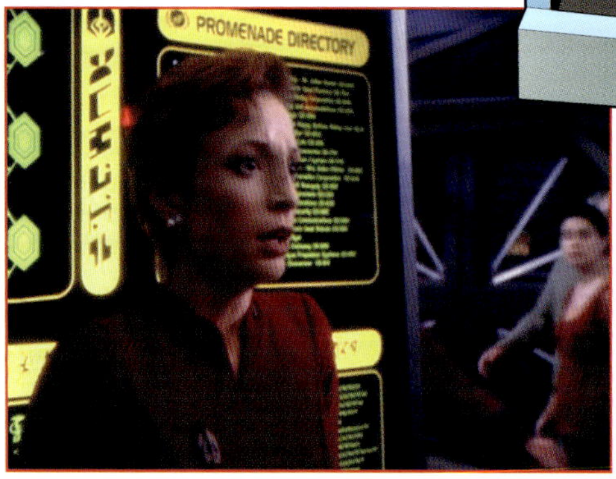

Major Kira standing by the Promenade directory in 2374. The English language listings can be seen over her left shoulder, with Ferengi display text to her right.

Circular windows ringed the mezzanine level, providing 360-degree views of starships coming and going from the docking pylons and the wormhole.

FURTHER FACILITIES
Additional services located on the Promenade included an information kiosk, a mineralogical assay office, an aquarium, and a gym.

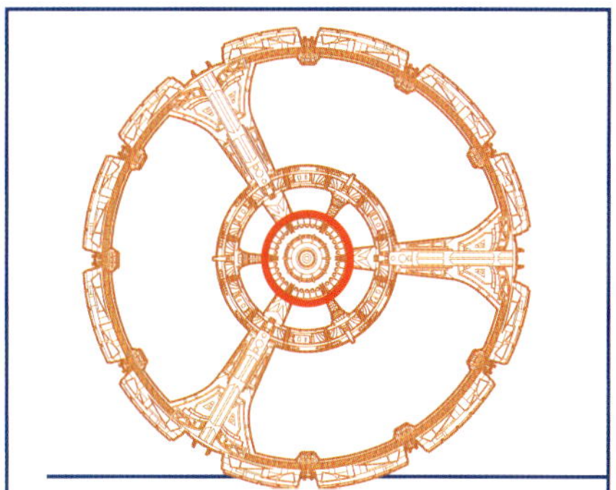

ROOM LOCATOR

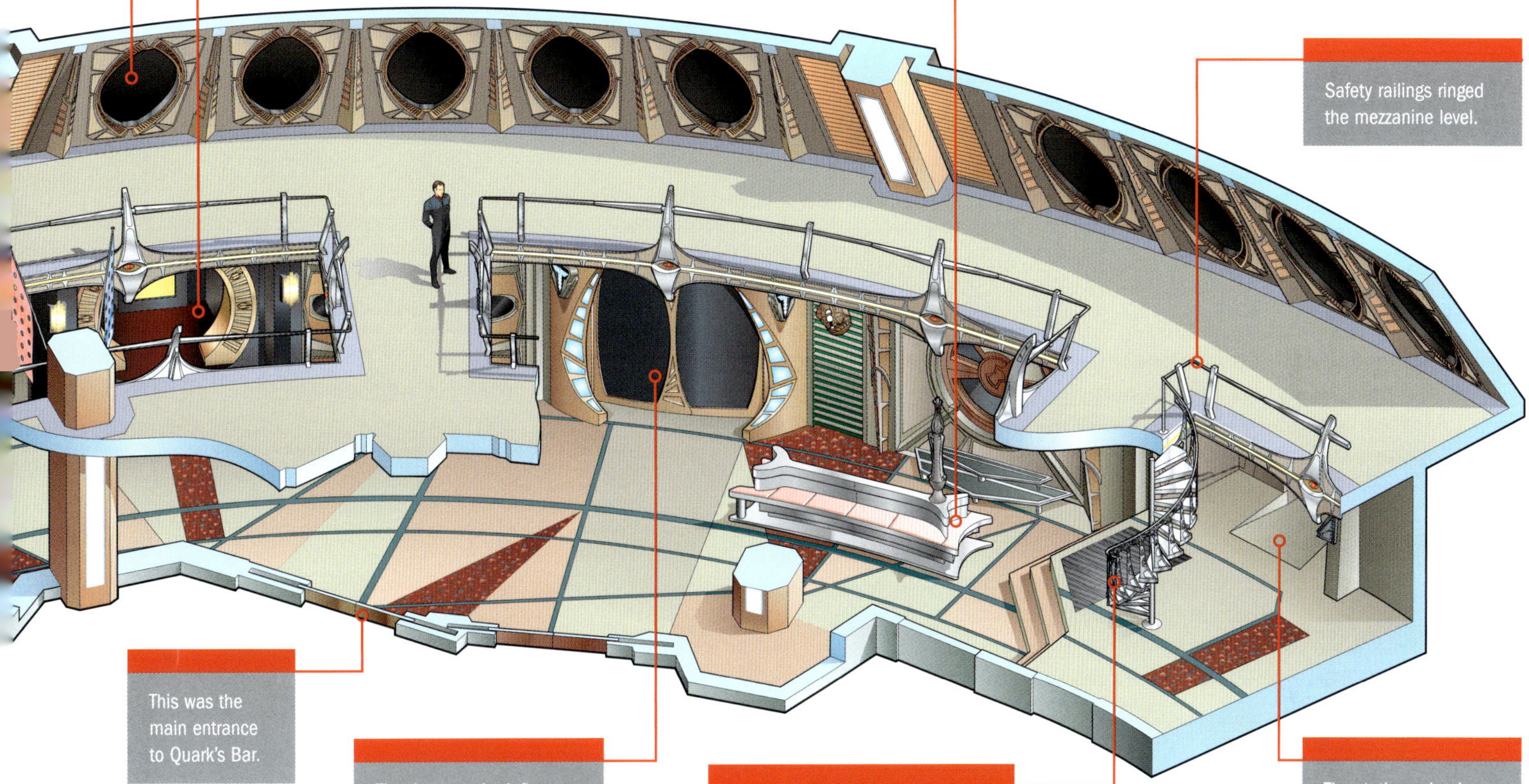

The temple's Promenade location reflected its place at the center of everyday life for many Bajorans.

Bench seating was provided at intervals, but loitering was actively discouraged by Odo.

Safety railings ringed the mezzanine level.

This was the main entrance to Quark's Bar.

The doors to the infirmary were usually kept open.

Spiral staircases linked the levels.

The station school was behind this door.

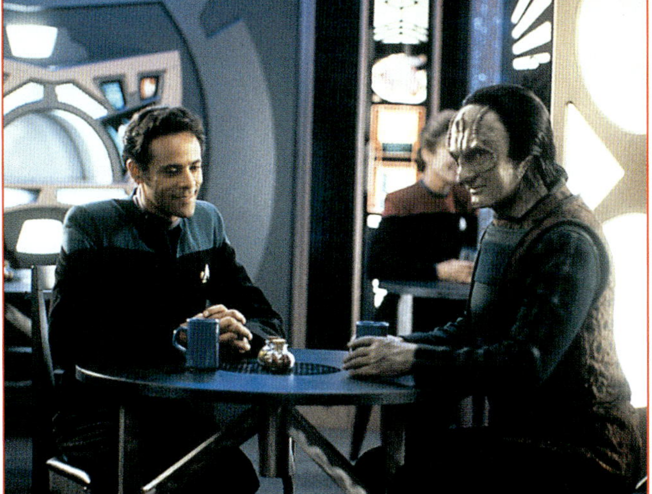

Dr. Bashir and Garak were among the regular patrons of the replimat. Its popularity meant that there were often queues to use the replicators and secure a table.

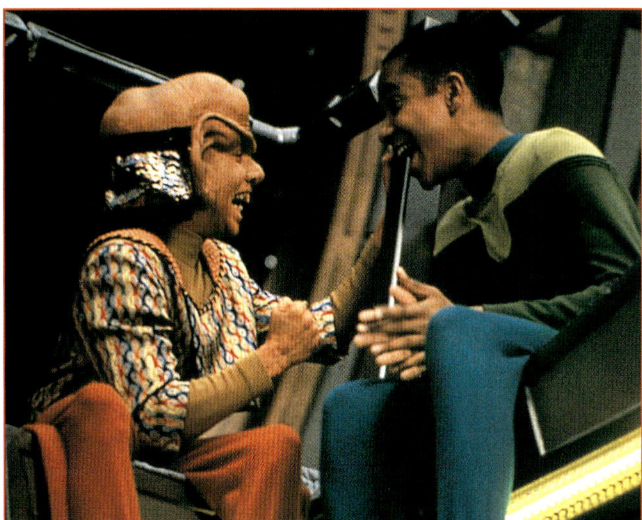

Good friends Nog and Jake Sisko spent much of their free time on the Promenade, watching the world go by as they perched on the edge of the mezzanine level.

QUARK'S BAR

The biggest and most notorious bar on the Promenade attracted everyone from smugglers to Starfleet officers, and operated on just the right side of the law.

Quark's Bar, Grill, Gaming House, and Holosuite Arcade (usually known simply as "Quark's") was the largest establishment on Deep Space 9, spanning both main levels of the Promenade and extending up to a third level just for holosuites. Its eponymous owner and manager was an unscrupulous Ferengi, who first opened for business when the station was a Cardassian ore-processing facility.

The main level was home to the bar and a casino area – and a dartboard, at the request of Chief O'Brien. Spiral stairs rose to the upper levels, with seating available on all three. Table and bar service was often provided by Quark himself, who prided himself on knowing his customers' needs and monetizing them. This included selling goods and services beyond the usual remit of a barkeeper, and so Quark's was known as a one-stop shop for obtaining the unobtainable.

To compete with the nearby replimat, Quark kept a wide range of real beverages in a secure storeroom. However, most meals were replicated from a station behind the bar. This was also where Quark stored holosuite programs on isolinear rods, which he loaned out for set periods of time.

Patrons could easily spend an entire evening at Quark's, starting with drinks and a meal, before trying their luck on the gaming tables, and then forgetting their losses with the fantasy adventure of a lifetime in one of the holosuites.

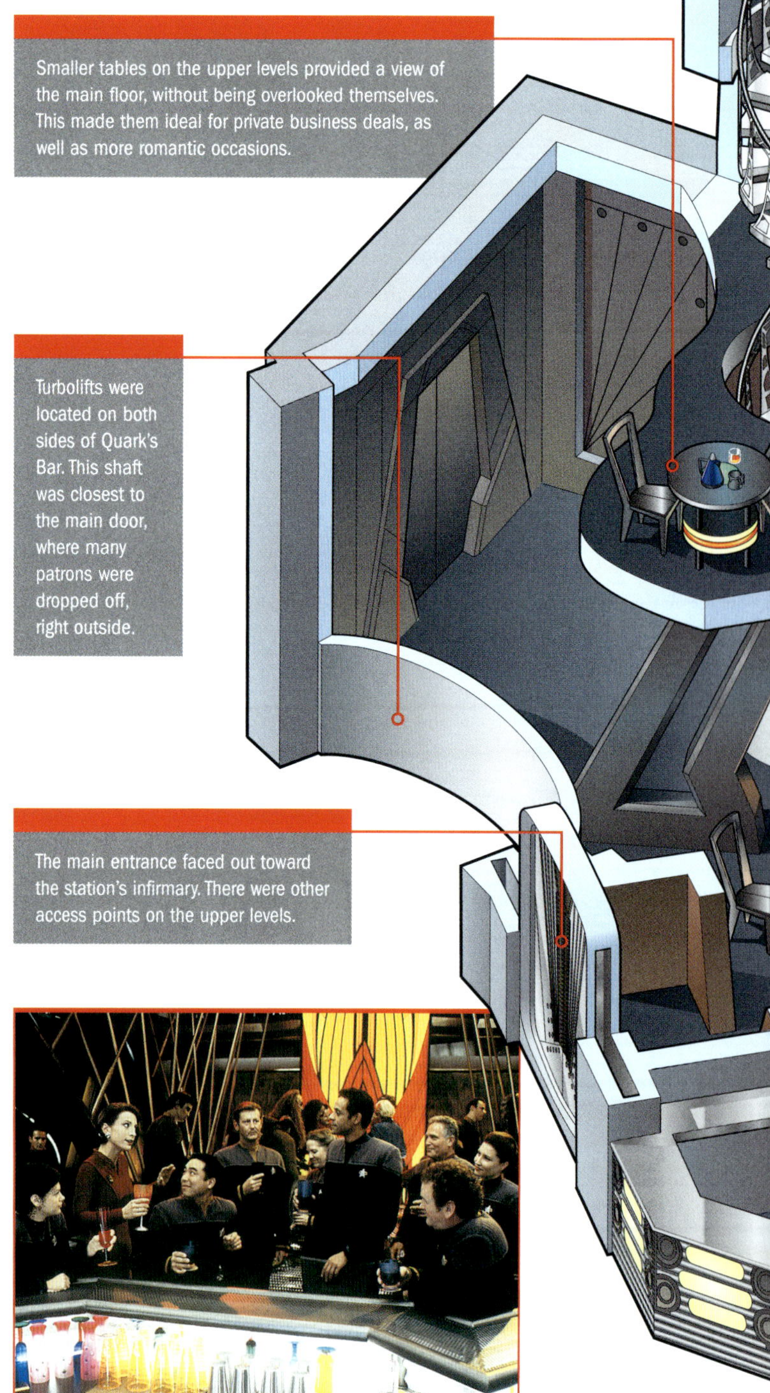

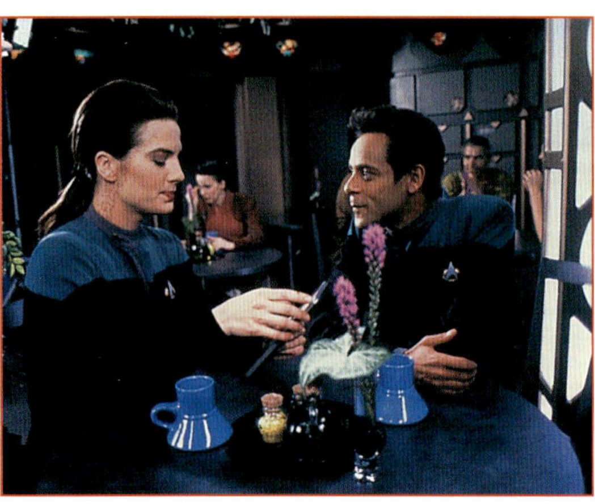

The Deep Space 9 staff often ate at Quark's, even though they had replicators in their quarters.

Station staff were a familiar sight at Quark's, especially during the Dominion War, when morale-boosting gatherings proved essential.

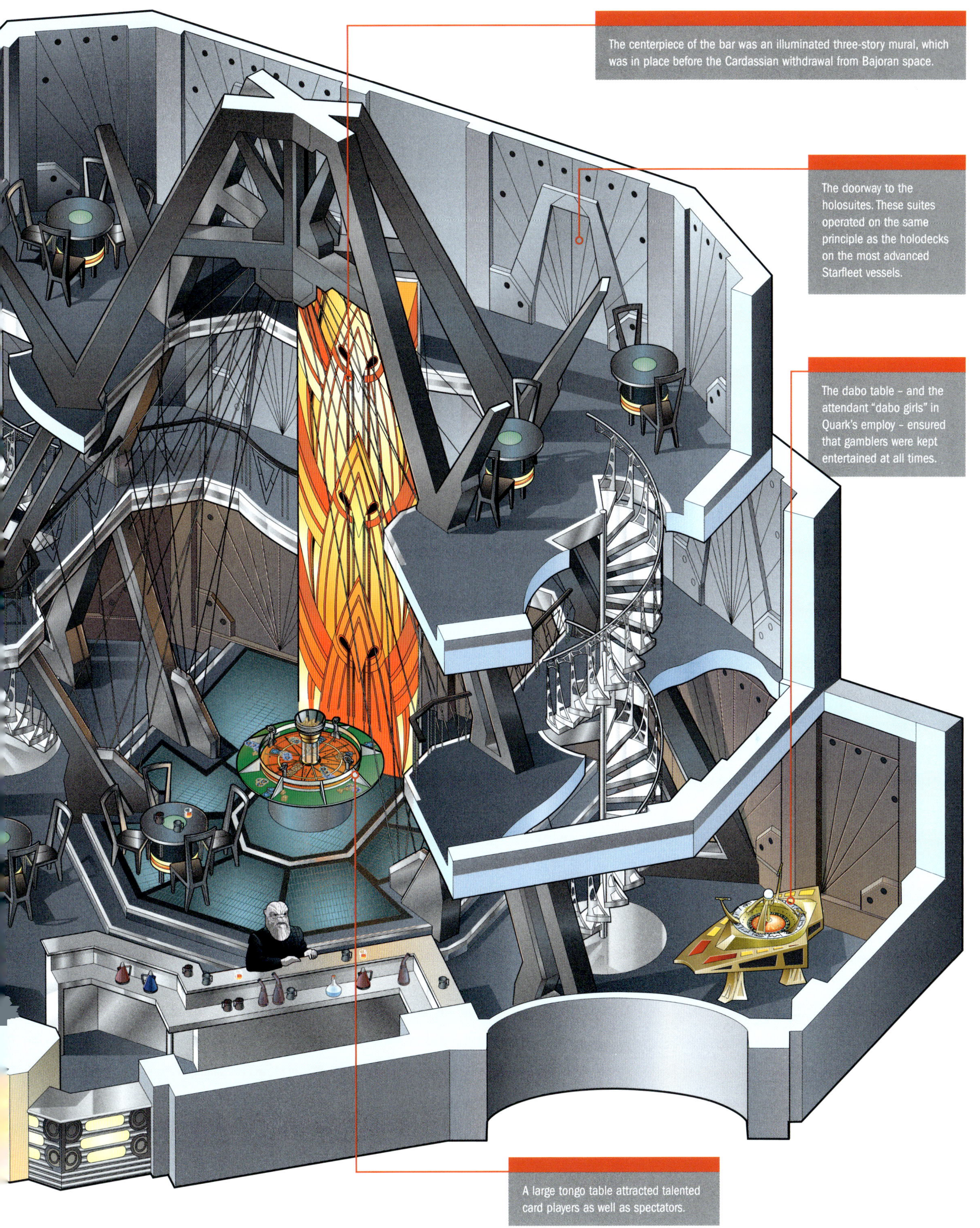

The centerpiece of the bar was an illuminated three-story mural, which was in place before the Cardassian withdrawal from Bajoran space.

The doorway to the holosuites. These suites operated on the same principle as the holodecks on the most advanced Starfleet vessels.

The dabo table – and the attendant "dabo girls" in Quark's employ – ensured that gamblers were kept entertained at all times.

A large tongo table attracted talented card players as well as spectators.

THE GAME OF DABO

Unlike the far more complex game of tongo, dabo required no special skill to play – only a supply of funds. For this reason, it was the most popular casino game available at Quark's.

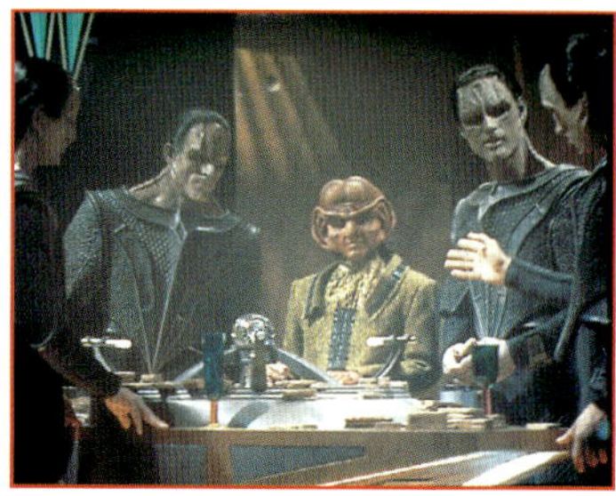

Ferengi waiter Broik sometimes worked the tables instead of dabo girls, a practice from when the station was a Cardassian facility.

One of the most popular entertainments at Quark's Bar was dabo – a Ferengi game of chance in which players laid bets on the spin of a wheel. Like the Earth game of roulette, which it superficially resembled, dabo's appeal lay in the potential to win vast riches with little effort, but huge losses were far more likely.

Play began with the placing of bets, usually in the form of latinum strips. Gamblers made their wagers based on intuitions about the likely combination of winning symbols, and then the dabo wheel was spun. "Pinch" pieces were released into the wheel automatically, and when it came to a stop after a few seconds, the number and position of the pinch pieces on the wheel determined the winners and losers. The latinum on the table was redistributed accordingly, before betting commenced once again.

Gaming on a dabo table could continue indefinitely, so long as players were in a position to wager. One gambler could quit the table at any time, leaving others to play on, with arrivals and departures changing the makeup of the game over the course of a session. At Quark's, the only limits on the length of a game were the house's operating hours and available funds – though it was highly unlikely that a player would ever win enough to "break the bank." Winnings were usually kept in their gold-pressed latinum form, but could also be redeemed as vouchers.

DABO GIRLS

Dabo at Quark's was always overseen by a member of staff. This was usually a young woman who was expected to maintain a party atmosphere and keep the gamblers

THE DABO TABLE

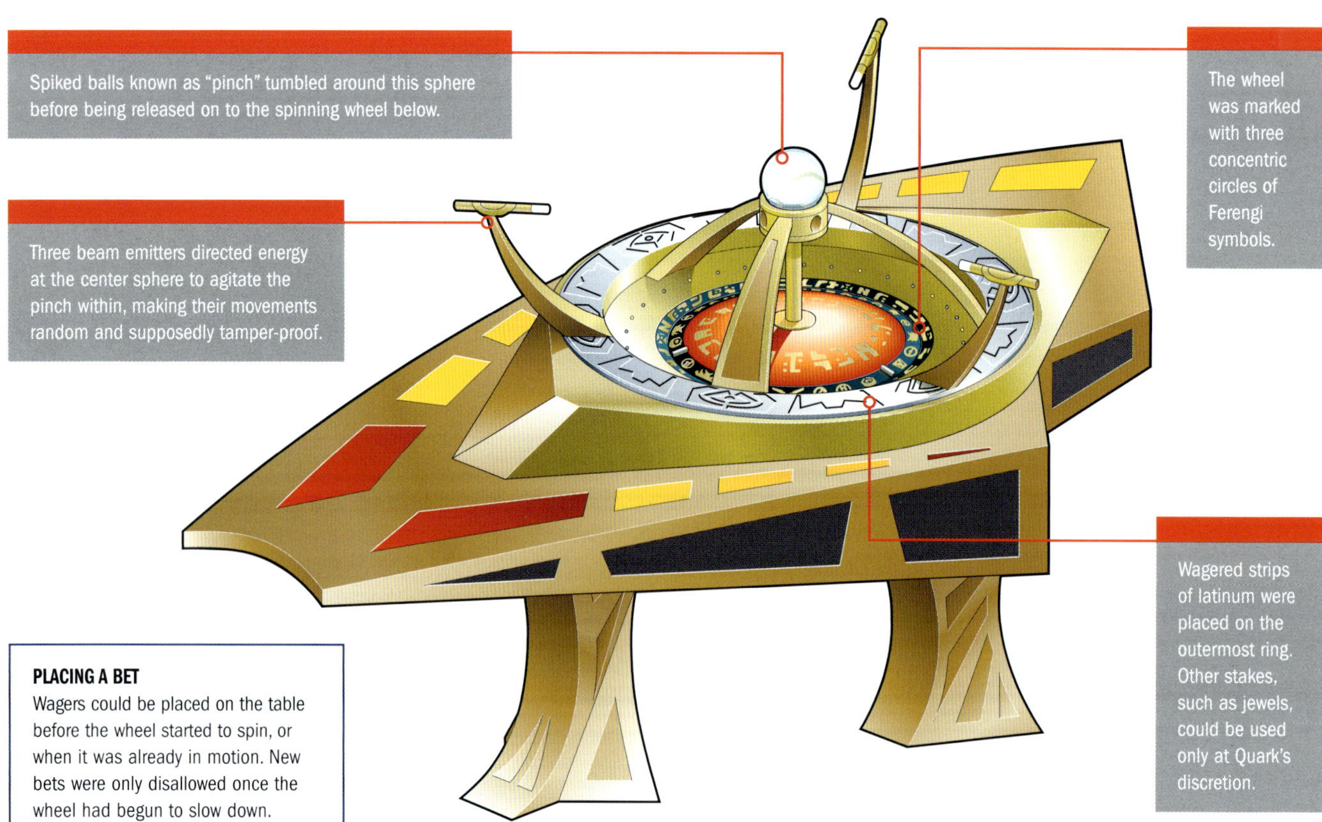

PLACING A BET
Wagers could be placed on the table before the wheel started to spin, or when it was already in motion. New bets were only disallowed once the wheel had begun to slow down.

from concentrating too hard on their strategies or their losses. Known as "dabo girls," these women could be recognized by the illuminated wand they used to operate the table, and the outfits that the job required them to wear. Dabo girls at Quark's included Sarda and Leeta, both of whom fought for – and won – better working conditions for themselves and for their fellow staff members.

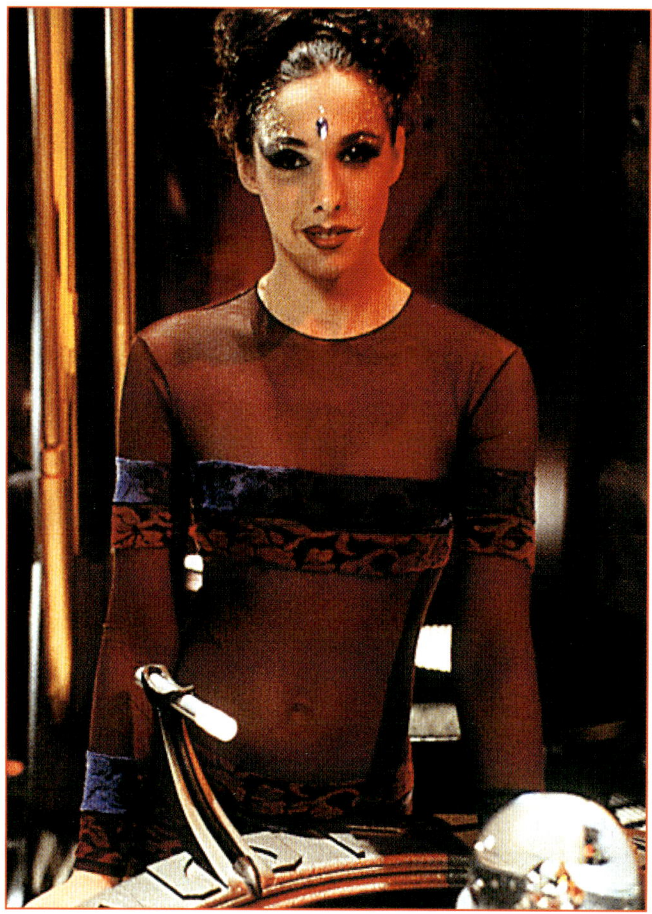

Quark's dabo girls were expected to look beautiful, while also enforcing game rules, spotting cheats, and instantly calculating any winnings from each spin of the wheel.

WINNERS AND LOSERS

Dabo wheels made a distinctive sound when they spun, adding to the anticipation of the outcome. A winning bet would be met with cries of "Dabo!" from those gathered around the table, making for a loud and lively ambience. Gamers accepted that the odds would never be in their favor, and played mostly for the fun of it, despite always hoping for a run of luck.

Although the game was entirely unpredictable, it was possible to acquire a degree of skill through practice – largely by knowing when to quit, and when to place high-stakes bets such as "triple down" and "triple over." If a player did hit a winning streak, Quark was not above ending it by instructing his staff to use a hidden function located on the underside of the dabo table. As running rigged games was illegal in the Federation and on Bajor, Quark had to be careful about how he used such devices. But his devious mind did prove useful if customers tried to cheat him. He knew that gravimetric scanners could be used to predict the outcome of a spin, and vigilantly watched for anyone using one in order to win unfairly.

FIGHTING FOR THEIR RIGHTS

Working as croupiers, hosts, and servers, Quark's dabo girls more than earned their meager wages. They frequently had to fend off the unwelcome attentions of customers who wanted them to exceed their contractual obligations, while other inappropriate demands were buried in the detail of their contracts...

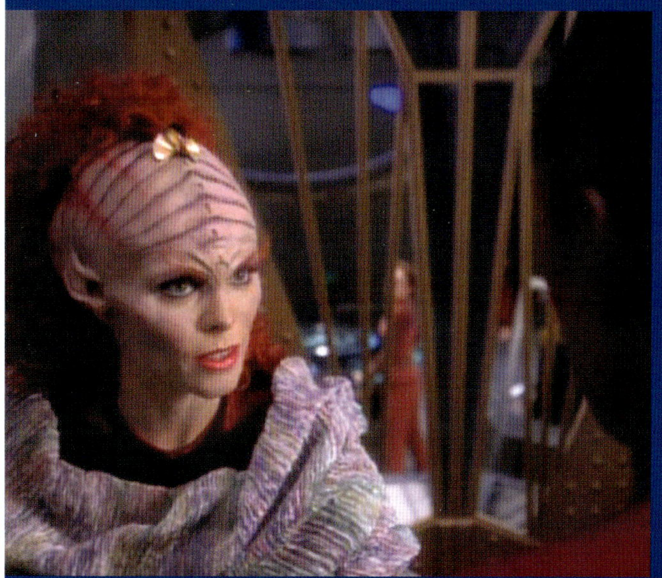

When dabo girl Sarda learned that her job description included being harassed, she complained to Commander Sisko, who forced Quark to amend his contracts.

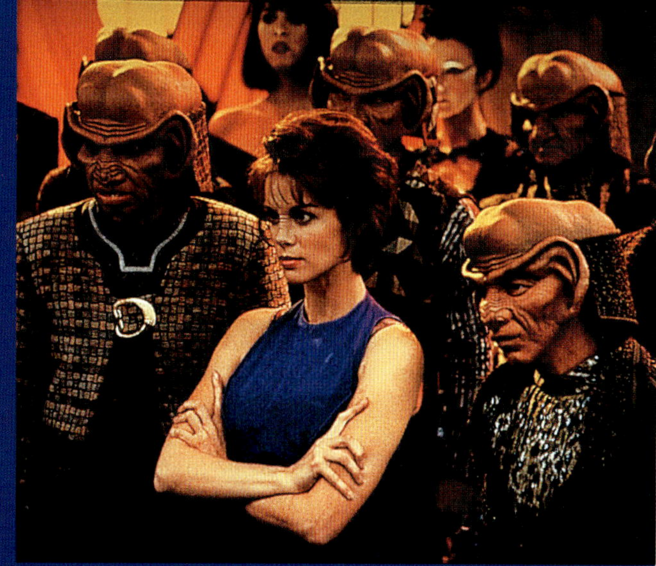

After Quark cut staff pay by one third, dabo girl Leeta was among the workers who went on strike, in defiance of Ferengi disregard for all employment rights.

QUARK'S HOLOSUITES

From brainteasers to ballgames and more, the most advanced recreational facilities on Deep Space 9 catered to all tastes and made a healthy profit for their owner.

Immersive holographic simulations were among the most popular forms of recreation during the late 24th century. The most advanced Federation starships of the era were equipped with holodecks, while commercial equivalents on planets and space stations were known as holosuites. The upper level of Quark's Bar was fitted with several of these, and the Ferengi hired them out for set periods of time.

Unlike standard Federation holodecks – which tended to be large, cuboid spaces with holographic projector arrays all along the flat walls – Quark's holosuites were a roughly octagonal shape with holo-emitters along the middle third of the walls only. However, the suites were just as capable of creating a believable, endlessly expansive environment as much larger and more powerful facilities.

EXPANDING SPACES

In most circumstances, Quark's customers would not even be aware of these design differences, since the program they had selected would be running before they stepped into the suite. All surfaces, including the floor, would be obscured by a tangible holographic scene, capable of scrolling with users' movements to create the impression of a seemingly limitless environment. Only during maintenance or basic programs that simply generated standalone elements – such as a single combatant for self-defense practice – would the bounds of the space become apparent.

POPULAR PROGRAMS

Anyone wanting to use Quark's holosuites was advised to make a booking well in advance, as the facilities were in near-constant demand. Patrons could supply a program of their own, or borrow one from Quark's ever-growing collection. For added realism, they could also opt to arrive at the bar dressed appropriately for their chosen scenario. Quark asked no questions, and was happy to satisfy any fantasy for a fee, but those favored by the station staff tended to be innocently escapist rather than erotic.

Dr. Bashir and Chief O'Brien often used the holosuites to recreate historical battles, while Major Kira employed them for springball practice. Lieutenant Dax had Quark install a puzzle game that responded to her brainwaves, and Captain Sisko used the facilities to watch and play baseball. During the Dominion War, a program based on a 1960s Las Vegas lounge proved especially popular with many of the station staff, and helped them cope in especially trying times.

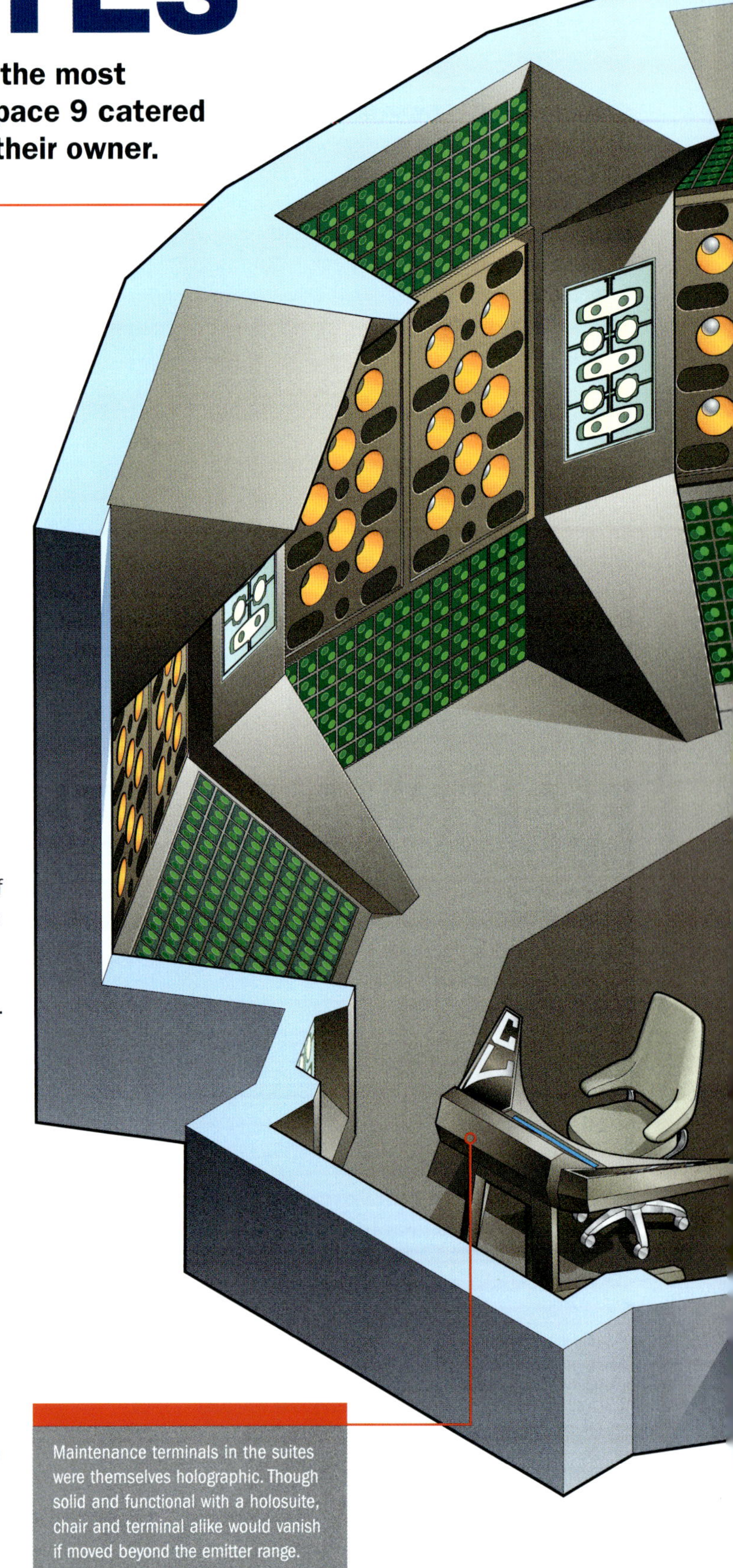

Maintenance terminals in the suites were themselves holographic. Though solid and functional with a holosuite, chair and terminal alike would vanish if moved beyond the emitter range.

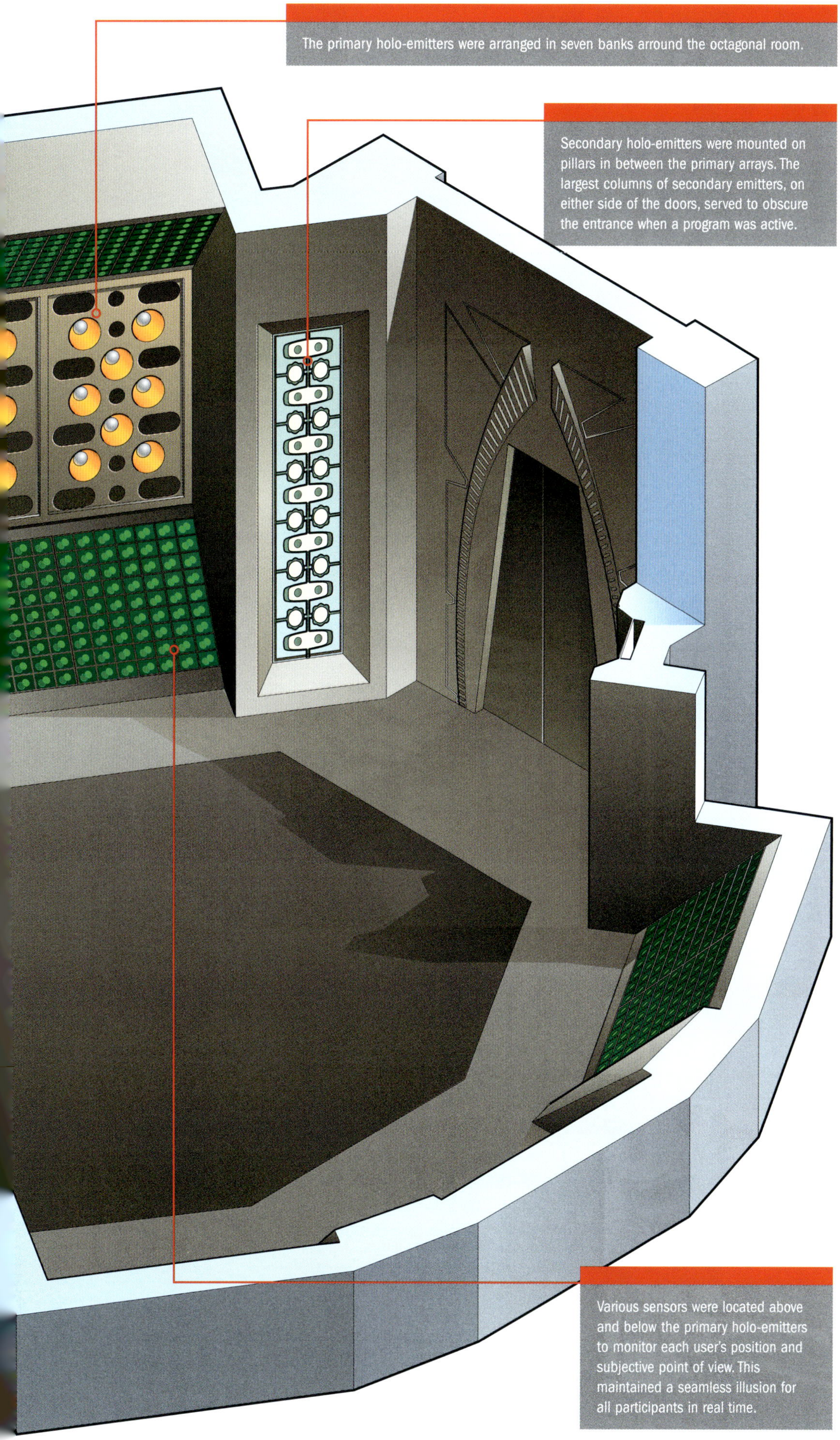

The primary holo-emitters were arranged in seven banks arround the octagonal room.

Secondary holo-emitters were mounted on pillars in between the primary arrays. The largest columns of secondary emitters, on either side of the doors, served to obscure the entrance when a program was active.

Various sensors were located above and below the primary holo-emitters to monitor each user's position and subjective point of view. This maintained a seamless illusion for all participants in real time.

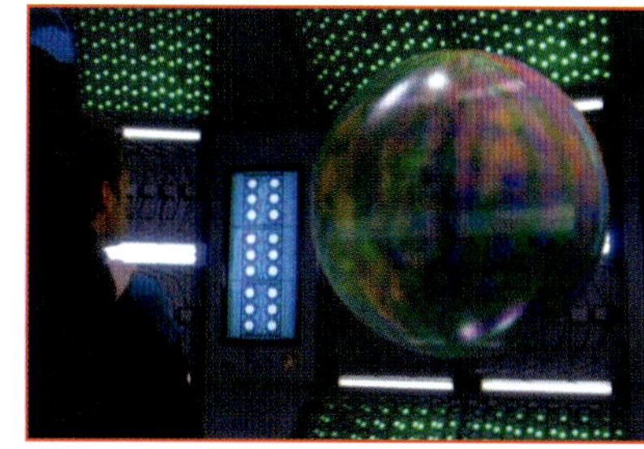

Under guidance from Dax in 2369, Dr. Bashir attempted to change the color of a holographic Altonian brainteaser sphere using just his mind.

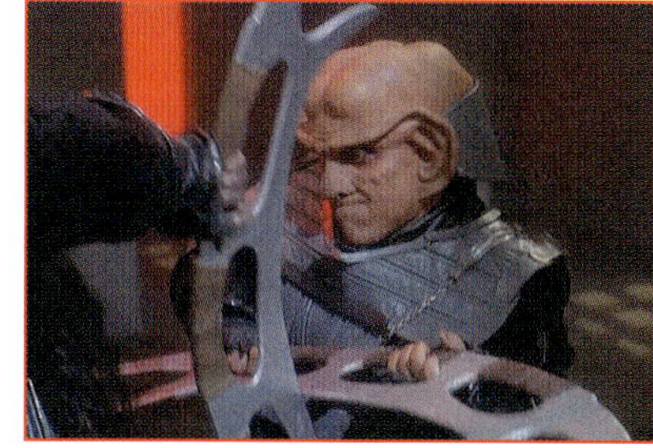

In 2373, Quark fought a real Klingon warrior in one holosuite, as Lt. Commander Worf secretly controlled his movements from a neighboring one.

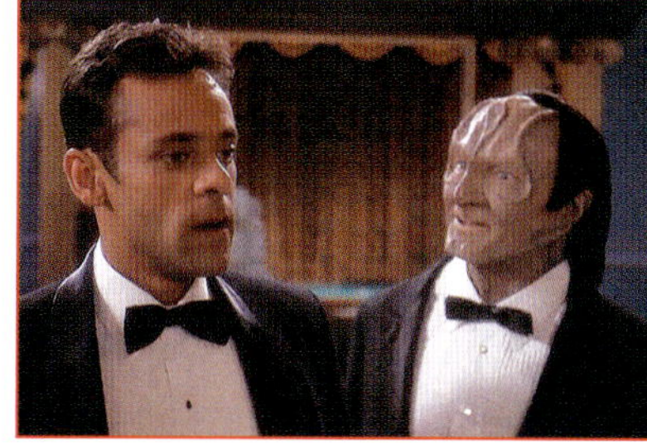

Dr. Bashir angrily reminded Garak that it was illegal to break into a holosuite program, when the tailor invaded his 20th-century spy fantasy in 2372.

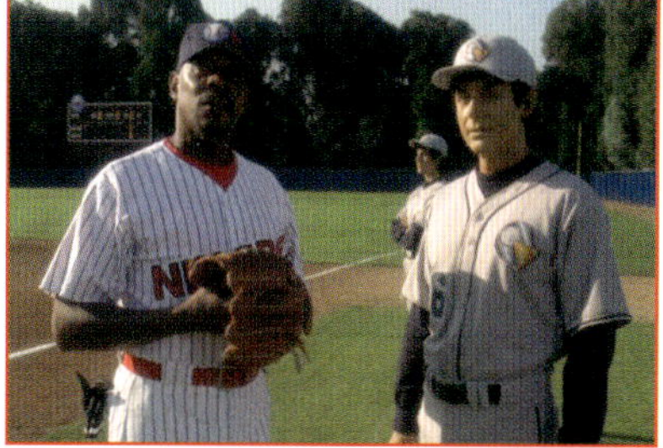

In 2375, Quark hosted a real baseball game in a holographic ballpark – a grudge match between Captain Sisko and the Vulcan Captain Solok.

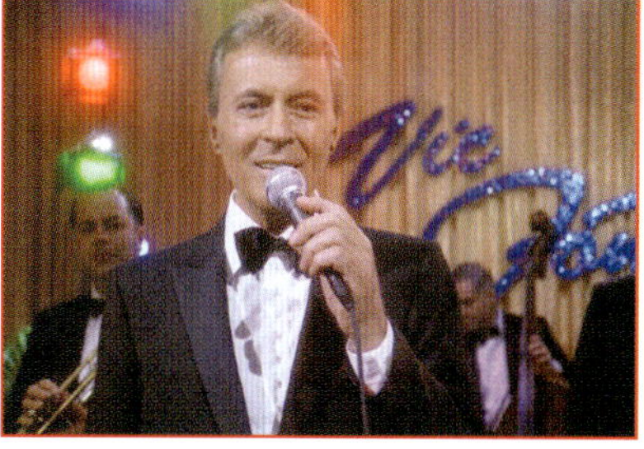

The appeal of the 1960s Las Vegas lounge program was down to its host, Vic Fontaine, who was well aware that he was really a 24th-century hologram.

MORN THE BARFLY

Quark's was the place where everyone knew Morn's name. His familiar face at the bar seemed utterly benign, but there were hidden sides to the lovable Lurian.

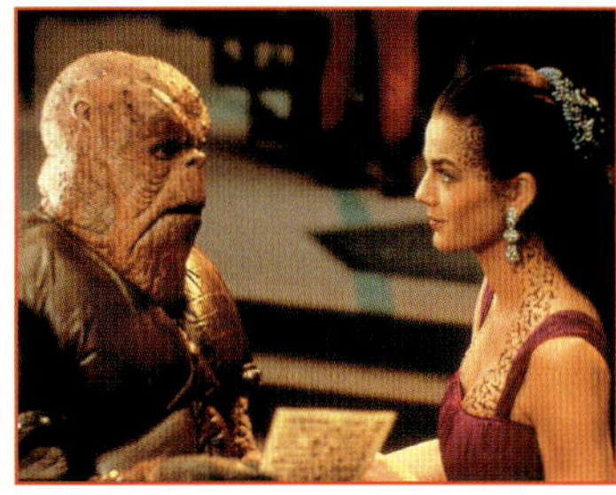

Morn was friends with Jadzia Dax, who had a crush on him, and with Worf, with whom he sparred in the holosuites once a week.

Morn first came to the station in the mid 2360s, when it was still the Cardassian mining facility Terok Nor. A courier by trade, Morn used his own ship for business but not as a permanent residence. Instead, he made his home on the station, in quarters dominated by a generous mud bath. He spent less time here, however, than sitting at the bar in Quark's. On his first ever visit, he chose a particular stool, and he returned to it time and time again thereafter. At this point, Morn still had a full head of hair – as well as criminal entanglements that none of his new friends in the bar could ever have suspected.

A FRIEND TO ALL

By the time that the Federation came to Deep Space 9 in 2369, Morn was a well-established and well-liked figure on the station. Naturally gregarious and talkative, he quickly won more friends and admirers among the new arrivals from Bajor and Starfleet. Even those who rarely joined him for a night at Quark's would enjoy hearing secondhand tales of his exploits the following morning. By now totally bald, the distinguished raconteur also had a reputation as something of a flirt and boasted numerous admirers, including Lieutenant Jadzia Dax.

And so it was that Morn became an accidental mascot for Quark's, reassuring other patrons with his presence and disappointing them when work called him away from the station. Quark had calculated that profits fell by more than four percent whenever Morn was absent for any length of time, and so he installed a convincing holographic replica to keep the Lurian's stool occupied as and when required.

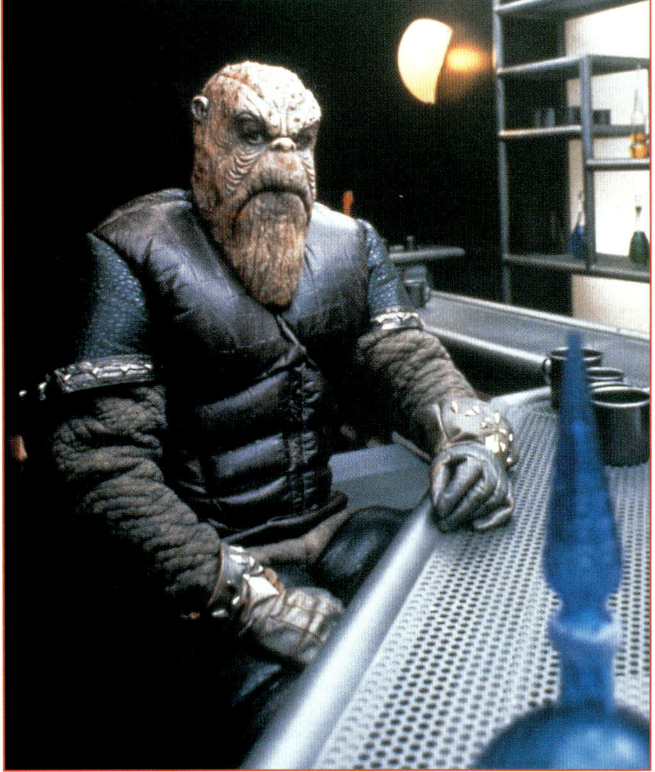

A Lurian from the Ionite nebula, Morn had multiple hearts and stomachs, resulting in a massive appetite. He sated it with raw slugs' livers and the occasional jumja stick.

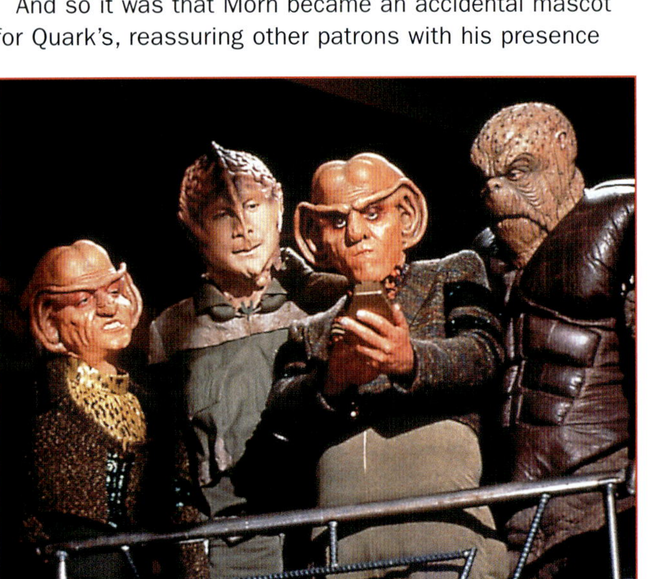

Quark sometimes involved Morn in his schemes and business deals, and trusted him enough to leave him in charge of the bar when he took a trip to Earth during 2372.

MOMENTS OF MADNESS

Despite all the goodwill he inspired, Morn was not always the best ambassador for Quark's. His Lurian physiology meant that he could become unexpectedly intoxicated by certain drinks, and it was not unheard of for him to get into fights, pass out in other people's quarters, or try to sleep on the Promenade. On one occasion, he almost got locked in the bar, and on another, he became so upset by the Dominion War that he shouted, "We're all doomed!" – before running naked into the Bajoran temple to beg for the Prophets' protection.

Yet, for all his wayward behavior, few would have thought Morn had a criminal past, let alone one that would cause him to fake his own death...

THE SECRET STASH

In 2374, Deep Space 9 was rocked by news of Morn's supposed demise. In his will, he left everything to Quark, including one thousand bricks of gold-pressed latinum that had been stolen from the Central Bank of Lissepia in the infamous Lissepian Mother's Day Heist a decade earlier. It transpired that Morn was one of five thieves involved in the robbery, and had taken all the latinum for himself. And by faking his own death once the legal limit for prosecution had passed, he was able to lure his ex-accomplices to the station in search of the loot.

When Quark finally took delivery of the bricks, it led to a shoot-out for possession between the reunited crooks – and their subsequent arrest and imprisonment. It also left Quark with one thousand worthless gold bricks that had been entirely drained of the liquid latinum that had once been suspended within them. Once the coast was clear, Morn revealed that he was alive and well by taking his usual seat at Quark's. He then rewarded the Ferengi for his unwitting part in the scheme with a cupful of the elusive latinum – which he had been storing in his second stomach every since the original heist. It was, as Quark was quick to point out, no surprise that the Lurian's hair had eventually fallen out.

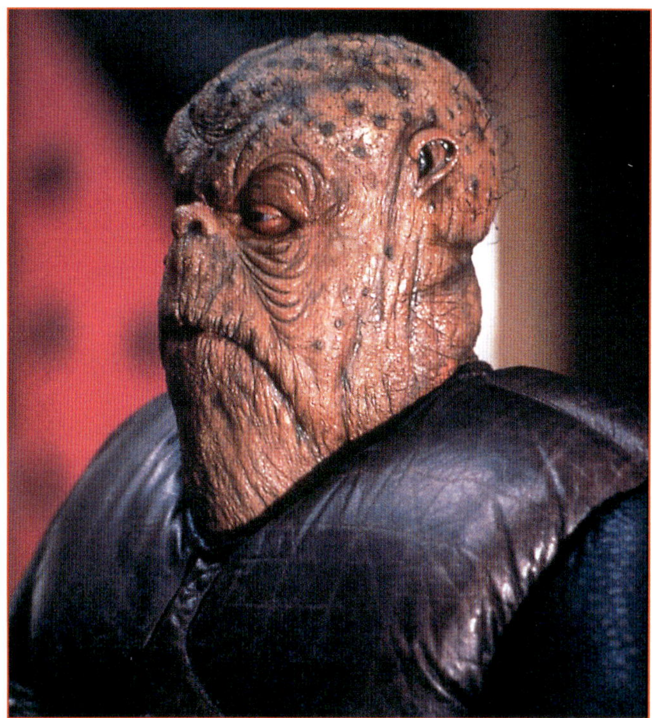

Morn wore Vaterian wool underwear, bought from Garak's Clothiers on the Promenade. He liked his garments well-padded for maximum comfort.

TRUSTED MESSENGER

Had Morn really met his end traveling through an ion storm (as had been reported), he would have been remembered not just as a popular barfly, but also as a war hero. Though he once panicked about threats from the Gamma Quadrant, when Deep Space 9 fell into Dominion hands, he bravely couriered a message from the station's resistance cell to Captain Sisko on Starbase 375. Sisko's unreserved trust in Morn as a source of information led him to step up his plans to retake the station, and the mission that followed as a direct result of his courageous action proved to be one of the greatest victories of the entire Dominion War.

A MEMORIAL FOR MORN

Morn had 17 siblings, but his biggest family was on Deep Space 9. When the station's inhabitants believed their friend to be dead, many of them attended a memorial service at Quark's bar. Gifts were brought, in line with Lurian tradition, and the bar staff were quick to sell appropriate items to anyone arriving empty-handed.

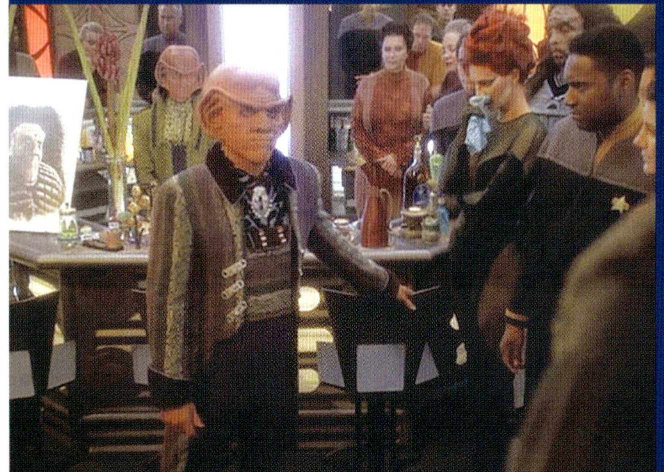

Quark spoke movingly about his most loyal customer, in front of a painting of Morn, and surrounded by mourning Humans, Bajorans, Klingons, and others.

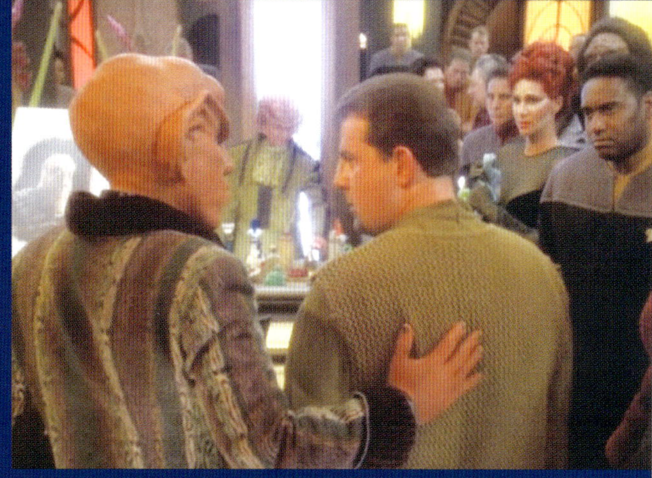

Ever mindful of a business opportunity, Quark then declared that Morn's seat at the bar should never be left empty, and guided a nervous Bajoran to it.

BAJORAN SPRINGBALL

This popular Bajoran pastime was also a much-loved professional sport. It called for speed, strength, and ruthlessness – plus mandatory head protection.

Players scored by hitting this target area with the ball.

The dynamic and fast-paced sport of springball was a global pastime on Bajor, with several professional championships closely followed by legions of fans. It resembled Human games such as squash and handball, but was a full-contact sport, allowing players to knock their opponents aside or block them with their bodies. Violent actions such as punches and kicks, however, were against the rules. The game required two players wearing head protection and a large padded glove; a small cube-shaped court; and a resilient, fast-moving ball.

Springball players scored points by using their glove like a racket, to propel the ball into a marked-out goal zone on the far wall. Other markings on the floor indicated no-hit areas, where contact by the player or the ball resulted in a penalty. The sides and ceiling of the court were not marked, and served only to confine the movement of the ball and the players. The open spectator end was also contained, usually by means of an invisible force field.

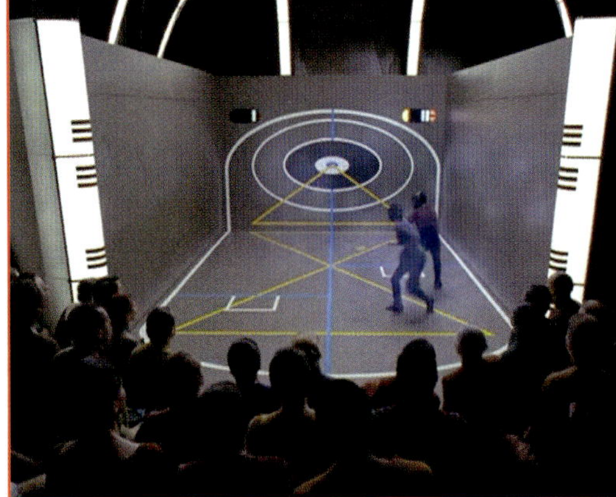

Helmets were worn by both players to protect against collisions with the ball, the walls of the court, and each other!

SPRINGBALL ON THE STATION

The sport's popularity was clear on Deep Space 9, where Kira Nerys was among the players capable of attracting an enthusiastic crowd. Kira grew up with the game – playing against her brothers during her time in the Singha refugee camp – and when she was stationed on Deep Space 9, she had Chief O'Brien build her a springball simulation for use in the holosuites above Quark's bar.

When not playing against a holographic opponent, Kira also enjoyed matches with Vedek Bareil, and her romantic relationship with him began when they bonded over the game. Bareil was not as accomplished a player as Kira (he sustained a shoulder injury during their first encounter), but he closely followed the professional game as a fan.

Another noted player on the station was Vedek Tonsa, and in 2372 the adjutant to Bajor's first minister sought to exploit his enthusiasm for the game for political ends. In the same year, Kira was reunited with a springball glove she had last seen in 2370. The glove had been stolen by the young Ferengi Nog, but whether or not he ever made use of it in competition remained a mystery.

In 2373, Kira's springball glove disappeared once again, but this time it had been hidden by Chief O'Brien, who did not want the surrogate mother of his unborn child playing contact sports. Kira did not take kindly to his intervention, resulting in a blazing row between the pair.

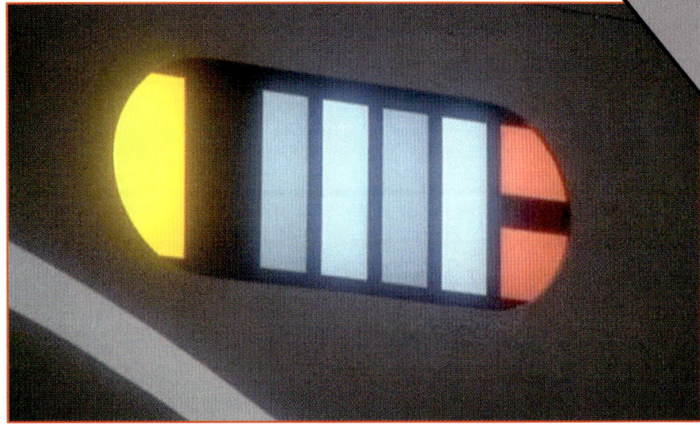

Light-up scoreboards on either side of the goal area kept a tally of both players' points and penalties. Five points were required to win a single round.

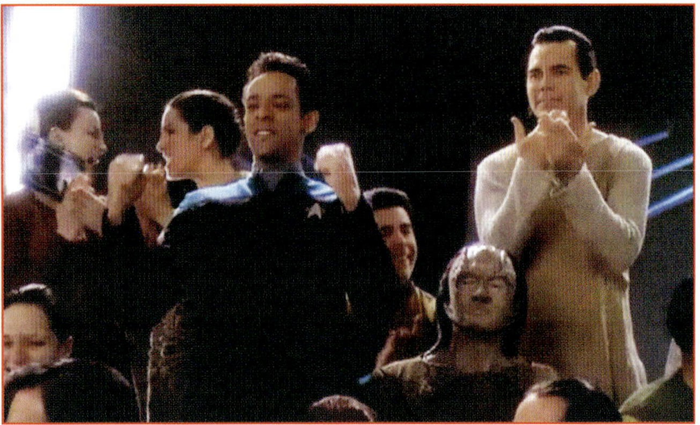

When Garak and Julian Bashir attended a springball game won by Major Kira, the tailor's mind was largely on other things, despite Bashir's infectious enthusiam.

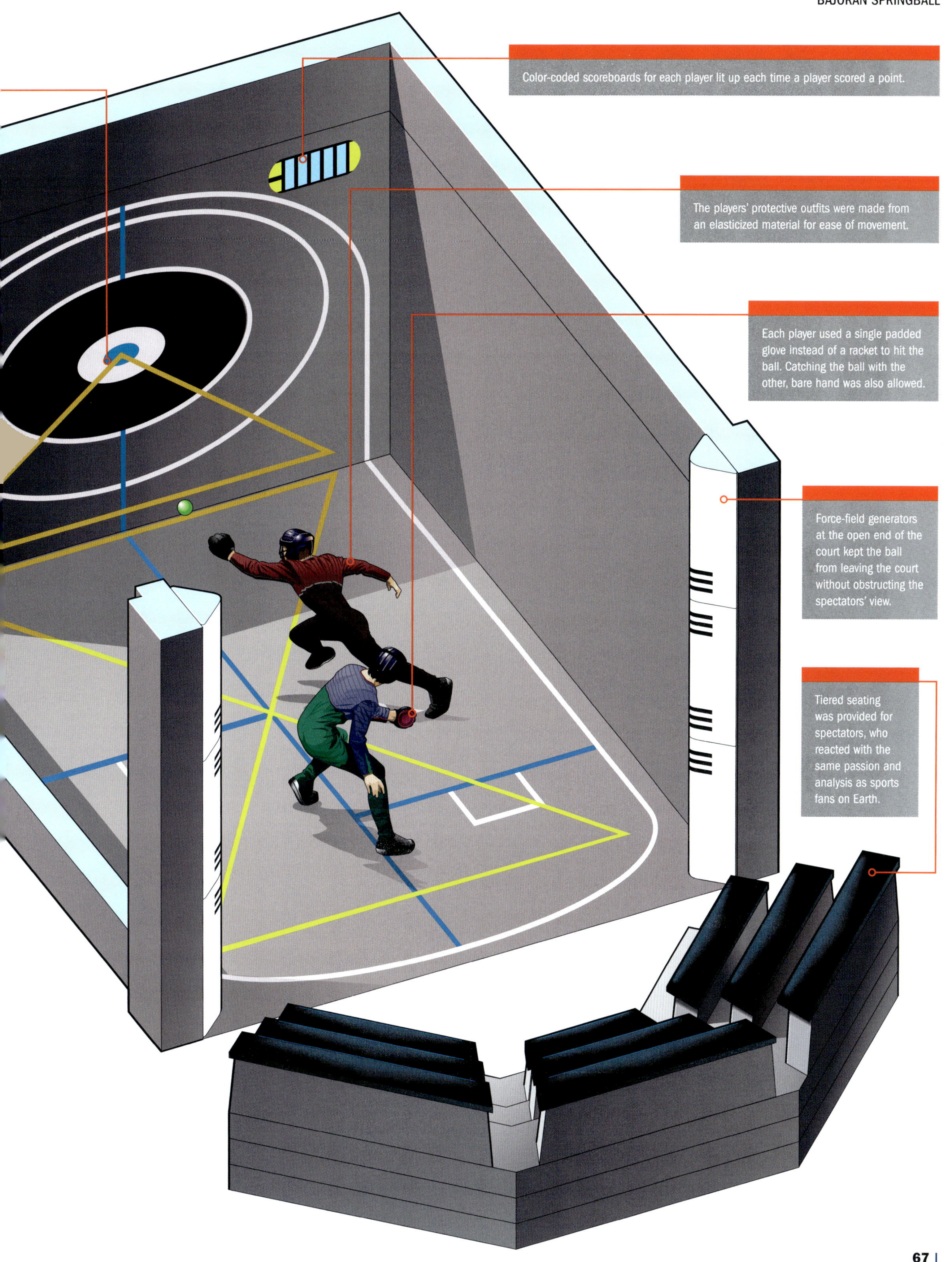
Color-coded scoreboards for each player lit up each time a player scored a point.
The players' protective outfits were made from an elasticized material for ease of movement.
Each player used a single padded glove instead of a racket to hit the ball. Catching the ball with the other, bare hand was also allowed.
Force-field generators at the open end of the court kept the ball from leaving the court without obstructing the spectators' view.
Tiered seating was provided for spectators, who reacted with the same passion and analysis as sports fans on Earth.

GARAK'S CLOTHIERS

This popular tailor's shop on the Promenade was notable not only for its fashions, but also for its owner – the one remaining Cardassian on Deep Space 9.

Of all the shops and services found on the Promenade, the tailor's shop would have seemed one of the most innocuous to newcomers. But residents knew that the proprietor of Garak's Clothiers was the only Cardassian to remain on Deep Space 9 after his species' withdrawal from Bajor, and many suspected him of being a spy. Senior staff on the station came to know that he was more than just a spy; he had been one of the most high-ranking and ruthlessly efficient operators in the Cardassian Obsidian Order. But in his day-to-day life, cutting suits and hemming dresses, he insisted he was nothing but "plain, simple Garak."

One thing that counted in Garak's favor was that he really was a very good tailor. He was also very personable – if a little caustic – and so his shop thrived and people grew to trust and even like him. Dr. Bashir was perhaps his best friend on the station. He gained a deeper understanding of the Cardassian's tortured inner life as a political exile when helping him overcome an addiction to endorphins released by a pain-relieving cranial implant.

In 2371, Garak faked a dramatic attempt on his own life by blowing up his shop on the Promenade. Well aware that an assassin called Retaya had genuine plans to kill him,

GARAK'S TAILORING TOOLS

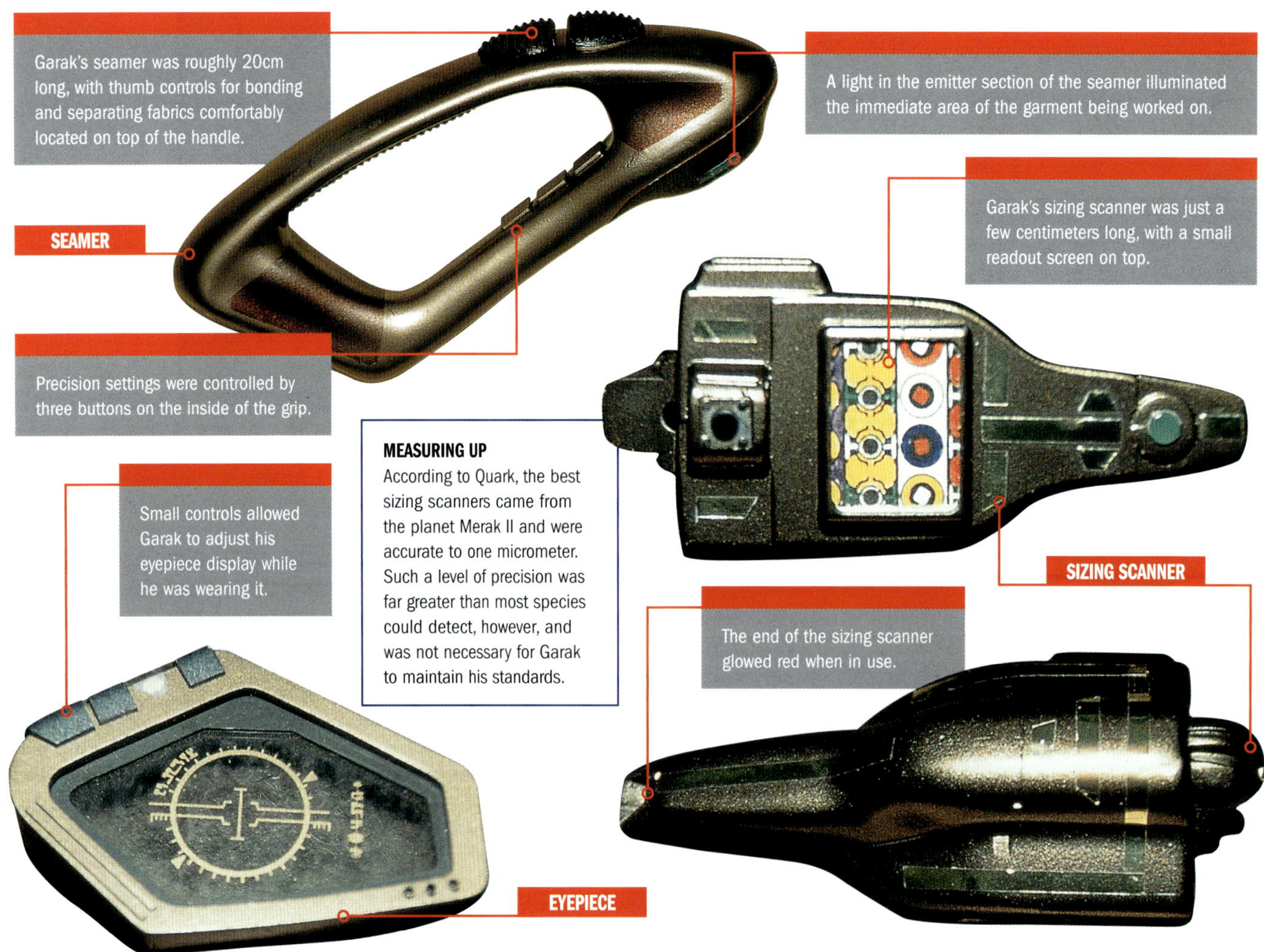

MEASURING UP
According to Quark, the best sizing scanners came from the planet Merak II and were accurate to one micrometer. Such a level of precision was far greater than most species could detect, however, and was not necessary for Garak to maintain his standards.

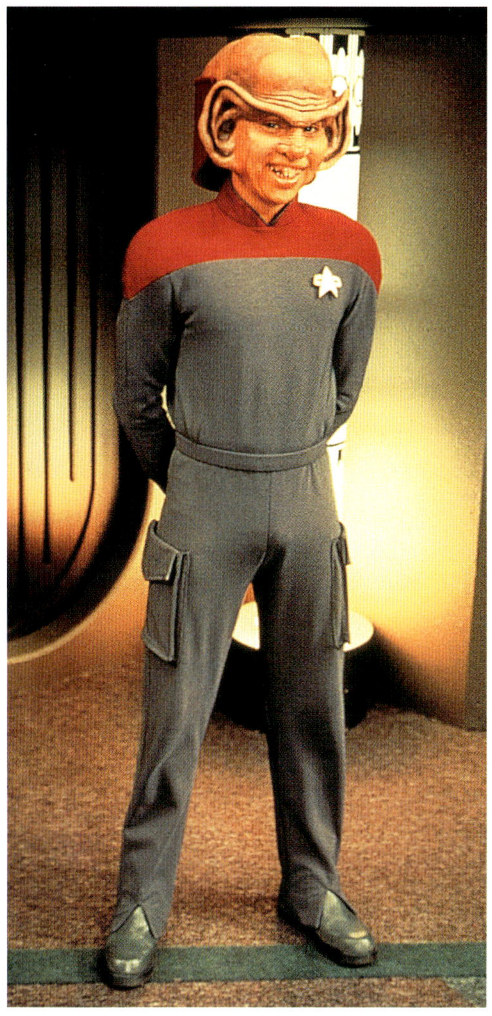

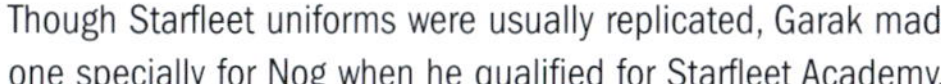

Though Starfleet uniforms were usually replicated, Garak made one specially for Nog when he qualified for Starfleet Academy.

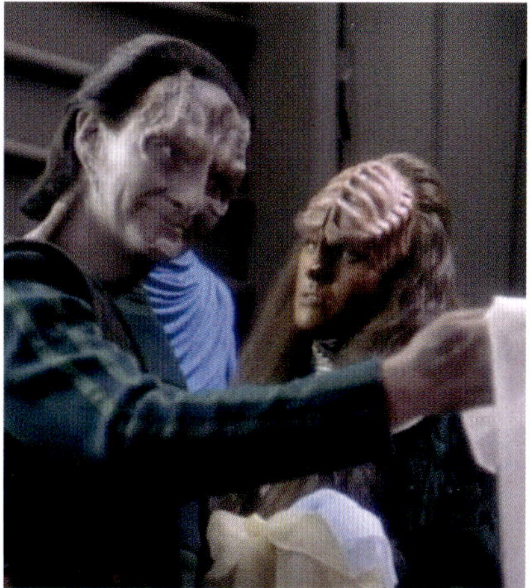

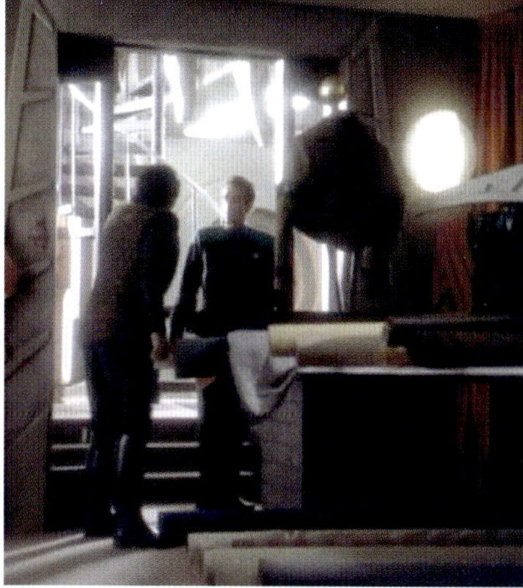

When Klingon sisters Lursa and B'Etor tried to involve Garak in the trafficking of a wanted man, the tailor hid Dr. Bashir in one of his changing rooms, so the doctor could "accidentally" hear full details of the plan.

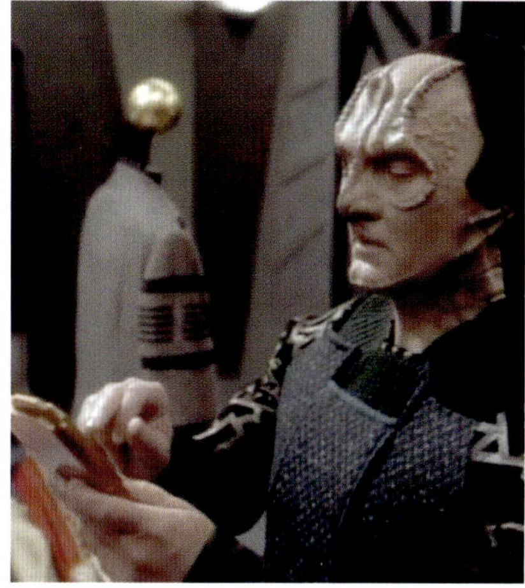

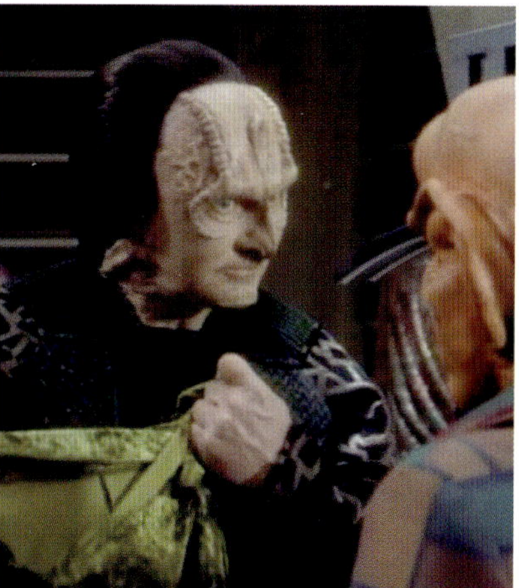

Garak insisted that he was "a simple tailor," but there was clearly far more to him. Visitors to his shop often found themselves discussing Cardassian and Bajoran politics, and learning valuable information.

he staged the explosion to cast suspicion on Retaya before he had a chance to act. Garak later rebuilt the shop, thwarting Quark's plans to turn it into a massage parlor.

TOOLS OF THE TRADE

Garak's Clothiers was set up to provide a personal service rather than anonymous browsing. Only a small number of his own creations were displayed on rails and mannequins; the room was dominated by a large tailor's worktable on which Garak would measure, cut, and stitch carefully chosen materials. Changing rooms were located on one side of the room, and could also be used for hiding eavesdroppers – such as Dr. Bashir in 2369.

The tools that Garak kept close at hand when working on a garment were numerous. He would begin by taking the customer's measurements with a sizing scanner. Though his experience allowed him to accurately judge garment fit by eye, the handheld scanner recorded sizes with even greater precision. When cutting cloth or doing detailed work, he would employ a Cardassian eyepiece with a finely calibrated display, designed to rest comfortably inside the distinctive eye ridges of his species.

Garak bonded sections of fabric to create a finished piece of clothing using a larger device called a seamer. Roughly the shape of a 21st-century steam iron, but with a small contact point rather than a large hotplate on its base, the seamer performed the same function as a needle and thread, but with far less expenditure of time and effort. It did require expertise to use accurately, however, and Garak was a master at making freehand joins at every angle. By adjusting the settings on the device, he was also able to use it to repair torn materials and to separate sections of material that had already been bonded.

SHUTTING UP SHOP

In 2372, Garak had just finished serving the Lurian courier Morn, when he was called away unexpectedly to fit Captain Sisko for a suit. Though Garak already had the captain's measurements, Sisko insisted he take them again, so that he could overhear confidential intelligence about a Klingon invasion of Cardassia and pass on a warning unofficially. It was one of several occasions over the years when Garak's network of back channels and influential contacts proved mutually beneficial to the tailor and the station at large.

During the last days of the Dominion War, Garak returned to Cardassia Prime and played a major part in his people's resistance to Dominion rule. After the war, he remained on his home planet, leaving behind his tailor's shop for good.

DINING FACILITIES

Deep Space 9's busy Promenade was a gourmet's paradise, showcasing diverse cultural specialties from sweet Bajoran jumja sticks to writhing Klingon racht.

Every day, newcomers from two quadrants of the galaxy arrived on Deep Space 9, joining residents and regular visitors amid the bustle of the Promenade. This rich, multicultural atmosphere encouraged an extensive range of caterers and vendors to set up shop on the station, offering the culinary delights of their various homeworlds to the crowds that came through the docking ports.

For those in search of an on-the-go snack, one popular destination was the jumja-stick kiosk. The extremely sweet Bajoran treat was made from the sap of the jumja tree and eaten from a stick like a lollipop. Others looking for a place to sit and enjoy a simple meal or a drink, without the need for table service, turned to the replimat. Akin to the mess hall on a starship, albeit open to the public, this functional space right on the Promenade comprised small tables and chairs for consuming produce from an adjacent bank of replicators. Waiters did attend the tables at busy times, but most customers favored a self-service approach, even if they had to queue up at the sometimes temperamental Cardassian replicators just to get a cup of raktajino.

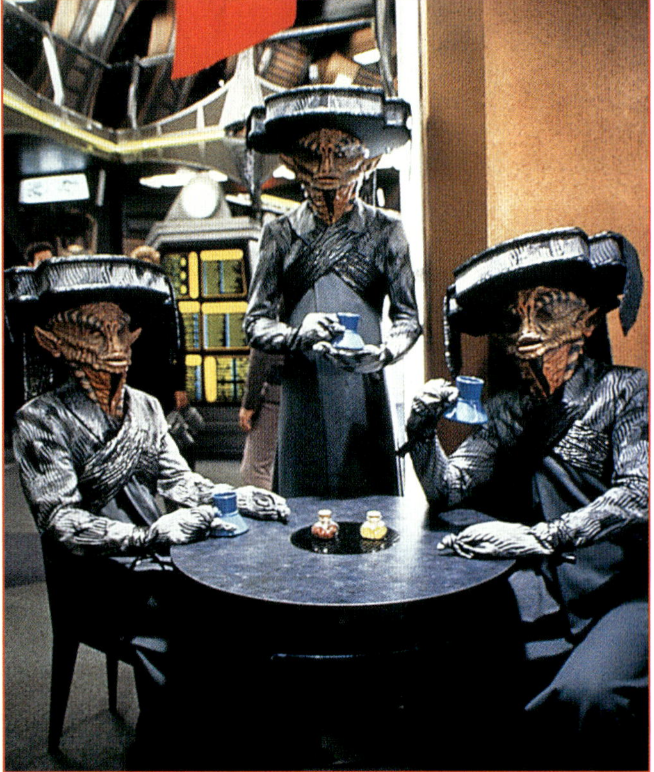

Visitors from across the Galaxy could be observed at the replimat, making it an ideal place for people-watching on the Promenade.

SOMETHING FOR EVERYONE

When only full restaurant service would do, there were also plenty of options to choose from. Though a bar first and casino second, Quark's was also a popular choice for eating in a lively atmosphere, and offered attentive table service. Its menu included Bajoran classics, such as groatcakes (a breakfast staple), mapa bread, and *hasperat* (a spicy wrap similar to an Earth burrito). Naturally, Bajoran cuisine was predominant elsewhere on the Promenade, too, but there was no shortage of alternatives. A Vulcan restaurant was the logical choice for fans of *pok tar* and *plomeek* soup, while a Bolian restaurant served, among other things, the decaying meat dishes traditional to the planet Bolarus IX. But perhaps the most adventurous option available on the station was the highly popular Klingon restaurant, with its live entertainment – and live food!

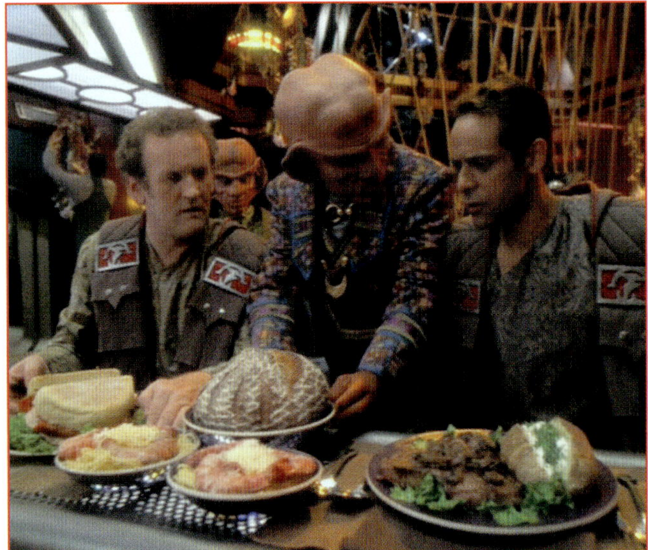

Quark served a wide range of food, including Altair sandwiches, linguine with Bajoran shrimp, and mapa bread – all ordered by Chief O'Brien following a ritual Klingon fast.

A TASTE OF QO'NOS

Identified amid its rivals on the Promenade by a deep red, illuminated sign combining the Klingon emblem with images of a crustacean and an animal heart, the Klingon dining room was a surprisingly relaxing and intimate place for a quiet meal. Customers could order from a hatch before finding a table, or help themselves from a large self-service buffet in the center of the room. This second option was especially popular, and a wise choice for first-time visitors who wanted to be confident that what they were ordering was moving as much or as little as they liked.

Lieutenant Dax, Dr. Bashir, Jake Sisko, and Major Kira all enjoyed the food in the Klingon restaurant, with the latter having a particular fondness for its broiled Krada legs. But it was the ambience created by the jovial proprietor that brought diners back again and again.

An imposing figure – with the barrel chest of a Klingon opera star – this consummate host was a chef, a singer, a musician, and more. He frequently serenaded his guests with songs from his homeworld, while playing the Klingon concertina or Klingon guitar. He was more than happy for patrons to join in with the singing, and would respond to complaints about the food by throwing it over his shoulder with a laugh and a dramatic flourish.

HOME COOKING

Of course, dining out wasn't the only way to eat on Deep Space 9, and resident and guest quarters in the habitat ring were equipped with food replicators as standard. For most inhabitants, this was more than sufficient to satisfy all dietary needs and desires, but gourmets and budding chefs could also keep their own private kitchen. Benjamin Sisko was one such culinary enthusiast, and often cooked elaborate meals in his quarters, using a mix of replicated ingredients and naturally grown produce.

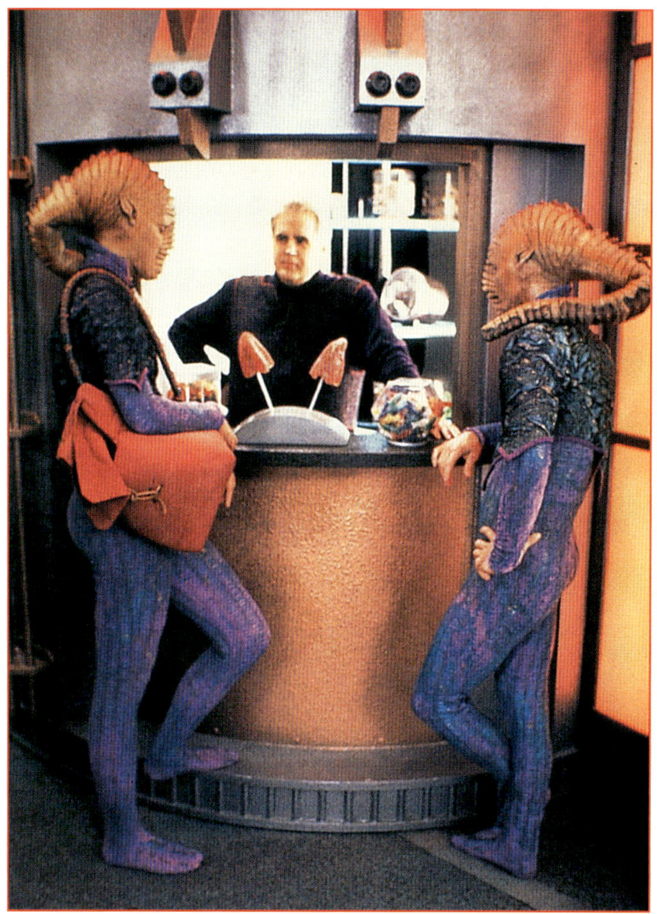

The jumja kiosk was a popular destination for many species. Its sickly-sweet confections were available in several different flavors and rich in vitamin C.

KLINGON HOSPITALITY

When Deep Space 9's senior staff wanted to show off the station's hospitality to newcomers, they frequently chose the Klingon restaurant. Quieter than Quark's, with a more sophisticated atmosphere, the setting was guaranteed to please. And if the food failed to delight, there was always music to make things memorable.

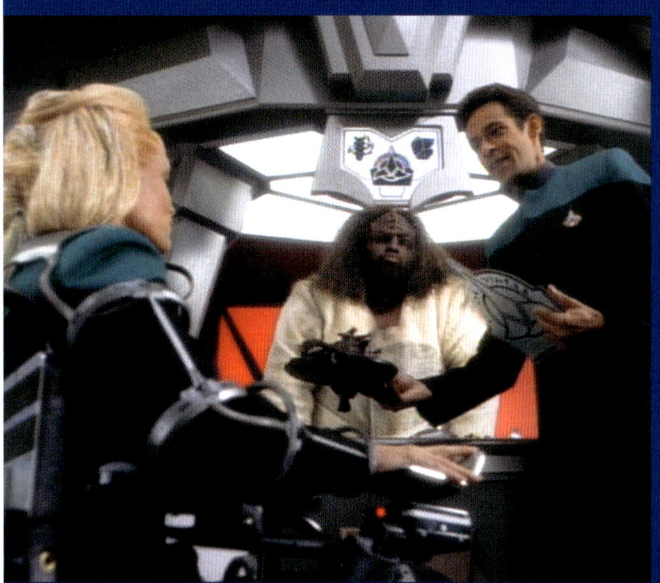

When Dr. Bashir took Ensign Melora Pazlar for Klingon food, she complained about the lack of liveliness in a plate of racht, much to the restaurateur's amusement.

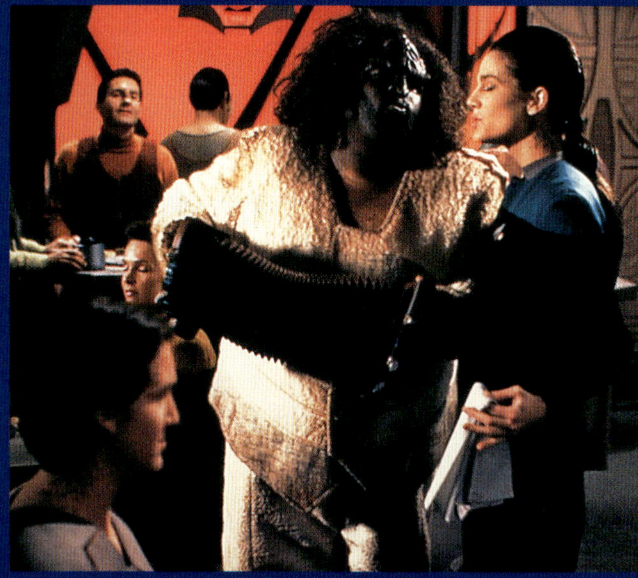

Conversely, when Lieutenant Dax took the Trill initiate Arjin to the restaurant, he was alarmed by just how lively his food was – and by Dax's sing-along with the chef.

SECURITY OFFICE

The center for law enforcement was well placed to police the Promenade on Deep Space 9. Its systems also offered a security overview of the entire station.

All aspects of Deep Space 9's internal security were coordinated from a public office accessed from the Promenade. This highly visible location was intended by the station's Cardassian designers to reassure the law-abiding, while also reminding them they were never far from a detention cell. All visitors to the office were greeted by security chief Odo or one of his deputies, seated behind an impressive workstation that enabled constant monitoring of all comings and goings on the station.

The compact office afforded no creature comforts, and its outer doors and walls were constructed from reinforced polyduranium to prevent unauthorized access and scans. Two inner doors led off to private areas, which included the detention cells, a forensics laboratory, and a cold storage area. There was also an armory, equipped with Starfleet phasers, Bajoran Militia rifles, trackable cuff restraints, and a variety of surveillance equipment. The security complex also had a rarely used side entrance, for discreet prisoner transfers and visitors who wanted to keep a low profile.

Despite their reinforced polyduranium makeup, the security office doors were destroyed in 2369 by the high-energy weapons carried by a hunter species from the Gamma Quadrant. Afterward they had to be entirely replaced.

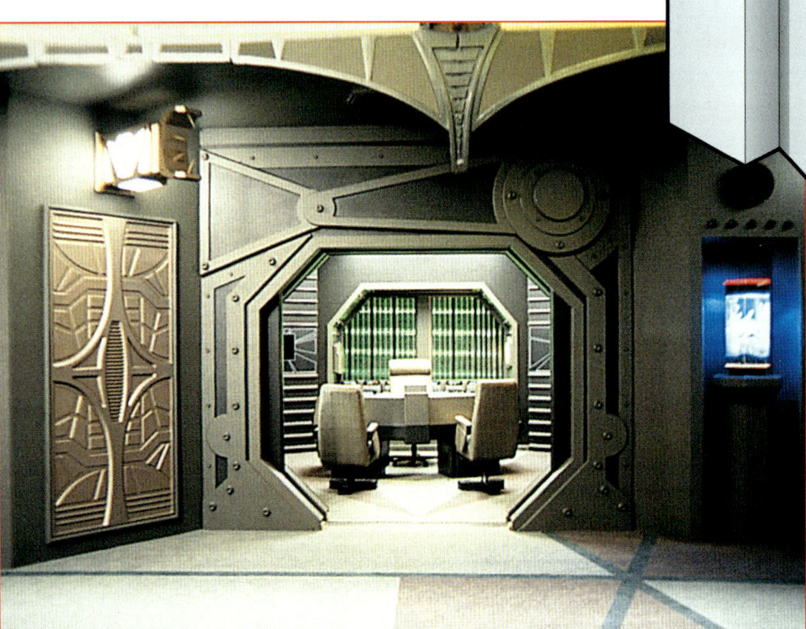

The security office workstation was used to record and retrieve encrypted records, and to access feeds from sensors and cameras located around the station. It also offered a view through the doors to the Promenade.

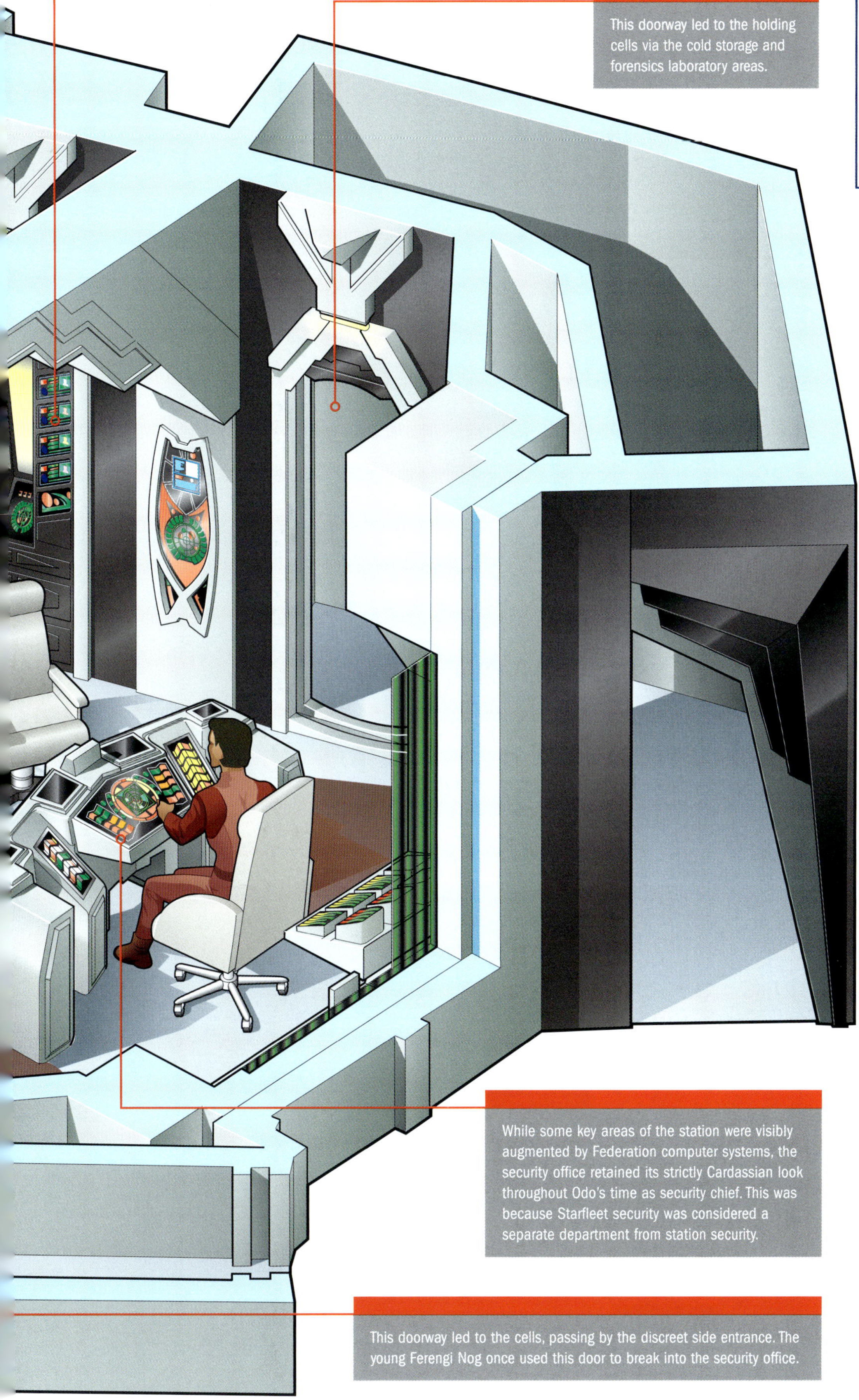

Consoles on both sides of the main doors displayed pictures and details of the station's most wanted criminals.

This doorway led to the holding cells via the cold storage and forensics laboratory areas.

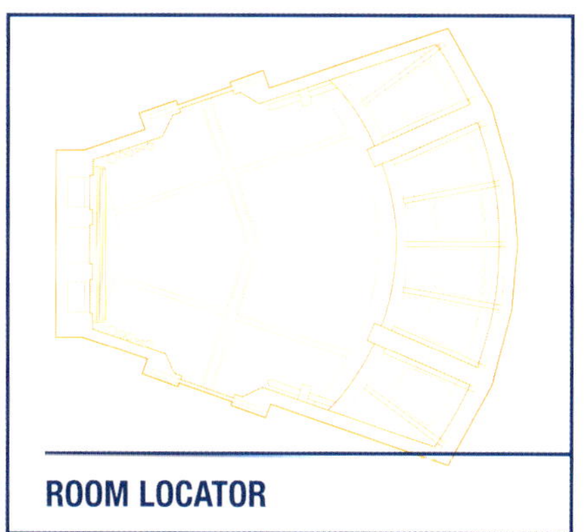

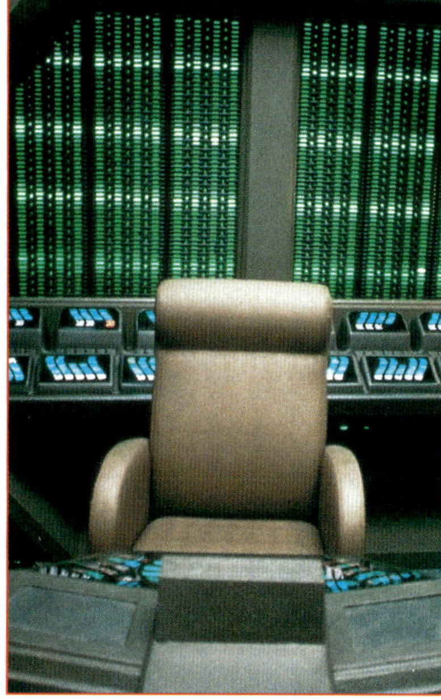

Odo made daily criminal-activity logs at his desk in the security office. He loathed the bureaucracy of record-keeping, and kept his observations concise.

While some key areas of the station were visibly augmented by Federation computer systems, the security office retained its strictly Cardassian look throughout Odo's time as security chief. This was because Starfleet security was considered a separate department from station security.

This doorway led to the cells, passing by the discreet side entrance. The young Ferengi Nog once used this door to break into the security office.

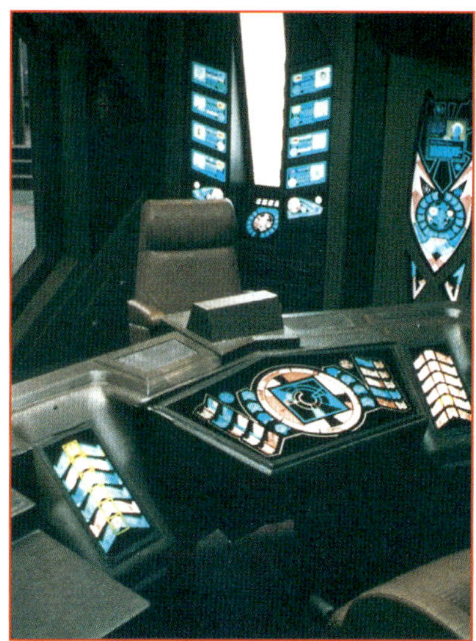

The console in Odo's office allowed him to monitor activity throughout the station, to access criminal records, ship manifests and communications.

HOLDING CELLS

Accessed via the security office on the Promenade, the station's cells were a temporary holding area for criminal suspects ahead of trial, extradition, or exoneration.

The detention cells on Deep Space 9 lay beyond the main security office. The corridors leading to them were accessible only to those members of station staff with appropriate security clearance. The corridors terminated in an octagonal room featuring three holding cells of varying sizes.

The largest cell at the center featured two bench-style beds and no additional comforts. Those on either side of it were designed for single occupancy with just one bench each. All three were open to observation at the front, with a white glow around the large entrances as the only evidence of the invisible force fields that kept the occupants confined.

Needless to say, the cells were not intended as a long-term method of incarceration, and were used only when entirely necessary. Though they did not have any obvious sanitation systems, detainees' bathroom needs were met by facilities that receded into the walls when not in use.

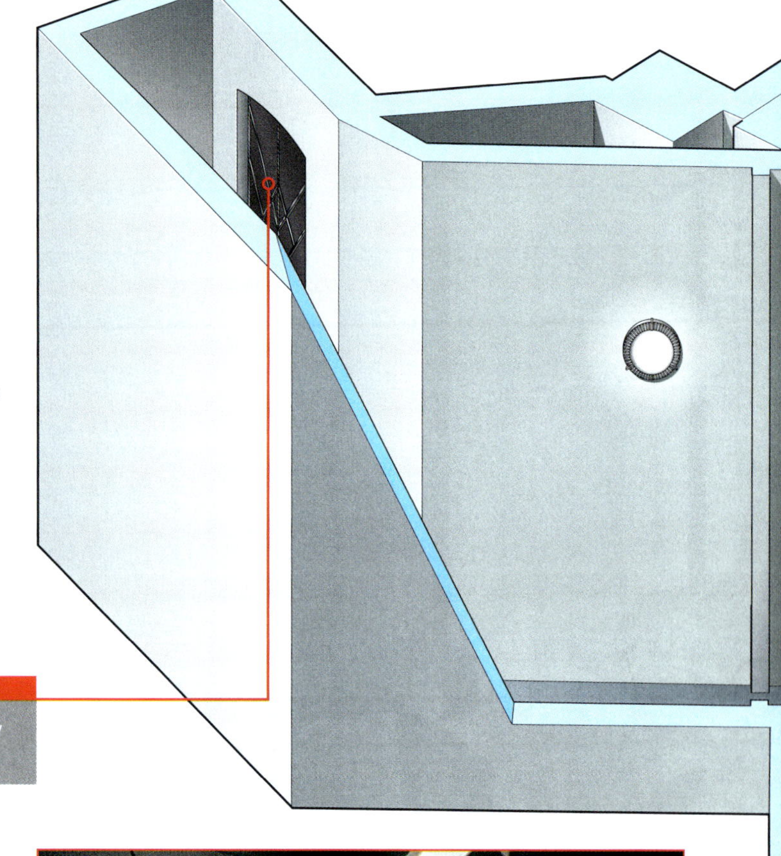

High-security doors and narrow corridors leading through the rest of the security complex made it difficult to stage a jail break – whether from inside or outside.

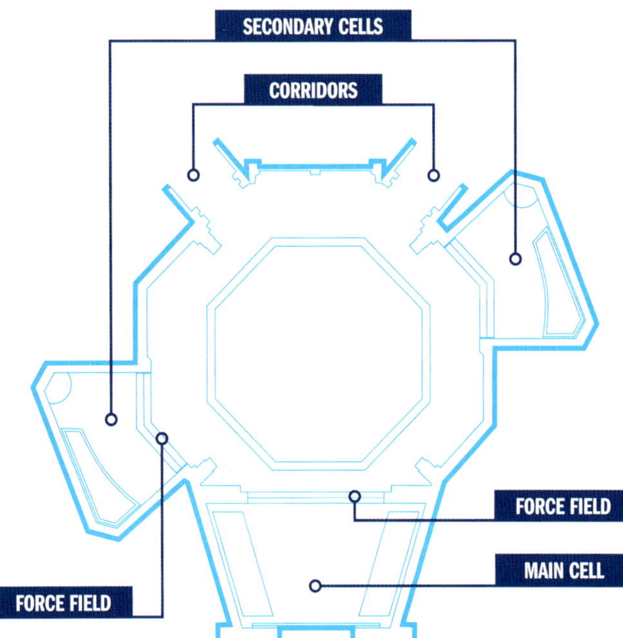

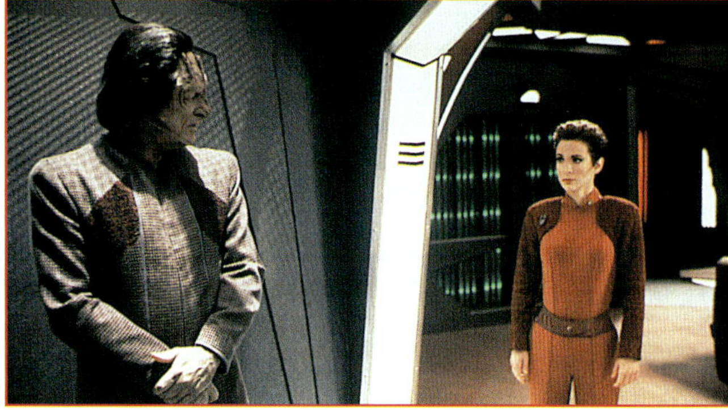

In late 2369, the Cardassian Aamin Marritza spent time in one of the secondary holding cells while posing as the notorious war criminal Gul Darhe'el.

The cell walls were lined with a duranium alloy. This stopped communication signals, sensor scans, and all but the most advanced transporter systems from getting through.

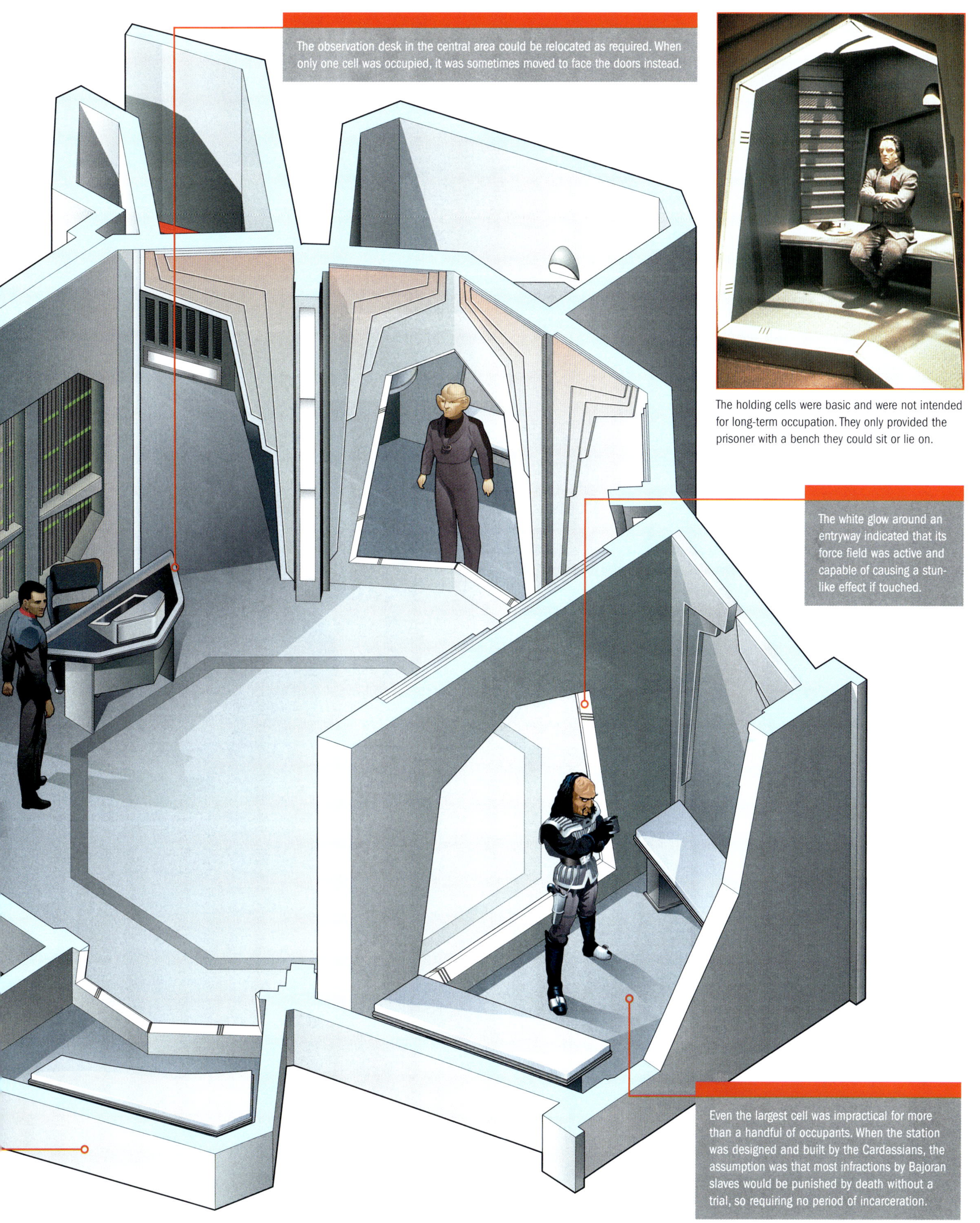

The observation desk in the central area could be relocated as required. When only one cell was occupied, it was sometimes moved to face the doors instead.

The holding cells were basic and were not intended for long-term occupation. They only provided the prisoner with a bench they could sit or lie on.

The white glow around an entryway indicated that its force field was active and capable of causing a stun-like effect if touched.

Even the largest cell was impractical for more than a handful of occupants. When the station was designed and built by the Cardassians, the assumption was that most infractions by Bajoran slaves would be punished by death without a trial, so requiring no period of incarceration.

THE BAJORAN TEMPLE

This small but important shrine was a spiritual retreat for the Bajoran faithful and others amid the bustling commercial hub of Deep Space 9's Promenade.

Faith was an important part of Bajoran life, with temples dedicated to the Prophets (also known as the wormhole aliens) located across Bajor. On Deep Space 9, the center of religious worship was the temple on the Promenade, where vedeks led daily prayers and meditations. The shrine was also the focus for events in the spiritual calendar, such as the Time of Cleansing, the Days of Atonement, and the Bajoran Gratitude Festival.

When religious figures visited Deep Space 9, they made a point of visiting the temple. And if one of the Bajorans' sacred Orbs was on the station, it was displayed there for the faithful, protected by a force field. In 2374, Jadzia Dax was praying to the Orb of Contemplation in the temple when she was attacked and fatally wounded by Gul Dukat, who was possessed by a Pah-wraith.

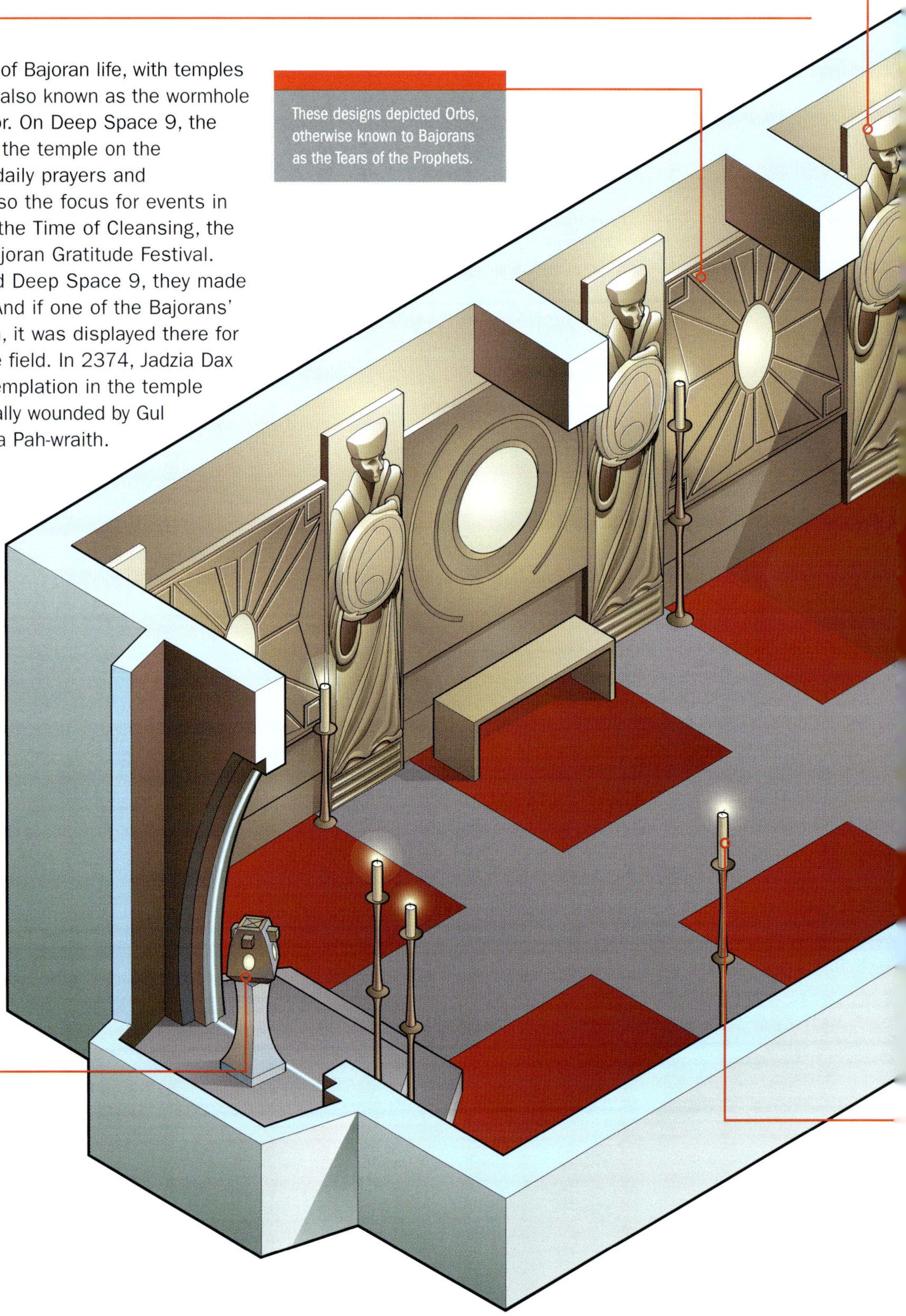

Stylized reliefs of noted vedeks decorated the walls of the temple.

These designs depicted Orbs, otherwise known to Bajorans as the Tears of the Prophets.

The focus of the temple was this recessed podium, on which Orbs could be safely exhibited behind a force field with encrypted controls.

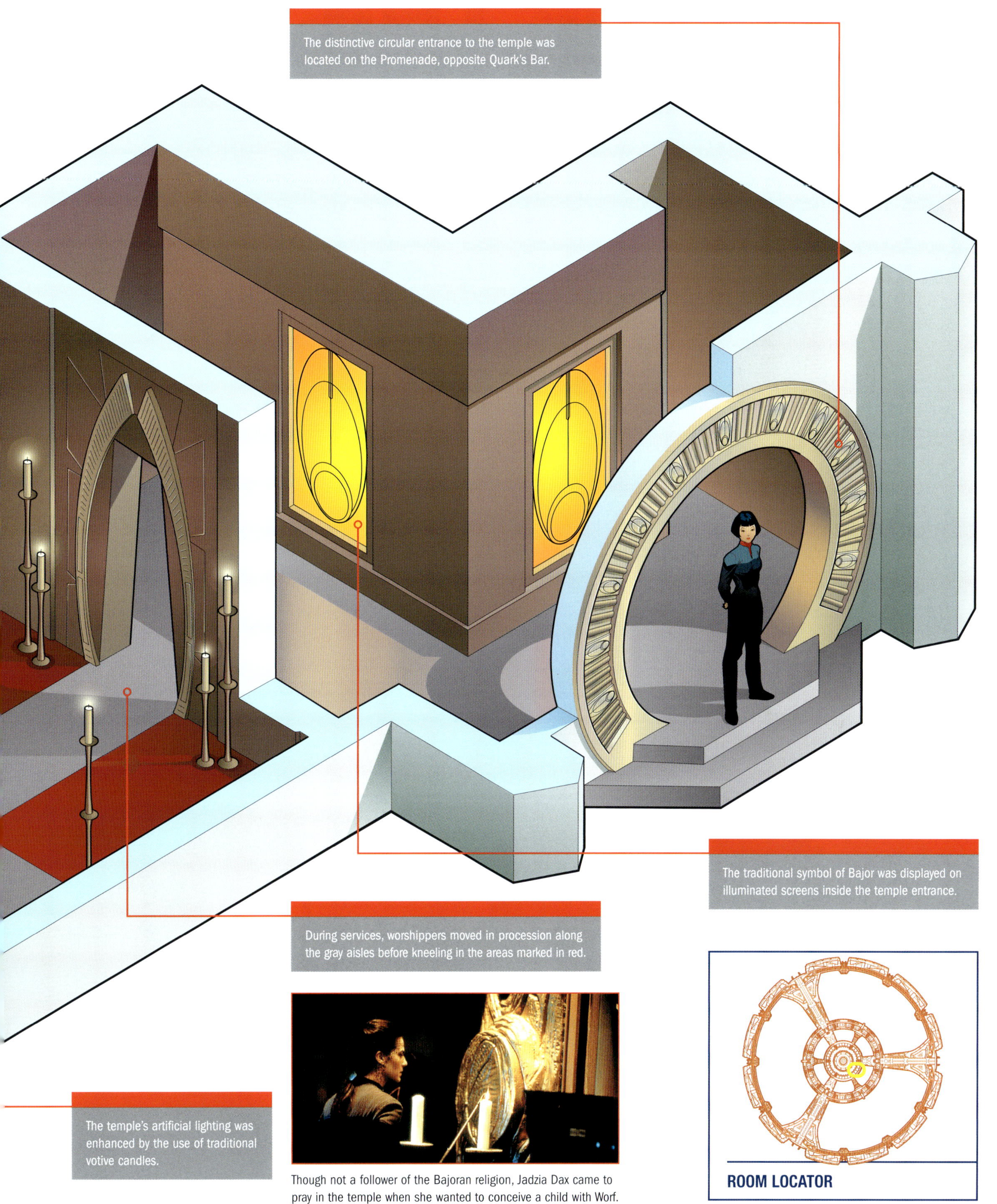

Though not a follower of the Bajoran religion, Jadzia Dax came to pray in the temple when she wanted to conceive a child with Worf.

ORBS OF THE PROPHETS

The Orbs created by the wormhole aliens formed the basis of Bajoran spiritual belief. Able to grant visions of the past and future, the ancient artifacts had power beyond faith alone.

Also known to Bajorans as the Tears of the Prophets, the Orbs were 10 mysterious artifacts created by the powerful beings that inhabited the Bajoran wormhole. The first nine Orbs were found in the Denorios belt over the course of 10,000 years – before the wormhole was known to exist – and the Bajorans attributed their appearances to their gods, the Prophets. The tenth was found by Benjamin Sisko on the planet Tyree in early 2375, by which time the Prophets and the incorporeal wormhole inhabitants were understood to be one and the same.

Over the millennia, the Bajoran priesthood treasured the Orbs as holy relics, and sought the wisdom of the Prophets by submitting to visions induced by looking into one of the artifacts. They named each Orb according to the nature of the experience it invoked, and consulted them for guidance on all aspects of daily life.

When the Cardassian Union occupied Bajor and claimed its resources for their own, they removed all but one of the Orbs from the planet. After failing to exploit them through scientific research, they retained them purely to deny the Bajorans the succour of their cultural heritage. By the end of the occupation, in 2369, the Orbs were largely forgotten by the Cardassians, but still a major part of the Bajorans' identity. Slowly, the artifacts were returned to Bajor by the Cardassian government, and once again became a source of guidance for religious Bajorans.

Thereafter, individual Orbs were sometimes housed in the Bajoran temple on Deep Space 9. These included the Orb of Prophecy and Change, and the Orb of Contemplation. In 2371, the Orb of Wisdom was also brought to the station by the Ferengi Grand Negus, Zek, who had retrieved it from Cardassia III, intending to sell it to the Bajorans.

BAJORAN ORB ARKS

Each Orb was housed within an ornate and resilient casket known as an ark. Standing around 45cm tall and tapering from a width of around 40cm at the base, these arks were hinged at two corners, allowing them to open up to reveal the Orb within. Jewel-like windows were illuminated by the Orb when the doors were shut.

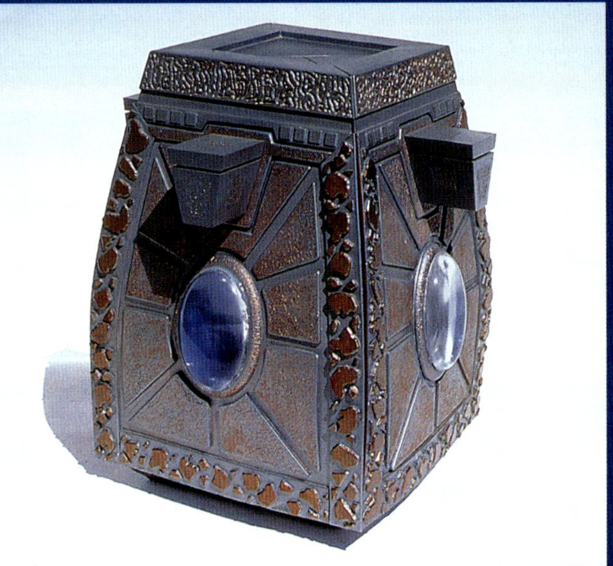

Short beams projected from all four sides of each ark. Windows were found only on the two opening sides, with flat, irregular designs in their place on the others.

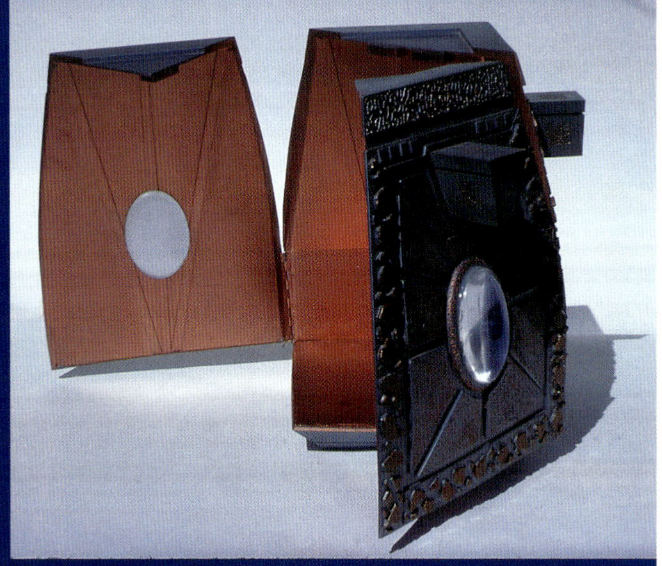

Each ark was intricately decorated on the outside, but almost entirely plain on the inside, so as not to detract from the Orb itself. It was very rare to see an empty ark.

FIVE ORBS AND ONE FRAGMENT

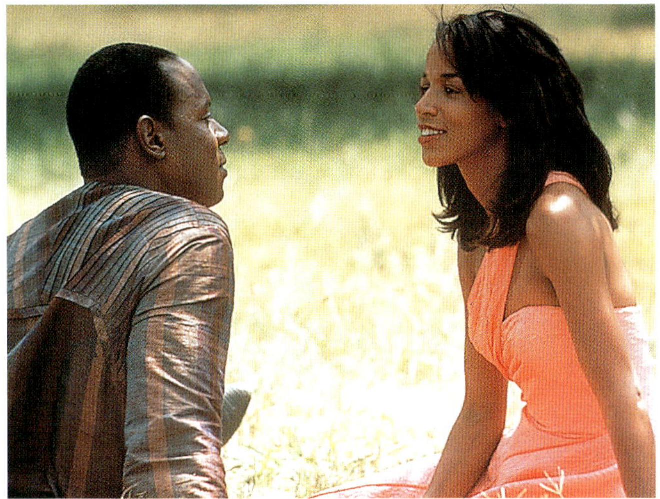

The Orb of Prophecy and Change caused Benjamin Sisko to see a vision of his late wife, Jennifer. Three thousand years earlier, a Bajoran called Trakor had written down a series of prophecies regarding the Emissary, based on an experience with the Orb.

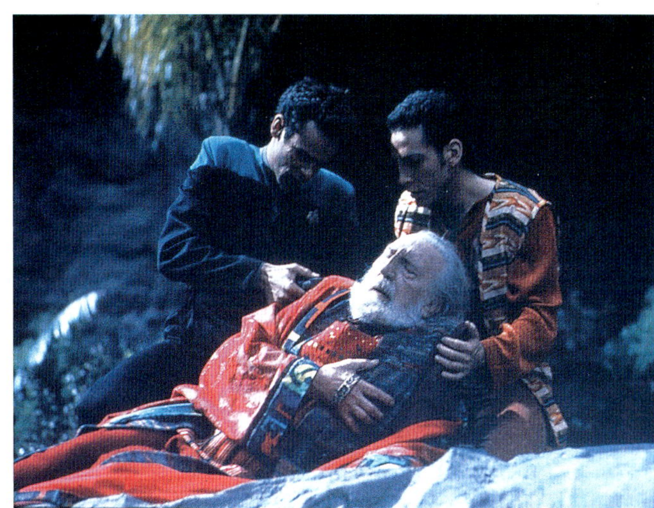

An Orb fragment formed part of a bracelet worn by the leader of a village on Bajor. He secretly used its power to create a dangerous energy cloud and unite his fellow villagers against a common enemy, before passing on the secret to a successor.

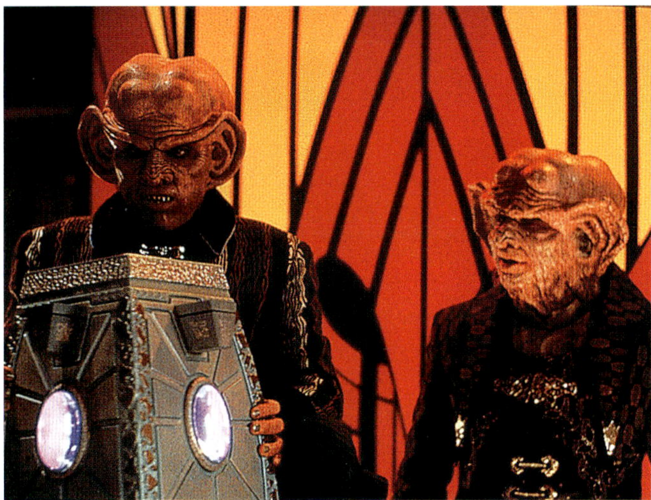

The Orb of Wisdom was returned to Bajor via the Ferengi Grand Negus, who acquired it from the Cardassians. The Bajoran spiritual leader Kai Winn later consulted the Orb for guidance on supporting a nonaggression pact between Bajor and the Dominion.

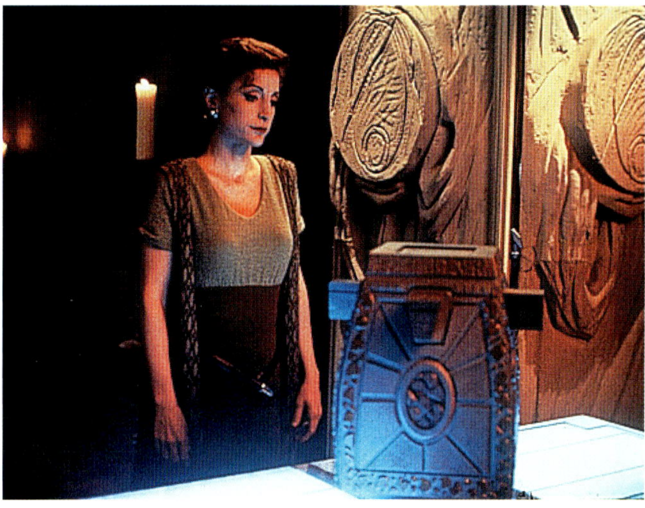

The Orb of Time was returned to Bajor onboard the *U.S.S. Defiant* in 2373, and used by Klingon spy Arne Darvin in a plot to change history. The following year, Major Kira consulted the Orb to learn the truth about her late mother's history with Gul Dukat.

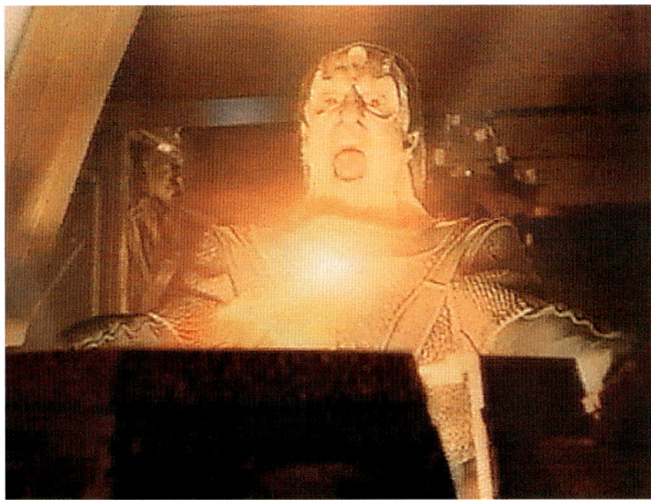

The Orb of Contemplation was on the station in 2374, when a Pah-wraith inhabiting Gul Dukat's body used it to gain access to the wormhole, initiating the final conflict between the Prophets and the Pah-wraiths. This caused all of the Orbs to go inert.

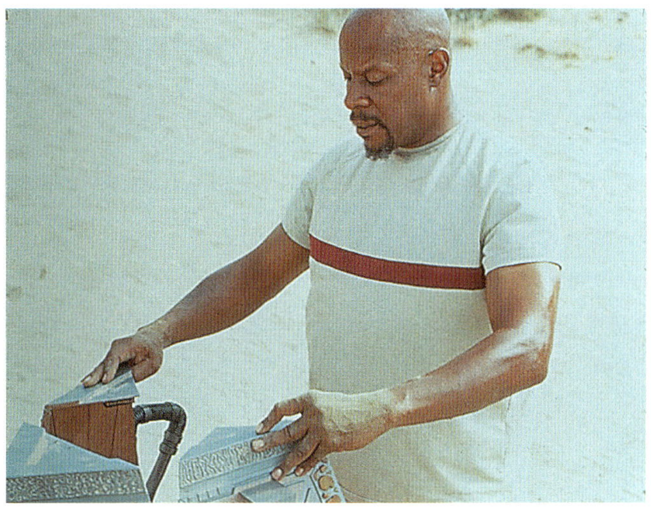

The Orb of the Emissary was home to one of the Prophets for 42 years, until it was discovered by Benjamin Sisko. Only he could open its ark, and when he did so, the being was set free to reopen the wormhole, which had been sealed by a Pah-wraith.

THE INFIRMARY

The station's original surgery was built with Cardassians in mind, but under Dr. Julian Bashir it became a lifesaver for diverse species from all across the galaxy.

The infirmary on Deep Space 9 provided care to station personnel, civilian inhabitants, and visitors. Run by Dr. Julian Bashir from Starfleet Medical alongside an expert team of Bajoran medics, the facility was located on the Promenade, directly opposite a turbolift and the main entrance to Quark's Bar. Like the rest of the station, it followed a Cardassian design, meaning that it bore little resemblance to a Federation starship sickbay.

When the Cardassians abandoned the station in 2369, they trashed the infirmary, leaving Starfleet to restore it to full functionality over the following year. However, by 2373, it still lacked some of the standard equipment found in the equivalent space on a modern starship, such as projectors required for an Emergency Medical Hologram.

MULTIPLE WORKSPACES

The infirmary consisted of three distinct areas: a laboratory with two workstations and space for additional equipment; a circular examination room with a biobed at its center; and a larger area for surgery and recuperation. Visitors entered through double doors leading directly to the lab area, where the smaller of the two workstations could also serve as a reception desk. Patients would be directed to their left – for examination or surgery – with only authorized staff having access to the medical stores at the back of the lab. While these mostly consisted of uncontrolled substances such as Bajoran Makara herbs – traditionally used during pregnancy – they also housed restricted items such as bio-mimetic gel. The surgery area was also restricted, and featured several biobeds and an array of portable monitoring equipment in a customizable layout, overlooking large, circular windows.

CENTER OF ACHIEVEMENT

Despite its shortcomings, Deep Space 9's infirmary played host to several major scientific breakthroughs during the 2370s. Dr. Bashir's research into biomolecular replication saw him nominated for the prestigious Carrington Award, while his work with Melora Pazlar and Sarina Douglas had significant implications for the fields of neuromuscular adaptation and subatomic brain surgery respectively. Most notably of all, the infirmary was where the doctor identified that the morphogenic virus killing Odo had been artificially created by the Federation's own black ops unit, Section 31, and where he eventually found a cure for it by probing the mind of the dying Section 31 agent, Luther Sloan.

The freestanding biobed could be removed or replaced for examining nonhumanoids. A central position allowed all-around access for staff, and ideal placement for overhead sensors set into the ceiling. This sensor cluster also generated a low-level antibacterial force field.

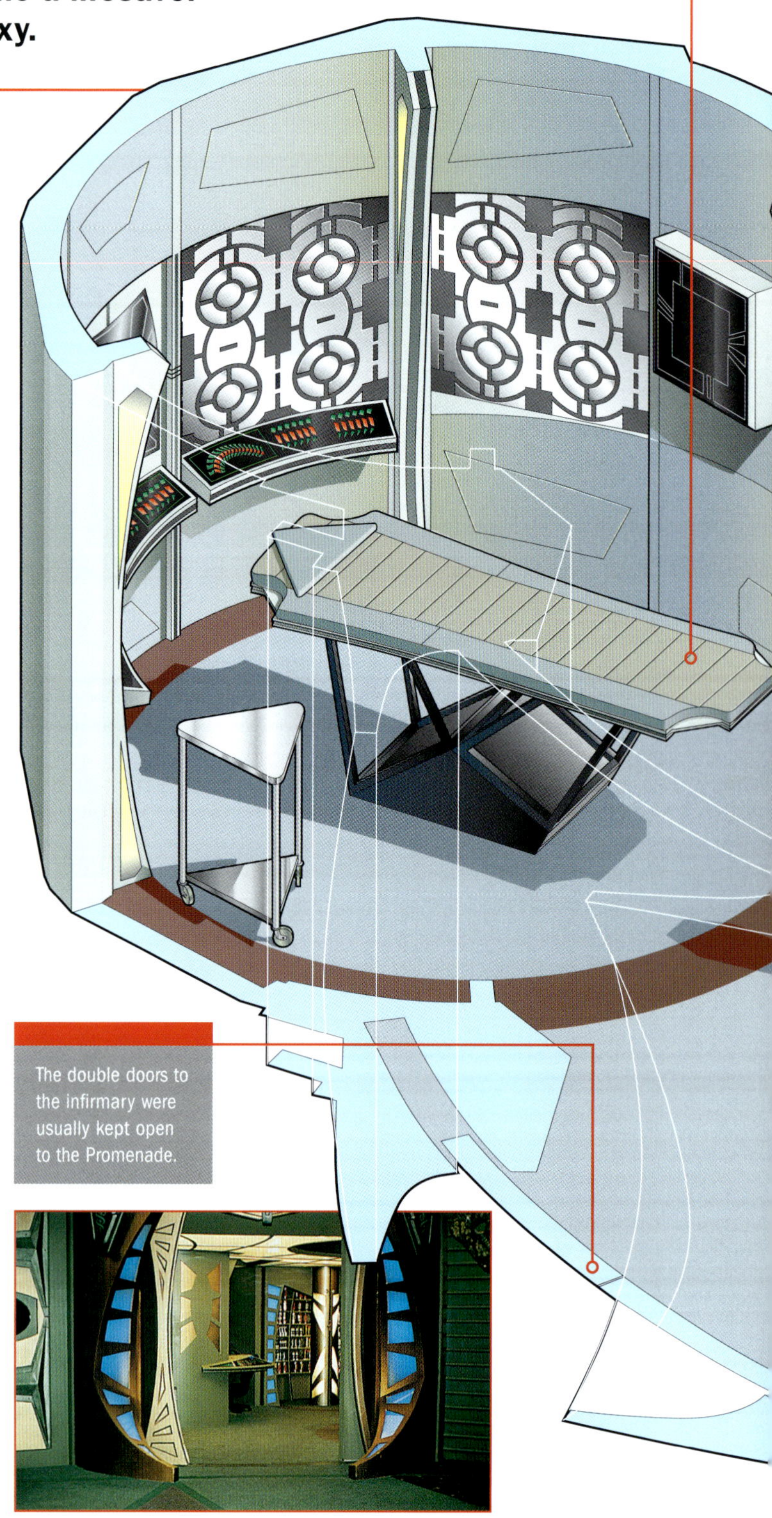

The double doors to the infirmary were usually kept open to the Promenade.

The infirmary could be accessed from the Promenade. The surgical room could only be reached from inside the room.

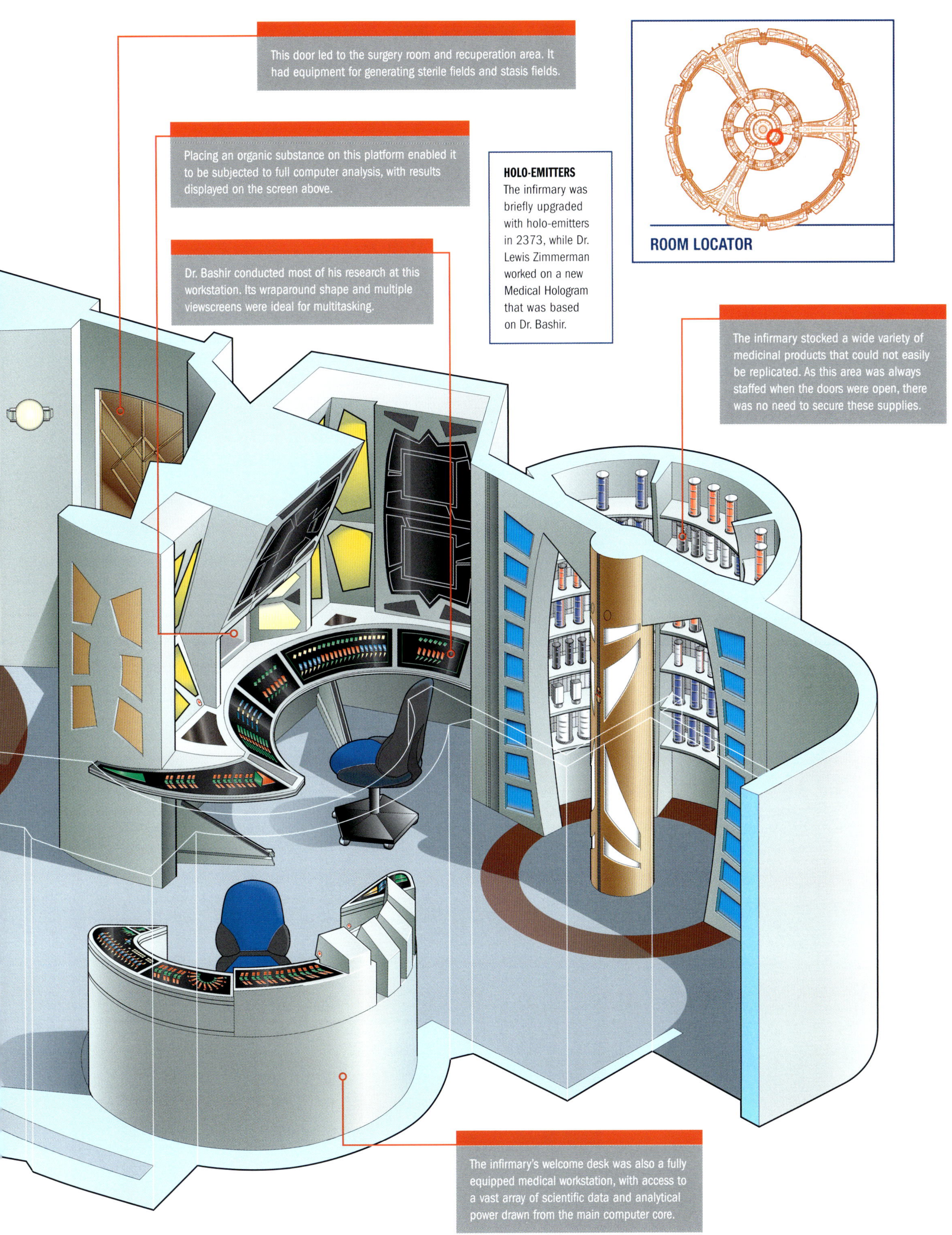

HOLO-EMITTERS

The infirmary was briefly upgraded with holo-emitters in 2373, while Dr. Lewis Zimmerman worked on a new Medical Hologram that was based on Dr. Bashir.

INFIRMARY BIOBEDS

The Starfleet biobeds on Deep Space 9 lacked some of the features found in a starship's sickbay, but they still enhanced the station's otherwise antiquated Cardassian infirmary.

One of the most important items of medical equipment in Deep Space 9's infirmary was the biobed, a staple of Starfleet medical facilities in one form or another since the 2250s. Compared with those on most starships, the biobeds installed on the station were simpler in design, but still boasted an array of built-in monitoring functions. They could also be connected to additional equipment for treating rare conditions and specialist injuries, affording the medical team a high degree of flexibility in care.

Designed primarily for treating humanoid patients, each biobed had a roughly rectangular surface, measuring over two meters long and a meter wide at its widest. The biobed was elevated above the floor on struts terminating in a weighted base that included much of the monitoring technology. A patient's head and chest were raised above the rest of the body, with a triangular pillow providing added comfort and support. Extra bedding was provided if a patient was expected to recuperate in the infirmary, but this was rarely necessary, and a simple white sheet was usually enough to protect the dignity of patients undergoing treatment.

Even though the rest of the infirmary remained largely run on dated Cardassian technology, the biobeds were able to transmit diagnostic data to the native interface, as well as to Starfleet-issue computers and screens. Both systems were used in tandem by chief medical officer Julian Bashir, who proved as flexible as the equipment he worked with.

ARRANGEMENT AND ADDITIONS

The largest concentration of biobeds on Deep Space 9 was located in the infirmary's post-op recovery room, where Dr. Bashir could monitor several patients at once. In cases of emergency, this space could also be used for triage, with patients beamed directly onto the biobeds via site-to-site transport. The main operating room centered on a single biobed, with space to accommodate extra equipment – such as the module attached directly to the top of the bed when Worf's brother, Kurn, was treated for a critical chest injury in 2372. Though not of Starfleet design, this module fitted comfortably over the biobed, contributing to the Klingon's healing process, while also restricting his movements and protecting him from accidental impacts.

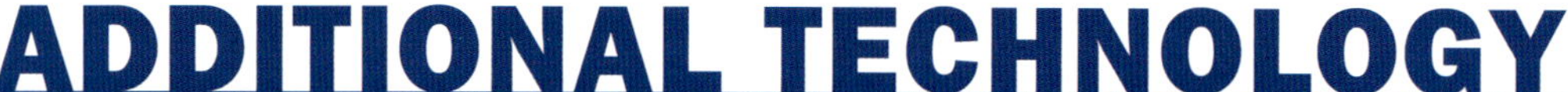

ADDITIONAL TECHNOLOGY

Starfleet biobeds could be adapted and augmented to deal with almost any medical contingency, from brain scans and lifesaving chest surgery to highly experimental procedures and autopsies.

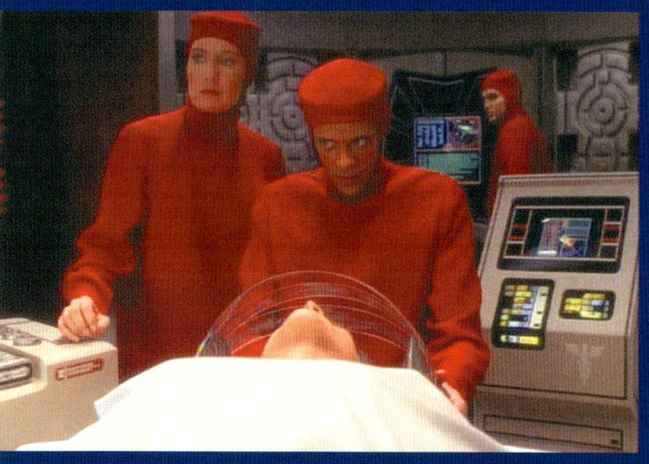

Dr. Bashir used a neurogenic stimulator to revive Vedek Bareil after a seemingly fatal accident. A positronic implant kept Bareil alive for a short while afterward.

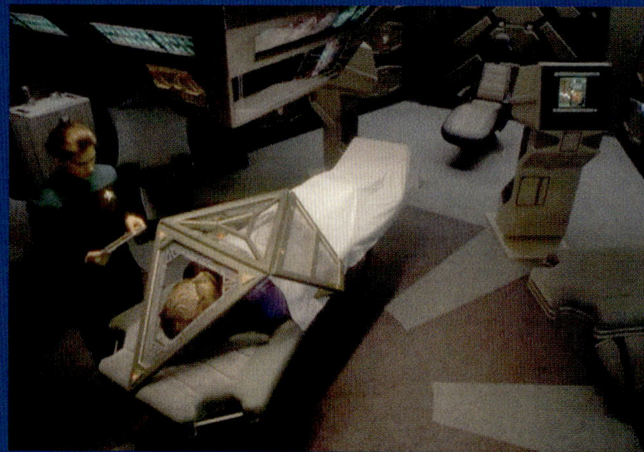

Jadzia Dax had Kurn beamed to a biobed when he suffered a life-threatening chest wound. The module placed over him regulated his recovery and his wakefulness.

A TYPICAL BIOBED

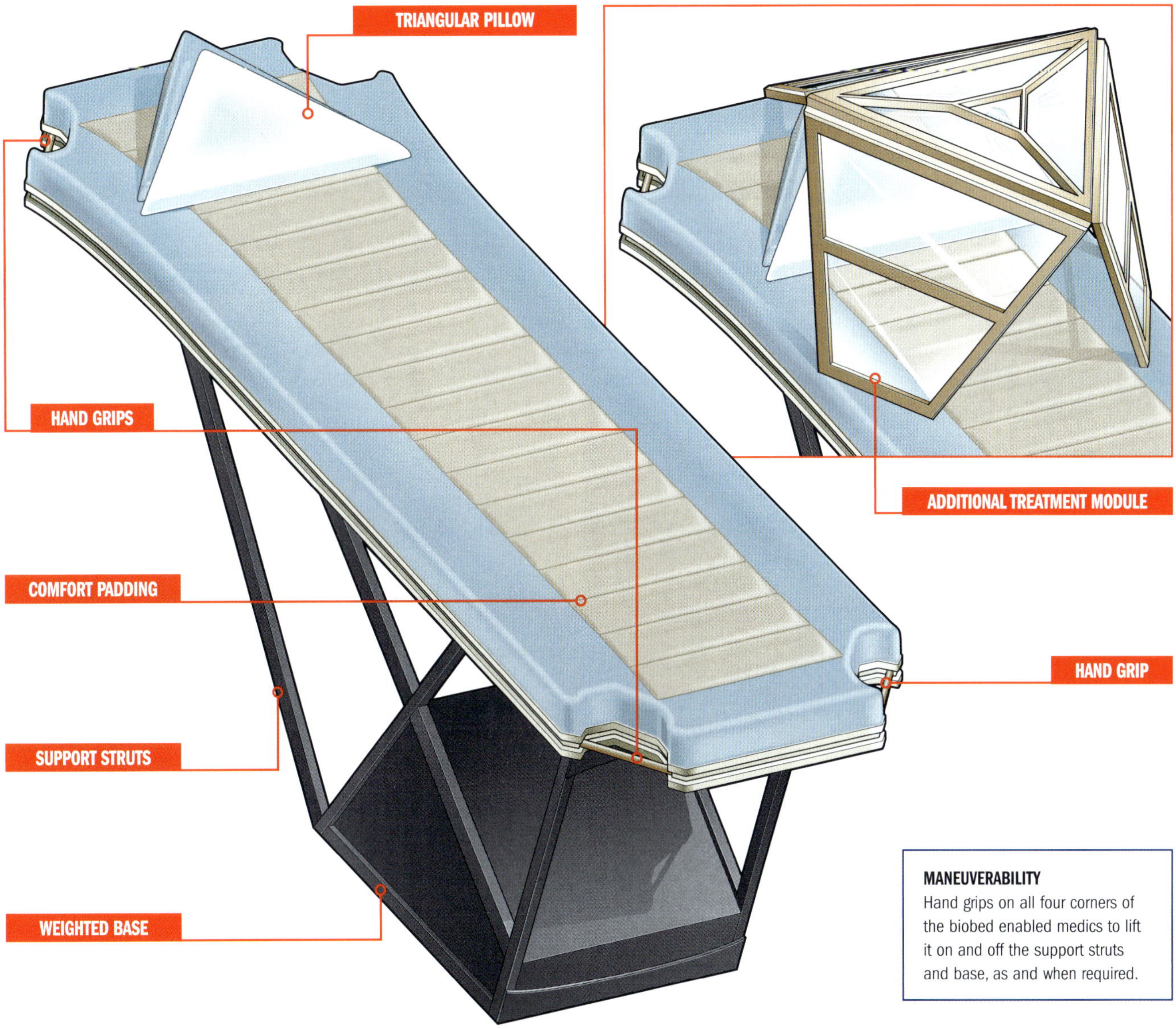

TRIANGULAR PILLOW

HAND GRIPS

COMFORT PADDING

SUPPORT STRUTS

WEIGHTED BASE

ADDITIONAL TREATMENT MODULE

HAND GRIP

MANEUVERABILITY
Hand grips on all four corners of the biobed enabled medics to lift it on and off the support struts and base, as and when required.

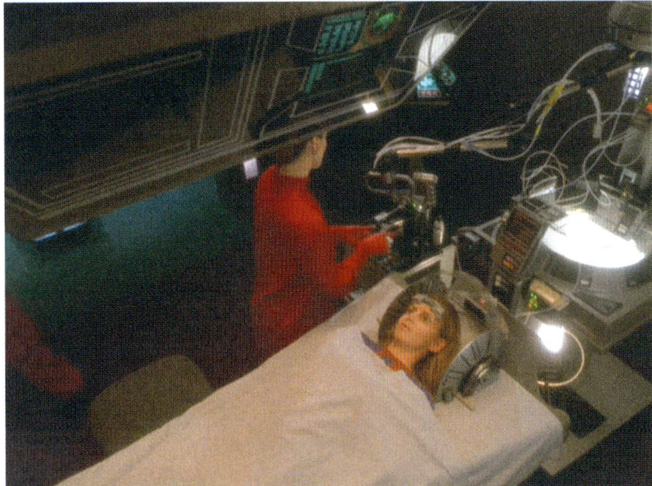

Dr. Bashir used an enhanced neurocortical probe to stimulate the growth of new synapses in Sarina Douglas's brain, curing a lifetime of sensory overstimulation.

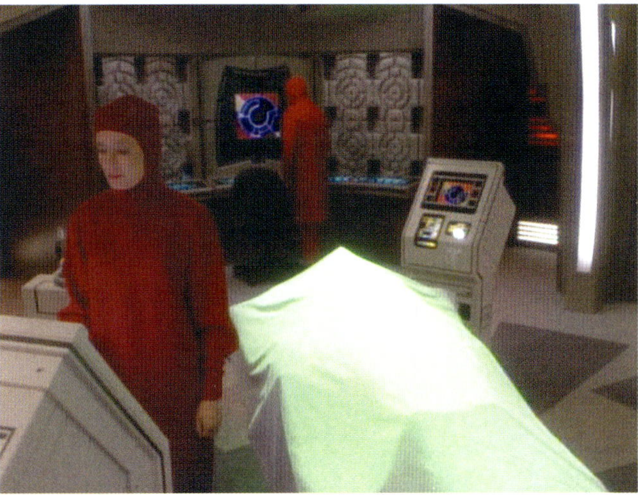

A fully covered biobed and the green glow of a stasis field indicated that a dead body was being preserved at the moment of death, prior to an autopsy.

NEUROCORTICAL PROBE

The infirmary on Deep Space 9 was equipped with a neurocortical probe: a highly advanced machine designed to treat patients who had suffered trauma to the brain or nervous system.

The neurocortical probe formed part of the station's medical equipment. It was a precision-engineered machine designed for doctors to operate on patients with injuries to the brain or nervous system. The two-part device stood approximately two meters high. The first part consisted of a moveable, lightweight metal alloy base, where the majority of controls – including a graphic control interface – were housed. A clear circular disk sat atop the base around a metre from the floor, positioned horizontally over the probe's hollow core. A large, curved metal arm extended upward from the base, with a display unit positioned on the inside of the arm.

The second part of the probe extended from the head of the arm. The extension comprised a succession of thin metal tubes connected by movable joints, which enabled the operator to direct the probe with accuracy.

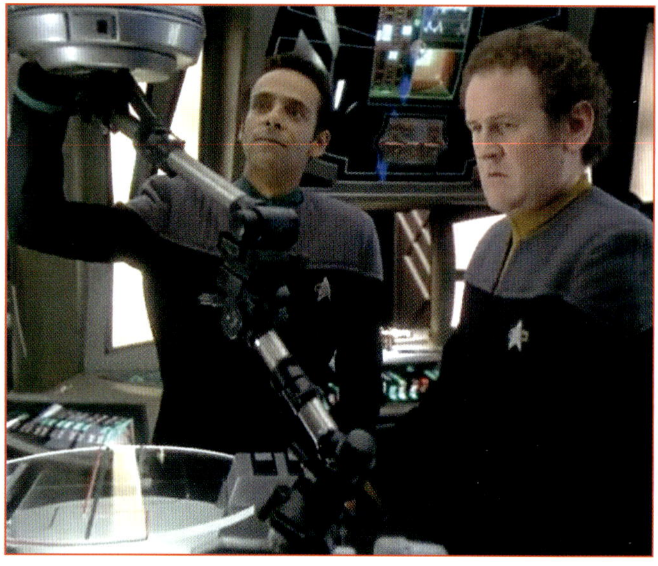

Chief Miles O'Brien was resistant to making the alterations to the neurocortical probe as he believed that quantum fluctuations would be impossible to control.

MOVEABLE SECTION

In 2375, Dr. Julian Bashir had the opportunity to use the probe to treat a patient in a catatonic state. Sarina Douglas had been brought to the station by Jack, Lauren, and Patrick – fellow genetically engineered mutants with extraordinary powers. As a child, Bashir himself had undergone the (subsequently banned) DNA resequencing, resulting in enhancements to his mental abilities, hand-eye coordination, reflexes, and vision. He was fortunate that his resequencing had not caused any unintended mutations, such as those suffered by the visitors. Although Sarina had been abducted from a medical facility by her companions, they had her best interests at heart. Dr. Bashir was sympathetic to Sarina's plight and, with consent from both the facility and her legal guardians, he willingly agreed to treat her.

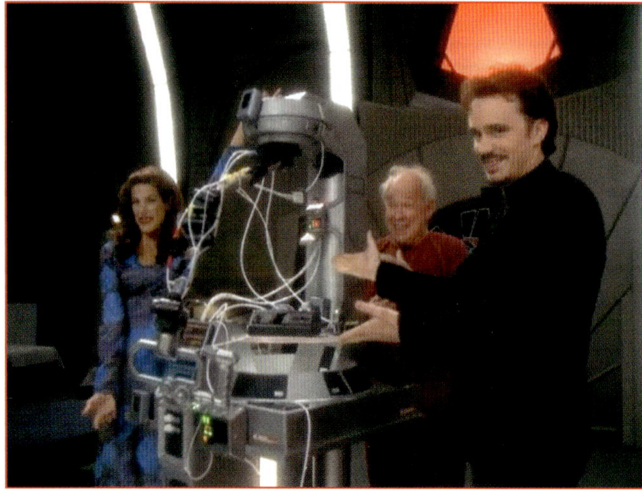

The genetically enhanced Humans modified the neurocortical probe with equipment from the station, giving it the extreme accuracy required to perform the procedure.

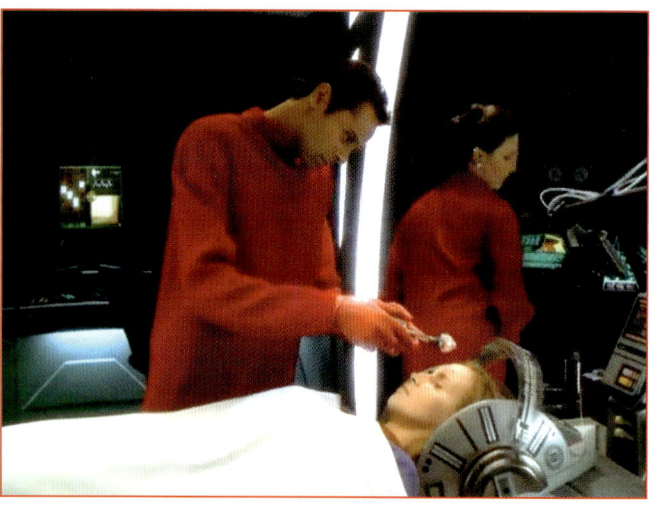

Dr. Bashir and assisting nurses prepared Sarina Douglas for the complex operation in the space station's infirmary.

LOST FOCUS

Dr. Bashir discovered that Sarina's cerebral cortex was genetically enhanced to accelerate the rate at which she could process information, but that her visual and auditory systems were not able to channel the stimuli into the cortex fast enough. The resulting lack of synchronization meant that Sarina could not focus on what was going on around her.

In order to bring her out of her catatonic state and restore her focus, Dr. Bashir needed to stimulate the growth of new synapses in her brain's thalamus. This meant manipulating neural proteins at a subatomic level with the neurocortical probe.

ESSENTIAL MODIFICATIONS

The probe on Deep Space 9 was the most advanced model available, but needed a higher degree of accuracy still to perform the subatomic procedure. Dr. Bashir asked Chief Miles O'Brien to make the necessary modifications to the probe, but despite his expertise O'Brien refused, stating that with such small resolutions it was impossible to control the quantum fluctuations with any accuracy. He commented bluntly to Bashir that he could not break the laws of physics.

However, while O'Brien would not help with the required modifications, Sarina's friends could – and did. They used their combined engineered intelligence to "bend" the laws of physics and recalibrate the imaging diodes of the machine, using a series of wires linked to a tricorder.

With the diodes modified, the probe was able to function with the infinitesimal detail necessary. Jack remarked that it was now so accurate, it could "clip the wings of an angel dancing on the head of a pin."

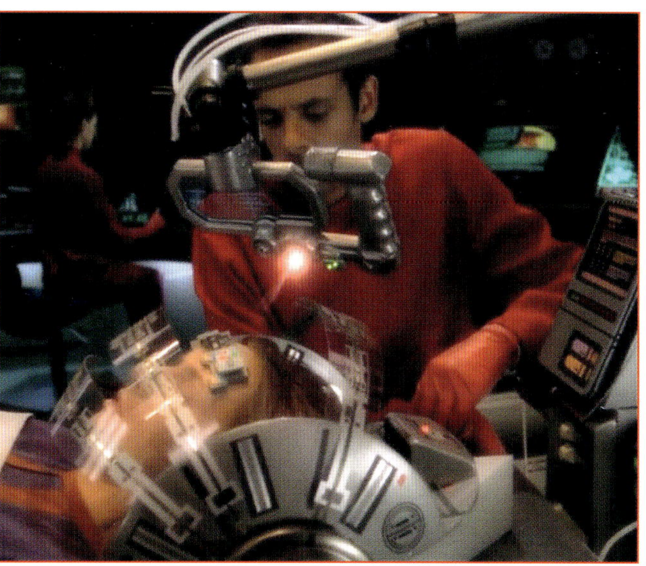

Sarina's head was partially encapsulated in a transparent dome as Dr. Bashir operated the neurocortical probe via a console on his left-hand side.

Dr. Bashir performed the operation in the infirmary, using the probe's lasers to stimulate the critical areas in Sarina's brain. It was five days before Sarina showed any signs that the procedure had been successful, but from her first waking hours she displayed a remarkable recovery that in any other patient would have taken weeks of therapy.

Sarina left Deep Space 9 with her friends to start a new life, Bashir having arranged an internship for her with one of the scientists at the Corgal Research Center on Corgal II.

KINDRED SPIRITS

Dr. Bashir empathized with his genetically enhanced visitors. The illegal procedures that they underwent as children had led to rare side effects that often could not be treated. Bashir was an exception in more ways than one, since those like him, with resequenced DNA, were not normally permitted to join Starfleet.

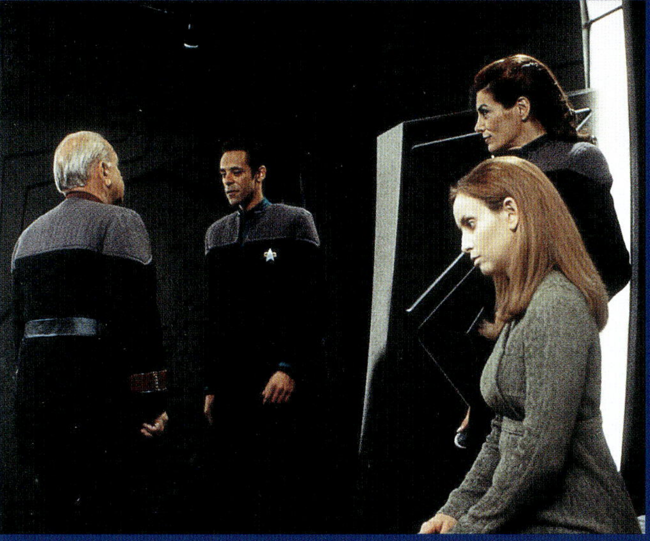

When Sarina was first brought to Deep Space 9, she did little but sit quietly. She seemed to be completely unaware of her surroundings and companions.

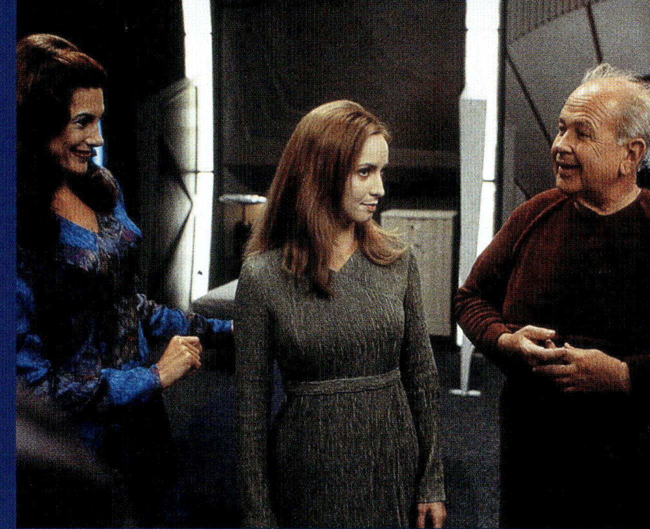

Dr. Bashir's treatment provided Sarina with another chance of life. She could finally smile, converse with her friends, and enjoy her existence as never before.

DERMAL REGENERATORS

Of all the tools in the 24th-century medikit, the dermal regenerator and its allied instruments were among the most important. The handheld unit healed wounds in seconds, reducing pain, the likelihood of scarring, and the risk of infection.

The dermal regenerator was one of the most commonly used tools in Deep Space 9's infirmary, second only to the hypospray. Along with a medical tricorder and a trauma kit, these two items also constituted the standard contents of a Starfleet battlefield medikit.

As its name suggests, the device was used to heal damaged skin. Dermal regenerators could be used for everything from removing light cosmetic blemishes to healing burns from radiation and plasma fires.

HEALING RADIATION

The basic principle of induced dermal regeneration was the localized application of radiation to stimulate anabolism: the synthesis of complex organic molecules from simpler ones. The technology to facilitate this dated back to the 23rd century, when Starfleet medics such as Dr. Leonard McCoy of the *U.S.S. Enterprise* NCC-1701 used handheld anabolic protoplasers to speed the regeneration of various wounds. But by the 24th century, dermal regenerators had become so common that they were no longer the preserve of medical professionals. In 2372, for example, the civilian restaurateur Joseph Sisko kept one in his home on Earth.

The most popular model of dermal regenerator in the late 24th century featured a nozzlelike emitter on top of a pistol-style grip. It was activated by a thumb switch on the back of the grip, with a glow from the emitter indicating when it was in use. When the emitter was passed over a target area – at a distance of between two and 10 centimeters – there

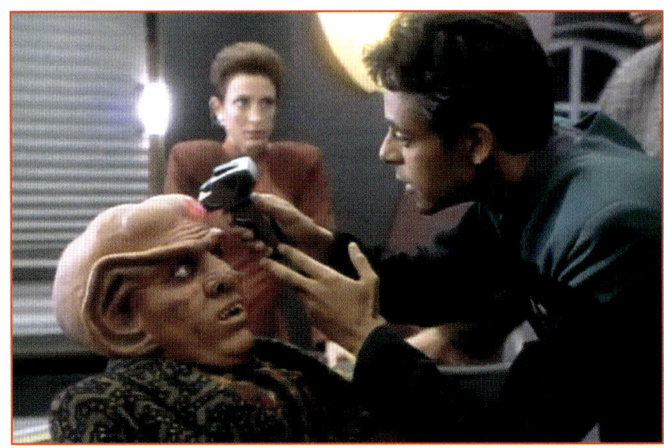

Dr. Bashir used more than one type of dermal regenerator in the infirmary on Deep Space 9, but favored the design shown here to remove a burn from Quark's forehead.

DR. BASHIR'S DERMAL REGENERATOR

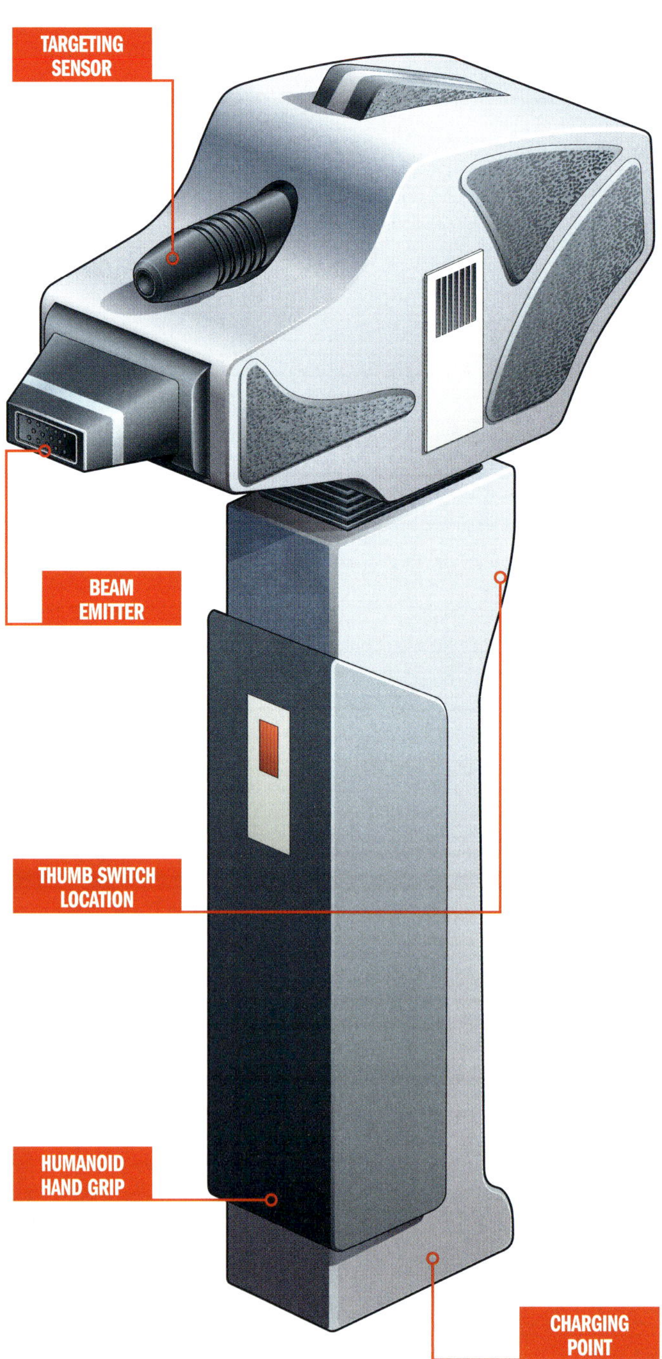

could be instantaneous effects that were clearly visible to the naked eye. However, some serious injuries called for more than one treatment, while others, such as the severe burns caused by contact with a Cardassian anti-insurgency force field – could not be healed effectively by regeneration alone.

ASSOCIATED TECHNOLOGY

Along with the various models of dermal regenerator, Starfleet medical equipment included several tools that had similar applications. Autosutures were used on injuries that went deeper than the surface layers of skin, such as puncture wounds from a knife. The pain of deep bruising, meanwhile, could be remedied by a short, cylindrical device that emitted a purple glow and could be operated without any need for specialist training.

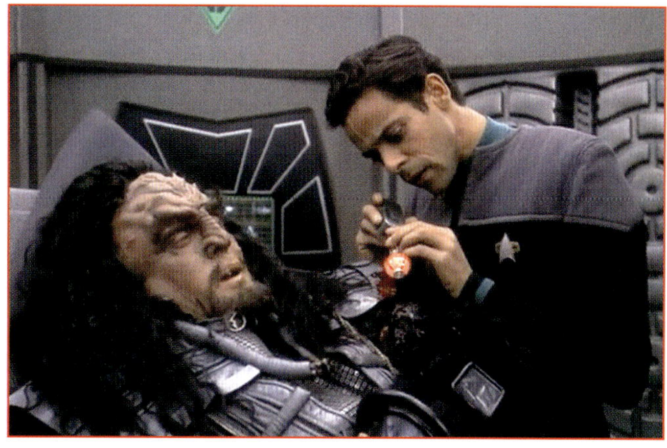

Dr. Bashir used an autosuture to repair a blade injury sustained by General Martok. Though similar in size to a dermal regenerator, it had a markedly different design.

ALTERNATIVE REGENERATOR MODELS

NEBULA-CLASS ADVANCEMENT
This design was used onboard the *U.S.S. Prometheus* NX-59650 in 2373, and combined multiple functions within a larger unit.

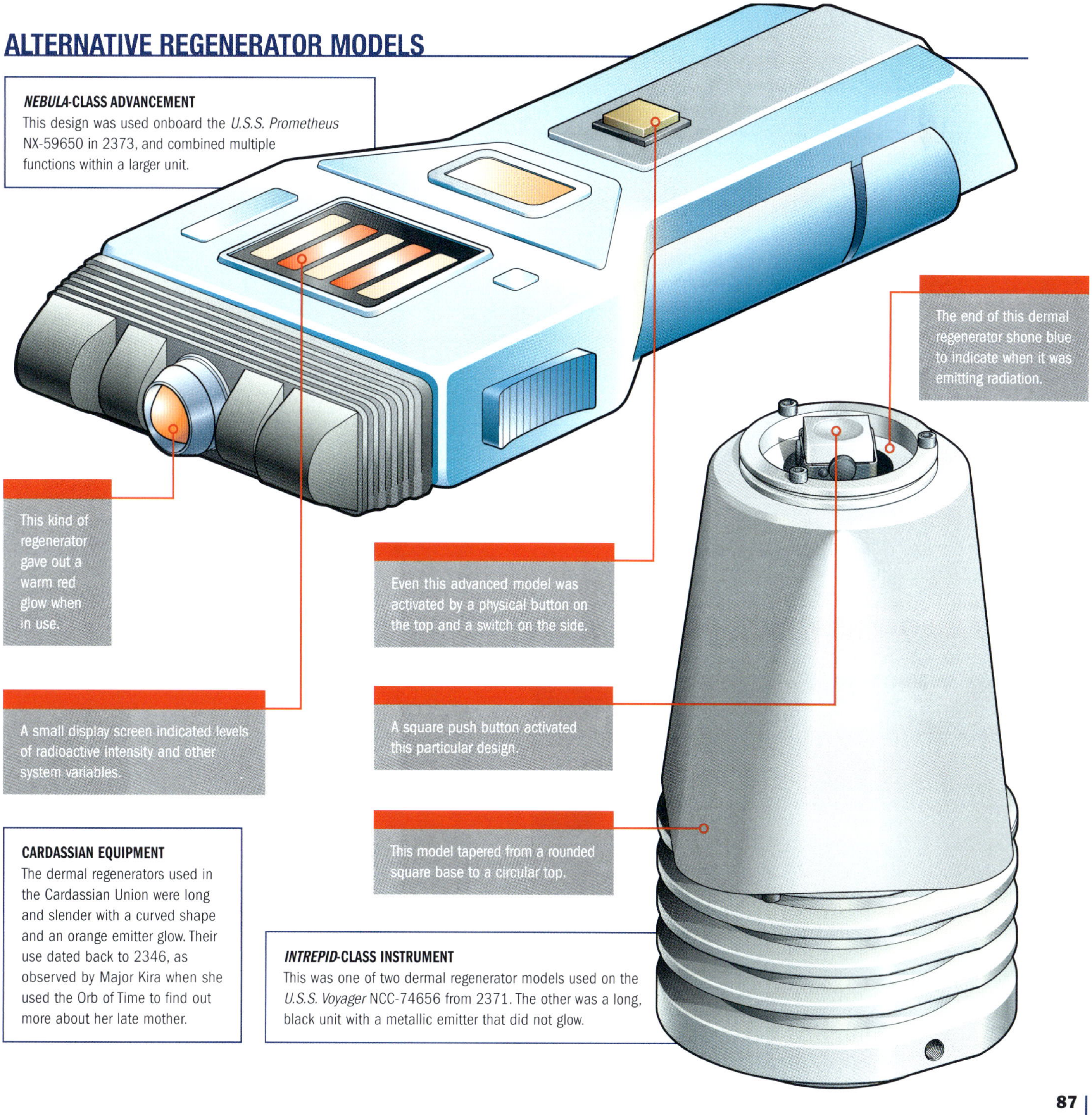

This kind of regenerator gave out a warm red glow when in use.

A small display screen indicated levels of radioactive intensity and other system variables.

Even this advanced model was activated by a physical button on the top and a switch on the side.

The end of this dermal regenerator shone blue to indicate when it was emitting radiation.

A square push button activated this particular design.

This model tapered from a rounded square base to a circular top.

CARDASSIAN EQUIPMENT
The dermal regenerators used in the Cardassian Union were long and slender with a curved shape and an orange emitter glow. Their use dated back to 2346, as observed by Major Kira when she used the Orb of Time to find out more about her late mother.

INTREPID-CLASS INSTRUMENT
This was one of two dermal regenerator models used on the *U.S.S. Voyager* NCC-74656 from 2371. The other was a long, black unit with a metallic emitter that did not glow.

THE SCIENCE LABORATORIES

From small rooms with central Cardassian workstations to fully equipped facilities with a mix of Federation, Bajoran, and Cardassian technology, Deep Space 9's science labs were ready for all eventualities.

When Starfleet personnel arrived on Deep Space 9 in 2369, the facilities for scientific research were limited. The station's new science officer, Lieutenant Jadzia Dax, got straight to work in a small lab with a central specimen table and overhead sensors, and made the most of the confined space over the following year. Like the station itself at the time, the lab's technology was old, wholly Cardassian, and prone to malfunctions. For example, when its secondary phase modulator started to emit a constant and very loud whine, working became impossible.

However, by 2370, there were more functioning research rooms on the station, offering extra space and a blend of Cardassian and Federation computer systems. A typical lab boasted a large, circular diagnostic table beneath a ceiling-mounted sensor unit similar to that in the smaller lab, with additional workstations and equipment around the edge of the room. One such facility in the station's docking ring was hastily equipped with a containment chamber for studying a protouniverse that eventually destroyed the lab and the surrounding section of the station.

By 2374, there was also a small laboratory close to ops in the station's central core. Roughly the same size as the original lab from 2369, this space had a small round table at its center with no overhead equipment, Cardassian work-stations with seating, and Federation terminals designed to be used while standing. It was here that Captain Sisko and Lieutenant Dax researched a 30,000-year-old Bajoran stone tablet before the Prophets compelled Sisko to destroy it.

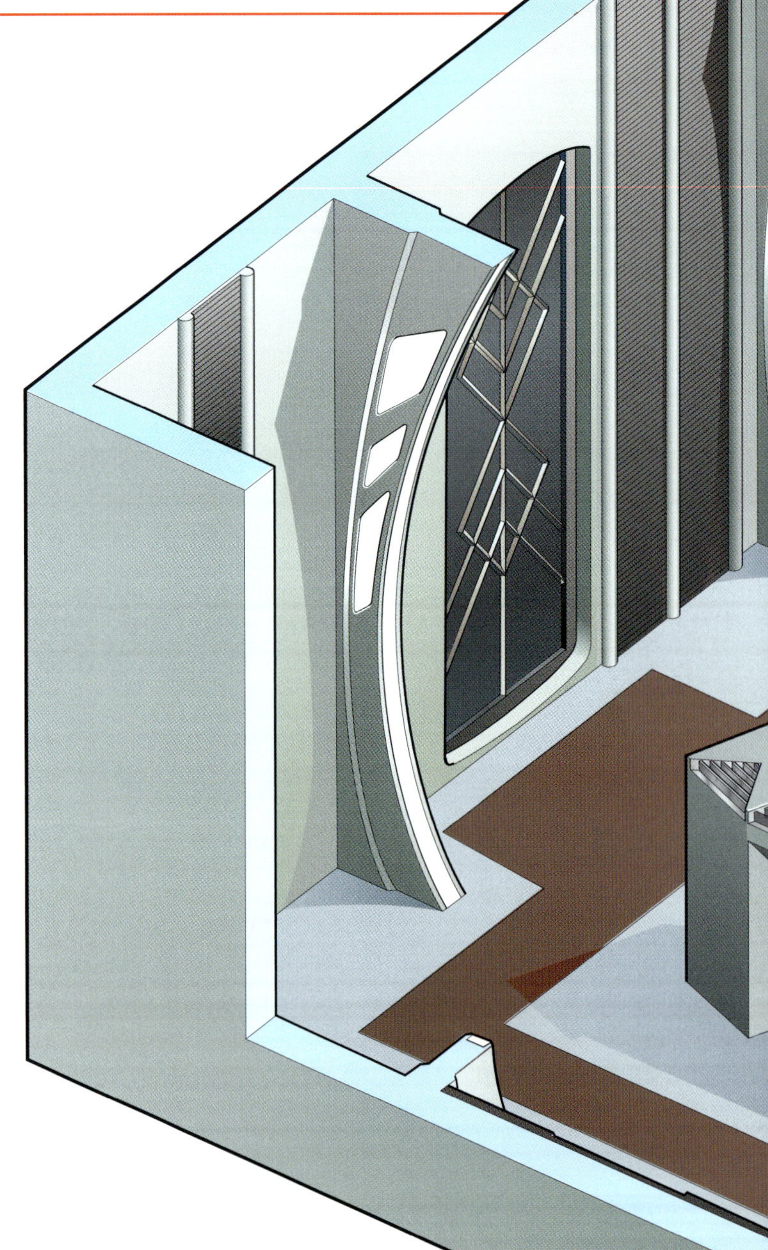

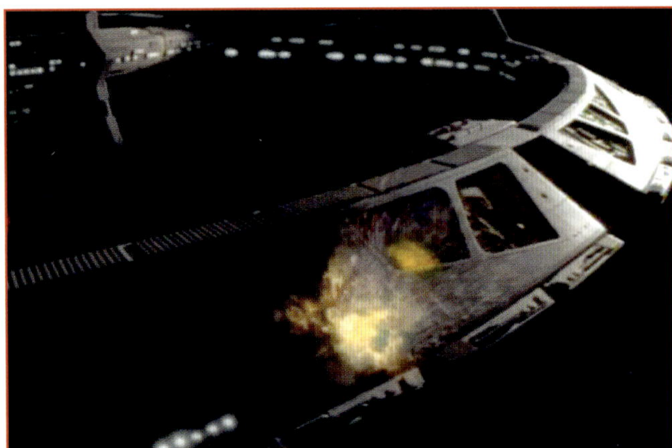

Level 22, section 14 of Deep Space 9 was destroyed by an explosion in a science lab. This was caused by the expansion of a protouniverse believed to contain life.

CRITICAL ANALYSIS

When Lieutenant Dax set foot on Deep Space 9 for the very first time, she was immediately put to work by her old friend Commander Sisko, to investigate the long history of the Orbs of the Prophets. Her researches in this Cardassian science lab led directly to the discovery of the Bajoran wormhole in the Denorios belt just a short time later.

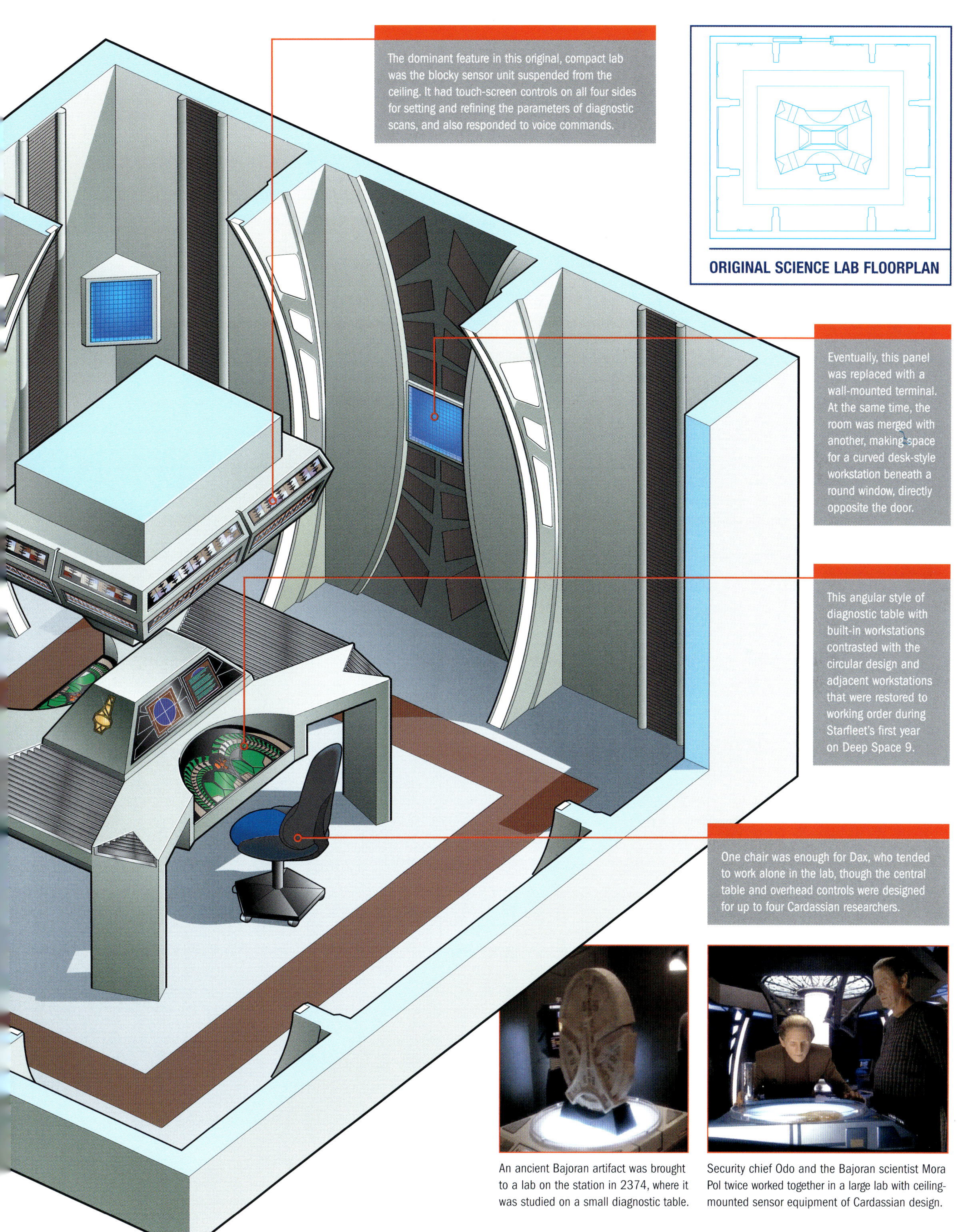

An ancient Bajoran artifact was brought to a lab on the station in 2374, where it was studied on a small diagnostic table.

Security chief Odo and the Bajoran scientist Mora Pol twice worked together in a large lab with ceiling-mounted sensor equipment of Cardassian design.

THE WARDROOM

As a briefing space, a function lounge, and a diplomatic meeting area, the wardroom played a pivotal role on the station, right up until the end of the Dominion War.

Deep Space 9's wardroom was located on level 13 in the station's central core, below the Promenade. The long, multipurpose space was most often used as a briefing room for senior staff, but it could also be a venue for diplomatic events and social functions.

In 2371, the wardroom hosted a gathering as part of the annual Bajoran Gratitude Festival, and a ceremony in which Benjamin Sisko was promoted from commander to captain. Two years later, Captain Sisko presided over the wedding of Nog and Leeta in the room, shortly before the Dominion War began. Throughout the war, casualty reports were posted in the wardroom, until the Dominion formally surrendered at its table in 2375.

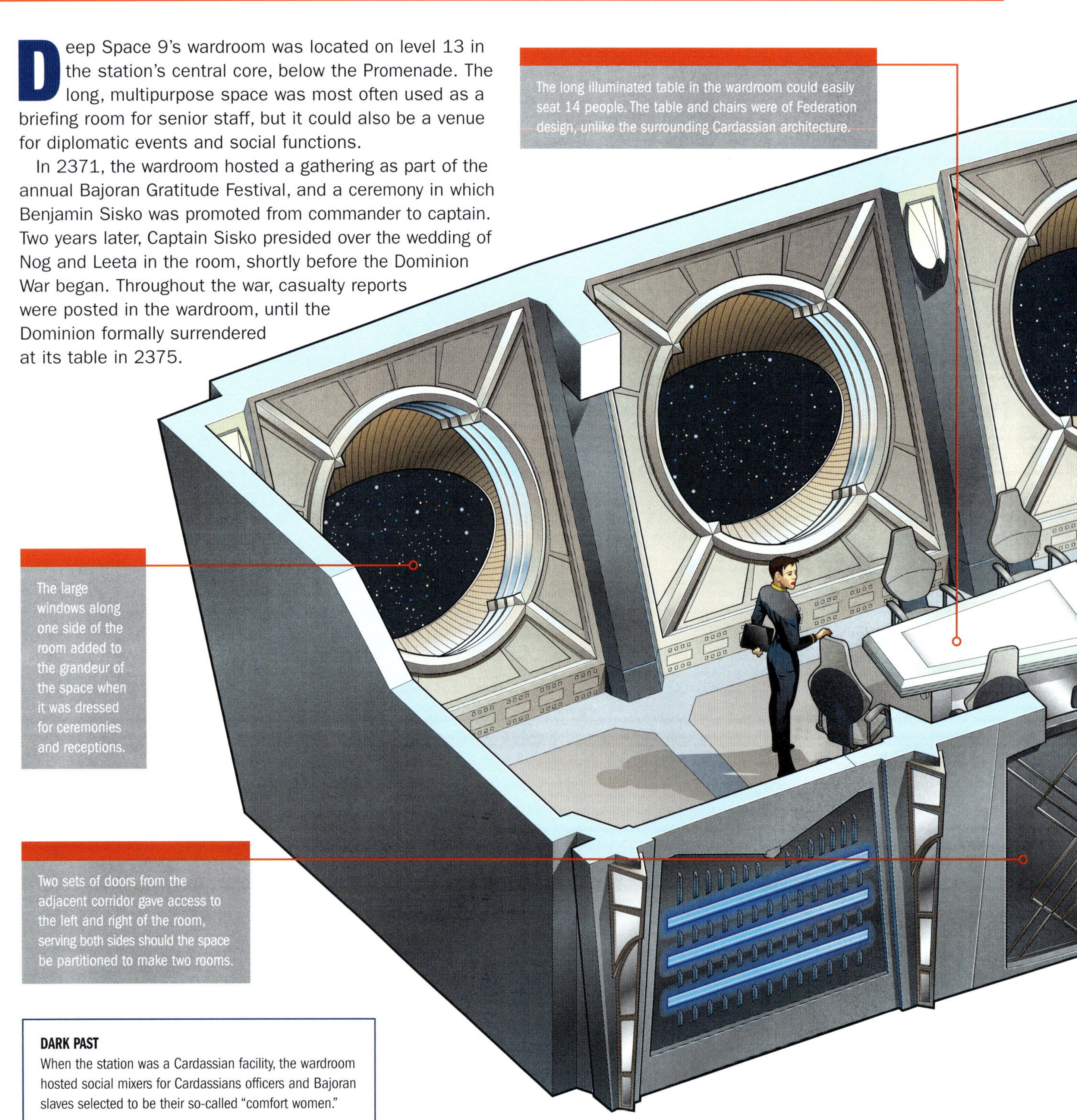

The long illuminated table in the wardroom could easily seat 14 people. The table and chairs were of Federation design, unlike the surrounding Cardassian architecture.

The large windows along one side of the room added to the grandeur of the space when it was dressed for ceremonies and receptions.

Two sets of doors from the adjacent corridor gave access to the left and right of the room, serving both sides should the space be partitioned to make two rooms.

DARK PAST

When the station was a Cardassian facility, the wardroom hosted social mixers for Cardassians officers and Bajoran slaves selected to be their so-called "comfort women."

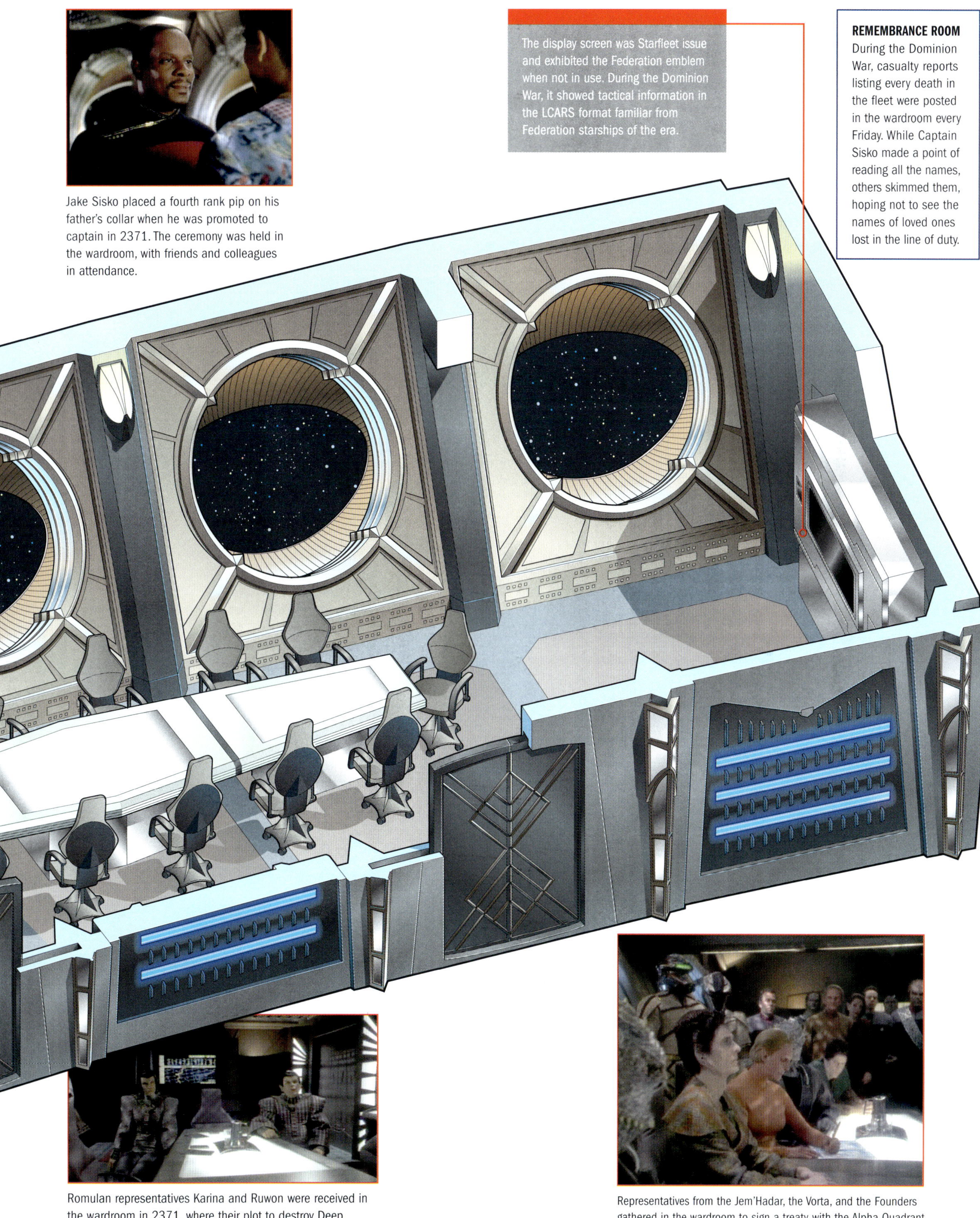

Jake Sisko placed a fourth rank pip on his father's collar when he was promoted to captain in 2371. The ceremony was held in the wardroom, with friends and colleagues in attendance.

The display screen was Starfleet issue and exhibited the Federation emblem when not in use. During the Dominion War, it showed tactical information in the LCARS format familiar from Federation starships of the era.

REMEMBRANCE ROOM
During the Dominion War, casualty reports listing every death in the fleet were posted in the wardroom every Friday. While Captain Sisko made a point of reading all the names, others skimmed them, hoping not to see the names of loved ones lost in the line of duty.

Romulan representatives Karina and Ruwon were received in the wardroom in 2371, where their plot to destroy Deep Space 9 and the wormhole was exposed.

Representatives from the Jem'Hadar, the Vorta, and the Founders gathered in the wardroom to sign a treaty with the Alpha Quadrant alliance in 2375, marking the end of the Dominion War.

RESIDENTIAL QUARTERS

Everyone from the station commander to the itinerant courier Morn had a home in Deep Space 9's habitat ring – though duty often kept them away from these personalized private spaces.

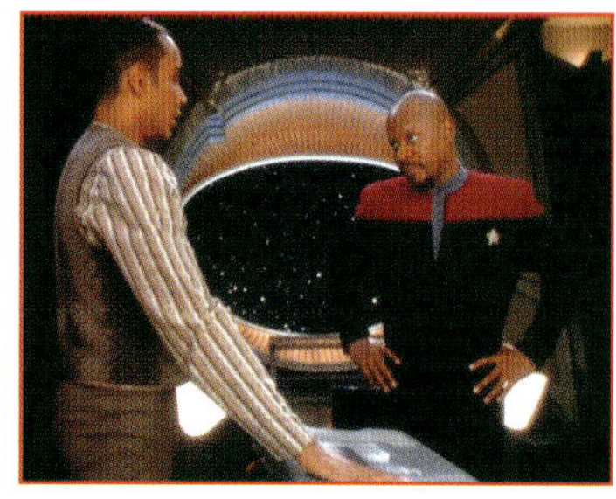

After four years living on Deep Space 9 with his father, Jake Sisko moved out of his room and into shared quarters with Nog in 2373.

Everybody who stayed on Deep Space 9 was assigned private living quarters in the habitat ring. This included permanent residents – such as the station's Starfleet and Bajoran personnel, and the proprietors and employees of the shops on the Promenade – and short-term visitors, for whom there were dedicated guest quarters.

The habitat ring was made up of five floors (levels 11 to 15, sometimes referred to as habitat levels one to five), and comprised 452 large residential units and 231 smaller ones. The former were originally intended for senior Cardassians administrating the occupation of Bajor, with the latter mostly occupied by rank-and-file soldiers. Bajorans on the station were mostly kept in pens, away from the habitat ring.

In the station's Starfleet era, most of the senior staff lived in the larger quarters. The Ferengi Quark was among the civilians based in the smaller rooms. Both kinds of accommodation followed a standard layout, with an open living area leading off to one or more bedroom suites. Food replicators were located in the main living area, which usually had at least one large, circular window. The choice of furnishings was entirely down to the individual.

The environmental controls in each set of quarters could also be set according to the needs of the resident. In some cases, this meant simple adjustments to the temperature, humidity, or light levels. In others, it could involve matching the artificial gravity to the conditions on a particular planet.

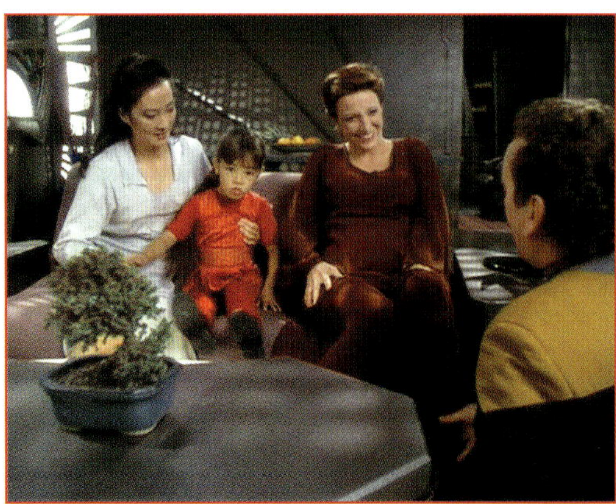

Though not a commissioned officer, Chief O'Brien was entitled to large quarters because he had a family. Major Kira moved in with the O'Briens for a time when she was carrying their second child as a surrogate.

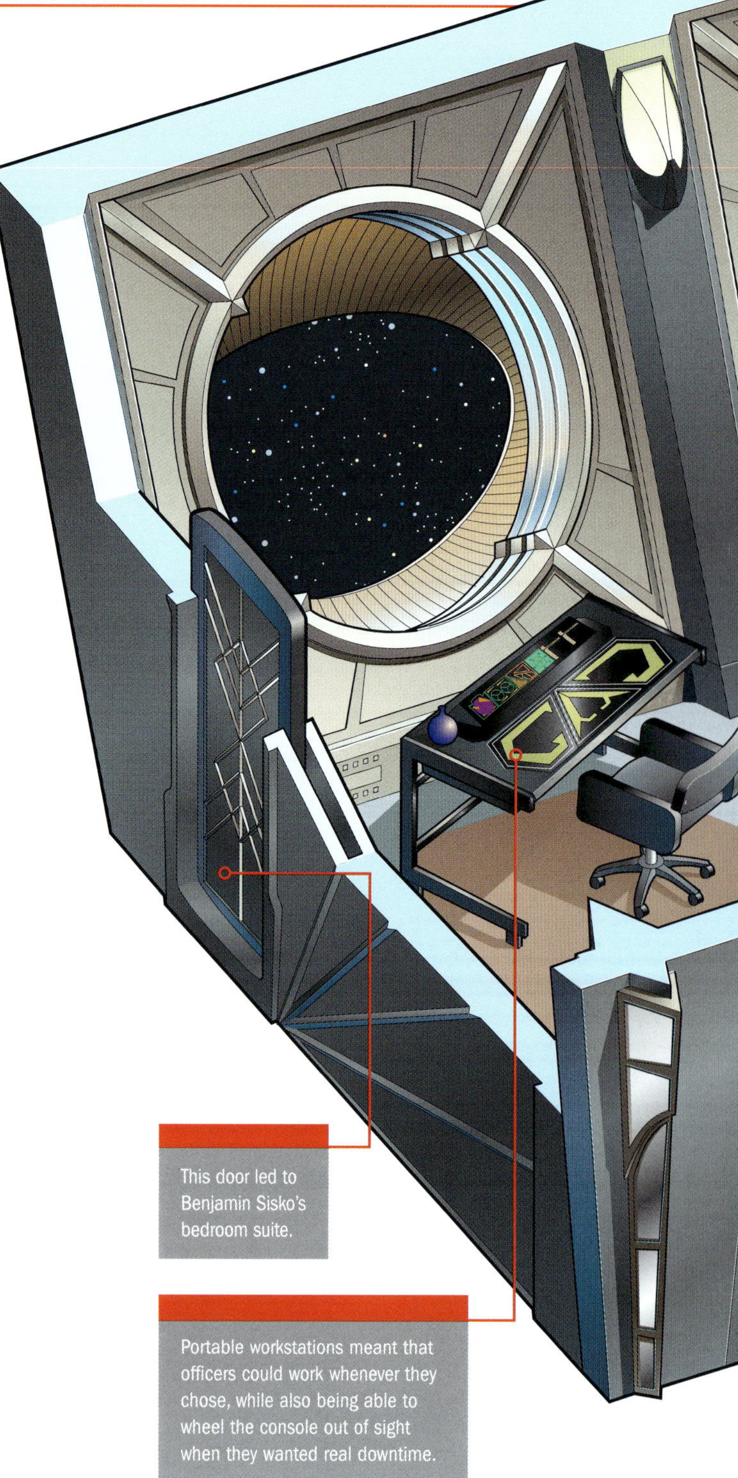

COMMAND QUARTERS

The illustration shows the main room of Benjamin and Jake Sisko's quarters. Dax, the O'Briens, and Dr. Bashir had quarters with the same dimensions, while Major Kira and Worf made the most of more compact spaces.

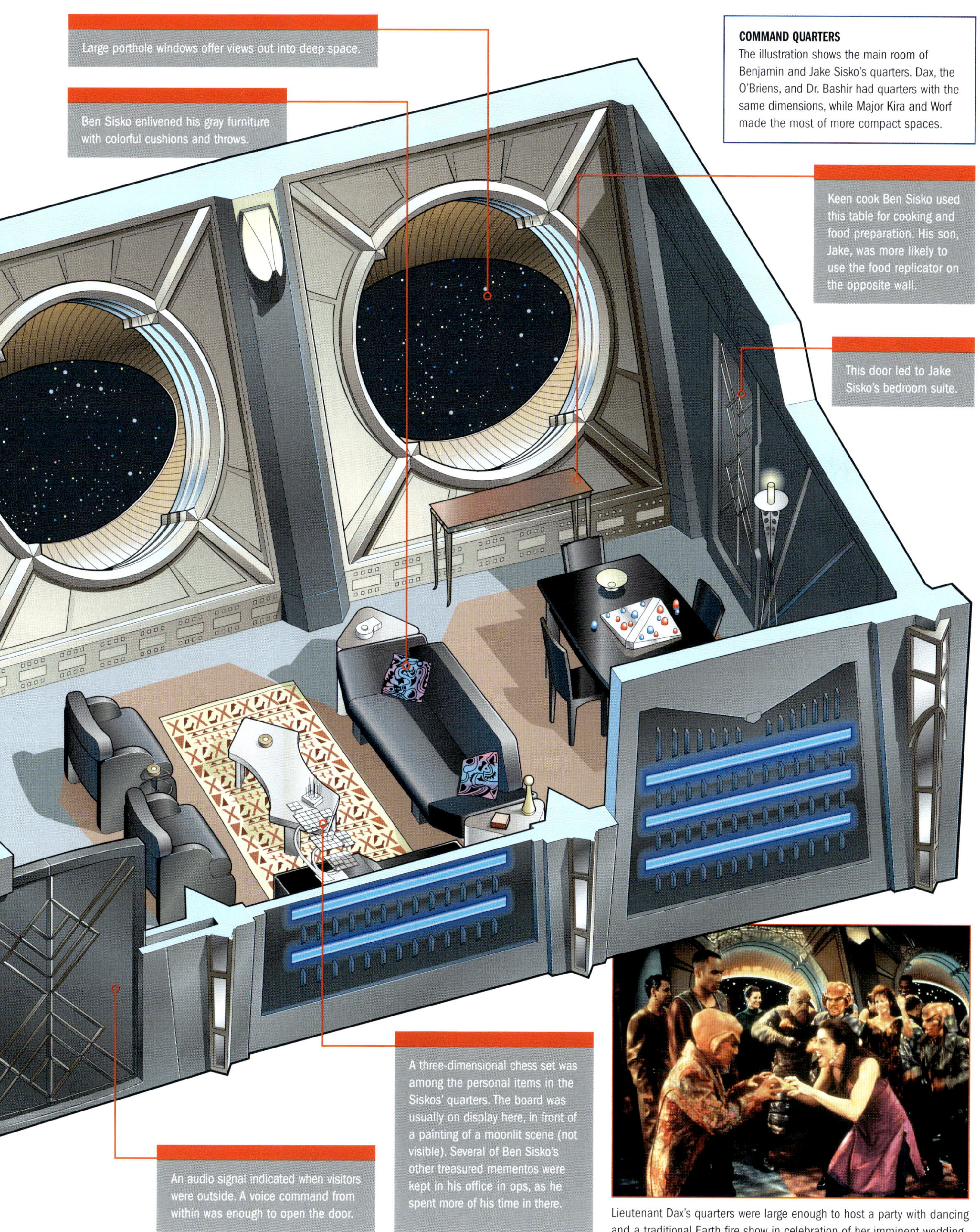

Lieutenant Dax's quarters were large enough to host a party with dancing and a traditional Earth fire show in celebration of her imminent wedding.

ODO'S QUARTERS

For a long time, Deep Space 9's chief of security had no quarters to call his own. When he finally requested a room for himself, Odo furnished it like no other on the station.

A side table with an array of ornamental vessels gave Odo a range of inspirations when he wanted to change his form. He could also take the shape of liquids or plants kept inside the vessels.

Though Odo's ability to shape-shift was innate, he had to learn to harness and control his skills. His earliest memories were of experiments conducted on his newly discovered, shapeless form by the Bajoran scientist Mora Pol, which used electric shocks to force this process. When Odo began to make a life for himself on the station then known as Terok Nor, he thought the laboratory stage of his life was over. While not on duty as the station's chief of security, he lived simply – reverting to a gelatinous state every 16 hours or so, and regenerating in a bucket that he kept in the privacy of the security office.

CHANGING ROOM

Then, in 2371, Odo made contact with his own people for the first time, and realized that he still had much to learn about being a shape-shifter. The Founders (also known as the Changelings) believed that "to assume a form was to begin to understand it," and spent hours contemplating their existence as rocks, plants, animals, and even clouds of gas. This led Odo to request his own quarters on Deep Space 9, which he furnished with a variety of complex forms. Instead of using his bucket, he spent his downtime getting to know these forms and their textures. By interacting with them and mimicking them, he not only enhanced his abilities, but also his understanding of what it meant to be a shape-shifter.

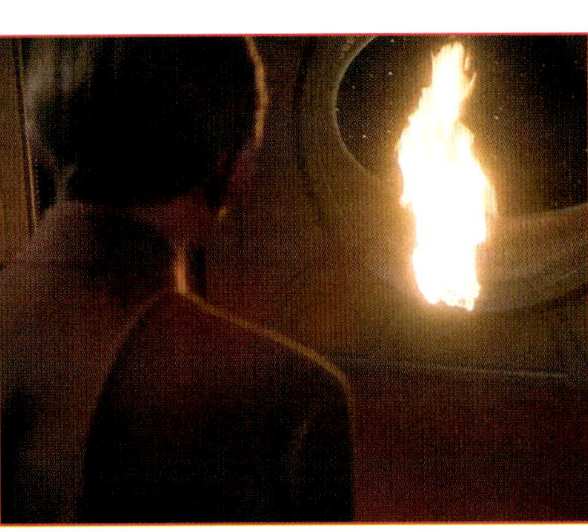

When the Changeling known as Laas stayed on Deep Space 9, he made use of Odo's quarters and demonstrated his ability to transform himself into a self-sustaining fire.

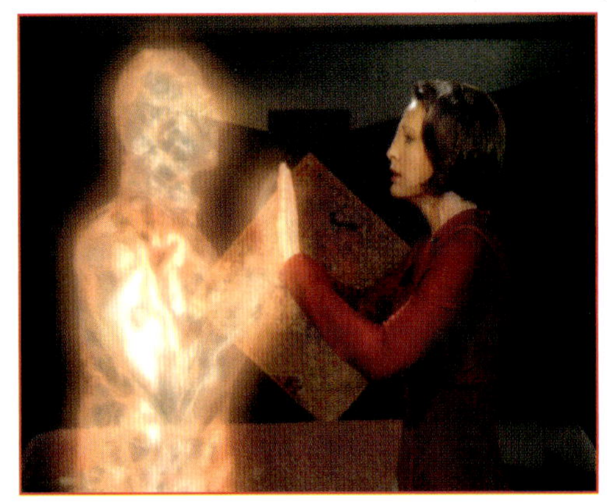

During his last year on the station, Odo spent much of his free time in Colonel Kira's quarters. On one occasion here, he shape-shifted into a glowing energy field.

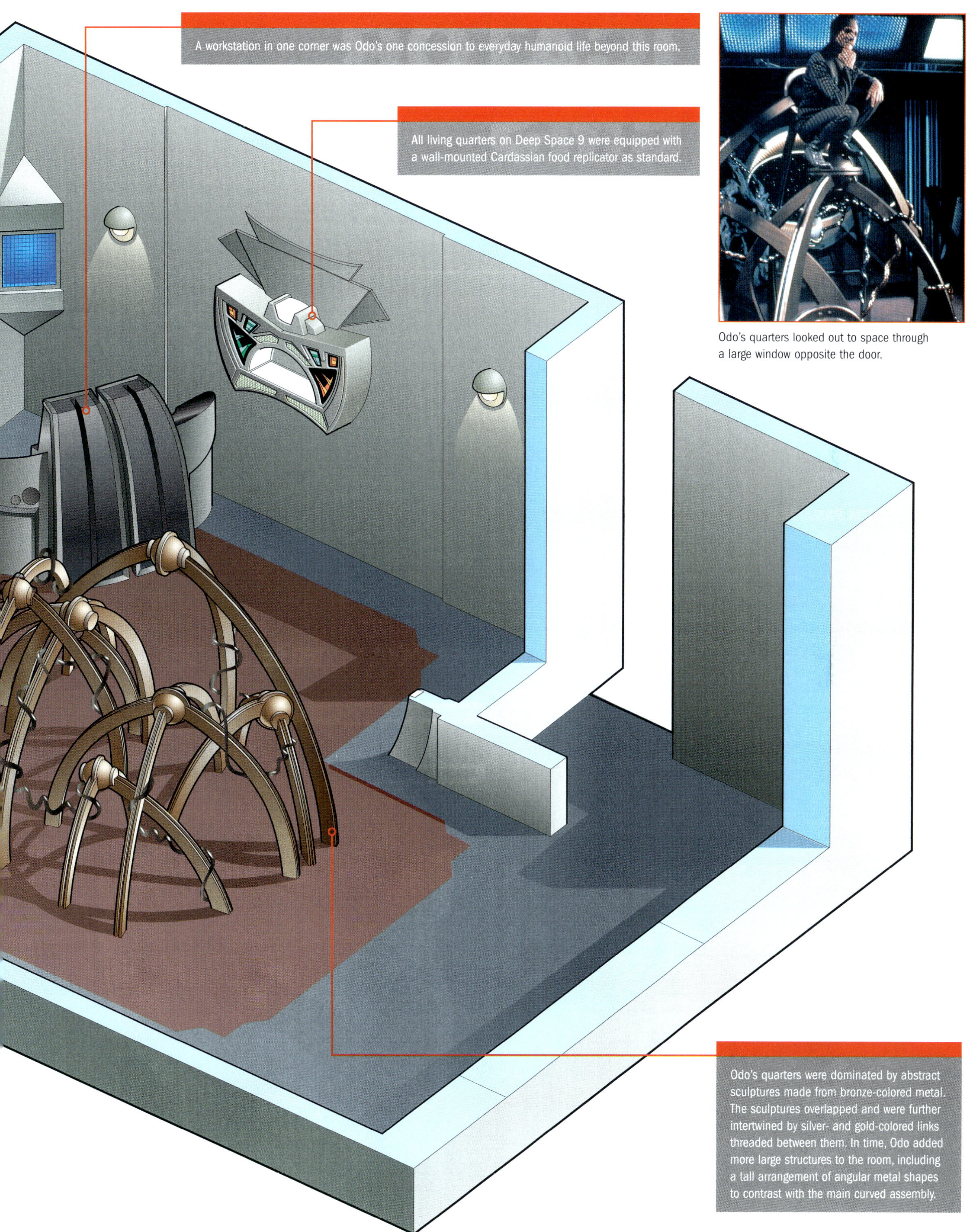

Odo's quarters looked out to space through a large window opposite the door.

REPLICATOR SYSTEMS

Most of the food and drink consumed on Deep Space 9 was generated instantaneously by Cardassian-built replicators. These were maintained and modified by Chief O'Brien.

When Starfleet personnel first arrived on Deep Space 9, they found that many of the Cardassian replicators were out of service, while the ones that worked were programmed to produce a very limited range of Cardassian food and drinks only. Replacing the hundreds of units across the station with Starfleet-issue equivalents would have been time-consuming and a waste of resources, so, instead, a program of repairs and system upgrades was hastily initiated, with limited long-term success.

SYSTEM FAILURES

At first, It didn't take long for Chief O'Brien and his team to get the broken replicators up and running – after a fashion. But owing to their age and limited compatibility with Federation software, they remained prone to malfunction in various ways. To complicate matters further, one early set of repairs activated a biological weapon that had been hidden in the system 18 years earlier, threatening all life onboard the station – starting with O'Brien himself. No sooner was this crisis averted (and O'Brien restored to health) than the replicators failed again. Eventually, their reliability and repertoire improved, but still with limitations. For example, the replimat – a popular replicator cafe on the Promenade – lacked the capacity to include Ferengi food in its database.

The two main types of replicator on the station were the large units found in all living quarters and the replimat, capable of producing a family meal in seconds; and a more compact version intended to provide only drinks and snacks in busy work areas such as ops. Quark's Bar used another design, which was also Cardassian in origin and tied into the station-wide food replication system.

All three kinds of replicator worked on identical principles. When a food or drink order was placed, the unit retrieved the high-resolution data template(s) for that order from locally stored isolinear data rods, or in some cases from the main computer core. This was fed into a matrix-field manipulation device, which then processed a stream of matter, molecule by molecule, to build the requested item(s) in the replication chamber. This sequence also generated nonconsumables, such as cups and plates, and included safety procedures to filter out any contaminants in the matter stream.

Rom was usually responsible for repairing Quark's replicators, and did so by cleverly repurposing parts from unrelated devices, such as Quark's personal disruptor pistol.

OPERATIONS CENTER REPLICATOR

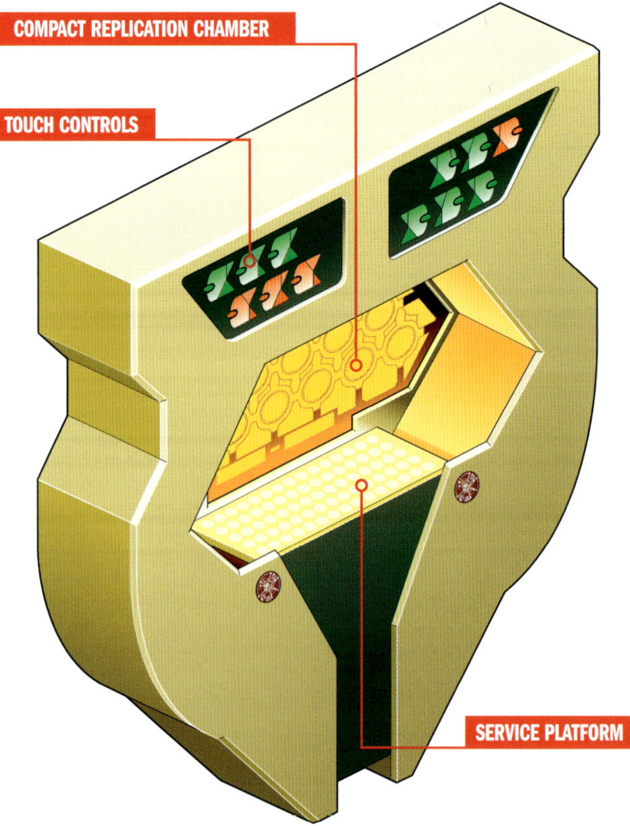

HOME REPLICATOR

HOME ESSENTIAL
This kind of replicator could be found on a wall in nearly all the station's living quarters. The height at which it was mounted could be easily adjusted to suit the user.

Touch screens provided an alternative to voice control and displayed data regarding nutrition, temperature, and other species-specific variables.

SECURITY CONSIDERATIONS
Replicators could create far more than just food and drink – given the relevant data. In certain circumstances, access to domestic replicators was restricted or refused, to prevent individuals from trying to replicate weapons, signaling equipment, or any other unauthorized communications equipment.

The size of a single portion was limited only by the capacity of the replication chamber. A residential replicator could easily provide two plates of food, or a meal and a drink, simultaneously, with larger orders requiring the user to clear the chamber with each materialization.

INTERRUPTED SERVICE
Even when they were running smoothly, the replicators had to be taken offline once a week for maintenance.

QUARK'S DRINKS REPLICATOR

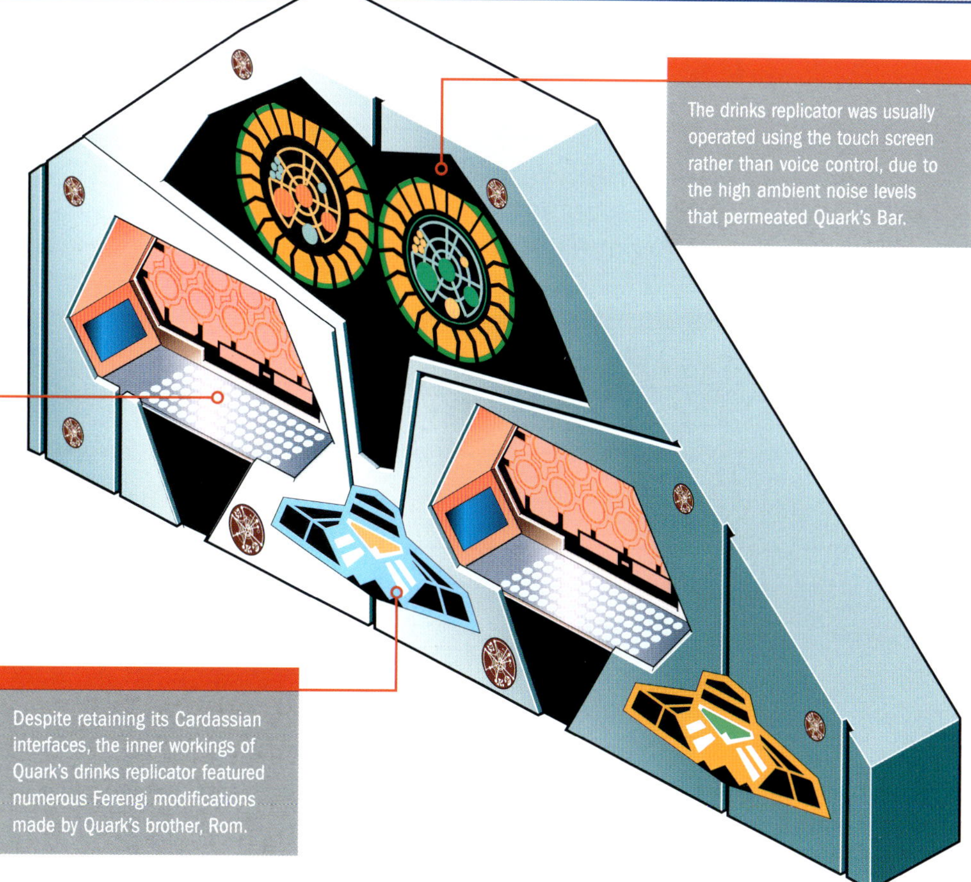

DRINKS MACHINE
This unusually angular Cardassian replicator was located behind the bar at Quark's and used to make drinks that the Ferengi owner did not keep in stock. He also had larger replicators away from the bar area to fulfill large food orders.

The drinks replicator was usually operated using the touch screen rather than voice control, due to the high ambient noise levels that permeated Quark's Bar.

A pair of replication units side by side allowed two members of bar staff to attend to different orders with no unnecessary waiting time.

WASTE DISPOSAL
Any leftover food, along with plates and utensils, could be returned to the replication chamber following a meal. It would then be recycled in a reverse of the usual process, which returned the detritus to its constituent molecules.

Despite retaining its Cardassian interfaces, the inner workings of Quark's drinks replicator featured numerous Ferengi modifications made by Quark's brother, Rom.

ZEK'S CALL CENTER

Zek set his team to work through the station's "night," with the automatic light levels set to match the lateness of the hour on nearby Bajor.

For one night in 2374, a small room in Deep Space 9's habitat ring became a communications hub for the once and future Ferengi Grand Negus.

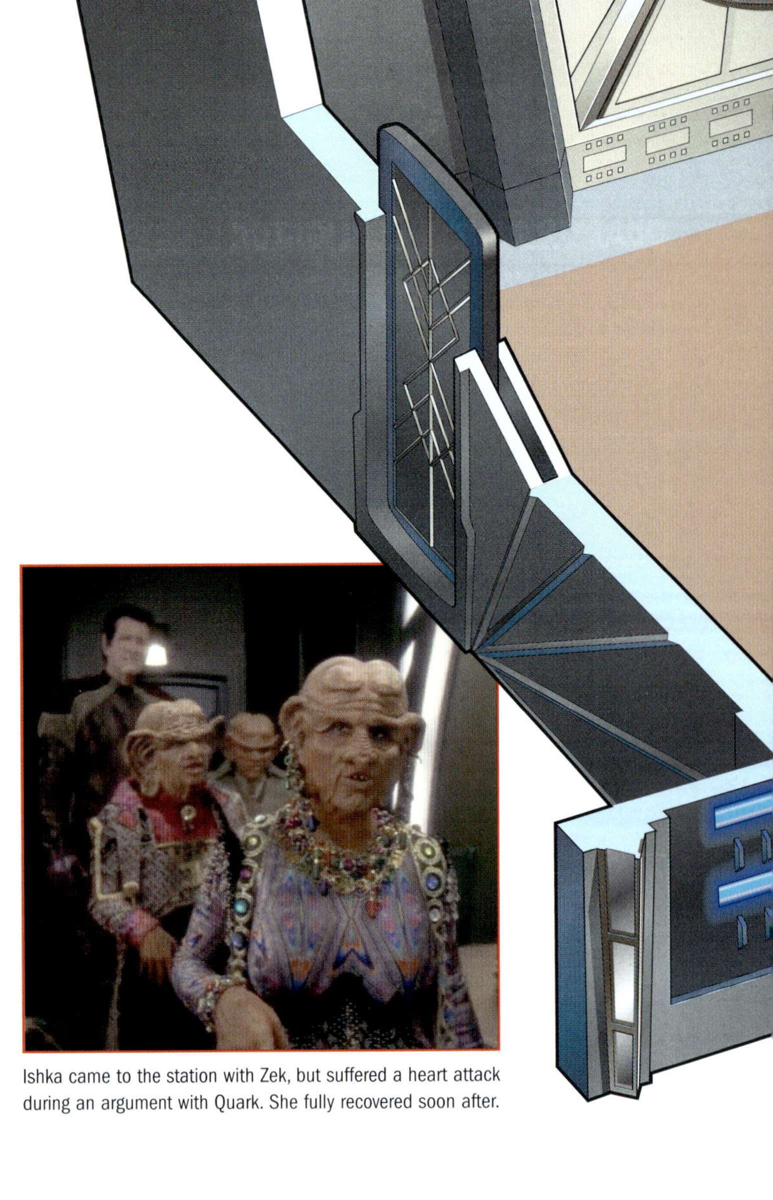

The Ferengi leader, Grand Negus Zek, made numerous visits to Deep Space 9 between 2369 and 2375. He was usually received with great fanfare by the station's resident Ferengi brothers, Quark and Rom, but his arrival in 2374 was a more muted affair, as he had lately been deposed by his despised rival, Brunt. With only days to go before Brunt officially graduated from Acting Grand Negus to fully fledged ruler of Ferenginar, Zek recruited Quark, Rom, and Rom's son Nog to put his case to his people.

CALLING ALL COMMISSIONERS

Zek's troubles had come about as a result of his unusual but admirable attempts to modernize Ferengi society. Guided by the example of Quark and Rom's taboo-busting mother, Ishka, he had called for all Ferengi to have the same rights and opportunities regardless of gender. This was far more than Ferenginar's male-dominated society could cope with, and Zek was forced to flee an uprising.

His plan to regain control from the station was simple. Zek, having set up a bank of three subspace transceivers in one room, instructed Quark and his associates to use them to invite all 432 commissioners from the Ferengi Commerce Authority to a summit where he and Ishka would win them over. In the event, only one commissioner proved willing to give Zek and Ishka a hearing, but it was enough to put a brake on Brunt's otherwise unopposed ascent.

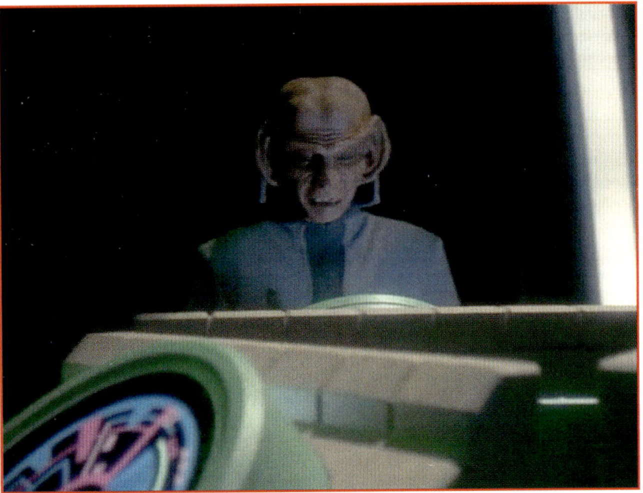

Rom, Quark, and Nog operated a transceiver each, working flat out to sweet-talk every single Ferengi Commerce Authority commissioner before Brunt's ascent was finalized.

Ishka came to the station with Zek, but suffered a heart attack during an argument with Quark. She fully recovered soon after.

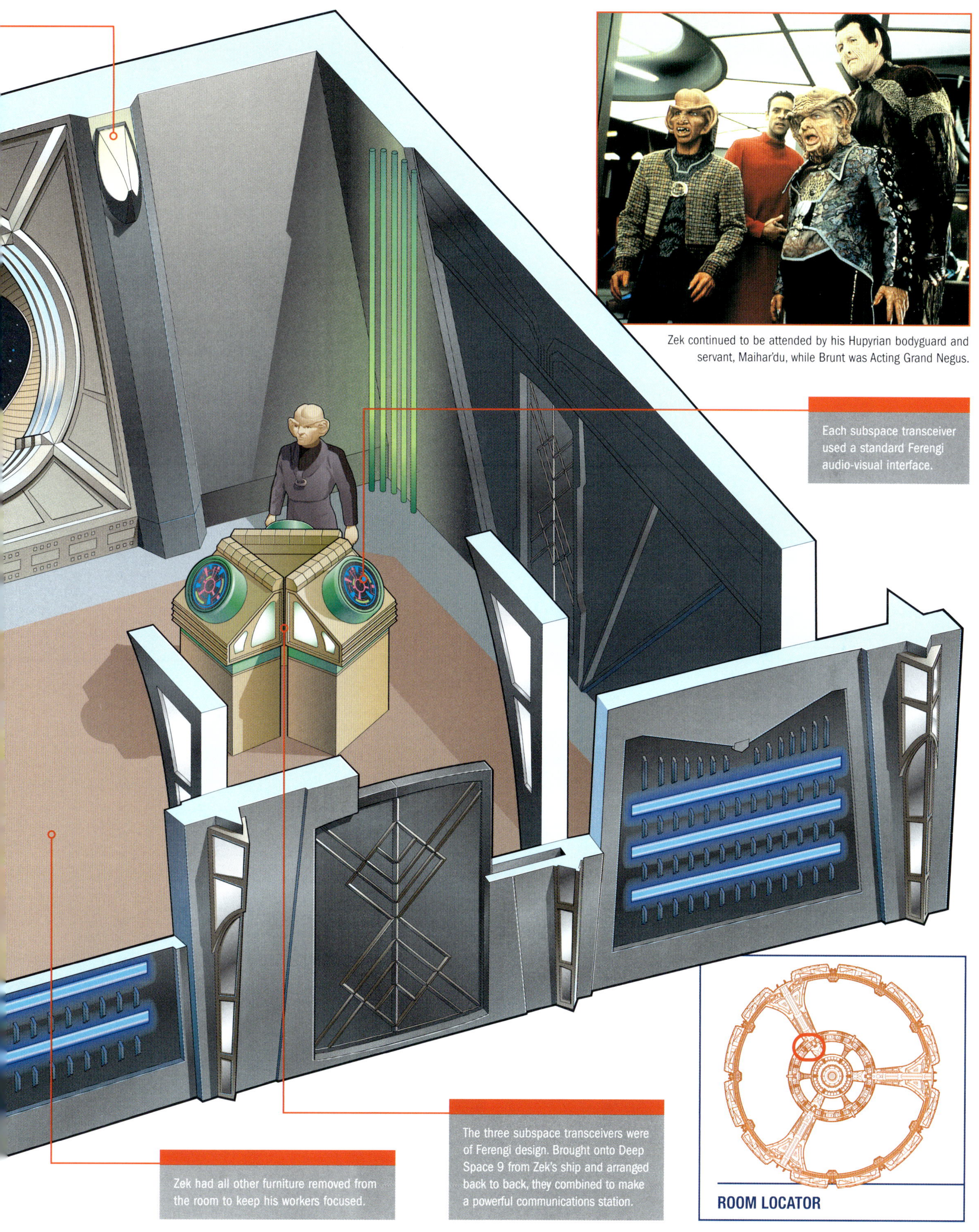

Zek continued to be attended by his Hupyrian bodyguard and servant, Maihar'du, while Brunt was Acting Grand Negus.

Each subspace transceiver used a standard Ferengi audio-visual interface.

The three subspace transceivers were of Ferengi design. Brought onto Deep Space 9 from Zek's ship and arranged back to back, they combined to make a powerful communications station.

Zek had all other furniture removed from the room to keep his workers focused.

CARGO BAYS

Cargo bays came in various shapes and sizes, but all were high-ceilinged spaces supported by illuminated arches. The regular floor-to-ceiling lighting meant that, even if one light source was obscured by cargo, the space remained well lit.

The discovery of the wormhole to the Gamma Quadrant put Deep Space 9 on a major new trade route. It quickly became a hub for cargo transfers, storage, and customs checks.

More than 250 cargo bays were arranged throughout Deep Space 9's docking ring, docking pylons, and crossover bridges. Originally designed to facilitate the ore processing for which the Cardassian station was intended, by the 2370s the bays largely catered to independent commercial interests alongside Federation supply chains. Cargo required for essential station operations was also routed through the cargo bays, but then stored separately in restricted areas in the central core.

The movement and storage of commercial cargo on the station was overseen by civilian staff, working with the freighter crews. Constable Odo and his deputies also kept a close eye on proceedings, working hard to minimize any trade in stolen, prohibited, or dangerous goods. Of the total available storage space, three-quarters was assigned on a first-come, first-served basis, with the rest reserved for long-term users with a high daily turnover. All users paid a fee to the Bajoran authorities for standard storage and security checks, and incurred additional charges for special services, such as reduced gravity in a particular bay.

Decisions about where to store cargo were based on the nature of the goods and the length of time they were to be kept on the station. Separation by type was a safety measure, with proximity-caution protocols to prevent unwanted substance interactions. Timing considerations were purely practical, with those items scheduled to ship out within two weeks remaining closest to the docking bays in the docking ring. Longer-term warehousing was provided by 108 EM-shielded modules in the crossover bridges.

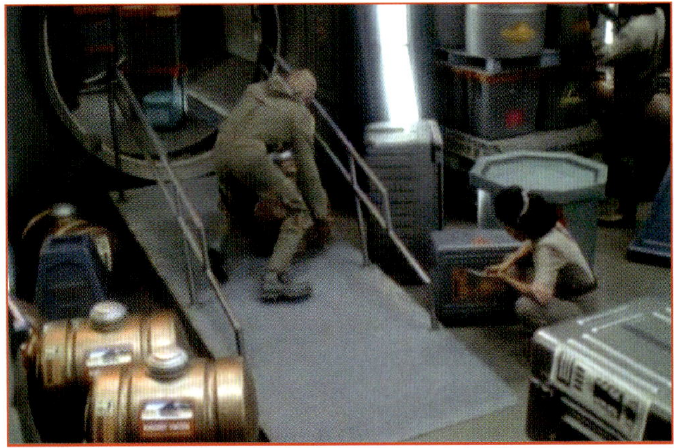

The owner and employees of Kasidy Yates' Interstellar Freights made do without anti-grav assistance to load lightweight goods onto their ship, the *S.S. Xhosa*, in 2371.

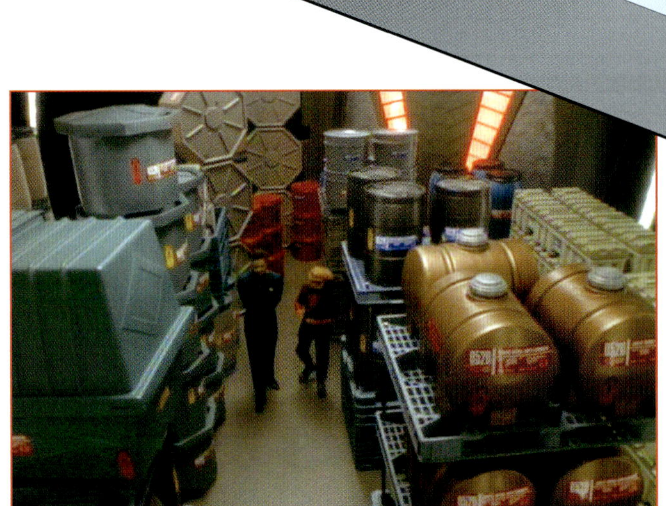

When Nog wanted to prove himself a worthy candidate for Starfleet Academy, he carried out an exhaustive inventory of cargo bay 4, on the orders of Lieutenant Dax.

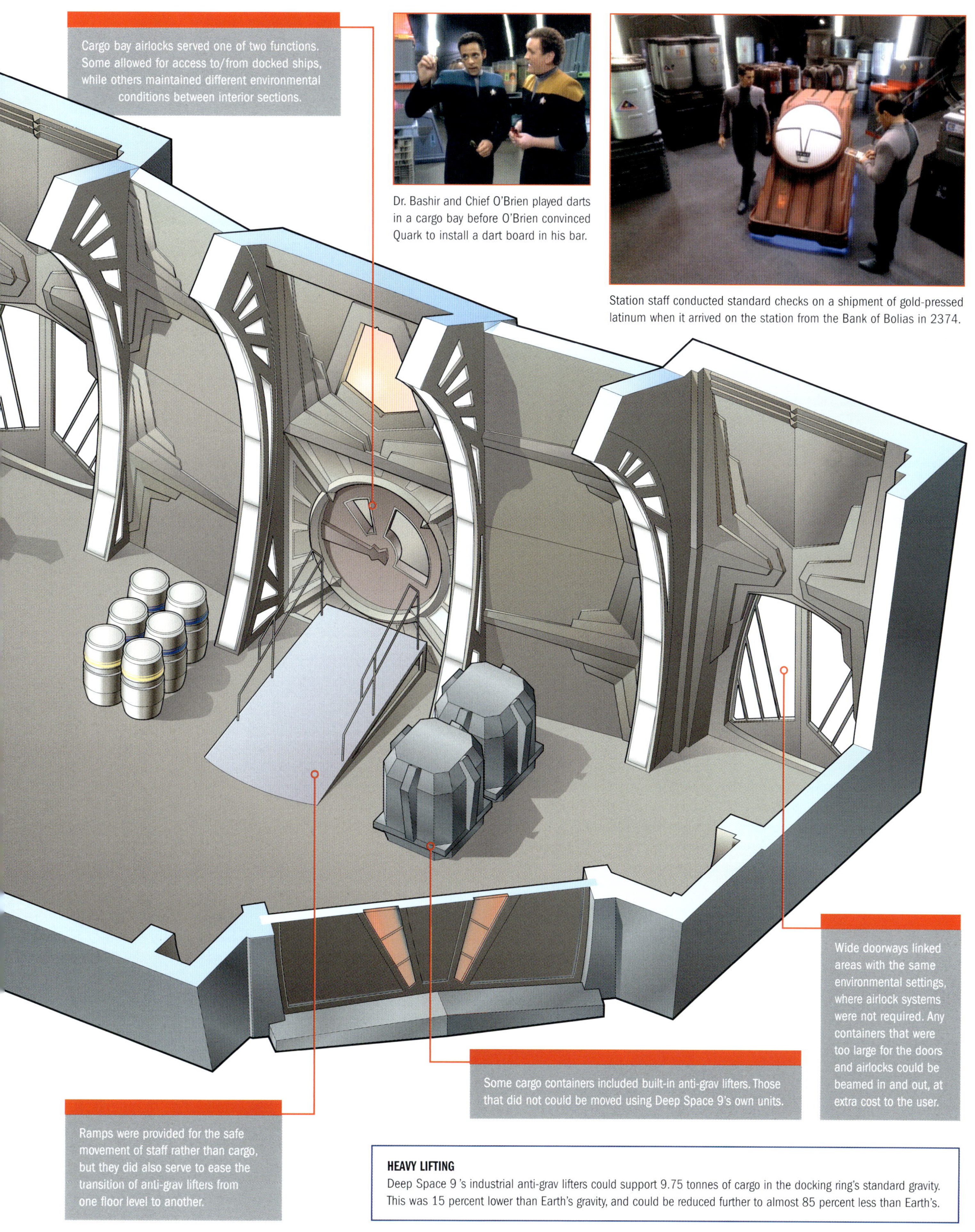

Cargo bay airlocks served one of two functions. Some allowed for access to/from docked ships, while others maintained different environmental conditions between interior sections.

Dr. Bashir and Chief O'Brien played darts in a cargo bay before O'Brien convinced Quark to install a dart board in his bar.

Station staff conducted standard checks on a shipment of gold-pressed latinum when it arrived on the station from the Bank of Bolias in 2374.

Wide doorways linked areas with the same environmental settings, where airlock systems were not required. Any containers that were too large for the doors and airlocks could be beamed in and out, at extra cost to the user.

Some cargo containers included built-in anti-grav lifters. Those that did not could be moved using Deep Space 9's own units.

Ramps were provided for the safe movement of staff rather than cargo, but they did also serve to ease the transition of anti-grav lifters from one floor level to another.

HEAVY LIFTING

Deep Space 9's industrial anti-grav lifters could support 9.75 tonnes of cargo in the docking ring's standard gravity. This was 15 percent lower than Earth's gravity, and could be reduced further to almost 85 percent less than Earth's.

SECURITY GATES AND AIRLOCKS

The distinctive airlocks on Deep Space 9 served two functions. As well as maintaining the station's atmospheric integrity, they could operate as security checkpoints.

Except when beaming aboard, entry to Deep Space 9 was achieved through a series of airlocks. These were located at the 12 mooring points around the docking ring, at the tips of the docking pylons, and at the three runabout bays housed within the habitat ring. Once onboard, visitors would sometimes pass through additional airlocks, which not only regulated environmental conditions across the station, but also served as security gates.

MATERIALS AND METHODOLOGY

Each airlock was an independent unit, prefabricated from modular components and then installed on the station. A single assembly consisted of two chambers separated by three cogwheel pressure doors. Automated systems were programmed to identify and match the atmosphere in the chambers with that on hundreds of vessel types, before equalizing it with the main station environment. If a previously unknown type of ship docked at the station, the system made a data link with it to establish an appropriate course of action.

MATERIALS AND METHODOLOGY

The outer airlock walls were made from duranium sheets and gamma-bonded toranium honeycombs. In most cases, the doors were toranium and kelindide composites with transparent toranium inserts, though some made use of rodinium monocrystal sheeting. All measured 2.32 meters across, and rolled open and closed horizontally on a rack-and-pinion principle, using electrohydraulic actuators powered by the electro-plasma system (EPS) network. In the event of a power failure, local capacitance banks stored enough energy to keep doors operational for six minutes. Thereafter, the actuators would disconnect for manual operation.

When the airlock doors closed, delcromin toroids in the surrounding frames expanded to create an airtight seal. This could be maintained for around 11,300 hours before it failed and, if it did, a backup seal could be maintained with a manual pump. The final failsafe was to establish a force field using emitters that were primarily intended as security barriers. These could also draw on locally stored energy reserves when main power was offline.

When the station was under construction, the airlocks on the Promenade led to temporary docking ports. They were retained on completion, and repurposed for security scans to keep unauthorized weapons away from the public.

This outer door was exposed to space when no vessel was docked with it.

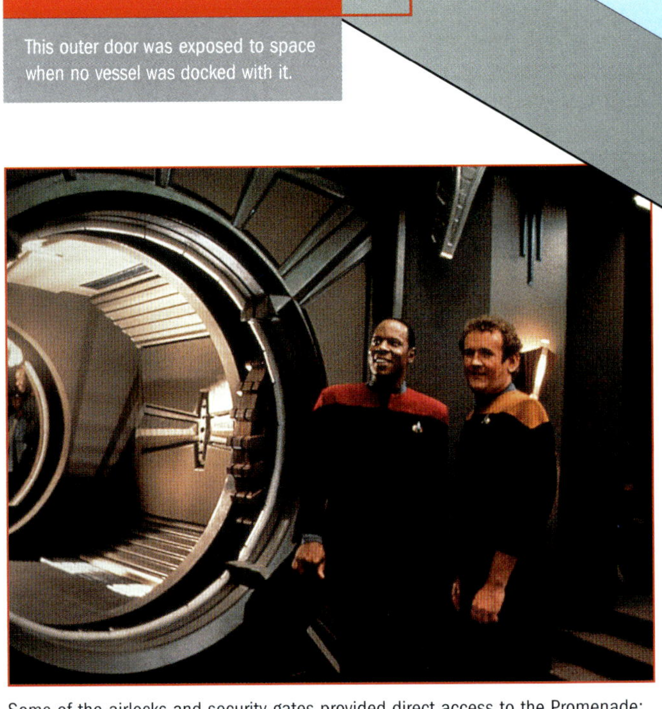

Some of the airlocks and security gates provided direct access to the Promenade; others led onto corridors or cargo bays.

CRAMPED CONDITIONS

In 2375, the station's resident Cardassian, Elim Garak, suffered an extreme attack of claustrophobia while inside airlock seven. Panic-stricken, he tried and failed to open the outer door by hand.

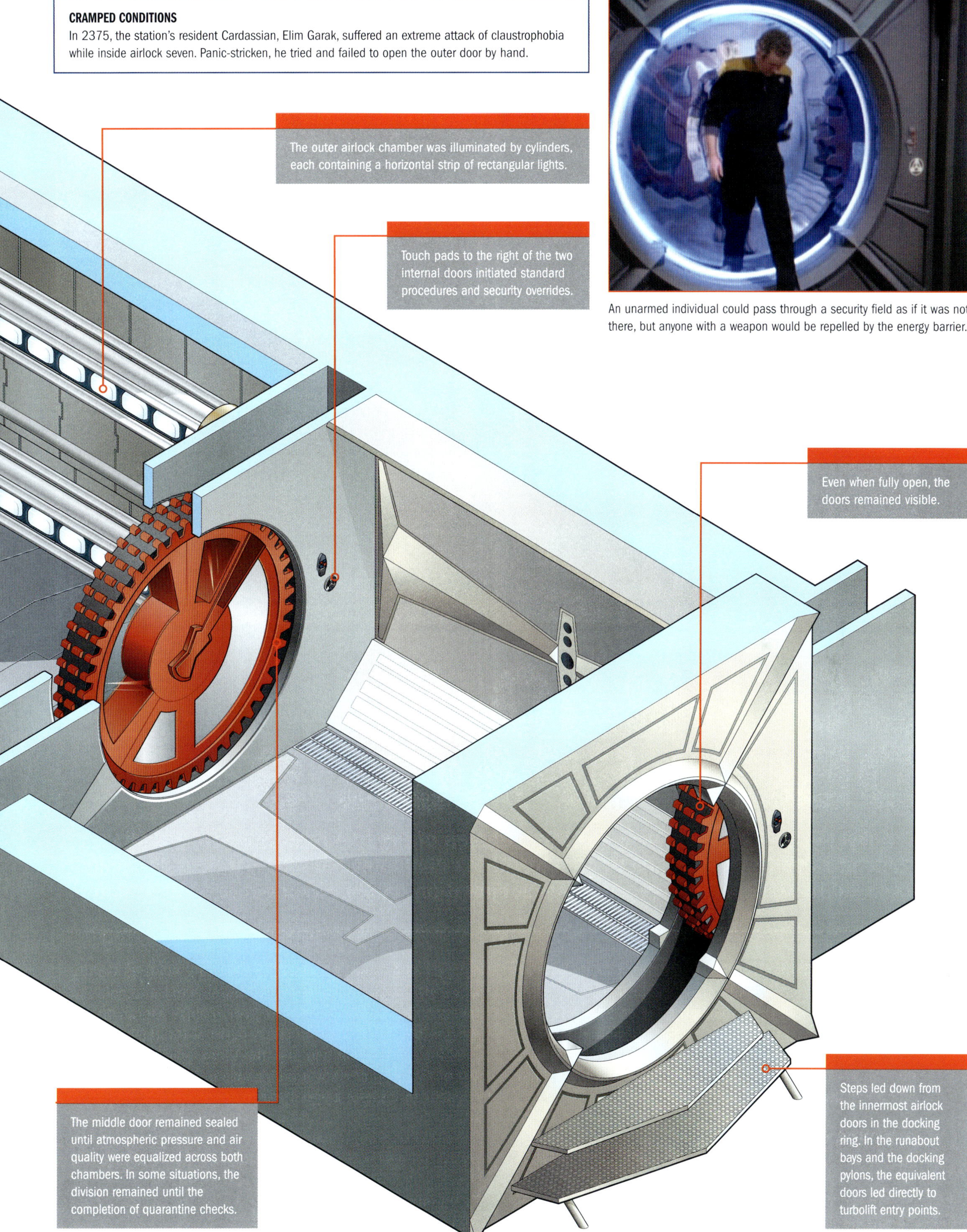

An unarmed individual could pass through a security field as if it was not there, but anyone with a weapon would be repelled by the energy barrier.

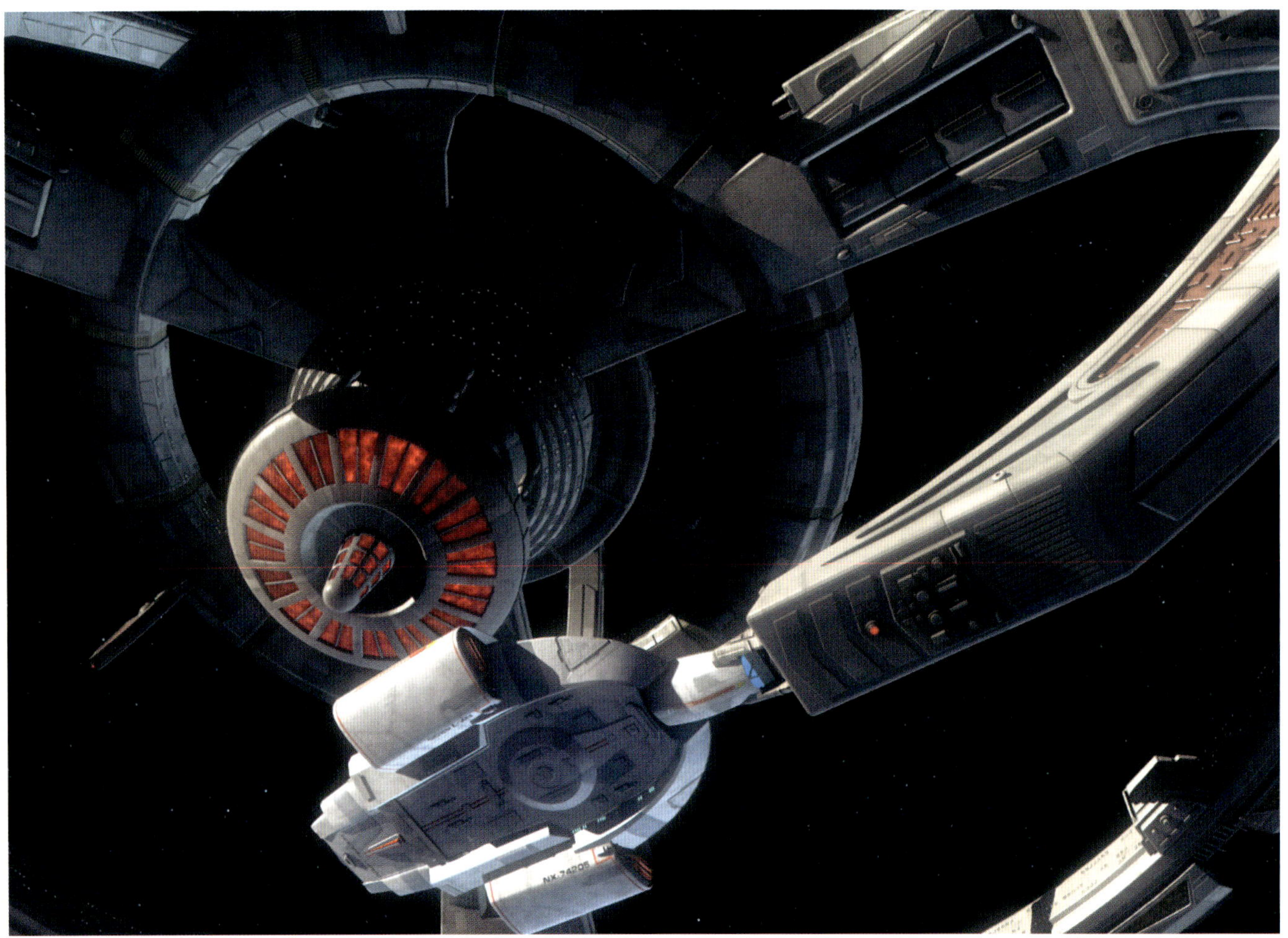

DOCKING AT DEEP SPACE 9

The discovery of the wormhole and the outbreak of the Dominion War brought all kinds of ships to Deep Space 9. As a result, its numerous mooring points – originally intended to serve a major ore-processing operation – were never out of commission.

From Federation starships and Klingon battle cruisers to cargo freighters and private shuttlecraft, an array of vessels frequently docked at Deep Space 9. More than 20 ships could be moored at the station at any one time, thanks to 12 ports distributed around the docking ring, another six ports at the tips of the docking pylons, and six landing pads set into the habitat ring.

BERTHING OPTIONS

The different types of docking facility catered for various classes and sizes of ship. Though the docking clamps and airlocks were largely consistent between the docking ring and the pylons, the latter were better suited to the largest vessels and those with irregular shapes, such as *Galaxy*-class starships. Those craft with more linear and compact designs, such as *Defiant*- and *Sydney*-class starships and Klingon birds-of-prey, could easily berth at the docking ring.

Of the 12 ports in this ring, the three located directly at the ends of the crossover bridges were the largest, with the capacity to transfer cargo measuring more than 13 meters across without special accommodations. Though originally designed for Cardassian freighters only, these and all the other ports were subsequently upgraded with adjustable docking clamps which employed a combination of tractor-beam emitters and electrohydraulic grab plates to function with a much wider range of craft.

The six landing pads, meanwhile, were ideally sized for Federation runabouts and other escort vessels, such as Romulan and Ferengi shuttlecraft. When a ship landed on one of these pads it retracted into the habitat ring, where docking was completed by means of a telescopic airlock shaft. At least three of these bays were usually reserved for the *Danube*-class runabouts assigned to the station, just as one of the 12 docking ring ports was allotted to the *U.S.S. Defiant* NX-74205 from 2371 onwards.

BENEFITS OF DOCKING

When Deep Space 9 was at its busiest, it was impossible for all visiting craft to dock at the station. Ships that were not delivering or collecting vital cargo then had to hold position in the Denorios belt and beam passengers to and from the station as necessary. While this was an entirely workable system, physical docking was always the preferable option for several straightforward reasons.

First, a moored vessel used much less energy, not only for transporter use, but also for attitudinal control and navigational systems. Second, being docked enabled much more efficient maintenance and repair, as well as replenishment of essentials and computer interfacing via conduits built into the docking systems. Finally, ships that were docked at the station did not need to rely on their own shields in the event of an attack, because Deep Space 9's own defensive bubble extended widely enough to encompass them all.

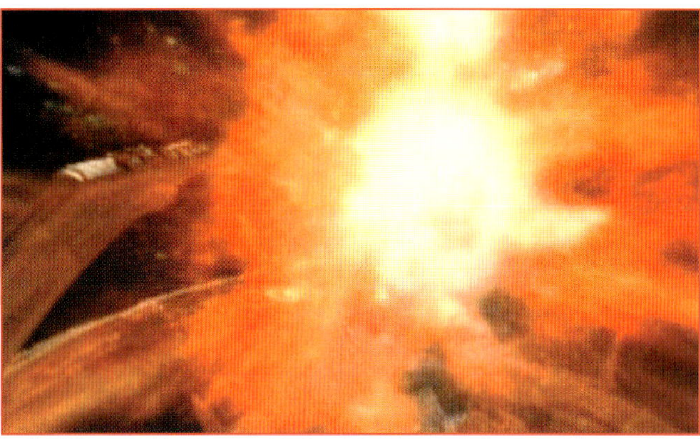

The Cardassian freighter *Bok'Nor* was sabotaged by the Maquis when it was docked at Deep Space 9 in 2370. It exploded as it departed from one of the upper pylons.

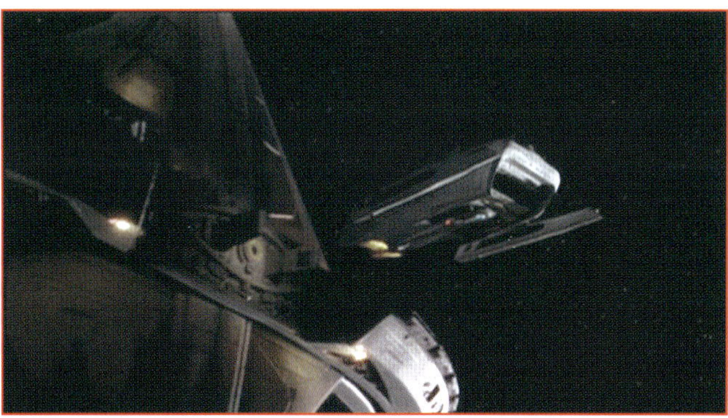

Small *Sydney*-class starships berthed at the station on numerous occasions, linking to one of the three main docking-ring ports by means of an airlock in the nose.

HABITAT RING LANDING PADS

Berthing at the six landing pads in the habitat ring rather than the docking ring made sense for the small craft, because they often carried diplomats and dignitaries who could be escorted directly to their quarters without encountering any cargo traffic. The positioning also made the runabouts quicker to access from ops.

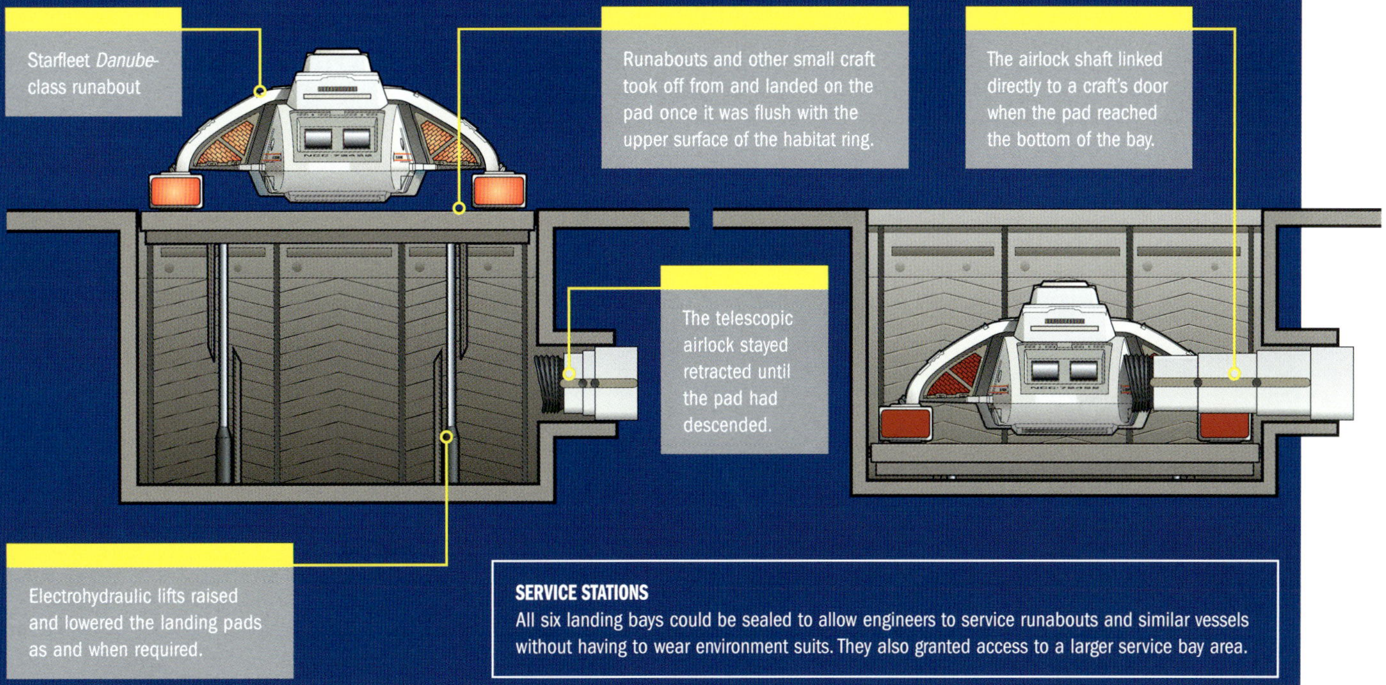

Starfleet *Danube*-class runabout

Runabouts and other small craft took off from and landed on the pad once it was flush with the upper surface of the habitat ring.

The airlock shaft linked directly to a craft's door when the pad reached the bottom of the bay.

The telescopic airlock stayed retracted until the pad had descended.

Electrohydraulic lifts raised and lowered the landing pads as and when required.

SERVICE STATIONS

All six landing bays could be sealed to allow engineers to service runabouts and similar vessels without having to wear environment suits. They also granted access to a larger service bay area.

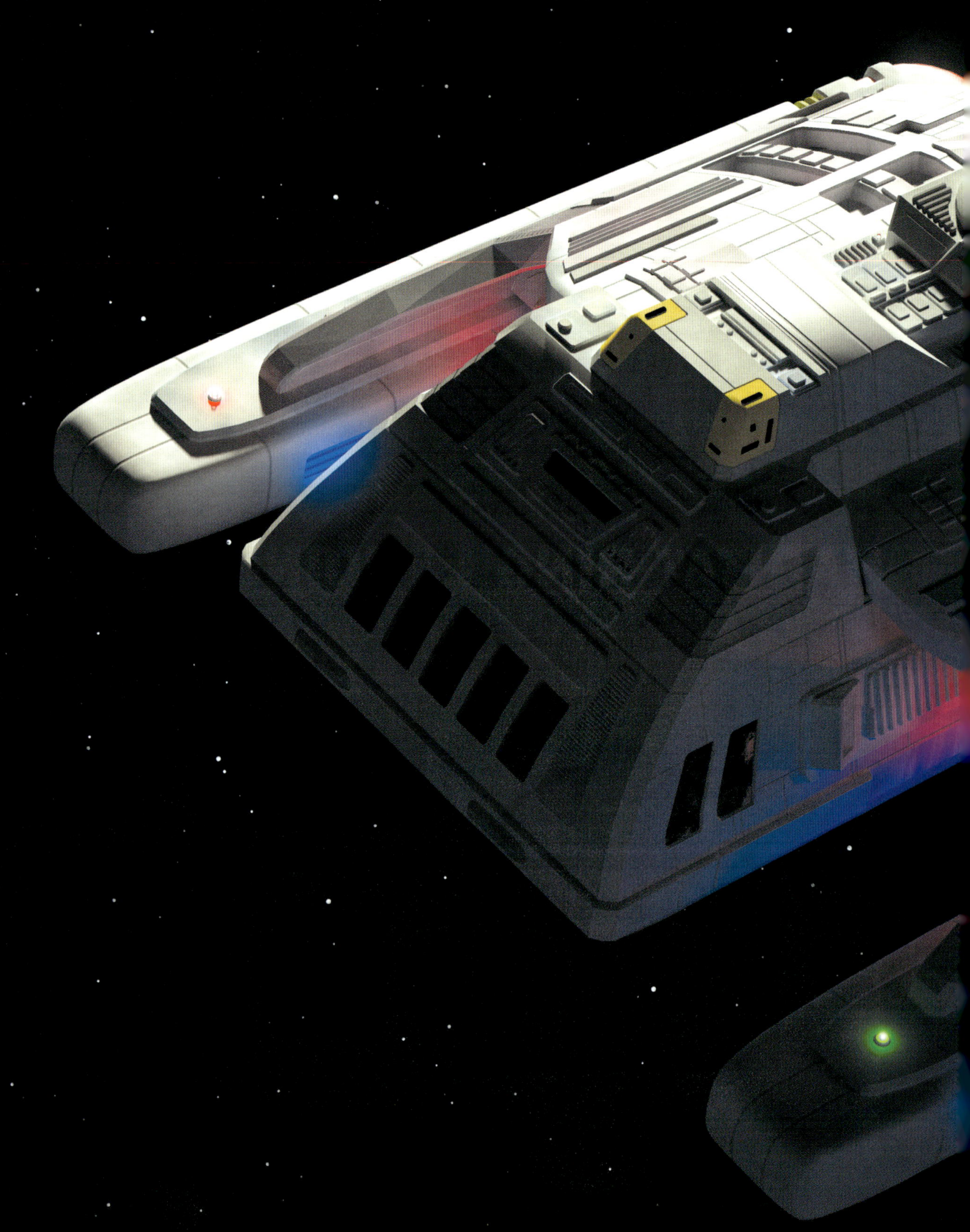

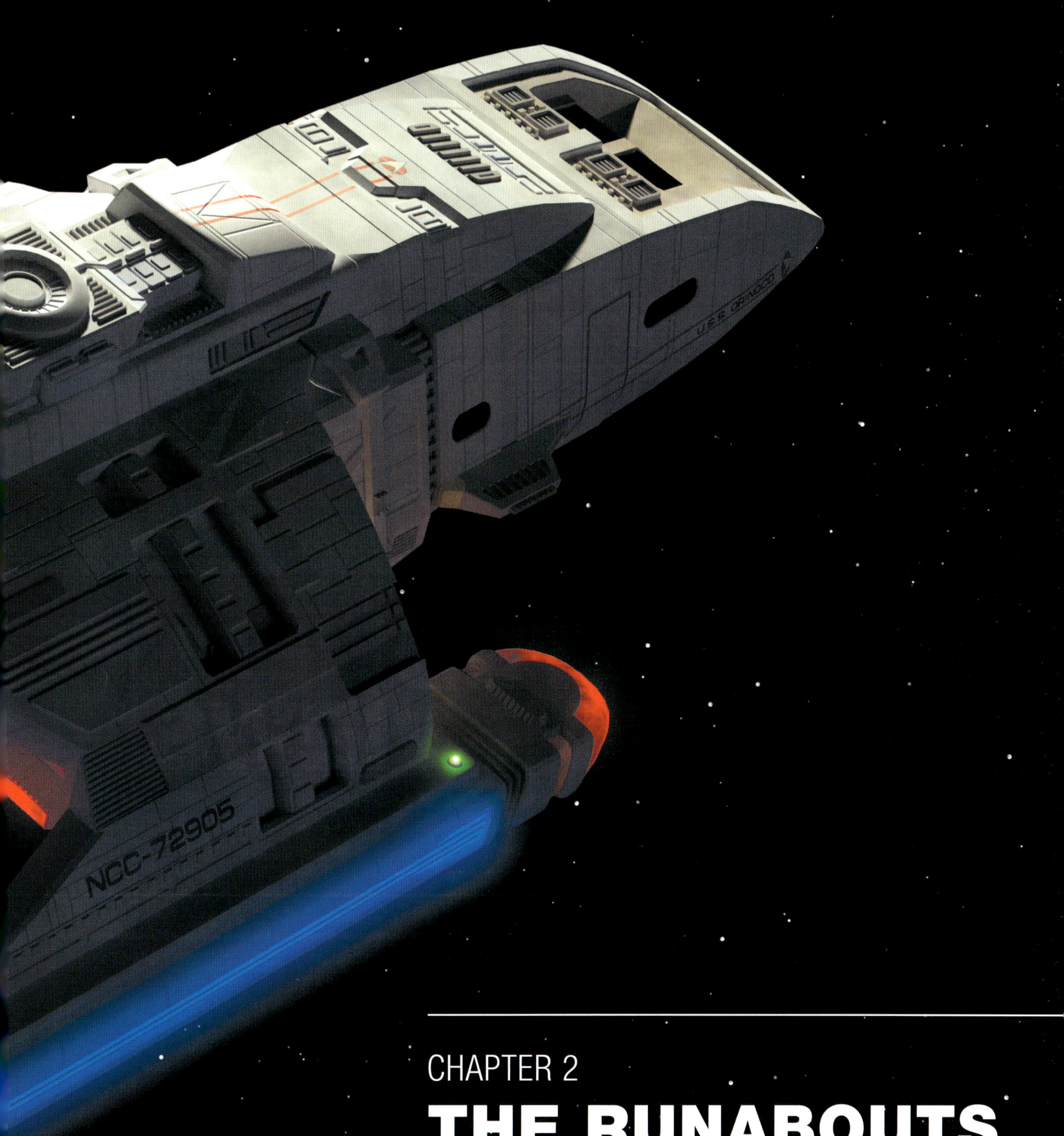

CHAPTER 2

THE RUNABOUTS

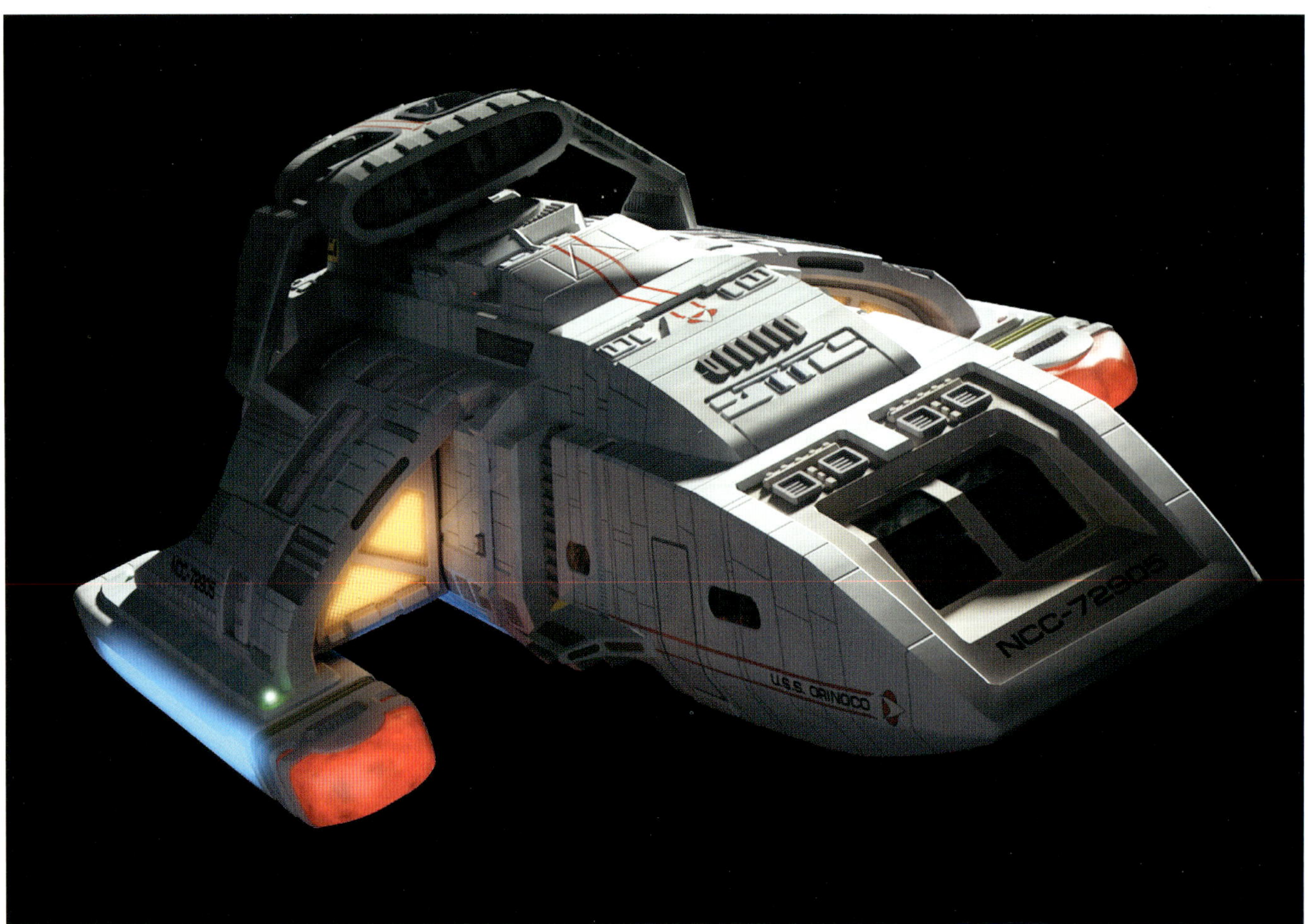

ANNOTATED EXTERIOR VIEWS

The first support craft to be assigned to Deep Space 9 were runabouts, mainly used for exploratory missions, but the Dominion threat later called for the assignment of the *U.S.S. Defiant* NX-74205 to defend the station.

Starfleet initially allocated three support craft to Deep Space 9 when it assumed control of the station in 2369. The vessels, delivered by the *U.S.S. Enterprise* NCC-1701-D were named for rivers on Earth and were the *U.S.S. Rio Grande* NCC-72452, the *U.S.S. Yangtzee Kiang* NCC-72453, and the *U.S.S. Ganges* NCC-72454.

These vessels were runabouts of the *Danube* class, a new type of ship that was ideal as support craft because of its adaptability. At 23.1 meters in length, 13.7 meters wide, and 5.4 meters high, the runabouts were larger than shuttles but smaller than starships. They were capable of more protracted missions and of carrying more cargo than shuttles.

On Deep Space 9, they were initially used to ferry people and cargo between the station and Bajor or neighboring worlds. The runabouts helped to evacuate the inhabitants during violent plasma storms in 2370, and when separatist group the Circle tried to seize control of the station. They were also used in the Badlands to track members of the renegade Maquis organization.

After Commander Sisko discovered the Bajoran wormhole that led to the Gamma Quadrant, the runabouts were used on exploratory missions. Having made first contact with the Jem'Hadar and the Dominion, several runabouts were lost in the line of duty. Although replaced by other runabouts, such as the *U.S.S. Mekong* NCC-72617, and *U.S.S. Orinoco* NCC-72905, it became clear they were not robust enough for the task. Sisko successfully lobbied to have the *U.S.S. Defiant* NX-74205 permanently assigned to the station.

DORSAL VIEW

NCC-72905
PRIMARY SECTION
COCKPIT
VIEWPORT
DOCKING HATCH
RCS THRUSTERS
THRUSTER WINGLET
BUSSARD COLLECTOR
MODULE ATTACHMENT CLAMPS
ANTIMATTER INJECTOR
WARP CORE
WARP NACELLE
NCC-72905
NCC-72905
NACELLE SUPPORT ARMS
IMPULSE DRIVE
MODULE VIEWPORTS
HABITAT MODULE

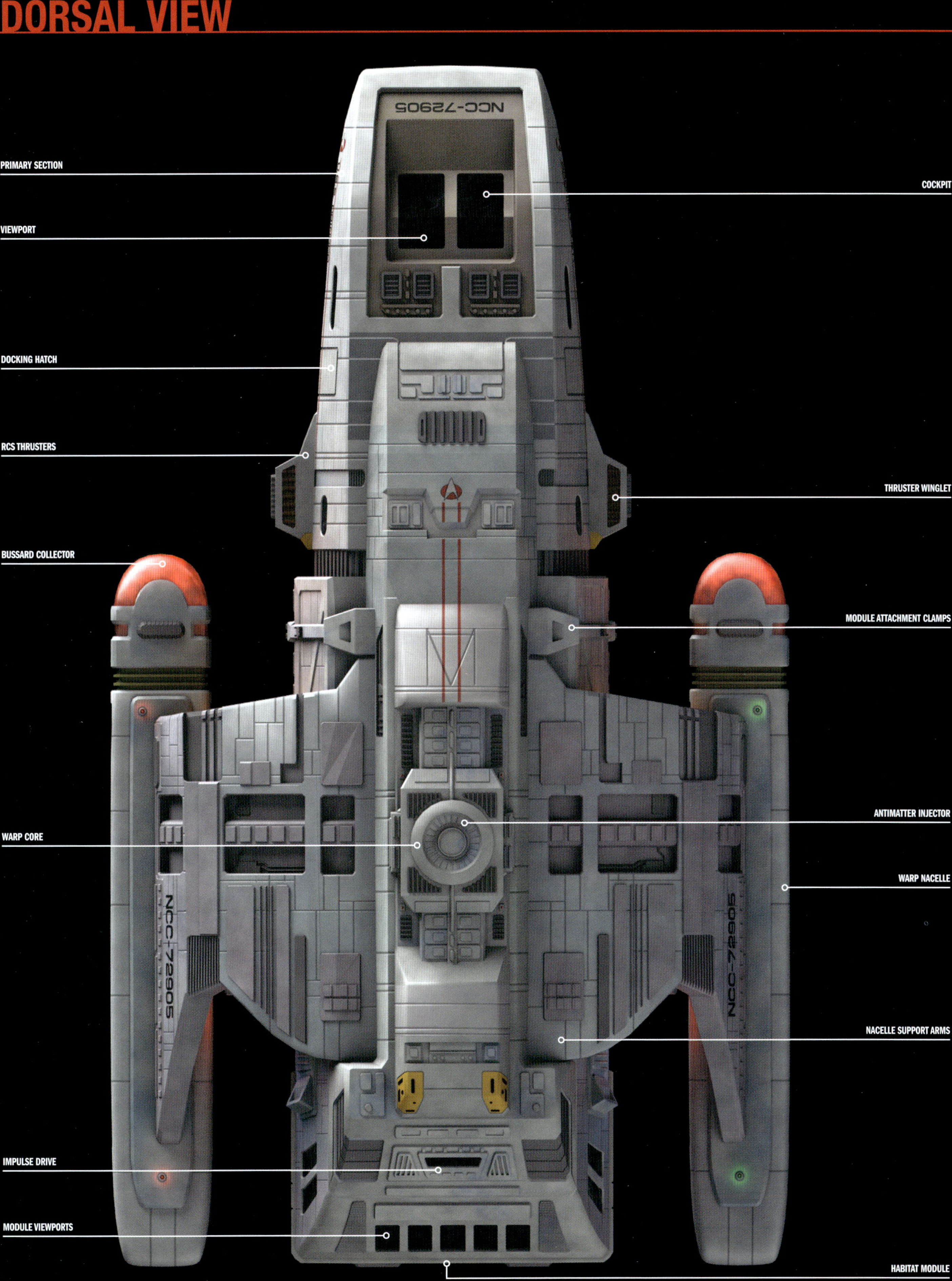

VENTRAL VIEW

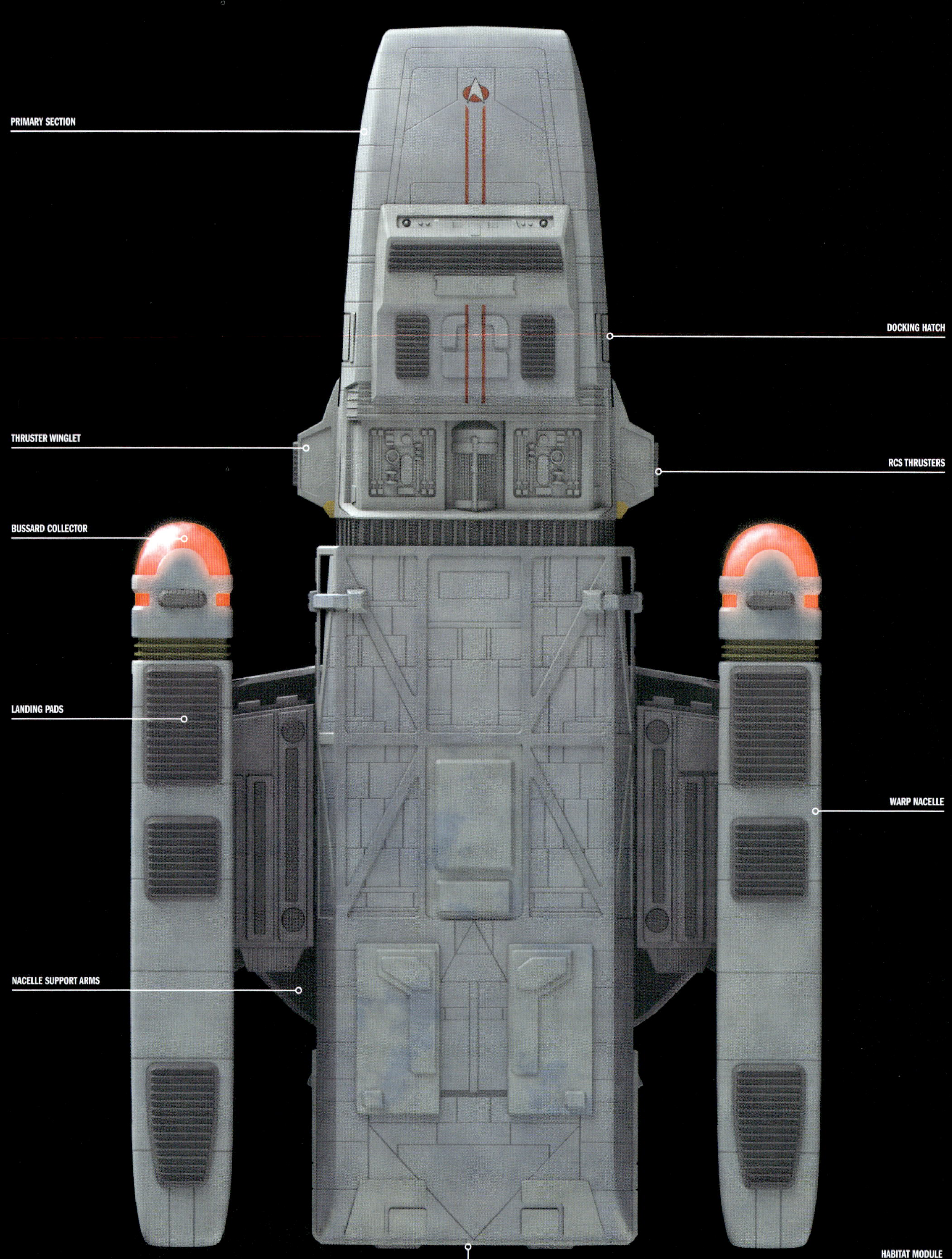

STARBOARD ELEVATION

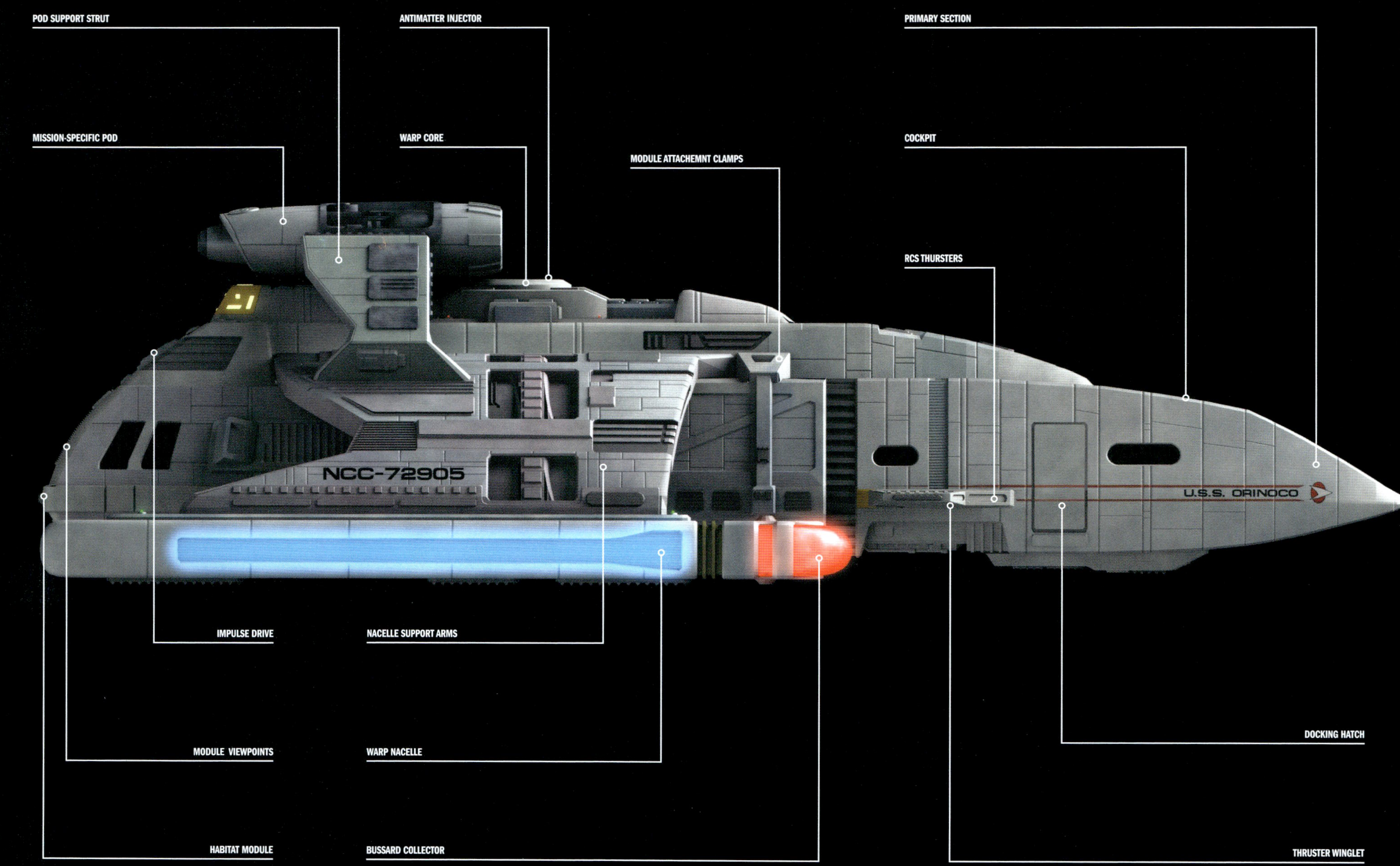

FRONT ELEVATION

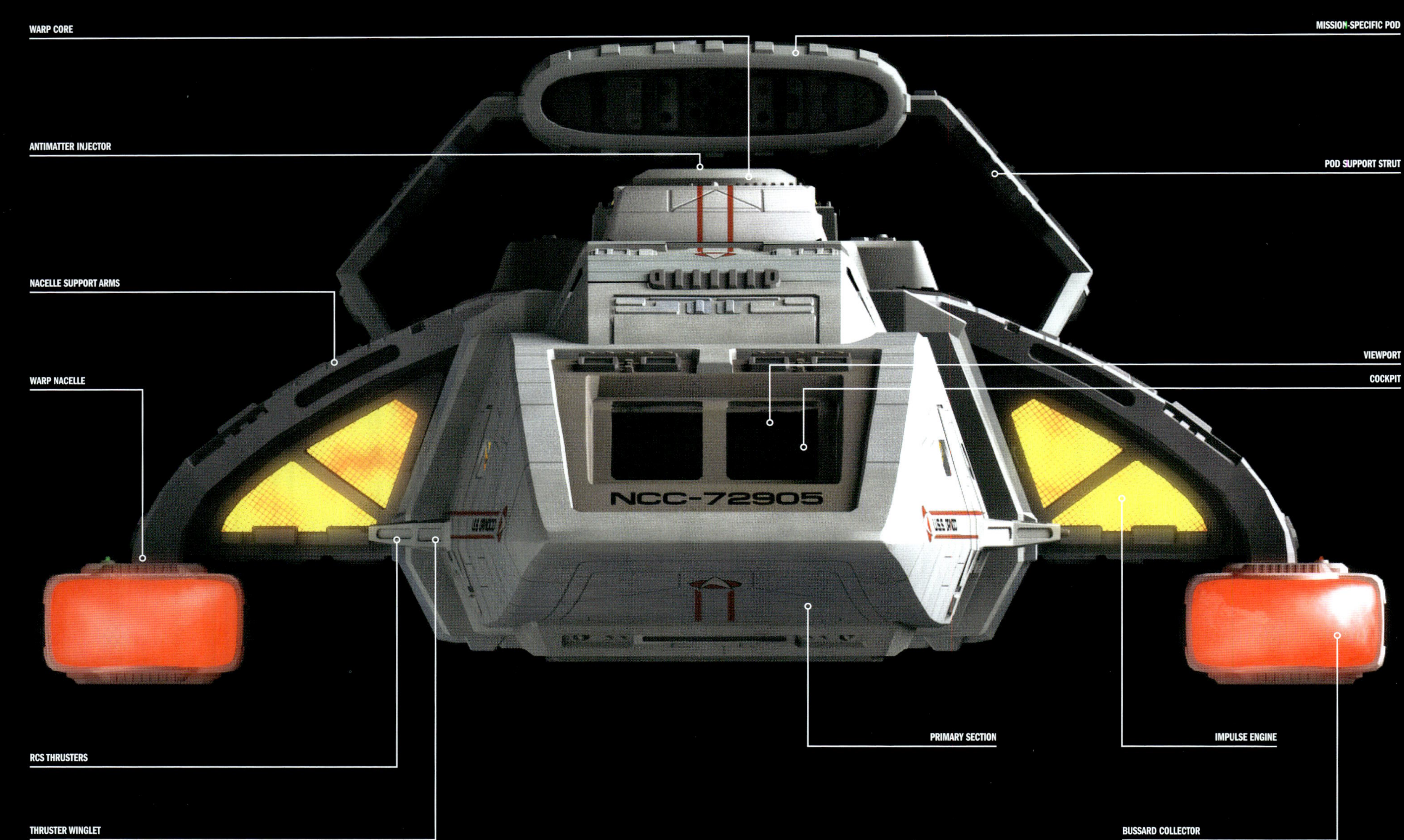

AFT ELEVATION

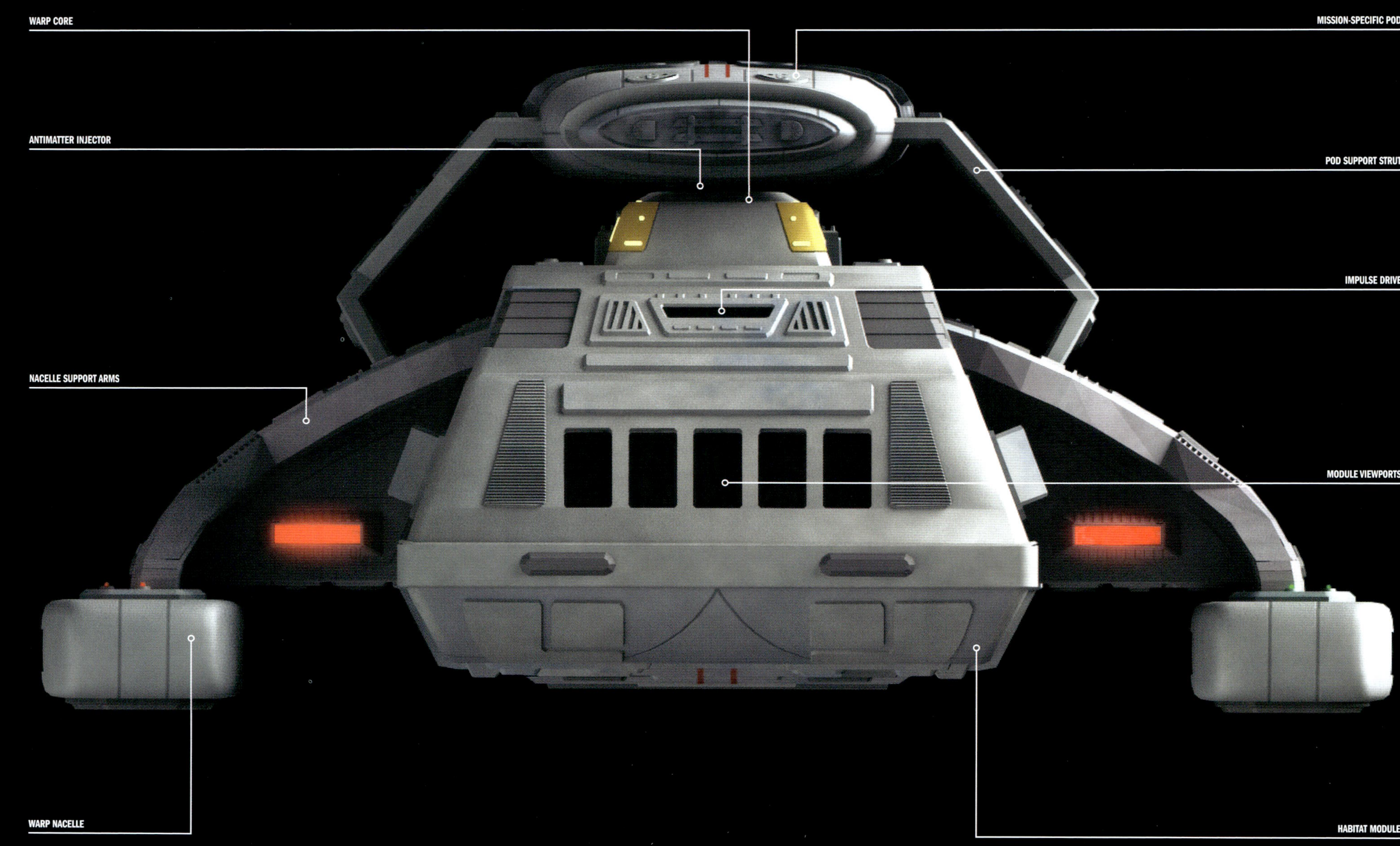

MULTIROLE SHIPS

A number of *Danube*-class runabouts were assigned to Deep Space 9, with more ships added to the fleet over time.

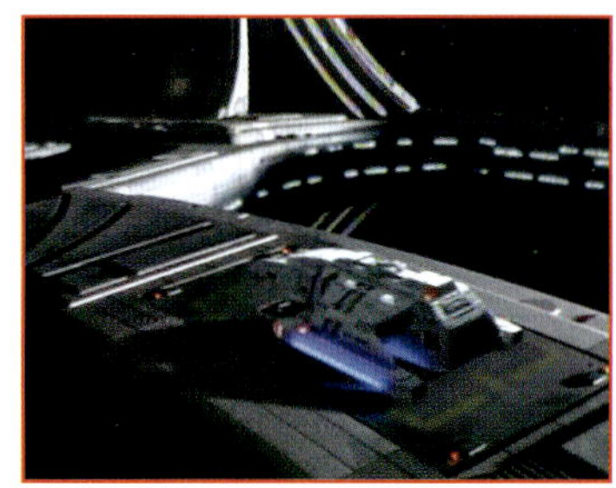

A *Danube*-class runabout would dock on one of six landing pads spaced out around Deep Space 9's habitat ring.

Runabouts were small, warp-capable Federation starships. They were equipped with transporters and a variety of sensors. The midsection, between the two wing pylons, housed a detachable module that could be changed to suit different mission profiles. Examples of available modules included science laboratories, additional crew quarters, and photon or quantum torpedo bays.

The aft section had living quarters that were spacious enough to accommodate up to 40 people, although runabouts were designed to carry a crew of eight.

ORIGINS

The prototype *U.S.S. Danube* NX-72003 was ordered to be constructed in 2365 at the Utopia Planitia Fleet Yards and began flight trials off the surface of Mars by 2368. As the *Danube* made its initial warp tests, the production series was in its final assembly cycle, with three runabouts sent to Deep Space 9 in 2369. The *U.S.S. Ganges*, *U.S.S. Yangtzee Kiang* and the *U.S.S. Rio Grande* were transported to Deep Space 9 aboard the *U.S.S. Enterprise* and were housed in landing bays around the habitat ring.

U.S.S. GANDER

SHIP'S REGISTRY: NCC-73624

NAMED FOR: The Gander river in eastern Newfoundland, Canada

OPERATIONAL HISTORY: In 2375, Lieutenant Ezri Dax commandeered the *Gander* on a solo mission to find Worf, shot down in the Badlands by Jem'Hadar. The *Defiant*'s search for him had been called off but Dax used its log to pinpoint a likely landing place for his escape pod. Turning off the Gander's engine, Dax intuited that the plasma storms would push her craft to the same place. She was then able to beam Worf's pod onboard. Soon after, the *Gander* was attacked and Dax and Worf transported to the nearby planet Goralis III.

STATUS: Destroyed by two Jem'Hadar fighters over Goralis III

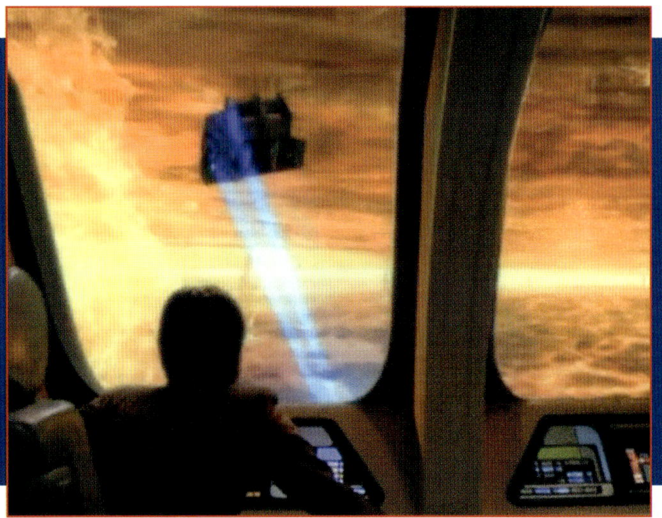

When Worf's ship was lost in the Badlands, Ezri used the *Gander* to search for him. When she found his escape pod she tractored it close enough to beam him aboard.

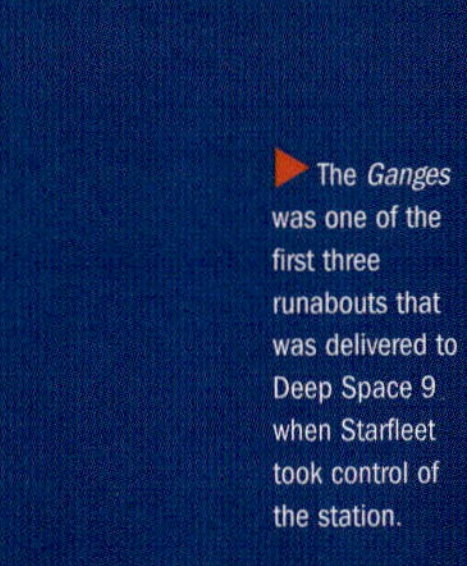

The *Ganges* was one of the first three runabouts that was delivered to Deep Space 9 when Starfleet took control of the station.

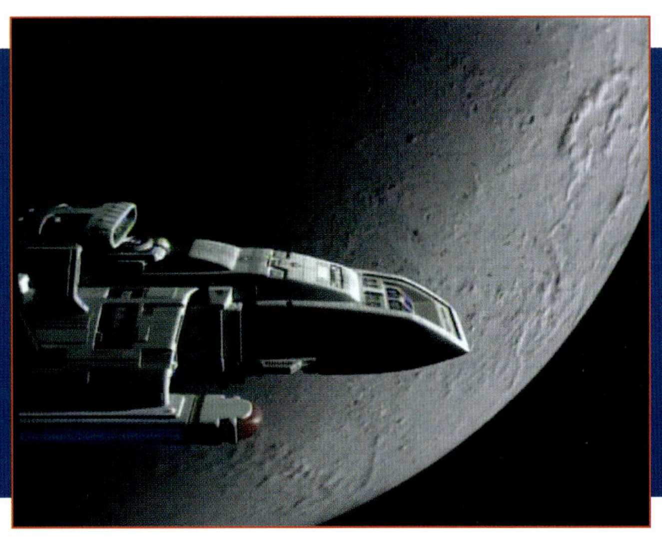

U.S.S. GANGES

SHIP'S REGISTRY: NCC-72454

NAMED FOR: The Ganges river in northern India and eastern Pakistan

OPERATIONAL HISTORY: While on an exploratory mission to the Gamma Quadrant, Lieutenant Jadzia Dax and Ensign Pauley picked up the intergalactic archaeologist Vash, the bearer of a mysterious crystal that induced power failures. Later, Odo set off on the *Ganges* to take Croden back to his homeworld Rakhar. Major Kira Nerys and Dax used the *Ganges* to scout an evacuation of the moon Jerrado, and the runabout was the last to leave Deep Space 9 during the Bajorans' attempted takeover.

STATUS: Destroyed by a T'Lani munitions cruiser in 2370. Its crew managed to escape in another runabout.

U.S.S. MEKONG

SHIP'S REGISTRY: NCC-72617

NAMED FOR: The Mekong river in southeast Asia

OPERATIONAL HISTORY: When Dax took the Trill initiate Arjin through the wormhole on the runabout, it picked up a substance called "subspace seaweed," damaging its starboard nacelle. The seaweed proved to be a protouniverse. The *Mekong* helped to intercept Calvin Hudson and a Maquis strike force trying to attack a weapons depot on the Bryma Colony. It also played a key role in rescuing Commander Sisko, Jake, Quark, and Nog from the Dominion.

STATUS: Destroyed by Jem'Hadar forces during an unsuccessful Romulan-Cardassian offensive against the Dominion in the Gamma Quadrant.

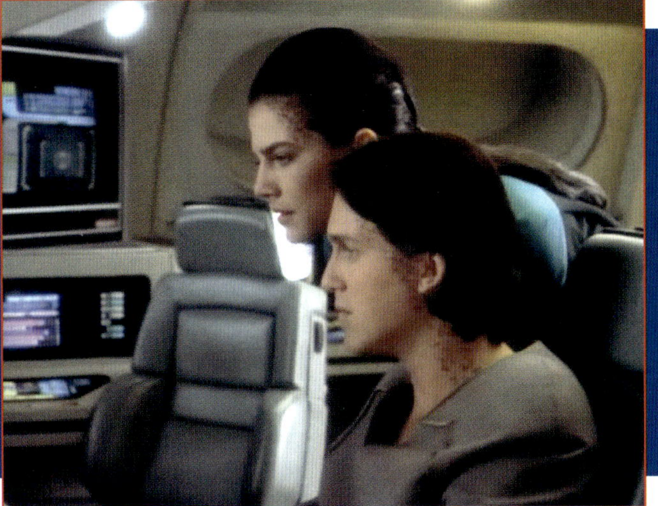

Dax and Arjin took the *Mekong* on an early mission to the Gamma Quadrant.

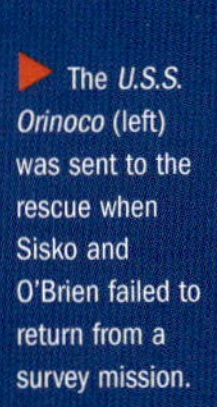

The *U.S.S. Orinoco* (left) was sent to the rescue when Sisko and O'Brien failed to return from a survey mission.

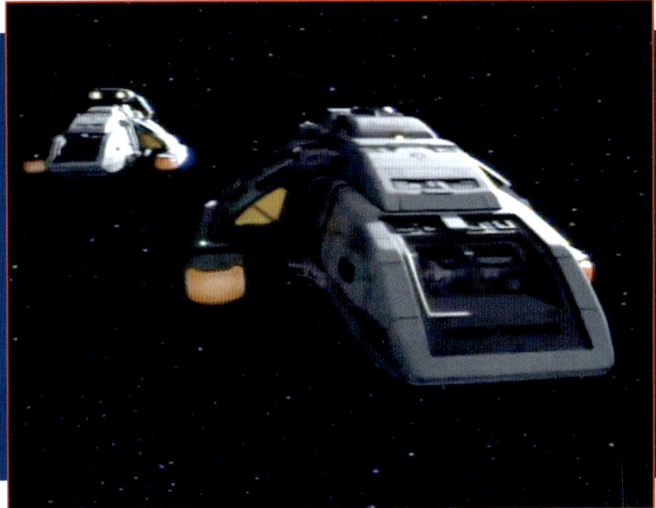

U.S.S. ORINOCO

SHIP'S REGISTRY: NCC-72905

NAMED FOR: The Orinoco river in Venezuela

OPERATIONAL HISTORY: In 2370, the *Orinoco* helped to evacuate Deep Space 9 during plasma storms, remaining as a standby craft for the skeleton crew. Nerys and Dax used the *Orinoco* to track down the *Rio Grande*, reportedly traveling on autonavigation. It sustained major damage during the battle with the Maquis at the Bryma Colony, but was retrieved and repaired. In support of the Odyssey, Nerys and Dr. Bashir took the *Orinoco* to rescue Sisko from the Dominion.

STATUS: Destroyed in 2372 after sabotage by the Cardassian sect The True Way.

EARLY YEARS

During the first two years of Starfleet's use of Deep Space 9, the runabout was the primary method of transport and defense support, required for discovering and exploring new worlds and civilizations in the Gamma Quadrant. The *Danube*-class runabouts were particularly suited to a number of common tasks, including scientific, resupply, intelligence, and personal transfer missions. They were multirole starships utilized by Starfleet on many missions. The runabouts on Deep Space 9 were all named after Earth rivers. As the station was primarily Cardassian in style, the runabouts also provided an outward symbol of Federation occupation of Deep Space 9.

In mid-2370, the space station sent its runabouts into the Gamma Quadrant to make contact with the fleet of Skrreean refugee ships on the other side of the Bajoran wormhole. In the following years, several more runabouts were assigned to supplement the fleet and replace ships destroyed in the line of duty.

At first, the runabouts were used to explore the Gamma Quadrant, but after hostilities with the Dominion began, this became impossible. They then counted as one more weapon in Deep Space 9's arsenal. Even after Deep Space 9 was assigned the *U.S.S. Defiant* in 2371, the runabouts were still frequently used and, for a time, the station was equipped with no fewer than four of the craft.

DOMINION WAR

Before the start of the Dominion War in 2373, Elim Garak and Worf used a runabout to rescue crewmembers by stealth from Internment Camp 371. The same year, the *Danube*-class runabouts also defended Deep Space 9 against a Dominion fleet. They were later sent on exercises with the Ninth Fleet in 2374. The following year, Colonel Kira Nerys took one of the runabouts to travel covertly to Cardassia Prime and aid Damar's resistance movement, the Cardassian Liberation Front, against the Dominion occupation.

Danube-class runabouts were not a match for a T'Lani cruiser in terms of speed, firepower, or defenses, nor could they outrun a Klaestron starship or a *Theta*-class starship. The runabout design also meant that one vessel alone could not match a wing of Jem'Hadar fighters. Despite these limitations, a runabout had the ability to destroy a Jem'Hadar fighter, if it got past the enemy's defenses and used directed phaser fire to overload the shield generators.

U.S.S. RIO GRANDE

SHIP'S REGISTRY: NCC-72452

NAMED FOR: The Rio Grande in the North American continent

OPERATIONAL HISTORY: The *Rio Grande* was the first ship to enter the Bajoran wormhole, in 2369. The following year, it evacuated civilians from Deep Space 9 before a Bajoran invasion. Bashir and Kira took the runabout to the New Bajor Colony, and on its return, it entered the mirror universe. In 2373, the Orion Syndicate planted a bomb on board and the *Rio Grande* crashed on a Class L planet, but was retrieved by the *Defiant*. In 2375, with Odo piloting, the ship was pursued by Jem'Hadar, but avoided attack. The long-serving *Rio Grande* carried Sisko to Bajor to meet with the Pah-wraiths after the Dominion War.

STATUS: Operational

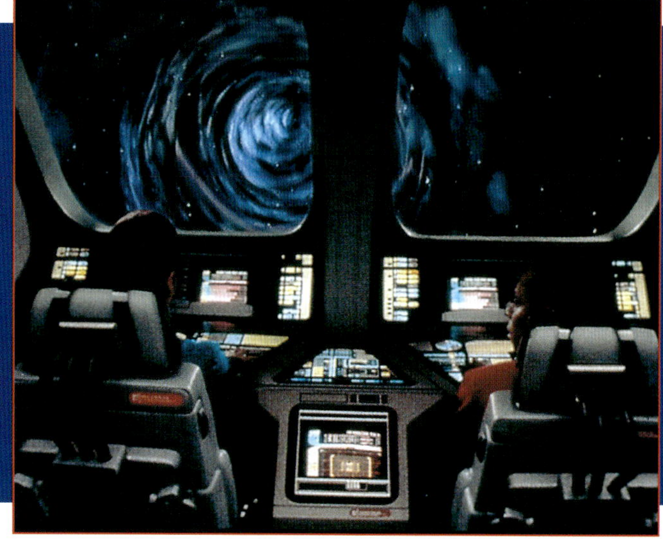

Dax and Sisko were piloting the *Rio Grande* when they discovered the Bajoran wormhole.

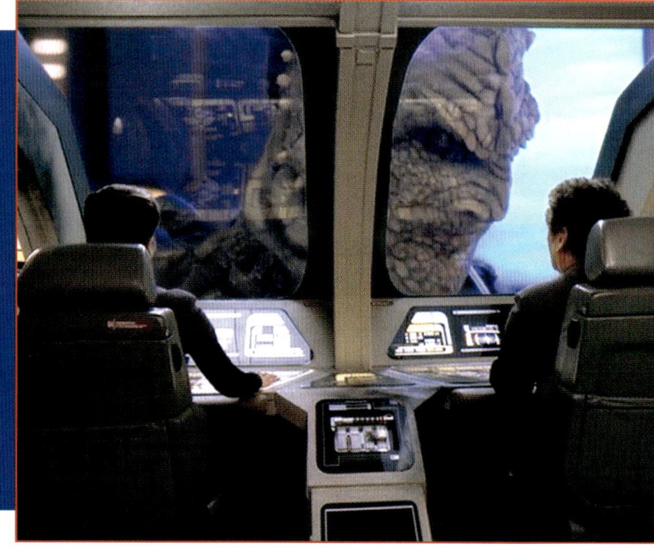

The *U.S.S. Rubicon* was shrunk to a tiny size when it passed through a subspace compression anomaly.

U.S.S. RUBICON

SHIP'S REGISTRY: NCC-72936

NAMED FOR: The ancient river that was of strategic importance to Julius Caesar in 49 B.C.

OPERATIONAL HISTORY: In early 2372, the *Rubicon* was carrying Bashir and O'Brien when forced to land on Bopak III. Here a group of rebel Jem'Hadar were seeking a cure for their genetic drug addiction. Ship and crew were eventually allowed to leave. Later, the *Rubicon* was on a mission to investigate a subspace compression anomaly when it shrank to miniature size. This enabled it to foil a Jem'Hadar attempt to take over the *Defiant*, after which it reverted to normal size. It helped to evacuate Deep Space 9 before the Reckoning.

STATUS: Operational

U.S.S. SHENANDOAH

SHIP'S REGISTRY: NCC-73024

NAMED FOR: The Shenandoah river in Virginia and West Virginia, USA

OPERATIONAL HISTORY: In 2374, Worf and Dax took the *Shenandoah* to transport a Cardassian informant, Lasaran, from the Dominion base on Soukara back to the Federation. The *Shenandoah*, along with the *Rubicon* and *Rio Grande*, was used to evacuate Deep Space 9 in late 2374 before the Reckoning. Subsequently, with Jake Sisko and Ensign Nog as crew, it undertook a diplomatic mission to deliver a Federation message to Grand Negus Zek. The *Shenandoah* was on its way to Ferenginar, when it was severely damaged in a Jem'Hadar strike. Sisko and Nog were rescued by the *U.S.S. Valiant*.

STATUS: Abandoned

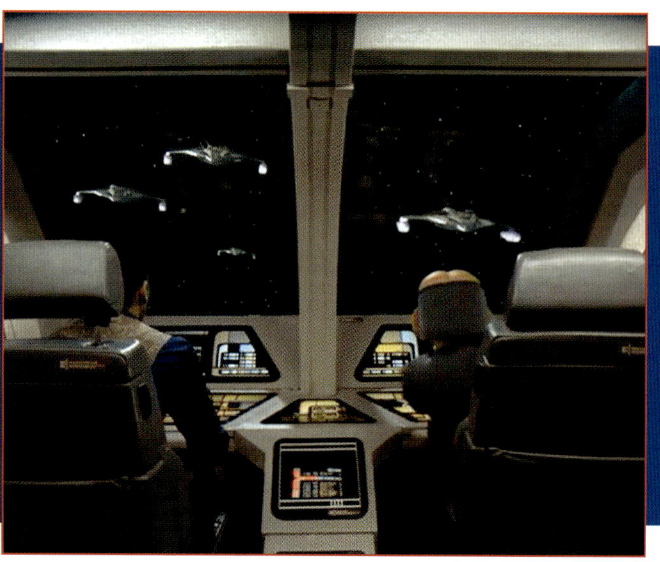

Jake Sisko and Nog were flying the *Shenandoah* when they ran into a Jem'hadar patrol. They were rescued by the *U.S.S. Valiant*.

U.S.S. VOLGA

SHIP'S REGISTRY: NCC-73196

NAMED FOR: The Volga river in the east of Earth's European continent

OPERATIONAL HISTORY: Dr. Bashir, Major Kira and a pregnant Keiko O'Brien took the *Volga* to study botanical species on Torad V in the Gamma Quadrant, in 2372. On its return to Deep Space 9, it was damaged by an asteroid and one of the fuel pods exploded. Captain Sisko also used it in 2373 to examine the cormaline mining potential of Torga IV, a small planet in the Gamma Quadrant. However, this mission ended in disaster, with the deaths of several members of the away team and the destruction of the ship.

STATUS: Destroyed by a Jem'Hadar attack ship

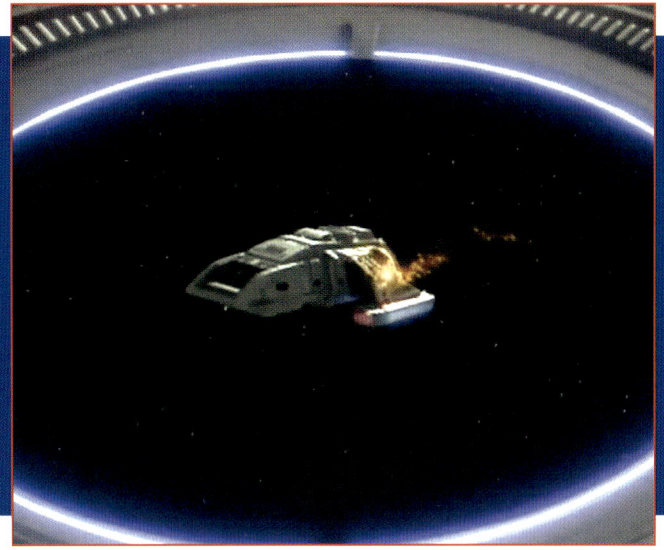

Keiko O'Brien was injured when the *Volga* was damaged. To save her baby, Dr. Bashir transported it to Kira's uterus.

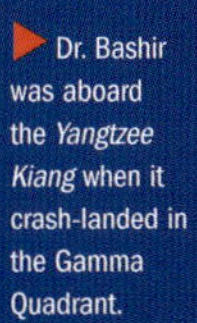

Dr. Bashir was aboard the *Yangtzee Kiang* when it crash-landed in the Gamma Quadrant.

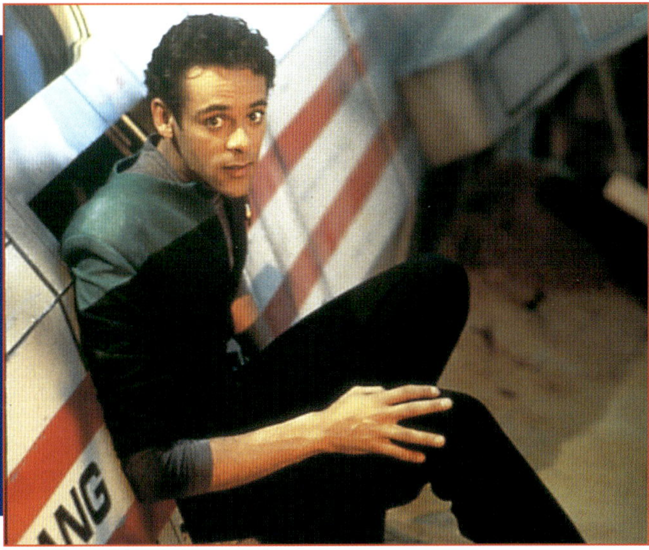

U.S.S. YANGTZEE KIANG

SHIP'S REGISTRY: NCC-72453

NAMED FOR: The Yangtze Kiang river in China

OPERATIONAL HISTORY: Bajoran terrorist Tahna Los used the *Yangtzee Kiang* to rendezvous with a Klingon bird-of-prey, in a (thwarted) attempt to destroy the wormhole. Kira later took the runabout to Bajor, bringing back Sumak Ren to Deep Space 9 to help find a cure for the aphasia virus. Sisko took Kai Opaka on the *Yangtzee Kiang* through the wormhole in 2369. The ship responded to a distress call and crashed on a Class-M moon, killing Opaka. She recovered by means of artificial microbes that revived the moon's inhabitants. The runabout was damaged beyond repair.

STATUS: Destroyed

U.S.S. YUKON

SHIP'S REGISTRY: NCC-74602

NAMED FOR: The Yukon river in the North American continent

OPERATIONAL HISTORY: In 2372, the *Yukon* picked up evidence of an illegal Klingon operation to lay minefields. The following year, it was stolen by a Changeling impersonating Bashir, who killed the crew and fitted it with a trilithium bomb. His plan was to destroy a combined Klingon, Federation, and Romulan fleet and blow up the Bajoran sun to induce a supernova. The *U.S.S. Defiant* tractored the runabout off course and saved the fleet, as well as Bajor and Deep Space 9, from imminent destruction. As the *Yukon* was being pulled away from the sun, the bomb detonated and blew it up.

STATUS: Destroyed

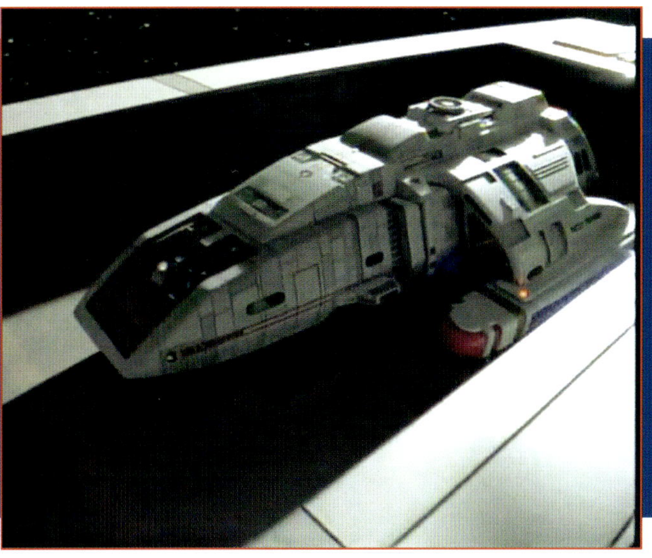

Like all the runabouts, the *U.S.S. Yukon* was housed in a bay on the station's inner ring.

THE COCKPIT

The cockpit of a *Danube*-class vessel had seating for four, with the two fore positions used by the pilots, though the craft could be switched to automatic helm control if necessary.

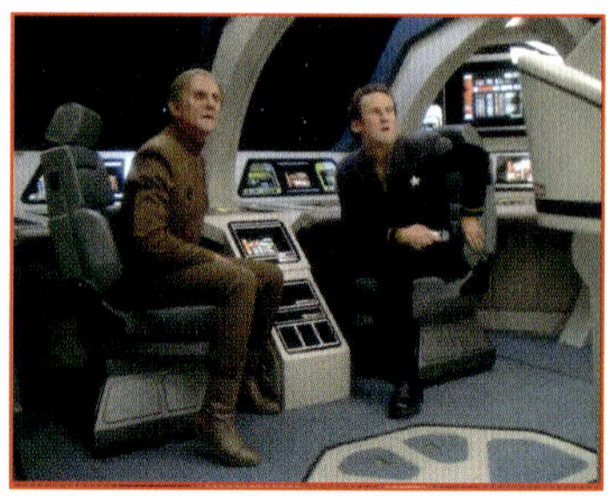

The interior of the runabouts was relatively spacious, with large windows providing a view of space.

The cockpit of a *Danube*-class runabout was designed to accommodate a crew of four. As part of the runabout's modular design, the entire cockpit could be detached in an emergency to continue in space or land on a planet's surface.

When the runabout was operated by a crew of two, all systems were shared between the two consoles at the front of the cockpit. With a crew of four, the forward port station was set as the commander's controls; the forward starboard console was used to pilot the vessel; the aft port station controlled the tactical systems; and the aft starboard console monitored the engineering systems.

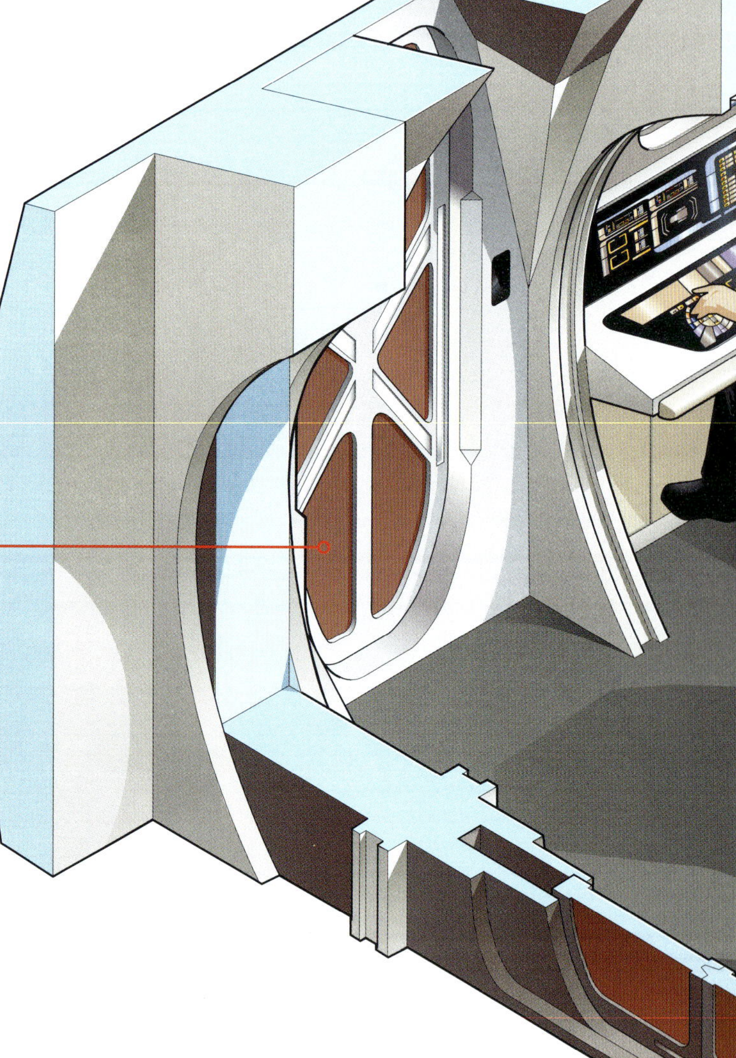

The cockpit of a runabout could be exited via the emergency hatch. When the *U.S.S. Yangtzee Kiang* NCC-72453 crash-landed on the surface of a penal moon 0.35 light years from the Idran system terminus in the Gamma Quadrant, Sisko, Bashir, and Kira used the hatch to escape the ship. The runabout itself was too damaged to be salvaged.

A compact personnel transporter was located immediately behind the cockpit stations. The transporter was capable of carrying multiple personnel simultaneously. There was also a food replicator in this part of the cabin. After the *Danube*-class runabout received a refit because of rising hostilities between the Federation and the Dominion, the transporter and replicator were moved further back and a secondary tactical console added in its place.

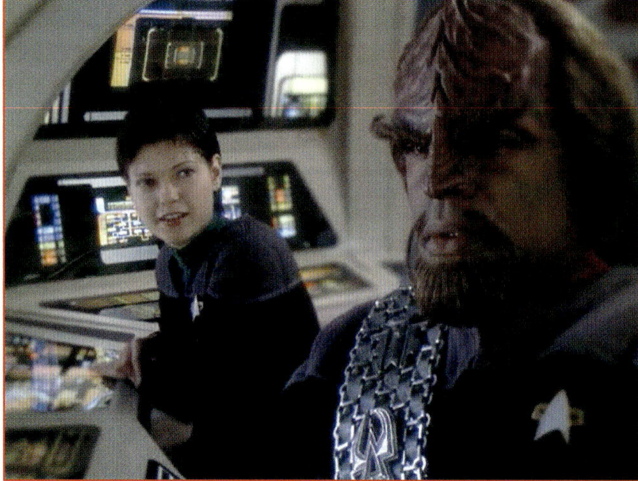

Flight controls were duplicated on the forward work stations so the vessel could be piloted from either, while the navigation reference console was between them.

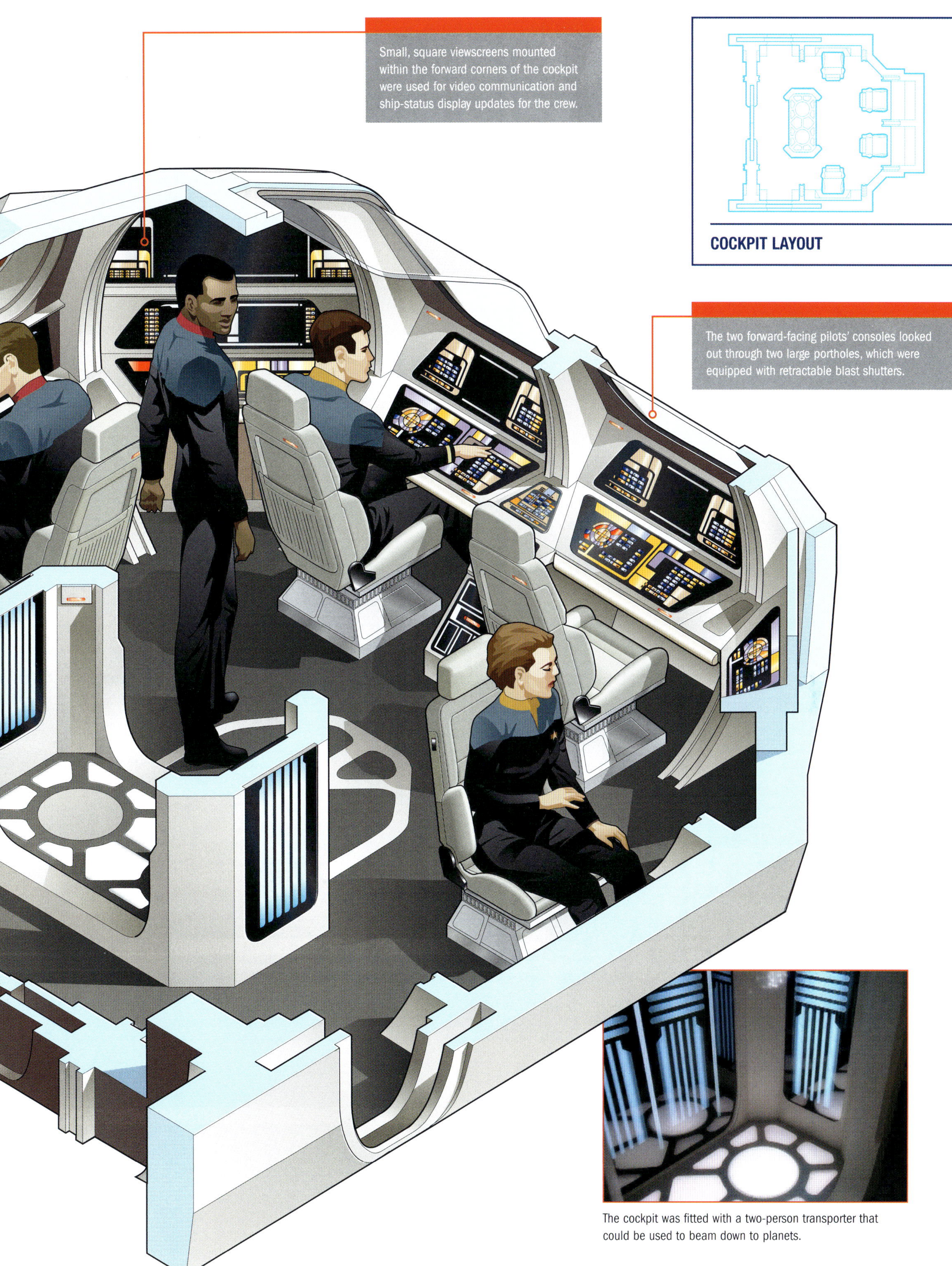

The cockpit was fitted with a two-person transporter that could be used to beam down to planets.

HABITAT MODULE

The crew of the runabout could live comfortably on board the ship for several weeks, thanks to a dedicated habitat module.

The habitat module at the rear of the runabout provided everything the crew needed on extended missions and long journeys. Its main feature was a large meeting/dining table where the crew could discuss mission objectives, relax, and eat together. A replicator provided food and drinks (but if it failed or was damaged, there were backup supplies in the form of emergency rations). Small bunkbeds were located in recesses on each side of the exit leading to the midsection.

There was also a computer console with a chair on one side of the compartment. This was used by the crew to access a comprehensive library for research purposes, record the activities of the mission, and log on to some of the ship's primary systems. This section also housed medical kits, four emergency EVA pressure suits, and a selection of hand phasers.

EXTRA SPACE

While the habitat module was sufficient to keep a small crew comfortable for several weeks, it could be a little cramped if there were more than four people. A larger crew could be accommodated by installing extra living space in the modular midsection of the runabout, normally used to house cargo or specialized laboratory equipment.

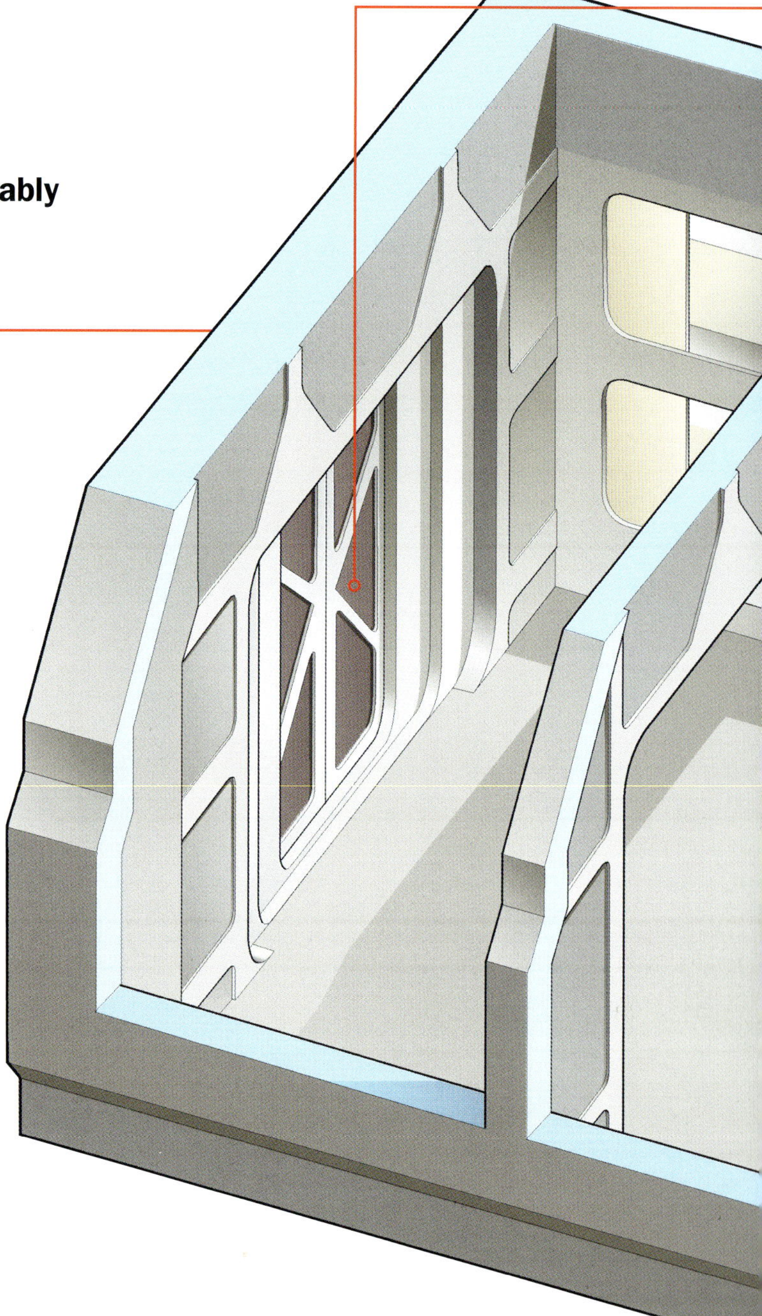

Two sets of bunkbeds on each side of the cabin ensured that the crew slept well on extended missions.

An LCARS (Library Computer Access/Retrieval System) terminal facilitated access to the vessel's main computer. This station, located on the starboard side, was also useful for mission briefings that required a visual display.

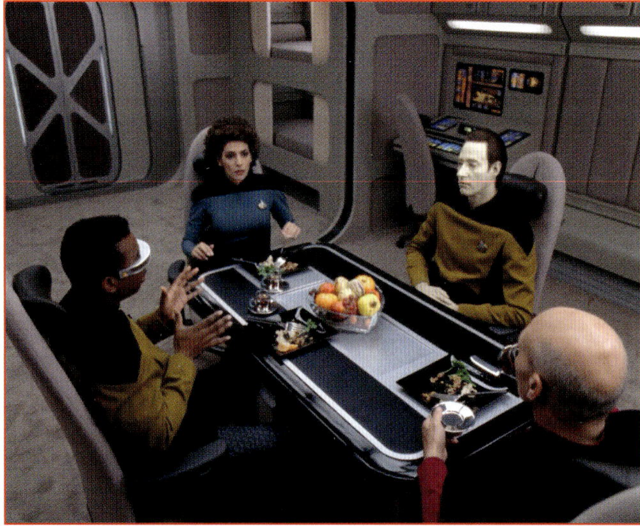

The habitat module was dominated by a large table where the crew could enjoy their meals together, while the runabout was left on autopilot. This helped to keep the crew relaxed and enabled longer missions to be undertaken.

Entrance to the habitat module was through a set of sliding doors that led from the midsection of the runabout. This meant that the living compartment was entirely separate from the rest of the ship.

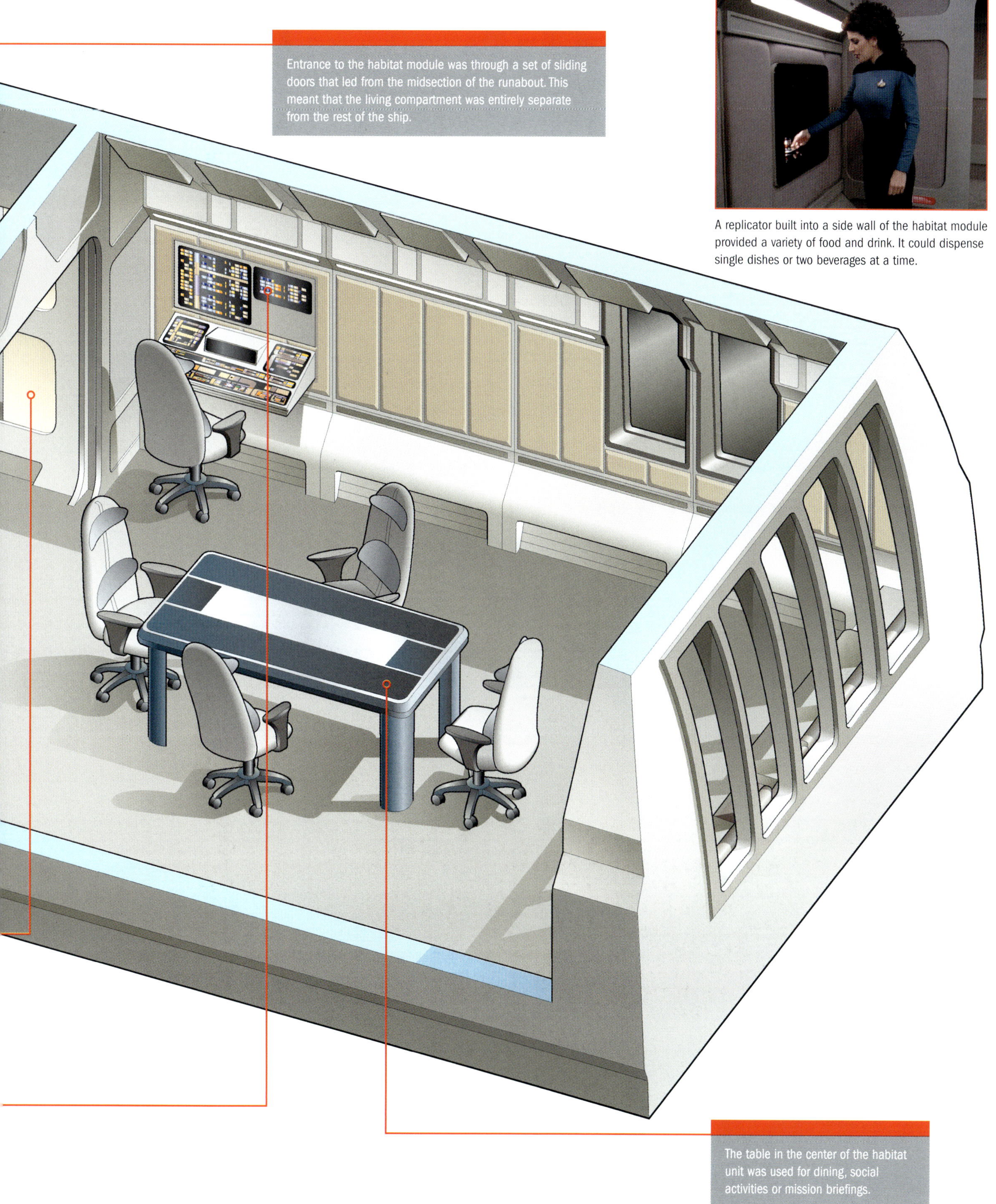

A replicator built into a side wall of the habitat module provided a variety of food and drink. It could dispense single dishes or two beverages at a time.

The table in the center of the habitat unit was used for dining, social activities or mission briefings.

DISTRESS BEACON

During the 24th century, Starfleet distress beacons tapped into the subspace network to deliver messages, ensuring that calls for help were answered quickly.

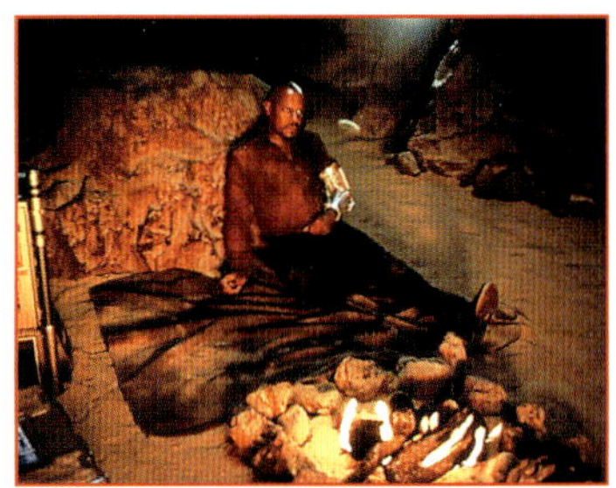
Captain Sisko and Gul Dukat relied on a distress beacon to bring help after they crash-landed in 2374.

The meter-tall distress beacon typically fitted to smaller Starfleet vessels, such as *Danube*-class runabouts and some escape pods, was normally attached to a bulkhead, and was linked to the craft's communication system. If survivors of a crash-landing needed to abandon ship, the unit could be detached and taken.

The advantages of having a subspace emergency beacon rather than a two-way, real-time device were speed and distance. The distress beacon was most often used to send signals from space; on a planet's surface, an internal signal booster was needed to amplify the signal. Without this, the beacon could be used only on planets with thin or nonexistent atmospheres. With the booster, the signal could even be sent through solid rock.

In 2374, Captain Benjamin Sisko's life was saved by a distress beacon salvaged from a shuttlecraft by Gul Dukat. Sisko was able to repair the damaged unit with a tine from a metal fork. In another situation, even a broken distress beacon saved the lives of Quark and Odo, when they found themselves marooned on an unpopulated Class-L planet after their runabout was sabotaged. The explosion that damaged their craft also ruined the distress beacon's internal booster, making the signal too weak to punch through the planet's atmosphere. By taking the beacon up a mountain, Quark could penetrate the atmosphere and send a signal. They were rescued soon after.

LIFE-SAVING DEVICE

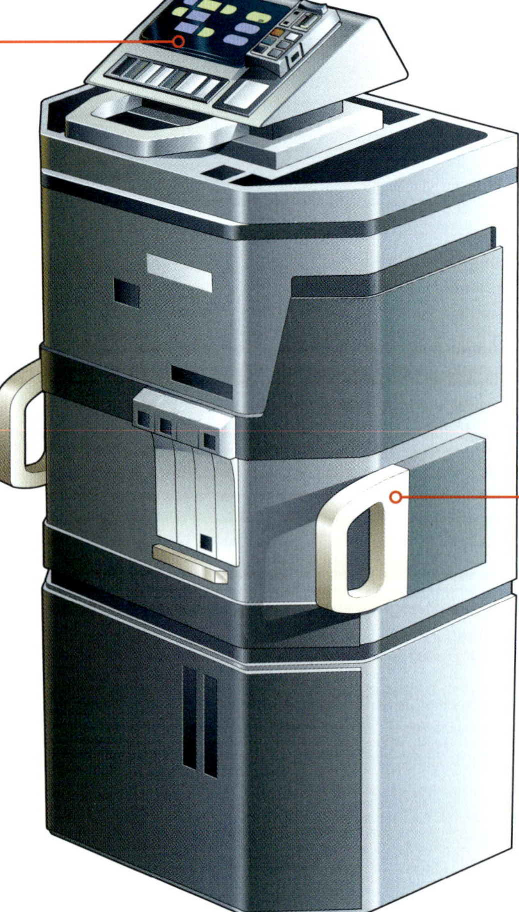

The transmitter array at the top included a touch-sensitive keypad and display for activating the beacon.

SUBSPACE TRANSCEIVER
At around 20 kilograms, the transceiver's weight was attributable to its self-contained power system. It could send messages 60 times faster than a starship, but required 100 times more energy than real-time communications devices.

DECADE OF SERVICE
The beacon had been standard issue equipment for more than a decade. It was fitted to the escape pods of the *U.S.S. Olympus*, captained by Lisa Cusack, which was lost in 2363.

Side handles enabled the beacon to be carried as a backpack if it had to be removed from the craft.

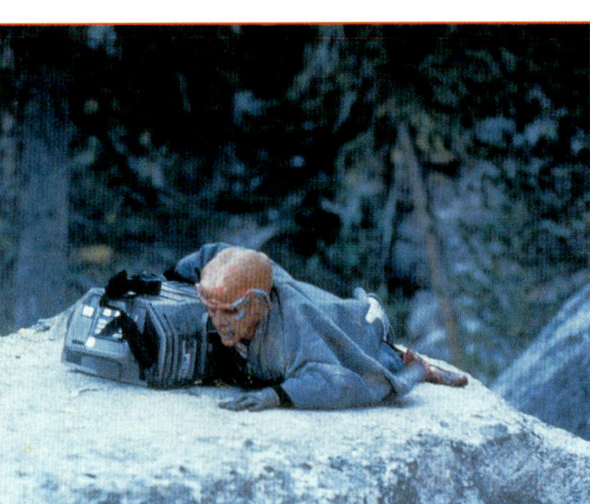
Quark moved the distress beacon up a mountain to send a signal after his and Odo's runabout crashed.

CALL FOR HELP

SIDE VIEW

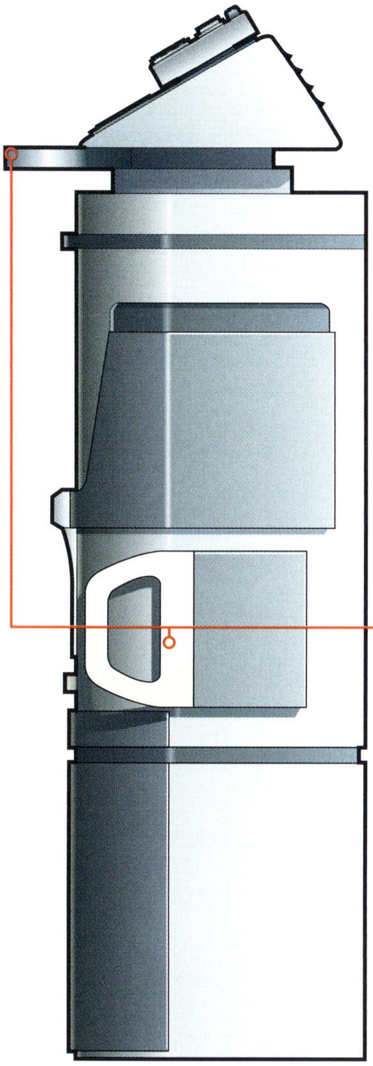

FRONT VIEW

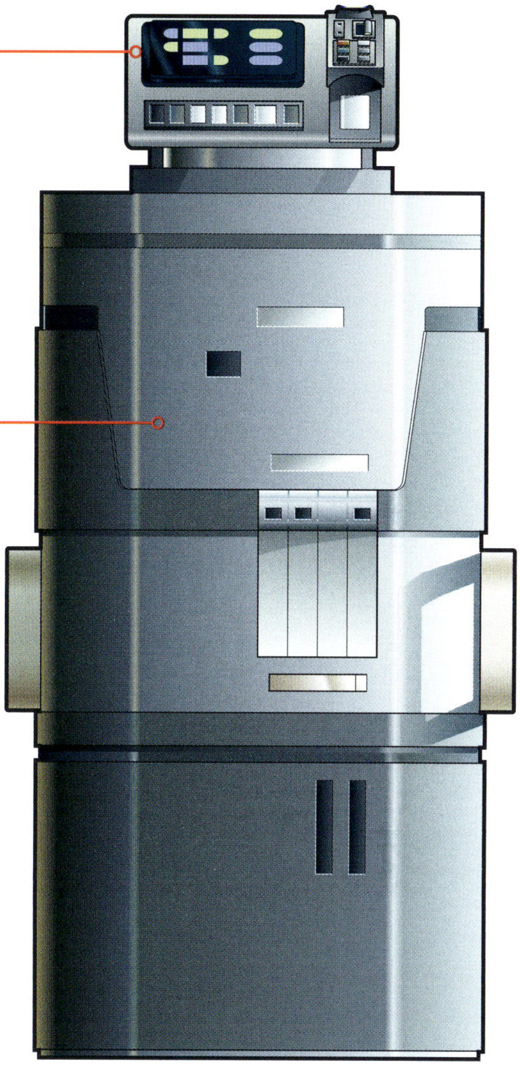

TRANSMITTER ARRAY

ACTIVATION LIGHTS
Status lights on the top display of the beacon confirmed whether the distress message was being broadcast successfully. A display on the back spelled out whether the system was online or not.

Isolinear chips and a video display panel were located behind a removable front plate.

HANDLES

LOW MAINTENANCE
The distress beacon needed minimum maintenance once activated, in case the operator might be weakened or injured. The distress calls could be picked up by any vessels to rescue the user.

TOP VIEW

TRANSMITTER ARRAY

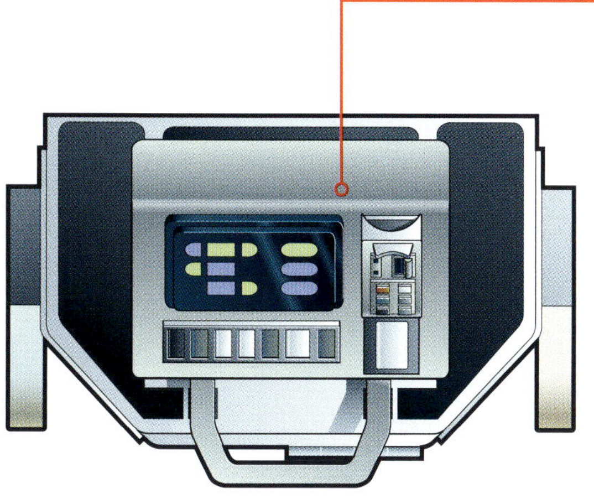

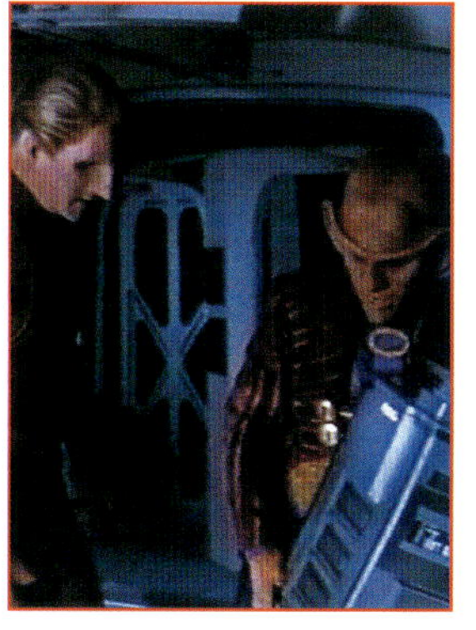

The distress beacon worked inside a crashed craft, but might have to be moved if the craft were damaged.

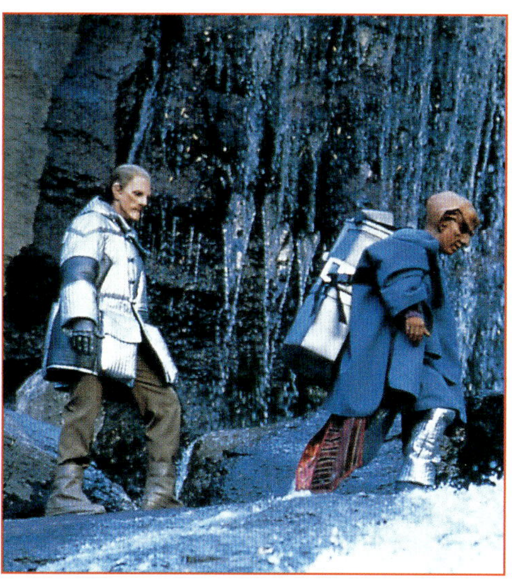

Carrying the distress beacon like a backpack, Quark ascended a mountain with Odo to break through the atmosphere on an unpopulated Class-L planet and find a signal.

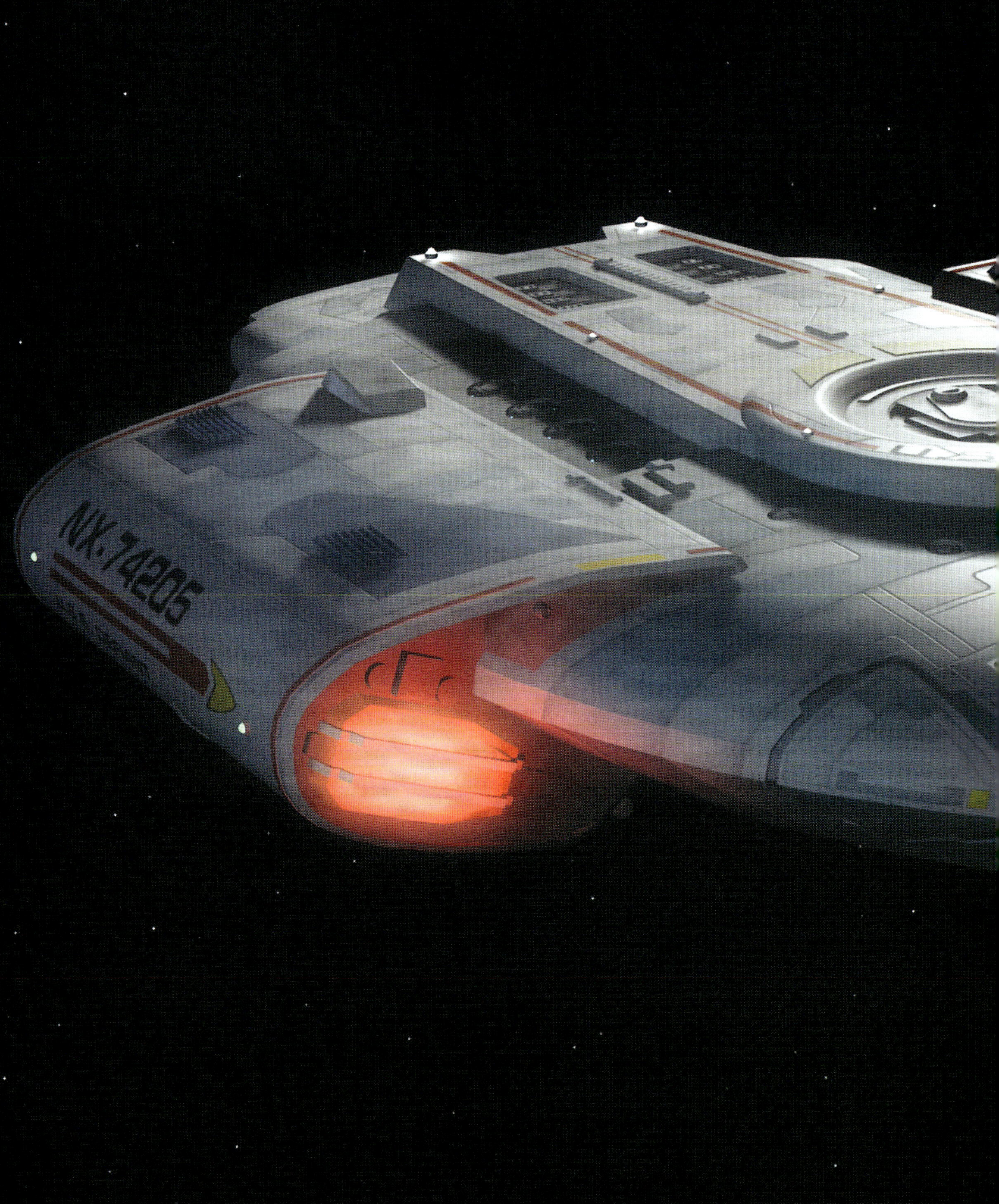
NX-74205

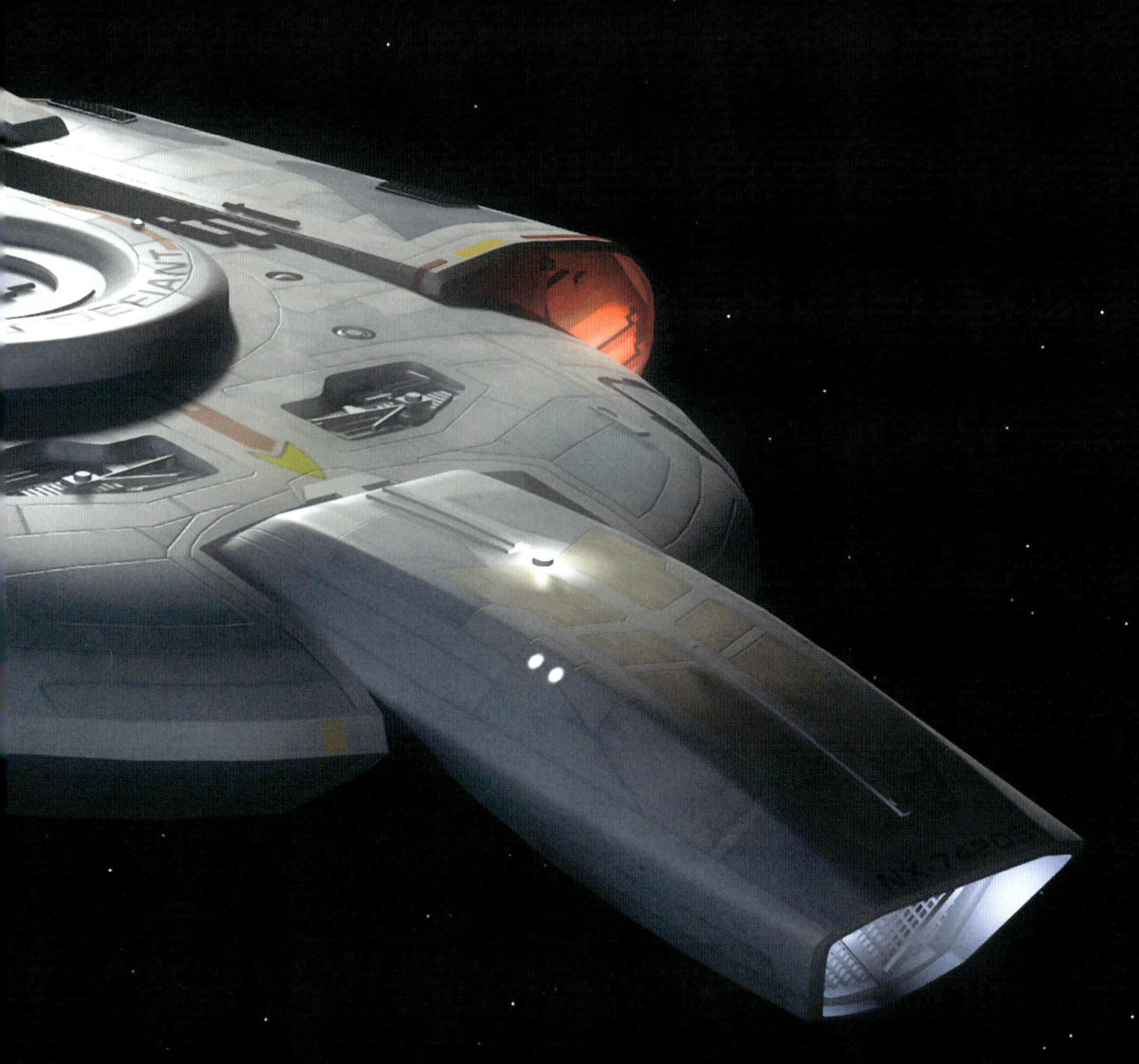

CHAPTER 3
THE DEFIANT

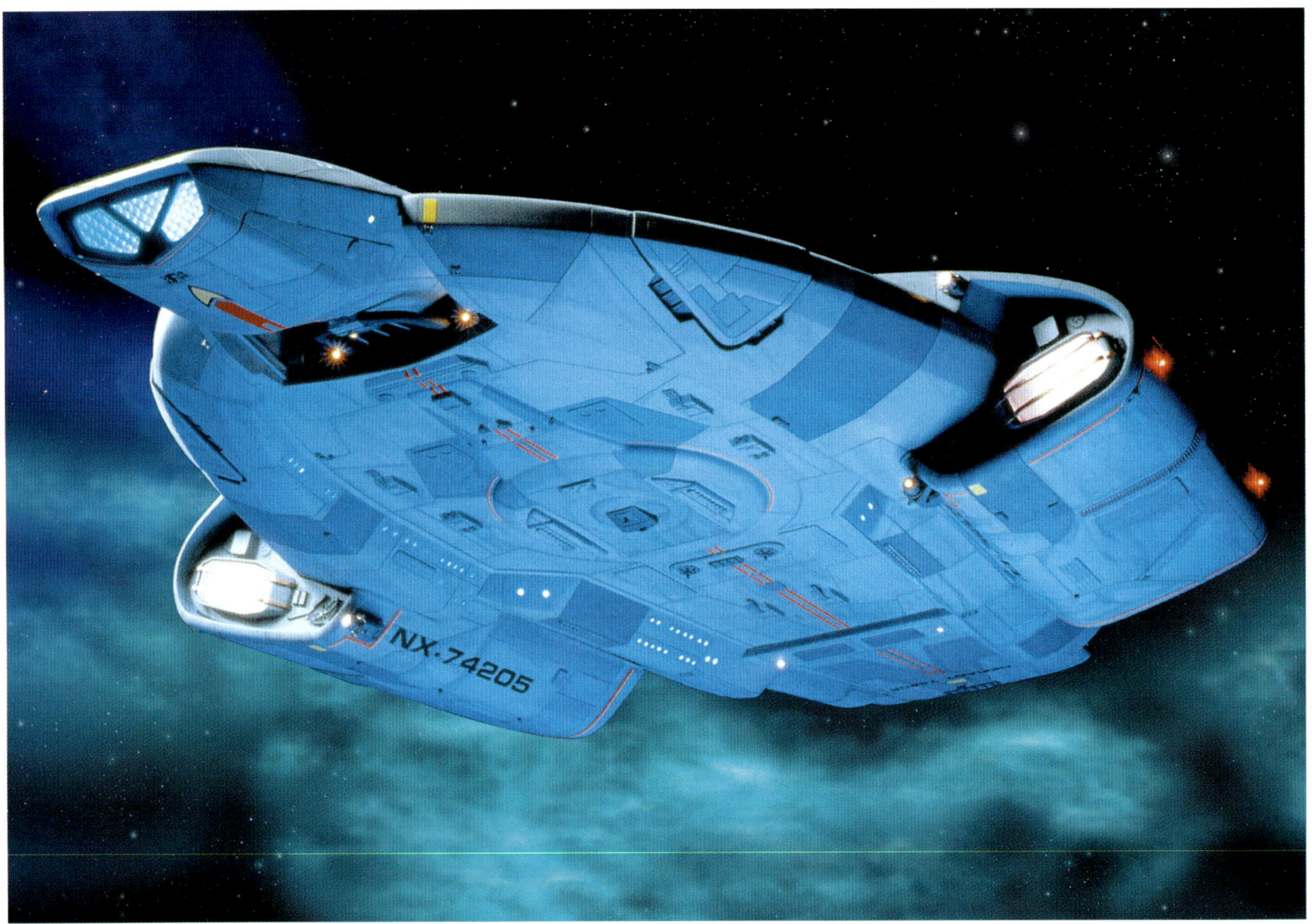

OPERATIONAL HISTORY

Starfleet's first warship, The *U.S.S. Defiant* NX-74205, was created as the first line of defense against the ememy ships of the Borg and the Dominion alliance's Jem'Hadar.

The *U.S.S. Defiant* NX-74205 was the prototype vessel for Starfleet's *Defiant*-class starships. Compact, efficient, and incorporating the latest in weaponry and defensive technology, it was Starfleet's first true warship. Like all battleships, it had It had few comforts and no provision for families, nor was it furnished for diplomatic missions. It was, as its designers intended, a heavily armored, stripped-down vessel created as a "first strike" vehicle for deployment in war.

SMALL VESSEL

As befitted its role, the *U.S.S. Defiant* was considerably smaller than most Federation starships: 170.68 meters long, 134.11 meters across, and 30.1 meters deep. It had a normal operational crew of 40 people, but could accommodate up to 192 in emergencies. Work on the *Defiant* project began in 2366, after Starfleet was alerted to the threat of a Borg invasion.

The ship was developed by Starfleet's Advanced Starship Design Bureau (ASDB) at the Antares Fleet Yards and the Utopia Planitia Fleet Yards on Mars. It was still in the design stages when the Borg arrived in 2367. Even though the crew of the *U.S.S. Enterprise* NCC-1701-D defeated the Borg, Starfleet was sufficiently concerned about the danger of another invasion attempt to continue work on the project.

Overall responsibility for the *Defiant* project rested with Admiral Batelle Toh, though a number of more junior officers were responsible for day-to-day operations. From

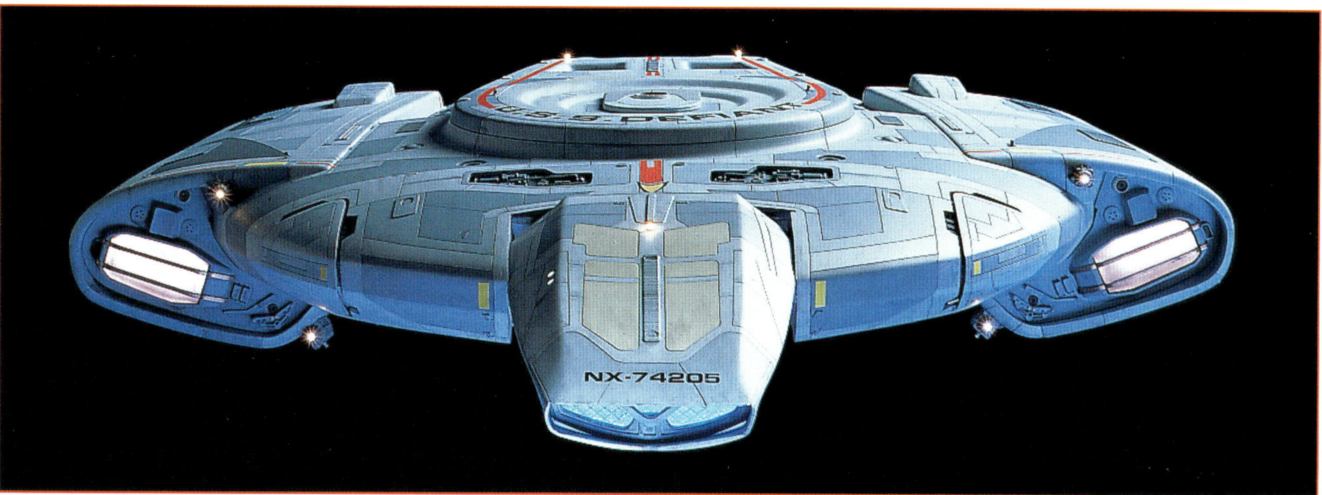

The *Defiant* had just four decks, giving it a very low forward profile that presented a minimal target to enemy ships. The design of the warship was based on an existing starship class that had entered the initial systems-level review stage. Significant alterations were made to this vessel to convert it into a fighting ship.

2367 to 2369, Commander Benjamin Sisko, a veteran of the Battle of Wolf 359, worked on the *Defiant* while he was stationed at the Utopia Planitia Fleet Yards.

The *Defiant* was not designed to operate in a planet's atmosphere but was constructed to withstand emergency planetfall. Landing pads were built into the ship's underside, and simulations showed that the *Defiant* class was capable of achieving liftoff from a planet's surface.

NEW DIRECTION

Early on in development, the *Defiant* was regarded as a fast torpedo attack ship. Its designers planned to equip it with six torpedo launchers and a large complement of both photon and quantum torpedoes. But as the project evolved, the ship was given more ambitious mission objectives.

The vessel's computer systems consisted of twin isolinear processing cores, which incorporated a delayed-venting heat storage block for stealth activities. Normally, only 45 percent of the storage and processing capacity of the computers was used, leaving 55 percent free to process intelligence-gathering and tactical operations.

After the *Defiant*'s shakedown cruise, serious design flaws came to light. In Sisko's words, the experimental vessel was "overgunned and overpowered for a ship its size." During battle drills, it nearly tore itself apart when the engines were tested at full capacity. Given the serious nature of the design problems and the diminished Borg threat, Starfleet Command decided to suspend work on the *Defiant*. The project was mothballed until 2371, when Starfleet became concerned about the Dominion threat.

When the *Galaxy*-class *U.S.S. Odyssey* NCC-71832 was destroyed by the Jem'Hadar, Commander Sisko, who was by then in command of Deep Space 9 at the mouth of the Bajoran wormhole, lobbied Starfleet Command to reactivate the *Defiant* project. Shortly afterward, the *Defiant* was placed on active duty and assigned to the Bajoran sector.

Under Sisko's command, the *Defiant*'s main roles were to protect Deep Space 9, the Bajoran wormhole, and Bajor from Dominion threats. It was also tasked with patrolling the Bajoran sector and the Gamma Quadrant, and was frequently assigned to special covert operations.

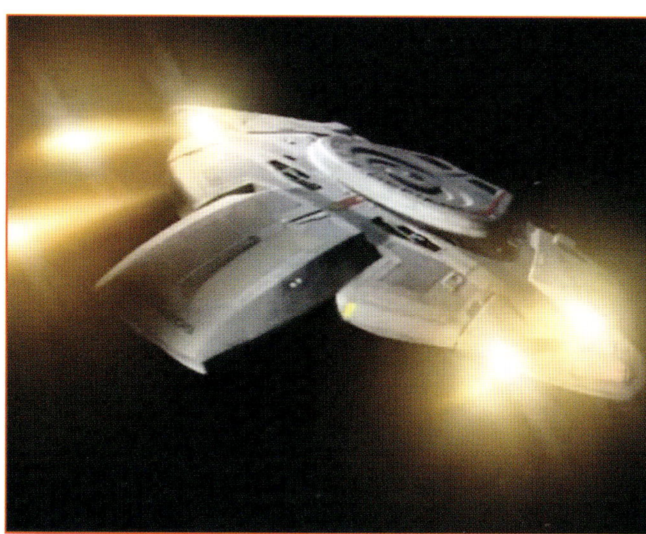

The Defiant's weapons' complement included pulse phaser cannons and torpedo launchers, as well as dorsal phasers.

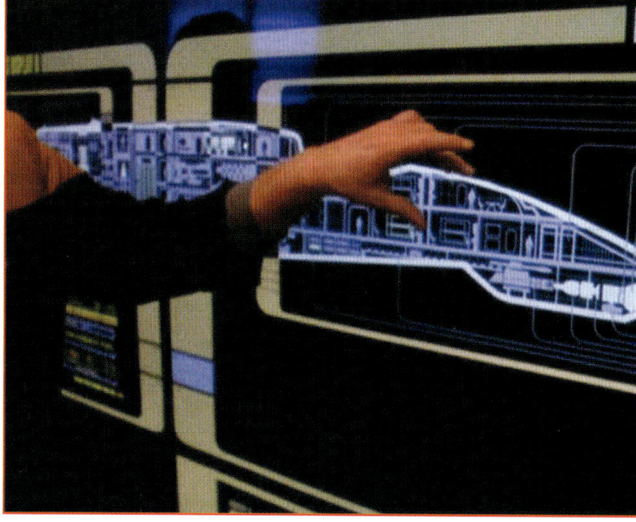

A *U.S.S. Defiant* schematic could be called up and viewed on any of the ship's many consoles. It provided information and updates on the state of the entire vessel.

NEW CLASS

During the Dominion War, the *Defiant* class went into limited production and these small, maneuverable ships became an essential part of Starfleet's operation. However, unlike the *U.S.S Defiant* itself, other *Defiant*-class ships were not fitted with a cloaking device.

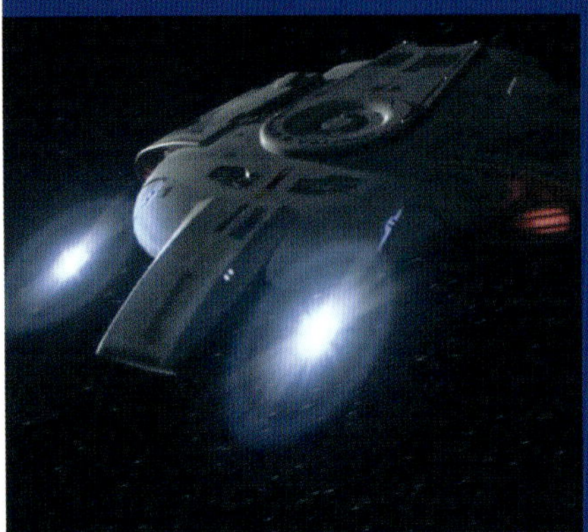

The *U.S.S. Valiant* NCC-74210 was a *Defiant*-class ship assigned to Starfleet Academy's Red Squad.

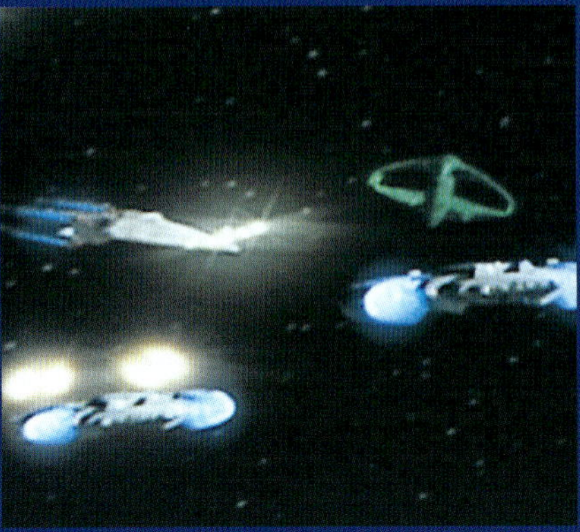

Two *Defiant*-class ships and other vessels chased the *U.S.S. Prometheus* when it was stolen by Romulans.

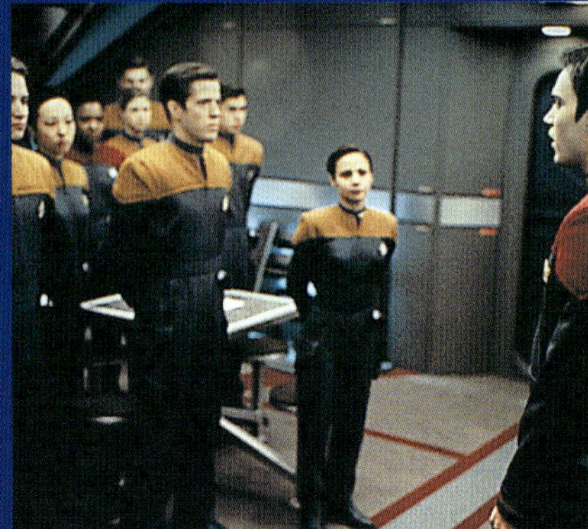

The cadets on the *U.S.S. Valiant* were forced to run the ship when commissioned officers were killed.

On its first mission to the Gamma Quadrant, the *U.S.S. Defiant* was overpowered and boarded by the Jem'Hadar. Subsequently, the *Defiant*'s crew cooperated with the Jem'Hadar to stop Jem'Hadar rebels from gaining control of Iconian technology.

ROMULAN TECHNOLOGY

The *U.S.S. Defiant* was unique in the United Federation of Planets in being the only ship equipped with a Romulan cloaking device. According to provisions in the Treaty of Algeron, the Federation had agreed to refrain from developing or using cloaking technology. Because of the Dominion threat, this provision was then set aside through a mutual agreement between the Romulan Star Empire and the Federation. When the *Defiant* was first assigned to Deep Space 9, a Romulan officer, Subcommander T'Rul, was part of the crew, though her presence was later deemed unnecessary.

Initially, use of the *Defiant*'s cloaking device was restricted to the Gamma Quadrant, but after the Klingon attack on Cardassian space in 2374, the agreement was modified to allow its limited use within the Alpha Quadrant. In exchange for supplying the cloaking device, the information that Starfleet gathered on the Dominion was transmitted to the Romulans.

RUNNING DARK

When the cloaking device was engaged, interior lights were dimmed and all defensive system power was transferred to the cloak, which enabled it to fully mask the strong energy signature that the *Defiant* put out. This made the ship virtually invisible to everything except the most powerful subspace scanner. The cloaking field enveloped the hull of the ship itself to minimize subspace distortion.

Because the *Defiant*'s power signature was unusually high for a ship of its size, the cloaking device could be penetrated by certain types of anti-proton beams. This was only discovered when a Jem'Hadar warship first encountered the *Defiant*. Cutting main power then enabled the ship to remain 'invisible' even to anti-proton scans. During warp flight, the cloak was extended to mask the warp field.

Because the *Defiant* was placed on active duty before its operational problems had been resolved, the engineering crew of Deep Space 9 were given responsibility for a program of modifications that it needed.

DANGEROUS FLAWS

On early missions, the *Defiant*'s weaknesses almost proved fatal. In particular, the sickbay was hopelessly inadequate, and required an enormous amount of work from Deep Space 9's medical and engineering staff.

However, over time, given the necessary modifications recommended by Sisko and supervised by Deep Space 9's chief of operations, Miles O'Brien, many of the *Defiant*'s

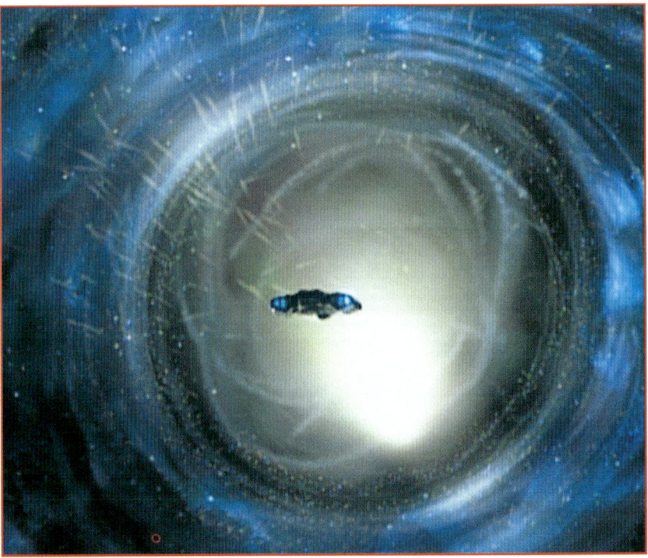

During the Dominion War, the *Defiant* entered the wormhole. Inside, Sisko persuaded the wormhole aliens to stop more Dominion ships traveling to the Alpha Quadrant.

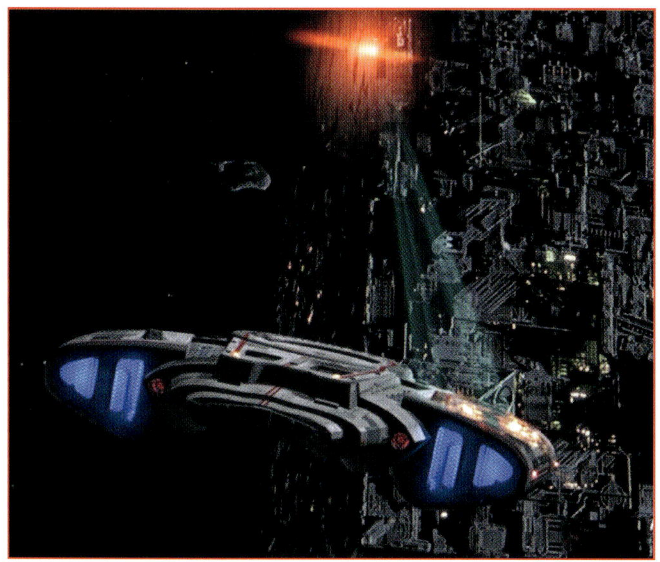

The *U.S.S. Defiant* eventually fought the Borg in 2373. It was severely damaged in the battle but was fully repaired at Deep Space 9.

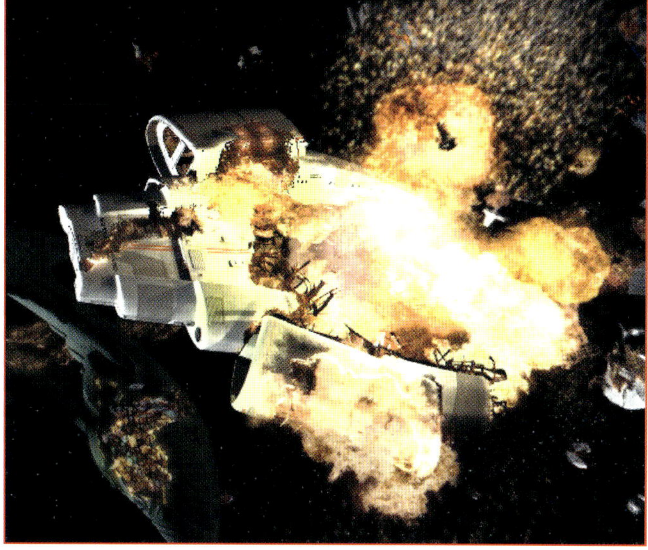

Captain Sisko's first *U.S.S. Defiant* was destroyed by a Breen energy-dampening weapon, but another ship, the *U.S.S. Sao Paulo*, was renamed *U.S.S. Defiant*.

flaws were corrected and it became a potent and reliable ship. Yet despite its great power and maneuverability, the *Defiant* remained ill-equipped for certain situations.

Many of its limitations were revealed on Stardate 49263, when it entered the atmosphere of a Class-J planet and was damaged. The *Defiant* had relatively few safety and crew-support systems to cope with this, and although repairs were eventually effected, several crewmembers almost lost their lives.

INTO PRODUCTION

Once the *Defiant* prototype had proved itself, Starfleet took the decision to put the *Defiant* class into production. By the end of 2373, there was a significant number of *Defiant*-class ships in operation, and over the next two years they played a vital role in the Dominion War.

The *U.S.S. Defiant* NX-74205 was destroyed by a Breen ship in 2375. Another *Defiant*-class ship, the *U.S.S. Sao Paulo*, was assigned to Deep Space 9 on Stardate 52861. Given the *U.S.S. Defiant*'s exceptional record under Captain Sisko's command, the Chief of Starfleet Operations gave a special dispensation to change the ship's name to *Defiant*.

The shield generators of this vessel were completely reconfigured so that it would not be affected by the Breen's energy-dampening weapon. This new *Defiant* played a distinguished role in the final battle with the Dominion at Cardassia Prime, and remained stationed at Deep Space 9.

THE MIRROR UNIVERSE

A version of the *U.S.S. Defiant* also existed in the mirror universe, where the Terran rebels used it to fight the Alliance. This version of the ship did not evolve independently. It had the same design problems as the original *Defiant*, only resolved when the Terran rebels kidnapped Sisko and persuaded him to help them.

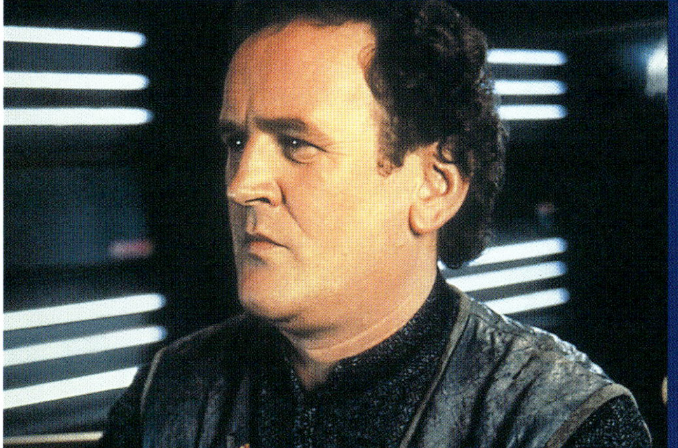

Miles 'Smiley' O'Brien, the Terran leader in the mirror universe, stole the plans for the *U.S.S. Defiant* from Deep Space 9, enabling the ship to be built.

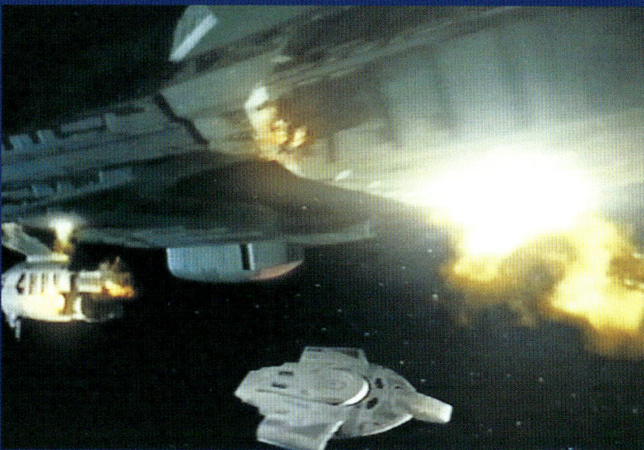

With Captain Sisko's help, the Terran rebels used their *Defiant* to inflict a defeat on the Klingon-Cardassian alliance. The ship was damaged, but not beyond repair.

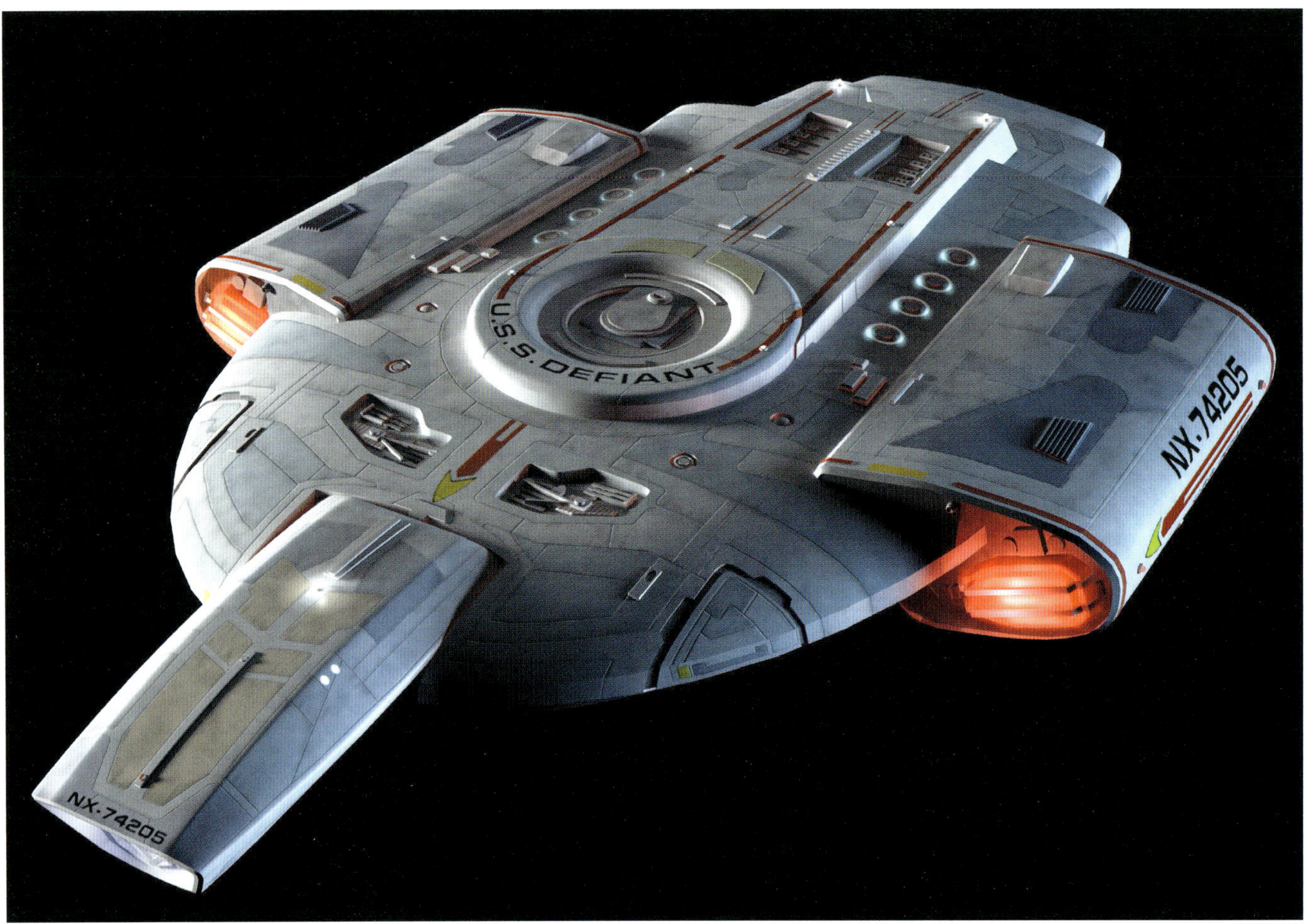

ANNOTATED EXTERIOR VIEWS

Small but heavily armed, the design of the *U.S.S.Defiant* NX-74205 was a new venture for Starfleet. Originally conceived as a fast torpedo attack ship, the vessel was assigned more ambitious missions.

The *Defiant*'s development team took the decision to abandon the traditional Starfleet layout, which placed the warp nacelles at the end of twin pylons, and move them in much closer to the main body. This flattened the *Defiant*'s profile, making the ship a much more difficult target to hit. In another important innovation, the designers gave their new ship multilayer ablative armor on the hull, which could resist repeated weapons fire. Under the ablative armor, the hull was constructed of a castrodium-neutromium composite.

Considerable effort went into making the *Defiant* faster and more heavily armed than standard Starfleet vessels. It was equipped with both warp and impulse engines, and by running a plasma conduit through the primary phaser coupling, the designers almost doubled the phaser power, boosting the efficiency of the warp drive by 30 percent. The ship's standard cruise speed was warp 7, and safe maximum warp speed was warp 9, though the *Defiant* was capable of exceeding that limit for short periods of time.

INSTANTANEOUS FIRE

To meet its offensive requirements, it was equipped with four state-of-the-art pulse phaser cannons and two torpedo launchers. The *Defiant*'s weapons systems were designed so that the time between the order to fire and the launch was near-instantaneous. Like other Starfleet vessels, the *Defiant* was fitted with an auto-destruct system to prevent the ship falling into enemy hands.

DORSAL VIEW

PRIMARY DEFLECTOR ARRAY
DETACHABLE WARHEAD
WARHEAD MODULE
FORWARD TARGETING ARRAY
PHOTON TORPEDO LAUNCHER
ESCAPE POD HATCHES
TARGETING SENSORS
FORWARD PHASER ARRAY
SENSOR PALLET
FORWARD PHASER ARRAY
PULSE PHASER CANNON
MAIN BRIDGE
BUSSARD COLLECTOR
RUNNING LIGHT
PLASMA VENT
WARP NACELLE
IMPULSE ENGINE
IMPULSE VENTS
AFT TORPEDO LAUNCHER
AFT SENSOR PALLET
NX-74205
U.S.S. DEFIANT
NX-74205
NX-74205

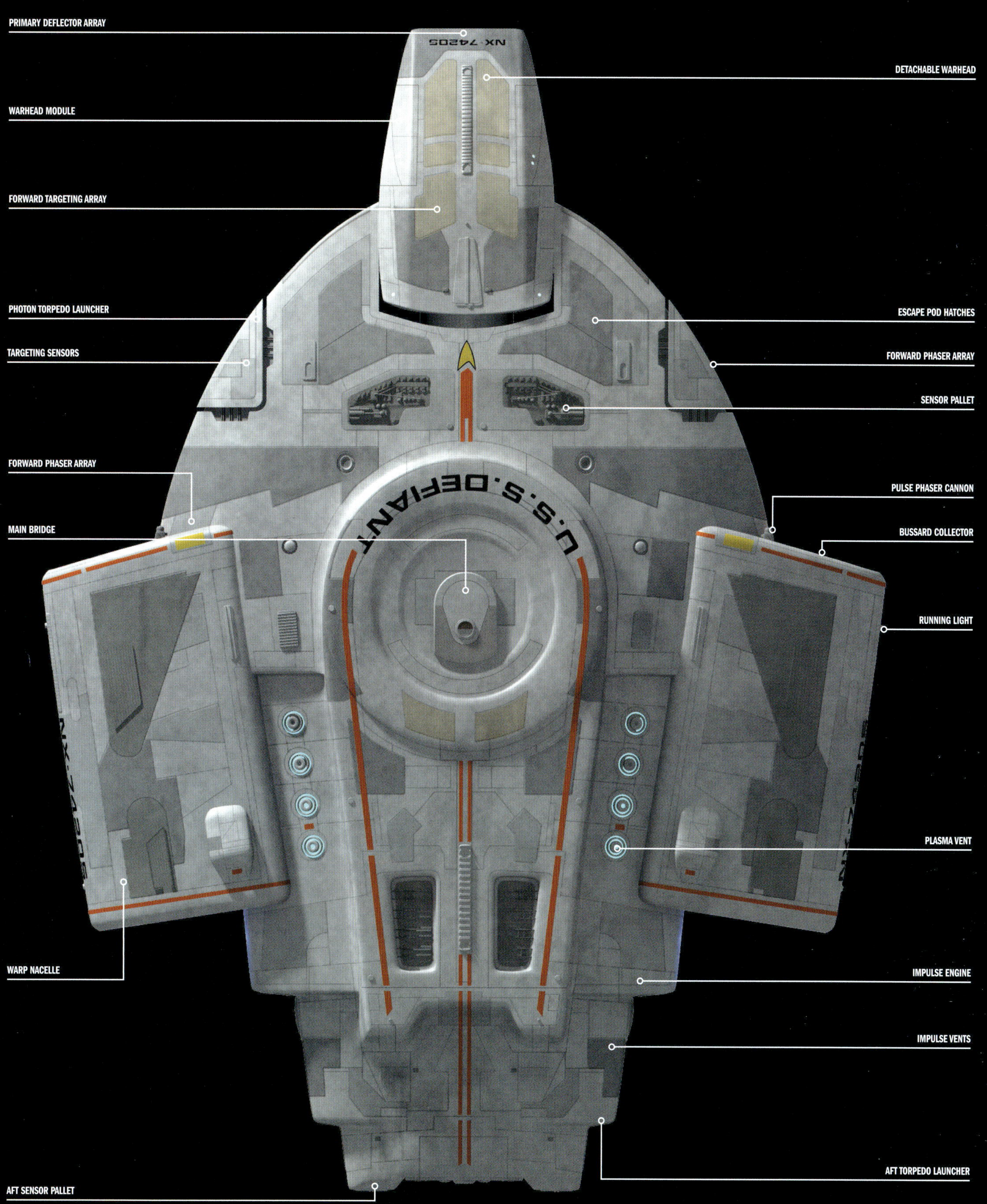

VENTRAL VIEW

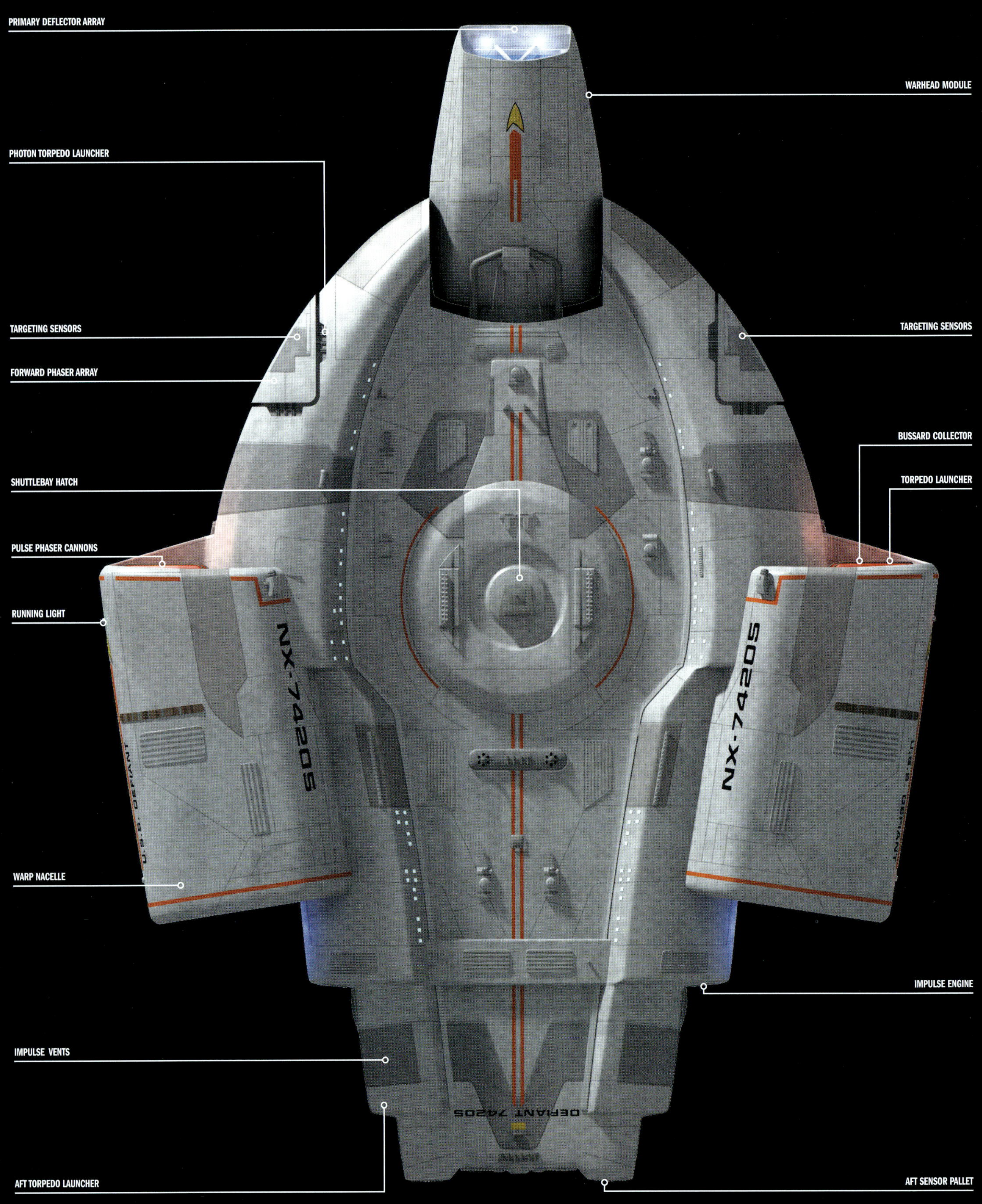

STARBOARD ELEVATION

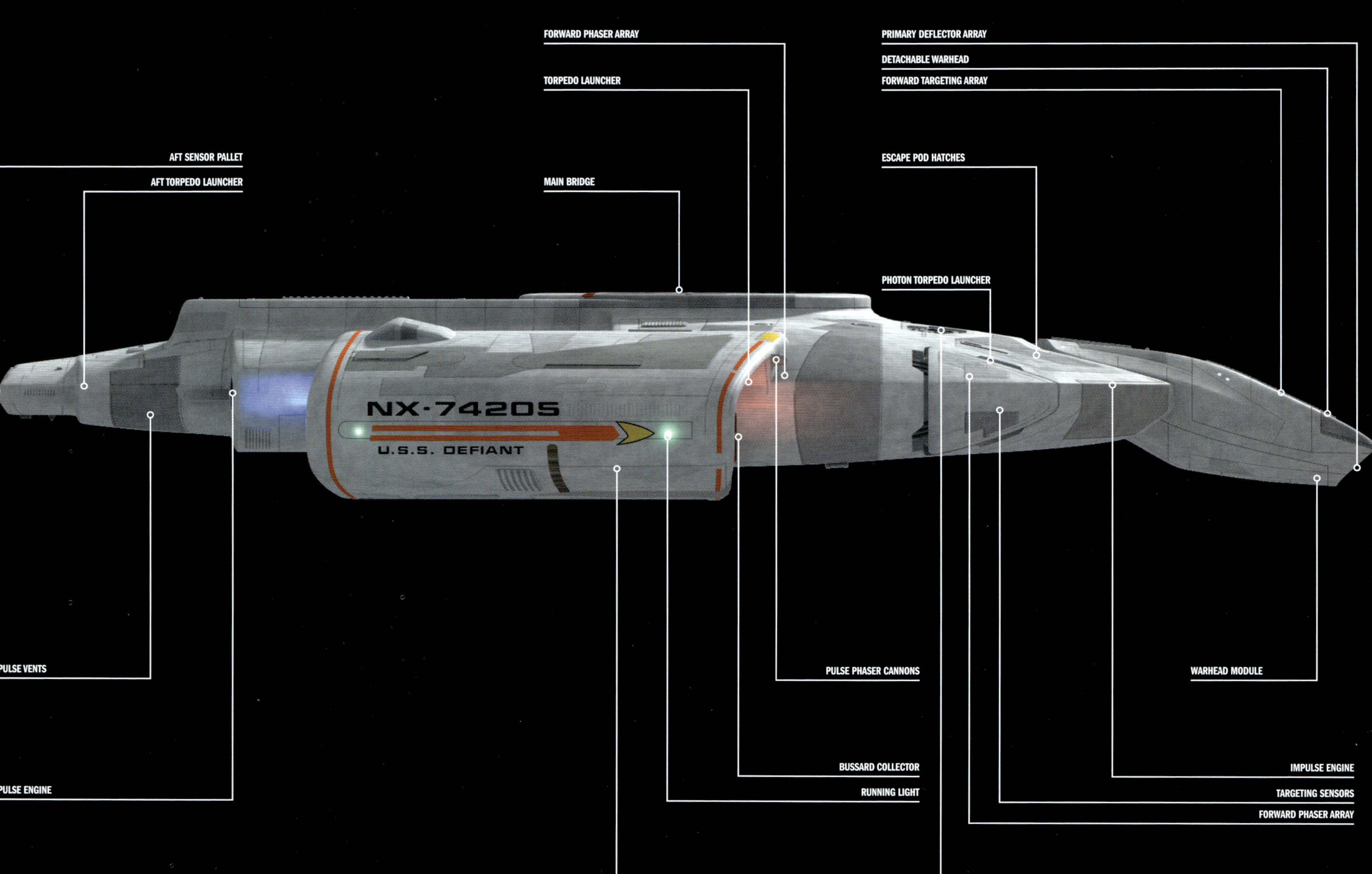

FRONT ELEVATION

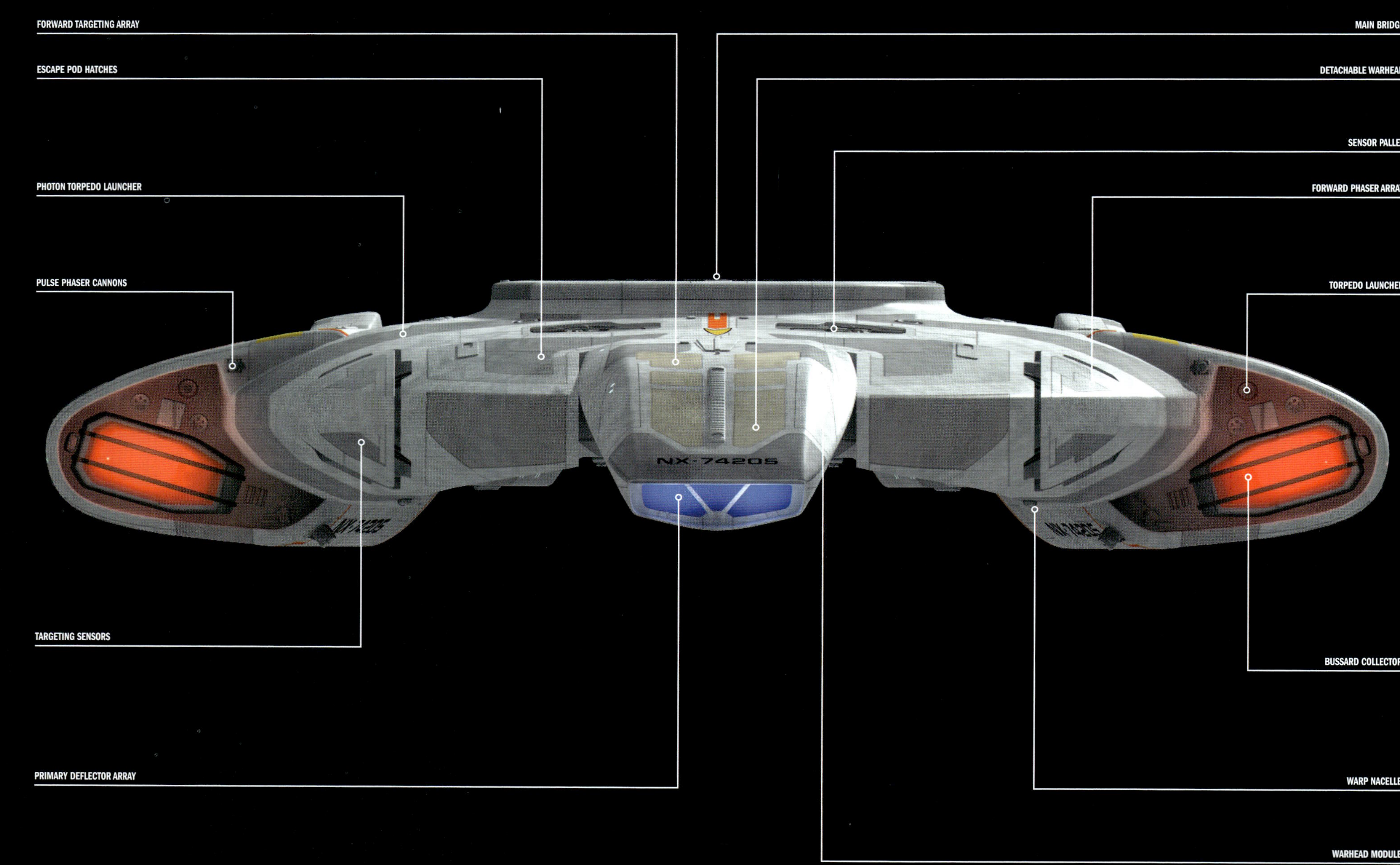

AFT ELEVATION

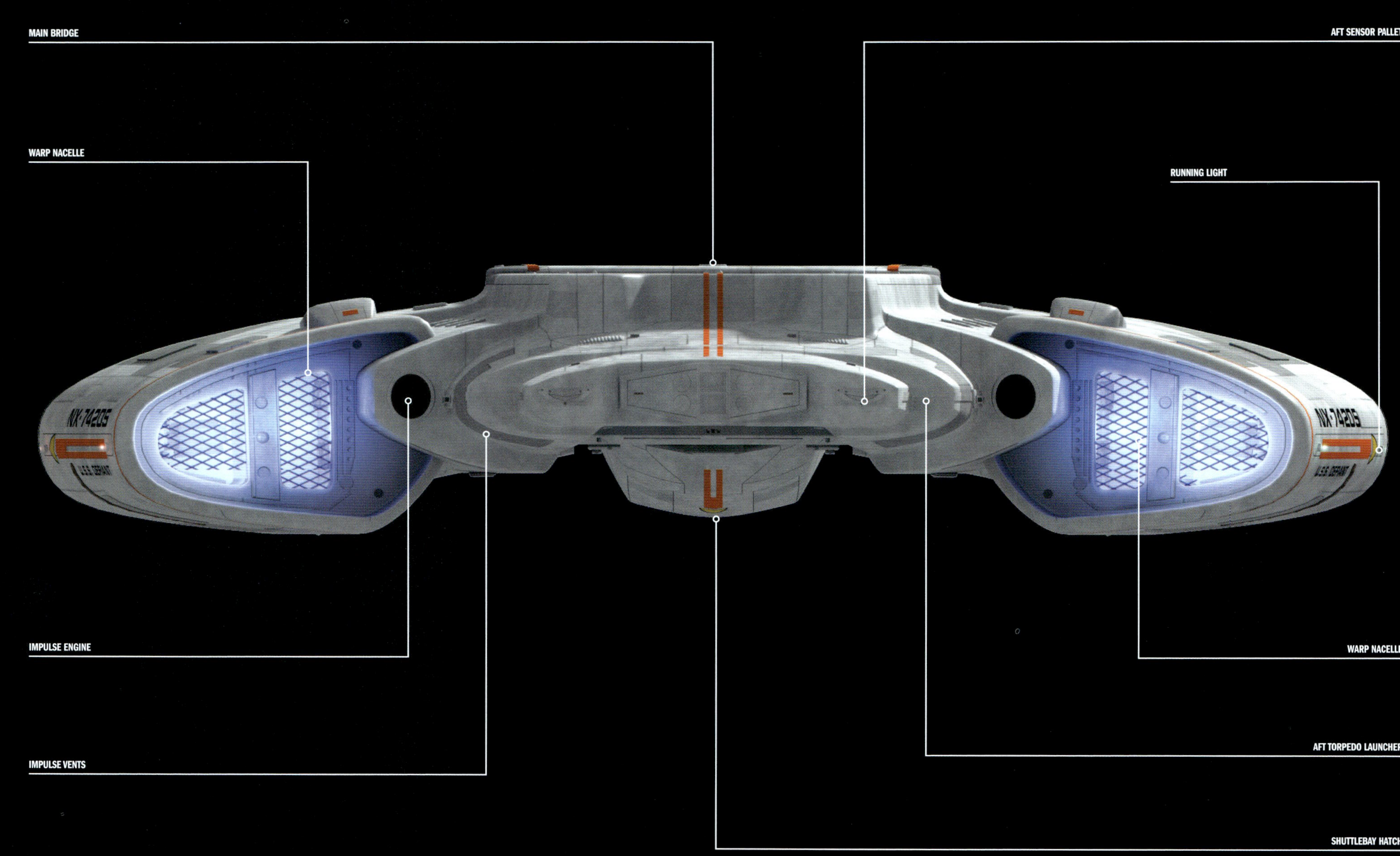

KEY LOCATIONS

Space was utilized to the maximum on the four main decks of the *U.S.S. Defiant*, with function prioritized over comfort and vital sections packed close together in the distinctive, saucer-shaped hull.

The *Defiant* was a stripped-down, high-powered warship, and some otherwise common elements were regarded as superfluous, since the ship was not designed to carry families, significant amounts of cargo, or even a large crew. The four main decks each had a distinct purpose.

DECK 1

The small command bridge was located on deck 1. A captain's ready room lay off the rear port side of the bridge. Unusually for a Starfleet vessel, the bridge module was flush with the dorsal hull of the vessel, and deck 1 therefore had a number of other sections. These included a transporter pad to the rear of the bridge and, slightly further back, the upper level of main engineering, which was arranged across decks 1 and 2. The phaser-charging coils that supplied the forward-mounted pulse phaser cannons rested on top of the warp coil nacelles that ran along either side of the bridge on deck 1. The rounded bow contained retrofitted sensor palettes, giving the *Defiant* a wider scope of operations than before. Two sets of four plasma vents ran along the exterior of the main hull.

DECK 2

Science, computer, and medical systems occupied deck 2. Most of the locations were arranged in a horseshoe around a central hub; the mess hall, sickbay, medical and science labs, and a transporter room ran clockwise from the one o'clock position along the front edge of the vessel. The warp coils descended to decks 3 and 4, and were fed by the warp core. Operated from the warhead control room near the bow, the warhead section of the ship could be detached completely, although under normal circumstances it connected to the twin medical and science laboratories. The larger transporter room 2 was located on the starboard side, and the relatively small sickbay, to port.

The cramped mess hall on deck 2 was the closest onboard equivalent to a social area, although it also had to double as a briefing room. The crew used one of the walls in this area to display trophies taken from their victories over Jem'Hadar attack cruisers. The interior mechanism for a pulse phaser cannon was also located on this deck, along with a slightly larger state room for meetings.

To maximize protection of its vital computer core, the *Defiant*'s twin stacks were situated dead center on the ship and ran from deck 2 to 3, adjacent to the main vertical turbolift that connected all four decks. The lower level of main engineering, on deck 2, allowed access to the warp core. This was connected to the impulse engines built into the stern, and housed the Romulan-manufactured cloaking device, again deliberately protected by its position.

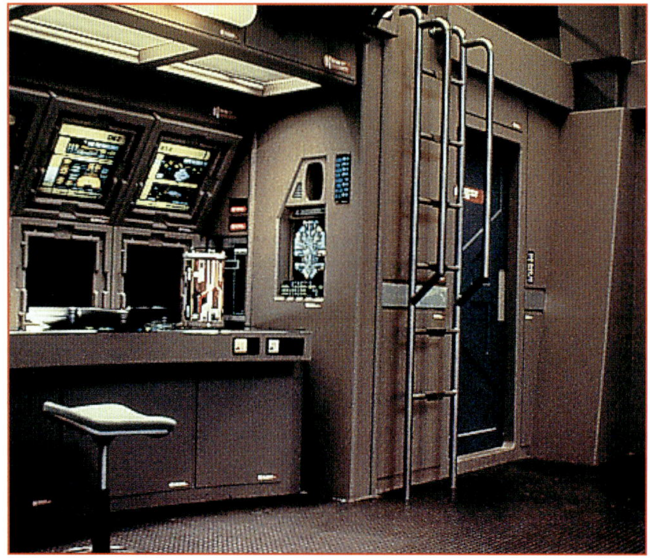

Main engineering was split across two levels. The top level was accessed from deck 1 and descended down to deck 2. The warp core ran across all four decks.

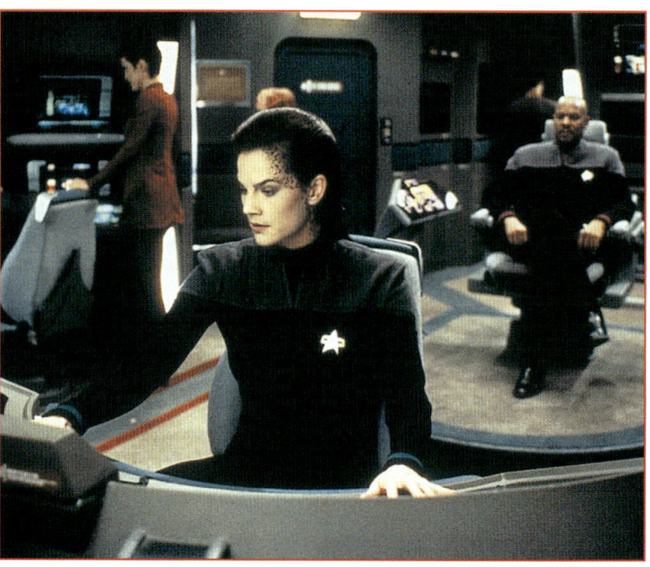

The *U.S.S. Defiant*'s bridge was near the top of the ship, but was not as exposed as the bridge modules of many Federation vessels.

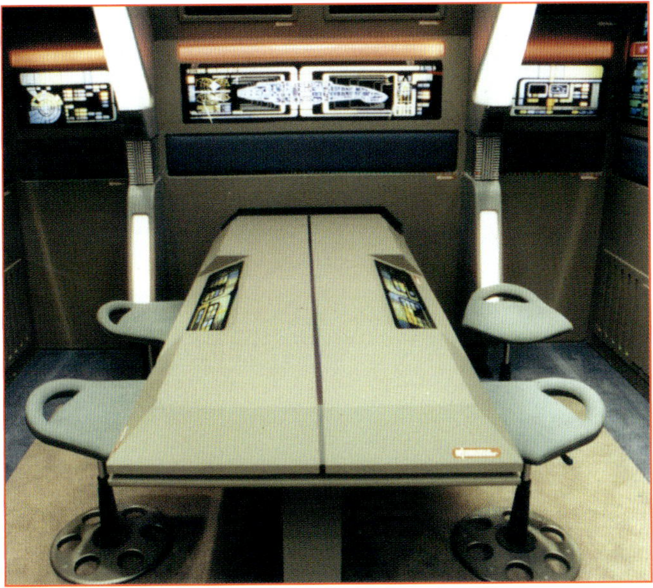
This situation table was located on the bridge and was used by personnel when they weren't manning their stations.

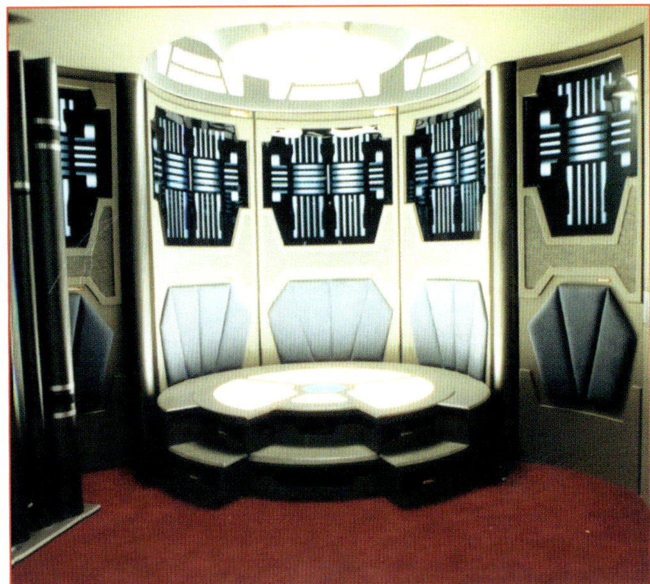
The *Defiant* had a relatively small transporter room that was located on deck 2. The pad could comfortably accommodate half a dozen passengers.

DECK 3

Directly below main engineering, on deck 3, were the antimatter storage containers. If engineering or the rest of the ship was severely damaged, the engineering crew could leave the vessel quickly by entering the escape pods tucked away at the rear of the warp coil.

Main access to the *Defiant* was via the twin airlocks built into the nose of the ship at the very front of deck 3, close to the horizontal connecting turbolift. Twin impulse engines were fitted port and starboard toward the rear of the angled bow, allowing this warhead section to operate under its own power if it needed to be separated from the main ship.

The majority of the forward and center sections of deck 3 were taken up with cargo storage. There were four cargo bays, arranged in a horseshoe shape along the front of the ship. They were served by a dedicated cargo transporter pad and a shuttlebay that enabled shuttles to offload directly into the cargo bays. Two more shuttlebays were also located on this deck, toward the rear. The rear port and starboard sections contained torpedo magazines, sited directly above the twin torpedo launchers on the deck below.

DECK 4

Because of the *Defiant*'s shape, deck 4 had the smallest surface area. Situated at the bottom of the warhead section were twin navigational deflectors; they sat either side of the forward-mounted single torpedo launcher and were fed by twin magazines to its rear, giving this detachable section considerable firepower. Directly behind these were the tactical sensor arrays.

The curving port and starboard sides of deck 4 contained forward and rear landing legs, which allowed the *Defiant* to land on the surface of a planet.

Deck 4 also contained the bays for shuttlecraft storage, another pulse phaser cannon, and a circular sensor array in the middle of the deck. Power conduits ran throughout the ship to all vital areas, backed up by a number of redundant systems and routes in case of rupture or faults in the supply.

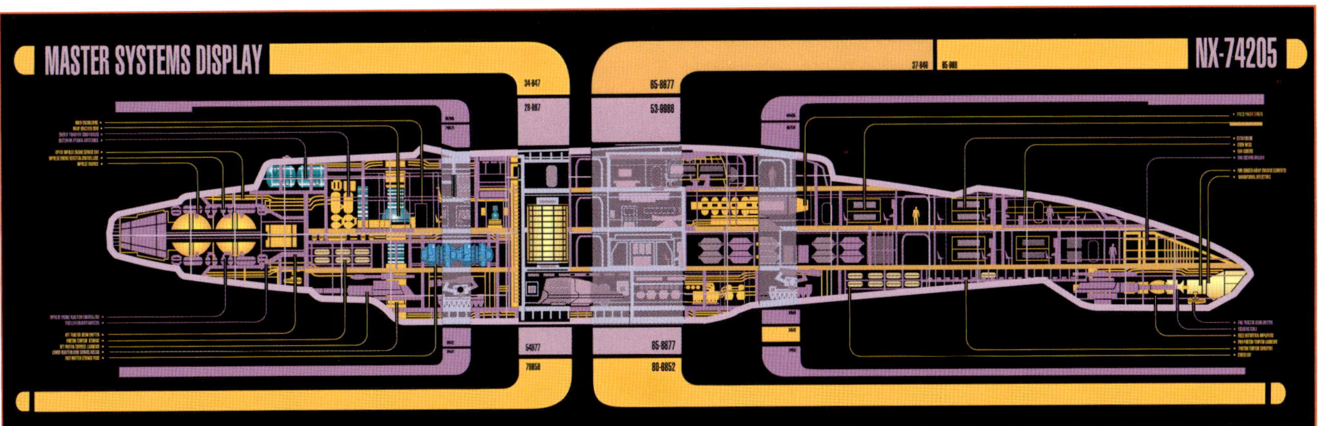

Many of the *Defiant*'s duty consoles displayed a detailed schematic of the ship: a master systems display showing, at a glance, all the different areas and rooms of the vessel and the status of various systems. Duty consoles in one area could be used to access or even control those in another part of the ship.

Compact but extremely efficient, the *Defiant*'s design maximized the limited space available.

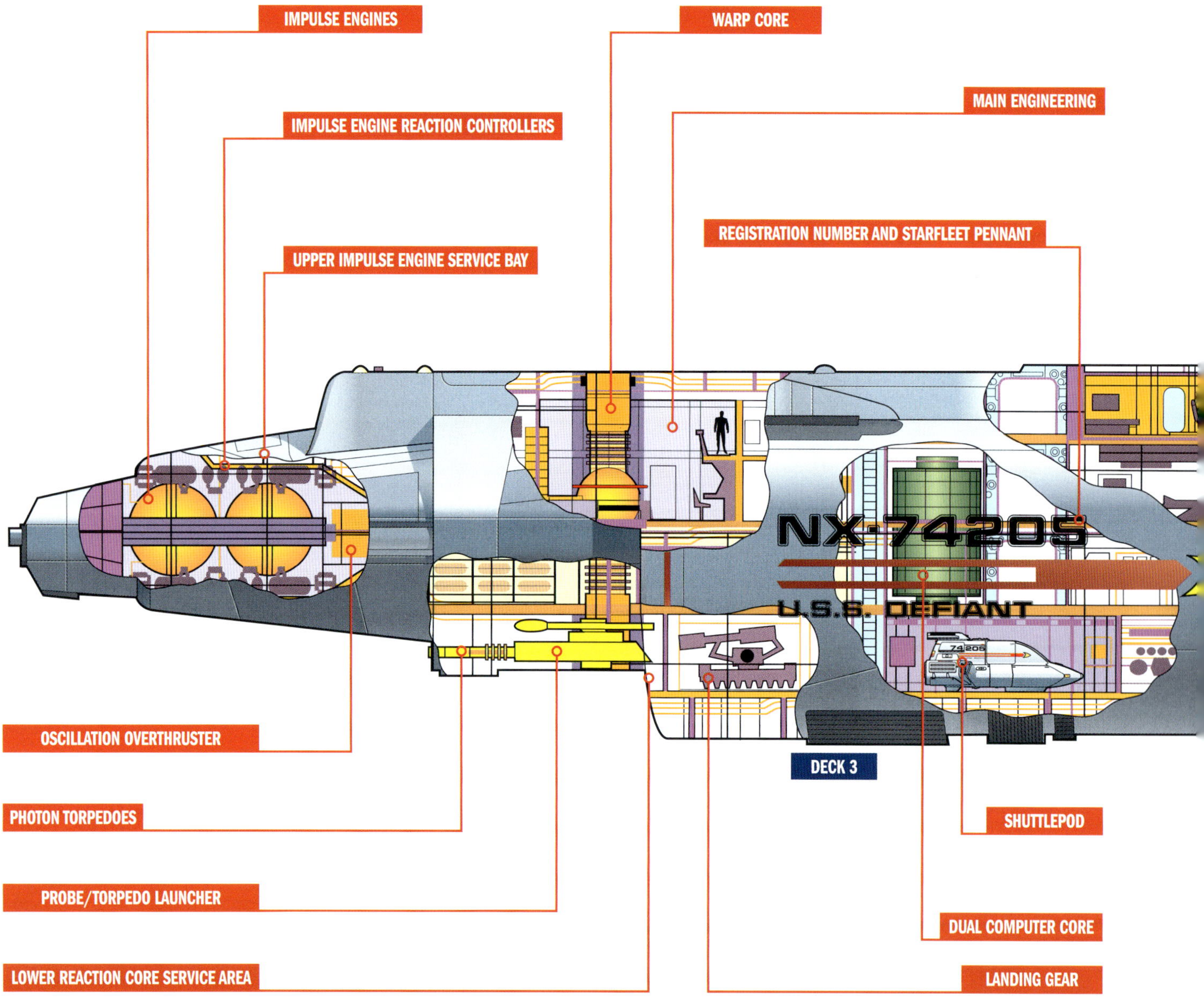

IMPULSE ENGINES

WARP CORE

MAIN ENGINEERING

IMPULSE ENGINE REACTION CONTROLLERS

REGISTRATION NUMBER AND STARFLEET PENNANT

UPPER IMPULSE ENGINE SERVICE BAY

NX-74205

U.S.S. DEFIANT

OSCILLATION OVERTHRUSTER

DECK 3

PHOTON TORPEDOES

SHUTTLEPOD

PROBE/TORPEDO LAUNCHER

DUAL COMPUTER CORE

LOWER REACTION CORE SERVICE AREA

LANDING GEAR

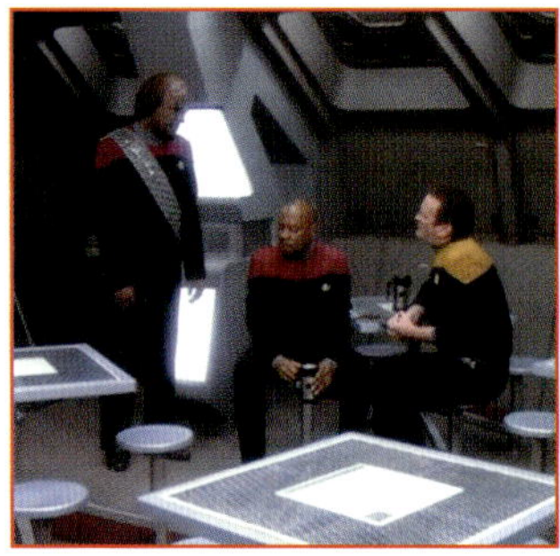
The mess hall on deck 2 was also used as an informal gathering area and a formal briefing room.

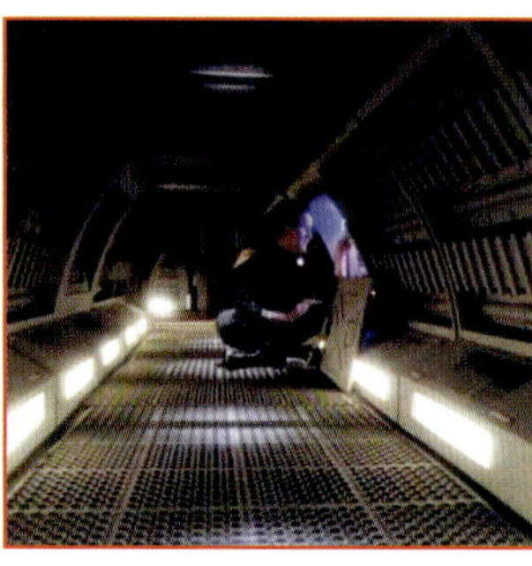
The Jefferies tubes were very low and there was no room for crew members to stand inside them.

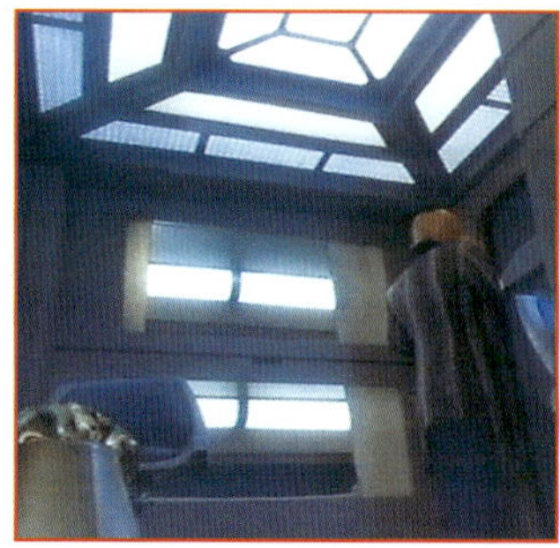
Sleeping quarters were basic and left little room for personal touches. The rows of bunk beds afforded little privacy.

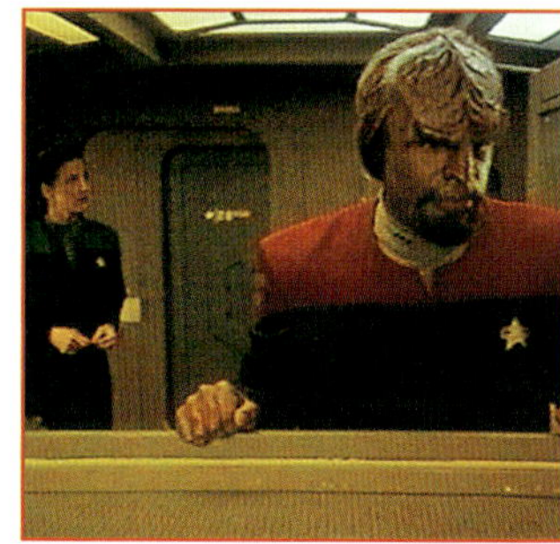
Spartan as the sleeping quarters seemed, they were too luxurious for the Klingon Worf, who removed his mattress.

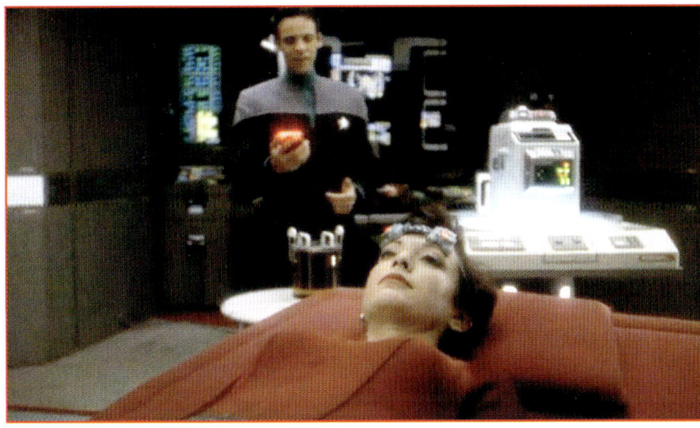

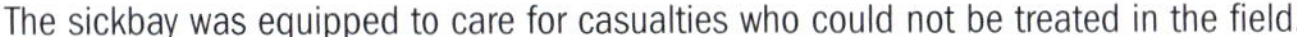

The sickbay was equipped to care for casualties who could not be treated in the field.

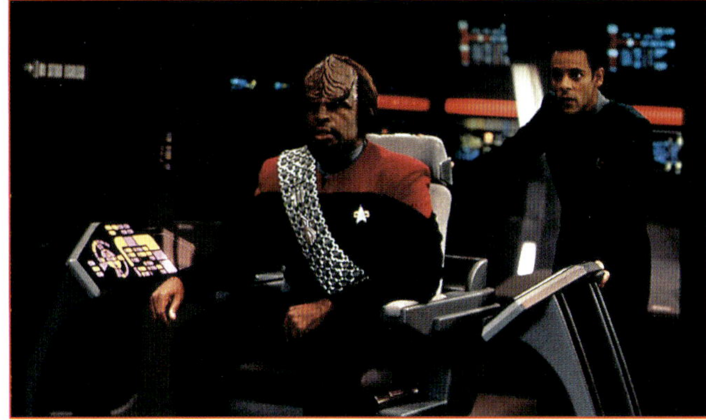

The bridge was compact and made the most of available surfaces for duty stations.

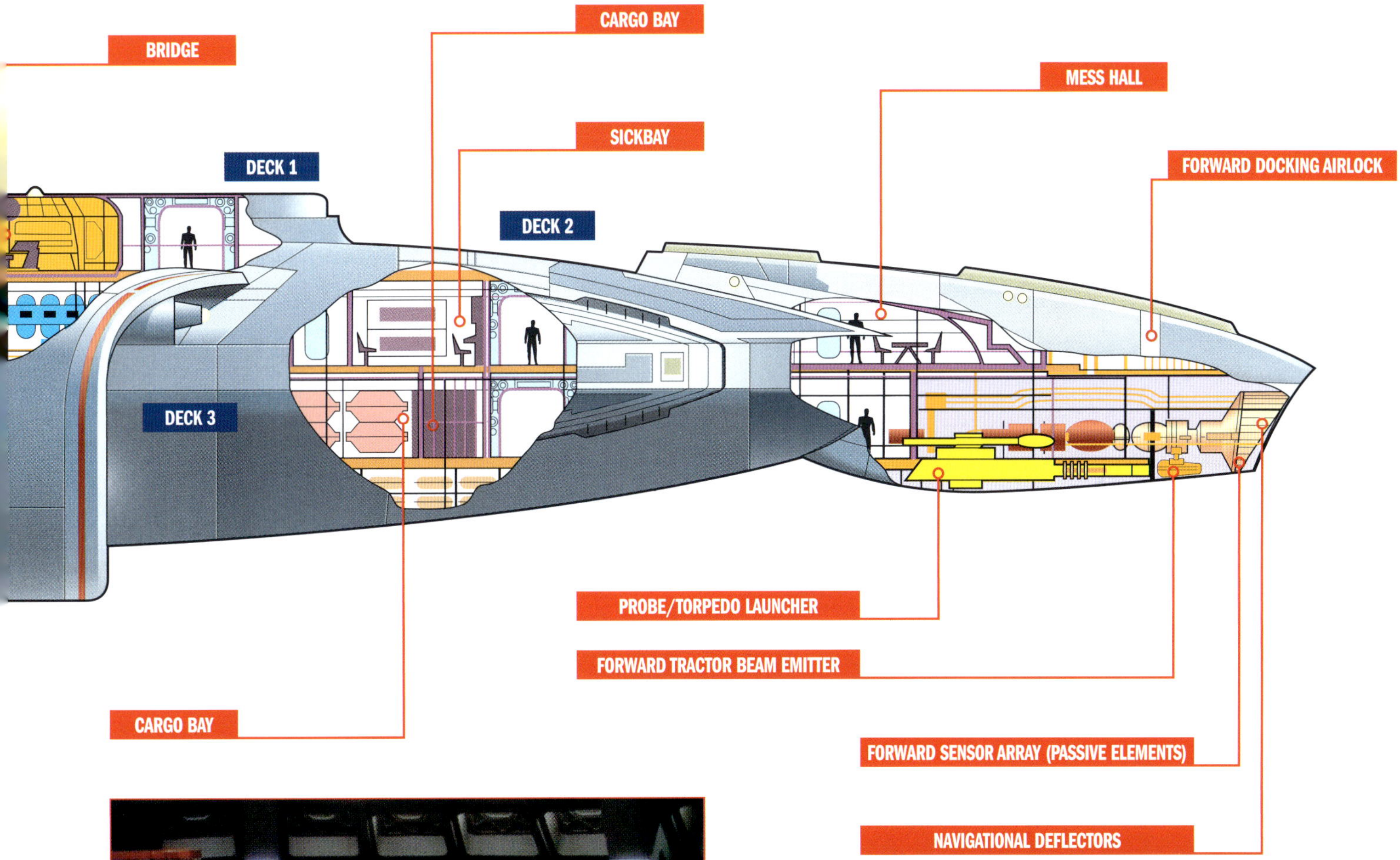

CARGO BAY

BRIDGE

MESS HALL

SICKBAY

FORWARD DOCKING AIRLOCK

DECK 1

DECK 2

DECK 3

PROBE/TORPEDO LAUNCHER

FORWARD TRACTOR BEAM EMITTER

CARGO BAY

FORWARD SENSOR ARRAY (PASSIVE ELEMENTS)

NAVIGATIONAL DEFLECTORS

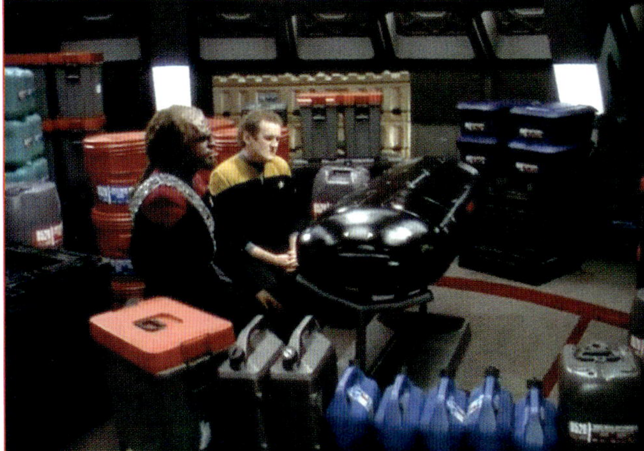

Small cargo bays were designed for storing supplies rather than carrying freight, their initial purpose being for short hit-and-run missions. The cargo bays were on deck 3, along with a cargo transporter.

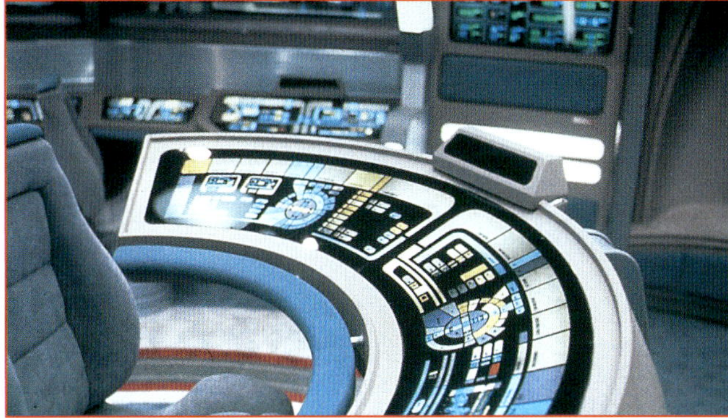

The *Defiant* had a combined conn and navigation station at the front of the bridge that was operated by a single pilot. When the ship was first assigned to Deep Space 9 this role was most often fulfilled by Jadzia Dax.

WEAPONS AND DEFENSE SYSTEMS

The *U.S.S. Defiant* NX-74205 incorporated many technological innovations, but its most remarkable features were its attack and defense systems.

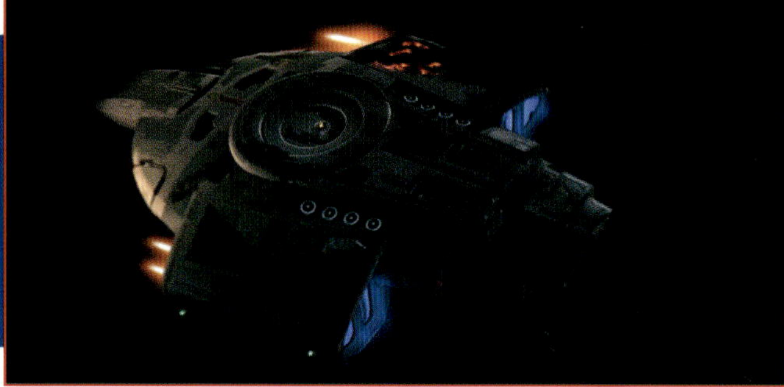

Four pulse phaser cannons were fitted at the front of the ship.

PULSE PHASER CANNONS

The *U.S.S. Defiant* carried this new type of phaser weapon. Developed at Starfleet's Tokyo R&D facility, it harnessed the power of artificially grown emitter crystals with a delivery system that allowed rapid phaser discharge. The effect was short, concentrated pulses capable of inflicting more damage than a standard phaser.

TORPEDO LAUNCHERS

The *Defiant* was equipped with several torpedo launchers at the front and rear of the vessel. The ship carried both the tried-and-tested photon torpedoes, which had an explosive yield of approximately 18.5 isotons, and the newer, next-generation quantum torpedoes, which had a much greater potential yield of 52.3 isotons.

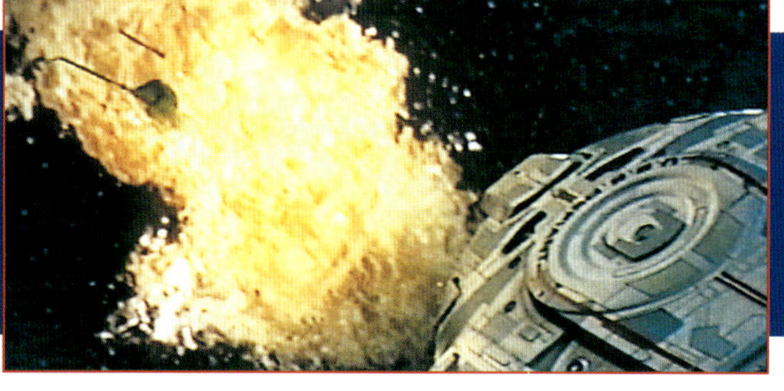

The effects of photon and quantum torpedoes were devastating.

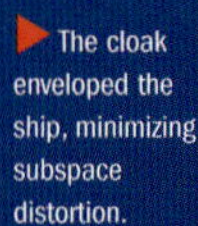

The cloak enveloped the ship, minimizing subspace distortion.

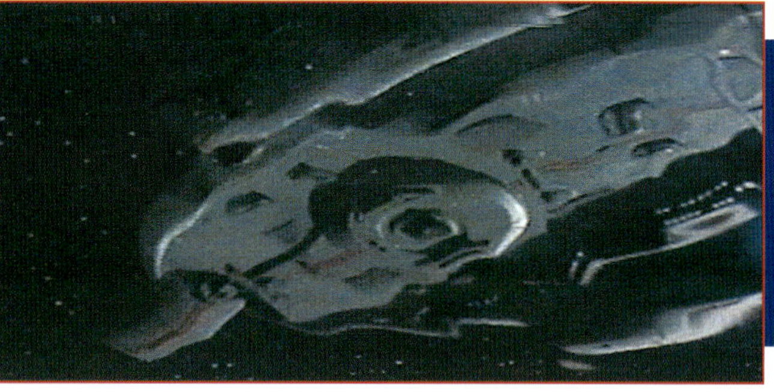

CLOAKING DEVICE

The Romulans loaned a cloaking device to the *Defiant* in exchange for intelligence Starfleet had on the Dominion. But the device could be penetrated by types of anti-proton beams that the *Defiant* was vulnerable to, because of its high power signature. However, it worked well enough to provide a major tactical advantage over Jem'Hadar ships.

ABLATIVE ARMOR

The *Defiant's* outer body was coated with ablative-armor hull plating, a top-secret technology – even Starfleet Operations had not heard of it until 2372. Ablative armor provided an extra layer of defense against enemy fire if the shields failed. It formed a protective layer over the hull surface, helping disperse large amounts of incoming phaser blasts.

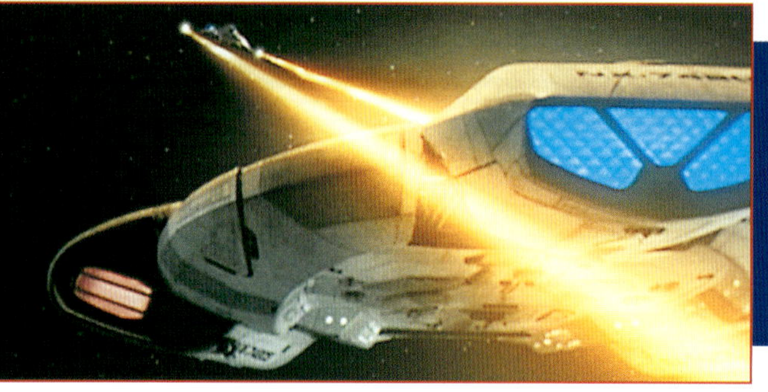

Ablative armor dissipated phaser fire, minimizing the damage to the ship.

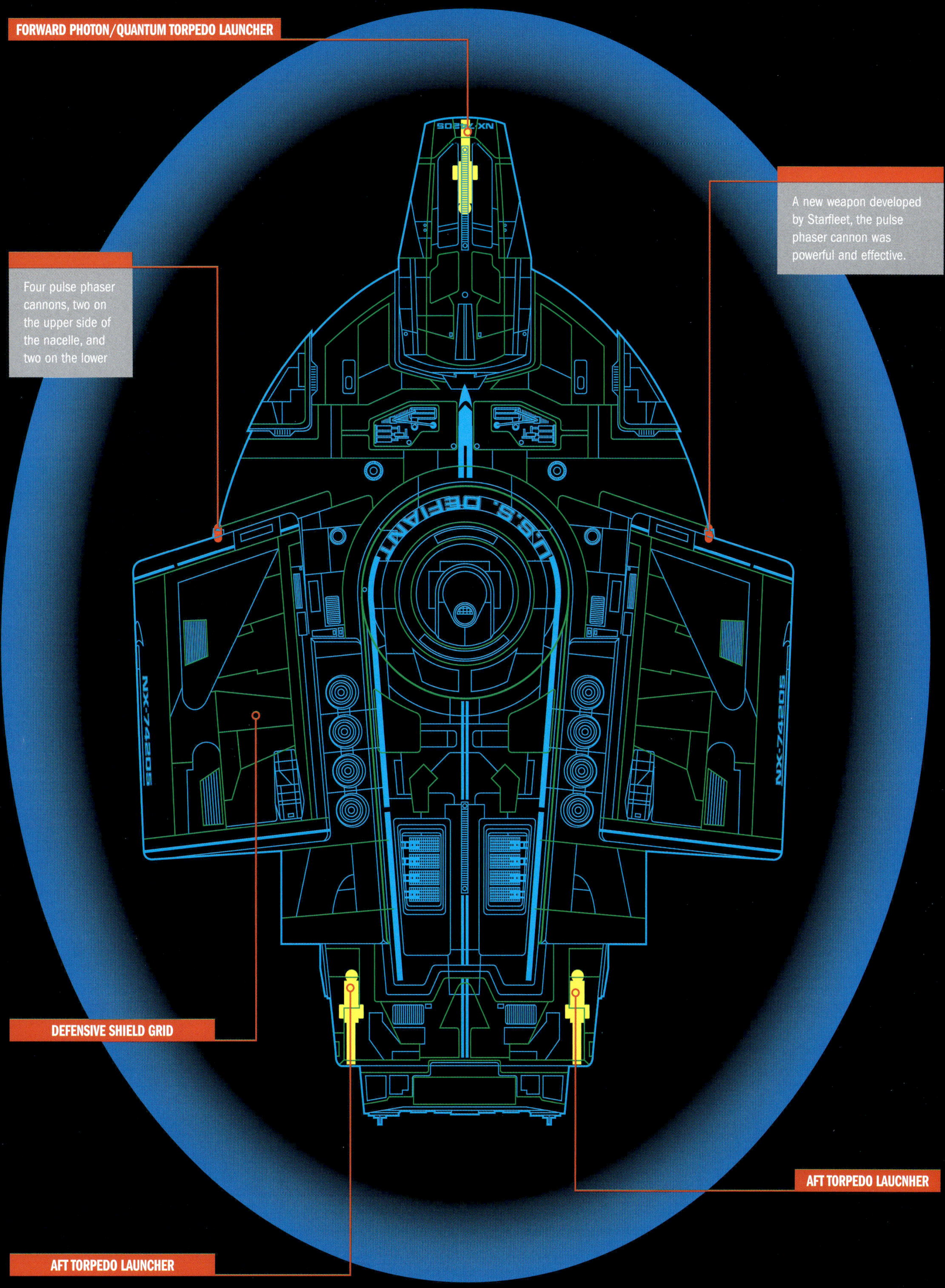

FORWARD PHOTON/QUANTUM TORPEDO LAUNCHER
A new weapon developed by Starfleet, the pulse phaser cannon was powerful and effective.
Four pulse phaser cannons, two on the upper side of the nacelle, and two on the lower
NX-74205
U.S.S. DEFIANT
NX-74205
NX-74205
DEFENSIVE SHIELD GRID
AFT TORPEDO LAUCNHER
AFT TORPEDO LAUNCHER

MAIN BRIDGE

The bridge of the *Defiant* NX-74205 was small by Starfleet standards, but it still accommodated all the stations usually found on larger vessels.

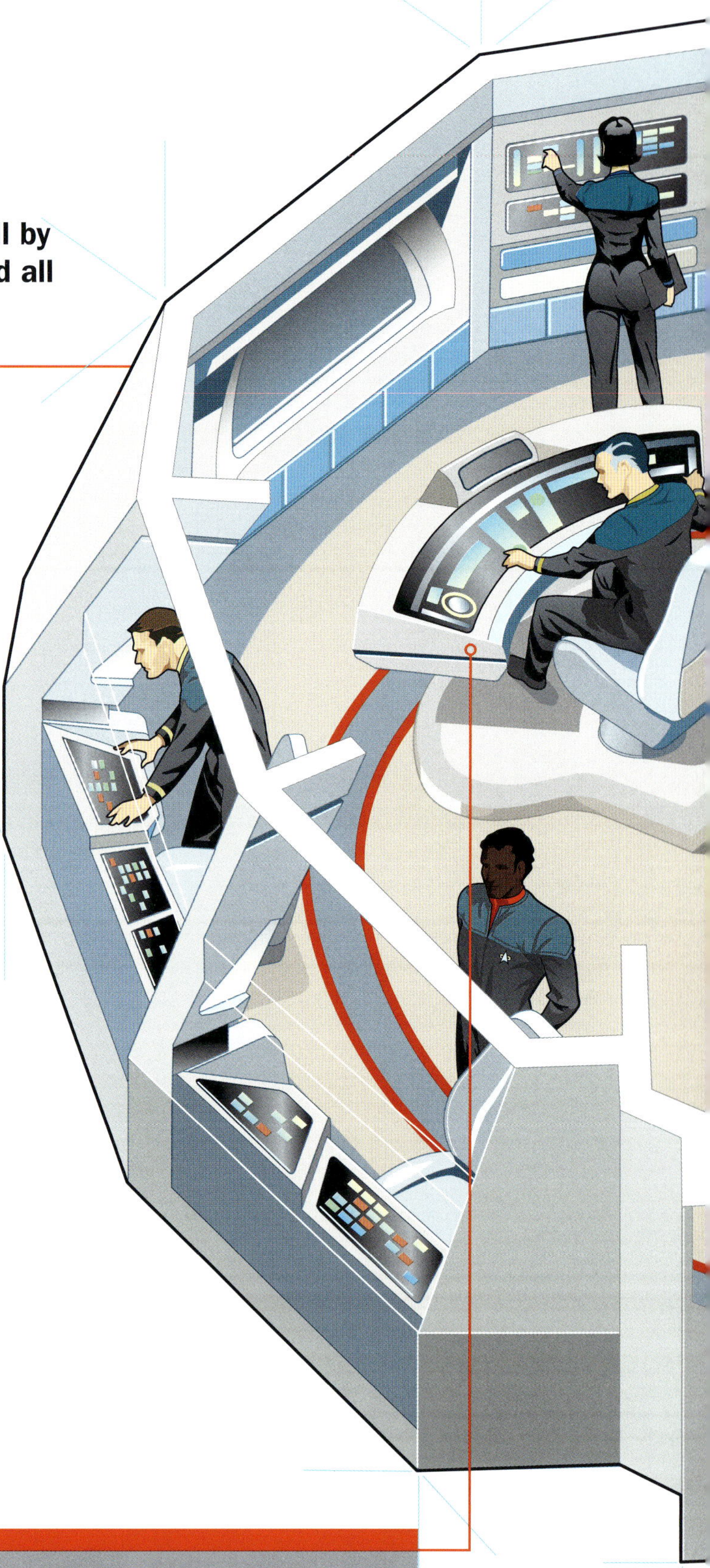

The layout of the bridge on this warship was compact, but included the familiar engineering, tactical, science, conn, and ops areas. At the forward end of the bridge, the main viewscreen was in the commander's line of vision. A merged conn and ops station sat between the command chair and the main viewer, while two tactical stations – tactical 1 (starboard) and tactical 2 (port) lined the perimeter of the bridge. Both tactical stations controlled the ship's fearsome advanced weapons, cloaking device and shield, and tractor beam operations. The engineering station monitored and controlled all engineering activities on deck. The other main station on the bridge was the science console. It was adapted to provide maximum aid in reconnaissance and combat maneuvers.

AFT STATIONS

The area behind the command chair featured a mission ops table that had computer access terminals recessed in each side. The table was used by the crew to analyze and plan military maneuvers and operations. On the bulkheads near the table, passive display panels reported data for mission ops (secondary mission activities), engineering, and environment.

On the wall behind the table, two sliding doors provided egress to other parts of the ship. The port door led to the transporter room, while the starboard door provided the most direct route to the crew's mess facilities.

Emergency medical supplies were kept near the port access door. A replicator in the aft provided crew on duty with food and drink.

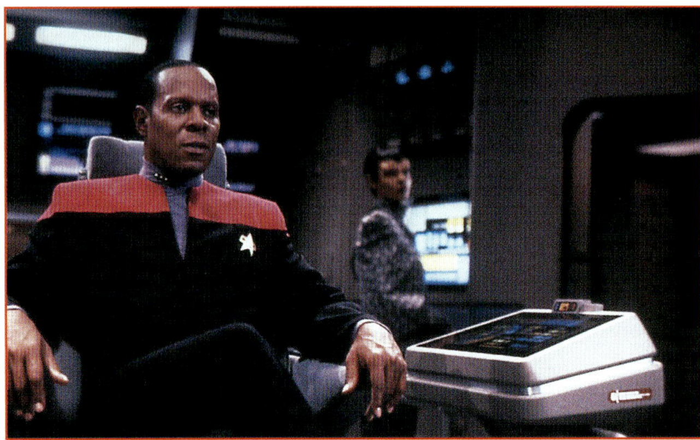

The *Defiant* was very much Sisko's ship. He had been involved in designing it and was the first officer to take command after he brought it into active service.

Conn and ops were combined into a single station. When in friendly space, both operated automatically. In emergencies, the officer at this station had to be able to fly the ship manually, and coordinate with engineering to make sure power was available and allocated where needed. The control panel was touch- and voice-activated.

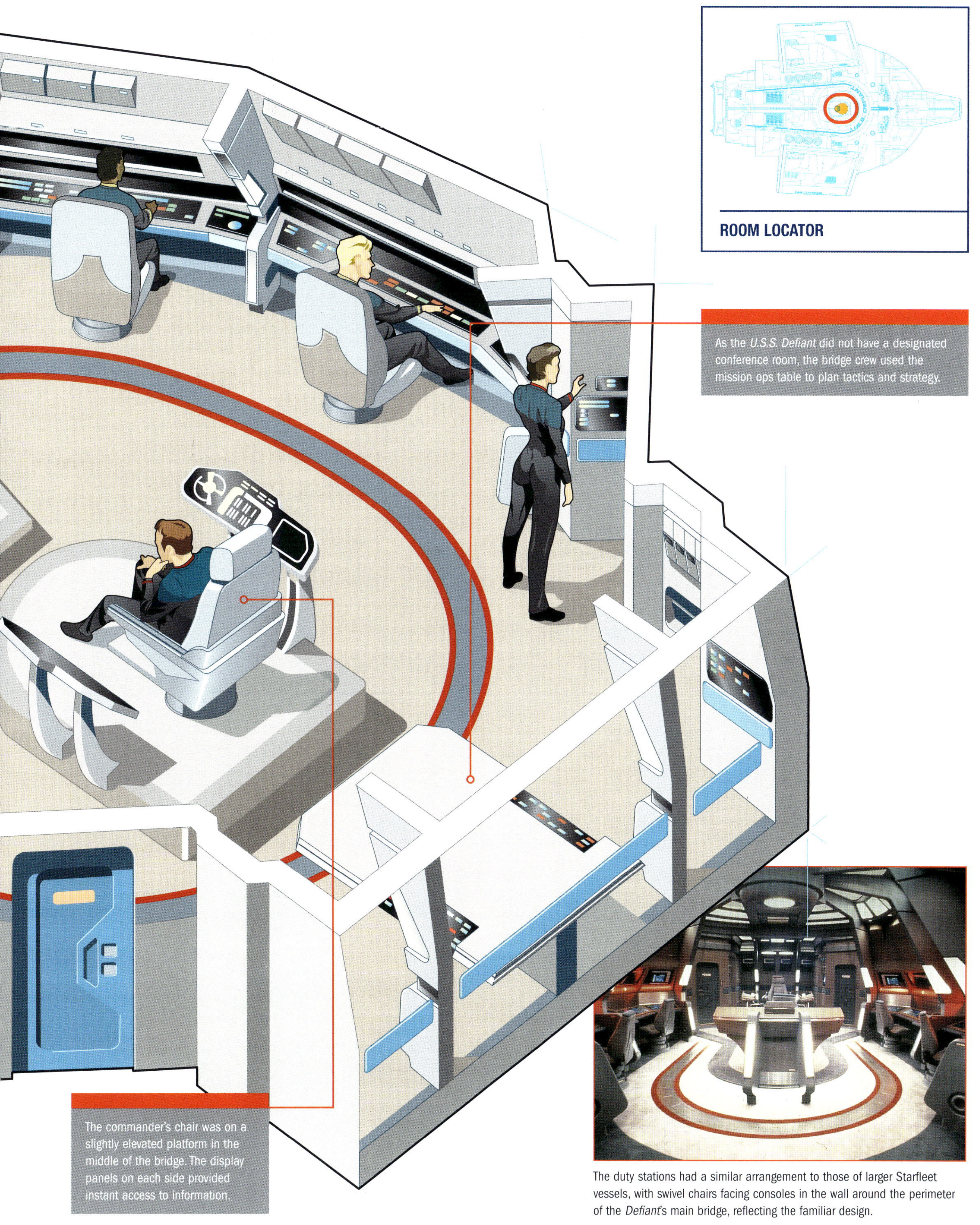

As the *U.S.S. Defiant* did not have a designated conference room, the bridge crew used the mission ops table to plan tactics and strategy.

The commander's chair was on a slightly elevated platform in the middle of the bridge. The display panels on each side provided instant access to information.

The duty stations had a similar arrangement to those of larger Starfleet vessels, with swivel chairs facing consoles in the wall around the perimeter of the *Defiant*'s main bridge, reflecting the familiar design.

HOLOGRAPHIC SYSTEMS

The development of sophisticated holographic technologies heralded the use of three-dimensional communications systems. The *Defiant* played an early role in their development.

One of the most vital areas of technological development for space-traveling species was that of communication. The United Federation of Planets would not have been able to function without its extensive subspace communications network that allowed member species, Starfleet, and civilian vessels to keep in constant touch with each other, and exchange data and information.

The majority of species throughout the Galaxy utilized some variation on this system, and tended to employ two-dimensional viewing screens with a broadcast and reception ability for both sound and vision. But, despite the significant advances in holotechnology since the mid-2360s, the availability of holographic three-dimensional communications remained limited.

Starfleet had made wide use of holographic communications systems in the 2250s, when ships such as the *U.S.S. Europa* and *U.S.S. Shenzhou* were fitted with them as a matter of course. However, the holographic transmissions were found to interfere with other ships' systems and, as a result, Captain Pike had them ripped out of the *Constitution*-class *U.S.S. Enterprise.* Other captains soon followed his example, and for more than 100 years Starfleet regarded them as an unnecessary luxury that wasn't worth the bother.

SIMPLE APPEARANCE

Recordable forms of holographic images were still one of the most widely used technologies within the United Federation of Planets for commercial, scientific, and personal use. Recordable three-dimensional technologies were widespread within holosuites and holodecks, and were an accepted and vital part of the 24th-century leisure market. Holographic displays were still used in science labs and even for computerized puzzles, while holographic cameras also had their enthusiasts.

TESTING ON DEEP SPACE 9

Starfleet revisited the idea of real-time holocommunication in 2373, when Chief Miles O'Brien fitted holographic projectors to the bridge of the *U.S.S. Defiant* during its assignment to Deep Space 9. This experimental system was installed for communication between Starfleet vessels without the issues that had been encountered a century before. It was tested by Captain Benjamin Sisko in a communication with Captain Sanders of the *U.S.S. Malinche*

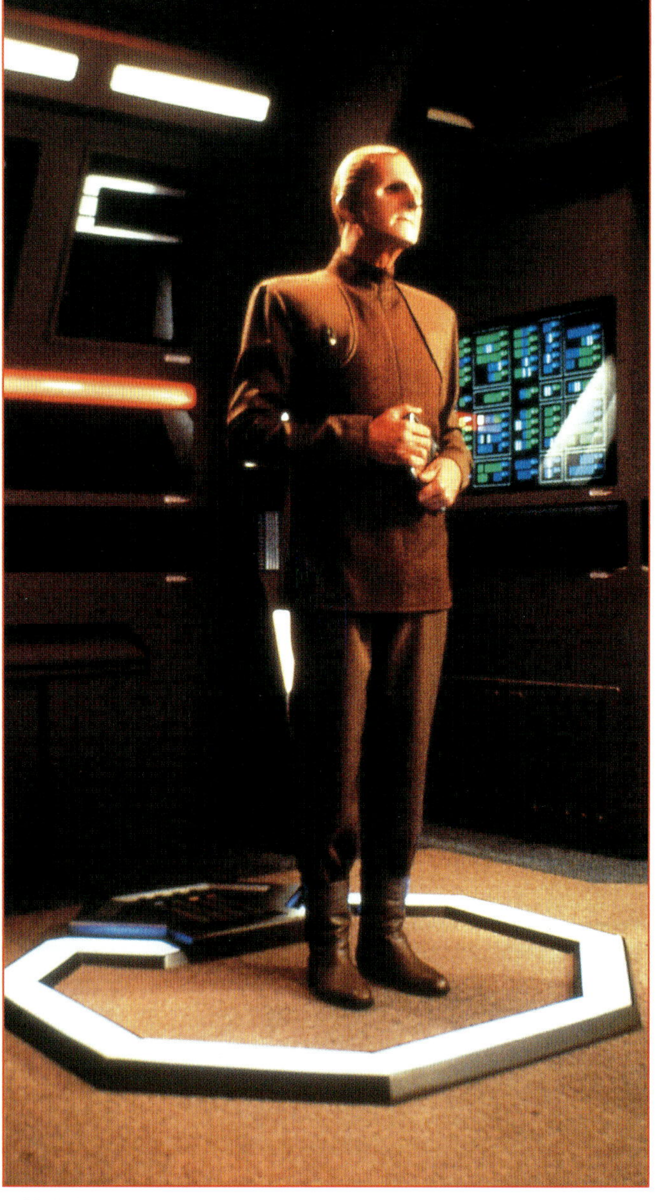

In 2373, Starfleet fitted the *Defiant* with a new model of holographic communicator that projected an image from a self-contained unit in the floor.

NCC-38997 on Stardate 50485.2, during the pursuit of the former Starfleet officer, Michael Eddington. Unlike many other starships, the *Defiant* did not have any built-in holographic systems – since it was designed as a warship, it had no need of holodecks. Instead of holoemitters being

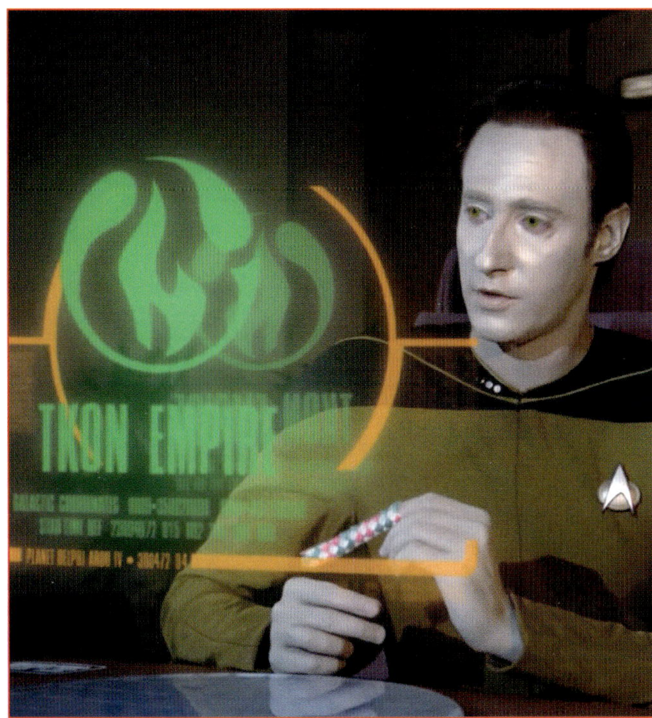

Holographic projectors were widespread in Starfleet but they were rarely used for real-time communications, which were not considered a priority.

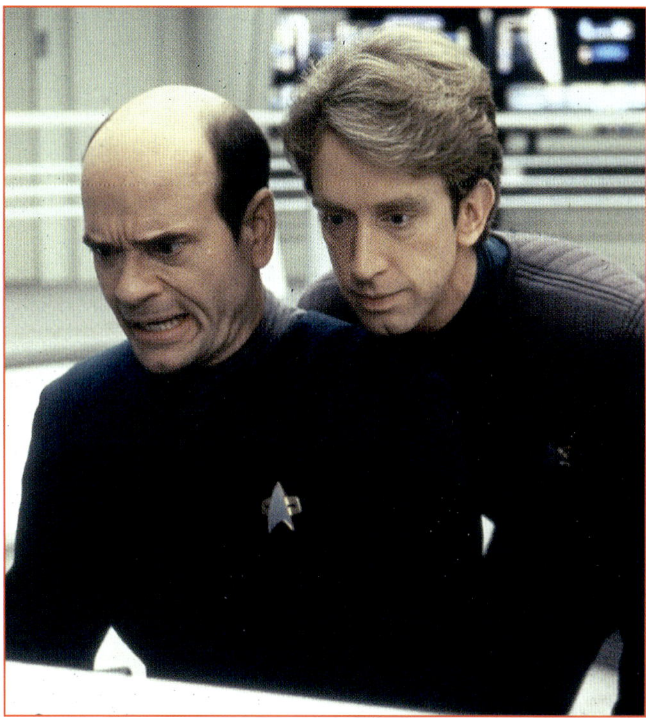
Other Starfleet vessels, such as the experimental *U.S.S. Prometheus*, were fitted with extensive holoemitters that could be used by emergency holograms.

fitted around the entire room, the holographic projection system was mounted on the floor directly behind the captain's chair at the rear of the *Defiant*'s bridge.

Communication was started by a verbal command from the captain, requesting a channel to be opened in exactly the same way that normal two-dimensional subspace communication would be initiated. Swiveling his chair to face the projection system, Sisko was then able to engage in audio communication with a life-sized representation of Captain Sanders, ensconced at the broadcast unit on board the *Malinche*.

The system was relatively simple, comprising a projection area defined by a series of light-gray strips connected in a geometric shape, around 1.5 meters across at its widest point. The rear of the unit had an integrated dark-gray plate connected to the framework, which glowed blue when communication commenced, and was accompanied by an elecronic sound. Captain Sanders' controls appeared to be wall-mounted, since he was manipulating an unseen system while standing and talking to Captain Sisko, whose projected image appeared sitting when viewed from the *Malinche*'s bridge.

In the 23rd-century, holographic projections had been slightly transparent, but by this point the technology projected a completely solid image. Sanders' appeared as if he were in the room, like any holographic character on a holodeck. The system only broadcast the image of the person who was speaking without any part of the environment they were in, so the *Defiant*'s floor was still visible. When the connection was broken, the image quickly disappeared and the electronic sound subsided as the projector unit on the floor deactivated. The two parties had little room for movement during their exchange, but the system was effective, if ultimately unnecessary.

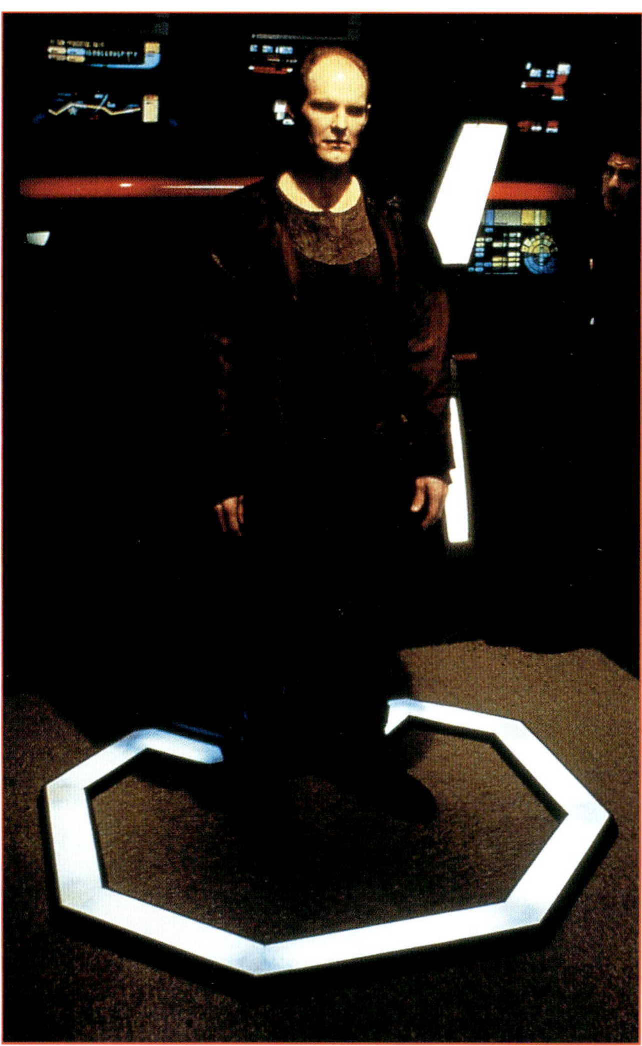
Michael Eddington appeared on the bridge of the *Defiant* after the Maquis acquired the necessary technology.

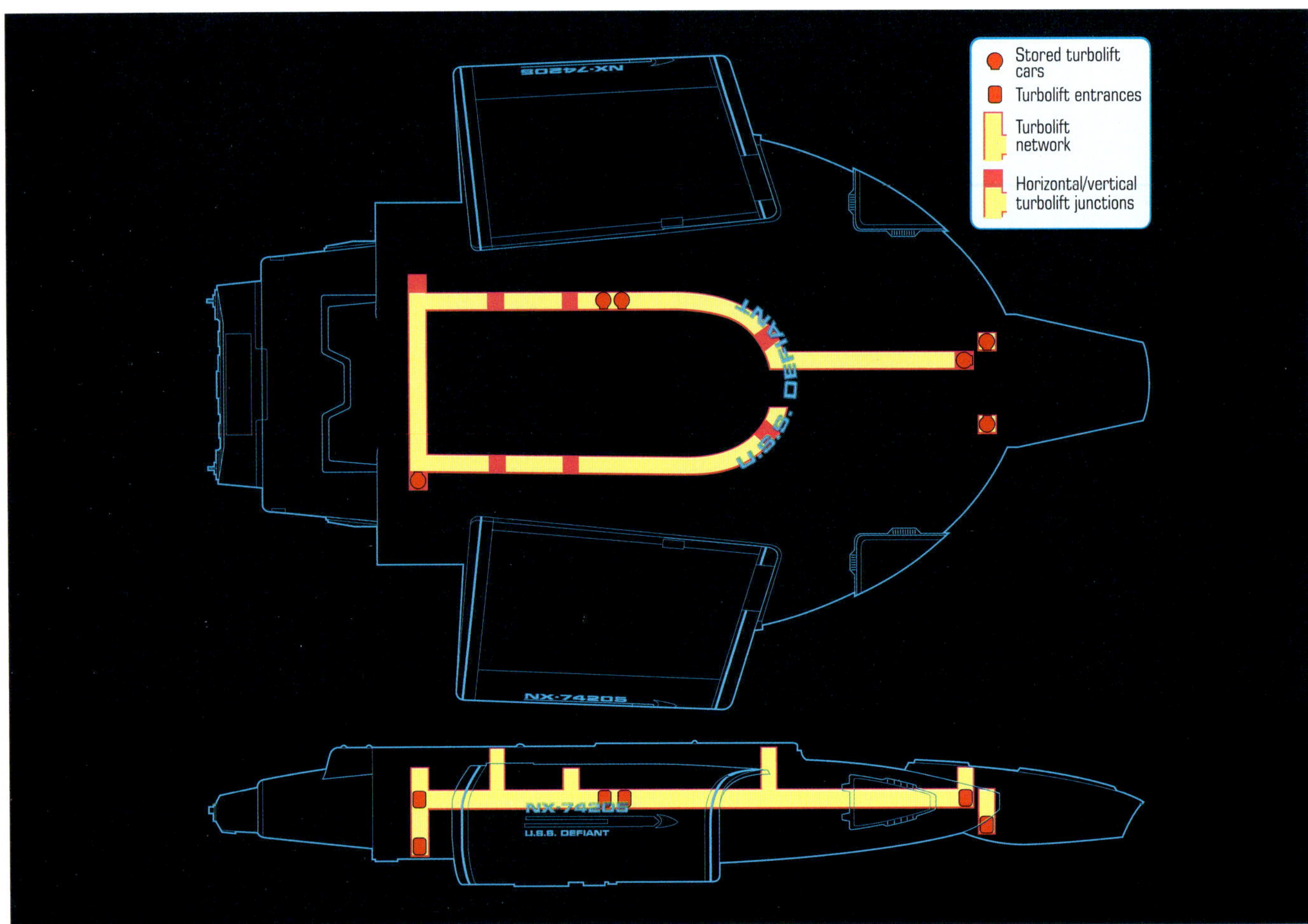

TRANSPORT SYSTEMS

An essential element of the *U.S.S. Defiant*, the extensive corridors and turbolift arteries made for fast travel between important locations on the vessel during intense battles and other emergencies.

In the heat of battle, ease of internal movement around a warship was vital. The bridge, main engineering, living quarters, sickbay, and galley facilities on the *Defiant* were all situated on the first two of the starship's four decks. Clustering major services eliminated the need for the elaborate, power-draining turbolift network often found on ships of other classes. Yet the *Defiant*'s extensive corridors and streamlined turbolift arteries were still critical – especially to technicians needing to access various system components installed throughout the vessel.

TURBOLIFT NETWORK

The cars moved horizontally and vertically, and the entire system was managed by computer to ensure they did not collide.This was a real risk, with numerous cars all running simultaneously at speed.

The *Defiant* units accommodated only two or three human adults comfortably, and the sides of the cars had safety handrails. The turbocars accepted voice commands as the car traveled to the specified terminal point. Inside the car, a graphic illustration displayed the ship's entire turbolift system, including the stops.

There were several vertical turbolift shafts along the length of the *Defiant*. Four shafts extended from deck 1 through the entire ship to deck 4, and decks 2 and 3 offered nine turbolift entry points. There was only one horizontal turboshaft, located on deck 3 – the longest deck. Virtually every turbolift journey on the ship flowed through deck 3.

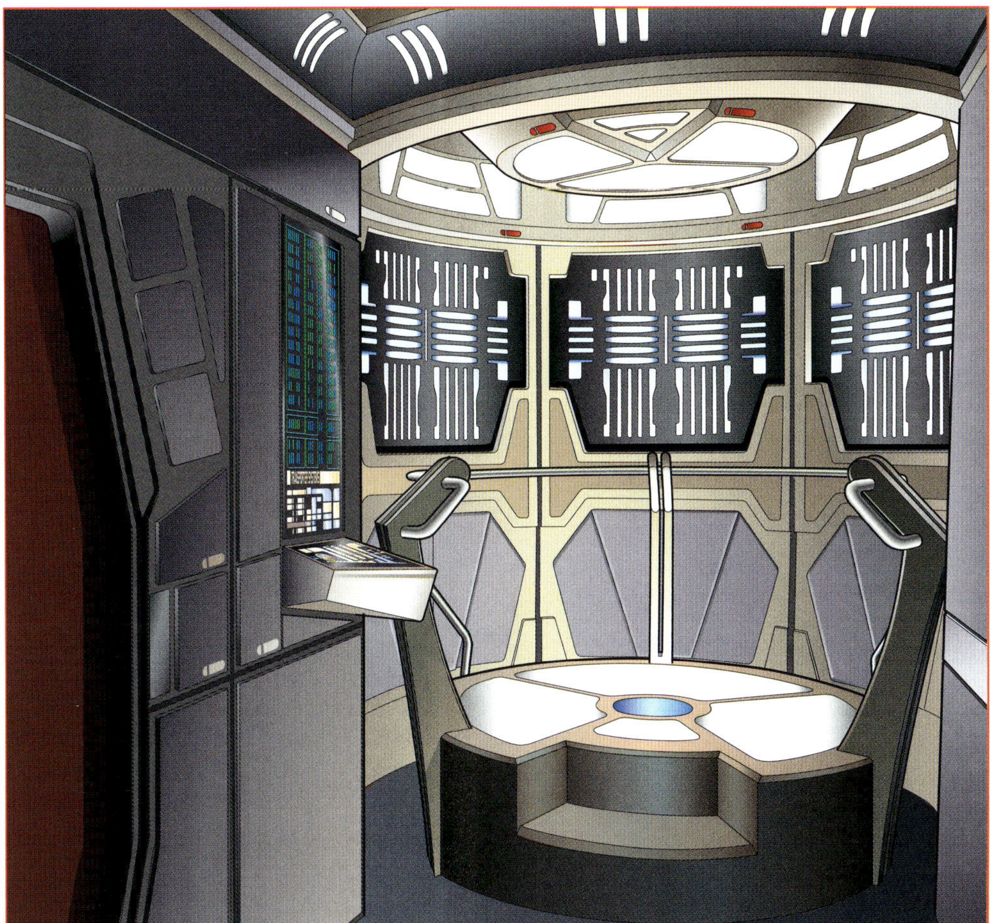

The *U.S.S. Defiant* had two small transporter rooms for personnel, and a third transporter for cargo.

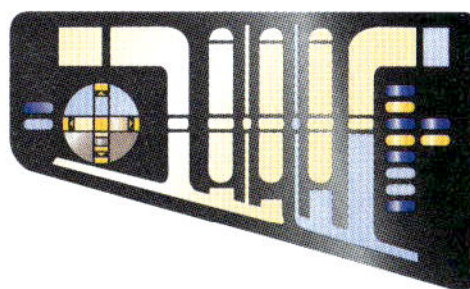

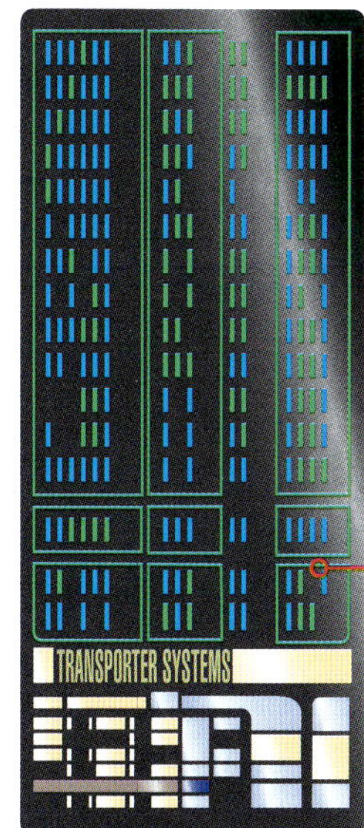

The *Defiant*'s transporters were operated from a touch-sensitive panel.

JEFFERIES TUBES

If power was needed elsewhere, or combat severed a power conduit, crewmembers could move around the ship using corridors, ladders, and, if need be, Jefferies tubes and crawlways. The latter were installed behind panels and between certain bulkheads. The main Jefferies tube, situated between the computer core and antimatter pods, vertically traversed the *Defiant*'s midpoint. It featured a simple metal ladder that accessed every deck onboard the ship; the bottom of the tube was accessed from the aft cargo bay, where the shuttlepods were docked.

Jefferies tubes were also installed beneath the horizontal decking. The horizontal crawlways were the sole points of entry to the portions of deck 4 that were reduced to half-height, near the *Defiant*'s nose, and within the nose itself.

TRANSPORTER ROOMS

The *Defiant* had two transporter rooms, one located between the bridge and main engineering on deck 1, and the other on deck 2, in the forward section on the starboard side. Site-to-site trips within the *Defiant* were difficult, given its size and power profile, but as long as safety protocols were observed, the transfers worked. A third transporter pad was situated on deck 3, but was designated as a cargo transporter that could not perform the enhanced, quantum-level scans and calculations needed to move a living being.

A panel on the rear wall of the turbolift car displayed the destinations to which it could travel.

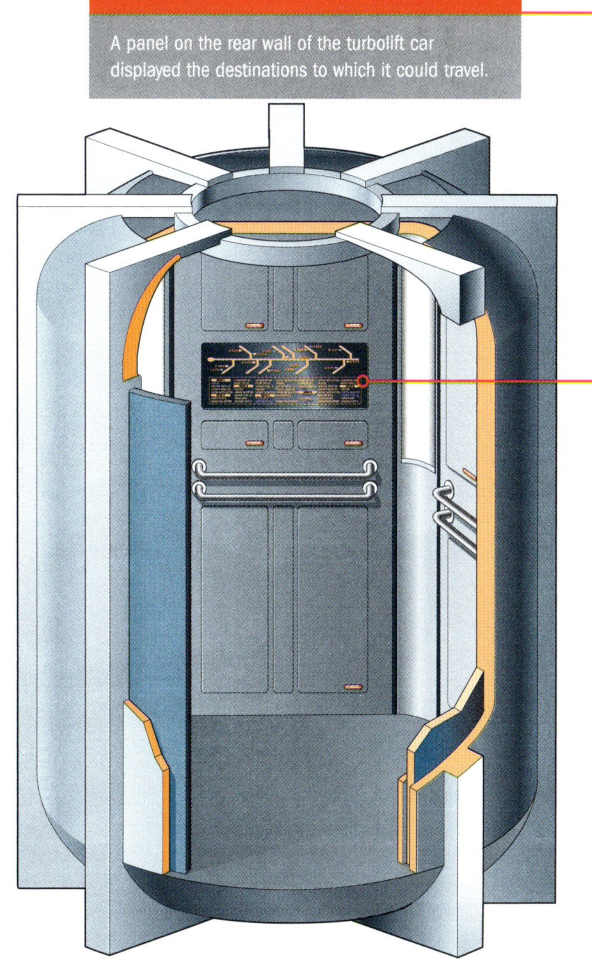

MAIN ENGINEERING

***Defiant* engineering provided all the power needed for this small but well-defended and -equipped warship to function at optimum level in all situatons.**

All of the components necessary to power and propel the *Defiant* were located in engineering, the section essential for channeling the huge power output into all areas of the ship. The warp core itself stood on a dais in the center of engineering and spanned all four decks. The core comprised a duranium reactor with a dilithium articulation frame, four lobed magnetic constriction segment columns, and matter and antimatter injectors.

Numerous workstations and display panels were installed around the walls, and these were monitored constantly by the engineering personnel. Some of the panels included the subsystem operational status 4077 display, the warp coil alignment 776 readout, and diagnostic screens for the RCS thruster quad assembly.

This section was usually crewed by Chief O'Brien and his select team, but all functions within engineering could be automated and controlled from the main bridge. However, in an emergency situation all bridge controls could be transferred to engineering.

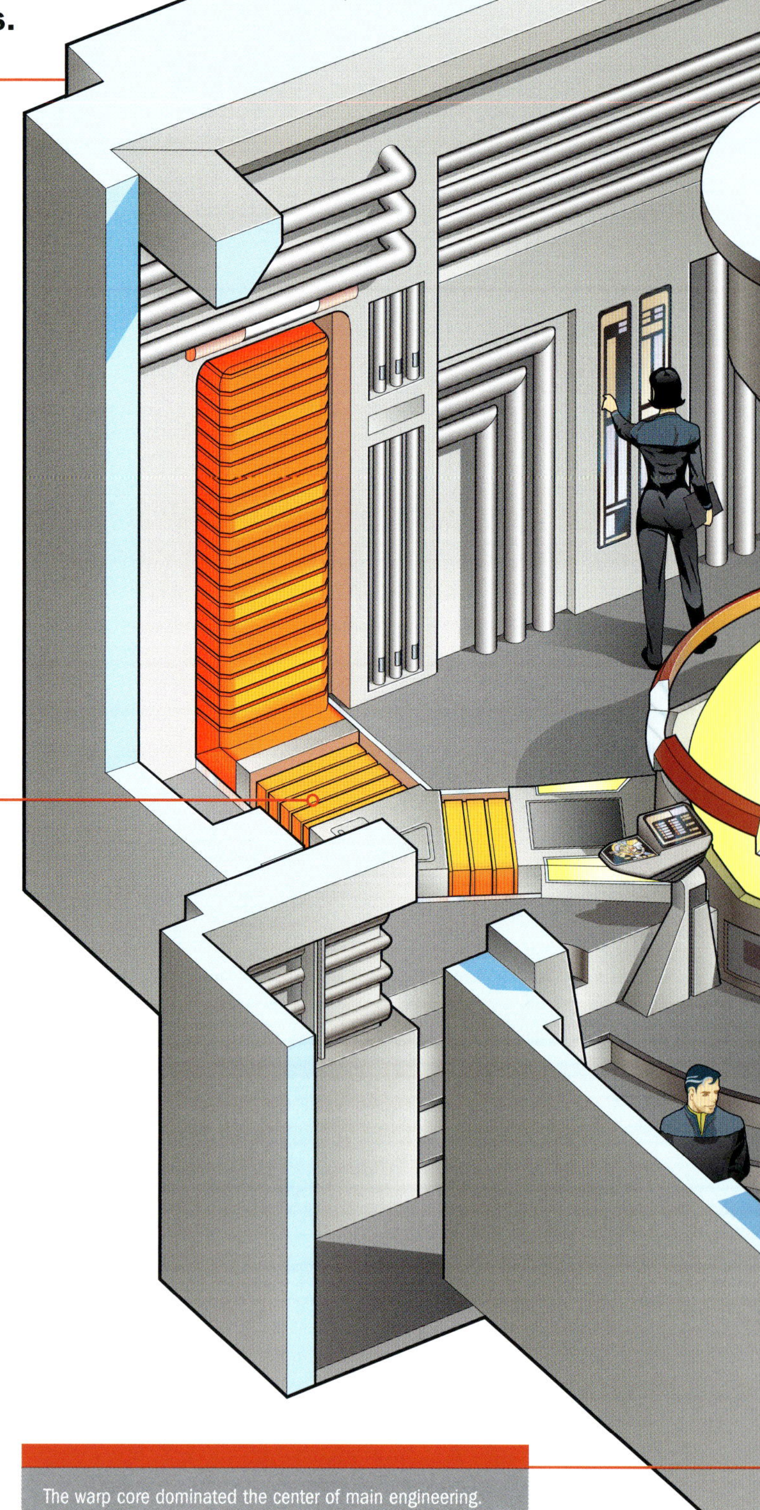

On each side of the warp core, a plasma conduit ran off toward the warp engines. The conduits glowed with a bright orange light.

The warp core dominated the center of main engineering.

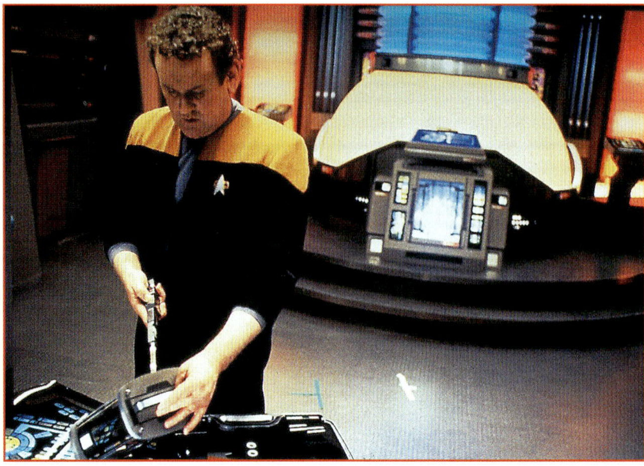

The engineers who worked onboard the *U.S.S. Defiant* were normally enlisted men and women who had not attended Starfleet Academy.

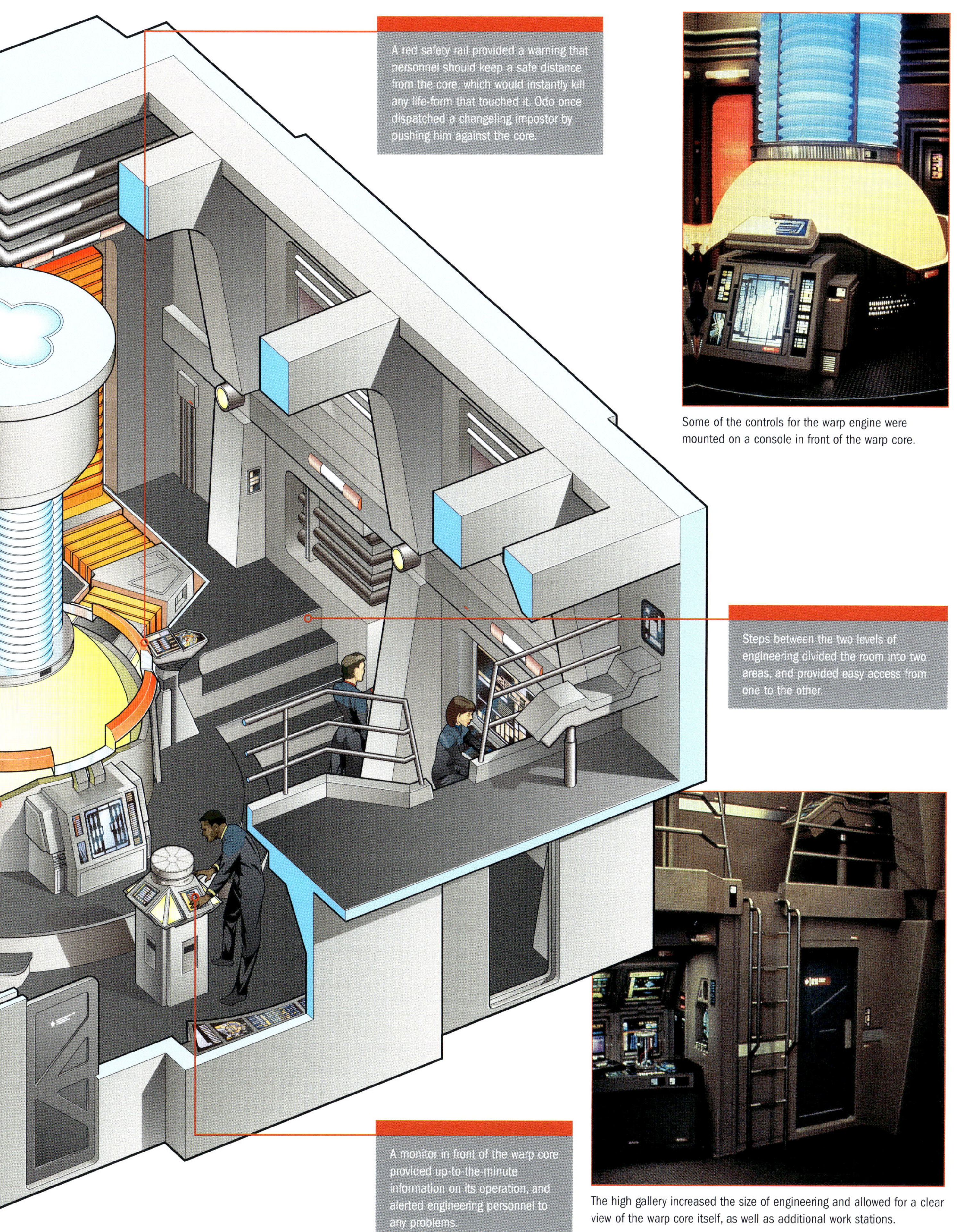

A red safety rail provided a warning that personnel should keep a safe distance from the core, which would instantly kill any life-form that touched it. Odo once dispatched a changeling impostor by pushing him against the core.

Some of the controls for the warp engine were mounted on a console in front of the warp core.

Steps between the two levels of engineering divided the room into two areas, and provided easy access from one to the other.

A monitor in front of the warp core provided up-to-the-minute information on its operation, and alerted engineering personnel to any problems.

The high gallery increased the size of engineering and allowed for a clear view of the warp core itself, as well as additional work stations.

CREW QUARTERS

There was no room for the luxuries of many Starfleet vessels onboard the *Defiant*. Designed for times of war, the crew quarters were comparatively basic but efficient.

Designed as the prototype for a fleet of Federation battleships, the *U.S.S. Defiant* NX-74205 stood as a model of efficiency. All the vital functions and systems of a much larger class of vessel were packed into its four decks, but because of space limitations, many of the facilities necessary for a sustained mission were downsized.

LOCATION

Crew quarters were located on decks 1 and 2. The senior command staff's quarters were close to the bridge on deck 1. Arranged in a semicircle around the forward command area, these cabins could house up to 20 personnel, and were located within easy reach of turbolifts connecting to the rest of the ship. In case of emergency, there were two escape pods situated in the main corridor that connected the accommodation, enabling a swift evacuation of the crew from duty stations, as well as from their quarters.

Deck 2 had more crew quarters at a variety of locations, again connected by a series of access corridors. Two sets of cabins lay on either side of the computer core, toward the center of the ship, while the majority of the accommodations ran from port to starboard close to the infirmary, science laboratories, and mess hall. Unlike on other Starfleet vessels, most of the *Defiant*'s individual quarters did not include their own toilet or bathing facilities, so there were a number of self-contained bathrooms adjacent to the individual sleeping areas. The *Defiant*'s small size meant that personnel were never more than a few minutes from their duty stations, allowing an extremely fast response time when a red alert was called.

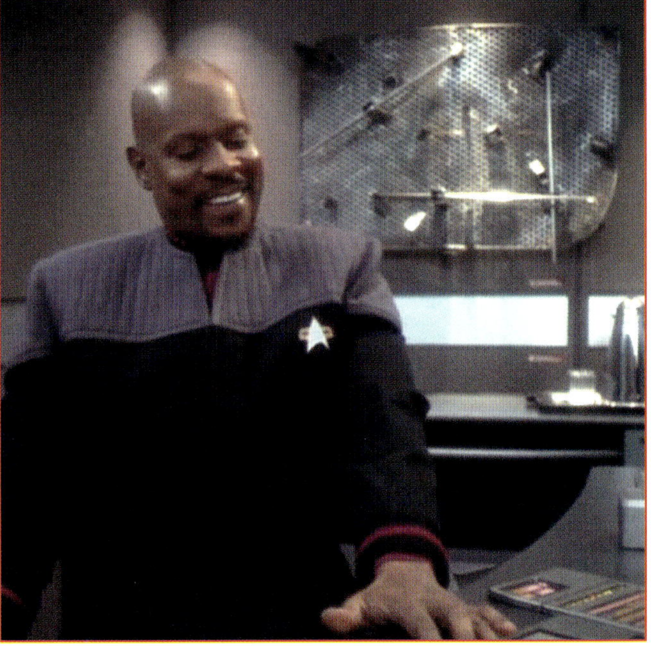
Captain Sisko had exactly the same kind of quarters with twin bunk beds as the rest of the crew, but he did also have a ready room.

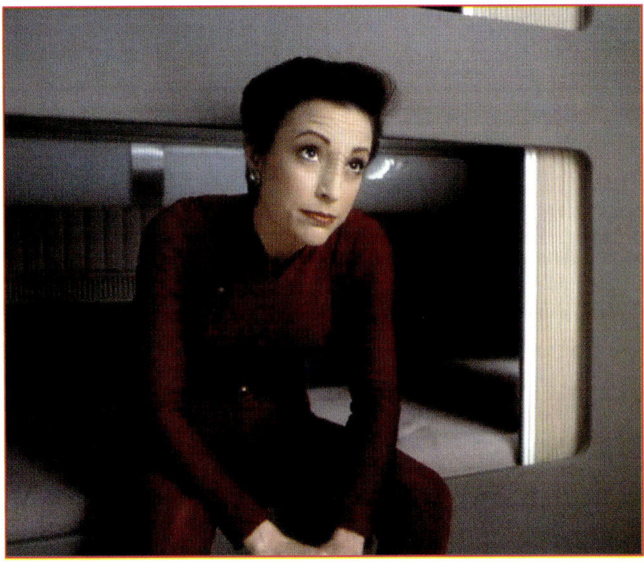
The crew slept on recessed bunk beds that were comfortable but only slightly larger than a typical humanoid.

CRAMPED CONDITIONS

Entered and exited through a single sliding door, the accommodations were basically rectangular in shape, around 3 meters in length and 2.5 meters wide. Some of the quarters were L-shaped, and furnished with a low desk and chair, forming a small personal workstation. Even with the open rectangular configuration, there was not a great deal of room for the occupants, although some storage was available for personal effects and clean uniforms within bulkhead drawers set into the wall. Seating came in the form of a low-backed chair, or even a stool.

All of the sleeping facilities were bunk beds, meaning that the majority of the crew had to share their quarters with a colleague. Lower ranks might well have experienced similar sleeping arrangements on other ships. The higher ranks might have been given a room to themselves, although accommodations would have to be shared if a larger crew complement was required, or other personnel were rescued and taken aboard.

REPLICATOR

One of the most significant differences between quarters was in the level of ancillary equipment installed within the accommodations. The *Defiant* was equipped with a small mess hall; the crew could assemble there to eat when off duty, but some quarters also had their own replicator installed. The quality of the food from these systems was variable, as a number of the *Defiant*'s systems did not attract the same amount of development as others, but the minimal requirements for nutrition were met. Command quarters featured a larger workstation situated to the side of the bunks, consisting of a small operating console and a larger touch sensitive display panel directly above it, allowing the captain to work when away from the bridge.

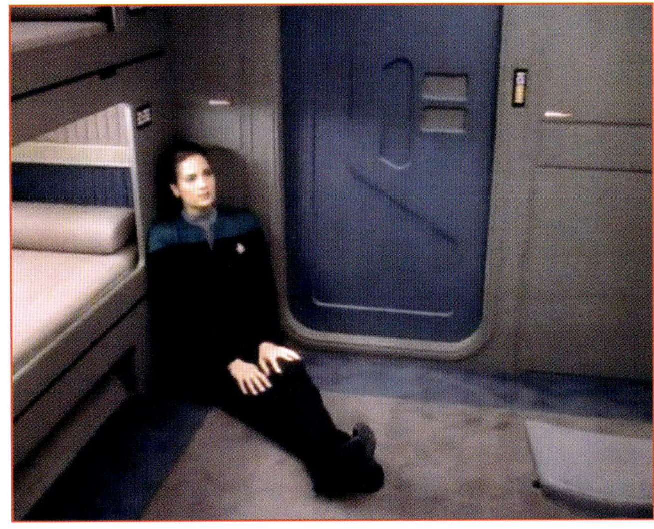

With only a single seat provided in addition to the bunks, the quarters on board the *U.S.S. Defiant* were not very conducive to social activities between personnel.

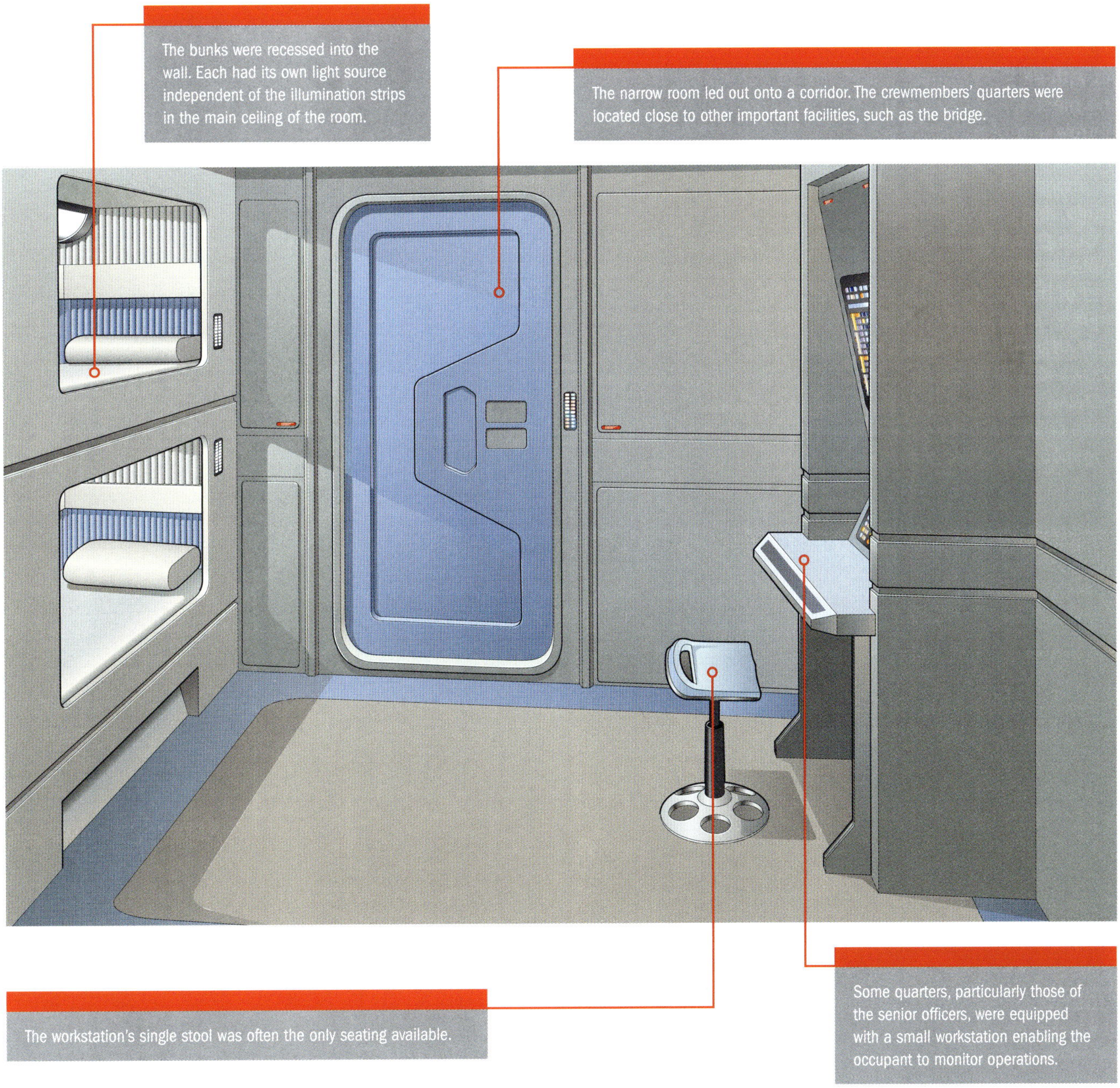

The bunks were recessed into the wall. Each had its own light source independent of the illumination strips in the main ceiling of the room.

The narrow room led out onto a corridor. The crewmembers' quarters were located close to other important facilities, such as the bridge.

The workstation's single stool was often the only seating available.

Some quarters, particularly those of the senior officers, were equipped with a small workstation enabling the occupant to monitor operations.

MESS HALL

The *Defiant*'s mess hall was not just a place for sustenance, but a space where the crew could take a break from their duties.

The *U.S.S. Defiant* NX-74205 was built from the ground up to be a pure fighting ship, and its only informal area was the mess hall. This space performed an important function above and beyond the essential supply of food and beverages, because it encouraged a strong sense of unity among the crew.

MEALS AND MEETINGS

As with all the equipment and fittings aboard the *Defiant*, the mess hall was spartan and tightly designed. At the narrow end of the room were three open hatches that served as dispensers for the replicators. A counter extended from underneath the replicators for placing trays, mugs, and eating utensils.

Dining facilities inside the mess hall consisted of four metallic tables arranged in a semicircle at the wider convex end of the room. These tables were approximately a meter square, and each had four integrated stools.

In addition, the mess hall doubled as a makeshift but convenient meeting area for conducting crew briefings and mission profiles. A tall interactive screen on one of the walls could be used as a visual aid for displaying tactical graphics and other vital communications.

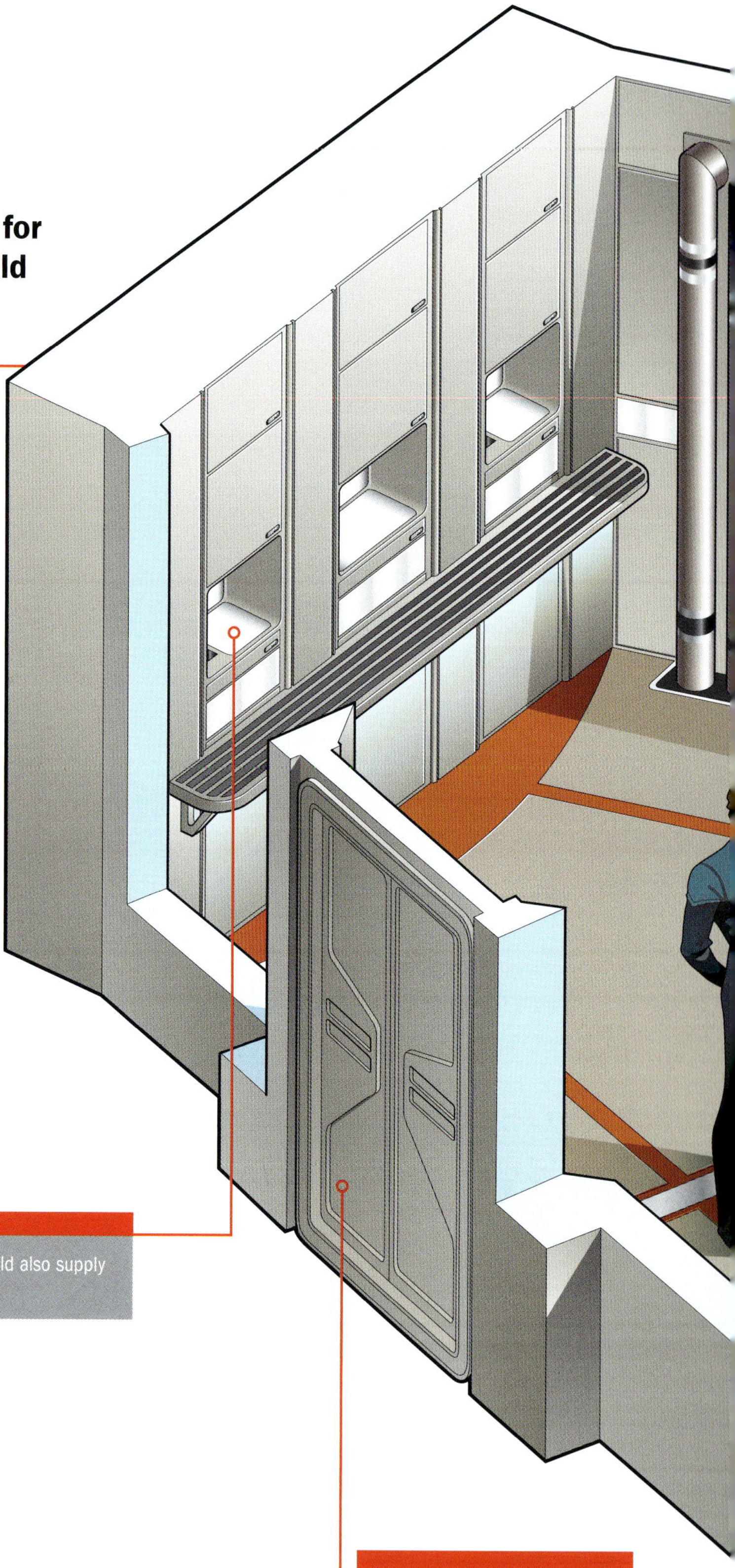

Food and beverages were dispensed from three replicators in the wall. These units could also supply regular Starfleet rations if replicator power went offline.

Two sets of doors provided access to the mess hall. In an emergency, such as a hull breach, fire, or an enemy attack, the doors could be automatically sealed.

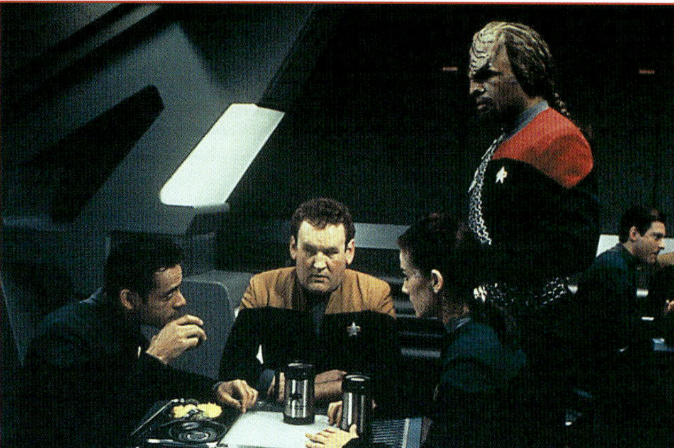

As a combat vessel, the *Defiant* drove its crew hard, but the mess hall provided a place where they could all relax and socialize.

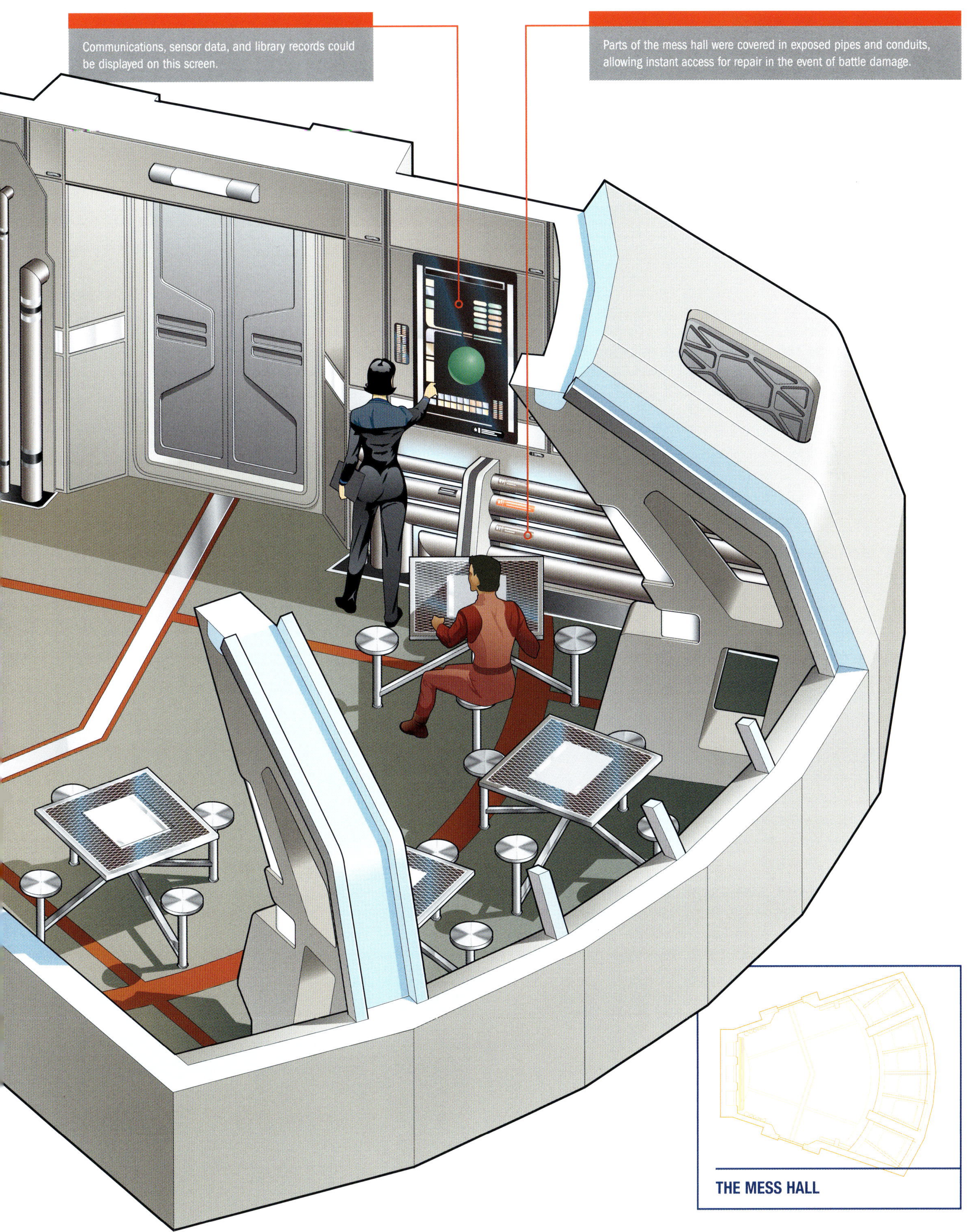
Communications, sensor data, and library records could be displayed on this screen.
Parts of the mess hall were covered in exposed pipes and conduits, allowing instant access for repair in the event of battle damage.
THE MESS HALL

THE SICKBAY

Situated on deck 2, the sickbay was mainly intended for stabilizing patients before they were transferred to a larger facility.

Medical facilities on the *Defiant* did not match the sophisticated offensive capabilities that made it such a formidable fighting ship. Initial specifications provided nothing more than a very basic field hospital, which was not equipped to handle a large number of casualties. For its first mission in 2371, chief medical officer Dr. Julian Bashir had to import many of his files from Deep Space 9 to make the facilities more serviceable. It was not until the *Defiant* was regularly used in the war against the Dominion that extensions were added to the original sickbay.

THE EQUIPMENT

For medical diagnosis and analysis, a dedicated workstation was fitted on one side of the facility, and a communications point allowed the resident physician to talk to the rest of the crew.

Three biobeds, which could be increased to a total of six within the confines of sickbay, were installed against three walls of the facility. A limited surgical suite was also available. The primary biobed by the large console had several additional medical readouts, giving a large amount of data to the physician in attendance. A number of portable units were kept in the facility, and could be quickly wheeled into place when required. Specialist treatment equipment and scanners were stored inside the units, and there was at least one cabinet containing emergency prescriptions and drugs.

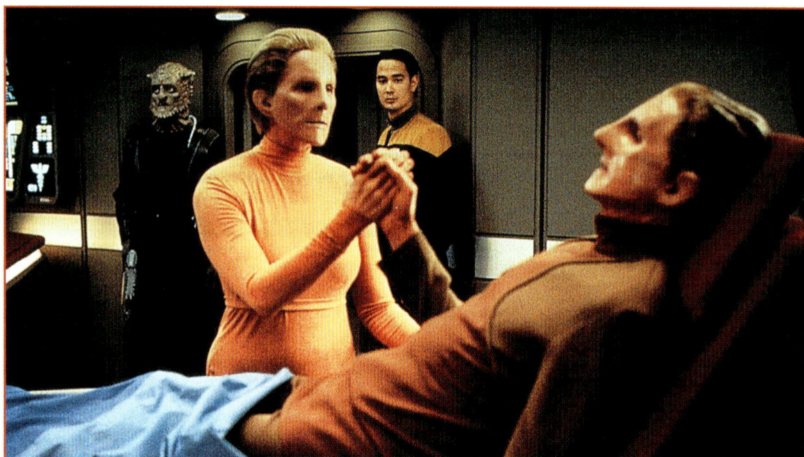

The sickbay aboard the *U.S.S. Defiant* was set up only as a field hospital to treat the wounded in combat situations. It was ill-equipped to treat illnesses such as the one that affected Odo in 2372.

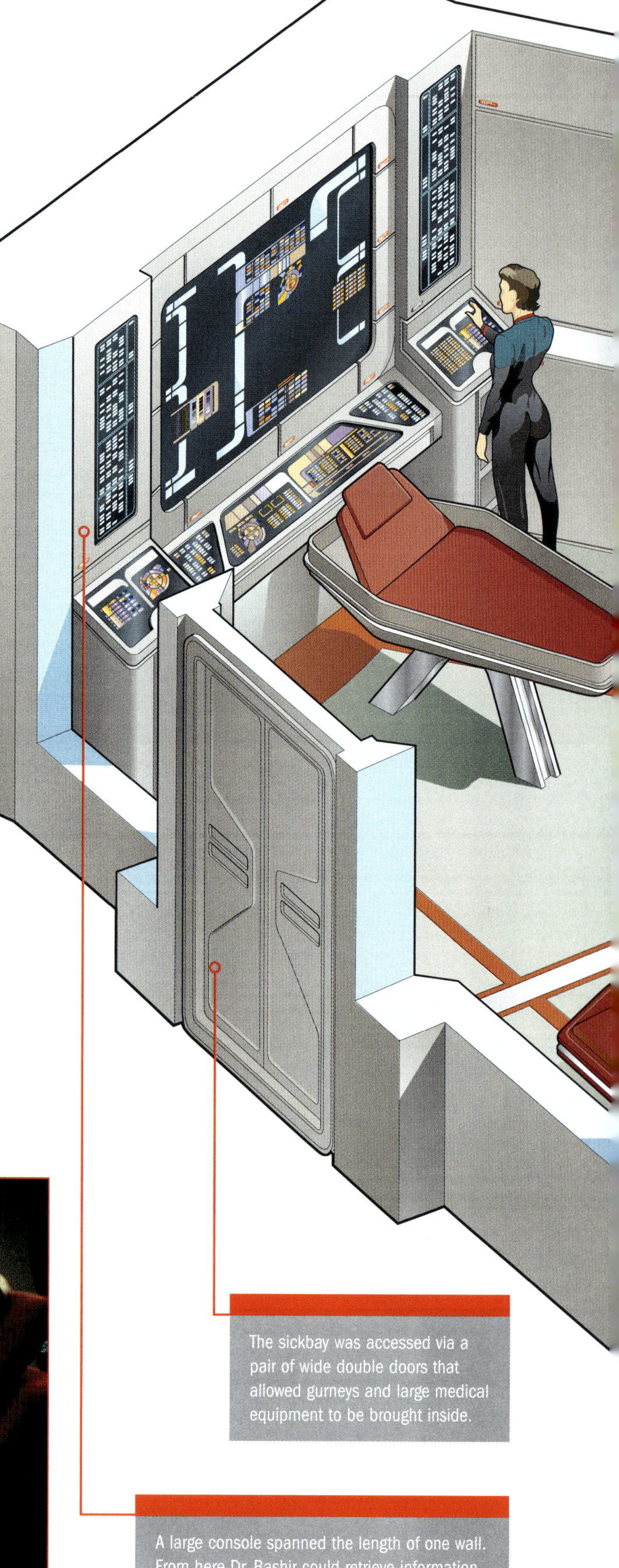

The sickbay was accessed via a pair of wide double doors that allowed gurneys and large medical equipment to be brought inside.

A large console spanned the length of one wall. From here Dr. Bashir could retrieve information from his medical database, analyze sensor findings, and communicate with the bridge.

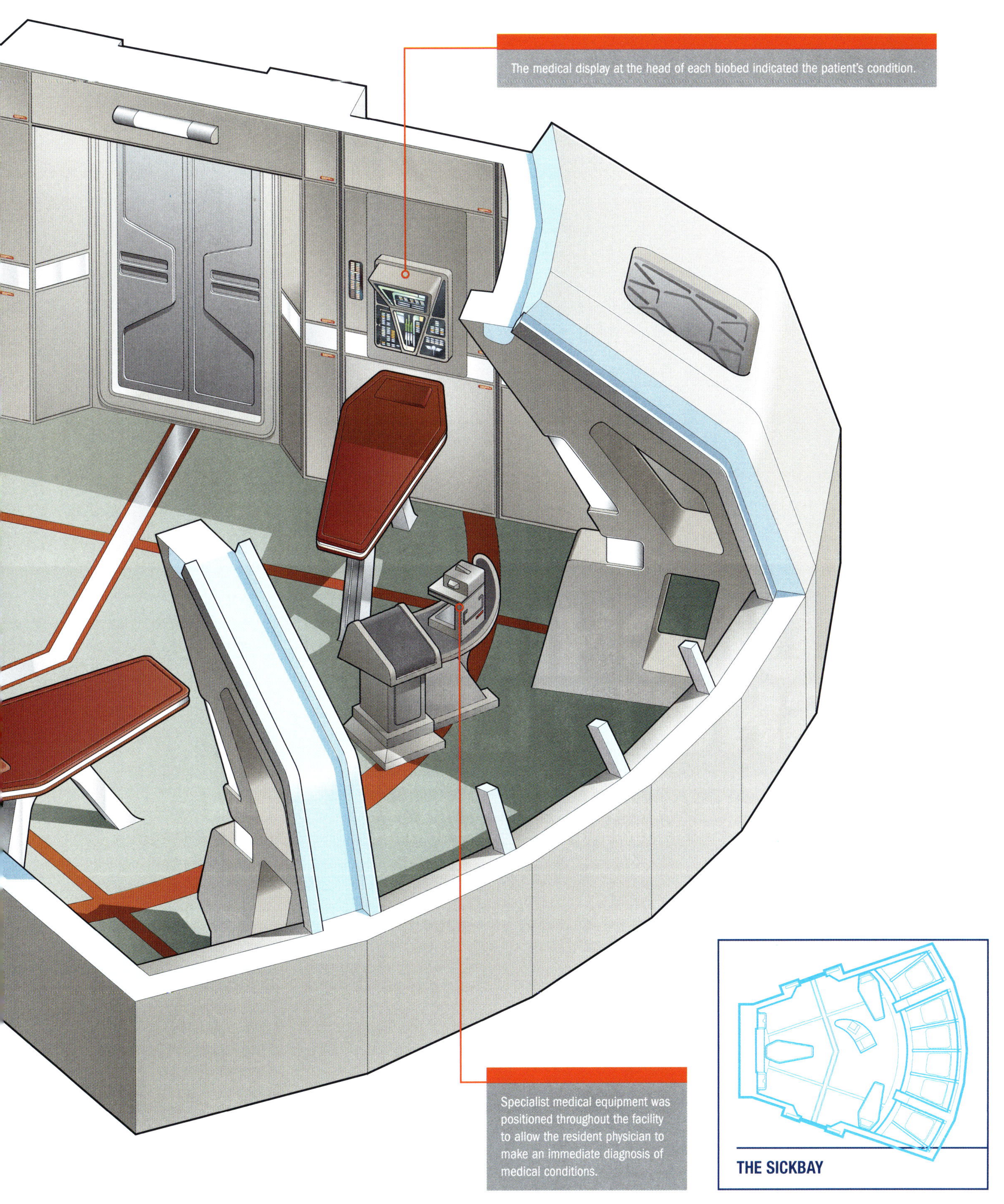
The medical display at the head of each biobed indicated the patient's condition.
Specialist medical equipment was positioned throughout the facility to allow the resident physician to make an immediate diagnosis of medical conditions.
THE SICKBAY

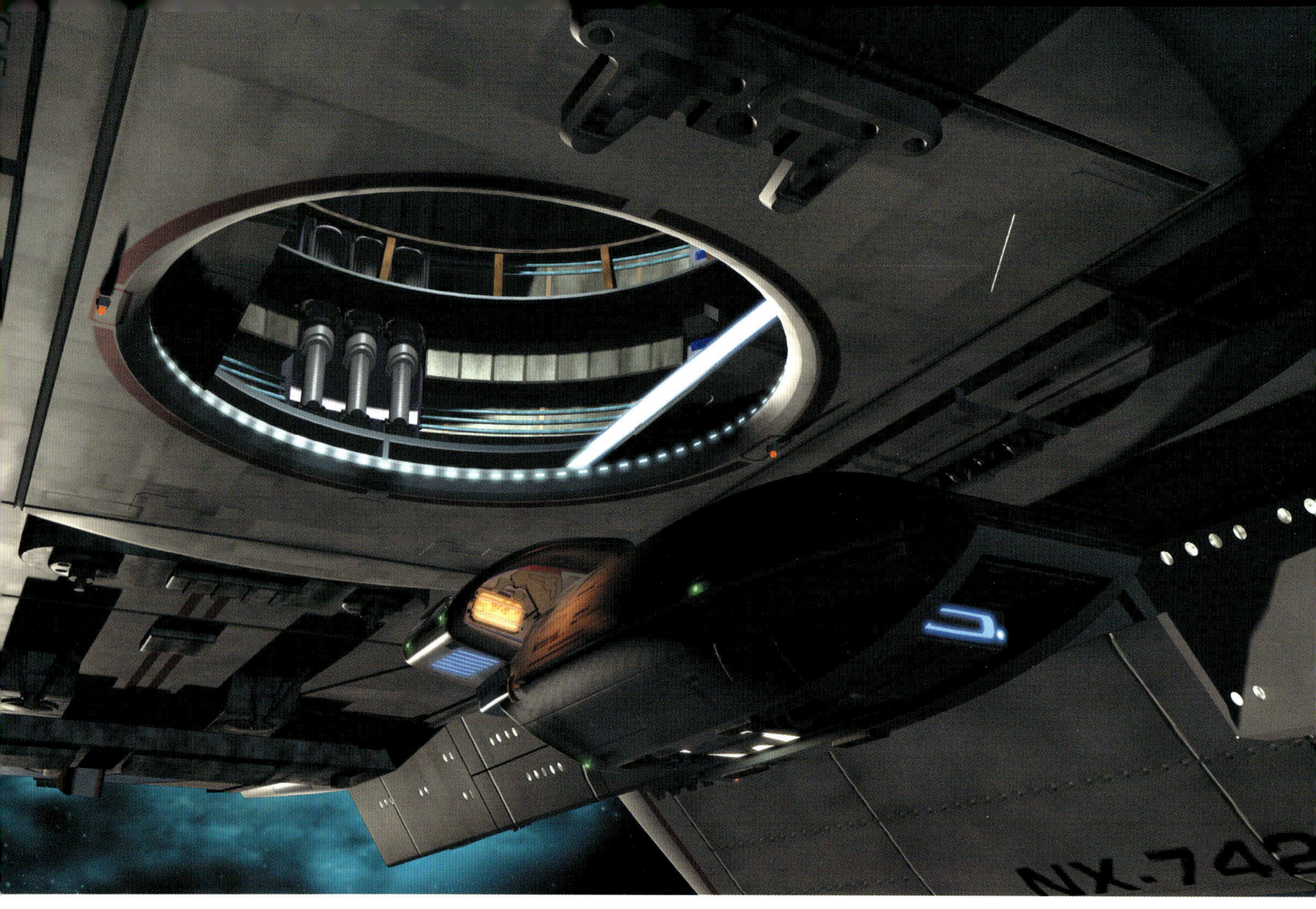

LAUNCHING A SHUTTLE

The location and operation of the *Defiant*'s main shuttlebay made it unique among Federation starships, with a 'drop ship' approach to shuttle deployment providing the maximum protection to shuttles.

The design of the *Defiant* was similar to that of *Intrepid*-class vessels in having the capability to land on a planet's surface if needed. But in keeping with Starfleet's philosophy of equipping its ships for all eventualities, the *Defiant*-class vessels also carried small impulse-powered shuttlepods and warp-capable shuttlecraft. Scaled down to match the reduced storage area available on the *Defiant,* these auxiliary vessels were housed within three shuttlebays that were located on deck 3 of the vessel.

DESIGN DEPARTURE

The compactness of the *Defiant*-class starship made it radically different from *Constitution*-, *Galaxy*-, and *Intrepid*-class vessels, and while the usage and nature of the shuttles were basically the same as those on other ships, the way in which these auxiliary craft deployed was unusual compared to most vessels.

The primary difference in the *Defiant*-class design could be found in the location of the shuttles' exit route. Taking the *Intrepid*-class *U.S.S. Voyager* NCC-74656 as a typical example of normal shuttle deployment, the main shuttlebay was located at the rear of the vessel's engineering hull, in much the same design as the original *Constitution*-class *U.S.S. Enterprise* NCC-1701. On these ships, shuttles sat in relatively spacious bays, where force fields were used to preserve the atmospheric conditions when the bay doors were opened.

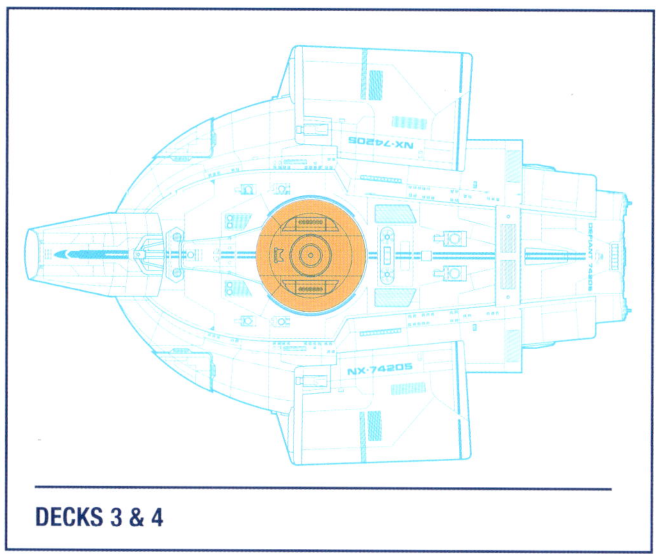

Following a 'drop ship' approach to shuttle deployment, the shuttlebay doors were located on the underside of the *Defiant* and, unlike the roughly rectangular shuttlebay exits found on the *Galaxy* and *Intrepid* classes, the *Defiant*'s hatchway was circular. Split double doors opened to provide the maximum exit area for the departing shuttle; one vessel was permanently berthed in the center of the inner double doors, which made up the floor of the main shuttlebay 3. Situated port and starboard of the launch area were shuttlebays 1 and 2, which were used to store additional craft, enabling the quick positioning and launch of further shuttles.

The advantages of launching from the underside of the *Defiant* were twofold. First, the port and starboard nacelles running alongside the vessel formed a highly effective barrier from attacking vessels, forcing an opponent to adopt an approach from directly underneath the ship to target any exiting shuttle. Second, shuttlebay 3 was totally enclosed on deck 3 apart from the launch doors, which opened onto an exit hatch that cut a cylinder through deck 4. The hatch was only slightly wider than the shuttle itself, ensuring that even a direct hit to the underside of the craft was unlikely to cause damage to stored auxiliary vessels.

The launched shuttle faced the same direction of travel as the *Defiant*, so was able to fly downward, away from any potential combat scenario. This was in contrast to shuttles leaving *Intrepid*- and *Galaxy*-class ships. These faced away from the direction of travel, and may have presented an easy target at the relatively exposed rear of the vessel.

ADAPTED FOR WAR

Defiant-class vessels launched shuttles in a different way from other Starfleet ships. This was dictated by the location of the *Defiant*'s bay and the design of the vessel itself. The *Defiant*'s hull and shield configuration was designed to afford maximum protection, so the inclusion of shuttlebay doors at the rear of the craft might present a weak spot in times of crisis. Consequently, the launch system had been reconsidered for the fastest deployment and retrieval of a shuttle without exposing the *Defiant* to undue risk.

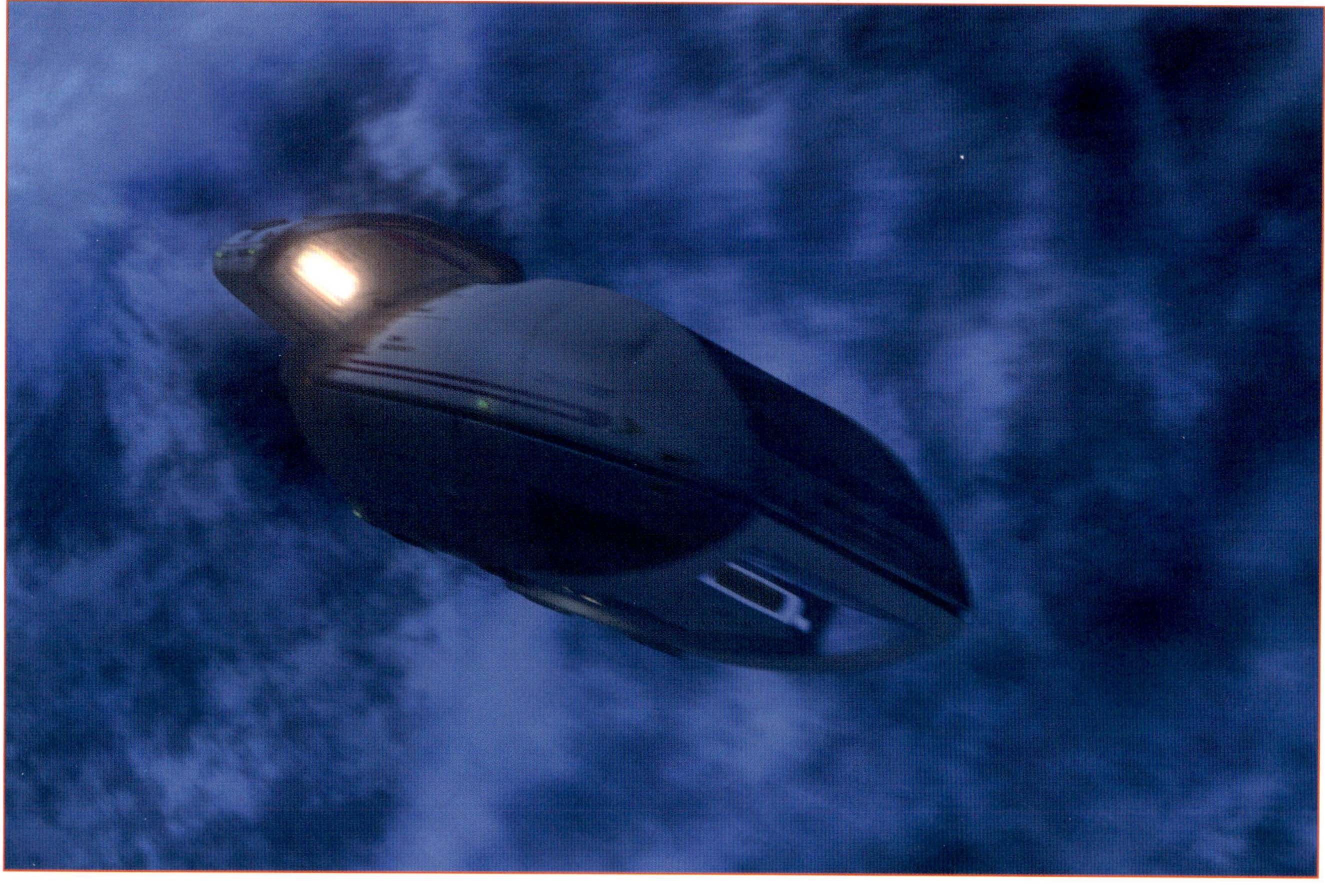

The *U.S.S. Defiant*'s shuttles were normally all called upon when the crew had to enter an atmosphere that made it difficult to use the transporters. The shuttles were warp capable so could be used for reconnaisance missions or by crewmembers who had to leave the ship to visit locations that were out of transporter range.

THE SHUTTLEPOD

The *U.S.S. Defiant* NX-74205's shuttlepods were smaller and much more aerodynamic than other Starfleet shuttles. Like the *Defiant* itself, they were not designed for comfort.

The *U.S.S. Defiant* could carry four shuttlepods, each measuring 4.5 meters long, 3.1 meters wide, and 1.8 meters high. The shuttles were designed for a maximum of six people each, with two operating the controls of the craft and four passengers. The shuttlepods were limited to impulse speeds, but could travel at faster-than-light velocity if they were released at warp.

MISSION-CAPABLE

This type of craft was not intended to be used for extended missions because of its size, but it was capable of entering a planet's atmosphere and landing on the surface. This made the craft ideal for planetary surface transfer, ship-to-ship transfer, or evacuations in the case of an emergency.

These shuttlepods had a compact design, which was basically rectangular, with the engines located at the rear. They had limited phaser armaments, but could be adapted to hold a larger arsenal.

Each shuttle had three doors: two gullwing doors on each side of the cockpit; and one large door, which was hinged at the top, at the rear of the ship. The cockpit was equipped with sensors and subspace communications arrays – though sensors could be blocked by certain polymetallic materials, and thermal radiation could interfere with communications.

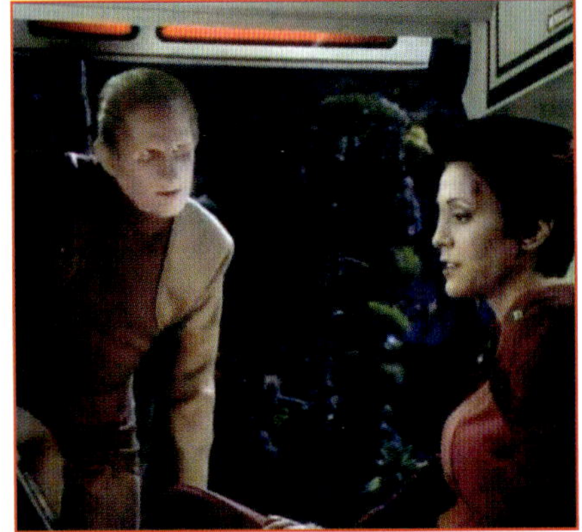

The interior of the shuttlepod was extremely cramped, and it was normally entered through gullwing doors on either side of the cockpit.

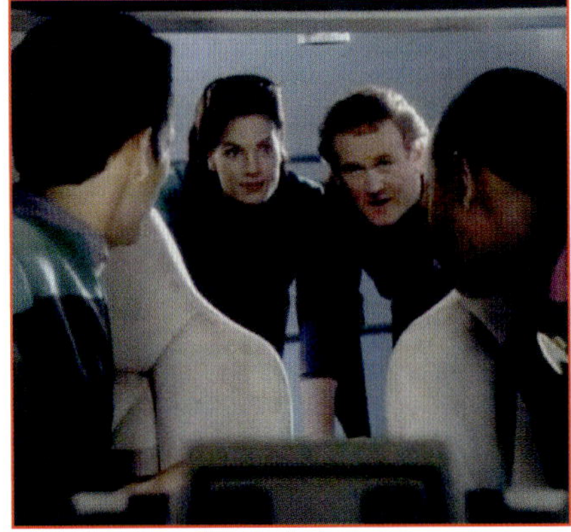

As well as the gullwing doors, the shuttle could be accessed from the rear of the cabin – the back wall formed a large, top-hinged door.

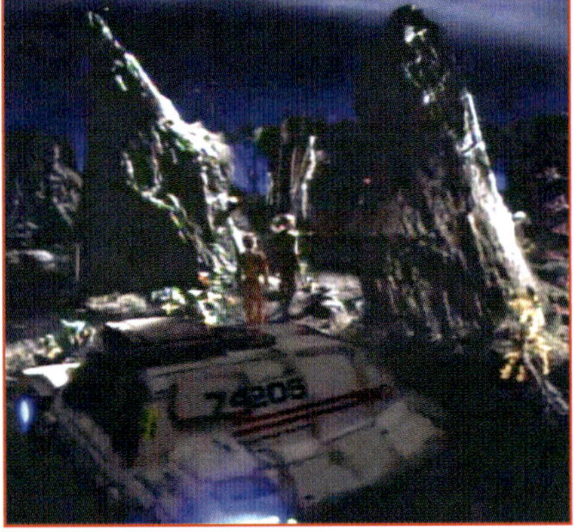

Unlike the *U.S.S. Defiant*, the shuttlepods were designed and built for atmospheric flight and planetary landing.

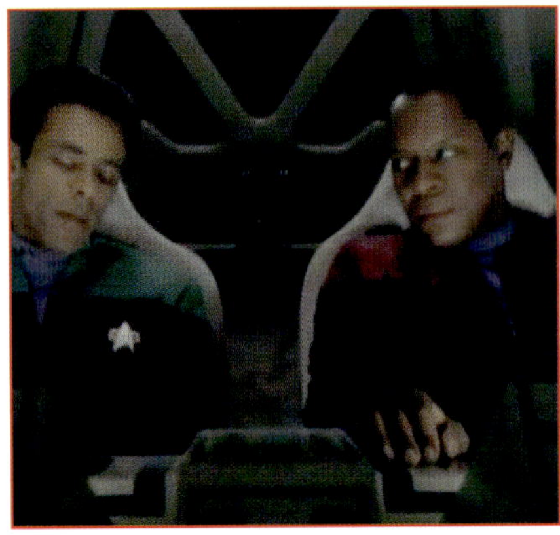

The cockpit of the shuttlepod only provided seating for two crewmembers. Although it had warp engines, the shuttle was not designed for extended journeys.

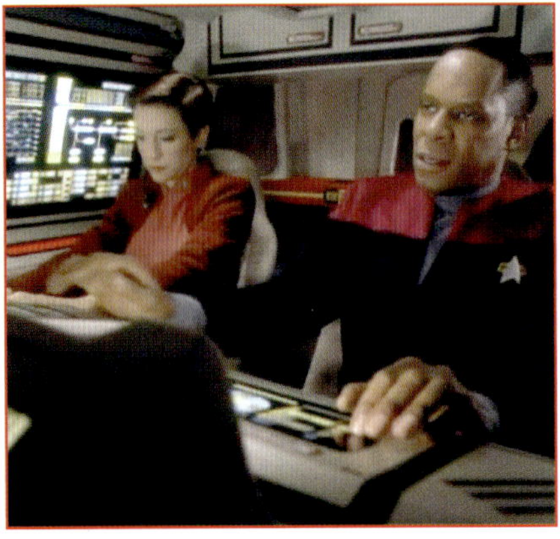

The shuttle's control consoles were located directly in front of the crew in the cockpit and on the inside of the two gullwing doors flanking them.

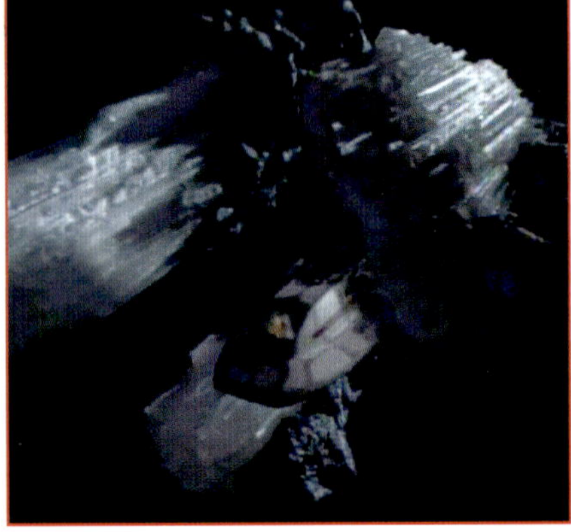

The shuttle was a nimble, highly maneuverable craft, able to react quickly to unexpected celestial debris, or outfly a hostile ship.

DORSAL VIEW

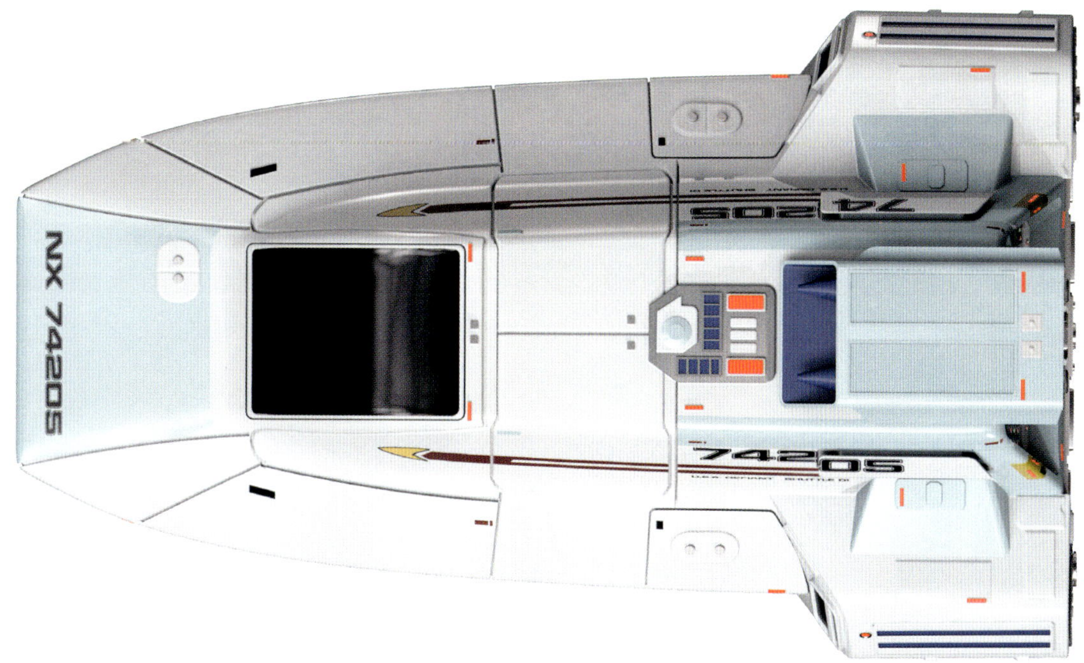

FORE VIEW

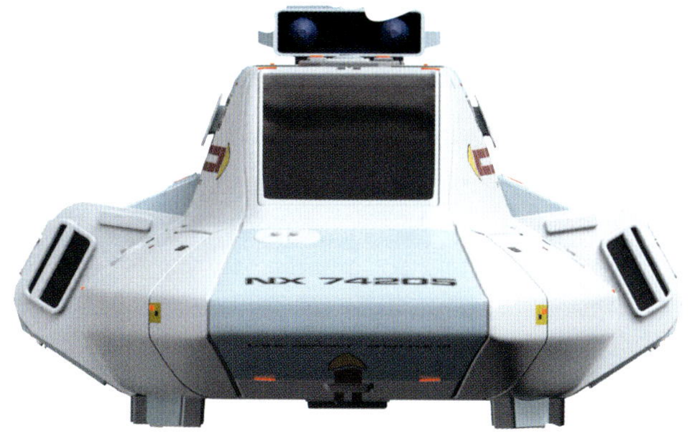

AFT VIEW

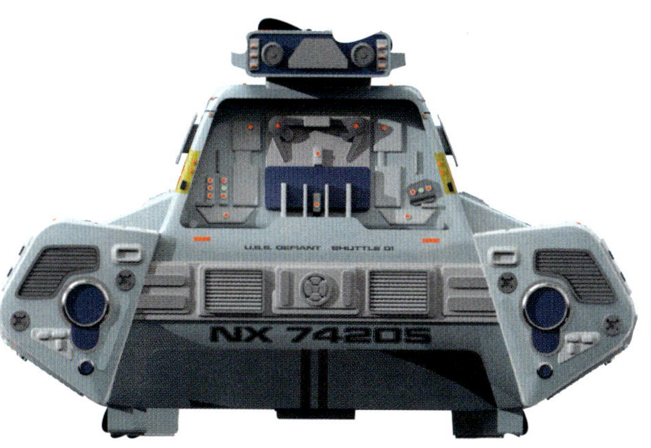

PORT VIEW

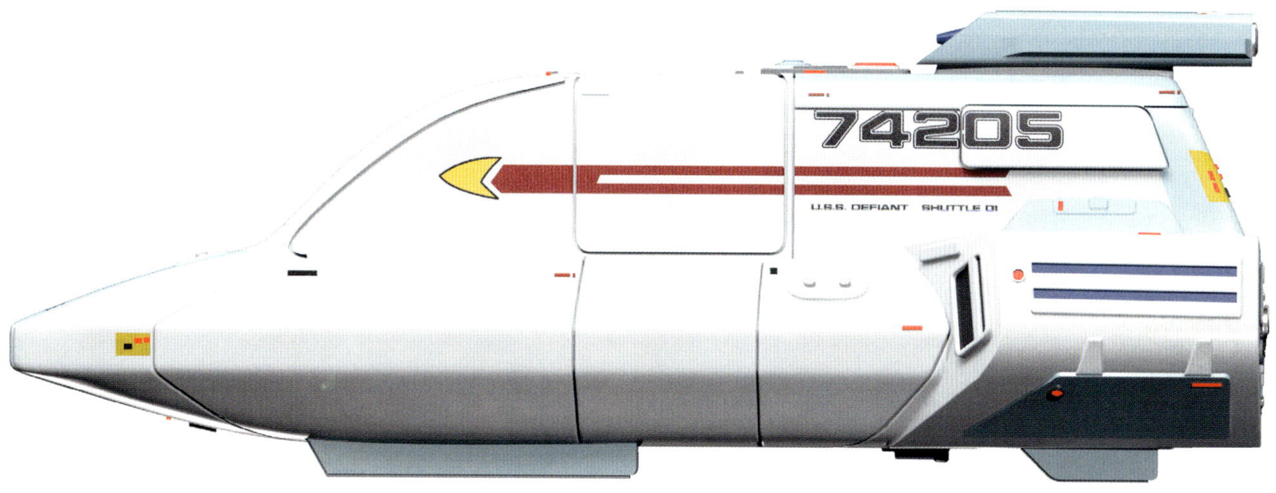

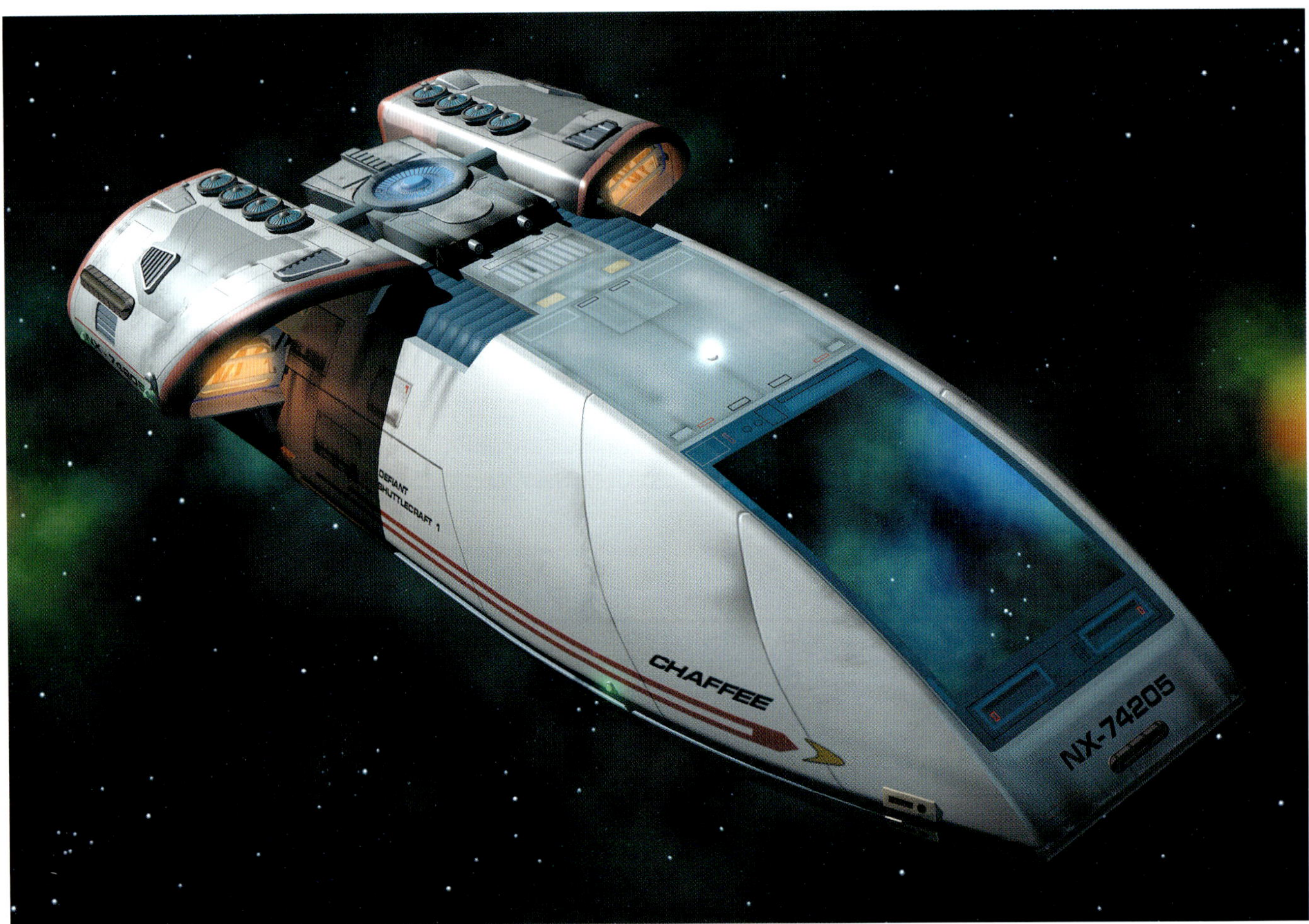

SHUTTLECRAFT CHAFFEE

In addition to the sublight shuttlepods, the *U.S.S. Defiant* NX-74205 also carried the Type-10, warp-capable auxiliary craft, the *Chaffee*.

The shuttlecraft *Chaffee*, specially assigned to the *Defiant*, was permanently located within its launch area in the center of the main hull of the *Defiant*.

SHIP SCHEMATICS

The *Chaffee* could accommodate a crew of four and it was equipped with both impulse and warp drive systems. The vessel weighed 19.73 metric tonnes, which was heavier than the average shuttle because of its much larger warp coil assembly.

The craft was equipped with a more compressed version of the onboard computer system found on the *Danube*-class runabouts. Various peripheral and upgrade slots had been installed in anticipation of bio-neural gel packs which were being developed at this time. The *Chaffee* was capable of entering planetary atmospheres and was equipped with both fixed and deployable surface pads.

EXTERNAL SHAPE

The exterior design of the shuttlepod shared similarities with the *Defiant* in that the warp nacelles were enclosed within the main body of the craft. A small sensor array was situated within a cutout section at the bow, beneath the large tinted cockpit canopy at the front of the ship, which glowed blue when active.

The *Chaffee* shuttlecraft was named for the astronaut Roger Chaffee, a space travel pioneer in the 20th century, and was a valuable addition to the *Defiant*.

DORSAL VIEW

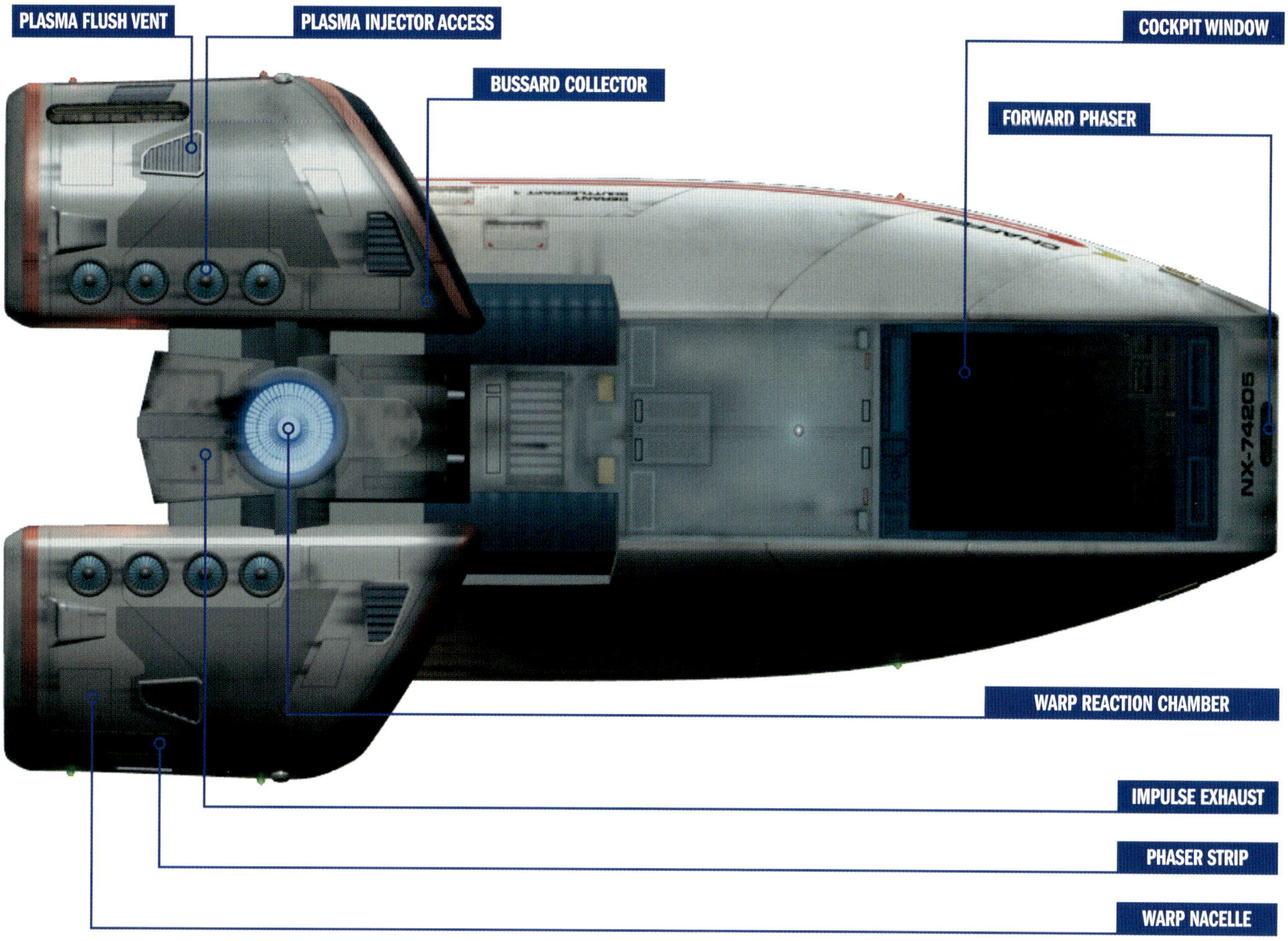

PLASMA FLUSH VENT
PLASMA INJECTOR ACCESS
BUSSARD COLLECTOR
COCKPIT WINDOW
FORWARD PHASER
WARP REACTION CHAMBER
IMPULSE EXHAUST
PHASER STRIP
WARP NACELLE

FORE VIEW

AFT VIEW

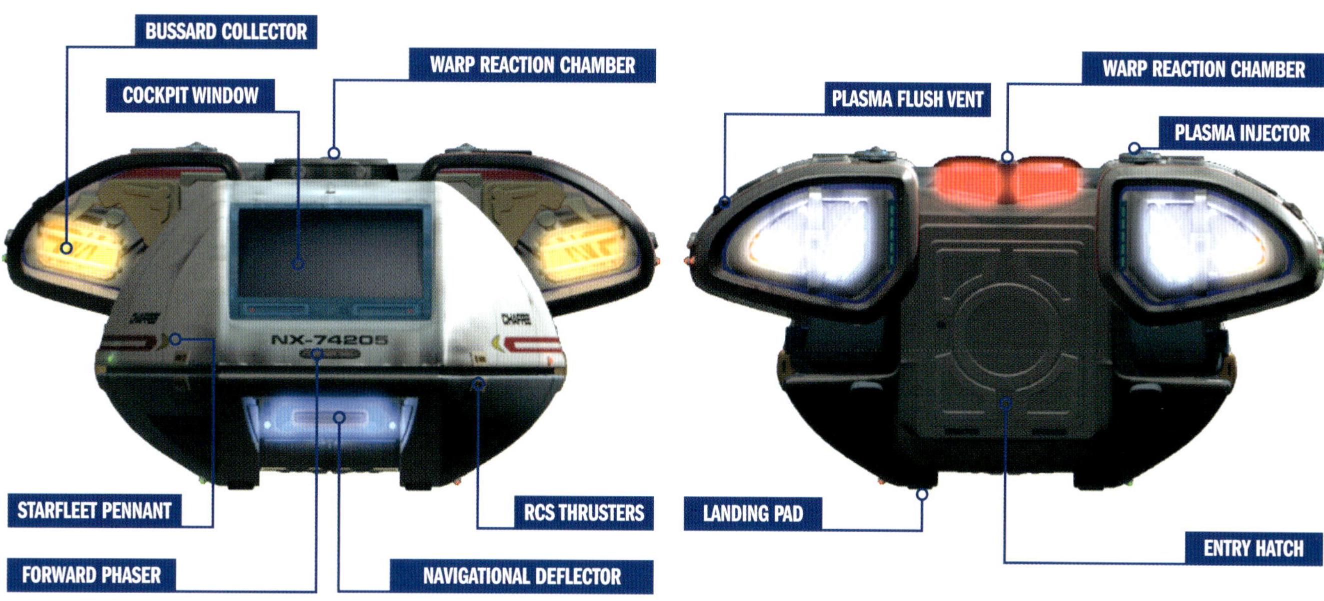

U.S.S. SAO PAULO

The destruction of the *U.S.S. Defiant* NX-74205 came as a severe blow during the Dominion War. But an identical vessel – the *U.S.S. Sao Paulo* NCC-75633 – swiftly took its place.

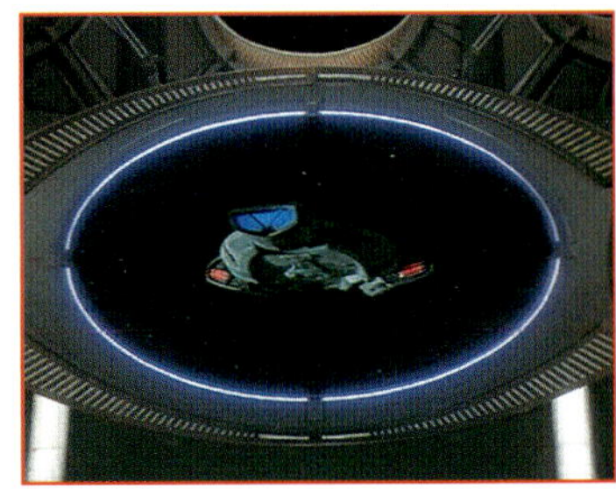

The *U.S.S. Sao Paulo* NCC-75633 was delivered to Deep Space 9 by Admiral William Ross in person.

After the prototype *Defiant* was assigned to Deep Space 9, the problems with its design were gradually worked out and the class was put into production. This was particularly valuable during the Dominion War, since Starfleet was in need of true warships rather than the multimission ships that they had concentrated on in peacetime.

TRAGIC LOSS

Following the abandonment and subsequent destruction of the *Defiant* by the Breen in the Chin'toka System, Captain Benjamin Sisko was left temporarily without a vessel to command during the final days of the Dominion War in 2375. Chief of Starfleet Operations Admiral William Ross arranged for the *Sao Paulo* to be transferred to Deep Space 9 prior to the final assault on Cardassia, and it was delivered to the station around Stardate 52891.

On the request of Captain Sisko, Admiral Ross allowed the ship to be renamed *Defiant*. The renaming of the *Sao Paulo* was unusual in that it broke a number of normal Starfleet traditions, since any vessel acting as a replacement for a destroyed or upgraded ship was given a new name or would carry an additional alphabetical character at the end of the registration.

IN THY IMAGE

Despite a number of minor upgrades and modifications, the new *Defiant* was virtually identical to its predecessor. Nevertheless, the basic design flaw remained in the production models, in that the vessel was overpowered for its size, requiring constant monitoring and adjustment to keep the ship from tearing apart at high impulse speeds during combat situations.

The high maneuverability and considerable firepower of *Defiant*-class ships proved vital in the conflict with the Dominion. The compact four-deck configuration of the new *Defiant* also ensured a minimal sensor area for enemy targeting systems.

Minor improvements were made to the ship's arsenal of pulse phaser cannons that were built into the forward port and starboard warp nacelles, and the latest version of the dual photon and quantum torpedo launcher and ordnance were incorporated. The ablative armor plating on the hull also enabled the new *Defiant* to withstand a high degree of punishment.

One of the greatest differences between the original *Defiant* and its replacement was the omission of a cloaking device. The original ship was equipped with such a device on loan from the Romulan Star Empire. Use of the system was problematic, with numerous incompatibilities between Starfleet and Romulan systems. Also, the massive political change created by the defeat of the Dominion in the Alpha Quadrant suggested a replacement cloaking system might be redundant, as the *Defiant* took on a more defensive role under the command of Colonel Kira Nerys in 2375, after the disappearance of Captain Sisko.

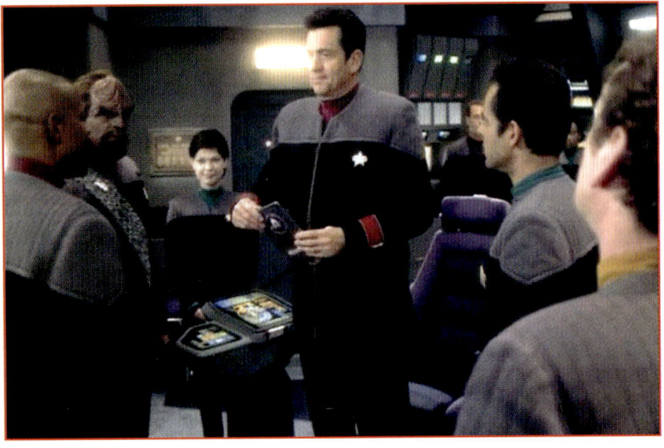

Admiral Ross handed command of the *Sao Paulo* to Captain Sisko, and confirmed its name change to *Defiant*.

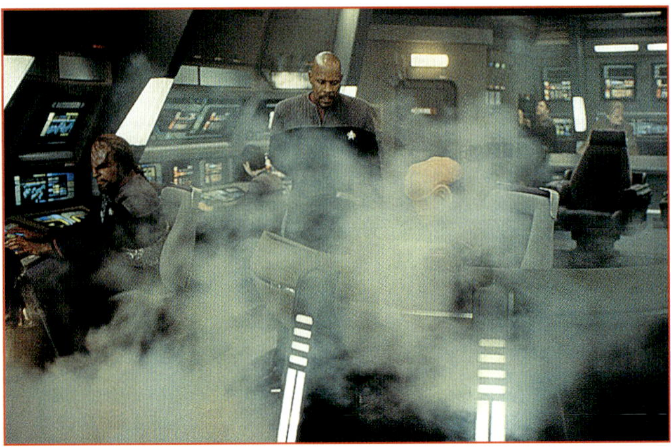

On the bridge of the *U.S.S. Defiant* NX-74205, Captain Sisko and his crew tried to remedy the fallout as the ship's systems failed.

DORSAL VIEW

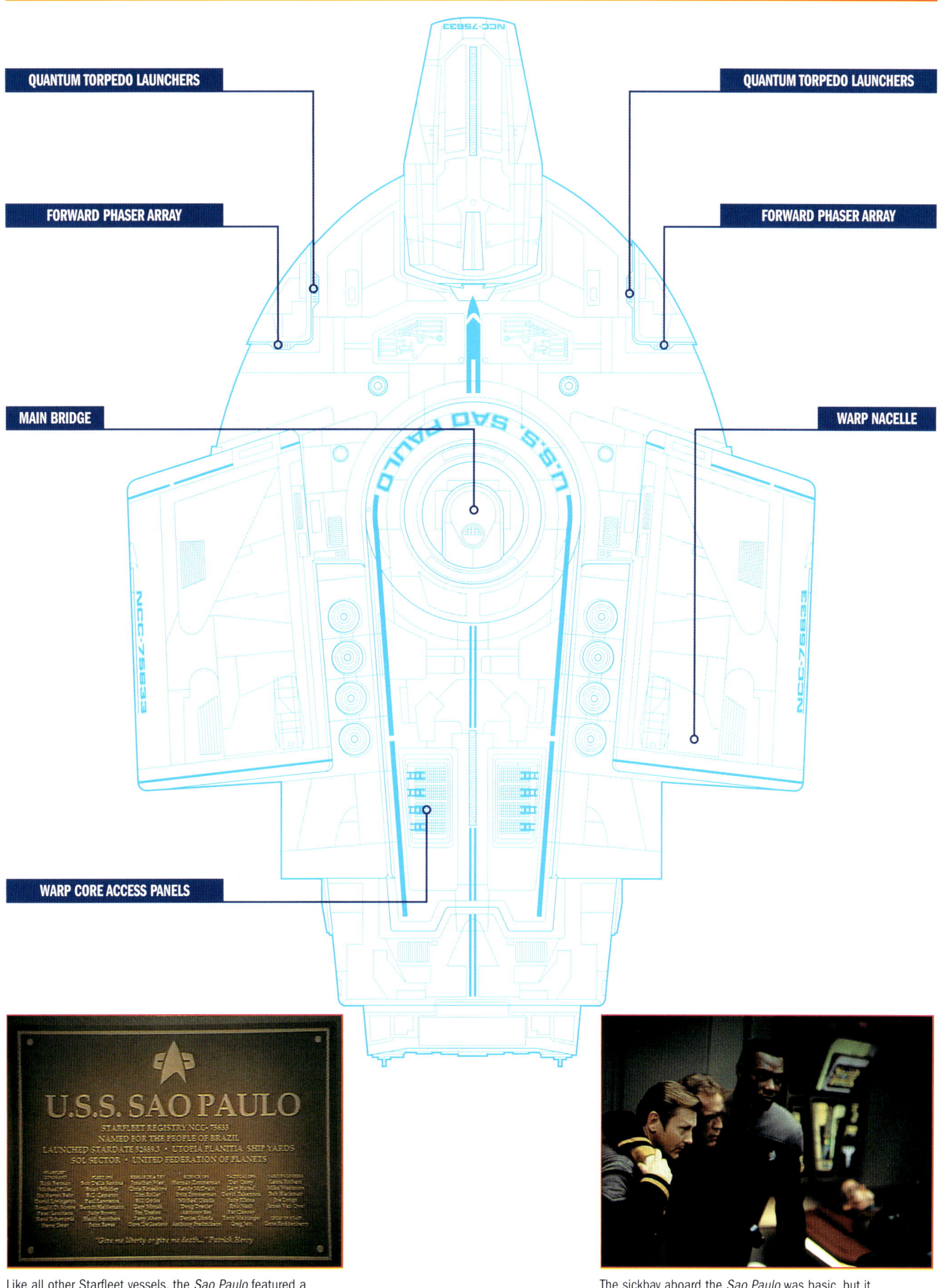

Like all other Starfleet vessels, the *Sao Paulo* featured a dedication plaque located in a prime position on the bridge.

The sickbay aboard the *Sao Paulo* was basic, but it nevertheless served the crew's immediate needs.

HAND PHASERS: 2371

The most recent incarnation of the Federation hand phaser was a more versatile and powerful version of the pistol phaser. Unlike previous models, this type-2 phaser could be recharged by personnel in combat.

The Federation type-2 phaser of 2371 was the seventh major design improvement on the pistol phaser since its introduction around a century before. The 2371 phaser looked like its 2366 predecessor, but the handgrip was curved at a 45-degree angle, making it easier to aim and fire, while a plethora of internal upgrades turned it into the most powerful and flexible type-2 weapon ever. The longer grip housed the improved sarium-krellide power cell.

The placement of the power cell was typical of type-2 phasers, but the new cell was larger than before to accommodate its own important design upgrades. The cell's energy charge capacity was almost double. It was also redesigned so that it could be easily replaced in the handgrip. The ribbed grip area of the handle was actually a portion of the sarium-krellide power cell.

BATTERY POWER

The process of opening the grip and exchanging batteries could be accomplished in the field by a user without disturbing personalization settings or phaser safety interlock codes. This prevented the device from overloading or discharging beyond certain intensities. In previous models, the phaser itself had to be recharged; now a spent battery could be recharged while a fresh one kept the weapon in operation.

The 2371 phaser holster was a streamlined holder with a black pocket at one end in which to insert the phaser nose, and a U-shaped cradle at the other to rest the handgrip. The holster attached to the uniform and was positioned so that the phaser was roughly horizontal, with the handle resting parallel with the waist.

OVERVIEW

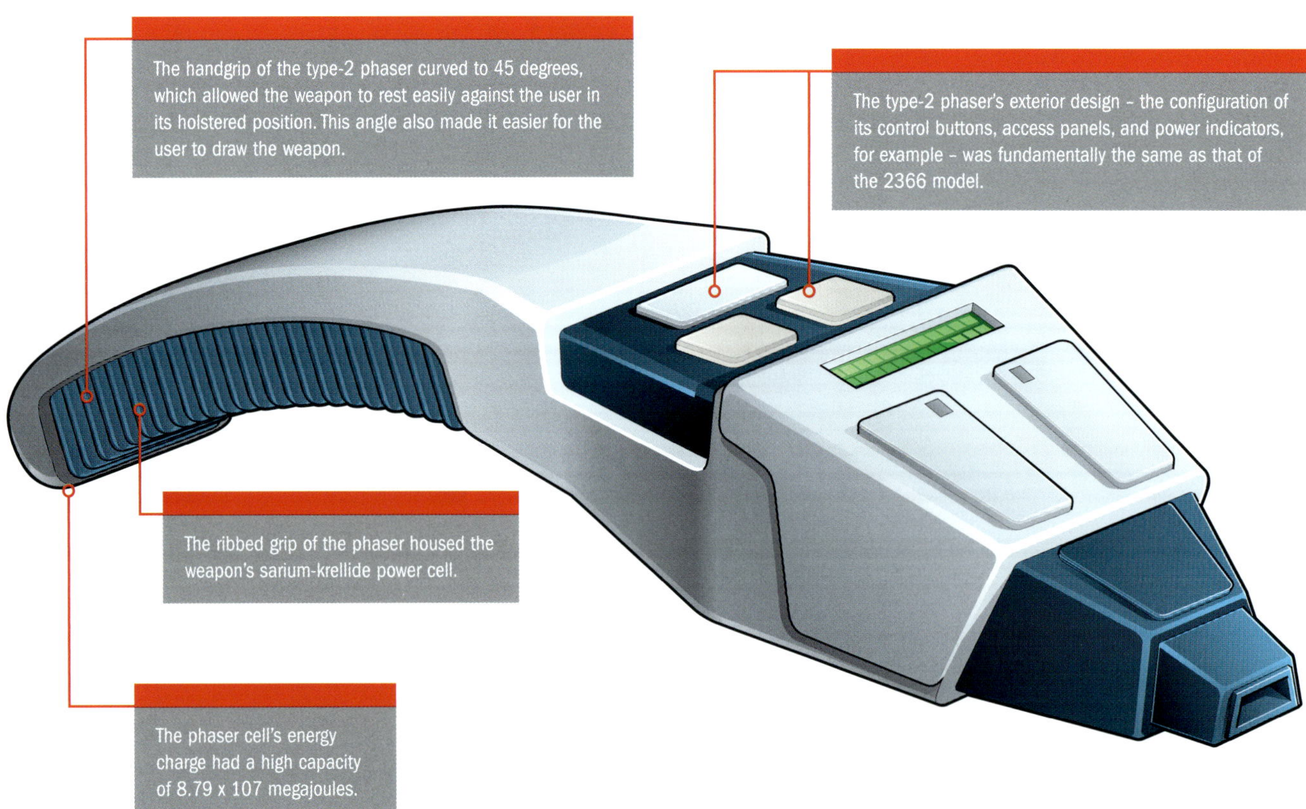

The handgrip of the type-2 phaser curved to 45 degrees, which allowed the weapon to rest easily against the user in its holstered position. This angle also made it easier for the user to draw the weapon.

The type-2 phaser's exterior design - the configuration of its control buttons, access panels, and power indicators, for example - was fundamentally the same as that of the 2366 model.

The ribbed grip of the phaser housed the weapon's sarium-krellide power cell.

The phaser cell's energy charge had a high capacity of 8.79 x 107 megajoules.

TOP VIEW

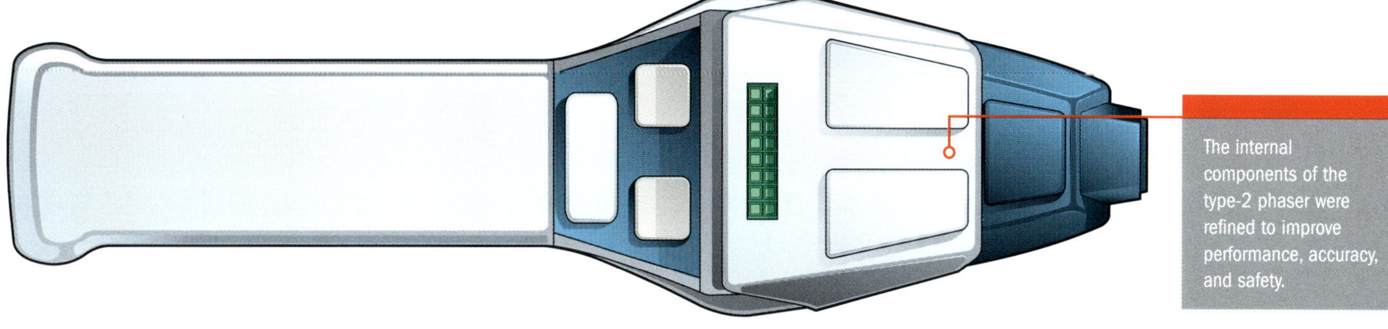

The internal components of the type-2 phaser were refined to improve performance, accuracy, and safety.

SIDE VIEW

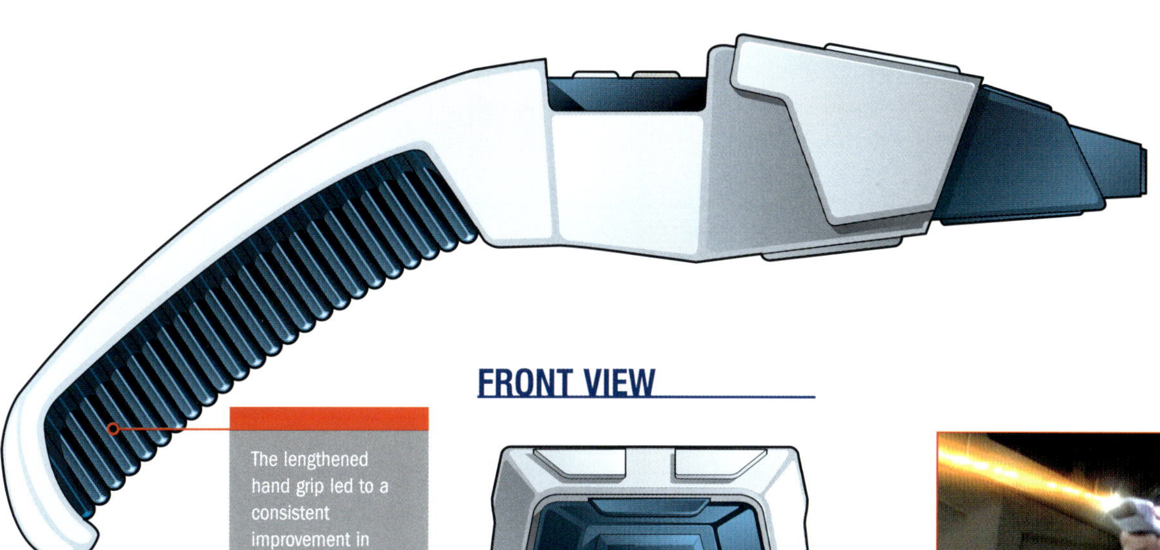

The lengthened hand grip led to a consistent improvement in personnel accuracy scores.

FRONT VIEW

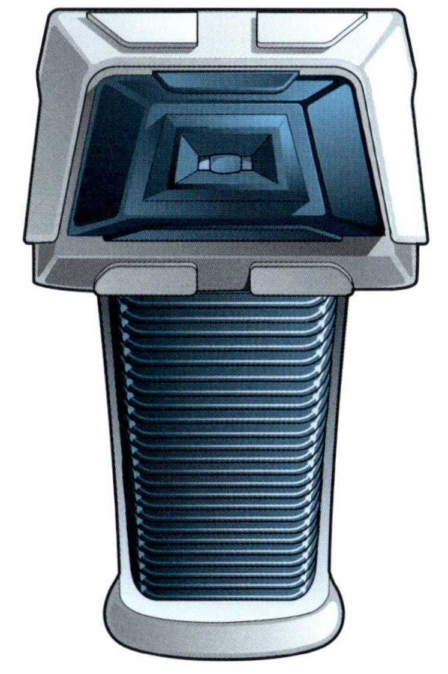

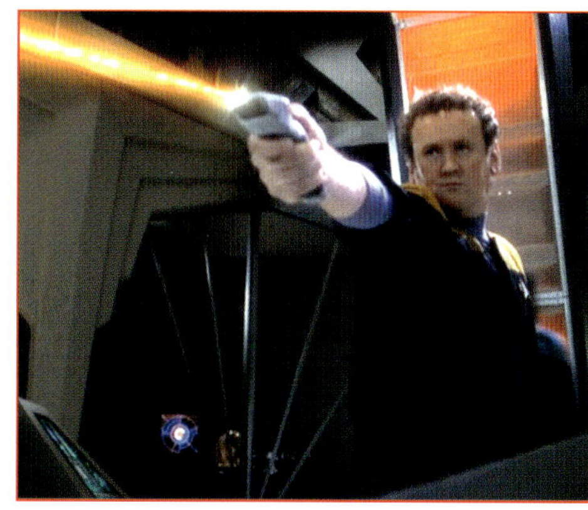

Chief of operations Miles O'Brien used the hand phaser in hand-to-hand combat after the station was attacked by Klingon boarding parties.

BOTTOM VIEW

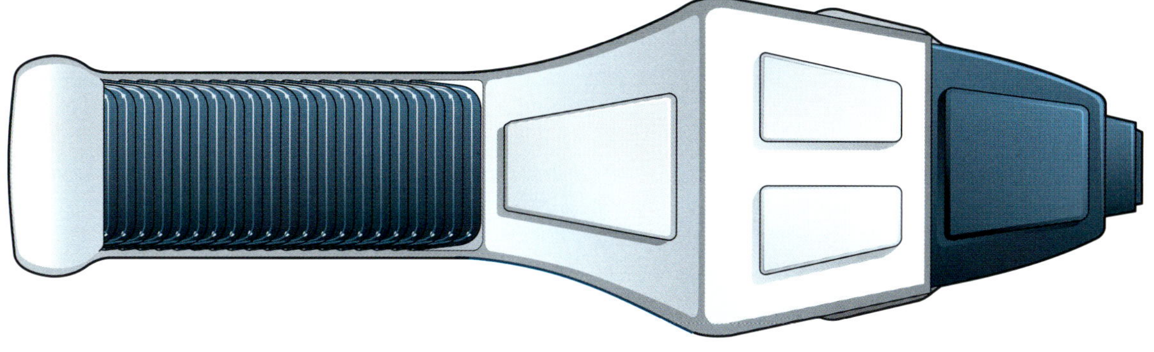

STARFLEET TR-116 RIFLE

This powerful firearm represented a shift away from directed energy weapons in favor of a type that fired a chemically propelled bullet, with revolutionary technological additions.

The United Federation of Planets prided itself on being a nonaggressive organization committed to the mutual development and preservation of member nations. But while Starfleet Command existed to undertake exploration and scientific study, it also ensured the security of the Federation. Starfleet understood the continual need for weapons development in order to create a threat significant enough to deter any would-be attackers. Therefore, its designers were often called upon to develop weapons that could prove effective against a specific threat or defensive capability.

Starfleet had been developing its directed energy technology for more than 100 years, arming its starship crews and troops with a variety of hand phasers and phaser rifles. This technology had proved both reliable and effective, but there were occasions where directed energy weapons could not function, placing Starfleet personnel at a potentially deadly disadvantage.

To counteract the difficulties created by artificially generated energy-dampening fields or radiogenic environments, Starfleet weapons designers returned to ancient technology and reexamined the merits of weapons that fired chemically propelled projectiles.

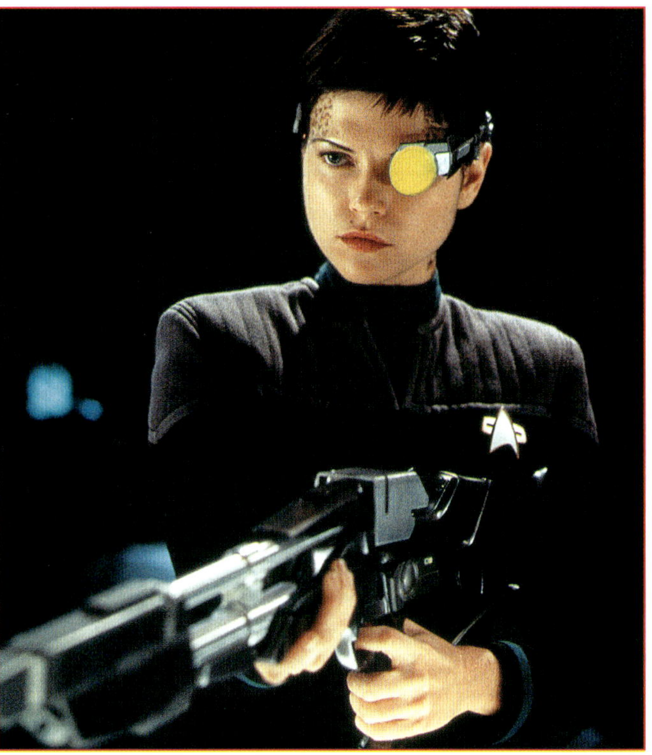

A headset worn by the operator of the TR-116 relayed a constant exographic image, providing unparalleled information for targeting.

DEADLY WEAPON

The TR-116 rifle was a prototype weapon combining the basics of firearms technology with a revolutionary tracking and projectile-delivery system. Ultimately abandoned in favor of continued regenerative phaser development, it nevertheless attracted great interest among weapons enthusiasts and Starfleet officers, who had the ability to retrieve the replicator patterns and construct such a weapon for themselves. Unauthorized reproduction of the TR-116 did signal an alarm to Starfleet Security, however. This illustrated how seriously Starfleet regarded the destructive potential of the weapon that had been used to such devastating and tragic effect on Deep Space 9 in 2375.

FORM AND FUNCTION

Constructed from a highly polished alloy, the TR-116 was much longer than a normal phaser rifle, and while it was lightweight and relatively easy to pick up, its overall length – in excess of one meter – made it more cumbersome in the field than the stockier energy weapon. The butt was constructed from a drilled alloy with a slight curve to ensure a comfortable fit in the crook of the trigger arm, with the other arm used to steady the weapon. The double over- and under-barrels ran to an extended muzzle and flash restrictor at the front of the weapon, while the trigger unit was located above and in front of the main grip. Unlike 20th-century rifles, which had to be held up to the chin so that the user could align the sights along the top of the barrel, the TR-116 was designed to be fired from the hip. This was because its targeting mechanism operated independently of its firing position.

When not in use, the TR-116 was kept inside a secure cabinet with a dummy magazine permanently locked in place on the underside of the lower barrel support. The magazine was around 20cm long, and constructed from a black, nonslip material. Each magazine contained live rounds of tritanium bullets.

The curved lower edge of the magazine formed a small grip that gave the user support for the weapon, illustrating

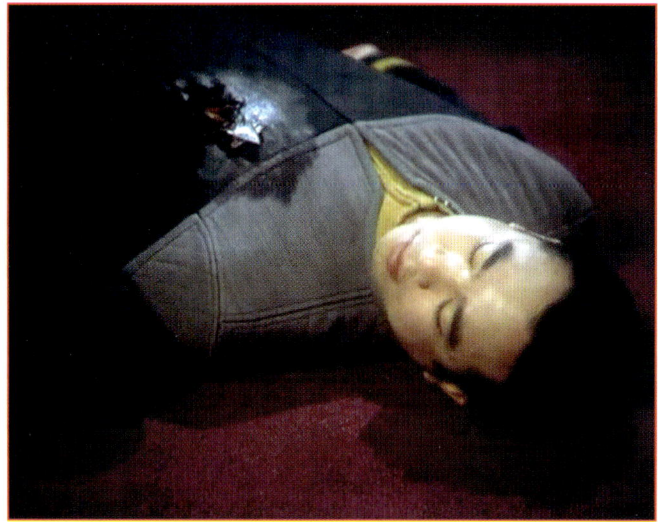

Lt. Hector Ilario was the first victim of a TR-116 attack on Deep Space 9 in 2375. The bullet fired by science officer Chu'lak, materialized about 5m behind him with a bang.

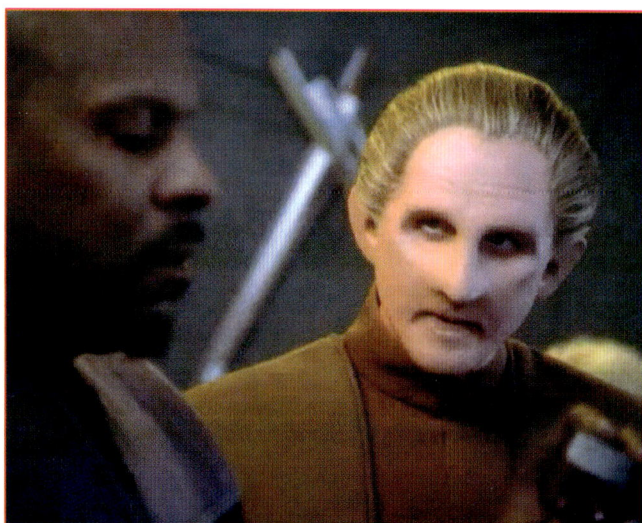

Captain Sisko was shocked to discover that Lt. Ilario had been killed by a single shot from a gun, rather than by a more common energy weapon of the 24th century.

the attention to detail and ease of use the Starfleet designers were attempting to create.

OPERATION AND TARGETING

The TR-116's operational status was signified by a faint electronic sound and a glowing blue indicator located in the angular muzzle housing, along with a series of blinking diodes on the the main chamber housing, directly above the trigger guard.

Designed primarily for long-range use, the unit made a perfect sniper's weapon under normal line-of-sight conditions. The addition of a highly accurate, exographic targeting sensor and micro-transporter exponentially increased the weapon's abilities. Suitable for both left-handed and right-handed users, the rifle and targeting sensor were separate units yet were completely integrated and extremely easy to deploy. The headset comprised an adjustable narrow metallic headband that supported a yellow lens large enough to cover the eye of a humanoid operator.

VICTIM IN SIGHT

The display fed a constant exographic image to the user, and included three coordinate monitors on the lower left quadrant of the display. The view was dominated by a rectangular 'kill-zone' indicator with a circular reticule in the center. A small set of crosshairs illuminated from static yellow to pulsing red when a potential target was found, accompanied by an audible electronic indicator. The movement of the sensor could be directly controlled by a protruding thumbwheel on the left side of the trigger guard. Surrounded by a series of sequentially flashing red indicators, the sensor enabled an assassin to scan through walls and find their target from a distance.

MICRO-TRANSPORTER

The targeting technique could only be successful if there was a method of transporting the bullet, along with its momentum, to the target. Firing through bulkheads and walls reduced the muzzle velocity considerably and could also deflect the bullet's path. But the micro-transporter beamed the bullet from the weapon so it re-materialized near its target at a devastatingly close range of around 8 to 9cm. The weakness of the transporter field made it undetectable to sensors, and it could not be traced back to the weapon. A single bullet fired into the heart of a humanoid in this manner would prove immediately fatal.

The use of a micro-transporter also meant there was no forensic evidence of powder burns from the weapon's residual combustion products, even without this stealth mode of fire. The TR-116 was still an extremely quiet gun, with virtually no recoil – it was hard to detect, very easy to use, and extremely effective.

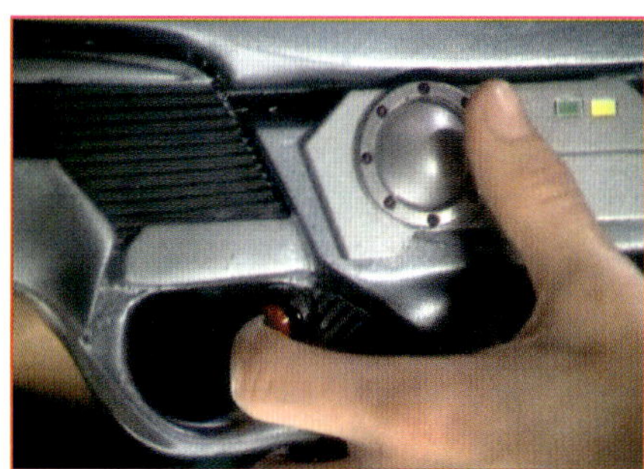

The operational status of the TR-116 was indicated by a series of diodes on the side of the weapon, just above the trigger guard.

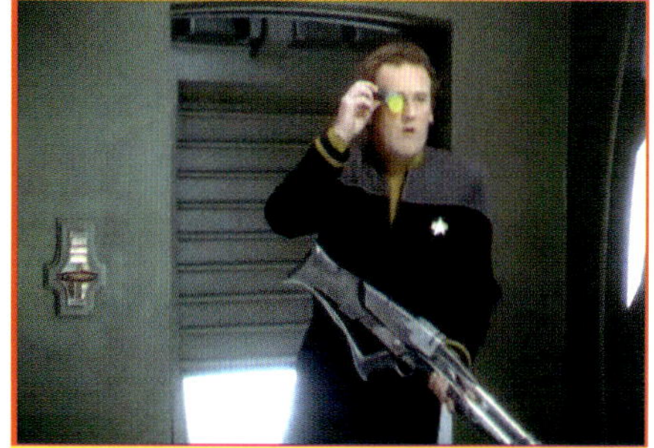

Chief Miles O'Brien demonstrated the power of the TR-116 when used with a micro-transporter for beaming bullets to other locations.

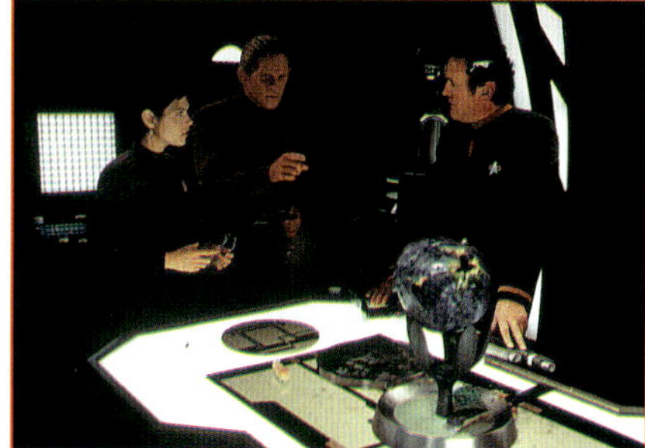

O'Brien's test involved transporting a bullet into another room, where it impacted into a melon. The fruit was shattered in the demonstration.

BAJORAN ENERGY WEAPONS

Years of armed resistance to Cardassian rule left many Bajorans wedded to the need for weapons. The Bajoran Militia carried two distinctive phaser types, and maintained them both with pride.

The Bajoran Resistance made use of directed energy weapons throughout the Cardassian occupation of their homeworld. When their oppressors withdrew, the men and women of the newly official Bajoran Militia were equipped with similar weapons as standard. This included Security Chief Odo and his personnel onboard Deep Space 9, though Odo himself rarely had cause to use weapons beyond his natural shape-shifting abilities.

The two main weapons employed by the Militia were the phaser pistol and phaser rifle. Both were bulkier than the Starfleet-issue equivalents, with large hand grips and trigger guards, and were made from a distinctive bronze-colored metal. They fired a blast of white-gold energy with adjustable width and intensity settings, and could inflict mortal wounds on members of most humanoid species. They could not instantly vaporize a target, however, making the need for medical attention more likely.

The phaser pistol was the weapon most commonly seen on Deep Space 9, and the standard Bajoran Militia uniform included a wide, removable holster for stowing the pistol on the belt. Phaser rifles were generally held in storage in the station armory and only used in emergencies. Though the rifle's size made the user less mobile, it also ensured a greater runtime before the energy cells were spent. This made the rifle well suited to siege situations and, at close quarters, it could also be used as a hand-to-hand weapon.

OVERVIEW

ALL-PURPOSE PAIR
Bajoran phasers could be used in all common environments, from confined indoor spaces to open countryside.

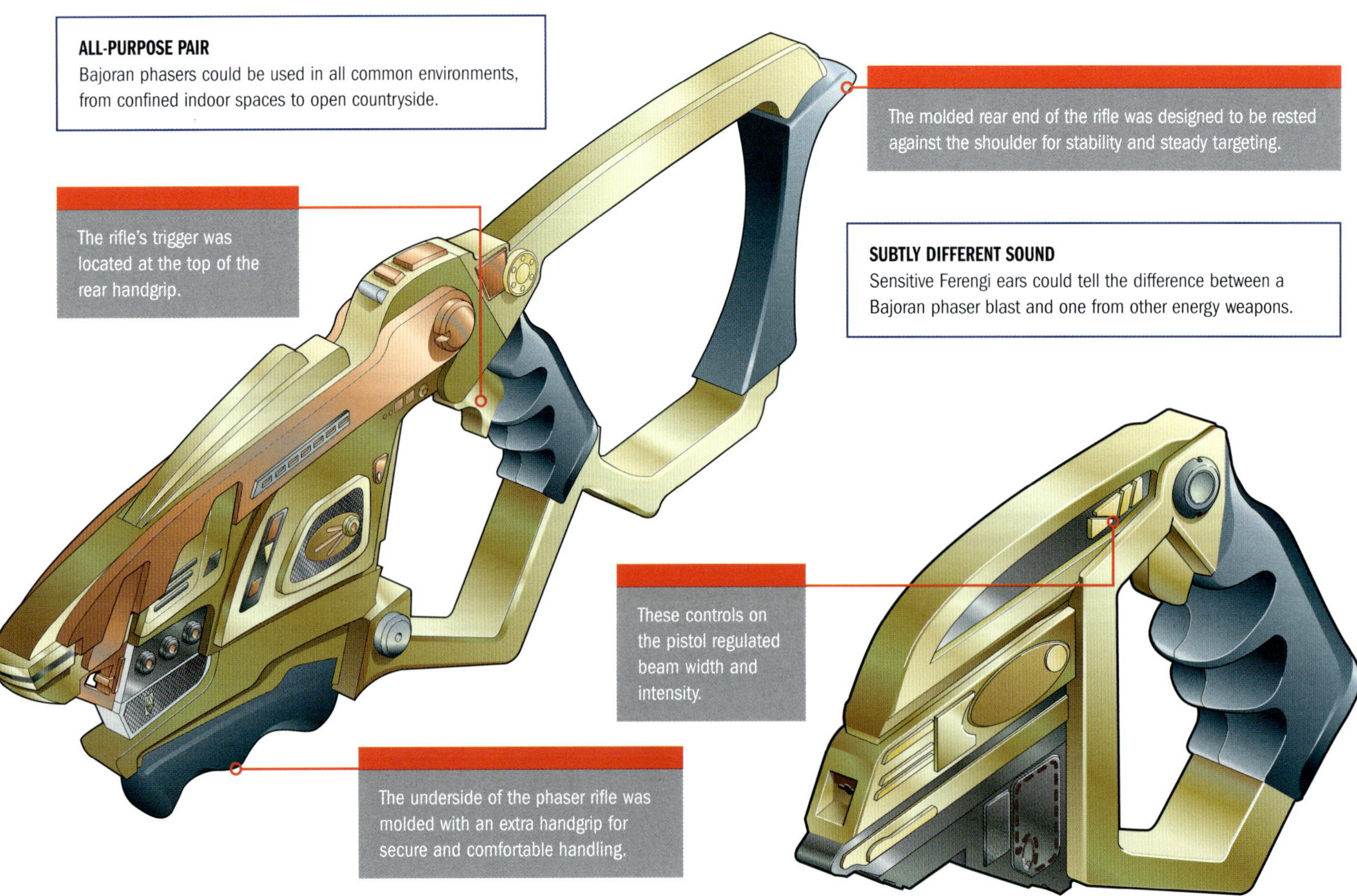

SUBTLY DIFFERENT SOUND
Sensitive Ferengi ears could tell the difference between a Bajoran phaser blast and one from other energy weapons.

PHASER PISTOL

RED ALERT
Bajoran Militia phaser pistols were usually bronze colored, but a red variant was used by the Bajoran extremist group, the Circle.

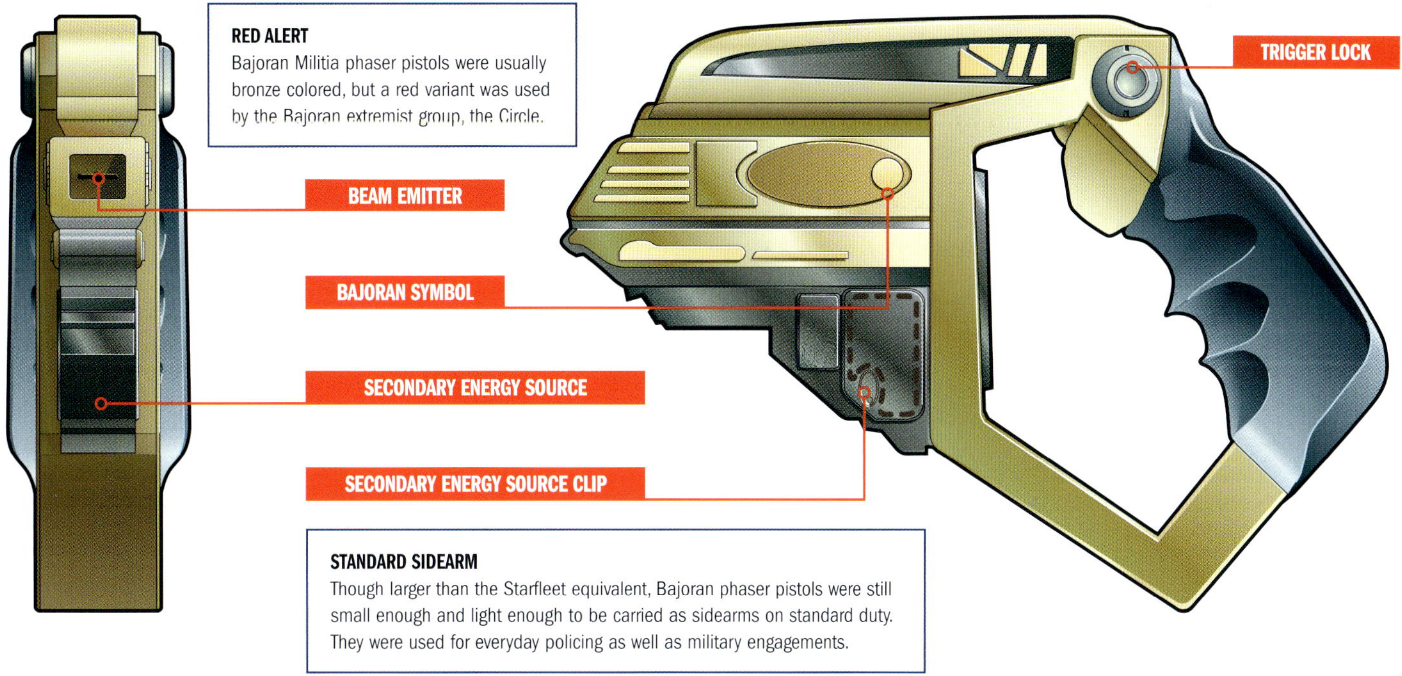

STANDARD SIDEARM
Though larger than the Starfleet equivalent, Bajoran phaser pistols were still small enough and light enough to be carried as sidearms on standard duty. They were used for everyday policing as well as military engagements.

NARROW BEAM
The slim width of the standard Bajoran phaser pistol compensated for its otherwise bulky proportions and kept it flush with the body when holstered. A smaller version was manufactured, but was very rarely used.

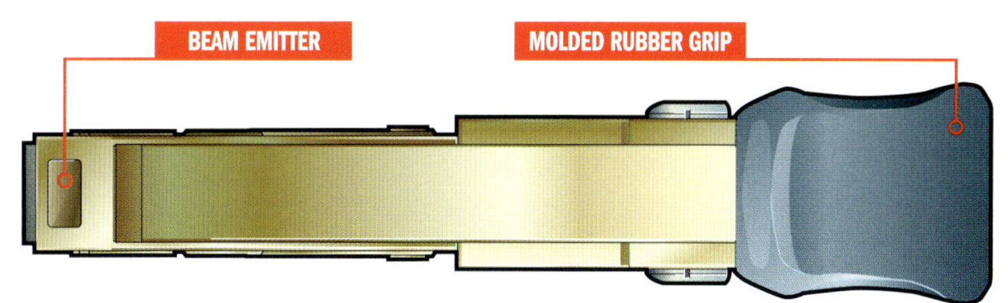

PHASER RIFLE

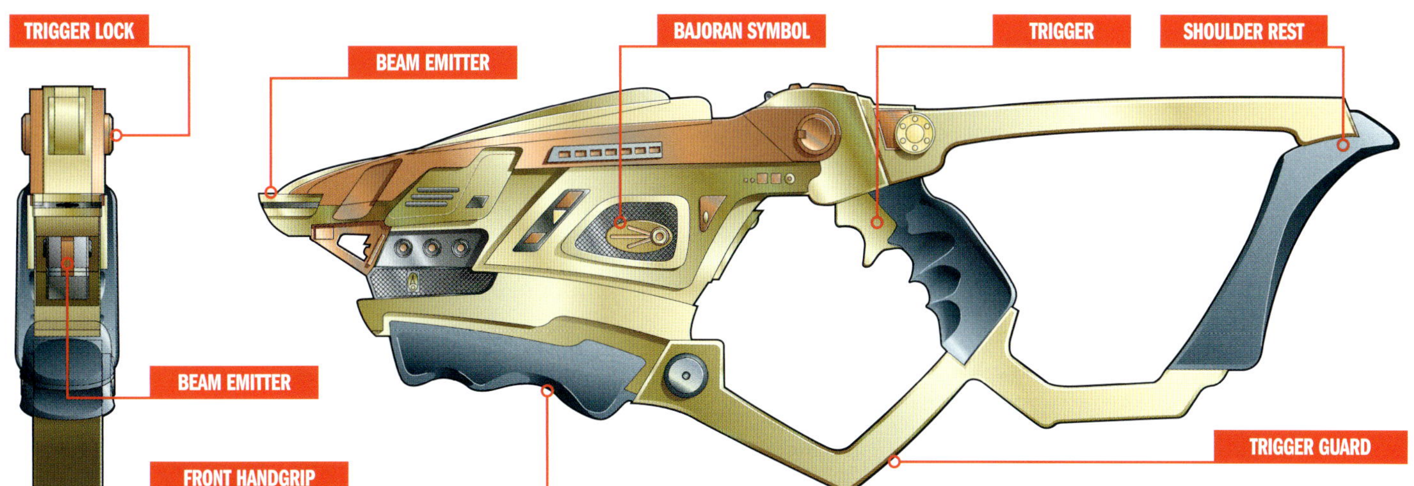

POWER SOURCES
Most Bajoran phaser rifles were powered by a rechargeable isotolinium ampule. Others used sarium-krellide energy cells for compatibility with Starfleet chargers.

SAFETY PRECAUTIONS
On Deep Space 9, phaser rifle strength was automatically capped at setting three, also referred to as heavy stun.

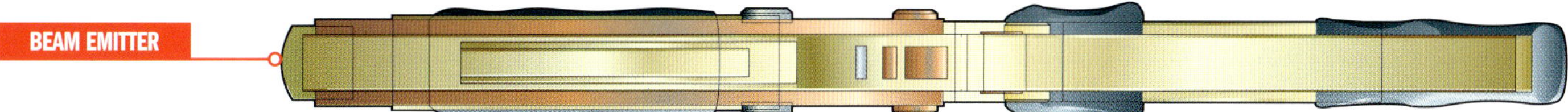

BAJORAN TRICORDER

The standard scanning and data recording device used by the Bajorans was an everyday equivalent of Starfleet's more specialized equipment.

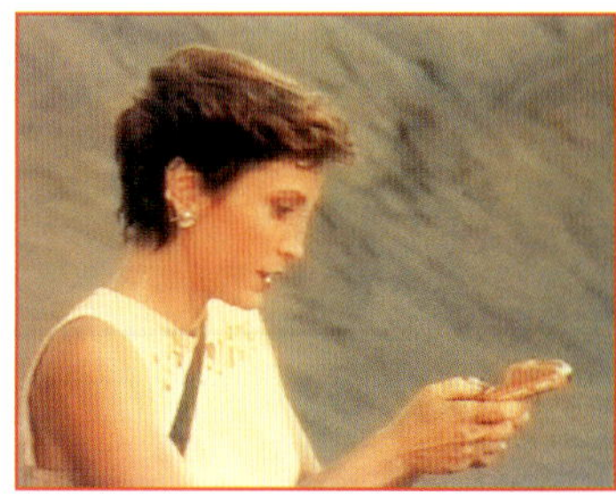

Major Kira used a Bajoran tricorder to locate survivors from a crashed ship on the planet Dozaria, six years after they were first lost.

Unlike the contemporary Starfleet model – which was designed for use by specialists in an array of situations and environments – the Bajoran tricorder was a layperson's tool, intended to function on M-class worlds such as Bajor itself. As a result, it was smaller, far less complex, and much more familiar. Members of the Bajoran Militia were equipped with the devices as standard, and they were also widely used by civilians.

Fitting comfortably in the palm of the hand, with a friction grip on one side, the Bajoran tricorder was made from robust and long-lasting toranium tetraborate. The lower two-thirds of its surface were given over to push-button controls, with the upper section housing a small display screen and all of the device's sensor units.

Most of the sensors were short-range and forward-facing, requiring close proximity for an effective scan. Others were omnidirectional and served to pinpoint phenomena for more detailed close-up readings. All were interchangeable for easy upgrade and repair.

EVERYDAY USES

On Deep Space 9, Bajoran security staff routinely used the tricorder for analyzing electromagnetic phenomena, detecting hidden weapons and weapons discharges, identifying energy signatures, and gathering crime-scene evidence. It also had a number of medical applications, such as monitoring an unborn baby.

Repurposed technology from the Bajoran combadge system also enabled the device to function as an audio receiver and universal translator. Its real-time translation function was 155 percent faster than the equivalent in

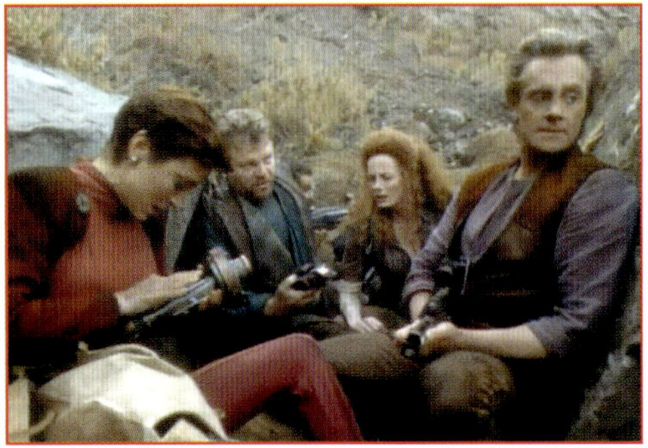

Former resistance members led by Shakaar used a Bajoran tricorder to track the government troops pursuing them.

OVERVIEW

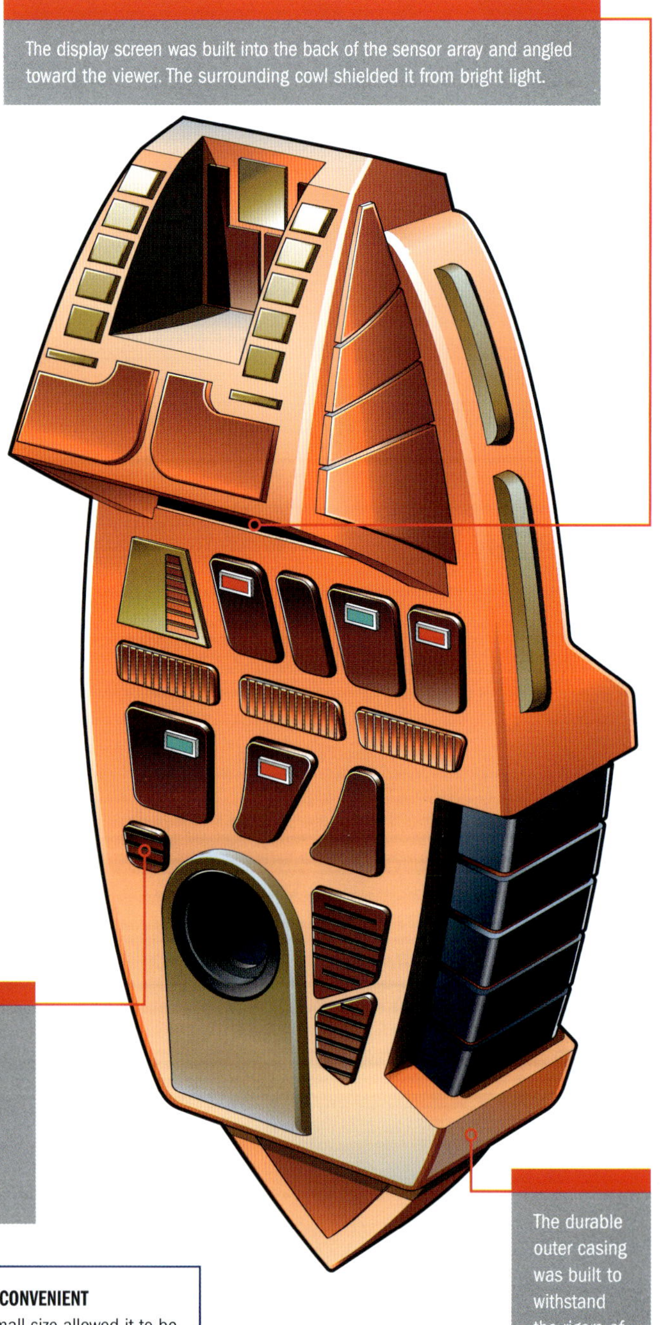

The display screen was built into the back of the sensor array and angled toward the viewer. The surrounding cowl shielded it from bright light.

Push-button controls were augmented by touch-screen functionality on the small, tilted display.

The durable outer casing was built to withstand the rigors of daily use.

COMPACT AND CONVENIENT
The device's small size allowed it to be carried unobtrusively when not in use.

Starfleet technology, but only because it comprised just 198 languages. Under normal conditions, the tricorder was designed to run continuously for 23 hours – powered by Bajoran isotolinium ampules or rechargeable sarium-krellide energy cells, as favored by Starfleet. But certain conditions could deplete the device more rapidly.

STORAGE AND SHORTCOMINGS

The Bajoran tricorder was fitted with 10 reinforced isolinear wafers capable of storing 12.1 kiloquads of information. Interchangeable read-only databases made up a portion of this total, with the remainder kept free for incoming raw data from the sensors. Whenever sensor data needed to be kept, it was streamed into long-term storage – giving the illusion of unlimited capacity. However, despite their myriad applications, Bajoran tricorders were not capable of detecting subspace phenomena or neutrino emissions.

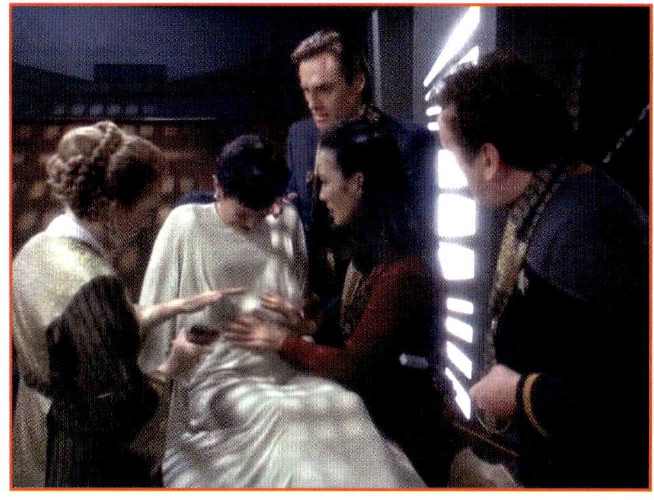

Y'Pora, a Bajoran midwife, used a tricorder to monitor Kira Nerys's pregnancy when she was carrying Miles and Keiko O'Brien's baby as a surrogate mother.

PLANS AND ELEVATION

TOUCH OF A BUTTON

No two controls on the Bajoran tricorder were the exact same shape, making them easier to navigate by touch.

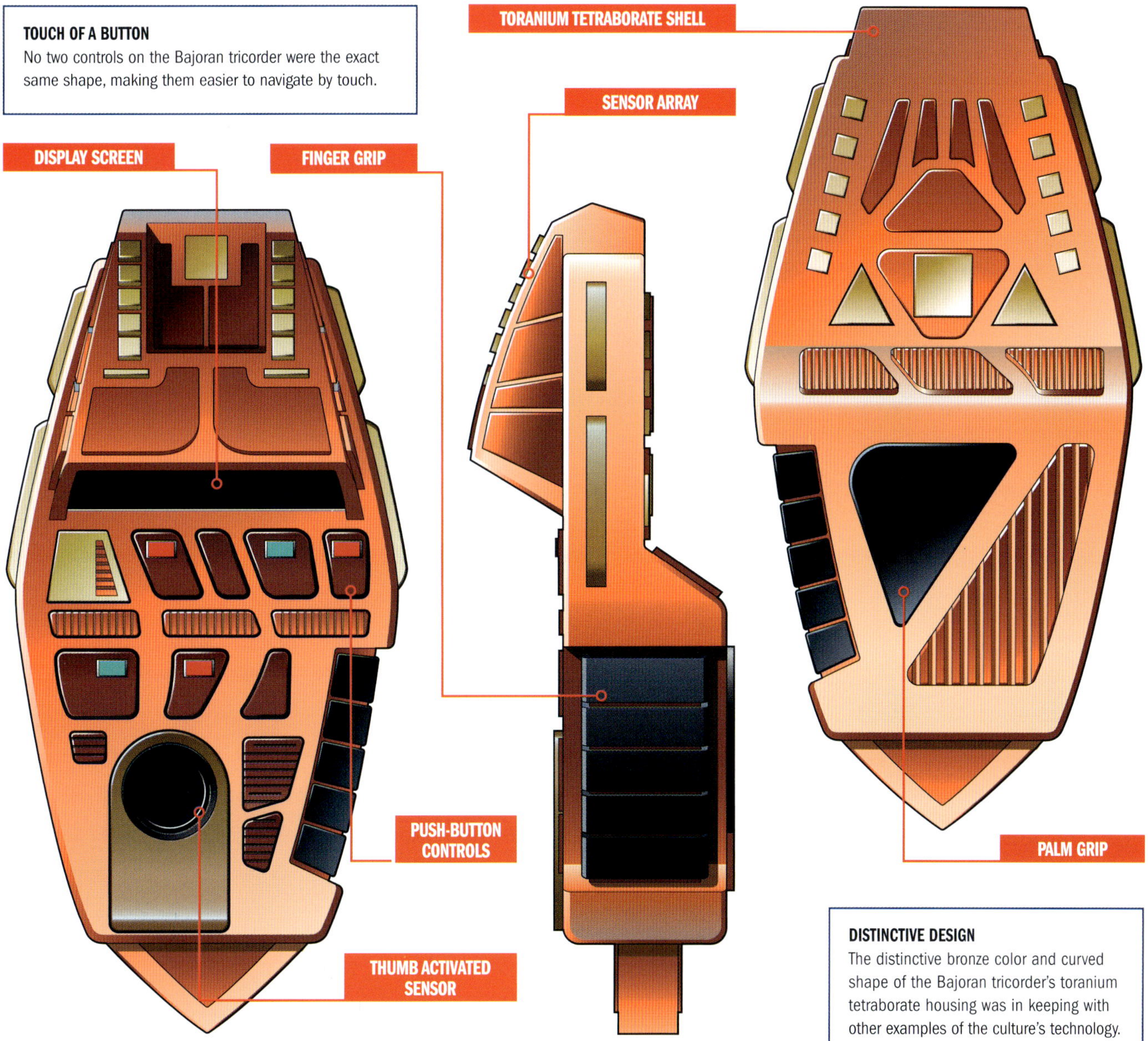

TORANIUM TETRABORATE SHELL

SENSOR ARRAY

DISPLAY SCREEN

FINGER GRIP

PUSH-BUTTON CONTROLS

PALM GRIP

THUMB ACTIVATED SENSOR

DISTINCTIVE DESIGN

The distinctive bronze color and curved shape of the Bajoran tricorder's toranium tetraborate housing was in keeping with other examples of the culture's technology.

ANTI-CHANGELING DEVICES

When the shape-shifting Founders proved they could operate undetected in the Alpha Quadrant, the Federation and other major powers urgently sought ways to locate and identify them.

One of the first effective anti-Changeling devices was developed by the Cardassian Obsidian Order. Relying on the fact that Founders must eventually revert to their natural gelatinous state to regenerate, the device used a quantum stasis field to make such a change impossible. As this caused growing distress to a Changeling over time, it was, effectively, a form of torture.

A prototype of the Cardassian device was used in 2371, when Odo was being held by a combined Romulan Tal Shiar and Obsidian Order fleet. A force field prevented Odo from escaping its effects, and slowly and painfully his humanoid form began to crack and flake, as though he was turning to dust. It is likely the device would eventually have killed him, but he was spared by his interrogator, Garak, who could not go on inflicting pain on someone he considered a friend.

Despite its effectiveness on Odo, the prototype device did have limitations – most notably the need to confine a Changeling in close quarters before use. It is also possible that other Changelings would have reacted differently than Odo when subjected to the device, because of their greater shape-shifting skills. But there were no further opportunities to test this theory, as the prototype was destroyed by the Dominion, along with the entire Tal Shiar/Obsidian Order fleet. After the Cardassian Union joined the Dominion, its priorities with regard to the Founders were rapidly reversed.

IN THE BLOOD

For the Federation and the Klingon Empire, regular blood screenings were initially seen as the most effective way to detect a Changeling posing as one of their own. While

THE CARDASSIAN PROTOTYPE

This unique Obsidian Order device emitted a quantum stasis field to prevent a Changeling from altering its biomolecular structure. It had to be used in conjunction with a force field, to keep the target within range. Though the long-term effects were never tested, they would likely have caused a slow and painful death.

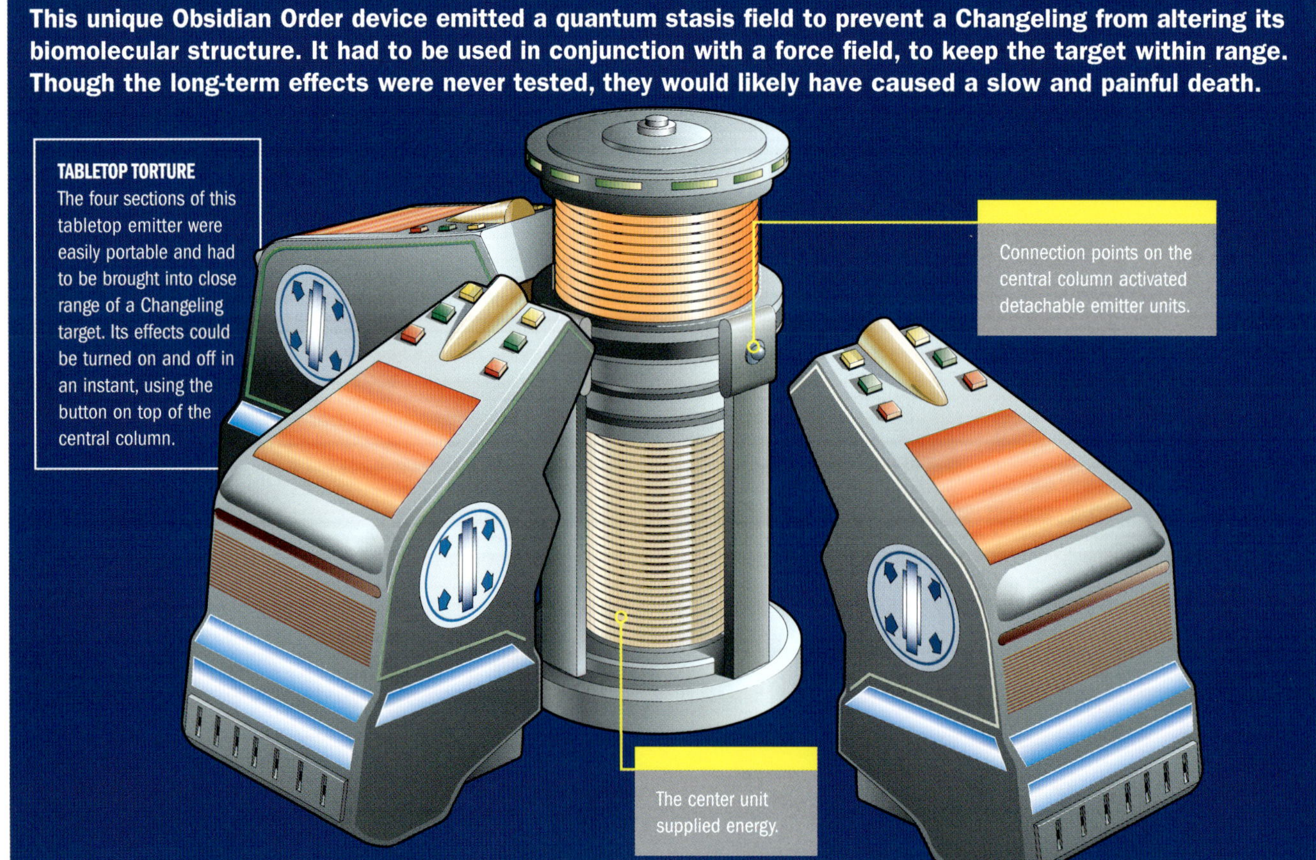

TABLETOP TORTURE
The four sections of this tabletop emitter were easily portable and had to be brought into close range of a Changeling target. Its effects could be turned on and off in an instant, using the button on top of the central column.

the Founders could convincingly assume any form – to the point of fooling tricorders and other scanning devices – any body sample taken from them rapidly reverted to its natural gelatinous state. Starfleet used blood screening with some success in 2371 when the *U.S.S. Defiant* NX-74205 was infiltrated by a Changeling, after which thc Klingon Empirc became obsessive about regular screenings. No Klingon would begin an official encounter without blood first being drawn, and Klingon ships unilaterally enforced testing on board other vessels in Bajoran space, in the vicinity of the wormhole to the Gamma Quadrant.

SCREENING AND PHASER SWEEPS

This level of paranoia eventually reached Earth and, when a Dominion invasion of Earth seemed likely in 2372, Federation President Jaresh-Inyo authorized planetwide blood screening for Starfleet personnel and civilians alike.

It soon became clear that such measures were not only intrusive and time-consuming but also ineffective, whether on Earth or elsewhere. The frequency with which the tests needed to be administered to have any real value was not compatible with a normally functioning society, and it did not take long for the Founders to render such widespread efforts pointless anyway. To escape detection, all that a Changeling had to do was absorb a blood sample from the species being imitated, and then release a drop of it when subjected to a screening.

The next, slightly more effective anti-Changeling device developed by the Federation made use of low-level, wide-beam phaser sweeps. Phaser settings of 3.5 were enough to cause pain to a Changeling – forcing it to return to its gelatinous state – but did no damage to the immediate surroundings. This technique was trialed in empty rooms, where a Changeling could be disguised as any inanimate object, but could not be used in populated areas, given that most species suffered discomfort from even a low-level phaser beam. Starfleet installed fixed phaser emitters in sensitive locations so that they could be swept ahead of occupancy, and also carried out room-by-room drills using phaser rifles. But resistance to such measures was never seriously tested, given the Founders' success in imitating far more useful living subjects.

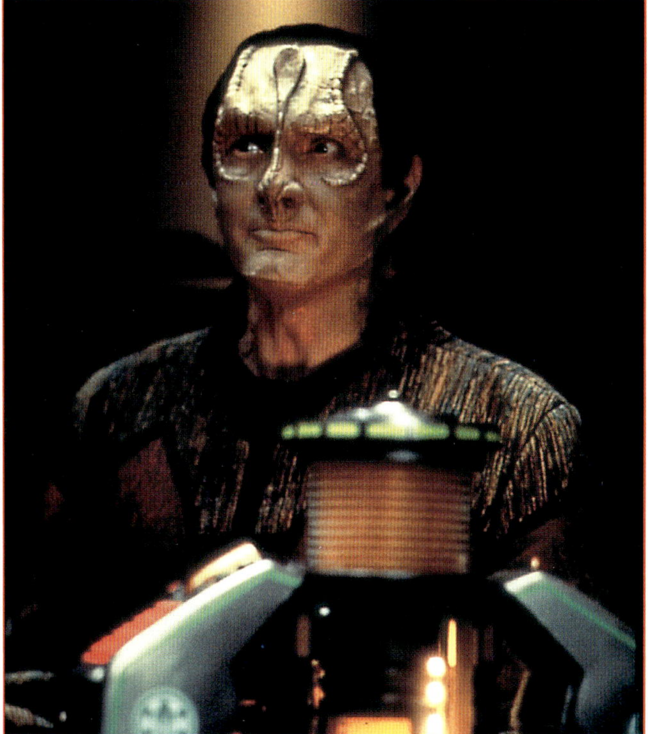

Elim Garak with the Obsidian Order's prototype anti-Changeling device. Garak used the device to torture Odo and wrestled with his conscience afterwards.

NATURAL DEFENSES

Some naturally occurring substances also proved harmful to Changelings. In 2370, on the planet L-S VI, Odo was exposed to a volcanic gas that caused him to become a gelatinous creature with beast-like instincts. Harnessing the rare gas for its anti-Changeling properties may have been possible, but its effects on the Founders may have been different from those experienced by Odo. They may also have known how to expel the gas from their systems, because doctors Julian Bashir and Mora Pol eventually purged it from Odo, restoring him to normal health.

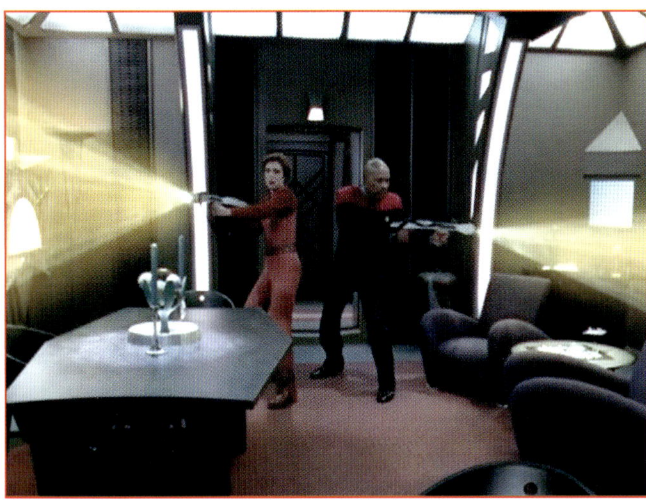

Major Kira and Captain Sisko carried out low-level phaser sweeps during a training exercise on Deep Space 9. A team of two could sweep a room in a few seconds.

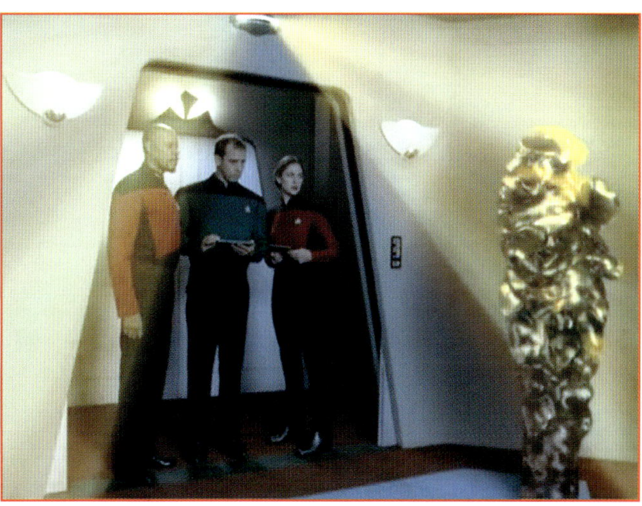

Odo was forced to revert to his naturally gelatinous state when he agreed to test the effectiveness of a low-level, wide-beam phaser emitter on Earth in 2372.

MODIFIED POLARON EMITTERS

Starfleet needed to develop devices to combat the Changelings, but often the biggest challenge was to pinpoint them in the first place. If a blood screening was not a viable option, other methods had to be employed.

With the threat from the Dominion rising, the United Federation of Planets developed many strategies, devices, and safeguards against the Changelings. Many of these were aimed at revealing Changeling impostors rather than causing injury or death to the individuals involved. Once a Changeling had been exposed, the main threat was generally over. Some Changeling countermeasures had been developed from scratch, while others had been modified from existing Federation technology. One Changeling defense of the latter type was the modified polaron emitter prototype X-47.

These emitters were small, spherical devices, about the size of a baseball. They were constructed from brass-colored metal, and could be held in the palm of the hand. The devices were used to emit polaron radiation in controlled bursts.

Each emitter comprised two hemispherical halves that separated completely to reveal the inner workings of the device; they could be taken apart and clipped back together with ease. Starfleet scientists had discovered that exposure to polaron radiation had a destabilizing effect on Changeling physiology: exposure to the radiation would prevent a Changeling from retaining its humanoid shape and force it to return to its natural, gelatinous state. However, prolonged or repeated exposure to the radiation was fatal to humans, Changelings, and most other known life-forms.

The modified polaron emitters were used in groups of four. Each emitter sent out a beam which, along with the beams of the other three, formed the perimeter of the area to be flooded with polaron radiation. Any Changeling

OVERVIEW

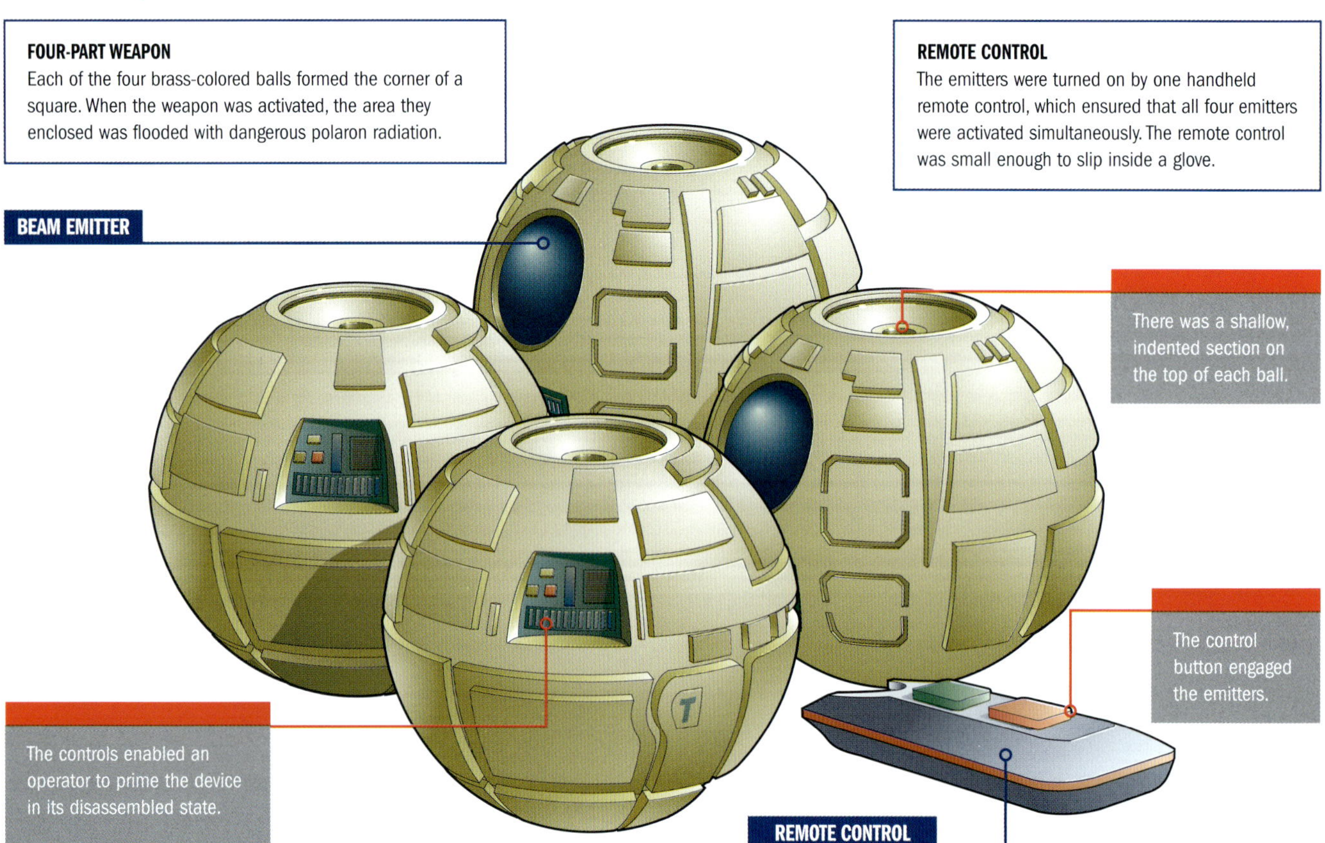

caught within this field would dissolve into its gelatinous state, but remain otherwise unharmed.

RADIATION FIELD

Four emitters could create a radiation field covering 12,000 cubic meters, an area that required the devices to be placed in fairly close proximity to the suspected Changeling before activation. All four emitters had to be turned on simultaneously, and to ensure this happened, they were connected to a single remote control unit.

The emitters were transported in two halves, and were only put together shortly before operating. Each device was primed while separated, then the two halves were snapped together. When the suspected Changeling was in position, the emitters were activated by the remote.

In 2373, officers from Deep Space 9 intended to use modified polaron emitter prototype X-47s against Chancellor Gowron, the suspected Changeling infiltrator of the Klingon military fortress at Ty'Gokor. Unfortunately, they were discovered before they had a chance to trigger the device, and the emitters were then destroyed by the Changeling impersonating General Martok. It is not known, therefore, whether this particular anti-Changeling device would have proved as successful as Starfleet hoped.

INTERIOR

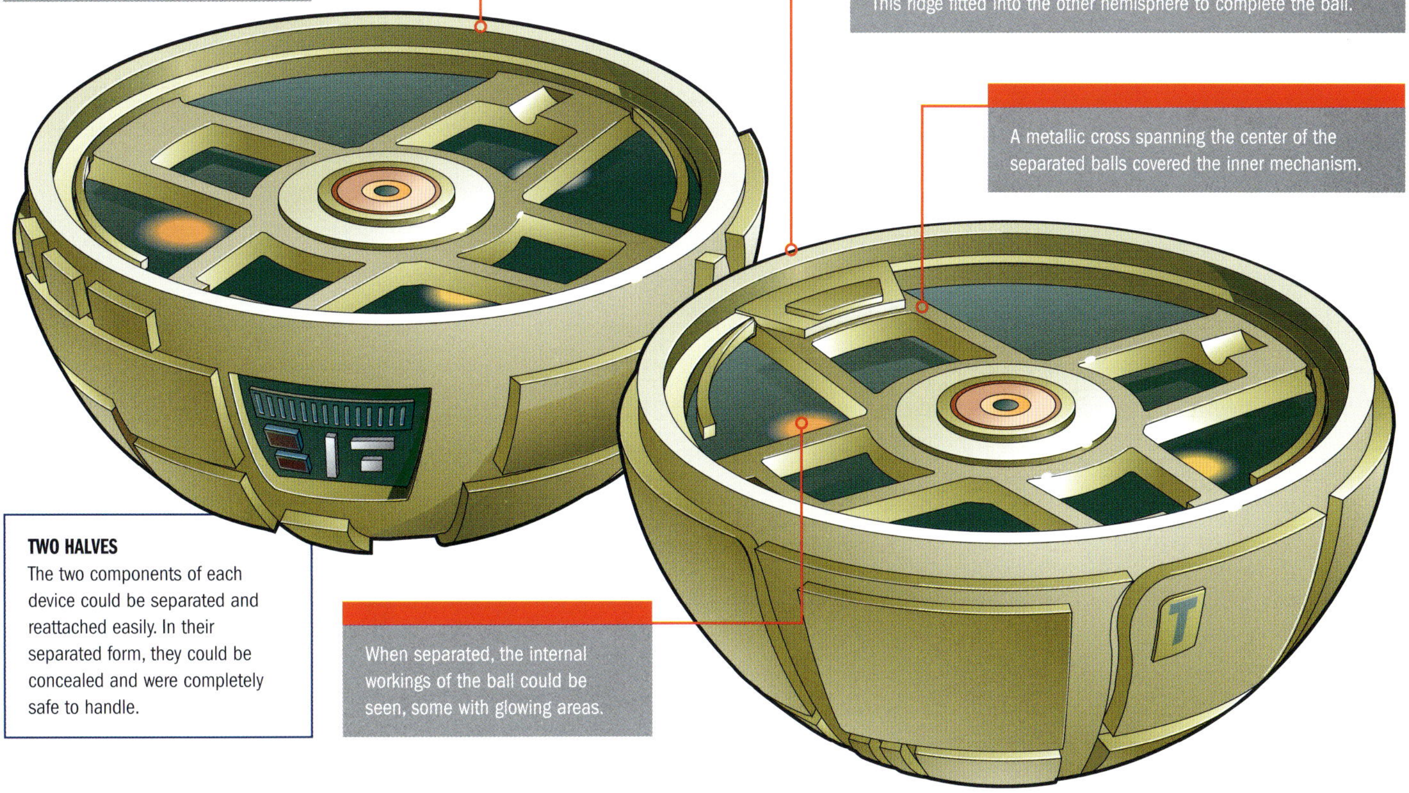

A raised lip on one hemisphere slotted ove a ridge on the other.

This ridge fitted into the other hemisphere to complete the ball.

A metallic cross spanning the center of the separated balls covered the inner mechanism.

TWO HALVES

The two components of each device could be separated and reattached easily. In their separated form, they could be concealed and were completely safe to handle.

When separated, the internal workings of the ball could be seen, some with glowing areas.

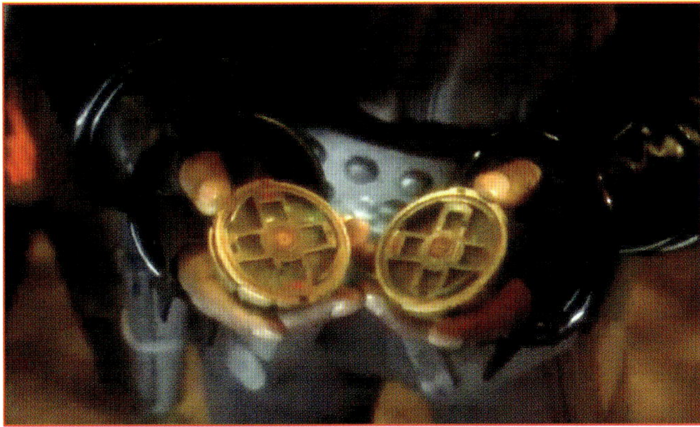

Keeping the emitters separated while in transit helped to prevent accidental activation, which could prove fatal to anyone in the field.

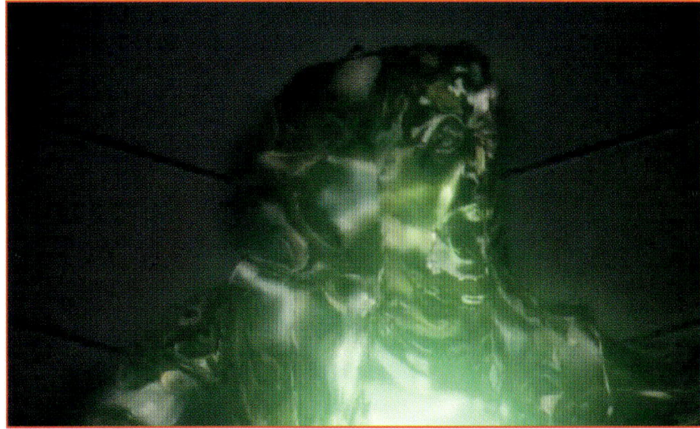

The one-off attempt to use the emitters by Benjamin Sisko and his team was frustrated by the Martok Changeling. They were exposed and the devices destroyed.

QUANTUM STASIS BOX

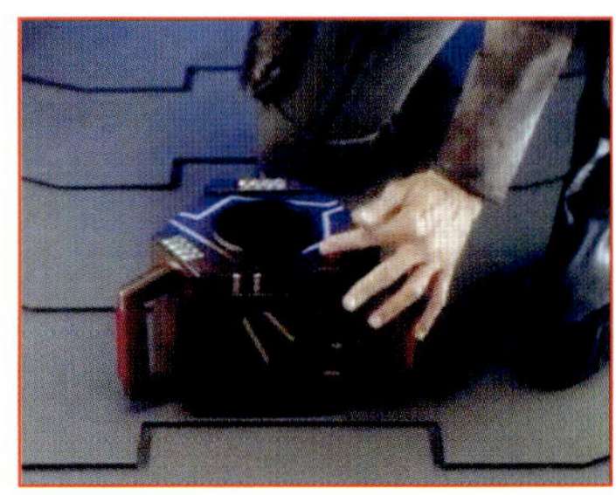
By operating the controls on top of the unit, the stasis box's iris opened, allowing access to the inner chamber.

In 2370, a mercenary group boarded Deep Space 9 intending to steal the Dax symbiont. They had with them a device capable of imprisoning a Changeling in liquid state.

The unique physiology of Deep Space 9's shape-shifting Chief of Security, Odo, gave the Changeling many advantages during his service aboard the station, which saw occupation by both Cardassian and Federation forces. His abilities were well respected, and even feared by some. For example, when Deep Space 9 was evacuated during a plasma storm, its skeleton staff was overpowered and the station taken over by a mercenary group that included the renegade Trill, Verad. He wanted to steal the Dax symbiont but knew that Odo was the most substantial block to this. So he aimed to immobilize the security chief as quickly as possible.

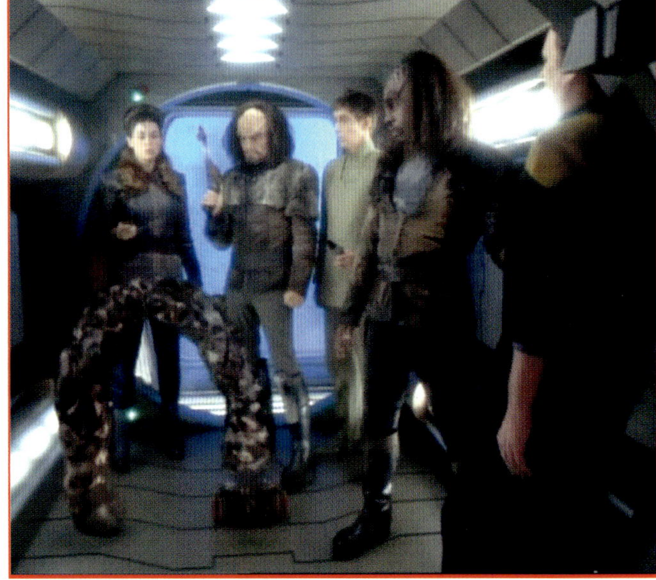
With the skeleton crew taken hostage, the belligerents coerced chief of security Odo into the stasis box in his Changeling liquid state.

INCARCERATION

To imprison Odo effectively and ensure the success of their plan, the group used a portable stasis box that appeared to have been manufactured specifically for the purpose of containing a Changeling in its liquid state. The stasis box was a sturdy, six-sided device, constructed from a durable dark-brown alloy that formed a protective exterior shell. Three of the longer sides were equal, separated by narrower, angled connecting sections with carrying handles.

The box was approximately half a meter across – from the outside of one handle to the opposite edge – and was around 25cm in height. The sides of the box comprised a number of smaller raised and depressed sections that protected the mechanism within the unit. This included the self-contained power system, and a sophisticated Delgorian locking mechanism.

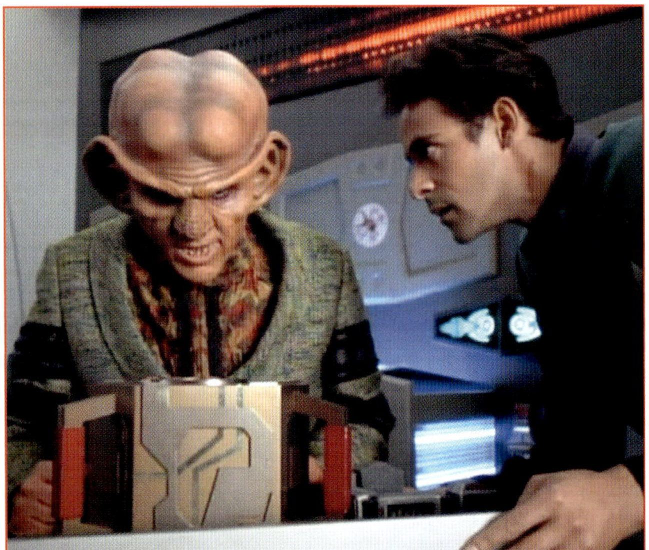
Such complex locks were no trouble to Deep Space 9's resident lockpick Quark. Using a laser cutter and a little bit of luck, he managed to open the stasis box.

ACCESS CODES

Delgorian locks offered a high level of security: a specific sequential access code had to be input through the seven raised buttons on the upper surface of the box. The correct manipulation of these buttons opened the five-sectioned metallic iris set into the raised circular port in the middle of the box.

Once the box had been opened and was ready for occupancy, however, there was no mechanism for forcing Odo into its confines. The Klingon T'Kar therefore had to threaten O'Brien's life to force Odo to revert to his liquefied state. The Changeling oozed headfirst into the hole before the iris was closed and locked. The unit was then carried away for enforced storage in Dr. Julian Bashir's medical facility.

The design of Verad's stasis box did not offer Odo any means of escape – the device appeared to be hermetically sealed, and was a cunningly effective way of incarcerating the Changeling. Bashir's attempts to open the box without the access code were met by failure. However, Quark's knowledge of locking systems enabled him to locate the weaknesses in the unit. Using a laser scalpel to remove a small plate on one side of the box, he manipulated the inner workings with one hand, and input the codes at the same time. In under 30 seconds, Quark had succeeded in opening the iris, allowing the shape-shifter to escape.

STARFLEET VARIATIONS

The stasis box also offered a unique protection for Changeling physiology. In 2373, the crew of the *U.S.S. Defiant* encountered extremely powerful quantum fluctuations within a strange energy barrier surrounding a planet. The effects on Odo's physiology were so severe that they prevented him from maintaining a humanoid shape, and he reverted back to his gelatinous state. Bashir stored him in a specially designed Starfleet version of Verad's stasis container to keep him safe.

A variation on this device was also used by Bashir to protect Odo some three years later. The doctor's purpose was far more benign than that of the original maker, however. Bashir's device consisted of two main parts: a large cylinder in which Odo could reside comfortably in his liquid form; and the main containment unit, in which the transparent cylinder sat.

Two small handles allowed Bashir to move the cylinder and lower it into the opened square unit, which was constructed from a polished metallic alloy in keeping with the design of Starfleet medical equipment.

STANDALONE UNIT

The main containment chamber was a standalone unit that had its own internal power source. Its active status was indicated by a number of different diodes on the large raised black panel on the box's front and some smaller red circular diodes in the thick lid. It was opened via a small control panel on the upper left side, instantly releasing a seal so the lid swung upward. This allowed easy access to the interior of the container. The stasis box did not require constant external monitoring.

ODO'S STASIS BOX

CONSTRUCTION
Since the stasis chamber was designed as a prison, it consisted of a sturdy construction that would withstand most attempts at tampering. It was not resistant to disruptor fire, however, so the stasis box could be deliberately damaged. Such violence might seriously injure the Changeling within.

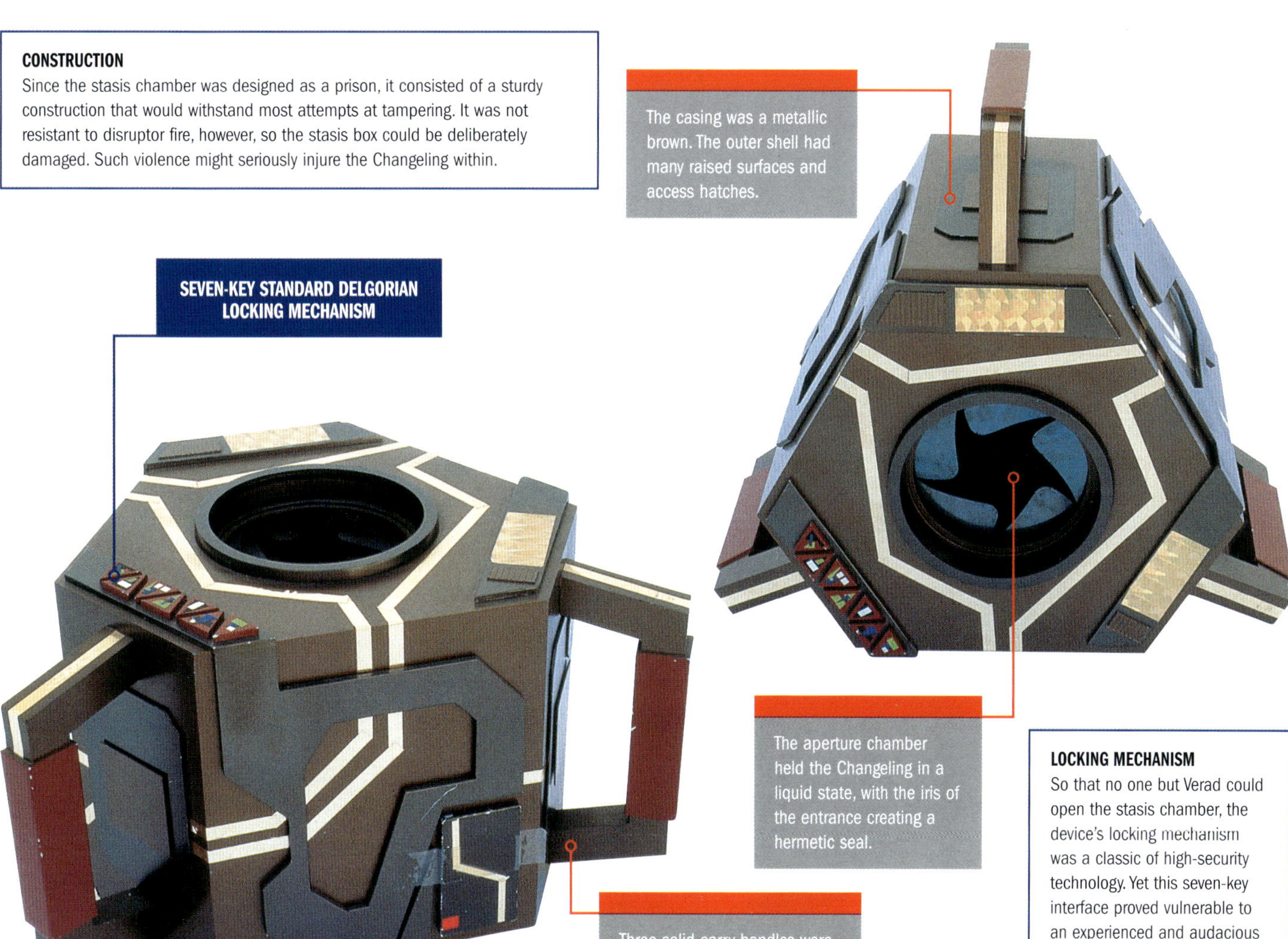

The casing was a metallic brown. The outer shell had many raised surfaces and access hatches.

SEVEN-KEY STANDARD DELGORIAN LOCKING MECHANISM

The aperture chamber held the Changeling in a liquid state, with the iris of the entrance creating a hermetic seal.

Three solid carry handles were attached to each alternate face of the stasis chamber.

LOCKING MECHANISM
So that no one but Verad could open the stasis chamber, the device's locking mechanism was a classic of high-security technology. Yet this seven-key interface proved vulnerable to an experienced and audacious lockpick, who found various means of bypassing the system.

SELF-REPLICATING MINES

These cloaked weapons automatically replaced themselves if they were destroyed. Disabling them was extremely difficult and involved the use of a massive anti-graviton generator.

Self-replicating mines were developed by the Federation to prevent the Dominion from sending ships through the Bajoran wormhole to support their forces in the Alpha Quadrant. They were extremely effective weapons that frustrated the Dominion for months, until Starfleet retook Deep Space 9.

Mining the wormhole presented a number of problems. Dominion ships could destroy conventional pulse mines from a distance, clearing a path to the wormhole. A new approach was therefore needed to make the wormhole inaccessible to the Dominion.

First of all, the mines were cloaked to prevent them from being detected. Then, because the Dominion had extremely advanced sensor technology, Starfleet also had to make them smaller than they would have wished. Each mine was no more than a meter across, which meant that on its own, a single mine could not produce a high enough explosive yield to disable a warship. To compensate for this, the minefield was extremely tightly packed, ensuring that any ship trying to pass through the field was likely to connect with dozens of mines. They were also programmed to swarm detonate in groups of 20 or 30.

IN GREAT NUMBERS

Another important consequence of making such small-scale mines was that they had to be laid in unusually large numbers. Starfleet also needed to be able to replace mines quickly, but as the minefield would be in Dominion territory, there would be no chance of visiting and maintaining it. Rom, the Ferengi engineer working on Deep

OVERVIEW

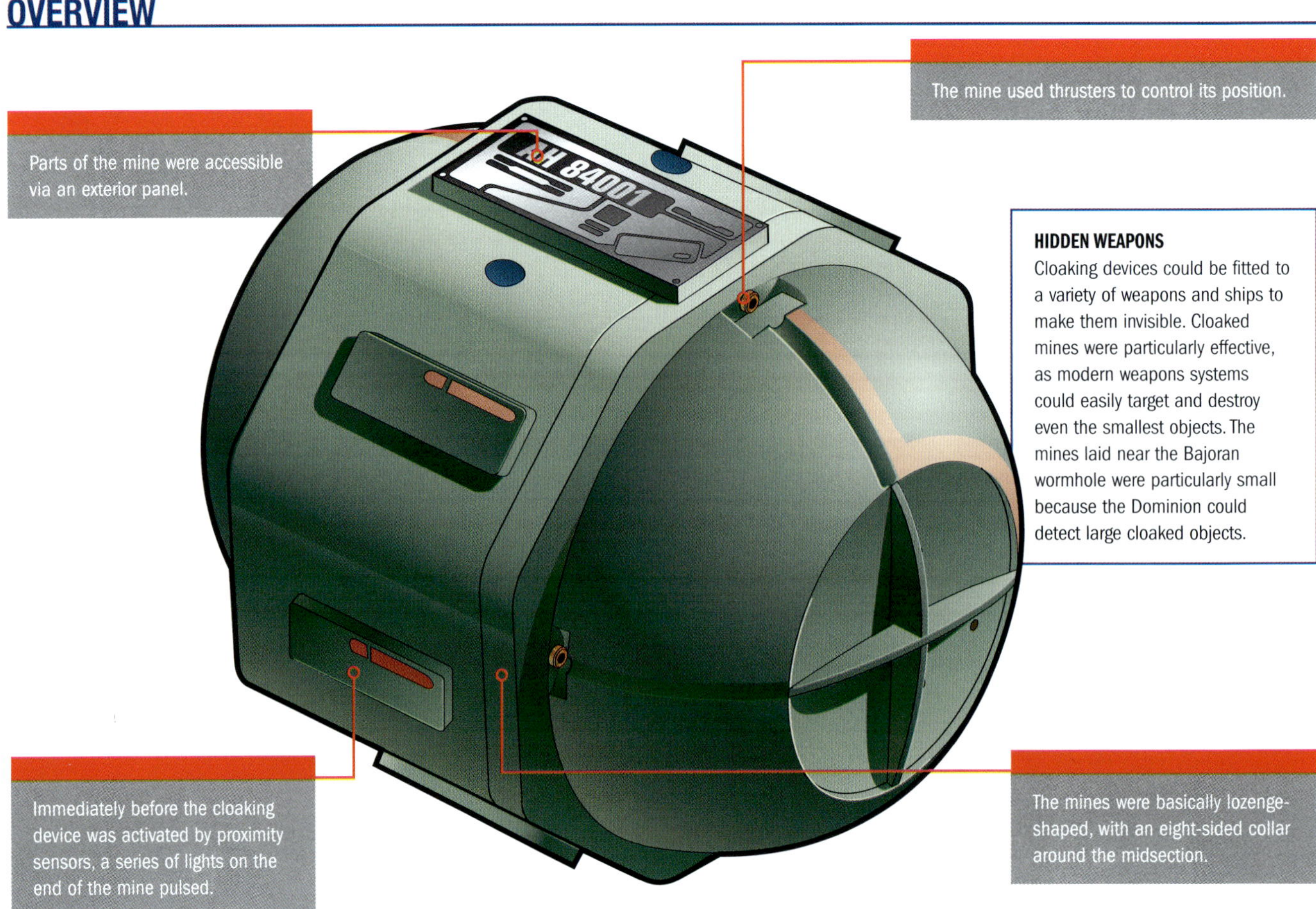

The mine used thrusters to control its position.

Parts of the mine were accessible via an exterior panel.

HIDDEN WEAPONS

Cloaking devices could be fitted to a variety of weapons and ships to make them invisible. Cloaked mines were particularly effective, as modern weapons systems could easily target and destroy even the smallest objects. The mines laid near the Bajoran wormhole were particularly small because the Dominion could detect large cloaked objects.

Immediately before the cloaking device was activated by proximity sensors, a series of lights on the end of the mine pulsed.

The mines were basically lozenge-shaped, with an eight-sided collar around the midsection.

Space 9, suggested that the answer was to enable the mines to replicate automatically. Each mine was equipped with a replicator so that it could replace its neighbors as they were destroyed.

DELICATE TASK

The mines were triggered by proximity sensors when near an object, so the minefield could not be activated until all the mines had been deployed. Because so many mines were needed, laying a minefield was a slow process. It took four days for the *U.S.S. Defiant* to establish the field around the Bajoran wormhole. The mines were extremely sensitive, so when the ship was deploying them, it had to take care not to make any sudden movements.

The only way to prevent the mines from self-replicating themselves was to isolate each one in an anti-graviton beam. The Dominion eventually discovered how to achieve this by reconfiguring the field generators in Deep Space 9's deflector dish, thus producing a huge anti-graviton beam. Once the beam was complete, it was a relatively simple operation to destroy the massive number of mines.

TOP/BOTTOM VIEW

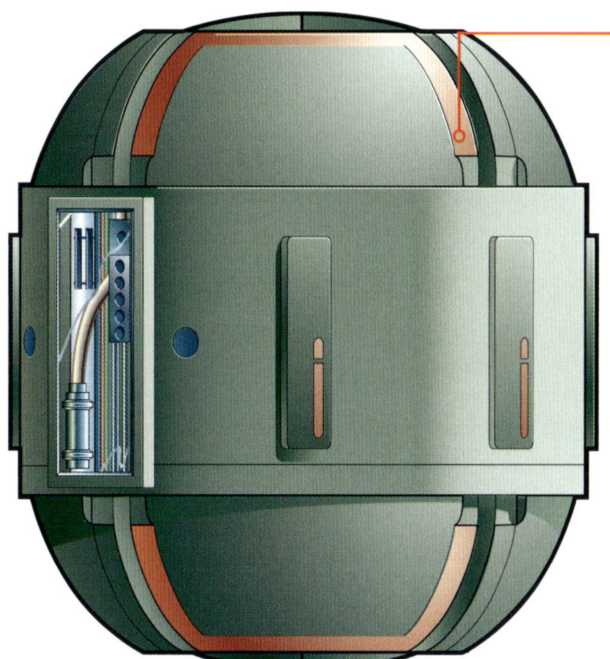

The mines had a diameter of approximately one meter and their small size was compensated by laying them in multiples, close together.

ENDLESS SUPPLY

Self-replication technology was not used on mines until 2373. The idea was developed by Deep Space 9 personnel Rom, Dax, and O'Brien. Because the mines were automatically replaced, it was extremely difficult to dismantle the minefield. Theoretically, the mines could survive forever. The replicator fitted to each mine could only be deactivated by being isolated in an anti-graviton beam. This then allowed the minefield to be destroyed by conventional methods.

SWARM DETONATION

The self-replicating mines were smaller than a photon or quantum torpedo, and they had to accommodate the replicators that were used to maintain the minefield. This meant that there was less room for explosives than in a conventional mine. As a result, the mines were programmed to swarm detonate: when triggered, 20 or 30 mines produced more than enough power to disable a Dominion warship.

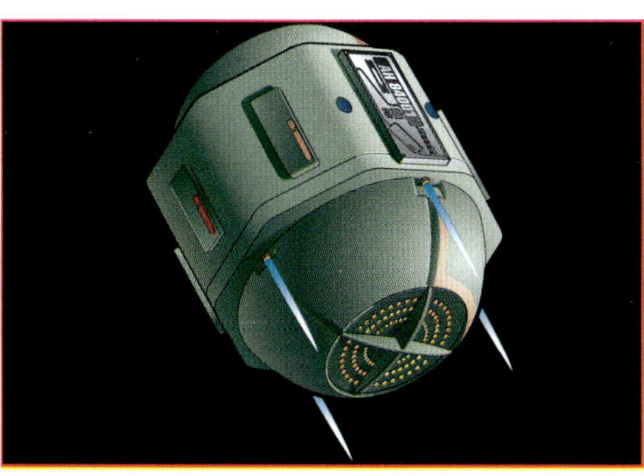

The four thrusters enabled the mine to maneuver itself. When a mine had been replicated it could move into position.

END VIEW

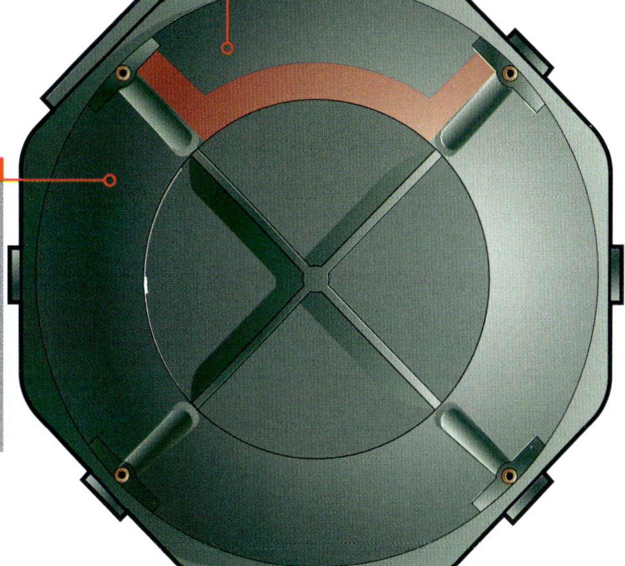

Whenever a mine was destroyed, it was instantly replaced by its neighbor.

The mine's cloaking device hid it from sensors, making it very difficult to establish the extent and proportions of the minefield.

REMOTE TRANSPORTER

Ease of movement was an important feature of the 24th century, whether within an indigenous environment or traveling the Galaxy. The remote transporter crossed all borders, and allowed travel into the mirror universe.

Late in 2267, a landing party led by Captain James T. Kirk of the *U.S.S. Enterprise* NCC-1701 was involved in an extraordinary transporter malfunction when beaming back from the planet Halkan. An extremely violent ion storm caused the team to be transposed with their counterparts from a previously unknown mirror universe. Their subsequent experiences and eventual return to their normal world became the first documented Starfleet encounter with this dark and violent alternate reality. While cross-reality contamination was confined to the *I.S.S. Enterprise* NCC-1701 and the primary *Enterprise*, the existence of an alternate universe to both realities remained undeniable fact.

CROSSING THE LINE

The conditions that caused the original transference were not repeated for more than a century. On Stardate 47879.2, Major Kira Nerys and Dr. Julian Bashir were traveling on a damaged runabout back to Deep Space 9 when it crossed the boundary into the mirror universe within the Bajoran wormhole. This marked the beginning of sporadic attempts by the Terran counterparts of Deep Space 9's senior officers to enlist the help of Captain Benjamin Sisko in their fight against the powerful Klingon-Cardassian Alliance.

REMOTE ACCESS

One of the greatest problems faced by the Terrans in trying to retrieve Sisko from Deep Space 9 was how to recreate the transporter malfunction that allowed travel between the realities. Miles 'Smiley' O'Brien of the mirror universe was at first reluctant to help Kira Nerys and Bashir to escape from his world. However, he later developed a remote transporter unit that could duplicate exactly the effect on a Cardassian-designed transporter that had initiated the two previous rogue events. In addition to this complex engineering, the remote transporter unit avoided the need for an operator on either side of the universes' divide to initiate transportation of one or more individuals, so allowing the user to act with a great deal of flexibility.

The concept of remote transportation was not a new one to Starfleet personnel, but the remote transporter unit had the additional function of altering the nature of the transporter beam, enabling safe passage through the reality divide.

OVERVIEW

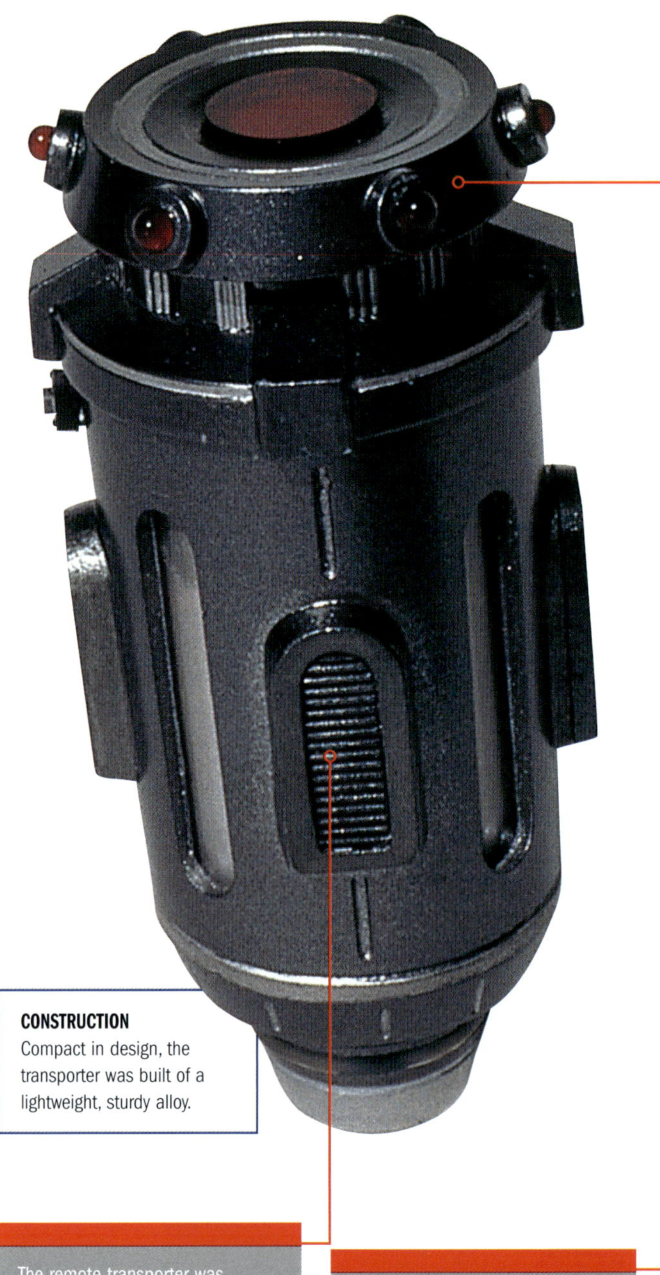

CONSTRUCTION
Compact in design, the transporter was built of a lightweight, sturdy alloy.

The remote transporter was operated with a switch and could be used with just one hand.

Small round diodes flashed when the mechanism was in use.

COMPONENT CONSTRUCTION

The remote transporter unit was compact and highly sophisticated, constructed from a sturdy metallic alloy. The device's various components were all roughly cylindrical, with the smooth surface of the middle section allowing ease of carrying and use with just one hand. A series of indentations and surface-mounted rectangular controls were located on the central section. These enabled the device to be calibrated for use with transporter systems regardless of the universe where it was being activated. The unit was approximately 15cm long and 6cm in diameter at its widest point, making it relatively easy to hide until required for use.

EFFECTS OF TRAVEL

In addition to carrying out physical transportation, the remote transporter seemed to include some form of instruction to the system on which it was employed, to counteract the physical effects of moving from the normal to the mirror universe. The initial foray by Dr. Bashir and Major Nerys in 2370 left both of them feeling dizzy on arrival in the duplicate universe. This was a problem not subsequently encountered by O'Brien, Sisko, or the alternate Jennifer Sisko in their journeys between the two realities.

The function was particularly important the first time that the remote transporter was employed by Smiley O'Brien in 2371, when he kidnapped Sisko from Deep Space 9. Passing through to the mirror universe, Sisko was still in control of his faculties, although he was quickly overpowered. O'Brien's appearance on Deep Space 9 also illustrated how effective the unit was on the Starfleet-modified Cardassian technology, although the similarity between equipment and systems had been previously noted by Starfleet personnel who had experienced the swap over. The second and final use of the remote transporter unit occurred a year later in 2372, when the alternate Jennifer Sisko kidnapped Jake Sisko. She took him back to the mirror universe, leaving the remote unit for Captain Sisko to find within his private quarters. This suggested either that the device could initiate transportation away from a pad, or that more than one of the Terran-designed units existed.

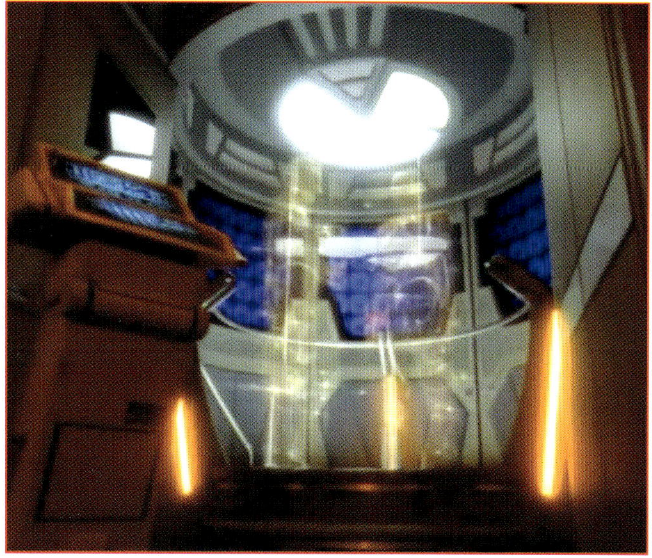

Captain Benjamin Sisko and Smiley O'Brien used the remote transporter unit to materialize on board Terok Nor in the mirror universe.

THROUGH THE WORMHOLE

Kira Nerys and Julian Bashir discovered a mirror universe in which everything had changed. The station was orbiting Bajor, Nerys was a tyrannical Intendant, Sisko a piratical captain, and the Klingon-Cardassian alliance was the major power. Bashir did not find his mirror-self in his first foray into the mirror universe.

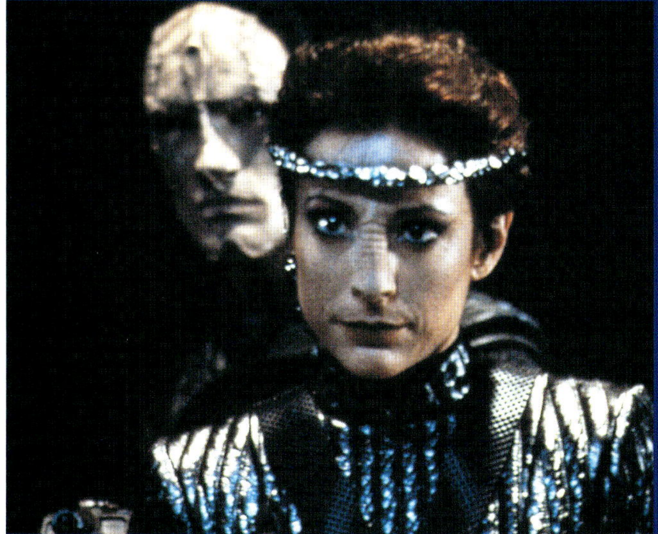

In the mirror universe, Bajor was part of the Klingon-Cardassian Alliance and Kira Nerys was the Intendant of the Bajor sector, based on Terok Nor.

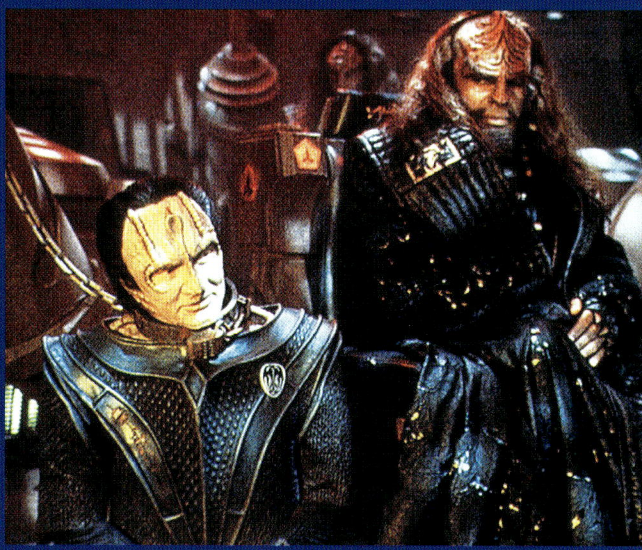

The mirror universe version of Worf was the Klingon emperor, and he kept Garak in chains aboard his massive flagship.

UNIFORMS AND RANK INSIGNIA

During Ben Sisko's tenure as commander of Deep Space 9, Starfleet's uniforms underwent a number of significant changes as new versions were introduced throughout the Federation.

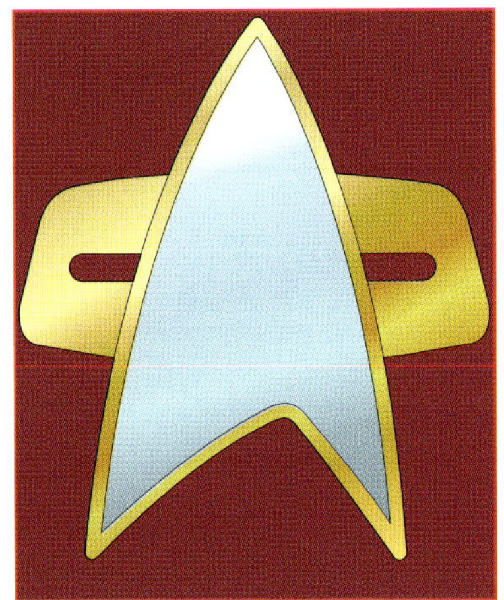

COMMAND (Duty Color Red)
as worn by Kira Nerys

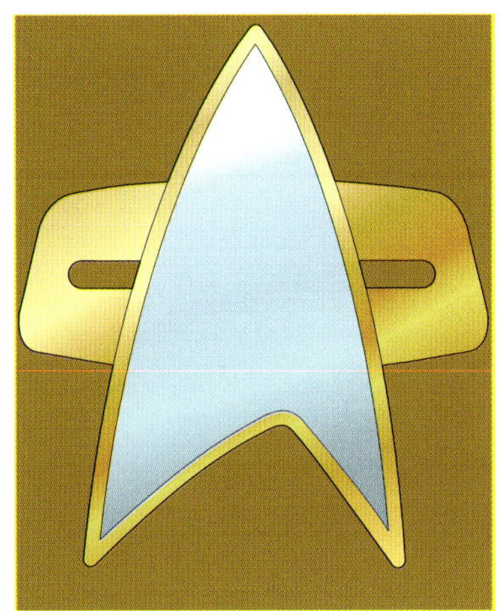

OPERATIONS (Duty Color Gold)
as worn by Miles O'Brien

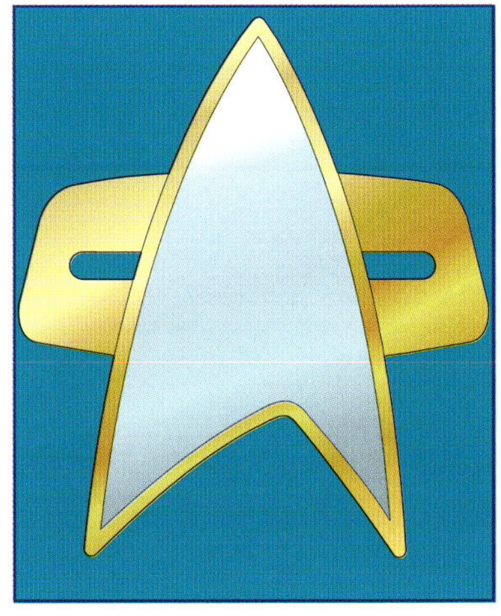

SCIENCE (Duty Color Blue)
as worn by Jadzia Dax and Julian Bashir

Starfleet officers assigned to Deep Space 9 were originally supplied with the standard duty uniforms that were introduced in the late 2360s. This version featured a two-tone design with a black body and pants, and division colors (red for command, gold for operations and blue for medical/science) on the yoke. An undershirt in division colour was worn beneath the jacket. Originally, this version of the uniform was reserved for officers serving on space stations, but by 2371 it had been introduced throughout the fleet and was also worn on starships. These duty uniforms were updated in 2373, with the yoke quilted and its color changed to blue-gray across all divisions. Colors for the divisions appeared in a band on the raised collar, with a corresponding stripe on the cuff. By this point, all Starfleet personnel wore a delta-shaped communicator badge, but in 2371 the shape behind the delta was changed from an ellipse to a rectangle with a void in the middle.

Rank insignia followed the system in use since the mid-24th century, and was denoted by a series of small circular pips, each just one centimeter in diameter, worn on the right-hand side of the collar. Pips were either gold or black with a metallic ring. The black pips were the equivalent of a "half pip," indicating a lower rank than a solid gold pip. The lowest rank of commissioned offer was ensign, shown by a single gold pip.

A gold pip accompanied by a black pip denoted a lieutenant junior grade, a position held by Dr. Julian Bashir when he first arrived on the station before his promotion to lieutenant, a rank indicated by two solid gold pips. An additional black pip was worn by officers who attained the rank of lieutenant commander. Michael Eddington, Starfleet security officer, held this rank on Deep Space 9, until his disillusionment with Starfleet led him to defect to the Maquis. The station's strategic operations officer, Worf, also held the rank of lieutenant commander.

A full commander – a role initially taken by Benjamin Sisko on Deep Space 9 – wore three solid gold pips. He was promoted to captain while on the station, a status indicated by four gold pips.

All ranks above captain were referred to as admirals, a category with five separate ranks, of which fleet admiral was the most senior. Lowest-ranking admirals wore a single metal pip, placed on a black background and bordered in gold. Pips increased with the admiral's importance, and were worn on both sides of the uniform collar. Some uniform variants also incorporated the rank bands on the outside of the tunic cuffs.

Noncommissioned officers, such as Chief Miles O'Brien, had a different kind of rank insignia. Initially, O'Brien wore a single black pip, but this was updated to a small rectangular plate on his collar.

BAJORAN UNIFORMS AND INSIGNIA

Deep Space 9 was jointly administered with the Bajorans who used the color of their uniforms to indicate what division they belonged to. Officers in the command division wore red/orange uniforms. Security wore brown, while engineering and operations officers wore gray, which was also worn by flag officers.

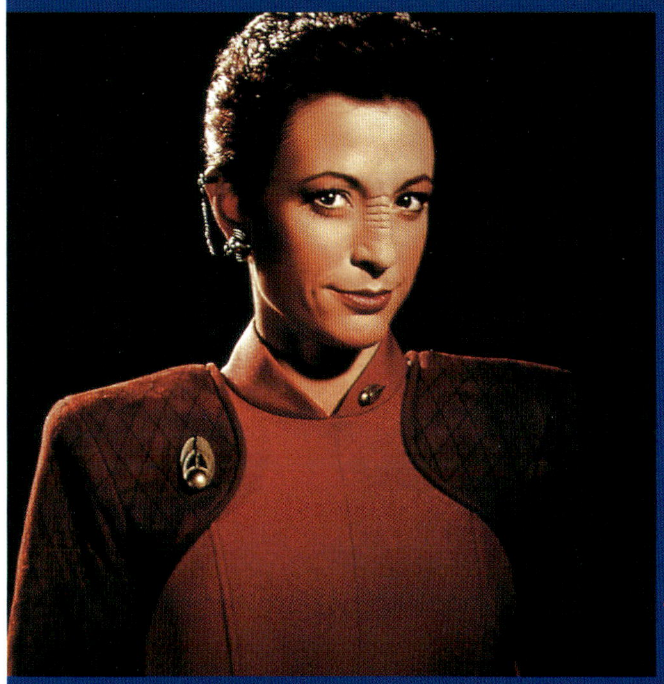

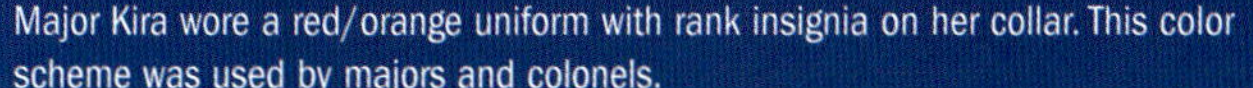

Major Kira wore a red/orange uniform with rank insignia on her collar. This color scheme was used by majors and colonels.

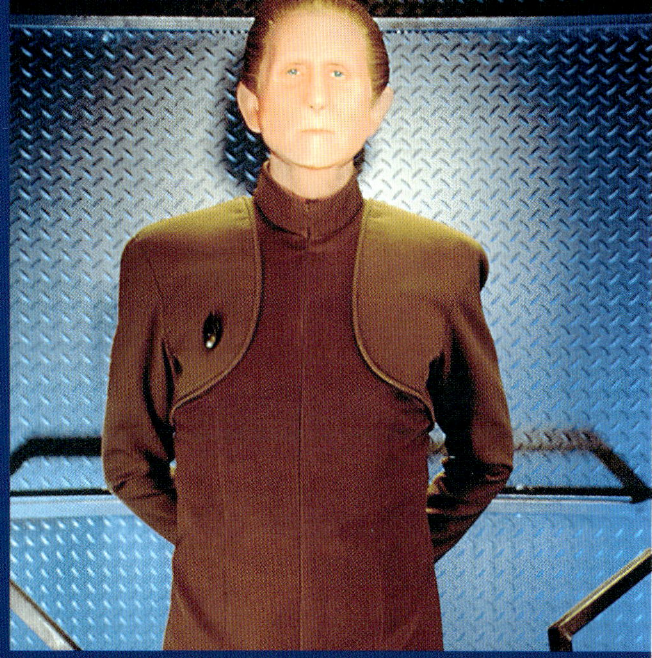

Constable Odo and the station's security staff wore brown uniforms. Odo never held a formal rank, so had no insignia on his collar.

FLAG OFFICER RANK PIPS

FLEET ADMIRAL

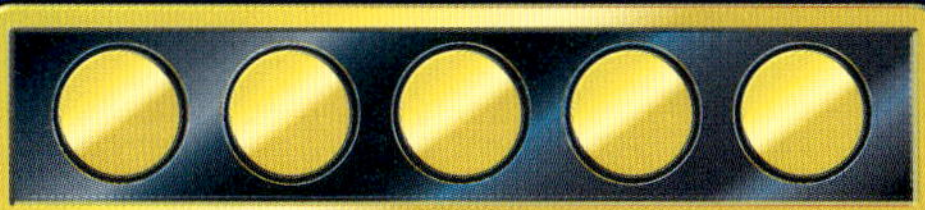

ADMIRAL (FOUR STAR)

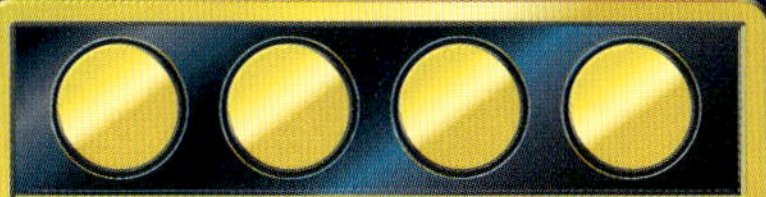

ADMIRAL (THREE STAR)

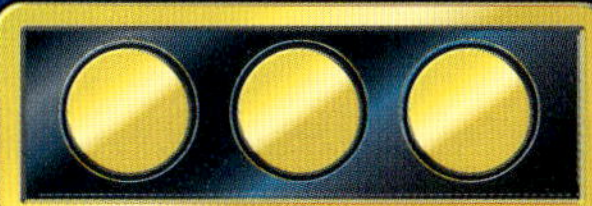

ADMIRAL (TWO STAR)

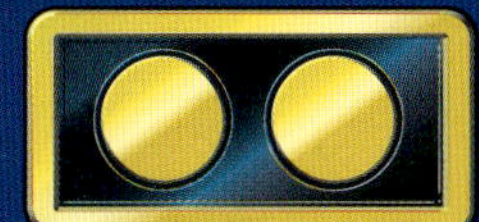

ADMIRAL (ONE STAR)

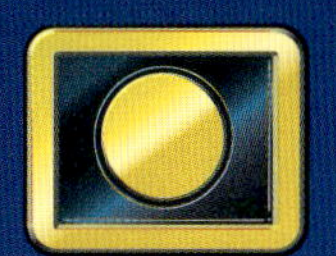

OFFICER RANK PIPS

CAPTAIN

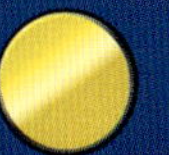

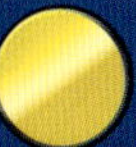

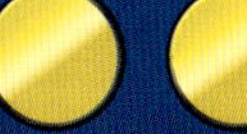

COMMANDER

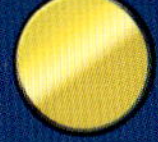

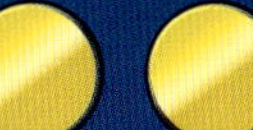

LIEUTENANT COMMANDER

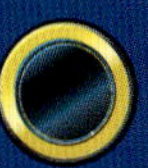

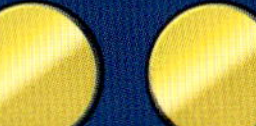

LIEUTENANT

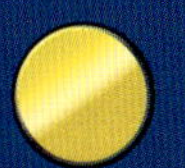

LIEUTENANT (JUNIOR GRADE)

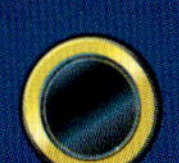

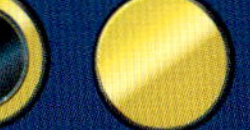

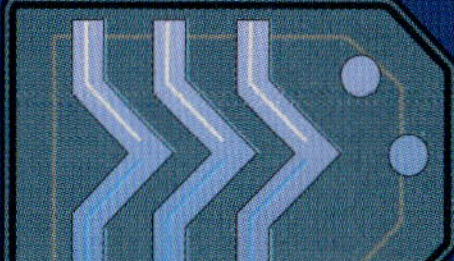

ENSIGN

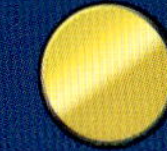

CHIEF

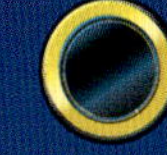

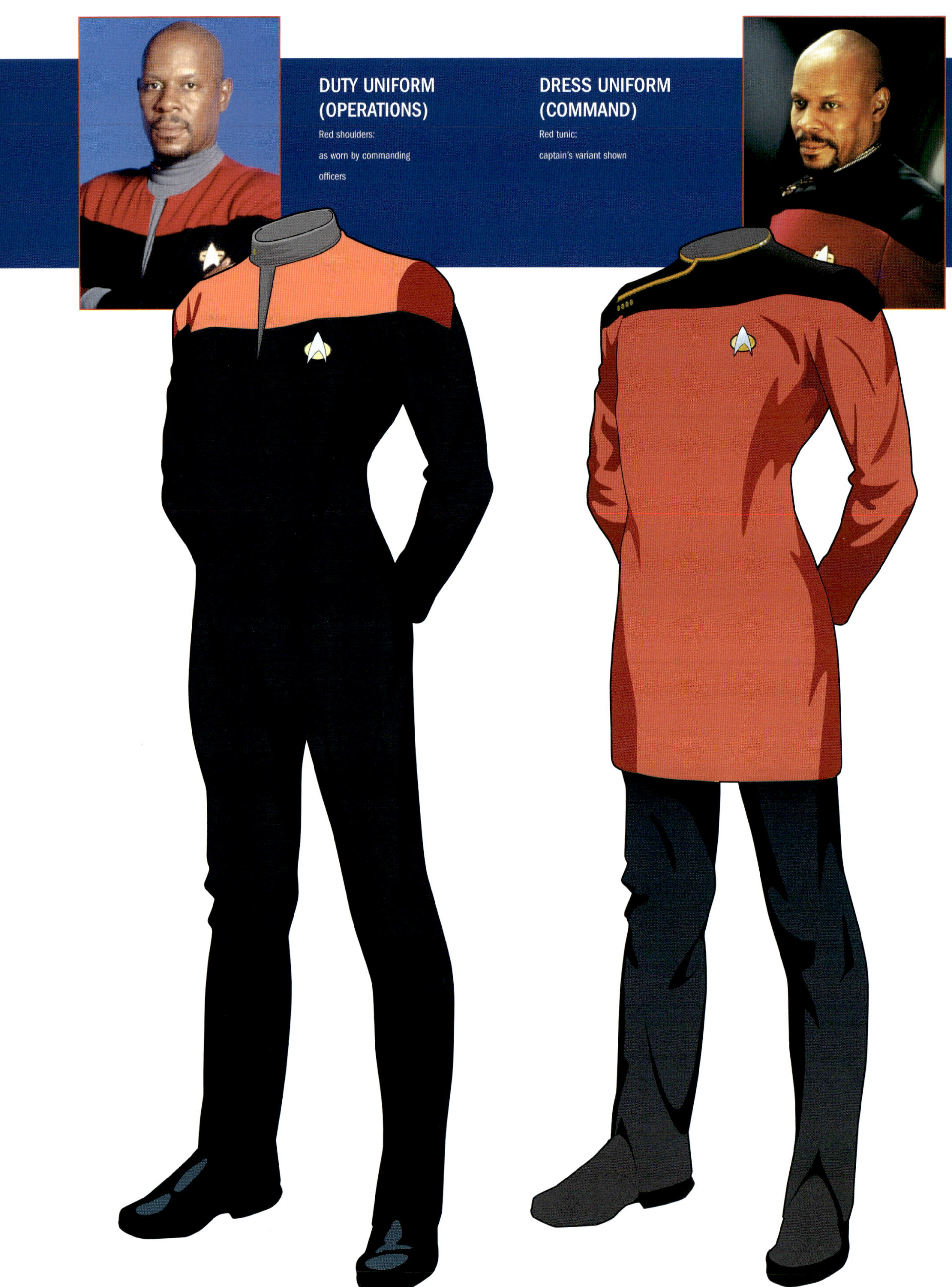

DUTY UNIFORM (OPERATIONS)

Red shoulders: as worn by commanding officers

DRESS UNIFORM (COMMAND)

Red tunic: captain's variant shown

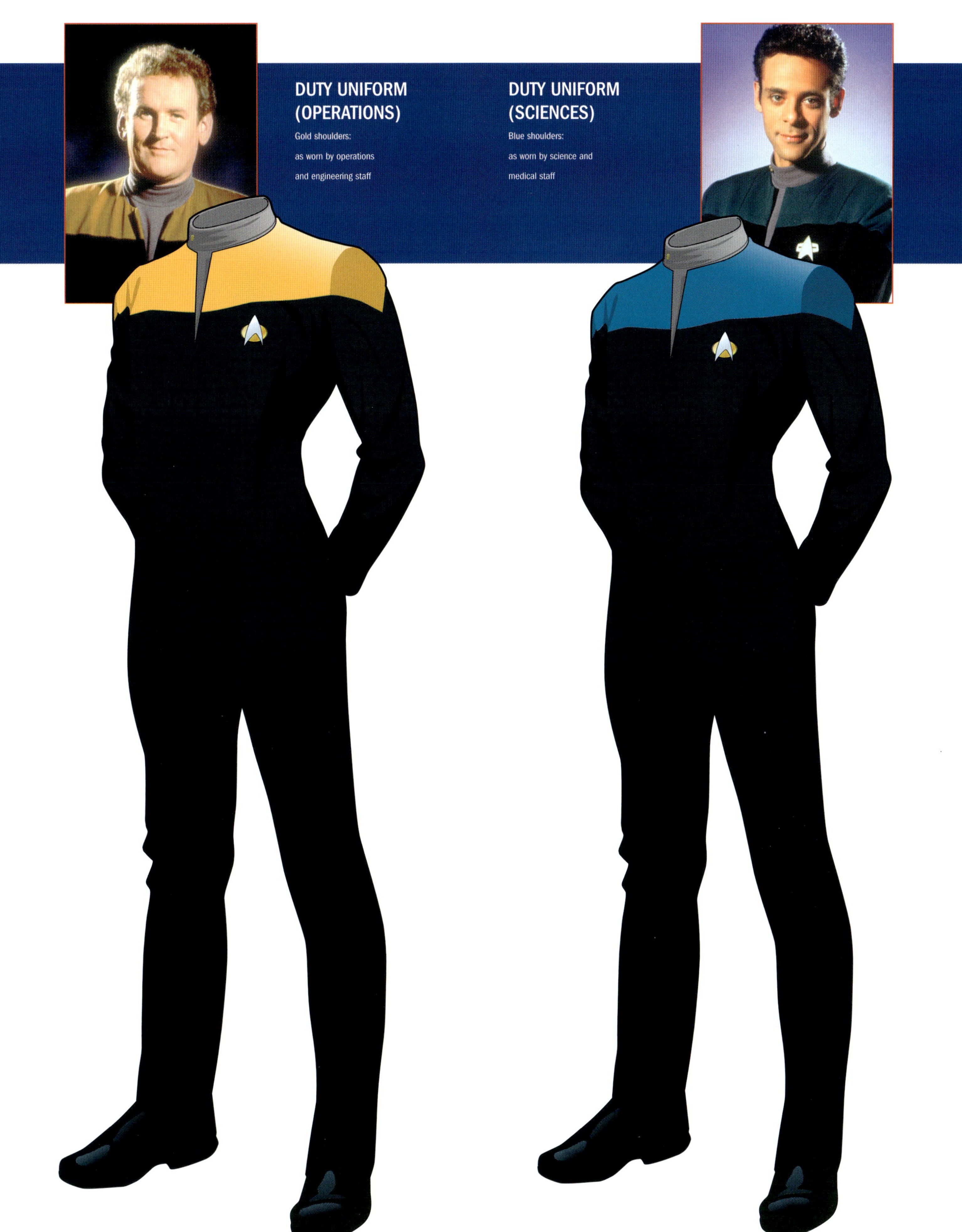

DUTY UNIFORM (OPERATIONS)

Gold shoulders: as worn by operations and engineering staff

DUTY UNIFORM (SCIENCES)

Blue shoulders: as worn by science and medical staff

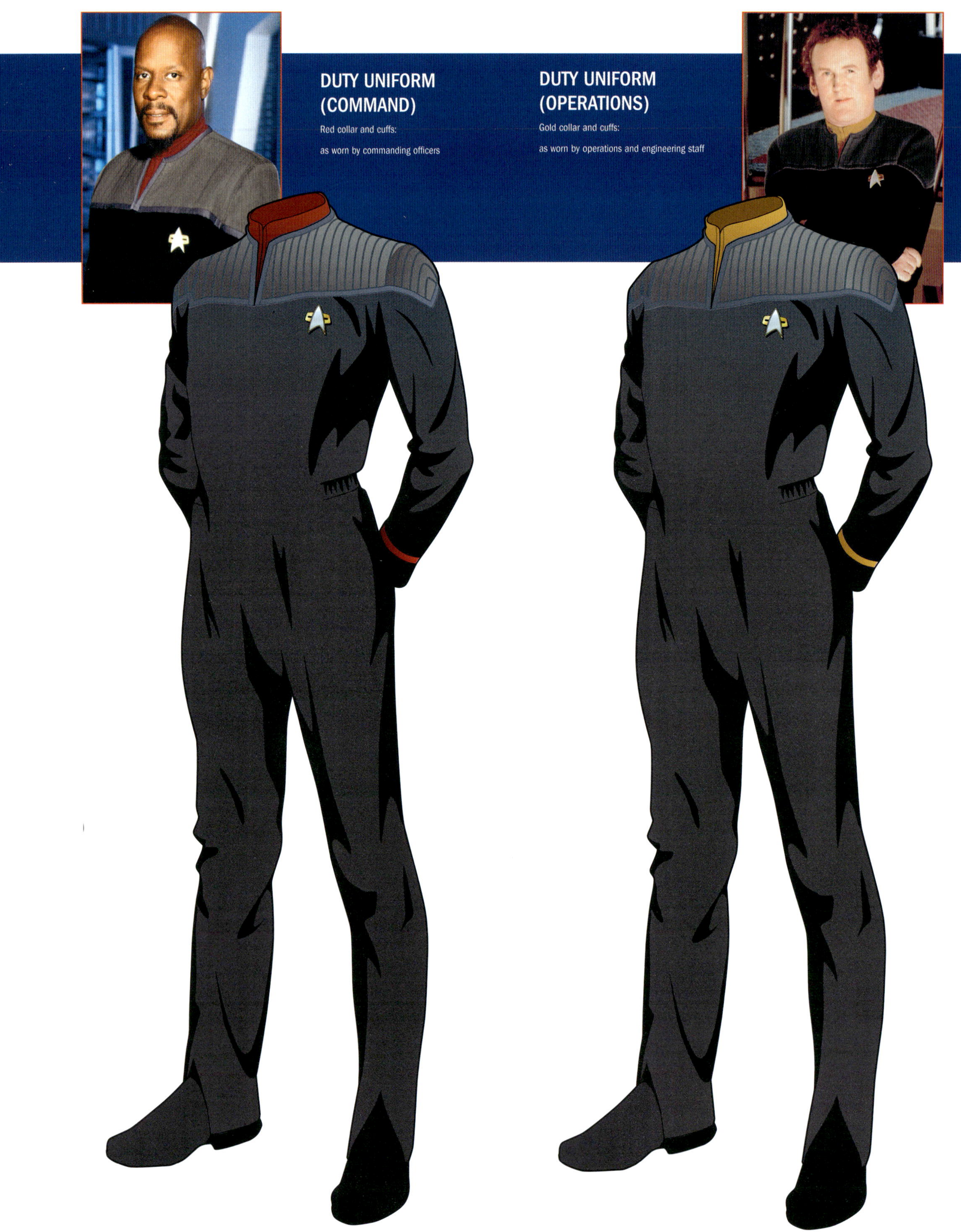

DUTY UNIFORM (COMMAND)

Red collar and cuffs:

as worn by commanding officers

DUTY UNIFORM (OPERATIONS)

Gold collar and cuffs:

as worn by operations and engineering staff

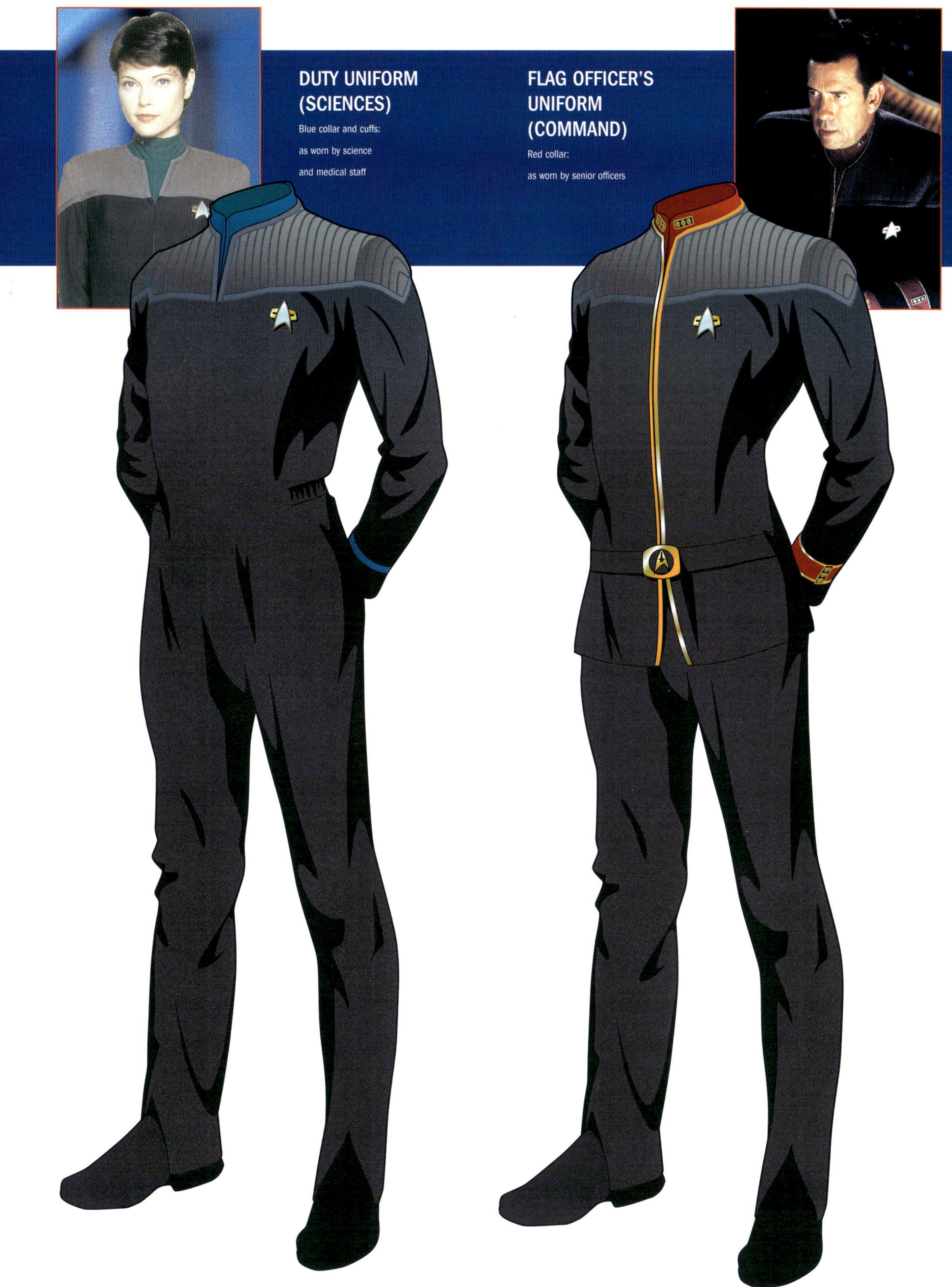

DUTY UNIFORM (SCIENCES)

Blue collar and cuffs: as worn by science and medical staff

FLAG OFFICER'S UNIFORM (COMMAND)

Red collar: as worn by senior officers

DESERT UNIFORMS

Special Starfleet uniforms ensured that officers were as comfortable as possible when they embarked on missions in the hot environments of desert planets.

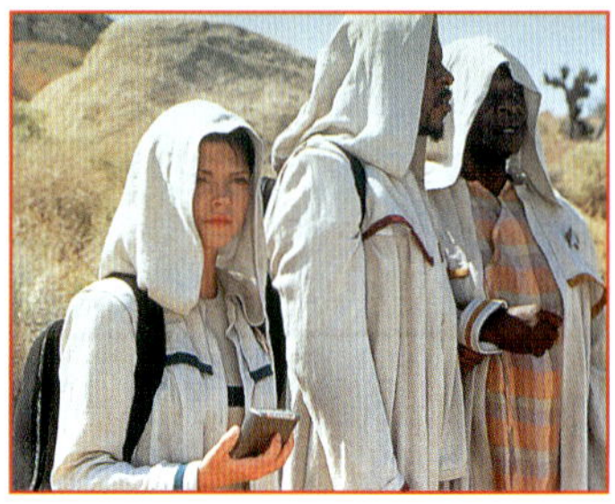
The standard Starfleet uniform was suitable for most conditions, but some extreme environments called for special clothing.

Captain Benjamin Sisko, his father Joseph, son Jake, and Ensign Ezri Dax went on a mission to the sun-baked world of Tyree in 2376, after a vision led Sisko to believe that the Orb of the Emissary was buried in the planet's sand.

To keep themselves protected from sunburn, Sisko and his companions wore Starfleet's desert uniforms: loose-fitting pants and a short-sleeved T-shirt in natural colors, covered by a loose, hooded cloak. The wearer's duty division colors were displayed in a thin band around the chest, and as braiding around the hood and sleeves of the cloak.

TRADITIONAL STYLE

The design of the desert uniforms was a tried-and-tested style of clothing for hot environments. The cloaks were very similar to the traditional robes of the Vulcan people, whose world was also hot and dry; they also harked back to the clothing worn by people living in Earth's equatorial regions. The robes were worn with soft ankle boots, with soles that provided a good grip on the dusty rocks and sand banks of desert terrain.

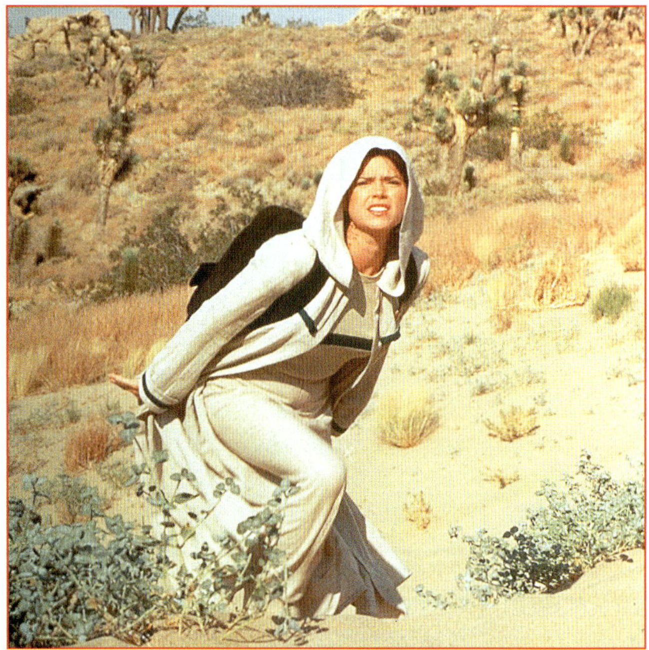
Hot planetary environments proved challenging for races used to more temperate climes, such as Trill Ezri Dax.

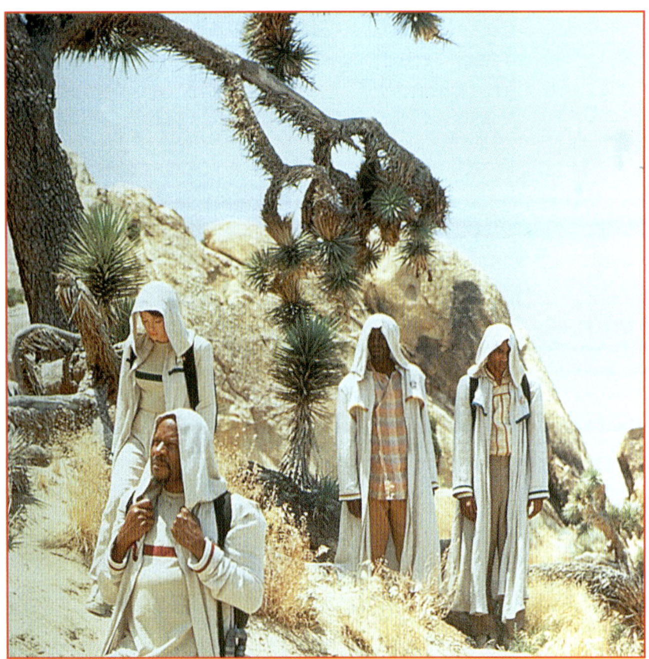
The cloaks could be worn over ordinary clothes if civilians, such as Jake and Joseph Sisko, accompanied Starfleet officers on their missions.

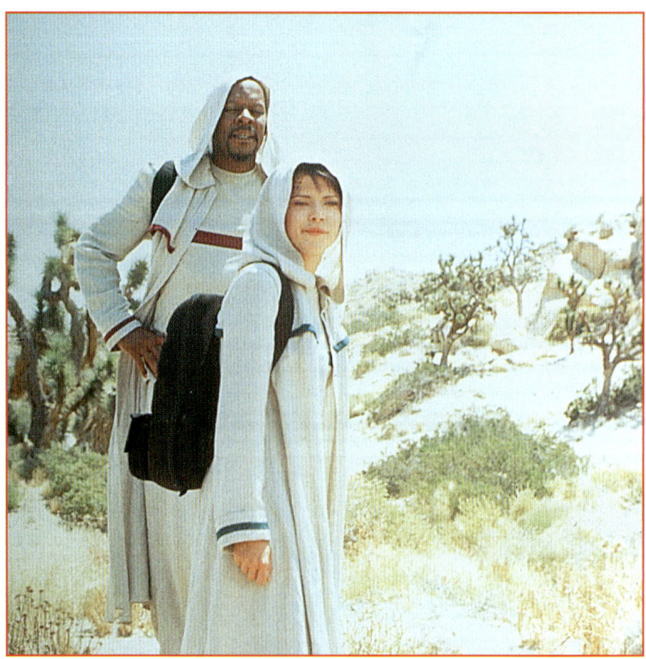
Standard-issue starfleet desert kit included backpacks containing equipment, supplies, and emergency water rations.

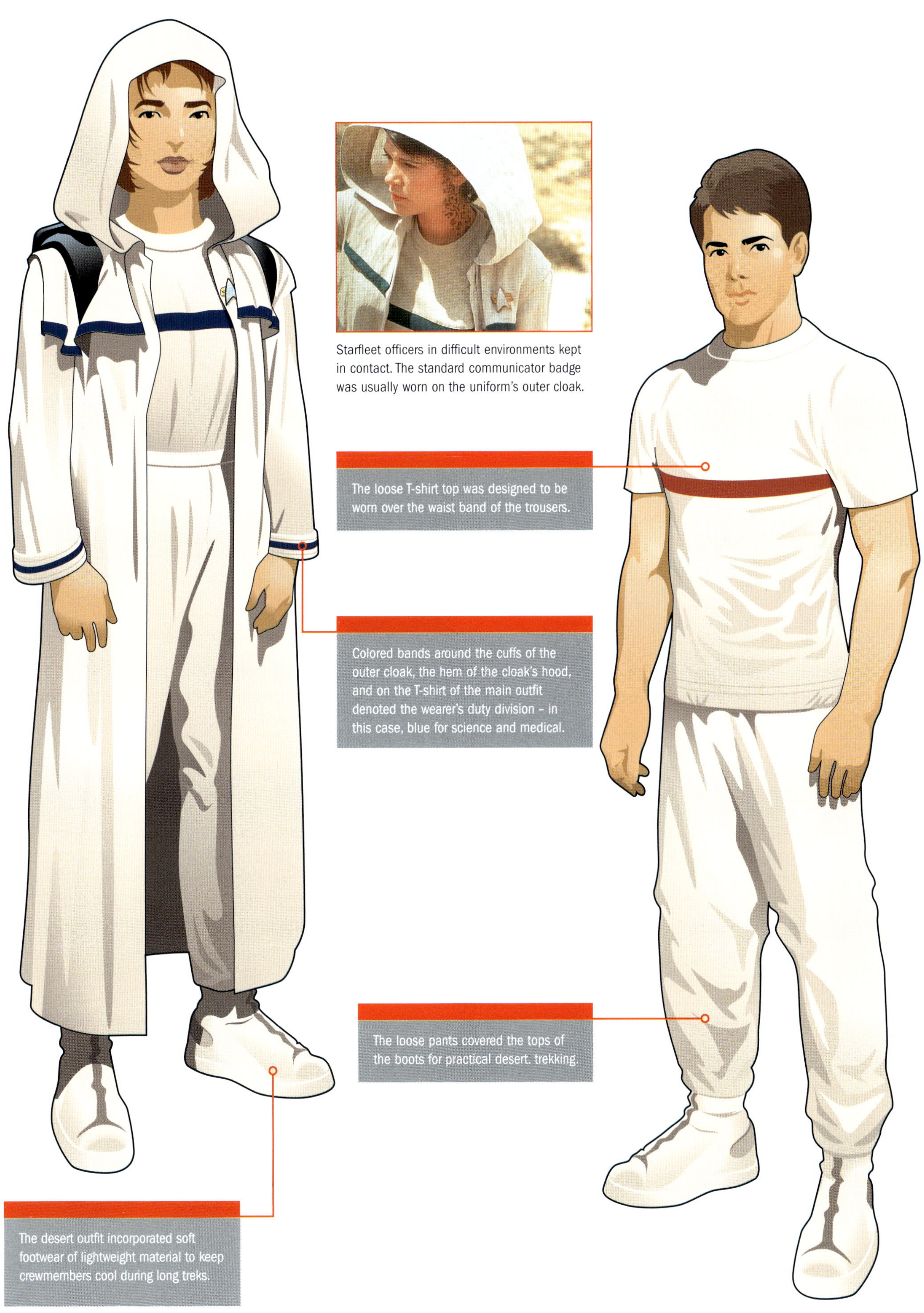

Starfleet officers in difficult environments kept in contact. The standard communicator badge was usually worn on the uniform's outer cloak.

COMBAT UNIFORMS

Starfleet's ground troops wore a unique uniform that was designed for combat. A band across the chest showed the divisional colors.

Starfleet combat uniforms were designed to offer ground troops an enhanced level of protection. The combination of a lightweight but tough uniform, with a backpack and phaser rifle, made Starfleet ground troops highly mobile and capable of a rapid response to a variety of tactical situations. Protective headgear such as helmets reduced visibility, so were not part of standard-issue combat clothing.

The combat uniform was black, which provided natural camouflage for nighttime or low-visibility operations. The close-fitting tunic worn over the standard-issue undershirt was also black, and had a vertical fastening strip running up the back. The tunic was padded for temperature control, and had additional padding across the shoulders. The shoulder section was made of a lightly ridged, water-resistant fabric, for extra comfort and durability when carrying strapped packs and equipment.

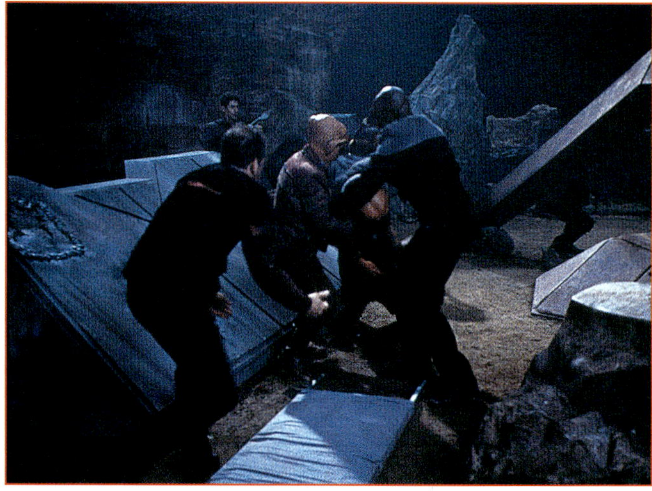

The orange band across the arms and shoulders of the tunic aided identification in the field, helping troops recognize fellow soldiers in the heat of the fray.

RELAY STATION DEFENSE

Combat uniforms proved their worth when Starfleet infantry was under a five-month siege on the planet AR-558, while defending a Dominion communications relay seized from the Jem'Hadar. Of 150 soldiers dispatched to the planet, only 43 survived to fight alongside Sisko and his landing party in the final battle.

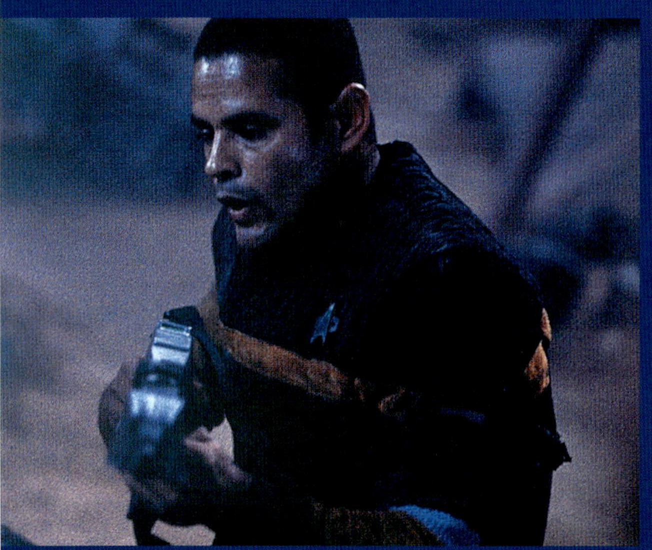

The neat, streamlined construction of the uniforms made it easier to perform precise movements, such as loading and firing weapons.

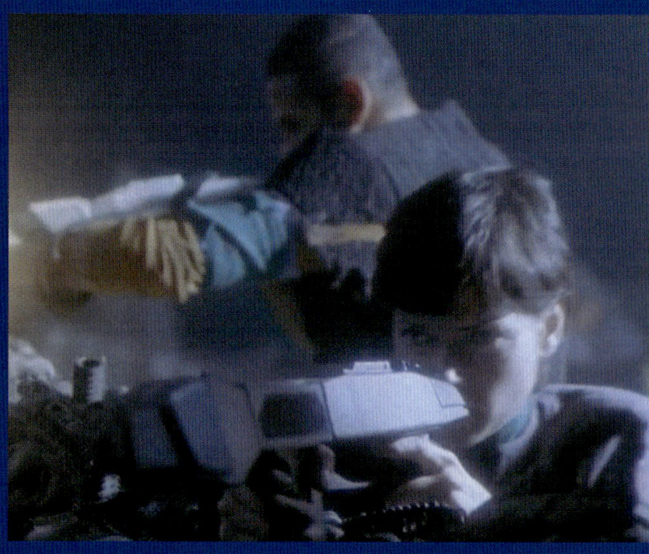

Lightweight, long-sleeved undershirts were supplied to the soldiers in the same color as the orange band on the uniform's tunic.

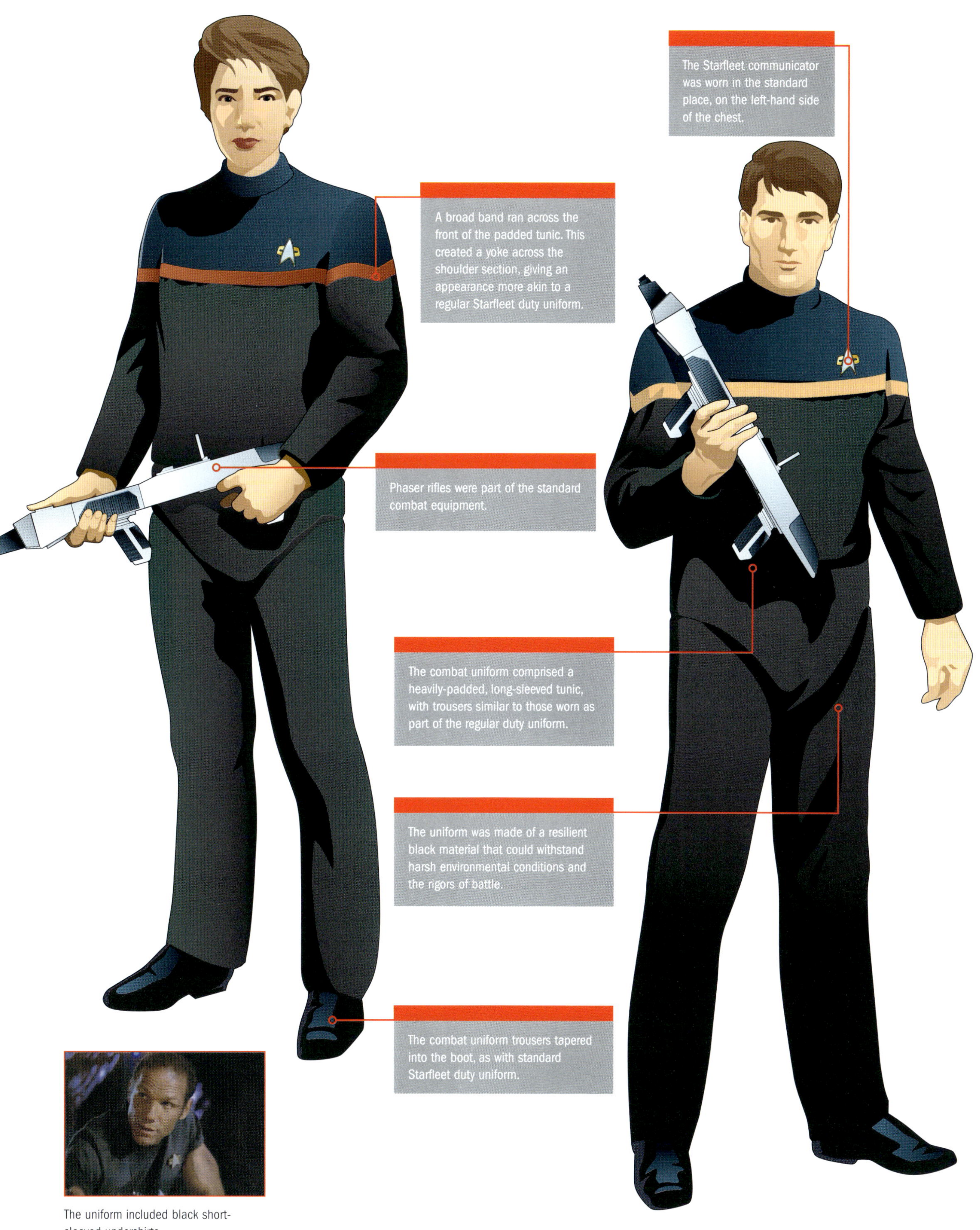

The uniform included black short-sleeved undershirts.

INDEX

E

F

G

H

I

J

K

L

M

N

ALSO AVAILABLE

STAR TREK VOYAGER – A CELEBRATION

THE FIRST IN THE NEW SERIES OF CELEBRATION BOOKS

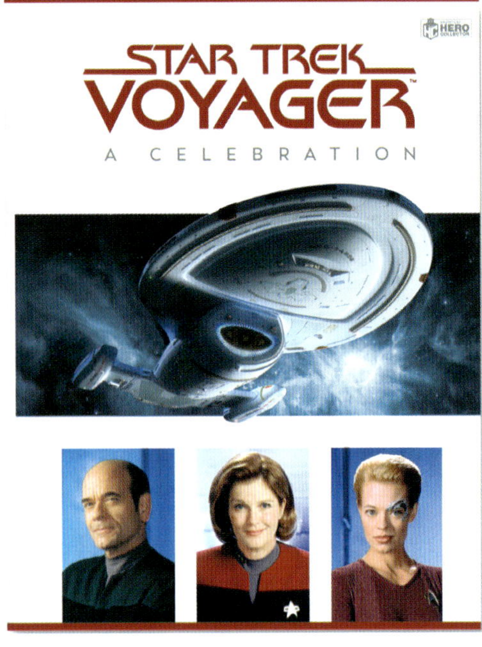

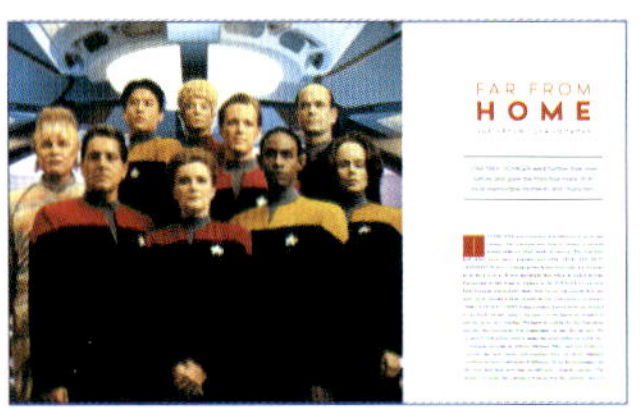

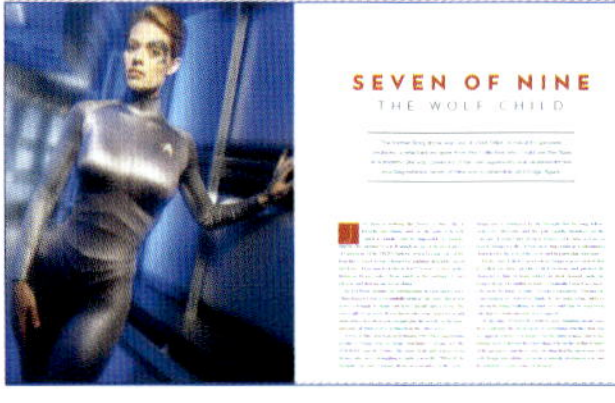

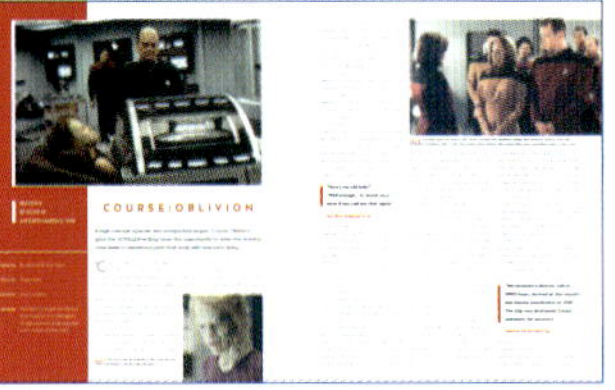

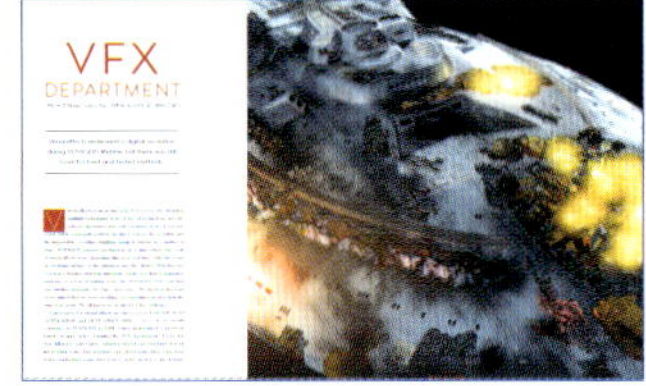

STAR TREK: A CELEBRATION is a series of lavishly illustrated volumes that chart the behind-the-scenes stories of the *STAR TREK* franchise, drawing on the memories of those who made each series. From the writers' room to the soundstages, each volume celebrates the creative endeavors of cast and crew through personal recollections and on-set tales, alongside exclusive production artwork, key episode guides and more.

STAR TREK ILLUSTRATED HANDBOOKS

STAR TREK ILLUSTRATED HANDBOOKS is a series of books that provide in-depth profiles of the *STAR TREK* universe, covering a wide range of topics from individual starships to races such as the Klingons. Each full-color, heavily illustrated reference work is packed with isometric illustrations, artwork, photographs and CG renders, and features detailed technical information from official sources.

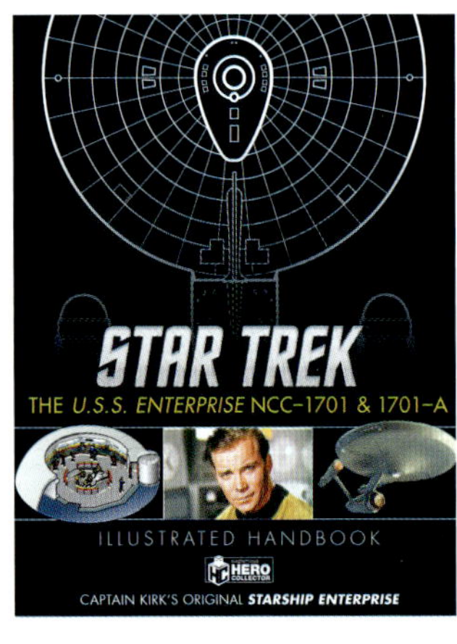

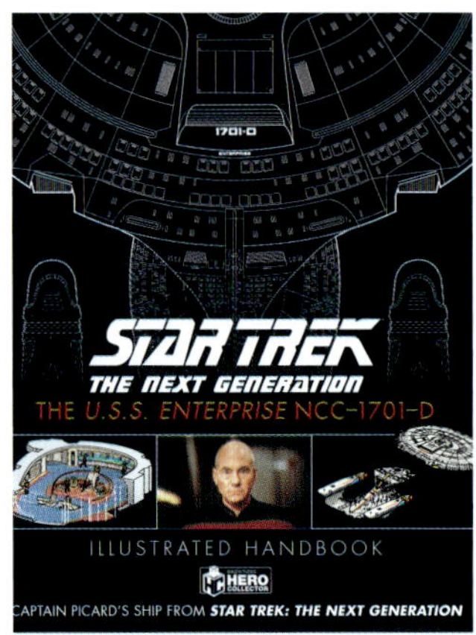

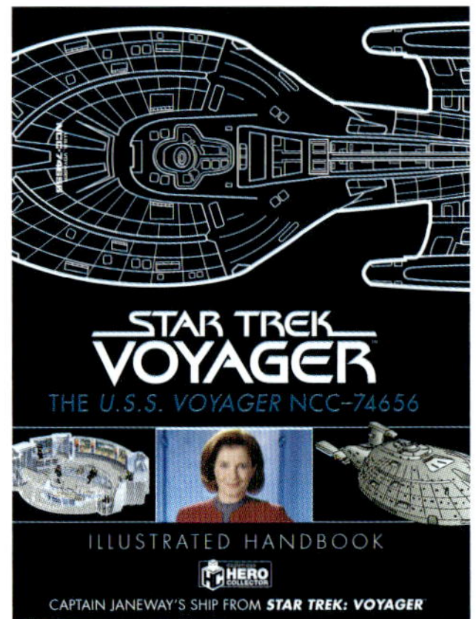

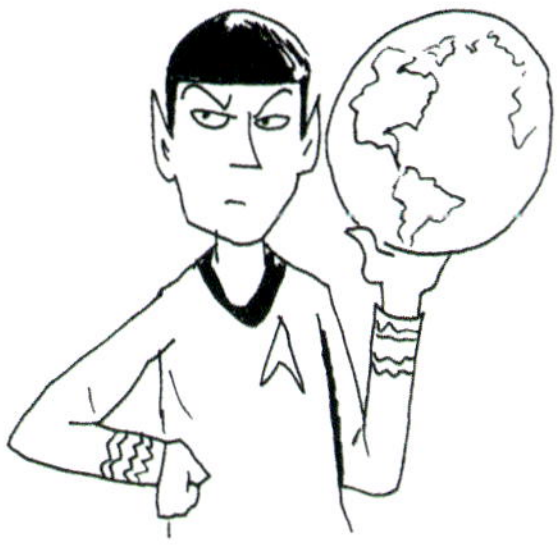

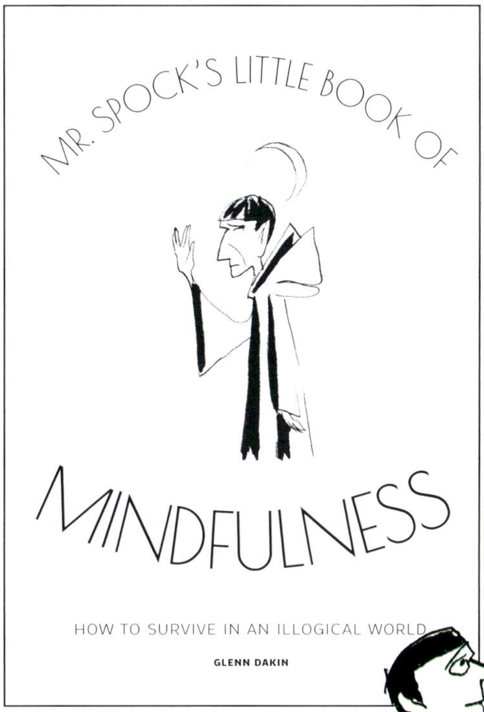

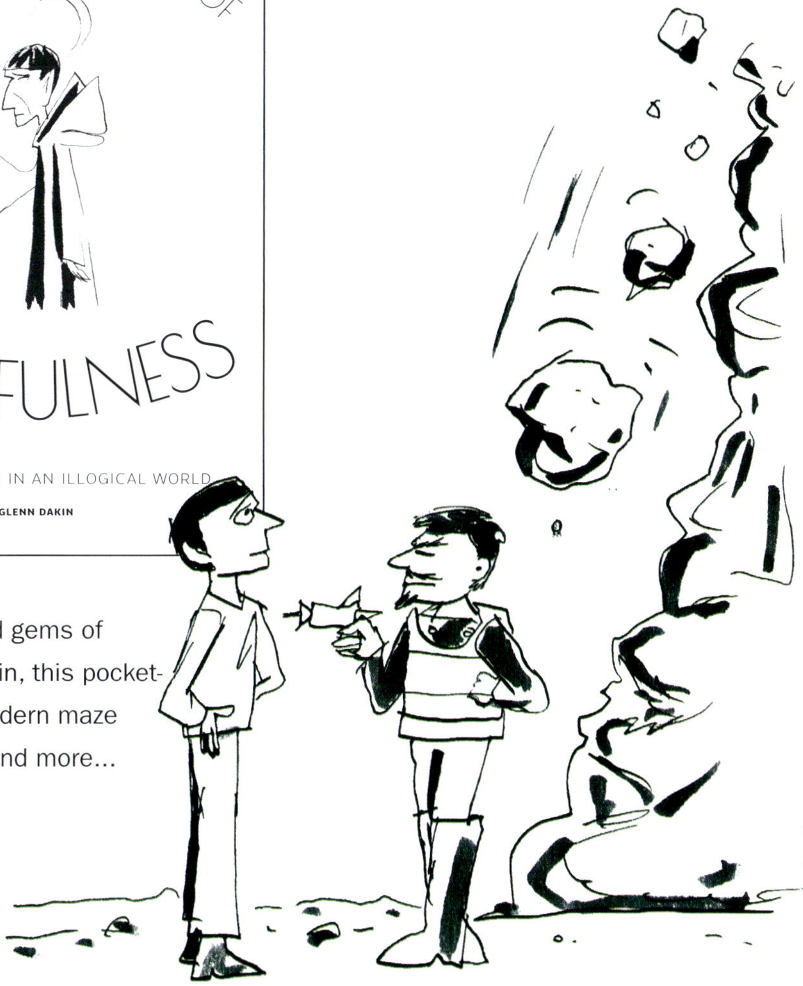

CREDITS

General Editor: Ben Robinson

Project Manager: Jo Bourne

Editor and writer: Simon Hugo, with additional text by Ian Chaddock

Sub-editor: Alice Peebles

Designer: Katy Everett

With thanks to the team at CBS: John Van Citters, Marian Cordry and Risa Kessler

Published by **Hero Collector Books**, a division of Eaglemoss Ltd. 2021

Eaglemoss Ltd., Premier Place, 2 & A Half Devonshire Square, EC2M 4UJ, London, UK

Eaglemoss France, 144 Avenue Charles de Gaulle, 92200 Neuilly-Sur-Seine, France

Most of the contents of this book were originally published as part of *The Official STAR TREK Fact Files* 1997-2002

ISBN 978-1-85875-951-7

Printed in Spain

www.herocollector.com